# INFINITY PLUS

## THE ANTHOLOGY

In 1997 the *infinity plus* website was launched at *www.infinityplus.co.uk* to showcase some of the best in SF, fantasy and horror fiction. This collection features the work of some of the site's major works—stories chosen by the writers themselves, stories dear to their hearts and deserving renewed attention. Contributors include:

Stephen Baxter

Michael Bishop

Terry Bisson

Eric Brown

Tony Daniel

Paul Di Filippo

Mary Gentle

Lisa Goldstein

James Patrick Kelly

Garry Kilworth

Ian R. MacLeod

Paul McAuley

Ian McDonald

Vonda N. McIntyre

Michael Moorcock

Kim Newman

Patrick O'Leary

Paul Park

Kit Reed

Adam Roberts

Kim Stanley Robinson

Lucius Shepard

Brian Stableford

Charles Stross

Michael Swanwick

Jeff VanderMeer

# INFINITY PLUS

## THE ANTHOLOGY

EDITED BY KEITH BROOKE
AND NICK GEVERS

**SOLARIS**

First published 2007 by Solaris
an imprint of BL Publishing
Games Workshop Ltd
Willow Road
Nottingham
NG7 2WS
UK

*www.solarisbooks.com*

ISBN 13: 978-1-84416-489-9
ISBN 10: 1-84416-489-6

10 9 8 7 6 5 4 3 2 1

A CIP catalogue record for this book is available from the British Library.

Designed & typeset by BL Publishing

*Grateful acknowledgement is made for permission to print the following material:*

"Radio Waves" by Michael Swanwick. Copyright 1995 Michael Swanwick. First appeared in *Omni*, Winter 1995.

"Lovestory" by James Patrick Kelly. Copyright 1998 James Patrick Kelly. First appeared in *Asimov's*, June 1998.

"Tomorrow Town" by Kim Newman. Copyright 2000 Kim Newman. First appeared on *SciFiction*, November 2000.

"The Second Window" by Patrick O'Leary. Copyright 2000 Patrick O'Leary. First appeared on *infinity plus*, April 2000.

"Ghost Dancing with Manco Tupac" by Jeff VanderMeer. Copyright 2000 Jeff VanderMeer. First appeared in *Imagination Fully Dilated II* (edited by Elizabeth Engstrom), 2000.

"Home Time" by Ian R. MacLeod. Copyright 1998 Ian R. MacLeod. First appeared in *The Magazine of Fantasy & Science Fiction*, February 1998.

"A Spy in the Domain of Arnheim" by Michael Bishop. Copyright 1981 Michael Bishop. First appeared in *Pictures at an Exhibition* (edited by Ian Watson), 1981.

"Memories of the Flying Ball Bike Shop" by Garry Kilworth. Copyright 1992 Garry Kilworth. First appeared in *Asimov's*, June 1992.

"Kitsune" by Mary Gentle. Copyright 1998 Mary Gentle. First appeared in *Odyssey 5*, 1998.

"Old Soldiers" by Kit Reed. Copyright 2001 Kit Reed. First appeared in *Infinity Plus One* (edited by Keith Brooke and Nick Gevers), 2001.

"God's Foot" by Tony Daniel. Copyright 1993 Tony Daniel. First appeared in *Asimov's*, May 1993.

"Jack Neck and the Worrybird" by Paul Di Filippo. Copyright 1998 Paul Di Filippo. First appeared in *Science Fiction Age*, July 1998.

# CONTENTS

# FOREWORD

So many good stories out there, so many fine authors—for speculative fiction still has a thriving short fiction market. To many, short stories are the heart of the genre. But what happens to these stories when a magazine's next issue comes along, or when an anthology goes out of print? Some are reprinted, of course, but many rapidly become hard to find. Perhaps authors should make more use of the Web to revive some of these stories... Perhaps we should get together and show off our work in the same place, sharing each other's readers around... That was the thinking of Keith Brooke, half of the current editorial team, way back in early 1997. And so the online science fiction and fantasy showcase, *infinity plus,* was born.

In our tenth year we passed several major landmarks: two million words of professional genre fiction, a hundred interviews with authors and editors, and a thousand book reviews, all available for free at *www.infinityplus.co.uk*. Contributors include Jack Vance, Michael Moorcock, Stephen Baxter, and Connie Willis and, month by month, the site continues to grow.

The anthology you have in your hands is a natural development of the website. If we devote so much of our efforts to promoting the best in short SF and fantasy it's inevitable that we should do this in print as well as online. Back in 2001 PS Publishing brought out an *infinity plus* anthology in a handsome limited edition hardback, each copy signed by all the contributors; in 2003 we teamed up with PS again to bring out a second signed limited edition anthology. The Solaris paperback edition you're now holding combines the contents of both of the PS volumes for the first time, and is published to coincide with the tenth anniversary of the thing that *infinity plus* has become. The contributors to this anthology have all played a prominent part in our Web presence, and our approach to them was the same as when we invite an author to contribute to the website: we selected the authors and asked each to nominate a story of their own—a story to which they are particularly attached, a story they feel deserves renewed attention, a story that may otherwise be hard to find. (Incidentally, we make no claim to originality in this approach: Josh Pachter did a similar thing with a series of anthologies two and a half decades ago—one of the inspirations for *infinity plus*.)

Some of the stories here first appeared in print magazines, anthologies or collections, only to later become hard to obtain; others appeared in print for the first time in one of the PS editions of this anthology— either new stories, or ones that first found publication on the Web. All are examples of speculative fiction that is intelligent, challenging, and, above all, entertaining.

*Keith Brooke and Nick Gevers*
*November 2006*

# RADIO WAVES

*Michael Swanwick*

I WAS WALKING the telephone wires upside down, the sky underfoot cold and flat with a few hard bright stars sparsely scattered about it, when I thought how it would take only an instant's weakness to step off to the side and fall up forever into the night. A kind of wildness entered me then and I began to run.

I made the wires sing. They leapt and bulged above me as I raced past Ricky's Luncheonette and up the hill. Past the old chocolate factory and the IDI Advertising Display plant. Past the body shops, past A. J. LaCourse Electric Motors-Controls-Parts. Then, where the slope steepened, along the curving snake of row houses that went the full quarter-mile up to the Ridge. Twice I overtook pedestrians, hunched and bundled, heads doggedly down, out on incomprehensible errands. They didn't notice me, of course. They never do.

The antenna farm was visible from here. I could see the Seven Sisters spangled with red lights, dependent on the Earth like stalactites. "Where are you running to, little one?" one tower whispered in a crackling, staticky voice. I think it was Hegemone.

"Fuck off," I said without slackening my pace, and they all chuckled.

Cars mumbled by. This was ravine country, however built-up, and the far side of the road, too steep and rocky for development, was given over to trees and garbage. Hamburger wrappings and white plastic trash bags rustled in their wake. I was running full out now.

About a block or so from the Ridge, I stumbled and almost fell. I slapped an arm across a telephone pole and just managed to catch myself in time. Aghast at my own carelessness, I hung there, dizzy and alarmed.

The ground overhead was black as black, an iron roof that somehow was yet as anxious as a hound to leap upon me, crush me flat, smear me to nothingness. I stared up at it, horrified.

Somebody screamed my name.

I turned. A faint blue figure clung to a television antenna atop a small, stuccoed brick duplex. Charlie's Widow. She pointed an arm that flickered with silver fire down Ripka Street. I slewed about to see what was coming after me.

It was the Corpsegrinder.

When it saw that I'd spotted it, it put out several more legs, extended a quilled head, and raised a howl that bounced off the Heaviside layer. My nonexistent blood chilled.

In a panic, I scrambled up and ran toward the Ridge and safety. I had a squat in the old Roxy, and once I was through the wall, the Corpsegrinder would not follow. Why this should be so, I did not know. But you learn the rules if you want to survive.

I ran. In the back of my head I could hear the Seven Sisters clucking and gossiping to each other, radiating television and radio over a few dozen frequencies. Indifferent to my plight.

The Corpsegrinder churned up the wires on a hundred needle-sharp legs. I could feel the ion surge it kicked up pushing against me as I reached the intersection of Ridge and Leverington. Cars were pulling up to the pumps at the Atlantic station. Teenagers stood in front of the A-Plus Mini Market, flicking half-smoked cigarettes into the street, stamping their feet like colts, and waiting for something to happen. I couldn't help feeling a great longing disdain for them. Every last one worried about grades and drugs and zits, and all the while snugly barricaded within hulking fortresses of flesh.

I was scant yards from home. The Roxy was a big old movie palace, fallen into disrepair and semi-converted to a skateboarding rink which had gone out of business almost immediately. But it had been a wonderful place once, and the terracotta trim was still there: ribbons and river gods, great puffing faces with pan pipes, guitars, flowers, wyverns. I crossed the Ridge on a dead telephone wire, spider-web delicate but still usable.

Almost there.

Then the creature was upon me, with a howl of electromagnetic rage that silenced even the Sisters for an instant. It slammed into my side, a storm of razors and diamond-edged fury, hooks and claws extended.

I grabbed at a rusty flange on the side of the Roxy.

Too late! Pain exploded within me, a sheet of white nausea. All in an instant I lost the name of my second daughter, an April morning when the world was new and I was five, a smoky string of all-nighters in Rensselaer Polytech, the jowly grin of Old Whatsisface the German who lived on LaFountain Street, the fresh pain of a sprained ankle out back of a Banana Republic warehouse, fishing off a yellow rubber raft with my old man on Lake Champlain. All gone, these and a thousand things more, sucked away, crushed to nothing, beyond retrieval.

Furious as any wounded animal, I fought back. Foul bits of substance splattered under my fist. The Corpsegrinder reared up to smash me down, and I scrabbled desperately away. Something tore and gave.

Then I was through the wall and safe among the bats and the gloom.

"*Cobb!*" the Corpsegrinder shouted. It lashed wildly back and forth, scouring the brick walls with limbs and teeth, as restless as a March wind, as unpredictable as ball lightning.

For the moment I was safe. But it had seized a part of me, tortured it, and made it a part of itself. I could no longer delude myself into thinking it was simply going to go away. "Cahawahawbb!" It broke my name down to a chord of overlapping tones. It had an ugly, muddy voice. I felt dirtied just listening to it. "Caw—" A pause. "—awbb!"

In a horrified daze I stumbled up the Roxy's curving patterned-tin roof until I found a section free of bats. Exhausted and dispirited, I slumped down.

"Caw aw aw awb buh buh!"

How had the thing found me? I'd thought I'd left it behind in Manhattan. Had my flight across the high-tension lines left a trail of some kind? Maybe. Then again, it might have some special connection with me. To follow me here it must have passed by easier prey. Which implied it had a grudge against me. Maybe I'd known the Corpsegrinder back when it was human. We could once have been important to each other. We might have been lovers. It was possible. The world is a stranger place than I used to believe.

The horror of my existence overtook me then, an acute awareness of the squalor in which I dwelt, the danger that surrounded me, and the dark mystery informing my universe.

I wept for all that I had lost.

Eventually, the sun rose up like God's own Peterbilt and with a triumphant blare of chromed trumpets, gently sent all of us creatures of the night to sleep.

WHEN YOU DIE, the first thing that happens is that the world turns upside down. You feel an overwhelming disorientation and a strange sensation that's not quite pain as the last strands connecting you to your body part, and then you slip out of physical being and fall from the planet.

As you fall, you attenuate. Your substance expands and thins, glowing more and more faintly as you pick up speed. So far as can be told, it's a process that doesn't ever stop. Fainter, thinner, colder... until you've merged into the substance of everyone else who's ever died, spread perfectly uniformly through the universal vacuum, forever moving toward but never arriving at absolute zero.

Look hard and the sky is full of the Dead.

Not everyone falls away. Some few are fast-thinking or lucky enough to maintain a tenuous hold on earthly existence. I was one of the lucky ones. I was working late one night on a proposal when I had my heart attack. The office was empty. The ceiling had a wire mesh within the plaster, and that's what saved me.

The first response to death is denial. *This can't be happening,* I thought. I gaped up at the floor where my body had fallen, and would lie undiscovered until morning. My own corpse, pale and bloodless, wearing a corporate tie and sleeveless gray Angora sweater. Gold Rolex, Sharper

Image desk accessories, and of course I also thought: *I died for THIS?*

By which of course I meant my entire life.

So it was in a state of both personal and ontological crisis that I wandered across the ceiling to the location of an old pneumatic message tube, removed and casually plastered over some fifty years before. I fell from the seventeenth to the twenty-fifth floor, and I learned a lot in the process.

Shaken, startled, and already beginning to assume the wariness that the afterlife requires, I went to a window to get a glimpse of the outer world. When I tried to touch the glass, my hand went right through. I jerked back. Cautiously, I leaned forward so that my head stuck out into the night.

What a wonderful experience Times Square is when you're dead! There is ten times the light a living being sees. All metal things vibrate with inner life. Electric wires are thin blue scratches in the air. Neon *sings*. The world is filled with strange sights and cries. Everything shifts from beauty to beauty.

Something that looked like a cross between a dragon and a wisp of smoke was feeding in the Square. But it was lost among so many wonders that I gave it no particular thought.

NIGHT AGAIN. I awoke with Led Zeppelin playing in the back of my head. "Stairway to Heaven." Again. It can be a long wait between Dead Milkmen cuts.

"Wakey-risey, little man," crooned one of the Sisters. It was funny how sometimes they took a close personal interest in our doings, and other times ignored us completely. "This is Euphrosyne with the red-eye weather report. The outlook is moody with a chance of existential despair. You won't be going outside tonight if you know what's good for you. There'll be lightning within the hour."

"It's too late in the year for lightning," I said.

"Oh dear. Should I inform the weather?"

By now I was beginning to realize that what I had taken on awakening to be the pressure of the Corpsegrinder's dark aura was actually the high-pressure front of an advancing storm. The first drops of rain pattered on the roof. Wind skirled and the rain grew stronger. Thunder growled in the distance. "Why don't you just go fuck your—"

A light laugh that trilled up into the supersonic, and she was gone.

I was listening to the rain underfoot when a lightning bolt screamed into existence, turning me inside out for the briefest instant then cartwheeling gleefully into oblivion. In the femtosecond of restoration following the bolt, the walls were transparent and all the world made of glass, its secrets available to be snooped out. But before comprehension was possible, the walls opaqued again and the lightning's malevolent aftermath faded like a madman's smile in the night.

Through it all the Seven Sisters were laughing and singing, screaming with joy whenever a lightning bolt flashed, and making up nonsense poems from howls, whistles, and static. During a momentary lull, the flat hum of a carrier wave filled my head. Phaenna, by the feel of her. But instead of her voice, I heard only the sound of fearful sobs.

"Widow?" I said. "Is that you?"

"She can't hear you," Phaenna purred. "You're lucky I'm here to bring you up to speed. A lightning bolt hit the transformer outside her house. It was bound to happen sooner or later. Your Nemesis—the one you call the Corpsegrinder, such a cute nickname, by the way—has her trapped."

This was making no sense at all. "Why would the Corpsegrinder be after her?"

"Why why why why?" Phaenna sang, a snatch of some pop ballad or other. "You didn't get answers when you were alive, what made you think you'd get any *now?*"

The sobbing went on and on. "She can sit it out," I said. "The Corpsegrinder can't—hey, wait. Didn't they just wire her house for cable? I'm trying to picture it. Phone lines on one side, electricity on the other, cable. She can slip out on his blind side."

The sobs lessened and then rose in a most unWidowlike wail of despair.

"Typical," Phaenna said. "You haven't the slightest notion of what you're talking about. The lightning stroke has altered your little pet. Go out and see for yourself."

My hackles rose. "You know damned good and well that I can't—"

Phaenna's attention shifted and the carrier beam died. The Seven Sisters are fickle that way. This time, though, it was just as well. No way was I going out there to face that monstrosity. I couldn't. And I was grateful not to have to admit it.

For a long while I sat thinking about the Corpsegrinder. Even here, protected by the strong walls of the Roxy, the mere thought of it was paralyzing. I tried to imagine what Charlie's Widow was going through, separated from this monster by only a thin curtain of brick and stucco. Feeling the hard radiation of its malice and need... It was beyond my powers of visualization. Eventually I gave up and thought instead about my first meeting with the Widow.

She was coming down the hill from Roxborough with her arms out, the inverted image of a child playing at tightrope walker. Placing one foot ahead of the other with deliberate concentration, scanning the wire before her so cautiously that she was less than a block away when she saw me.

She screamed.

Then she was running straight at me. My back was to the transformer station—there was no place to flee. I shrank away as she stumbled to a halt.

"It's you!" she cried. "Oh God, Charlie, I knew you'd come back for me, I waited so long, but I never doubted you, never, we can—" She lunged forward as if to hug me. Our eyes met.

All the joy in her died.

"Oh," she said. "It's not you."

I was fresh off the high-tension lines, still vibrating with energy and fear. My mind was a blaze of contradictions. I could remember almost nothing of my post-death existence. Fragments, bits of advice from the old dead, a horrifying confrontation with... something, some creature or phenomenon that had driven me to flee Manhattan. Whether it was this event or the fearsome voltage of that radiant highway that had scoured me of experience, I did not know. "It's me," I protested.

"No, it's not." Her gaze was unflatteringly frank. "You're not Charlie and you never were. You're—just the sad remnant of what once was a man, and not a very good one at that." She turned away. She was leaving me! In my confusion, I felt such a despair as I had never known before.

"Please..." I said.

She stopped.

A long silence. Then what in a living woman would have been a sigh. "You'd think that I—well, never mind." She offered her hand, and when I would not take it, simply said, "This way."

I followed her down Main Street, through the shallow canyon of the business district to a diner at the edge of

town. It was across from Hubcap Heaven and an auto-
motive junkyard bordered it on two sides. The diner was
closed. We settled down on the ceiling.

"That's where the car ended up after I died," she said,
gesturing toward the junkyard. "It was right after I got the
call about Charlie. I stayed up drinking and after a while
it occurred to me that maybe they were wrong, they'd
made some sort of horrible mistake and he wasn't really
dead, you know? Like maybe he was in a coma or something, some horrible kind of misdiagnosis, they'd gotten
him confused with somebody else, who knows? Terrible
things happen in hospitals. They make mistakes.

"I decided I had to go and straighten things out. There
wasn't time to make coffee so I went to the medicine cabinet and gulped down a bunch of pills at random, figuring
*some*thing among them would keep me awake. Then I
jumped into the car and started off for Colorado."

"My God."

"I have no idea how fast I was going—everything was a
blur when I crashed. At least I didn't take anybody with
me, thank the Lord. There was this one horrible moment
of confusion and pain and rage and then I found myself
lying on the floor of the car with my corpse just inches
beneath me on the underside of the roof." She was silent
for a moment. "My first impulse was to crawl out the window. Lucky for me I didn't." Another pause. "It took me
most of a night to work my way out of the yard. I had to
go from wreck to wreck. There were these gaps to jump.
It was a nightmare."

"I'm amazed you had the presence of mind to stay in the
car."

"Dying sobers you up fast."

I laughed. I couldn't help it. And without the slightest
hesitation, she joined right in with me. It was a fine warm
moment, the first I'd had since I didn't know when. The

two of us set each other off, laughing louder and louder, our merriment heterodyning until it filled every television screen for a mile around with snow.

My defenses were down. She reached out and took my hand.

Memory flooded me. It was her first date with Charlie. He was an electrician. The people next door were having the place rehabbed. She'd been working in the back yard and he struck up a conversation. Then he asked her out. They went to a disco in the Adam's Mark over on City Line Avenue.

She wasn't eager to get involved with somebody just then. She was still recovering from a hellish affair with a married man who'd thought that since he wasn't available for anything permanent, that made her his property. But when Charlie suggested they go out to the car for some coke—it was the Seventies—she'd said sure. He was going to put the moves on her sooner or later. Might as well get this settled early so they'd have more time for dancing.

But after they'd done up the lines, Charlie had shocked her by taking her hands in his and kissing them. She worked for a Bucks County pottery in those days and her hands were rough and red. She was very sensitive about them.

"Beautiful hands," he murmured. "Such beautiful, beautiful hands."

"You're making fun of me," she protested, hurt.

"No! These are hands that *do* things, and they've been shaped by the things they've done. The way stones in a stream are shaped by the water that passes over them. The way tools are shaped by their work. A hammer is beautiful, if it's a good hammer, and your hands are too."

He could have been scamming her. But something in his voice, his manner, said no, he really meant it. She squeezed his hands and saw that they were beautiful too. Suddenly she was glad she hadn't gone off the pill when she broke up with Daniel. She started to cry. Her date looked alarmed and baffled. But she couldn't stop. All the tears she hadn't cried in the past two years came pouring out of her, unstoppable.

Charlie-boy, she thought, you just got lucky.

ALL THIS IN an instant. I snatched my hands away, breaking contact. "*Don't do that!*" I cried. "Don't you *ever* touch me again!"

With flat disdain, the Widow said, "It wasn't pleasant for me either. But I had to see how much of your life you remember."

It was naive of me, but I was shocked to realize that the passage of memories had gone both ways. But before I could voice my outrage, she said, "There's not much left of you. You're only a fragment of a man, shreds and tatters, hardly anything. No wonder you're so frightened. You've got what Charlie calls a low signal-to-noise ratio. What happened in New York City almost destroyed you."

"That doesn't give you the right to—"

"Oh be still. You need to know this. Living is simple, you just keep going. But death is complex. It's so hard to hang on and so easy to let go. The temptation is always there. Believe me, I know. There used to be five of us in Roxborough, and where are the others now? Two came through Manayunk last spring and camped out under the El for a season and they're gone too. Holding it together is hard work. One day the stars start singing to you, and the next you begin to listen to them. A week later they start to make sense. You're just reacting to events—that's not good enough. If you mean to hold on, you've got to know why you're doing it."

"So why are *you?*"

"I'm waiting for Charlie," she said simply.

It occurred to me to wonder exactly how many years she had been waiting. Three? Fifteen? Just how long was it possible to hold on? Even in my confused and emotional state, though, I knew better than to ask. Deep inside she must've known as well as I did that Charlie wasn't coming. "My name's Cobb," I said. "What's yours?"

She hesitated and then, with an odd sidelong look, said, "I'm Charlie's widow. That's all that matters." It was all the name she ever gave, and Charlie's Widow she was to me from then onward.

I ROLLED ONTO my back on the tin ceiling and spread out my arms and legs, a phantom starfish among the bats. A fragment, she had called me, shreds and tatters. No wonder you're so frightened! In all the months since I'd been washed into this backwater of the power grid, she'd never treated me with anything but a condescension bordering on contempt.

So I went out into the storm after all.

The rain was nothing. It passed right through me. But there were ion-heavy gusts of wind that threatened to knock me right off the lines, and the transformer outside the Widow's house was burning a fierce actinic blue. It was a gusher of energy, a flare star brought to earth, dazzling. A bolt of lightning unzipped me, turned me inside out, and restored me before I had a chance to react.

The Corpsegrinder was visible from the Roxy, but between the burning transformer and the creature's metamorphosis, I was within a block of the monster before I understood exactly what it was I was seeing.

It was feeding off the dying transformer, sucking in energy so greedily that it pulsed like a mosquito engorged with blood. Enormous plasma wings warped to either side, hot blue and transparent. They curved entirely around the Widow's house in an unbroken and circular wall. At the resonance points they extruded less detailed versions of the Corpsegrinder itself, like sentinels, all facing the Widow.

Surrounding her with a prickly ring of electricity and malice.

I retreated a block, though the transformer fire apparently hid me from the Corpsegrinder, for it stayed where it was, eyelessly staring inward. Three times I circled the house from a distance, looking for a way in. An unguarded cable, a wrought-iron fence, any unbroken stretch of metal too high or too low for the Corpsegrinder to reach.

Nothing.

Finally, because there was no alternative, I entered the house across the street from the Widow's, the one that was best shielded by the spouting and stuttering transformer. A power line took me into the attic crawl space. From there I scaled the electrical system down through the second and first floors and so to the basement. I had a brief glimpse of a man asleep on a couch before the television. The set was off but it still held a residual charge. It sat quiescent, smug, bloated with stolen energies. If the poor bastard on the couch could have seen what I saw, he'd've never turned on the TV again.

In the basement I hand-over-handed myself from the washing machine to the main water inlet. Straddling the pipe, I summoned all my courage and plunged my head underground.

It was black as pitch. I inched forward on the pipe in a kind of panic. I could see nothing, hear nothing, smell nothing, taste nothing. All I could feel was the iron pipe beneath my hands. Just beyond the wall the pipe ended in a T-joint where it hooked into a branch line under the drive. I followed it to the street.

It was awful: like suffocation infinitely prolonged. Like being wrapped in black cloth. Like being drowned in ink. Like strangling noiselessly in the void between the stars.

To distract myself, I thought about my old man.

When my father was young, he navigated between cities by radio. Driving dark and usually empty highways, he'd twist the dial back and forth, back and forth, until he hit a station. Then he'd withdraw his hand and wait for the station ID. That would give him his rough location—that he was somewhere outside of Albany, say. A sudden signal coming in strong and then abruptly dissolving in groans and eerie whistles was a fluke of the ionosphere, impossibly distant and easily disregarded. One that faded in and immediately out meant he had grazed the edge of a station's range. But then a signal would grow and strengthen as he penetrated its field, crescendo, fade, and collapse into static and silence. That left him north of Troy, let's say, and making good time. He would begin the search for the next station.

You could drive across the continent in this way, passed from hand to hand by local radio, and tuned in to the geography of the night.

I went over that memory three times, polishing and refining it, before the branch line abruptly ended. One hand groped forward and closed upon nothing.

I had reached the main conduit. For a panicked moment I had feared that it would be concrete or brick or even one of the cedar pipes the city laid down in the nineteenth century, remnants of which still linger here and there beneath the pavement. But by sheer blind luck, the system had been installed during that narrow window of time when the pipes were cast iron. I crawled along its underside first one way and then the other, searching for the branch line to the Widow's. There was a lot of crap under the street. Several times I was blocked by gas lines or by the high-pressure pipes for the fire hydrants and had to awkwardly clamber around them.

At last I found the line and began the painful journey out from the street again.

When I emerged in the Widow's basement, I was a nervous wreck. It came to me then that I could no longer remember my father's name. A thing of rags and shreds indeed!

I worked my way up the electrical system, searching every room and unintentionally spying on the family who had bought the house after the Widow's death. In the kitchen a puffy man stood with his sleeves rolled up, elbow-deep in the sink, angrily washing dishes by candlelight. A woman who was surely his wife expressively smoked a cigarette at his stiff back, drawing in the smoke with bitter intensity and exhaling it in puffs of hatred. On the second floor a pre-adolescent girl clutched a tortoiseshell cat so tightly it struggled to escape, and cried into its fur. In the next room a younger boy sat on his bed in earphones, Walkman on his lap, staring sightlessly out the window at the burning transformer. No Widow on either floor.

How, I wondered, could she have endured staying in this entropic oven of a blue-collar row house, forever the voyeur at the banquet, watching the living squander what she had already spent? Her trace was everywhere, her presence elusive. I was beginning to think she'd despaired and given herself up to the sky when I found her in the attic, clutching the wire that led to the antenna. She looked up, silenced and amazed by my unexpected appearance.

"Come on," I said. "I know a way out."

Returning, however, I couldn't retrace the route I'd taken in. It wasn't so much the difficulty of navigating the twisting maze of pipes under the street, though that was bad enough, as the fact that the Widow wouldn't hazard the passage unless I led her by the hand.

"You don't know how difficult this is for me," I said.

"It's the only way I'd dare." A nervous, humorless laugh. "I have such a lousy sense of direction."

So, steeling myself, I seized her hand and plunged through the wall.

It took all my concentration to keep from sliding off the water pipes, I was so distracted by the violence of her thoughts. We crawled through a hundred memories, all of her married lover, all alike.

Here's one:

Daniel snapped on the car radio. Sad music—something classical—flooded the car. "That's bullshit, babe. You know how much I have invested in you?" He jabbed a blunt finger at her dress. "I could buy two good whores for what that thing cost."

Then why don't you, she thought. Get back on your Metroliner and go home to New York City and your wife and your money and your two good whores. Aloud, reasonably, she said, "It's over, Danny, can't you see that?"

"Look, babe. Let's not argue here, okay? Not in the parking lot, with people walking by and everybody listening. Drive us to your place, we can sit down and talk it over like civilized human beings."

She clutched the wheel, staring straight ahead. "No. We're going to settle this here and now."

"Christ." One-handed he wrangled a pack of Kents from a jacket pocket and knocked out a cigarette. Put the end in his lips and drew it out. Punched the lighter. "So talk."

A wash of hopelessness swept over her. Married men were supposed to be easy to get rid of. That was the whole point. "Let me go, Danny," she pleaded. Then, lying, "We can still be friends."

He made a disgusted noise.

"I've tried, Danny, I really have. You don't know how hard I've tried. But it's just not working."

"All right, I've listened. Now let's go." Reaching over her, Daniel threw the gearshift into reverse. He stepped on her foot, mashing it down on the accelerator.

The car leapt backwards. She shrieked and in a flurry of panic swung the wheel about and slammed on the brake with her free foot.

With a jolt and a crunch, the car stopped. There was the tinkle of broken plastic. They'd hit a lime-green Hyundai.

"Oh, that's just perfect!" Daniel said. The lighter popped out. He lit his cigarette and then swung open the door. "I'll check the damage."

Over her shoulder, she saw Daniel tug at his trousers' knees as he crouched to examine the Hyundai. She had a sudden impulse to slew the car around and escape. Step on the gas and never look back. Watch his face, dismayed and dwindling, in the rearview mirror. Eyes flooded with tears, she began quietly to laugh.

Then Daniel was back. "It's all right, let's go."

"I heard something break."

"It was just a taillight, okay?" He gave her a funny look. "What the hell are you laughing about?"

She shook her head hopelessly, unable to sort out the tears from the laughter. Then somehow they were on the Expressway, the car humming down the indistinct and warping road. She was driving but Daniel was still in control.

WE WERE COMPLETELY lost now and had been for some time. I had taken what I was certain had to be a branch line and it had led nowhere. We'd been tracing its twisty passage for blocks. I stopped and pulled my hand away. I couldn't concentrate. Not with the caustics and poisons of the Widow's past churning through me. "Listen," I said. "We've got to get something straight between us."

Her voice came out of nowhere, small and wary. "What?"

How to say it? The horror of those memories lay not in their brutality but in their particularity. They nestled into empty spaces where memories of my own should have been. They were as familiar as old shoes. They *fit*.

"If I could remember any of this crap," I said, "I'd apologize. Hell, I can't blame you for how you feel. Of course you're angry. But it's gone, can't you see that, it's over. You've got to let go. You can't hold me accountable for things I can't even remember, okay? All that shit happened decades ago. I was young. I've changed." The absurdity of the thing swept over me. I'd have laughed if I'd been able. "I'm dead, for pity's sake!"

A long silence. Then, "So you've figured it out."

"You've known all along," I said bitterly. "Ever since I came off of the high-tension lines in Manayunk."

She didn't deny it. "I suppose I should be flattered that when you were in trouble you came to me," she said in a way that indicated she was not.

"Why didn't you tell me then? Why drag it out?"

"Danny—"

"Don't call me that!"

"It's your name. Daniel. Daniel Cobb."

All the emotions I'd been holding back by sheer force of denial closed about me. I flung myself down and clutched the pipe tight, crushing myself against its unforgiving surface. Trapped in the friendless wastes of night, I weighed my fear of letting go against my fear of holding on.

"Cobb?"

I said nothing.

The Widow's voice took on an edgy quality. "Cobb, we can't stay here. You've got to lead me out. I don't have the slightest idea which way to go. I'm lost without your help."

I still could not speak.

"*Cobb!*" She was close to panic. "I put my own feelings aside. Back in Manayunk. You needed help and I did what I could. Now it's your turn."

Silently, invisibly, I shook my head.

"God damn you, Danny," she said furiously. "I won't let you do this to me again! So you're unhappy with what a jerk you were—that's not my problem. You can't redeem your manliness on me any more. I am not your fucking salvation. I am not some kind of cosmic last chance and it's not my job to talk you down from the ledge."

That stung. "I wasn't asking you to," I mumbled.

"So you're still there! Take my hand and lead us out."

I pulled myself together. "You'll have to follow my voice, babe. Your memories are too intense for me."

We resumed our slow progress. I was sick of crawling, sick of the dark, sick of this lightless horrid existence, disgusted to the pit of my soul with who and what I was. Was there no end to this labyrinth of pipes?

"Wait." I'd brushed by something. Something metal buried in the earth.

"What is it?"

"I think it's—" I groped about, trying to get a sense of the thing's shape. "I think it's a cast-iron gatepost. Here. Wait. Let me climb up and take a look."

Relinquishing my grip on the pipe, I seized hold of the object and stuck my head out of the ground. I emerged at the gate of an iron fence framing the minuscule front yard of a house on Ripka Street. I could see again! It was so good to feel the clear breath of the world once more that I closed my eyes briefly to savor the sensation.

"How ironic," Euphrosyne said.

"After being so heroic," Thalia said.

"Overcoming his fears," Aglaia said.

"Rescuing the fair maid from terror and durance vile," Cleta said.

"Realizing at last who he is," Phaenna said.

"Beginning that long and difficult road to recovery by finally getting in touch with his innermost feelings," Auxo said.

Hegemone giggled.

"What?" I opened my eyes.

That was when the Corpsegrinder struck. It leapt upon me with stunning force, driving spear-long talons through my head and body. The talons were barbed so that they couldn't be pulled free and they burned like molten metal. "Ahhhh, Cobb," the Corpsegrinder crooned. "Now this is *sweet.*"

I screamed and it drank in those screams, so that only silence escaped into the outside world. I struggled and it made those struggles its own, leaving me to kick myself deeper and deeper into the drowning pools of its identity. With all my will I resisted. It was not enough. I experienced the languorous pleasure of surrender as that very will and resistance were sucked down into my attacker's substance. The distinction between *me* and *it* weakened, strained, dissolved. I was transformed.

I was the Corpsegrinder now.

MANHATTAN IS A virtual school for the dead. Enough people die there every day to keep any number of monsters fed. From the store of memories the Corpsegrinder had stolen from me, I recalled a quiet moment sitting cross-legged on the tin ceiling of a sleaze joint while table dancers entertained Japanese tourists on the floor above and a kobold instructed me on some of the finer points of survival. "The worst thing you can be hunted by," he said, "is yourself."

"Very aphoristic."

"Fuck you. I used to be human too."

"Sorry."

"Apology accepted. Look, I told you about Salamanders. That's a shitty way to go, but at least it's final. When they're done with you, nothing remains. But a Corpsegrinder is a parasite. It has no true identity of its own, so it constructs one from bits and pieces of everything that's unpleasant within you. Your basic greeds and lusts. It gives you a particularly nasty sort of immortality. Remember that old cartoon? This hideous toad saying 'Kiss me and live forever—you'll be a toad, but you'll live forever.'" He grimaced. "If you get the choice, go with the Salamander."

"So what's this business about hunting myself?"

"Sometimes a Corpsegrinder will rip you in two and let half escape. For a while."

"Why?"

"I dunno. Maybe it likes to play with its food. Ever watch a cat torture a mouse? Maybe it thinks it's fun."

From a million miles away, I thought: So now I know what's happened to me. I'd made quite a run of it, but now it was over. It didn't matter. All that mattered was the hoard of memories, glorious memories, into which I'd been dumped. I wallowed in them, picking out here a winter sunset and there the pain of a jellyfish sting when I was nine. So what if I was already beginning to dissolve? I was intoxicated, drunk, stoned with the raw stuff of experience. I was high on life.

Then the Widow climbed up the gatepost looking for me.

"Cobb?"

The Corpsegrinder had moved up the fence to a more comfortable spot in which to digest me. When it saw the Widow, it reflexively parked me in a memory of a gray drizzly day in a Ford Fiesta outside of 30th Street Station. The engine was going and the heater and the windshield wiper too, so I snapped on the radio to mask their noise. Beethoven filled the car, the Moonlight Sonata.

"That's bullshit, babe," I said. "You know how much I have invested in you? I could buy two good whores for what that dress cost."

She refused to meet my eyes. In a whine that set my teeth on edge, she said, "Danny, can't you see that it's over between us?"

"Look, babe, let's not argue in the parking lot, okay?" I was trying hard to be reasonable. "Not with people walking by and listening. We'll go someplace private where we can talk this over calmly, like two civilized human beings."

She shifted slightly in the seat and adjusted her skirt with a little tug. Drawing attention to her long legs and fine ass. Making it hard for me to think straight. The bitch really knew how to twist the knife. Even now, crying and begging, she was aware of how it turned me on. And even though I hated being aroused by her little act, I was. The sex was always best after an argument; it made her sluttish.

I clenched my anger in one hand and fisted my pocket with it. Thinking how much I'd like to up and give her a shot. She was begging for it. Secretly, maybe, it was what she wanted; I'd often suspected she'd enjoy being hit. It was too late to act on the impulse, though. The memory was playing out like a tape, immutable, unstoppable.

All the while, like a hallucination or the screen of a television set receiving conflicting signals, I could see the Widow, frozen with fear half in and half out of the ground. She quivered like an acetylene flame. In the memory she was saying something, but with the shift in my emotions came a corresponding warping-away of perception. The train station, car, the windshield wipers and music, all faded to a murmur in my consciousness.

Tentacles whipped around the Widow. She was caught. She struggled helplessly, deliciously. The Corpsegrinder's emotions pulsed through me and to my remote horror I found that they were identical to my own. I *wanted* the Widow, wanted her so bad there were no words for it. I wanted to clutch her to me so tightly her ribs would splinter and for just this once she'd know it was real. I wanted to own her. To possess her. To put an end to all her little games. To know her every thought and secret, down to the very bottom of her being.

No more lies, babe, I thought, no more evasions. You're mine now.

So perfectly in synch was I with the Corpsegrinder's desires that it shifted its primary consciousness back into the liquid sphere of memory, where it hung smug and lazy, watching, a voyeur with a willing agent. I was in control of the autonomous functions now. I reshaped the tentacles, merging and recombining them into two strong arms. The claws and talons that clutched the fence I made legs again. The exterior of the Corpsegrinder I morphed into human semblance, save for that great mass of memories sprouting from our back like a bloated spider-sack. Last of all I made the head.

I gave it my own face.

"Surprised to see me again, babe?" I leered.

Her expression was not so much fearful as disappointed. "No," she said wearily. "Deep down, I guess I always knew you'd be back."

As I drew the Widow closer, I distantly knew that all that held me to the Corpsegrinder in that instant was our common store of memories and my determination not to lose them again. That was enough, though. I pushed my face into hers, forcing open her mouth. Energies flowed between us like a feast of tongues.

I prepared to drink her in.

There were no barriers between us. This was an experience as intense as when, making love, you lose all track of which body is your own and thought dissolves into the animal moment. For a giddy instant I was no less her than I was myself. I was the Widow staring fascinated into the filthy depths of my psyche. She was myself witnessing her astonishment as she realized exactly how little I had ever known her. We both saw her freeze still to the core with horror. Horror not of what I was doing.

But of what I was.

I can't take any credit for what happened then. It was only an impulse, a spasm of the emotions, a sudden and unexpected clarity of vision. Can a single flash of decency redeem a life like mine? I don't believe it. I refuse to believe it.

Had there been time for second thoughts, things might well have gone differently. But there was no time to think. There was only time enough to feel an upwelling of revulsion, a visceral desire to be anybody or anything but my own loathsome self, a profound and total yearning to be quit of the burden of such memories as were mine. An aching need to *just once* do the moral thing.

I let go.

Bobbing gently, the swollen corpus of my past floated up and away, carrying with it the parasitic Corpsegrinder. Everything I had spent all my life accumulating fled from me. It went up like a balloon, spinning, dwindling... gone.

Leaving me only what few flat memories I have narrated here.

I screamed.

And then I cried.

I don't know how long I clung to the fence, mourning my loss. But when I gathered myself together, the Widow was still there.

"Danny," the Widow said. She didn't touch me. "Danny, I'm sorry."

I'd almost rather that she had abandoned me. How do you apologize for sins you can no longer remember? For having been someone who, however reprehensible, is gone forever? How can you expect forgiveness from somebody you have forgotten so completely you don't even know her name? I felt twisted with shame and misery. "Look," I said. "I know I've behaved badly. More than badly. But there ought to be some way to make it up to you. For, you know, everything. Somehow. I mean—"

What do you say to somebody who's seen to the bottom of your wretched and inadequate soul?

"I want to apologize," I said.

With something very close to compassion, the Widow said, "It's too late for that, Danny. It's over. Everything's over. You and I only ever had the one trait in common. We neither of us could ever let go of anything. Small wonder we're back together again. But don't you see, it doesn't matter what you want or don't want—you're not going to get it. Not now. You had your chance. It's too late to make things right." Then she stopped, aghast at what she had just said.

But we both knew she had spoken the truth.

"Widow," I said as gently as I could, "I'm sure Charlie—"

"Shut up."

I shut up.

The Widow closed her eyes and swayed, as if in a wind. A ripple ran through her and when it was gone her features were simpler, more schematic, less recognizably human. She was already beginning to surrender the anthropomorphic.

I tried again. "Widow…" Reaching out my guilty hand to her.

She stiffened but did not draw away. Our fingers touched, twined, mated. "Elizabeth," she said at last. "My name is Elizabeth Connelly."

WE HUDDLED TOGETHER on the ceiling of the Roxy through the dawn and the blank horror that is day. When sunset brought us conscious again, we talked through half the night before making the one decision we knew all along that we'd have to make.

It took us almost an hour to reach the Seven Sisters and climb down to the highest point of Thalia.

We stood holding hands at the top of the mast. Radio waves were gushing out from under us like a great wind. It was all we could do to keep from being blown away.

Underfoot, Thalia was happily chatting with her sisters. Typically, at our moment of greatest resolve, they gave us not the slightest indication of interest. But they were all listening to us. Don't ask me how I knew.

"Cobb?" Elizabeth said. "I'm afraid."

"Yeah, me too."

A long silence, and then she said, "Let me go first. If you go first, I won't have the nerve."

"Okay."

She took a deep breath—funny, if you think about it—and then she let go, and fell into the sky.

First she was like a kite, and then a scrap of paper, and finally she was a rapidly tumbling speck. I stood for a long time watching her falling, dwindling, until she was lost in the background flicker of the universe, just one more spark in infinity.

She was gone and I couldn't help wondering if she had ever really been there at all. Had the Widow truly been Elizabeth Connelly? Or was she just another fragment of my shattered self, a bundle of related memories that I had to come to terms with before I could bring myself to finally let go?

A vast emptiness seemed to spread itself through all of existence. I clutched the mast spasmodically then, and thought: *I can't!*

But the moment passed. I've got a lot of questions, and there aren't any answers here. In just another instant, I'll let go and follow Elizabeth (if Elizabeth she was) into the night. I will fall forever and I will be converted to background radiation, smeared ever thinner and cooler across the universe, a smooth, uniform, and universal message that has only one decode. Let Thalia carry my story to whoever cares to listen. I won't be here for it.

It's time to go now. Time and then some to leave. I'm frightened, and I'm going.

Now.

# LOVESTORY

*James Patrick Kelly*

### ONE

MAM SHOULD HAVE guessed something was wrong as soon as the father entered the nursery. His ears were slanted back, his ruby fur fluffed. He smelled as sad as a cracked egg. But Mam ignored him, skimming her reading finger down the leaf of her lovestory. It was about a family just like theirs, except that they lived in a big house in the city with a pool in every room and lots of robot servants. That family loved one another, but bad people kept trying to drive them apart.

"How's the scrap tonight?" The father shut the door behind him as if it were made of glass.

It was then that Mam realized the mother wasn't with him. "What is it?" She bent the corner of the leaf back to mark her place. The father and mother always visited together. She loosened her grip on the lovestory and it rewound into its watertight case.

"Wa-wa, it's the lucky father!" The scrap tumbled out of the dark corner where she had been hiding and hugged the father's legs. "Luck always, Pa-pa-*pa!*" The father staggered, almost toppled onto the damp, spongy rug, but then caught himself. The scrap had been running wild all night, talking back to the jokestory she was only half-watching on the tell, choreographing battles with her mechanical ants, making up nonsense songs, trying to crawl in and out of Mam's pouch for no good reason. It was almost dawn and the scrap was still skittering around the nursery like a loose button.

"Oh, when the father swims near," sang the scrap, "and he comes up for air, all the families cheer."

He reached down, scooped her into his arms and smoothed her silky brown fur, which was wet where it had touched the floor. It had only been in the last month that the scrap had let anyone but Mam hold her. Now she happily licked the father's face.

"Who's been teaching you rhyme?" he said. "Your mam?" He laughed then, but his wide, yellow eyes were empty.

"Mam is fat and Mam is slow. If I'm a brat, well, she don't know."

"Hush, little scrap," said the father. "Your tongue is so long we might have to cut some off." He snipped two fingers at her.

"Eeep!" The scrap wriggled in his arms and he set her down. She scrambled across the room to Mam's settle and would've wormed into her pouch, but Mam was in no mood and cuffed her lightly away. The scrap was almost a tween, too old for such clowning. Soon it would be time for them to part; she was giving Mam stretch marks.

"Silmien, what *is* it?" Mam waved at the tell to turn the scrap's annoying jokestory off. "Something has happened."

The father stiffened when she named him. This was no longer idle family chatter; by saying his name, she had made a truth claim on her mate. For a moment, she thought he might not answer, as was his right. But whatever it was, he must have wanted to tell her or why else had he come to them?

"It's Valun," he said. "She's gone."

"Gone?" said Mam. "Where?"

"To Pelotto." There was an angry stink to the father now. "She went to Pelotto, to live with the aliens."

"Pelotto?" Mam was confused. "But the scrap is almost weaned."

"Obviously," said the father. "She knows that."

Mam was confused. If she knew, then how could she leave? "What about her patients?"

"Gone?" The scrap whimpered. "Mother gone, mother?"

"Who will give the scrap her name?" Mam reached an arm around the little one to comfort her. "And it's time to quicken the new baby. The mother, Valun and I have to…" She paused, uneasy talking about birthing with the father. "What about the baby?" she said weakly.

"Don't you understand? She has left us." The father's anger was not only in his scent, but spilled over into his words. "You. Me. She has left the family. She's an out, now. Or maybe the aliens are her family."

Mam rose from her settle. She felt as if she were hefting a great weight; if she did not bear the load, the whole house might collapse around them. "This is my fault," she said. "She does not trust me to carry the baby, nurse it into a scrap."

"It's not you!" the father shouted. "It's *her*." The scrap shrank from the crack of his voice. "We're still here, aren't we? Where is she?"

Mam stooped to let the scrap wriggle into the pouch.

"She thinks I'm stupid," said Mam. She felt the moisture in the rug creep between her toes. "She has nothing to say to me anymore."

"That's not true."

"I heard her tell you. And that all I read are lovestories."

The father squished across the room to her then, and she let him stroke the short fur on her foreleg. She knew he meant to comfort, but this unaccustomed closeness felt like more weight that she must bear. "This has gone very badly," he said. He brought his face up to hers. "I'm sorry. It's probably *my* fault that she's gone." He smelled as sincere as newly split wood and Mam remembered when she had fallen in love with them, back at the gardens. Then it was only Valun and Silmien and her. "Something I did, or didn't do. Maybe we should've stayed in the city, I don't know. It has nothing to do with you, though. Or the scrap."

"But what will happen to the new baby?" Mam said. Her voice sounded very small, even to her.

"I love you, Mam." The father pricked his ears forward, giving her complete attention. "Maybe Valun loves you too, in her way. But I don't think you and I will ever see that baby."

Mam felt the scrap shiver inside her.

The father lingered for a few moments more, although everything important had been said. Mam coaxed the scrap out of hiding and she slipped her head from the pouch. She stared at the father as he rubbed the fluff around her nose, saying nothing. The scrap had just started her tween scents, another sign that it was time for them to part; she gave off the thin, bright smell of fear, sharp as a razor. The father made warbling sounds and her edge dulled a little. Then he licked the side of her face. He straightened and took Mam by surprise when he gave her an abrupt good-day lick, too. "I'm sorry, Mam," he said, and then he was gone.

Mam collapsed onto her settle. The heated cushion was blood hot, but did little to ease the chill that gripped her neck. For a moment she sat, brittle as ice, unsure what to do. The next ten minutes without Valun were harder to face than the next ten years. In ten years they'd probably be dead, Mam and the father and the mother, their story forgotten. But just now Valun's absence was a hole in Mam's life that was too wide to cross over. Then the scrap stirred restlessly against her.

"Time to sleep," Mam said, tugging at the scrap's left ear. "Almost dawn." No matter what happened, she was still this one's mam.

The scrap shook her head. "Not tired not."

"You want the sun to scratch your eyes out?" Mam rippled her stomach muscles, squeezing her from the pouch like a seed. The scrap mewled and then slopped across the wet rug as if she had no bones. "You pick up your things and get ready." Mam gave the scrap a nudge with her foot. She might have indulged the little one; after all, the scrap had just lost her mother. But then Mam had just lost her mate and there was nobody to indulge her. "Make sure you clear all your projects off the tell."

The scrap formed up her ants and marched the little robots back into the drawer of her settle. She ejected her ID from the tell, flipped it onto the tangle of ants and shut the drawer. She sorted the pillows she had formed into a nest. She turned off the pump that circulated water through her rug, dove into the nursery's shallow egg-shaped pool at the narrow end and immediately slid out at the wide end. "Does this mean I can't go to the gardens?" She shook the water from her fur.

"Of course not. This has nothing to do with growing up. You'll be a tween soon, too big for the pouch."

"But what about my name?"

"The father will give you one. I'll help him."

"Won't be the same."

"No." Mam hesitated. "But it will be enough."

The scrap smoothed the fur flat against her chest. She was almost two and her coat had begun to turn the color of her mother's: blood red, deepening like a sunset. "They're the parents," she said. "They were supposed to take care of us."

Mam tried not to resent her. The scrap *had* been taken care of. She was about to leave the family, go off to the gardens to live. She'd fall in love with a father and a mam and start a new family. It was Mam who had not been taken care of, Mam and the new baby. "They did their best."

"I wish she was dead," said the scrap. "Dead, red, spread on a bed." She was careful as she wriggled into Mam's pouch. "Do you think she'll come to visit me at the gardens?"

"I don't know." Mam realized then that she didn't know anything about Valun. The mother had always been restless, yes, and being a doctor in this little nowhere had only made things worse. But how could aliens be more important than the family? "But I'll come visit."

"You have to, you," said the scrap. "You're my old, fat Mam."

"That's right." Mam tickled her behind the ears. "And I will never leave you." Although she knew that the scrap would leave her soon enough, just like she had left her mam.

Mam got up to darken the windows against the rising sun. It was a chore getting around; the scrap bobbed heavily against her belly as she crossed the room. In the last few days, the scrap had begun to doze off on her own settle; Mam was once again getting used to the luxury of an uninterrupted day's sleep. But it felt right to carry the little one just now, to keep her close.

Mam waddled back to her settle through the soothing gloom. She wasn't tired and with the scrap in the pouch, it was hard to find a comfortable position. The scrap was fidgety too. Mam wondered whether the father was sleeping and decided he was probably not. He'd be making a story about what had happened, trying to understand. And the mother? No, Valun wasn't a mother any more. She was an out. Mam focused on the gurgle of water in the pool and tried to let the sound quench her thoughts.

There were never aliens in the kinds of lovestories Mam liked to read. Fathers and mothers might run off to be an out for a while, but everyone would be so unhappy that they'd come back at the end. Of course, mams never ran. Or else one of the three mates might die and the others would go to the city and try to find a good out to take their place.

She started when the scrap's lips brushed the tender skin near her nipple. At first she thought it was an accident, but then she felt it again, tentative but clearly deliberate, a question posed as loving touch. Her first impulse was to push her away; the scrap had fed that afternoon. But as the nubbly little tongue probed the edges of her aureole, Mam knew that it wasn't hunger that the scrap sought to ease. It was grief. Mam shivered and the underfur on her neck bristled. Had the scrap tried to nurse out of turn on any other day, Mam would certainly have shaken her from the pouch. But this day they had each been wounded; this feeding would ease not only the scrap's pain but Mam's as well. It was something they could do for each other— maybe the only thing. With a twitch of excitement, she felt her milk letting down. It wasn't much, it wasn't time, but the scrap had such a warm, clever mouth.

"Oh," said Mam. "*Oh*."

The father had told her once that, when she nursed, chemicals flooded her brain and seeped into her milk. He said this was how Mam was making the scrap into who she was. He told her the names of all the chemicals, but she had forgotten them. Mam had a simpler explanation. She was a mam, which meant that her emotions were much bigger than she was, so they spilled onto whoever was nearest. The mother always used to say that she was a different person when she was with Mam, because of her smell. Even the father relaxed when the family came together. But it was the scrap Mam was closest to, into whom she had most often poured the overflow of feelings. Now, as they bonded for one of the last times, perhaps *the* last time, Mam was filled with ecstasy and regret. Of all the pleasure the scrap had given her, this was the most carnal. When she sucked, she made a wet, little sound, between a squeak and a click, that made the top of Mam's head tingle. Mam enfolded her bulging pouch with both arms and shifted the scrap slightly so that she came at the nipple from a different angle. She could smell the bloom of her own excitement, heady as wine, thick as mud. She thought she might scream—but what would the father say if he heard her through the walls? He would not understand why she was taking pleasure with the scrap on this night of all nights. He would... not... understand. When the urgent sound finally welled up from the deepest part of her, she closed her throat and strangled it. "My... little," she gasped, and it was as if Valun had never gone, the aliens had never come to plague the families with their wicked wisdom. "My little... *scrap.*"

The weight lifted from her and for a brief, never-ending moment, she felt as light as air.

## Two

SILMIEN WAS PROUD of his scrap. "Tevul," he corrected himself, cupping the name he had given her on his tongue. He was so proud that losing her mother almost didn't matter anymore. He spotted her and some of her friends splashing in the pond across the bone garden. She was so quick, so carefree, so beautiful in the chill, blue light of the mothermoon.

"What?" Mam had stopped to smell the sweetbind that wound through the skeleton of someone's long dead ancestor; she hurried over to him. "What?"

He pointed. Mam was already nearsighted from spending so much time indoors, the curse of the nursery. Distance seemed to confuse her. "She hasn't seen us yet," he said.

"The scrap?"

"The tween," said Silmien. "Tevul."

Silmien was proud of Mam, too. She had been a good parent, considering everything that had happened. After all, Tevul was their firstborn. Silmien knew just how lonely the long rainy season had been for Mam, especially since she didn't exactly understand about Valun and the aliens.

But that wasn't right. Silmien was always surprised at how much Mam understood, even though she did not follow the news or query the tell. She engaged the world by means that were mysterious to him. If she did not always reach for the complex, her grasp of essentials was firm. Silmien drew strength from her trust in him—and her patience. Even though it was a burden on her not to be nursing a scrap, she had never once nagged him to start looking for a mother to take Valun's place.

"I'm glad you came tonight, Mam." He wanted to put an arm around her, but he knew that would make her uncomfortable. She was a mam, not a mother. Instead he stooped and picked a pink buttonbright and offered it to her. She accepted it solemnly and tucked it behind her ear.

There was something about visiting the gardens that revived Silmien, burned troubles away like morning mist. It was not only nostalgia for that simple time when Valun had chosen him and he had found Mam. It was the scent of the flowers and ponds, of mulch and moss, of the golden musk of old parents, the sharp, hormone-laden perfume of tweens and the round, honest stink of chickens. It was the fathermoon chasing the mothermoon across an enormous sky, the family obelisks pointing like fingers toward the stars. Valun always used to tease him about being such a romantic, but wasn't that a father's job, to dream, to give shape to the mud? The garden was the place where families began and ended, where futures were spun, lives honored.

"Over here!" Tevul had finally caught sight of them. "Come meet my friends!"

Silmien waved back. "More introductions," he whispered to Mam. "I don't recognize a single face in this batch." It was only his second visit of the dry season, but he was already having trouble keeping them all straight. Although he was glad Tevul was popular, he supposed he resented these fortunate tweens for stealing his little scrap away from him. Tevul, he reminded himself again, Tevul. At home, he and Mam still called her *the scrap*. "Come along, Mam. Just a long smile and short bow and we'll have her to ourselves."

"Not me," said Mam. "You."

Silmien blinked in surprise. There was that odd smell again, a dusty staleness, like the corner of an empty closet. If Valun had been here, she would have known immediately what to do, but then if she were here, Mam wouldn't be. "Nonsense," said Silmien. "We're her family."

Mam crouched abruptly, making herself as small as possible. "Doesn't matter." She smoothed her sagging pouch to her belly self-consciously.

"Why did you come then," said Silmien, "if not to see Tevul?"

"You wanted me."

"Mam, the scrap wants you too."

"I'm not here." Mam was staring at her feet.

They had to stop arguing then, because a clutch of old parents entered the garden, giggling and stroking the bones. One, a father with thin, cement-colored fur, noticed the buttonbright behind Mam's ear and bent to pick one for himself. His companions teased him good-naturedly about acting his age. Then a shriveled mam popped one of the flowers into her mouth, chewed a few times, and spat it at the father. Everyone laughed except Silmien and Mam. Ordinarily, he enjoyed the loopy antics of the old, but now he chafed at the interruption.

"I'll bring Tevul to you," he whispered to Mam. "Is that what you want?"

She made no reply. She curled her long toes into the damp soil as if she were growing roots.

Silmien grunted and left her. Mam was not getting any easier to live with. She was moody and stubborn and often reeked of self-loathing. Yet he had stuck by her, given her every consideration. Not once, since he had first told her about Valun, had he let his true feelings show. It struck him that he ought to be proud of himself, too. It was small comfort, but without a mate to share his life, all he had were glimmers and wisps.

"Pa-pa-*pa*." Tevul hauled herself partly out of the pond and perched on the grassy bank. "My father, Silmien." Her glistening coat clung to her body, making her as streamlined as a rocket. She must have grown four or five centimeters since the solstice. "Here is Mika. Tilantree. Kujalla. Karmi. Jotan. And Putket." Tevul indicated each of her friends by splashing with her foot in their direction. Karmi and Jotan and Putket were standing in the shallows and acknowledged him with polite but not

particularly warm bows. Kujalla—or was it Tilantree?—
was treading water in the deep; she just stared at him.
Only Mika clambered up the bank of the pond to greet
him properly.

"Silmien," said Mika as they crossed hands. "It is truly
an honor to meet you."

"It is you who honor me," Silmien murmured. The
tween's effusiveness embarrassed him.

"Tevul tells us that you write stories."

Silmien shot Tevul a glance; she returned his gaze innocently. "I write many things," he said. "Mostly histories."

"Lovestories?" said Mika.

Tilantree's head disappeared beneath the surface of the
pond.

"I wouldn't call them lovestories, exactly," Silmien said.
"I don't like sentiment. But I do write about families sometimes, yes."

Tilantree surfaced abruptly, splashing about and making
rude, blustery sounds. The three standing tweens smirked
at her.

"Silmien has been on the tell," said Tevul. "Write,
bright, show me the light."

"My mam was on the tell last year," said one of the
standing tweens, "and she's a stupid old log."

"Even aliens get on the tell now," said another.

"Have you written any lovestories about aliens?" Mika
was smirking too.

With a sick lurch, Silmien realized what was going on.
The tweens were making fun of him—and Tevul. Only
his trusting little scrap didn't get it. He wondered if the
reason she was always in the middle of a crowd was not
because she was popular, but because she was a freak.

"Can't write lovestories about aliens." Tilantree rolled
onto her back.

"Why not?" said Tevul.

She did not reply. Instead, she sucked in a mouthful of pond water and then spat it straight up in the air. The three standing tweens spoke for her.

"Their mothers are mams."

"*Perverts.*"

"Two, few, haven't a clue. Isn't that right, Tevul?"

The air was suddenly vinegary with tween scorn. Tevul seemed taken aback by the turn of the conversation. She drew her knees to her chest and looked to Silmien, as if he could control things here in the gardens the way he had at home.

"No," he said, coming around the pond to Tevul. "I haven't written about the aliens yet." His voice rose from the deepest part of him. "But I've thought a lot about them." He could feel his scent glands swell with anger and imagined his stink sticking its claw into them. "Unlike you, Tilantree." He singled out the floating tween as the leader of this cruel little gang. "Maybe you should try it." He reached Tevul, tugged her to her feet, and pulled her to him. "You see, they're our future. They're calling us to grow up and join the universe, all of us, tweens and families and outs and the old. If they really are perverts as you say, then that's what we will be, someday. I suppose that's a big thought to fit into a small mind." He looked down at his scrap. "What do you say, Tevul?"

"I don't know what you're talking about." Her eyes were huge as the mothermoon.

"Then maybe we should discuss this further." He bowed to the others. "Luck always." He nudged Tevul toward the bone garden.

Silmien heard the tweens snickering behind him. Tevul heard it too; her gait stiffened, as if she had sand in her joints. He wondered if the next time he visited her, she might be like them. Tilantree and her friends had the next four years to twist his scrap to their shallow thinking. The family had made her a tween, but the garden would make her into a mother. Silmien felt removed from himself as they passed the wall built of skulls that marked the boundary of the bone garden. No Tevul. No Valun. Mam a stranger. He could not believe that he had defended the aliens to the tweens. That was Valun talking, not him. He hated the aliens for luring her away from him. It was almost as if they had seduced her. He shivered; maybe they *were* perverted. Besides, he must have sounded the pompous fool. Who was he to be speaking of small minds? He was as ordinary as a spoon.

"Well?" said Tevul.

"Well what?"

"Pa-*pa*, you embarrassed me, pa."

He sighed. "I suppose I did."

"Is this the way you're going to be?" said Tevul. "Because if it is..."

"No, I'll mind." He licked two fingers and rubbed them on her cheekbone. "But are you sure they're your friends?"

"*Silmien!*"

"I just thought I'd ask."

"If they're not, it's your fault." She skipped ahead down the path and then turned on him, blocking his way. "Why do you always have to bring Mam?"

"What do you mean, always?" He looked over her shoulder. The old parents had doddered off, but Mam had not moved. Even though she was still a good thirty meters away, he lowered his voice. "It's only been three times and she wanted to see you."

"Why can't she wait until I come home for a visit? Besides, I don't have anything to say to her. What am I supposed to do, play a game of fish and snakes? Climb into her fruity old pouch? I'm not a scrap anymore!"

"She's unhappy, Tevul. She feels unwanted, useless."

"Don't use *my* name, because there's nothing *I* can do about that." Tevul's ears went flat against her head. "It's strange, you two here together. When the others have visitors, they get their mothers and fathers. She's not my mother."

"No," he said, "she's not."

Tevul's stern facade crumbled then and she broke down, quietly but completely, just as her mother had on the night she had left him. And he hadn't seen it coming; Silmien cursed himself for having stones up his nose and knotholes for eyes. Tevul's body was wracked by sobs and she keened into his chest so that Mam wouldn't hear. "They say such mean things. They say that Mam picked my name, not you, and that she named me after a character in a stupid lovestory. I try to joke along with them so they won't make a joke of me, but then they start in about my mother, they say that because she's a doctor... that the aliens..." She turned a scared face up to him, her scent was bitter and smoky. "What happened to the baby, pa-pa? Is he still in her? I want to *know*. It's not fair that I never got to see you pull him from mother and bring him to Mam, that's what's supposed to happen, isn't it, not all the disgusting things they keep saying, and I'm supposed to be there, only I wasn't because *she* went to the aliens, it's not *my* fault, I'm tired of being different, I want to be the same, in a real family like Tilantree, the same." She caught her breath, sniffed, and then rubbed her face into his stubby fur on his chest. "No blame, no shame," she said. "The same." She shuddered, and the hysterics passed, as cleanly as a summer squall.

He bent down and licked the top of her head. "Are you unhappy here, my beautiful little Tevul?"

She thought about it, then sniffed and straightened her dignity. "This is the world," she said. "There is nowhere else."

The orange fathermoon was up now, resuming his futile chase of the mothermoon. It was the brightest part of the night, when the two parent moons and their billion star scraps cast a light like spilled milk. A stirring along a hedge of bunchbead, where a farmbot was harvesting the dangling clusters of fruit, distracted Silmien momentarily.

"I am proud of you," he said. It wasn't what he wanted to say, but he couldn't think of anything better. When the robot passed them, he dipped into its hopper, pulled out a handful of bunchbead, and offered them to Tevul. She took some and smiled. Silence slid between them. Somewhere in the distance, the chickens were singing.

Tevul watched the stars as she ate. "Where is Mars?" she said at last.

"It's too far away." Silmien looked up. "We can't see it,"

"I know that, but where is it?"

"Kadut showed me their star last week." He came up behind her and, resting his elbow on her shoulder, pointed so that she could sight along his forearm. "It's in The Mask, there."

"Why did they come, the aliens?"

"They want to help, I guess. That's what they say."

"I have to get back soon," said Tevul. "Let's go see Mam."

Tevul was very polite to Mam and Silmien could see that the visit cheered Mam up. Mam insisted on waiting while Silmien walked Tevul back to her burrow, but he finally understood that this was what both of them wanted. Back at the burrow, Tevul showed him a lifestory she was working on. It was about Ollut, the scientist who had first identified oestrophins, the hormones that determined which females became mothers and which mams. Silmien was impressed by Tevul's writing and how much she had absorbed from the teaching tells in just one season. She was quick, like her mother. Tevul promised to copy her working draft onto the tell, so he could follow along with her research. As he was getting ready to leave, her roommate Laivan came in. To his relief, Silmien remembered her name. They chatted briefly. Silmien was on his guard for any sign of mockery, but there wasn't any. Laivan seemed to like Tevul and, for her sake, tolerated his intrusion into their privacy.

"Luck always," he said. "To both of you." And then he left.

It was only later that his anger caught up with him. Mam had fallen asleep, lulled by the whoosh of the go-to through the tunnels, so there was no one to notice when he began to wring his hands and squirm on his seat. First he was angry at himself, then Tilantree, then Tevul's teachers, then at himself again, until finally his outrage settled on Valun.

She had been the leader of their family. Where she jumped, they followed, even if they landed in mud. It had been her idea to move to the paddies, where the air was thick and the water tasted of the swamp. Farmers needed doctors, too, she said. She had been the one who healed the family's wounds as well, the one they all talked to. Yet when she left them, she wouldn't say exactly why she was going, only that there was something important she had to find out from the aliens. Valun had ripped his life apart, left him incomplete, but he had tried not to hurt her the way she had hurt him. Speakers from the tell had interviewed him about Valun and about his life now. In all his statements, he had protected her. Her work with the aliens was important, he said, and he supported it, as all the families must. There were so many diseases to be cured, so much pain to be eased. It was an honor that she had been chosen. If he had followed a different path, it was because he was a different person, not a better one. He had done all this, he realized now, not because it was the right thing to do, but because he still loved her.

Only Silmien had not realized how much she had hurt Tevul. Valun hadn't visited the gardens, hadn't even copied a message to the tell. Silmien had long since decided that Valun left the family because she had been bored with him, and maybe he could understand that. But no mother ought to be bored with her own tween. For an hour, his thoughts were as blinding as the noonday sun.

Eventually, Silmien had to calm himself. Their stop was coming up and he'd have to rouse Mam soon. What was it Tevul had said? *This was the world.* What did he have to give to it? A new family? The truth was he couldn't imagine some poor out taking Valun's place. But life was too short, twenty years from pouch to bone garden. A new family then—and afterward, he'd give the world his story. He would need to get some distance from Valun; he could see that. But eventually he would write of how she had hurt him and Mam and Tevul. He would tell how he had borne the pain, like a mam carries a scrap. He paused, admiring the image. No, not a lovestory—the story of how he had suffered. Because of her.

Because of Valun and the aliens.

### THREE

VALUN THOUGHT SHE could feel the baby swimming inside her. Impossible. The baby was no bigger than her thumb. He was blind and hairless and weak and brainless, or nearly so. Couldn't swim, didn't even know that he was alive.

The baby wasn't moving; she knew that the waves she felt were made by the muscles of her own uterus. The contractions weren't painful, more like the lurch of flying through turbulence. Only this was predictable turbulence, a storm on a schedule. The contractions were coming more frequently, despite her fierce concentration. It was what distressed her most about giving birth. Valun had gotten used to being in control, especially of her own body.

The humans had almost complete control of their bodies; it was their astonishing medicine that had drawn her to them. They had escaped from nature, vanquished diseases, stretched life spans to the brink of immortality. They managed their emotions, commanded their thoughts, summoned inspiration at will. And on those rare occasions when they reproduced... well, they could play their genome like a flute. There were no stupid humans, no wasted space in their population. No mother was inconvenienced by labor...

Another lurch. Too soon for another contraction. Then she realized that it was the go-to decelerating. Coming to a station. The readout in the front bulkhead lit up. Uskoon. Less than half an hour until she was home. Plenty of time.

She didn't want to be traveling while she was in labor, but this was the only way to have the baby on her terms. Mothers were supposed to give birth in the nursery with their happy families gathered around them. She would be in the nursery soon enough, only she doubted that the family would be all that happy to see her. Mam would be vastly relieved—maybe that was within sight of happiness. Silmien, however, would be furious that she was forcing this baby on him and then leaving him to care for it with Mam. He'd strike the martyr's pose, maybe even write about it. The scrap? She probably hated Valun. Valun would've hated *her* mother, had she done something like this when she was a tween. Tweens' deepest feelings were for themselves; she'd grow out of it. Valun had heard that he had named her Tevul, after the heroine of that story he liked so much. Was it *Drinking the Rain?* No, the other one. But then Silmien liked too many stories too much. The world was not a story.

Thinking about them made Valun feel like the loneliest person in the universe. Part of her desperately wanted to go back to stay. She longed to sleep and eat and breathe again with her family. But not to talk; if she told them what she had learned it might destroy them. Living with the humans had not made her happy at all. Indeed, most of the outs in Pelotto were miserable.

Valun now knew what she had only suspected when she left the family. The world they had been born into was a lie. There was no reason for the laws of birth order. No reason why she or Silmien or Mam or their little scraps should have such brutally short life spans. Mams could be mothers, mothers could nurse, outs could have babies.

No reason why there had to be families at all.

Of course, the humans did not advocate change. They offered only information; it was up to each intelligent species to decide how to use it. Except their message was corrosive as acid. Everything was negotiable. Reality was a decision—and no one here was making it.

This idea had infected Valun's imagination. Even if all the families took from the humans was the ability to prolong lives, the rigid structure of their culture must surely crumble. She wasn't sure what would come after, or who. Perhaps those people—those outs—would be happy. But how could anyone alive today bear to watch the families collapse? Valun didn't want to inflict that future on Silmien and Mam and the scrap, so she had exercised her right of silence and cut them off entirely. If they wanted to learn what she had, they would have to choose, as she had chosen. But her silence had isolated Valun from the ones she loved most. She belonged to no family now, only to herself. She was alone, but it was not what she had wanted. Alone. She drifted alone on the whisper of the go-to.

And dreamed of smells. The sweetness of rain brushing her nose like a lace veil. The honeycup he had put behind her ear; he loved to pick flowers and give them to her. The velvet scent of grass crushed beneath the weight of warm bodies. It had been so long ago that they had made this baby—much more than the traditional two years—that she had forgotten where it happened. Under the moons, out in the fields and her head filled with the husky father smell that was like a lick between the legs. Then the hot, silky bouquet of sex. She felt as if there were a hand inside her, squeezing. The pressure was not cruel, but rather the firm grip of a lover. "Silmien." His name caught in her throat.

Valun started awake at the sound of her own voice. The seat beneath her was damp with the yeasty soup of her birth waters. "Oh, no," she said. Ten more minutes. She focused all her attention on the knot under her belly and the pressure eased—a little. Lucky there were no other passengers in the compartment. *Luck always,* Silmien had said on the night she had left him. Why did he keep popping into her head? Concentrate. She was thinking womb thoughts when the go-to stopped at their station and she walked on candystick legs to their burrow and announced herself to their doorbot.

"*Valun.*" Silmien flung the door open. "I can't believe…" His nostrils flared as he took in her scent. "What have you done?"

"Come home for the holidays." She was trying for a light touch, but when she stepped into the burrow, her body betrayed her and she stumbled. Like crunching through a skim of ice, except that ice seemed to have formed in her head too. When Silmien caught her, she slumped into his arms. She knew she ought to be embarrassed for losing control. But not now—tomorrow, maybe. Felt good not to be standing on her own.

"Tevul!" Silmien shouted. "Mam!"

They carried her to the nursery and laid her on Mam's settle. The ice in her head cracked and began to melt. Something different about the nursery, but she couldn't pick it out at first. The water rug still brimmed, its damp breath filling the room. Lovestory next to Mam's settle. Wedding picture above the pool: Mam and Valun and Silmien. The tell murmured in its familiar corner. Then Valun realized the obvious. No toys, no lines of ants marching up the walls, no miniature settle in the corner. As she had expected, the scrap was home from the gardens for the lunar eclipse, but she was a visitor now and would certainly *not* be staying in the nursery. She was probably sleeping in Valun's settle, next to Silmien. And where would Valun sleep that night?

She shivered and saw her whole family gathered around her, as if she had just fallen out of a tree. Valun giggled. That seemed to fluster them even more. "Tevul." She nodded at the scrap. "Sweet name. Fills the tongue."

Tevul stared as if she thought her mother insane.

"I'm sorry I wasn't at your naming," Valun said. "Life in the gardens agrees with you?"

"It's all right."

"You're learning a lot? Making new friends?"

"What do you want?" said Silmien. "What has happened?"

"Valun, did *they* do this to you?" said Mam. "The aliens?"

"What?" said Tevul. "Someone tell me what's going on."

"She's having the baby," said Silmien. "Smell it!"

"She can't." Tevul looked from Silmien to Mam and finally at Valun. "We just learned that in biology. You have to be exposed to all Mam's pheromones in order to bring an embryo out of latency. You're still supposed to be in diapause."

"This is *their* work," Mam said.

Choosing what to tell them was the hardest thing Valun had ever done. She didn't explain how she had lied about being invited to live with the humans. She had simply gotten tired of waiting and had gone to them on her own. It turned out that was the only way to gain access. The humans never actually invited *anyone;* all the outs in Pelotto were self-selected. Self-condemned. Nor could she tell them about the longevity treatments, the first reward for those who sought human knowledge. The problem was that pregnant mothers could not be rejuvenated, even if their embryos were latent. She said nothing of how the humans had offered to remove the embryo from her womb, and how she had almost left Pelotto then. That was too much story; her time was getting short. She could feel her womb knotting again.

"By the end of the rainy season," she said, "I started to worry that some other family's pheromones might be similar enough to yours to trigger a quickening. But by then, the scrap had already left for the gardens."

"I'm Tevul," said the scrap. "You can say my name."

"So I had already missed the weaning," Valun continued, "and the chance to share scents with all of you. The humans told me that they could end diapause artificially, so I could control when I had the baby. I was sure that you all still wanted him, so I agreed. And here I am. I timed him for the eclipse so that we could all, as a family, I mean..." There was a sudden, vast and inevitable loosening inside of her, and once again she felt her body slipping from her control. Something trickling, tickling through her birth canal.

"You should have told us." Silmien's scent was bitter as a nut. "Why did this have to be a surprise?"

"Because she isn't staying," said Mam. "You want to go back to the aliens, isn't that it? Your *humans*." She made it sound like a curse. "Who are you having this baby for, us or yourself?"

"Mam, I..." Valun pumped her knees together convulsively, then spread them apart wide. "The baby..." She kneaded her belly. "Help, Silmien!"

Silmien and Tevul rallied to her. No question that she could feel the baby now, wriggling, pulling himself into her vagina with his ridiculous little arms. It occurred to her that at this moment in time she had family inside and out. What odd thoughts she was having tonight! She giggled again. The scrap was licking her face and sobbing, "Ma-ma-*ma*. Oh, ma!" Valun could feel Silmien's hands on her vulva, delicately opening her as he had opened her just once before, controlling her as only a father should, fingers basketed to catch the baby. She had forgotten how much pleasure there was in giving birth, ecstasy of mind and body to smell hot, wet life scrabbling toward the world. "*Oh,*" she said, as the final dribble of birth waters leaked out of her, and Silmien held the baby high, offering it to the moons. "Oh."

Silmien brought the baby down so that she and Tevul could see. He was just four centimeters long and almost lost in the palm of his proud father's hand.

"He's so tiny, so pink," said Tevul. "Where are his eyes?"

"They'll grow." Silmien's voice was husky. He brought the baby to his face and cleaned him gently with the tip of his tongue. The baby's mouth opened and closed. The arms wriggled uselessly.

"Stop." The harshness of Mam's voice startled Valun. "What are you doing?"

"Washing the baby," said Silmien.

"There is no baby."

Valun propped herself on an elbow, her head savagely cleared of the moist joy of birth. Mam's scent was like a hook up her nose; Valun had never smelled anyone so angry.

"Here." Silmien offered it to her. "See it."

"A baby has a mother," said Mam. "There is no mother here, only a father. This is an experiment by the humans. Take it back to them. Tell them that it has failed."

"Mam, no, Mam!" said Tevul. "He can only live outside a few minutes. He has to start crawling to your pouch now. Look, he's already shivering."

"Mam," said Silmien. "Our baby will die."

"Then put it on her." Mam turned contemptuously to Valun. "Let her open her pouch. Let *her* love it."

"I have no pouch, Mam," said Valun. "Only you can take care of him." She could see that the baby was distressed. "Please, tell me what you want." He curled into a ball and unrolled with a spasm. "Mam, I'll do anything!" Whatever crumb of brain the baby had must have registered that something was wrong. He should already be threading through his Mam's fur, not still flailing across his father's hand.

"I have nothing to say to an out," said Mam. "I will talk to its mother. Does anyone know where she is?"

"There's no time for this," said Silmien.

"What do you want from me, Totta?" Valun could tell that it had been a long time since anyone had used Mam's name. "I'm Valun. The mother."

Mam's eyes narrowed. "I want you to care about someone else other than yourself," she said. "I want your story to be a lovestory, Valun."

Valun struggled up off the settle. The world spun crazily for a few seconds, but she got it under control. She cupped her hands and extended them to Silmien. "Give him to me."

He brought his hands on top of hers and opened them. Silmien was sobbing as the baby slid onto her palm. Valun had never held a baby before. It weighed less than a berry and yet it was as heavy a burden as she had ever carried. "Will you take my place, Totta?" She nodded at the settle.

Mam hesitated for a moment, but then stretched out, facing Valun. She kept her legs closed, however, and clutched her knees to her chest to cover her pouch. Valun held the baby just above her.

"Totta, Silmien, Tevul, I will stay with you and be this one's mother." Valun astonished herself. In just one season the humans had taught her more about her own biology than she had learned in a lifetime of study. How could she turn away from that knowledge? "I'll be here to give him his name," she continued, "and I won't leave until he has come out of the gardens with his own family. I will do this for the love of him and against my best interests. But I will not sleep with you, Silmien, and there will be no mam baby from this family. No more babies at all. I can't be what you want, and you must all accept that. When Tevul and this scrap are grown up, I will go back to Pelotto again and study with the humans. I hope it won't be too late. Until then, I will study patience."

Mam did not unbend. "I heard many words, but hardly anything of love. What kind of mother are you?"

The baby was on the move again, scrambling up the side of Valun's cupped hands. "I will love this baby because I have given up so much for him," she said. "That is the truth, by my name."

"It's not a happy ending." Mam was still not convinced.

"Totta," said Silmien, "this is not a story."

"Mam." Valun tilted her hands to show her the baby's blunt head. "Someone's hungry."

Mam closed her eyes. Her face was hard with grief as she opened her legs. Valun laid her hands on Mam's belly and let the baby slip through her fingers. He landed on his back but flipped himself immediately. Driven by instinct, guided by scent, he crawled unerringly for the pouch. With each heroic wriggle forward that the baby took, Mam's face softened. When she opened her eyes again, they were bright as stars. Valun tried to imagine herself as a mam. A difference in her family's birth order and it could have been.

Valun could smell the buttery scent of relief melting from Silmien and Tevul. And once the baby had found the nipple, Mam's nursing bliss filled Valun's nose like spilled perfume. All these happy smells made Valun a little ill. This had certainly not turned out the way she had wanted. She wondered what fool had made all those promises. How could Valun keep them?

How could she not?

"Ma-ma-*ma!*" Tevul hugged Valun, just like she used to, but then she was still a tween and had so much to learn about being a mother.

# TOMORROW TOWN

*Kim Newman*

## This way to the Yeer 2000

THE MESSAGE, IN Helvetica typeface, was repeated on
arrow-shaped signs.

"That'll be us, Vanessa," said Richard Jeperson, striding
along the platform in the indicated direction, toting his
shoulder-slung holdall. He tried to feel as if he were about
to time-travel from 1971 to the future, though in practice
he was just changing trains.

Vanessa was distracted by one of the arrow signs, fresh
face arranged in a comely frown. Richard's associate was
a tall redhead in hot pants, halter top, beret, and stack-
heeled go-go boots—all blinding white, as if fresh from the
machine in a soap-powder advert. She drew unconcealed
attention from late-morning passengers milling about the
railway station. Then again, in his lime Day-Glo blazer

edged with gold braid and salmon-pink bell-bottom trousers, so did he. Here in Preston, the fashion watch-word, for the eighteenth consecutive season, was "drab."

"It's misspelled," said Vanessa. "Y-double-E-R."

"No, it's F-O-N-E-T-I-K," he corrected. "Within the next thirty years, English spelling will be rationalized."

"You reckon?" she pouted, skeptically.

"Not my theory," he said, stroking his mandarin mous-taches. "*I* assume the lingo will muddle along with magical illogic as it has since the Yeer Dot. But ortho-graphic reform is a tenet of Tomorrow Town."

"Alliteration. Very Century 21."

They had traveled up from London, sharing a rattly first-class carriage and a welcome magnum of Bollinger with a liberal bishop on a lecture tour billed as "Peace and the Pill" and a working-class playwright revisiting his slag-heap roots. To continue their journey, Richard and Vanessa had to change at Preston.

The arrows led to a guarded gate. The guard wore a British Rail uniform in shiny black plastic with silver high-lights. His oversized cap had a chemical lighting element in the brim.

"You need special tickets, Ms and Mm," said the guard.

"Mm," said Vanessa, amused.

"Ms," Richard buzzed at her.

He searched through his pockets, finally turning up the special tickets. They were strips of foil, like ironed-flat chocolate bar wrappers with punched-out hole patterns. The guard carefully posted the tickets into a slot in a metal box. Gears whirred and lights flashed. The gate came apart and sank into the ground. Richard let Vanessa step through the access first. She seemed to float off, arms out for balance.

"Best not to be left behind, Mm," said the guard.

"Mm," said Richard, agreeing.

He stepped onto the special platform. Beneath his rubber-soled winkle-pickers, a knitted chain mail surface moved on large rollers. It creaked and rippled, but gave a smooth ride.

"I wonder how it manages corners," Vanessa said.

The moving platform conveyed them toward a giant silver bullet. The train of the future hummed slightly, at rest on a single gleaming rail which was raised ten feet above the gravel railbed by chromed tubular trestles. A hatchway was open, lowered to form a ramp.

Richard and Vanessa clambered through the hatch and found themselves in a space little roomier than an Apollo capsule. They half-sat, half-lay in over-padded seats which wobbled on gyro-gimbals. Safety straps automatically snaked across them and drew tight.

"Not sure I'll ever get used to this," said Richard. A strap across his forehead noosed his long, tangled hair, and he had to free a hand to fix it.

Vanessa wriggled to get comfortable, doing a near-horizontal dance as the straps adjusted to her.

With a hiss the ramp raised and became a hatch-cover, then sealed shut. The capsule-cum-carriage had berths for eight, but today they were the only passengers.

A mechanical voice counted down from ten.

"Richard, that's a Dalek," said Vanessa, giggling.

As if offended, the voice stuttered on five, like a record stuck in a groove, then hopped to three.

At zero, they heard a rush of rocketry and the monorail moved off. Richard tensed against the expected g-force slam, but it didn't come. Through thick-glassed slit windows, he saw green countryside passing by at about twenty-five miles per hour. They might have been on a leisurely cycle to the village pub rather than taking the fast train to the future.

"So this is the transport of tomorrow?" said Vanessa.

"A best-guess design," explained Richard. "That's the point of Tomorrow Town. To experiment with the lives we'll all be living at the turn of the century."

"No teleportation then?"

"Don't be silly. Matter transmission is a fantasy. This is a reasonable extrapolation from present-day or in-development technology. The Foundation is rigorous about probabilities. Everything in Tomorrow Town is viable."

The community was funded partially by government research grants and partially by private sources. It was projected that it would soon be a profitable concern, with monies pouring in from scientific wonders developed by the visioneers of the new technomeritocracy. The Foundation, which had proposed the "Town of 2000" experiment, was a think tank, an academic-industrial coalition dedicated to applying to present-day life lessons learned from contemplating the likely future. Tomorrow Town's 2,000-odd citizen-volunteers ("zenvols") were boffins, engineers, social visionaries, health food cranks, and science fiction fans.

Three years ago, when the town was given its charter by the Wilson government, there had been a white heat of publicity: television programs hosted by James Burke and Raymond Baxter, picture features in all the Sunday color supplements, a novelty single ("Take Me to Tomorrow" by Big Thinks and the BBC Radiophonic Workshop) which peaked at Number 2 (prevented from being Top of the Pops by The Crazy World of Arthur Brown's "Fire"), a line of "futopian fashions" from Carnaby Street, a heated debate in the letter columns of *New Scientist* between Arthur C. Clarke (pro), Auberon Waugh (anti), and J. G. Ballard (hard to tell). Then the brouhaha died down and Tomorrow Town was left to get on by itself, mostly forgotten. Until the murder of Varno Zhoule.

Richard Jeperson, agent of the Diogenes Club—least-known branch of the United Kingdom's intelligence and investigative services—was detailed to look into the supposedly open-and-shut case and report back to the current Prime Minister on the advisability of maintaining government support for Tomorrow Town.

He had given Vanessa the barest facts.

"What does the murder weapon of the future turn out to be?" she asked. "Laser beam? Poisoned moon rock?"

"No, the proverbial blunt instrument. Letting the side down, really. Anyone who murders the co-founder of Tomorrow Town should have the decency to stick to the spirit of the game. I doubt if it's much comfort to the deceased, but the offending bludgeon was vaguely futurist, a stylized steel rocket ship with a heavy stone base."

"No home should be without one."

"It was a Hugo Award, the highest honour the science fiction field can bestow. Zhoule won his murder weapon for Best Novelette of 1958, with the oft-anthologized *Court Martian*."

"Are we then to be the police of the future? Do we get to design our own uniforms?"

"We're here because Tomorrow Town has no police force as such. It is a fundamental of the social design that there will be no crime by the year 2000."

"Ooops."

"This is a utopian vision, Vanessa. No money to steal. No inequality to foster resentment. All disputes arbitrated with unquestionable fairness. All zenvols constantly monitored for emotional instability."

"Maybe being 'constantly monitored' leads to 'emotional instability.' Not to mention being called a 'zenvol.'"

"You'll have to mention that to Big Thinks."

"Is he the boss-man among equals?"

Richard chuckled. "He's an *it*. A computer. A very large computer."

Vanessa snapped her fingers.

"Ah-ha. There's your culprit. In every sci-fi film I've ever seen, the computer goes power-mad and starts killing people off. Big Thinks probably wants to take over the world."

"The late Mm Zhoule would cringe to hear you say that, Vanessa. He'd never have deigned to use such a hackneyed, unlikely premise in a story. A computer is just a heuristic abacus. Big Thinks can beat you at chess, solve logic problems, cut a pop record, and make the monorail run on time, but it hasn't got sentience, a personality, a motive, or, most importantly, arms. You might as well suspect the fridge-freezer or the pop-up toaster."

"If you knew my pop-up toaster better, you'd feel differently. It sits there, shining sneakily, plotting perfidy. The jug-kettle is in on it, too. There's a conspiracy of contraptions."

"Now you're being silly."

"Trust me, Richard, it'll be the Brain Machine. Make sure to check its alibi."

"I'll bear that in mind."

THEY FIRST SAW Tomorrow Town from across the Yorkshire Dales, nestled in lush green and slate gray. The complex was a large-scale version of the sort of back-garden space station that might have been put together by a talented child inspired by Gerry Anderson and instructed by Valerie Singleton, using egg boxes, toilet roll tubes, the innards of a broken wireless, pipe cleaners, and a lot of silver spray-paint.

Hexagonal geodesic domes clustered in the landscape, a central space covered by a giant canopy that looked like an especially aerodynamic silver circus tent. Metallized roadways wound between trees and lakes, connecting the domes. The light traffic consisted mostly of electric golf carts and one-person hovercraft. A single hardy zenvol was struggling along on what looked like a failed flying bicycle from 1895 but was actually a moped powered by wing-like solar panels. It was raining gently, but the town seemed shielded by a half-bubble climate control barrier that shimmered in mid air.

A pylon held up three sun-shaped globes on a triangular frame. They radiated light and, Richard suspected, heat. Where light fell, the greenery was noticeably greener and thicker.

The monorail stopped outside the bubble, and settled a little clunkily.

"You may now change apparel," rasped the machine voice.

A compartment opened and clothes slid out on racks. The safety straps released them from their seats.

Richard thought for a moment that the train had calculated from his long hair that he was a Ms rather than a Mm, then realized the garment on offer was unisex: a lightweight jumpsuit of semi-opaque polythene, with silver epaulettes, pockets, knee- and elbow-patches, and modesty strips around the chest and hips. The dangling legs ended in floppy-looking plastic boots, the sleeves in surgeon's gloves.

"Was that 'may' a 'must'?" asked Vanessa.

"Best to go along with native customs," said Richard.

He turned his back like a gentleman and undressed carefully, folding and putting away his clothes. Then he took the jumpsuit from the rack and stepped into it, wiggling his feet down into the boots and fingers into the gloves. A seam from crotch to neck sealed with Velcro strips, but he was left with an enormous swathe of polythene sprouting from his left hip like a bridal train.

"Like this," said Vanessa, who had worked it out.

The swathe went over the right shoulder in a toga arrangement, passing under an epaulette, clipping on in a couple of places, and falling like a waist-length cape.

She had also found a pad of controls in the left epaulette, which activated drawstrings and pleats that adjusted the garment to suit individual body type. They both had to fiddle to get the suits to cope with their above-average height, then loosen and tighten various sections as required. Even after every possible button had been twisted every possible way, Richard wore one sleeve tight as sausage skin while the other was loose and wrinkled as a burst balloon.

"Maybe it's a futopian fashion," suggested Vanessa, who—of course—looked spectacular, shown off to advantage by the modesty strips. "All the dashing zenvols are wearing the one-loose-one-tight look this new century."

"Or maybe it's just aggravated crackpottery."

She laughed.

The monorail judged they had used up their changing time, and lurched off again.

THE RECEIVING AREA was as white and clean as a bathroom display at the Belgian Ideal Home Exhibition. A deputation of zenvols, all dressed alike, none with mismatched sleeves, waited on the platform. Synthesized Bach played gently and the artificial breeze was mildly perfumed.

"Mm Richard, Ms Vanessa," said a white-haired zenvol, "welcome to Tomorrow Town."

A short oriental girl repeated his words in sign language.

"Are you Georgie Gewell?" Richard asked.

"Jor-G," said the zenvol, then spelled it out.

"My condolences," Richard said, shaking the man's hand. Through two squeaking layers of latex, he had the impression of a sweaty palm. "I understand you and Varno Zhoule were old friends."

"Var-Z is a tragic loss. A great visioneer."

The oriental girl mimed sadness. Other zenvols hung their heads.

"Jesu, Joy of Man's Desiring" segued into the "Dead March" from *Saul*. Was the Muzak keyed in somehow to the emotional state of any given assembly?

"We, ah, founded the Foundation together."

Back in the 1950s, Varno Zhoule had written many articles and stories for science fiction magazines, offering futuristic solutions to contemporary problems, preaching the gospel of better living through logic and technology. He had predicted decimal currency and the vertical-takeoff airplane. Georgie Gewell was an award-winning editor and critic. He had championed Zhoule's work, then raised finances to apply his solutions to the real world. Richard understood the seed money for the Foundation came from a patent the pair held on a kind of battery-powered circular slide rule that was faster and more accurate than any other portable calculating device.

Gewell was as tall as Richard, with milk-fair skin and close-cropped snow-white hair. He had a deep smile and frown lines and a soft, girlish mouth. He was steadily leaking tears, not from grief but from thick, obvious Reactolite contact lenses that were currently smudged to the darker end of their spectrum.

The other zenvols were an assorted mix, despite their identical outfits. Most of the men were short and tubby, the women lithe and fit—which was either Big Thinks's recipe for perfect population balance or some visioneer's idea of a good time for a tall, thin fellow. Everyone had hair cut short, which made both Richard and Vanessa obvious outsiders. None of the men wore facial hair except a red-faced chap who opted for the Puritan beard-without-a-moustache arrangement.

Gewell introduced the delegation. The oriental girl was Moana, whom Gewell described as "town speaker," though she continued to communicate only by signing. The beardie was Mal-K, the "senior medico" who had presided over the autopsy, matched some bloody fingerprints, and seemed a bit put out to be taken away from his automated clinic for this ceremonial affair. Other significant zenvols: Jess-F, "arbitrage input tech," a hard-faced blonde girl who interfaced with Big Thinks when it came to programming dispute decisions, and thus was the nearest thing Tomorrow Town had to a human representative of the legal system—though she was more clerk of the court than investigating officer; Zootie, a fat little "agri-terrain rearrangement tech" with a bad cold for which he kept apologizing, who turned out to have discovered the body by the hydroponics vats and was oddly impressed and uncomfortable in this group, as if he weren't quite on a level of equality with Gewell and the rest; and "vocabulary administrator" Sue-2, whom Gewell introduced as "sadly, the motive," the image of a penitent young lady who "would never do it again."

Richard mentally marked them all down.

"You'll want to visit the scene of the crime?" suggested Gewell. "Interrogate the culprit? We have Buster in a secure store-room. It had to be especially prepared. There are no lockable doors in Tomorrow Town."

"He's nailed in," said Jess-F. "With rations and a potty."

"Very sensible," commented Richard.

"We can prise the door open now you're here," said Gewell.

Richard thought a moment.

"If you'll forgive me, Mr. Jep—ah, Mm Richard," said Mal-K, "I'd like to get back to my work. I've a batch of anti-virus cooking."

The medico kept his distance from Zootie. Did he think a streaming nose reflected badly on the health of the future? Or was the artificial breeze liable to spread sniffles around the whole community in minutes?

"I don't see any reason to detain you, Mm Mal-K," said Richard. "Vanessa might pop over later. My associate is interested in the work you're doing here. New cures for new diseases. She'd love to squint into a microscope at your anti-virus."

Vanessa nodded with convincing enthusiasm.

"Mal-K's door is always open," said Gewell.

The medico sloped off without comment.

"Should we crack out the crowbar, then?" prompted Gewell.

The co-founder seemed keen on getting on with this: to him, murder came as an embarrassment and an interruption. It wasn't an uncommon reaction. Richard judged Gewell just wanted all this over with so he could get on with things, even though the victim was one of his oldest friends and the crime demonstrated a major flaw in the social design of Tomorrow Town. If someone battered Vanessa to death, he didn't think he'd be so intent on putting it behind him—but he was famous for being sensitive. Indeed, it was why he was so useful to the Diogenes Club.

"I think as long as our putative culprit is safely nailed away, we can afford to take our time, get a feel for the place and the set-up. It's how I like to work, Mm Gewell. To me, understanding why is much more important than knowing who or how."

"I should think the why was obvious," said Gewell looking at Sue-2, eyes visibly darkening.

She looked down.

"The arbitration went against Buster, and he couldn't accept it," said Jess-F. "Though it was in his initial contract that he abide by Big Thinks's decisions. It happens sometimes. Not often."

"An arbitration in a matter of the heart? Interesting. Just the sort of thing that comes in a box marked 'motive' and tied with pink string. Thank you so much for mentioning it early in the case. Before we continue the sleuthing, perhaps we could have lunch. Vanessa and I have traveled a long way, with no sustenance beyond British Rail sandwiches and a beverage of our own supply. Let's break bread together, and you can tell me more about your fascinating experiment."

"Communal meals are at fixed times," said Gewell. "The next is not until six."

"I make it about six o'clock," said Richard, though his watch-face was blurred by the sleeve-glove.

"It's only f-five by our clock," said Sue-2. "We're on two daily cycles of ten kronons. Each kronon runs a hundred sentikronons."

"In your time, a kronon is seventy-two minutes," explained Gewell. "Our six is your…"

Vanessa did the calculation and beat the slide rule designer, "Twelve minutes past seven."

"That's about it."

Richard waved away the objection.

"I'm sure a snack can be rustled up. Where do you take these communal meals?"

Moana signaled a direction and set off. Richard was happy to follow, and the others came too.

THE DINING AREA was in the central plaza, under the pylon and the three globes, with zinc-and-chrome sheet-and-tube tables and benches. It was warm under the globes, almost Caribbean, and some zenvols wore poker players' eye-shades. In the artificially balmy climate, plastic garments tended to get sticky inside, which made for creaky shiftings in seats.

An abstract ornamental fountain gushed nutrient-enriched, slightly carbonated, heavily fluoridated water. Gewell had Moana fetch a couple of jugs for the table, while the meek Sue-2 hustled off to persuade "sustenance preparation" techs to break their schedule to feed the visitors. Vanessa cocked an eyebrow at this division of labor, and Richard remembered Zhoule and Gewell had been planning this futopia since the 1950s, well before the publication of *The Female Eunuch*. Even Jess-F, whom Richard had pegged as the toughest zenvol he had yet met, broke out the metallized glass tumblers from a dispenser by the fountain, while Gewell and the sniffling Zootie sat at their ease at table.

"Is that the building where Big Thinks lives?" asked Vanessa.

Gewell swiveled to look. Vanessa meant an imposing structure, rather like a giant art deco refrigerator decorated with Mondrian squares in a rough schematic of a human face. Uniformly dressed zenvols came and went through airlock doors that opened and closed with hisses of decontaminant.

Gewell grinned, impishly.

"Ms Vanessa, that building *is* Big Thinks."

Richard whistled.

"Bee-Tee didn't used to be that size," said Jess-F. "Var-Z kept insisting we add units. More and more complicated questions need more and more space. Soon, we'll have to expand further."

"It doesn't show any telltale signs of megalomania?" asked Vanessa. "Never programs Wagner for eight straight hours and chortles over maps of the world?"

Jess-F didn't look as if she thought that was funny.

"Bee-Tee is a machine, Ms."

Sue-2 came back with food. Colored pills that looked like Smarties but tasted like chalk.

"All the nutrition you need is here," said Gewell, "in the water and the capsules. For us, mealtimes are mostly ceremonial, for debate and reflection. Var-Z said that some of his best ideas popped into his head while he was chatting idly after a satisfying pill."

Richard didn't doubt it. He also still felt hungry.

"Talking of things popping into Zhoule's head," he said, "what's the story on Buster of the bloody fingerprints?"

Jess-F looked at Sue-2, as if expecting to be contradicted, then carried on.

"Big Thinks assessed the dispute situation, and arbitrated it best for the community if Sue-2 were to be pair-bonded with Var-Z rather than Buster."

"Buster was your old boyfriend?" Vanessa asked Sue-2.

"He is my husband," she said.

"On the outside, in the past," put in Jess-F. "Here, we don't always acknowledge arbitrary pair-bondings. Mostly, they serve a useful purpose and continue. In this instance, the dispute was more complicated."

"Big Thinks arbitrated against the arbitrary?" mused Richard. "I suppose no one would be surprised at that."

He looked from face to face and fixed on Sue-2, then asked: "Did you leave Buster for Mm Zhoule?"

Sue-2 looked for a cue, but none came.

"It was best for the town, for the experiment," she said.

"What was it for you? For your husband?"

"Buster had been regraded. From 'zenvol' to 'zenpass.' He couldn't vote."

Richard looked to Jess-F for explication. He noticed Gewell had to give her a teary wink from almost-black eyes before she would say anything more.

"We have very few citizen-passengers," she said. "It's not a punishment category."

"Kind of you to clarify that," said Richard. "I might have made a misconclusion otherwise. You say zenpasses have no vote?"

"It's not so dreadful," said Gewell, sipping nutrient. "On the outside, in the past, suffrage is restricted by age, sanity, residence, and so on. Here, in our technomeritocracy, to register for a vote—which gives you a voice in every significant decision—you have to demonstrate your applied intelligence."

"An IQ test?"

"Not a quotient, Mm Richard. Anyone can have that. The vital factor is application. Bee-Tee tests for that. There's no personality or human tangle involved. Surely, it's only fair that the most useful should have the most say?"

"I have a vote," said Zootie, proud. "Earned by applied intelligence."

"Indeed he does," said Gewell, smiling.

"And Mm Jor-G has fifteen votes. Because he applies his intelligence more often than I do."

Everyone looked at Zootie with different types of amazement.

"It's only fair," said Zootie, content despite a nose-trickle, washing down another purple pill.

Richard wondered whether the agri-terrain rearrangement tech was hovering near regrading as a zenpass.

Richard addressed Sue-2. "What does your husband do?"

"He's a history teacher."

"An educationalist. Very valuable."

Gewell looked as if his pill was sour. "Your present is our past, Mm Richard. Buster's discipline is surplus."

"Doesn't the future grow out of the past? To know where you're going you must know where you've been."

"Var-Z believes in a radical break."

"But Var-Z is in the past too."

"Indeed. Regrettable. But we must think of the future."

"It's where we're going to spend the rest of our lives," said Zootie.

"That's very clever," said Vanessa.

Zootie wiped his nose and puffed up a bit.

"I think we should hand Buster over to you," said Gewell. "To be taken outside to face the justice of the past. Var-Z left work undone that we must continue."

"Not just yet," said Richard. "This sad business raises questions about Tomorrow Town. I have to look beyond the simple crime before I make my report. I'm sure you understand and will extend full cooperation."

No one said anything, but they all constructed smiles.

"You must be economically self-supporting by now," continued Richard, "what with the research and invention you've been applying intelligence to. If the Prime Minister withdrew government subsidies, you'd probably be better off. Free of the apron strings, as it were. Still, the extra cash must come in handy for something, even if you don't use money in this town."

Gewell wiped his eyes and kept smiling.

Richard could really do with a steak and kidney pie and chips, washed down with beer. Even a Kit-Kat would have been welcome.

"Have you a guest apartment we could use?"

Gewell's smile turned real. "Sadly, we're at maximum optimal zenvol residency. No excess space wastage in the living quarters."

"No spare beds," clarified Zootie.

"Then we'll have to take the one living space we know to be free."

Gewell's brow furrowed like a rucked-up rug.

"Zhoule's quarters," Richard explained. "We'll set up camp there. Sue-2, you must know the way. Since there are no locks we won't need keys to get in. Zenvols, it's been fascinating. I look forward to seeing you tomorrow."

Richard and Vanessa stood up, and Sue-2 followed suit. Gewell and Jess-F glared. Moana waved bye-bye.

"WHAT ARE YOU looking for?" Vanessa asked. "Monitoring devices?"

"No," said Richard, unsealing another compartment, "they're in the light fittings and the communicator screen, and seem to have been disabled. By Zhoule or his murderer, presumably."

There was a constant hum of gadgetry in the walls and from behind white-fronted compartments. The ceiling was composed of translucent panels, above which glowed a steady light.

The communicator screen was dusty. Beneath the on-off switch, volume and brightness knobs, and channel selector was a telephone dial, with the Tomorrow Town alphabet (no Q or X). Richard had tried to call London but a recorded voice over a cartoon smiley face told him that visiphones only worked within the town limits. Use of the telephone line to the outside had to be approved by vote of zenvol visioneers.

In a compartment, he found a gadget whose purpose was a mystery. It had dials, a trumpet, and three black rubber nipples.

"I'm just assuming, Vanessa, that the co-founder of Tomorrow Town might allow himself to sample the forbidden past in ways denied the simple zenvol or despised zenpass."

"You mean?"

"He might have real food stashed somewhere."

Vanessa started opening compartments too.

It took a full hour to search the five rooms of Zhoule's bungalow. They discovered a complete run of *Town*

*Magazeen,* a microfilm publication with all text in fonetik, and a library of 1950s science fiction magazines, lurid covers mostly promising Varno Zhoule stories as backup to Asimov or Heinlein.

They found many compartments stuffed with ring-bound notebooks which dated back twenty years. Richard flicked through a couple, noting Zhoule had either been using fonetik since the early Fifties or was such a bad speller that his editors must have been driven to despair. Most of the entries were single sentences, story ideas, possible inventions, or prophecies. *Tunel under Irish See. Rokit to Sun to harvest heet. Big lift to awbit. Stoopids not allowd to breed. Holes in heds for plugs.*

Vanessa found a display case, full of plaques and awards in the shapes of spirals or robots.

"Is this the murder weapon?" Vanessa asked, indicating a needle-shaped rocket. "Looks too clean."

"I believe Zhoule was a multiple Hugo winner. See, this is Best Short Story 1957, for 'Vesta Interests.' The blunt instrument was..."

Vanessa picked up a chunk of ceramic and read the plaque, "Best Novelette 1958." It was a near-duplicate of the base of the other award.

"You can see where the rocket ship was fixed. It must have broken when the award was lifted in anger."

"Cold blood, Vanessa. The body and the Hugo were found elsewhere. No blood traces in these quarters. Let's keep looking for a pork pie."

Vanessa opened a floor-level compartment and out crawled a matt-black robot spider the size of an armored go-kart. The fearsome thing brandished death-implements that, upon closer examination, turned out to be a vacuum cleaner proboscis and limbs tipped with chamois, a damp squeegee, and a brush.

"Oh, how useful," said Vanessa.

Then the spider squirted hot water at her and crackled. Electrical circuits burned out behind its photo-eyes. The proboscis coughed black soot.

"Or maybe not."

"'I have seen the future, and it works,'" quoted Richard. "Lincoln Steffens, on the Soviet Union, 1919."

"'What's to become of my bit of washing when there's no washing to do,'" quoted Vanessa. "The old woman in *The Man in the White Suit,* on technological progress, 1951."

"You suspect the diabolical Big Thinks sent this cleaning robot to murder Varno Zhoule? A Frankensteinian rebellion against the Master-Creator?"

"If Bee-Tee is so clever, I doubt it'd use this arachnoid doodad as an assassin. The thing can't even beat as it sweeps as it cleans, let alone carry out a devilish murder plan. Besides, to use the blunt instrument it would have to climb a wall, and I reckon this can't manage stairs."

Richard poked the carapace of the machine, which wriggled and lost a couple of limbs.

"Are you still hungry?"

"Famished."

"Yet we've had enough nourishment to keep body and spirit together for the ten long kronons that remain until breakfast time."

"I'll ask medico Mal-K if he sees many cases of rickets and scurvy in futopia."

"You do that."

Richard tried to feel sorry for the spider, but it was just a gadget. It was impossible to invest it with a personality.

Vanessa was thinking.

"Wasn't the idea that Tomorrow Town would pour forth twenty-first-century solutions to our drab old 1970s problems?"

Richard answered her. "That's what Mr. Wilson thought he was signing up for."

"So why aren't Mrs. Mopp Spiders on sale in the Charing Cross Road?"

"It doesn't seem to work all that well."

"Lot of that about, Mm Richard. A monorail that would lose a race with Stephenson's Rocket. Technomeritocratic *droit de seigneur.* Concentrated foods astronauts wouldn't eat. Robots less functional than the wind-up ones my nephew Paulie uses to conquer the playground. And I've seen the odd hovercraft up on blocks with 'Owt of Awder' signs. Not to mention Buster the Basher, living incarnation of a society out of joint."

"Good points all," he said. "And I'll answer them as soon as I solve another mystery."

"What's that?"

"What are we supposed to sleep on?"

Around the rooms were large soft white cubes which distantly resembled furniture but could as easily be tofu chunks for the giants who would evolve by the turn of the millennium. By collecting enough cubes into a windowless room where the lighting panels were more subdued, Richard and Vanessa were able to put together a bed-shape. However, when Richard took an experimental lie-down on the jigsaw-puzzle affair, an odd cube squirted out of place and he fell through the gap. The floor was covered with a warm fleshy plastic substance that was peculiarly unpleasant to the touch.

None of the many compartment-cupboards in the bungalow contained anything resembling twentieth-century pillows or bedding. Heating elements in the floor turned up as the evening wore on, adjusting the internal temperature of the room to the point where their all-over condoms were extremely uncomfortable. Escaping from the Tomorrow Town costumes was much harder than getting into them.

It occurred to Richard and Vanessa at the same time that these spacesuits would make going to the lavatory awkward, though they reasoned an all-pill diet would minimize the wasteful toilet breaks required in the past. Eventually, with some cooperation, they got free and placed the suits on hangers in a glass-fronted cupboard which, when closed, filled with colored steam. "Dekontaminashun Kompleet," flashed a sign as the cabinet cracked open and spilled liquid residue. The floor was discolored where this had happened before.

Having more or less puzzled out how the bedroom worked, they set about tackling the bathroom, which seemed to be equipped with a dental torture chamber and a wide variety of exotic marital aids. By the time they were done playing with it all, incidentally washing and cleaning their teeth, it was past midnight and the lights turned off automatically.

"Nighty-night," said Richard.

"Don't let the robot bugs bite," said Vanessa.

HE WOKE UP, alert. She woke with him.

"What's the matter? A noise?"

"No," he said. "No noise."

"Ah."

The Tomorrow Town hum, gadgets in the walls, was silenced. The bungalow was technologically dead. He reached out and touched the floor. It was cooling.

Silently, they got off the bed.

The room was dark, but they knew where the door—a sliding screen—was and took up positions either side of it.

The door had opened by touching a pad. Now that power was off, they were shut in (a flaw in the no-locks policy), though Richard heard a winding creak as the door lurched open an inch. There was some sort of clockwork backup system.

A gloved hand reached into the room. It held an implement consisting of a plastic handle, two long thin metal rods, and a battery pack. A blue arc buzzed between the rods, suggesting lethal charge.

Vanessa took the wrist, careful not to touch the rods, and gave a good yank. The killing-prod, or whatever it was, was dropped and discharged against the floor, leaving a blackened patch and a nasty smell.

Surprised, the intruder stumbled against the door.

As far as Richard could make out in the minimal light, the figure wore the usual Tomorrow Town suit. An addition was an opaque black egg-shaped helmet with a silver strip around the eyes which he took to be a one-way mirror. A faint red radiance suggested some sort of infrared see-in-the-dark device.

Vanessa, who had put on a floral bikini as sleepwear, kicked the egghead in the chest, which clanged. She hopped back.

"It's armored," she said.

"All who defy Buster must die," rasped a speaker in the helmet.

Vanessa kicked again, at the shins, cutting the egghead down.

"All who defy Buster must die," squeaked the speaker, sped-up. "All who de... de... de... de..."

The recorded message was stuck.

The egghead clambered upright.

"Is there is a person in there?" Vanessa asked.

"One way to find out," said Richard.

He hammered the egghead with a bed-cube, but it was too soft to dent the helmet. The intruder lunged and caught him in a plastic-and-metal grasp.

"Get him off me," he said, kicking. Unarmored, he was at a disadvantage.

Vanessa nipped into the ensuite bathroom and came back with a gadget on a length of metal hose. They had decided it was probably a water-pick for those hard-to-clean crannies. She stabbed the end of the device at the egghead's neck, puncturing the plastic seal just below the chin-rim of the helmet, and turned the nozzle on. The tappet-key snapped off in her fingers and a high-pressure stream that could have drilled through cheddar cheese spurted into the suit.

Gallons of water inflated the egghead's garment. The suit self-sealed around the puncture and expanded, arms and legs forced out in an X. Richard felt the water pressure swelling his captor's chest and arms. He wriggled and got free.

"All who defy Buster…"

Circuits burned out, and leaks sprouted at all the seams. Even through the silver strip, Richard made out the water rising.

There was a commotion in the next room.

Lights came on. The hum was back.

It occurred to Richard that he had opted to sleep in the buff and might not be in a decorous state to receive visitors. Then again, in the future taboos against social nudity were likely to evaporate.

Georgie Gewell, the ever-present Moana, and Jess-F, who had another of the zapper-prod devices, stood just inside the doorway.

There was a long pause. This was not what anyone had expected.

"Buster has escaped," said Gewell. "We thought you might be in danger. He's beyond all reason."

"If he was a danger to us, he isn't any longer," said Vanessa.

"If this is him," Richard said. "He was invoking the name."

The egghead was on the floor, spouting torrents, super-inflated like the Michelin Man after a three-day egg-eating contest.

Vanessa kicked the helmet. It obligingly repeated "All who defy Buster must die."

The egghead waved hands like fat starfish, thumbing toward the helmet, which was sturdier than the rest of the suit and not leaking.

"Anybody know how to get this thing off?" asked Richard.

The egghead writhed and was still.

"Might be a bit on the late side."

Gewell and Jess-F looked at each other. Moana took action and pushed into the room. She knelt and worked a few buttons around the chin-rim of the helmet. The egghead cracked along a hitherto unsuspected crooked seam and came apart in a gush of water.

"That's not Buster," said Vanessa. "It's Mal-K, the medico."

"And he's drowned," concluded Richard.

"A USEFUL RULE of thumb in open-and-shut cases," announced Richard, "is that when someone tries to murder any investigating officers, the case isn't as open-and-shut as it might at first have seemed."

He had put on a quilted double-breasted floor-length jade green dressing gown with a Blakeian red dragon picked out on the chest in sequins.

"When the would-be murderer is one of the major proponents of the open-and-shut theory," he continued, "it's a dead cert that an injustice is in the process of being perpetrated. Ergo, the errant Buster is innocent and someone else murdered Mm Zhoule with a Hugo Award."

"Perhaps there was a misunderstanding," said Gewell.

Richard and Vanessa looked at him.

"How so?" Richard asked.

Wheels worked behind Gewell's eyes, which were amber now.

"Mm Mal-K might have heard of Buster's escape and come here to protect you from him. In the dark and confusion, you mistook his attempted rescue as an attack."

"And tragedy followed," completed Jess-F.

Moana weighed invisible balls and looked noncommittal.

It was sixty-eight past six o'kronon. The body had been removed and they were in Zhoule's front room. Since all the cubes were in the bedroom and wet through, everyone had to sit on the body-temperature floor. Vanessa perched decorously, see-through peignoir over her bikini, on the dead robot spider. Richard stood, as if lecturing.

"Mm Jor-G, you were an editor once," he said. "If a story were submitted in which a hero wanted to protect innocent parties from a rampaging killer, would you have allowed the author to have the hero get into a disguise, turn off all the lights and creep into the bedroom with a lethal weapon?"

"Um, I might. I edited science fiction magazines. Science fiction is about *ideas*. No matter what those New Wavers say. In sf, characters might do anything."

"What about 'All who defy Buster must die'?" said Vanessa.

"A warning?" Gewell ventured, feebly.

"Oh, give up," said Jess-F. "Mal-K was a bad 'un. It's been obvious for desiyears. All those speeches about 'expanding the remit of the social experiment' and 'assuming pole position in the larger technomeritocracy.' He was in a position to doctor his own records, to cover up instability. He was also the one who matched Buster's fingerprints to the murder weapon. Mm and Ms, congratulations, you've caught the killer."

"Open-and-shut-and-open-and-shut?"        suggested Richard.

Moana gave the thumbs-up.

"I'm going to need help to convince myself of this," said Richard. "I've decided to call on mighty deductive brain-power to get to the bottom of the mystery."

"More yesterday men?" said Jess-F, appalled.

"Interesting term. You've been careful not to use it before now. Is that what you call us? No, I don't intend to summon any more plods from the outside."

Gewell couldn't suppress his surge of relief.

"I've decided to apply the techniques of tomorrow to these crimes of the future. Jess-F, I'll need your help. Let's take this puzzle to Big Thinks, and see how your mighty computer does."

Shutters came down behind Jess-F's eyes.

"Computer time is precious," said Gewell.

"So is human life," answered Richard.

THE INSIDE OF the building, the insides of Big Thinks, was the messiest area Richard had seen in Tomorrow Town. Banks of metal cabinets fronted with reels of tape were connected by a spaghetti tangle of wires that wound throughout the building like colored plastic ivy. Some cabinets had their fronts off, showing masses of circuit boards, valves, and transistors. Surprisingly, the workings of the master brain seemed held together with a great deal of Sellotape, string, and Blu Tack. Richard recognized some components well in advance of any on the market, and others that might date back to Marconi or Babbage.

"We've been making adjustments," said Jess-F.

She shifted a cardboard box full of plastic shapes from a swivel chair and let him sit at a desk piled with wired-together television sets. To one side was a paper towel dispenser which coughed out a steady roll of graph paper with lines squiggled on it.

He didn't know which knobs to twiddle.

"Ms Jess-F, could you show me how a typical dispute arbitration is made. Say, the triangle of Zhoule, Buster, and Sue-2."

"That documentation might be hard to find."

"In this a futopia of efficiency? I doubt it."

Jess-F nodded to Moana, who scurried off to root through large bins full of scrunched and torn paper.

Vanessa was with Gewell and Zootie, taking a tour of the hydroponics zone, which was where the body of Varno Zhoule had been found. The official story was that Buster (now, Mal-K) had gone to Zhoule's bungalow to kill him but found him not at home. He had taken the Hugo from its display case and searched out the victim-to-be, found him contemplating the green gunk that was made into his favorite pills, and did the deed then and there. It didn't take a computer to decide it was more likely that Zhoule had been killed where the weapon was handy for an annoyed impulse-assassin to reach for, then hovercrafted along with the murder weapon to a public place so some uninvolved zenvol clot could find him. But why ferry the body all that way, with the added risk of being caught?

"Tell you what, Ms Jess-F, let's try Bee-Tee out on a hypothetical dispute? Put in the setup of *Hamlet,* and see what the computer thinks would be best for Denmark."

"Big Thinks is not a toy, Mm."

Moana came back waving some sheaves of paper.

Richard looked over it. Jess-F ground her teeth.

Though the top sheet was headed "Input tek: Buster Munro," this was not the triangle dispute documentation. Richard scrolled through the linked print-out. He saw maps of Northern Europe, lists of names and dates, depositions in non-phonetic English, German and Danish, and enough footnotes for a good-sized doctoral thesis. In fact, that was exactly what this was.

"I'm not the first to think of running a hypothetical dispute past the mighty computer," said Richard. "The much-maligned Buster got there before me."

"And wound up recategorized as a zenpass," said Jess-F.

"He tried to get an answer to the Schleswig-Holstein Question, didn't he? Lord Palmerston said only three men in Europe got to the bottom of it—one who forgot, one who died, and one who went mad. It was an insanely complicated argument between Denmark and Germany, over the governance of a couple of border provinces. Buster put the question to Big Thinks as if it were a contemporary dispute, just to see how the computer would have resolved it. What did it suggest, nuclear attack? Is that why all the redecoration? Buster's puzzle blew all the fuses."

Richard found the last page.

The words "forgot died mad" were repeated over and over, in very faint ink. Then some mathematical formulae. Then the printer equivalent of scribble.

"This makes no sense."

He showed it to Jess-F, hoping she could interpret it. He really would have liked Big Thinks to have got to the bottom of the tussle that defeated Bismarck and Metternich and spat out a blindingly simple answer everyone should have seen all along.

"No," she admitted. "It makes no sense at all."

Moana shrugged.

Richard felt a rush of sympathy for Jess-F. This was painful for her.

"Bee-Tee can't do it," said Richard. "The machine can do sums very fast, but nothing else?"

Jess-F was almost at the point of tears.

"That's not true," she said, with tattered pride. "Big Thinks is the most advanced computer in the world. It can solve any logic problem. Give it the data, and it can deliver accurate weather forecasts, arrange schedules to optimize efficiency of any number of tasks..."

"But throw the illogical at it, and Bee-Tee just has a good cry."

"It's a machine. It can't cry."

"Or arbitrate love affairs."

Jess-F was in a corner.

"It's not fair," she said, quietly. "It's not Bee-Tee's fault. It's not my fault. They knew the operational parameters. They just kept insisting it tackle areas outside its remit, extending, tampering, overburdening. My techs have been working all the hours of the day..."

"Kronons, surely?"

"...all the bloody kronons of the day, just trying to get Big Thinks working again. Even after all this, the ridiculous demands keep coming through. Big Thinks, Big Thinks, will I be pretty, will I be rich? Big Thinks, Big Thinks, is there life on other planets?"

Jess-F put her hands over her face.

"'They'? Who are 'they'?"

"All of them," Jess-F sobbed. "Across all disciplines."

"Who especially?"

"Who else? Varno Zhoule."

"Not any more?"

"No."

She looked out from behind her hands, horrified.

"It wasn't me," she said.

"I know. You're left-handed. Wrong wound pattern. One more question: what did the late Mm Mal-K want from Big Thinks?"

Jess-F gave out an appalled sigh.

"Now, he *was* cracked. He kept putting in these convoluted specific questions. In the end, they were all about taking over the country. He wanted to run the whole of the United Kingdom like Tomorrow Town."

"The day after tomorrow, the world?"

"He kept putting in plans and strategies for infiltrating vital industries and dedicating them to the cause. He didn't have an army, but he believed Big Thinks could get all the computers in the country on his side. Most of the zenvols thought he was a dreamer, spinning out a best-case scenario at the meetings. But he meant it. He wanted to found a large-scale Technomeritocracy."

"With himself as Beloved Leader?"

"No, that's how mad he was. He wanted Big Thinks to run everything. He was hoping to put Bee-Tee in charge and let the future happen."

"That's why he wanted Vanessa and me out of the story. We were a threat to his funding. Without the subsidies, the plug is pulled."

"One thing Bee-Tee can do is keep track of figures. As a community, Tomorrow Town is in the red. Enormously."

"There's no money here, though."

"Of course not. We've spent it. And spent money we don't have. The next monorail from Preston is liable to be crowded with dunning bailiffs."

Richard thought about it. He was rather saddened by the truth. It would have been nice if the future worked. He wondered if Lincoln Steffens had any second thoughts during the Moscow purge trials?

"What threat was Zhoule to Mal-K?" he asked.

Jess-F frowned. "That's the oddest thing. Zhoule was the one who really encouraged Mal-K to work on his coup plans. He did see himself as, what did you call it, 'Beloved Leader.' All his stories were about intellectual supermen taking charge of the world and sorting things out. If anything, he was the visioneer of the tomorrow takeover. And he'd have jumped anything in skirts if femzens wore skirts here."

Richard remembered the quivering Sue-2.

"So we're back to Buster in the conservatory with the Hugo award?"

"I've always said it was him," said Jess-F. "You can't blame him, but he did it."

"We shall see."

Sirens sounded. Moana put her fingers in her ears. Jess-F looked even more stricken.

"That's not a good sign, is it?"

THE COMMUNAL MEAL area outside Big Thinks swarmed with plastic-caped zenvols, looking up and pointing, panicking and screaming. The three light-heat globes, Tomorrow Town's suns, shone whiter and radiated hotter. Richard looked at the backs of his hands. They were tanning almost as quickly as an instant photograph develops.

"The fool," said Jess-F. "He's tampered with the master controls. Buster will kill us all. It's the only thing he has left."

Zenvols piled into the communally owned electric carts parked in a rank to one side of the square. When they proved too heavy for the vehicles, they started throwing each other off. Holes melted in the canopy above the globes. Sizzling drips of molten plastic fell onto screaming tomorrow townies.

The sirens shrilled, urging everyone to panic.

Richard saw Vanessa through the throng.

She was with Zootie. No Gewell.

A one-man hovercraft, burdened with six clinging zenvols, chugged past inch by inch, outpaced by someone on an old-fashioned, non-solar-powered bicycle.

"If the elements reach critical," said Jess-F, "Tomorrow Town will blow up."

A banner-like strip of paper curled out of a slit in the front of Big Thinks.

"Your computer wants to say goodbye," said Richard.

SURKIT BRAKER NO. 15.

"Not much of a farewell."

Zootie walked between falling drips to the central column, which supported the three globes. He opened a hatch and pulled a switch. The artificial suns went out. Real sunlight came through the holes in the canopy.

"Now that's what computers can do," said Jess-F, elated. "Execute protocols. If this happens, then that order must be given."

The zenvol seemed happier about her computer now.

Richard was grateful for a ditch-digger who could read.

"THIS IS WHERE the body was?" he asked Zootie. They were by swimming-pool-sized tanks of green gunk, dotted with yellow and brown patches since the interruption of the light source. "Bit of a haul from Zhoule's place."

"The body was carried here?" asked Vanessa.

"Not just the body. The murder weapon too. Who lives in that bungalow?"

On a small hill was a bungalow not quite as spacious as Zhoule's, one of the mass of hutches placed between the silver pathways, with a crown of solar panels on the flat roof, and a dish antenna.

"Mm Jor-G," said Moana.

"So you do speak?"

She nodded her head and smiled.

GEWELL SAT ON an off-white cube in the gloom. The stored power was running down. Only filtered sunlight got through to his main room. He looked as if his backbone had been removed. All the substance of his face had fallen to his jowls.

Richard looked at him.

"Nice try with the globes. Should have remembered the circuit-breaker, though. Only diabolical masterminds construct their private estates with in-built self-destruct systems. In the future, as in the past, it's unlikely that town halls will have bombs in the basement ready to go off in the event that the outgoing Mayor wants to take the whole community with him rather than hand over the chain of office."

Gewell didn't say anything.

Vanessa went straight to a shelf and picked up the only award in the display. It was another Hugo.

"Best Fan Editor 1958," she read from the plaque.

The rocket ship came away from its base.

"You killed him here," said Richard, "broke your own Hugo, left the bloody rocket ship with the body outside. Then, when you'd calmed down a bit, you remembered Zhoule had won the same award. Several, in fact. You sneaked over to his bungalow—no locks, how convenient—and broke one of his Hugos, taking the rocket to complete yours. You made it look as if he were killed with his own award, and you were out of the loop. If only you'd got round to developing the glue of the future and fixed the thing properly, it wouldn't be so obvious. It's plain that, though you've devoted your life to planning out the details of the future, your one essay in the fine art of murder was a rushed botch-up job done on the spur of the moment. You haven't really improved on Cain. At least, Mm Mal-K made the effort with the space suit and the zapper-prod."

"Mm Jor-G," said Jess-F, "*why?*"

Good question, Richard thought.

After a long pause, Gewell gathered himself and said, "Varno was destroying Tomorrow Town. He had so many... so many *ideas*. Every morning, before breakfast, he had four or five. All the time, constantly. Radio transmitters the size of a pinhead. Cheap infinite energy from tapping the planet's core. Solar-powered personal flying machines. Robots to do everything. Robots to make robots to do everything. An operation to extend human lifespan threefold. Rules and regulations about who was fit to have and raise children, with gonad-block implants to enforce them. Hats that collect the electrical energy of the brain and use it to power a personal headlamp. Non-stop, unrelenting, unstoppable. Ideas, ideas, ideas…"

Richard was frankly astonished by the man's vehemence. "Isn't that what you wanted?"

"But Varno did the easy bit. Once he'd tossed out an idea, it was up to *me* to make it work. Me or Big Thinks or some other plodding zenvol. And nine out of ten of the ideas didn't work, couldn't ever work. And it was always our fault for not making them work, never his for foisting them off on us. This town would be perfect if it hadn't been for his ideas. And his bloody dreadful spelling. Back in the Fifties, who do you think tidied all his stories up so they were publishable? Muggins Gewell. He couldn't write a sentence that scanned, and rather than learn how he decreed the language should be changed. Not just the spelling, he had a plan to go through the dictionary crossing out all the words that were no longer needed, then make it a crime to teach them to children. It was something to do with his old public school. He said he wanted to make gerunds extinct within a generation. But he had these wonderful, wonderful, ghastly, terrible *ideas*. It'd have made you sick."

"And the medico who wanted to rule the world?"

"Him too. He had ideas."

Gewell was pleading now, hands fists around imaginary bludgeons.

"If only I could have had ideas," he said. "They'd have been *good* ones."

Richard wondered how they were going to lock Gewell up until the police came.

THE MONORAIL WAS out of commission. Most things were. Some zenvols, like Jess-F, were relieved not to have to pretend that everything worked perfectly. They had desiyears—months, dammit!—of complaining bottled up inside, and were pouring it all out to each other in one big whine-in under the dead light-heat globes.

Richard and Vanessa looked across the Dales. A small vehicle was puttering along a winding, illogical lane that had been laid out not by a computer but by wandering sheep. It wasn't the police, though they were on the way.

"Who do you think this is?" asked Vanessa.

"It'll be Buster. He's bringing the outside to Tomorrow Town. He always was a yesterday man at heart."

A car-horn honked.

Zenvols, some already changed out of their plastic suits, paid attention. Sue-2 was excited, hopeful, fearful. She clung to Moana, who smiled and waved.

Someone cheered. Others joined.

"What is he driving?" asked Vanessa. "It looks like a relic from the past."

"For these people, it's deliverance," said Richard. "It's a fish 'n chip van."

# THE SECOND WINDOW

*Patrick O'Leary*

"TWENTY MINUTES. TWENTY minutes for a damn Big Mac!"

"Dad," my son says.

"What are they doing in there? Making buns? Inventing beef?"

"Geeze, Dad. At least we get to spend this quality time together."

I look at him and crack up. He's always surprising me. The silent type who waits for your guard to drop then smacks you between the eyes with a ball-peen hammer. This blond ten-year-old who seems to regard the world as a homework assignment he has to put up with. I don't recall when he became a wise child. And I take no credit for it.

Finally, we're at the second window, and a brown arm hands me my change.

I sputter. "Excuse me, but there must be some mistake."

"Sir?" the polite black woman asks; the warm draft of burger on the grille wafts past her, into the cold December night, into my car.

"You just gave me a hundred dollar bill."

"That's right. It's our way of saying thanks for being a customer."

"Cool," my son says, as if the world has finally transformed into someplace worthy of his attention.

"I can't take this!"

"Dad," he explains. "Shuttup."

"I can't take this."

"Sir, consider it our way of apologizing."

"Apologizing?"

"Yes, for all those times we got your order wrong."

"Well," I admit in so many words how irritating it's been to come home to discover your happy meal has mutated into a Spicy Chicken Extra Value Meal with Biggie Fries. But how could she have known that?

"That's very... courteous of you, but I can't believe this is a sensible way to run a business."

"We want our customers happy. Our service has been pretty slack lately. We realize that none of us will have jobs if our customers aren't satisfied."

"That's true," I say. How many times have I bemoaned the lackadaisical attitude of our minimum wage help?

"We figure we owe a lot of people a lot of money for their inconvenience."

"Yes. That's fine. That's noble, even. But how do you make any profit handing out hundred dollar bills?"

"Actually, they're counterfeit. But most people don't find that out until they try to cash them."

I look at the bill and it does indeed seem a bit half-hearted in its attempt to mimic a Federal Reserve note.

"It's the thought that counts," my son comments, grasping the logic of it.

Somebody's horn ponks behind me.

"Is there anything else, Sir?"

"Yes. Well. Our food?"

"That'll be up shortly. Wayne is depressed tonight and it's all he can do just to separate the cheese. And Felicia just had an abortion so she's sort of slow. And me," The woman holds back a sob, "Me—I got problems of my own."

"Like what?" my son says quickly and she leans on both her elbows until she is almost eye level with us. Dark dark circles around her dark brown eyes.

I hand her back the hundred and say, "Keep it. You look like you need it more than I do."

She receives the bill in her pink fingers and tucks it into her apron pocket. "Thanks."

"Wanna talk about it?" my son says, before I can stop him. He has yet to learn the limits of empathy. Or the timing.

"Nahh," she says. "It's grown up stuff. Sex and bills and family." She turns to the crew behind her and yells, "Come on people! Put some mantra into it!"

"Mantra?"

"New company policy. Each franchise has a mantra. Helps morale. Holds focus. Keeps your mind off the fact that you're in a dead-end job serving swill to ungrateful customers." She catches herself. "Sorry. That's in the handbook, but not for public consumption."

"What's a mantra?" my curious son asks.

She nods. "'Burn it. Squirt it. Wrap it. Sell it.' Try saying that a thousand times a night."

"That's kind of a weird mantra," I admit.

"It's realism. The first of seven principles. 'You are what you are. You do what you do. Do it and get it over with.

Don't complain. Don't explain. Say thanks. And wash your hands after you use the restroom.'"

"Sounds pretty bleak," I say.

The car behind me ponks its horn. I hold up my hands in the universal non-offensive gesture of helplessness. That road-rage seminar is really paying off.

"Bleak?" she squinches up her face as if those weren't the exact words she'd have used. She sighs. "Yeah, I guess it's bleak." She looks at my son. "Hey, boy? You want a few hundreds?"

"Sure!" my son says perkily. "I'll take 'em!"

"No, you won't," I say, putting a hand on his leg.

"It's a job, you know? It beats roadwork. Try walking on an incline all day on the side of a freeway. Nothing but a scythe in your hand." She tilts her head side to side like those dogs you see in the back windows of cars. "Wish, wish, wish."

"I'd like that job," my son says. "You get to wear those neon jackets, don't you?"

"Yeah, but it's murder on your ankles."

"Listen," I say. "Let's just forget the order. You guys have a nice night."

"Hookay," she says. "Thanks for listening."

I pull away into the cold dark to see the guy behind me giving me the finger. Wonder what he'll do with his hundred.

"She was nice," my son says. "But I'm still hungry."

"At least we got to spend this quality time together," I joke and he smiles at the verbal return. And the quote.

I pull over to the side of the road. I feel the father-need coming on and the opportunities to instruct are so few and far between that I relish the moment. I keep the car running, the heater going, and I turn in my seat to address him, to present the accumulated wisdom of my fifty years upon his delicate mind. I say this.

"Son. It is a crazy world. Nobody understands it. They just pretend to. People hurt you and there's nothing you can do. There will always be someone more broken than you. Someone with less advantages. And barring any major upheaval, like a revolution or something, we're just kind of stuck here. And it doesn't make much sense." I sigh, relieved to be unburdened of this truth, finally, having carried it for many years, waiting for the chance to tell it, relieved that I no longer have to lie, and prevaricate, convinced he can handle this awesome unsettling news.

"I know that, Dad," he says.

He said much the same thing when I finally explained the mechanics of sex, assuring him that it all made sense later when vaginas and ejaculation were no longer technical terms but passwords to the realm of desire and pain.

"We just have to do the best we can. And try not to hurt anyone along the way."

"Like the way you hurt Mom?"

"Exactly," I say, after a moment, proud of him. I see forgiveness and a slangy shrug of acceptance in his brown eyes and expensive jacket.

"I figured it was something like that. Hey, Dad. You know what I wanna be when I grow up?"

I brace myself. They never tell you how often this happens to parents. How crevices will open before you and offer a whole new realm of terror and disappointment and possible failure. And how much, no matter how hard you try to be calm about it, how much you care.

"I want to be happy," he says, smiling.

Oh, god, I think—not for the first time. He hasn't heard a word I've said.

# GHOST DANCING WITH MANCO TUPAC

### Jeff VanderMeer

*Ghost dancing was not simply a phenomenon central to the North American Indian mythos, but also an integral part of the ritual of the indigenous South American populations, particularly to the descendants of the Incas. The primary difference between the North and South American versions of the ghost dance is that the Incas danced more for remembrance than renewal. To the Inca, the future, unknowable, was considered to be at a person's back and the past, known, opened up before a person to be seen clearly.*

—Sir Richard Bambaugh, *Inca Ritual*, 1986, Harper & Row

## I

AT TIMES IT seems to the reporter as she scribbles notes in the dim light that this is his last breath, that the lungs will collapse in mid-sentence; the arms—hands twig-like

111

but supple—will punctuate his stories with a flourish
and then convulse, become limp, cold, languid. The
eyes, shining from the sunken orbits, will dim to the
color of weathered turquoise. The mouth will die a
hummingbird's death, slackening in a final flutter of
lips. Already a smell, old as parchment and strong as
vinegar, has begun to coat the hotel room. Outside,
Cuzco's moonlit streets are silent.

She can taste his death on her tongue: a bitterness
softened by the sweet-sour of incense burning in a bowl.
Her pen falters on the page, then hurries forward ghoul-
ishly, to catch his essence before it vanishes into the air.

But he does not die that evening, despite the heaving of
his breaths, the pauses and halts which disrupt the urban-
ity of his voice and its subtle hints of accent, none of which
can quite break the surface of syntax.

Behind him, black machinery sputters and jerks as it
feeds his lungs. At times he is lost within the machines that
engulf him, their own cough-cough threatening to drown
out his words, or snatch them before they can reach the
reporter's ears, and by extension, her pen.

She thinks it odd that a machine, a collection of cogs
and wires and bellows, should keep a man's soul in his
body, the two having no natural connection, nor even a
common meeting ground. Yet, when she looks up from
her page, he appears to have melted into the machines,
no longer a figure draped in sheets, lying placid on a
wooden bed.

Then, too, she finds it odd she should be here, having
closer kinship to the machinery than the man. At least she
can understand the machinery. Peru stonewalls her. It has
nothing to do with who she is or what she desires from
life. The hotel, for example, carved into the mountainside,
and the hotel room with its small window that winks from
the wall opposite her chair. The window, during daylight

hours, shows a cross-section of mosses and lichens, the loamy soil alive with beetles. Now it is just another shadow, rectangular amid deeper shadows.

The window reminds her of the grave and, staring again at Manco Tupac, last true descendant of the Inca emperors, she realizes just how small, how bird-like, he is. She had expected a giant, with the sinewy, leathery health of a man who claims to have survived one hundred forty winters in a country that already has her gasping for breath, ears popping. The man lying on the bed looks as though a breeze could strip the flesh from his ribs.

Her expectations have often led her astray; her vision of New York City before she moved there from Florida was of a citadel of shining chrome and steel—evenings at the Met, operas at the Lincoln Center, walks in Central Park. Cultural Eden. It was an image that, as her editor at *Vistas: Arts and Culture Monthly,* often says, "Got turned on its ass."

When her thoughts stray, as now, to home, or the hypnotic movement of his hands lulls her toward sleep, his *words,* muscular and tight, bring her back to her notes, to the physical sensation of the pen in her hand, to the nerves in her wrist that tense, untense, tense again.

Already she has been writing for an hour, her tape recorder broken and discarded an isthmus away in Mexico, her wrist ready to break on her now, with no money to replace that, either. She feels a spark of resentment toward the old man in front of her and then rebukes herself. She asked for it. It was the type of assignment her rival freelancers regularly had orgasms over as they drummed up articles from their pathetic little stomping grounds in Manhattan and the Bronx: interviewing the last of a breed, with all the echoes of faded glory, lost triumphs, a hitherto-overlooked pocket of nostalgia that readers and award judges alike could fawn over. Dramatic headlines dance through her head: BRUTAL IRONY: LAST DESCENDANT OF THE INCAS DYING OF ASTHMA; THE SECRET HISTORY OF THE 20TH CENTURY, AS REVEALED BY THE LAST OF THE INCAS. She does not know much more—yet. She knows that the old man requested the interview and that he holds an honorary degree from the National University of Lima at Cuzco. Beyond this, nothing. A void as black as the window carved into the mountainside.

"Do you think you have transcribed my words accurately thus far? It must be difficult."

His voice startles the reporter, because now it is directed at her. She squints at the page. Her eyes blur. The words become hieroglyphics. What did it mean, really, as a whole? Where is the article she dreamed up while still in New York? The perfect story and yet, almost indefinably, she can sense it going sour, going south.

"Yes, I think so," she says, smiling, looking up at him. Even her feet and ankles ache, a healthy, well-used ache, as if she has just swum ten laps at her local gym.

"Good," he says, and spins out the dry reed of his voice until it is impossibly thin, impossibly tight, tighter than the quipu knots his ancestors wove into compact messages: scrolls of knots sent across the Empire by fleet-footed men with muscles like knots beneath their skin.

She has only her pen.

## II

IN 1879, WHEN I met the man who called himself Pizarro, though Pizarro had been dead for over 300 years, I knew the Inca knots better than the Español of the usurper. I had not yet left my village for renown on the Brazilian coast, nor infamy in the United States, where I would spend many years being hunted by Pancho Villa over one misunderstanding and two exaggerations. I had yet to become known by the moniker of "Jimmy Firewalker," and still relied upon my given name, Manco Tupac, which I have returned to in these later years.

And also in 1879 my mother and father were still living. My parents, my four brothers and two sisters, and myself all worked the land, never owning the land, although we were allowed to plant some crops for our family's use. The hours were hard and we had few pleasures in our lives, but, for better or worse, I was always scheming to do better, to get out of our ruined hut of a house, to be *someone*. For the man you see before you is dissipated and jaded from too many years traveling this world, but in 1879 I was very, very *young*...

THE MAN WHO would be Conquistador again entered my village, two miles from this very city, as winter began to settle over the land. The trees had lost their few leaves, the sun had a watery, distant quality, and in the far off mountains, I heard the raw sound of avalanches as falling snow dislodged packed ice.

The man who would be Conquistador again rode up the old Inca road from Cuzco. He rode a nag, was himself a nag of a man: thin to a shadow, arms like poles of balsa wood, and his age above sixty. Wedged into the wrinkles of his face, his blue eyes shone with a self-assurance that beggared the decay of his other parts. He wore a rusted helmet from the past century, such as the men of the Peruvian viceroyalty wore before Bolivar swept them into the sea. At his side hung a rusty sword in a scabbard and a flintlock rifle, aging but oiled and shiny. Supplies weighted down his horse—blankets, water skins, bread, and dried beef—and it was the banging and clanging of these supplies that alerted me to his presence.

As this oddity approached, I sat idly in a chair outside our leaky house and pretended not to see him. Our family had just eaten our noontime meal and everyone was already in the fields, my father yelling for me to join them. I pretended not to see him either.

The stranger's shadow fell across my body. The voice that addressed me held no trace of quaver, more akin to the Damascus steel in his eyes than the ruins that surrounded them.

"Manco Tupac?"

"Yes," I replied.

"I am called Pizarro. I require a guide."

I stared up at him, saw the yellow cast to his face, smelled the quinoa berries on his breath.

"Where?"

He pointed to the mountains.

"Up where Tupac Amaru used to rule. I seek the Lost Treasure of the Incas." He said this with precision, capitalizing the phrase. "In Cuzco they say you are the best guide, that your ancestors are descended from Tupac."

I nodded and folded my arms. I was not the best guide. I was cheap. I had gained my meager reputation from my name, which combined the names of the two last and greatest Incan emperors, this an act of bravery on the part of my mother. It had been several months since anyone had requested my services due, no doubt, to the landowner wars that sputtered and flared like brushfires across most of the lower country.

"I have a map."

I stifled laughter. They all had maps in those days, whether it was black-clad Dominicans searching for treasure for European dioceses, or the newly coined "archaeologists" who dug up our graves, or common thieves from Lima and Quito. Maps on parchment, lamb's skin, papyrus, even tattooed on their skin. Never once had I heard of their quests turning up anything more profound than pottery shards, skulls, or abandoned mercury mines.

I nodded and stated my fee for such a venture.

"Of course." He inclined his head, an odd gesture of deference that almost made me forget he claimed the inheritance of Pizarro.

OUR QUEST BEGAN amicably enough. I said goodbye to my family, my father stern, his brow furrowed with worry, as he handed me his own set of bolas, with which I could bring down wild game. My mother, feigning indifference, had already returned to the fields by the time I left with the Spaniard. I cannot pretend they did not fear for me, but the money I earned would keep us fed and clothed through the winter. All the while, Pizarro upon his nag looked neither left nor right, harmless as statuary from another age.

We set out into a morning sharp and bright enough to cut our eyes, he upon his horse, myself following on foot. We traversed the Incan highway, still intact after 400 years, which ran from Cuzco into the mountains. The road was pockmarked with rubble, shot through with sweet-smelling grasses. We would not leave the highway until well near the end of his quest.

Every few miles, my companion would point proudly to the etched initials of a Spaniard immortalized in stone. Some of the crudest carvings dated back to Pizarro's original few score men.

As we traveled, he spoke to me of his ancestors, of what they had endured to bring my ancestors into the light of Christendom.

"It was a time of great energy! A time of great industry, unlike today, when Spain has fallen back on its haunches like a toothless lion." He grimaced at the thought, but then he brightened. "Perhaps a time will again come when..." He trailed off, as if realizing to whom he spoke.

"You are Christian, are you not?" he asked.

"I am not," I said.

"But you have been baptized?"

"I have not," I replied.

"Your parents?"

"They have not."

He shook his head, as if this did not make sense to him.

"There is but one true God," he said, in a lecturing tone, "and His Son, who died for our sins, is Jesus Christ. If you do not believe in Jesus Christ, you shall be eternally damned."

"What do you hope to find?" I asked. I had no religion, only a faith in the myths my mother had whispered to me even as a baby at her breast, a faith in the confident way she told them. It gave me secret pride that such tales had outlived the Spanish conquest, for the Christian God was by contrast colorless.

"What do you hope to find?"

A one word answer.

The only honest answer, ever.

"Gold."

WE DID NOT converse much after that first brittle exchange, but contented ourselves with watching the countryside unfold, always ascending along the winding road. The mountains surrounded us ever more and if we looked at them for too long, perspective seemed to place them within reach, as if we had only to clutch at the glittering domes of snow and they would be ours. But when we let our gaze drop to the ground beneath our feet—and we did this rarely—we quickly noted the precariousness of the path: our feet often came to the edge of open air, almost stepping out into a sky that could plunge us a thousand, two thousand feet to a valley floor, a river bed. Pizarro developed the habit of glancing down, then over at me, as if he wondered whether I would lead him into an abyss.

Near dusk of the third day, weary and ready to sleep, we came upon a troupe of Ghost Dancers. They danced around the ruined spire of an old Inca guard tower. The tooth of stone had served as a home to animals for at least 300 years, but they danced to restore the guard tower to its former glory and purpose. The bittersweet smell of sweat and exertion was a testament to their faith, their hope—a dream I could not share, for I found it impractical at that age. It would have accomplished much more, in my view, to rebuild the tower and refit the stones into the highway.

The dancers had adorned themselves in the rags of old ceremonial dress, clothing that still glittered with iridescent reds and greens, where it was not torn and re-sewn. The women, stooped and folded in on themselves, stank from years of labor in the mercury mines. Miraculous that they walked at all, and they danced like scarecrows on a puppeteer's strings, their jerky strides worn down to a caricature of normal human motion. To me they appeared bewitched, their twitches and stumbles those of a people caught forever in trance.

The men blended in with the women, except for one, who looked up at Pizarro astride his horse. Age had hardened this man until his true nature had retreated into the wrinkles and taut skin around the bone: one last rearguard against death. One could not guess whether he was happy or sad or merely indifferent, for his face had become such a mask that even ennui was a carefully guarded secret. And yet, if one discounted the faded rags, the dull eyes, this man resembled Pizarro closely enough to be his brother—and Pizarro must have recognized this, for he turned quickly away and muttered to me, "Do not stop here. Do not stop. Go on. Go on!," and urged his nag forward, at a pace I could hardly match.

When, after several strides, I glanced back, I saw that the man stood in the middle of the highway, staring at us. His gaze stabbed into my proud Pizarro's back like a dagger blunted by ill use, though why the similarity in their faces should frighten the Spaniard I did not know.

That night we camped in the sandy soil beside a patch of thorny yuccas. Though our clothing barely protected us from the chill, the Conquistador refused to unpack the blankets. He seemed to invite the cold, to embrace it, as if seeking penance. But for what? Because a mirror had been held up to him?

He remained awake for a long time, watching the stars glint like the eyes of gods. In his face, I still saw the ghost of the men from the dance, and realized they haunted him. His prayers that night, conducted in a whisper I strained to understand, were for his wife and children in Spain.

EVER UPWARDS WE climbed. I led now, despite his map, for the road contained treacherous potholes, overgrown with eelgrass and other weeds that disguised ruts until too late. On the fifth day, I brought down a wild pig with my bolas to supplement his supplies. Always we went higher. Always higher. However we traveled—slow or fast, on foot or leading his horse—we went higher.

"The air is thinner here," he said, wheezing.

"Yes, it is."

"How much longer?"

He asked this question often and I had no ready reply. Who could predict what obstacles we might encounter? Our conversations consisted of little else, and this depressed me, for I was normally talkative and animated with my clients. But when I asked Pizarro, he had no stories, no descriptions of his country. At most he might say, "Where I live it is beautiful this time of year." Or, "Churches are the only bastions of faith left, the only strength left in Spain." Once he said, "You will never go to Spain. Why do you ask?" He said this so matter-of-factly that I determined that I would travel to Spain, if only to spite this stupid old man who really thought his map and his alone led to the lost treasure of the Incas.

Now the mists began to roll in: thick soups that our weak eyes could not penetrate. We traveled through this underworld with no anchor to secure our senses. In the absence of taste, touch, hearing, we became each a ghost to the other, a form in the mist. Only sharp sounds—the jingle of bit and harness, the creak of leather saddle—pierced the whiteness. It did not, of course, affect our camaraderie, because our camaraderie would have fit into the space between his saddle and his horse's back.

Pizarro's nose bled copiously in the thin air. He tried, and failed, to staunch the flow with his spare shirt. The white fabric was soon clotted red as if he had suffered a fatal wound.

I had many strange thoughts. Disembodied by the mist, not even able to see our own feet, I found that my imagination tried to compensate for the loss of sight. Soon, every tree root under my tread was a human bone—here a thigh bone, there a neck bone. Helmets, too, I found aplenty with my feet, no doubt only rocks.

The only relief from the mist came in the form of lakes so blue and deep that they seemed black; so thickly placid that a skipping stone would only "plunk" and disappear, leaving no ripple to mark its entrance. The bones and treasure of many Inca lay at the bottom of such lakes, and I felt in my heart that a man would fare no better than the stones. The lakes were all graveyards without markers.

I told this to the Conquistador and he laughed.

"Think of the gold," he said. "If only we could find a way to raise the gold."

I began to fear his determination, his single-mindedness, his refusal to make camp until after the moon rose high above the mountain peaks. He was old and yet by strength of will refused to allow his body to betray him.

On the seventh day, when the silence and the mist made me both jumpy and melancholy, he asked me to tell him a story. I told him it was an odd request.

I thought I saw him shrug through the mist as he said, "My father once told me stories to pass the time when we went out into the fields—to oversee the men. This mist unsettles me." And then, in a whisper, "Please." I wondered if he saw the ghost dancer in his dreams, if the man stood in the ruins of the old Incan highway and stared at Pizarro, night after night.

I thought for a moment and then said, "I shall tell you a tale from the beginning of the end of our reign."

He nodded, motioned for me to continue.

And so, I launched into my tale, determined to drive away the mist that clotted my eyes and stole my breath...

## III

THEY JOURNEYED TO see the toad who lived in the maggot-cleansed eye of an eagle. This eagle had died high above a granite canyon, and already on the trek all seven llamas had been lost to thirst and fatigue. The meat was rationed by the seven Quechua who walked the ancient paths. These paths had been laid down long before the Inca rulers had arrived at Macchu Picchu and built the city of Vilcapampa. They never remained the same—carefully chosen stones led the uninitiated to ravines, or places where the earth buckled, cracked, as mountains tossed and turned in fitful sleep.

One Quechua, Melchor Arteaga, was a lunatic. He danced the dance of the Emerald Beetle, Conchame, bringer of drunkenness and shortened breath. Twelve days before, Melchor had been struck by a Spanish musket load near Vitcos, where even now refugees straggled in ahead of the conquerors. The left side of the lunatic's head had darkened; he moved jerkily. His eyes darted back and forth, perhaps following a hummingbird's frantic flight from flower to flower. By nightfall, Melchor would be dead. By nightfall, the toad would have told them what they wished to know.

Two men, nobles, had already died, but three strong men carried the corpses on shrouded litters, muscles straining, faces long since stripped of any fat. Captain Rimachi Yupanqui, oldest of them all, had suffered through Inca Atahualpa's capture by Pizarro. He of narrow eye and hawkish nose had seen the old king butchered once he filled a room with gold. Rimachi remembered the delicate butterflies, beetles, alpacas: children's toys. The metal work had bought nothing. It never would. Rimachi walked with a soldier's sense of fixed steps. His companions, Sayric Tupac and Titi Cusi, sons of the seventh man, had witnessed excesses themselves on the fields outside Cuzco; they listened with hatred when Rimachi spoke of Pizarro, the man who had robbed them of their birthright. All three carried bolas at their waists, the stones flaked with dried blood.

The seventh man was the king, Manco. His army awaited his return, bearing the oracle of the toad. The toad had always decided the punishment of the worst evil-doers. Manco staggered forward, clutching his side, Rimachi supporting him at intervals. The wound would heal in time. But the king's eyes were hollow and the clear, cold air cut through his robes. He shivered.

"Treachery," Manco muttered, speaking to the sky. After raising the banner of revolt, many Quechua had joined him. But the Spanish had routed Manco near Cuzco and he had fled to the Urubamba Valley; the safety of fortress-capital Vilcapampa reassured him. Steep drops, raging rivers, and passes three miles high would hinder pursuit. But his forces needed a sign as the Spaniards approached, stripping bodies of metal, their thirst for gold unslaked. Manco made this pilgrimage because his captains had lost faith, and he himself refused to be ruler over the solitary mountain peak of Macchu Picchu. Manco still hoped the toad that watched from the eagle's eye, the oracle of the Quechua, would shed some wisdom on this crisis. Certainly the resident priest could help him understand.

So, sliding and stumbling, seven men lost themselves on the paths. Squinting, Manco pressed forward in the glare of the morning sun. Melchor followed, giggling and clutching his broken head. Behind both, the king's sons and his captain dragged the dead nobles; they would be placed near the oracle, buried under rocks. No one spoke, though once or twice Rimachi would mutter a word to Titi, staring with concern at Manco. They ate as they moved, llama meat and quinoa, the cereal-like seeds kept in waist pouches. The sun eclipsed Melchor's face. Manco allowed himself a smile, his callused feet lifting more easily with each step. They were close. Rimachi smiled too, a guarded smile. He knew the odds, had known them since Manco had cast off the role of puppet king.

They reached the bridge that joined the two sides of the canyon. Its liana cords made it durable, but the ropes swung and groaned in the wind. Manco crossed first, bracing himself against the gusts, planting one foot in front of the other. Melchor ran across, nearly ramming a foot through the webbing. When everyone had reached the other side, Manco said, "We will cut the bridge once we cross over again. We will cut every bridge…" He looked to Rimachi, who nodded his approval. Manco glanced at his sons, then moved forward.

The stone hut next to the bridge was empty. The priest who had stood guard was discovered by Rimachi, who pointed downward to the base of the cliffs. The man was dead, sprawled with arms outstretched, his robes a blur of blood. Manco frowned, and said, "Leave him."

Together, they made their way to the toad's alcove, their bolas held ready. The alcove lay in a grotto which had been hollowed out at eye level above a shelf of rock. From the shelf, the men could see the stacked range of mountains fading into the distance, clouds stalking from above. The valleys beneath them were green smudges, the rivers sinuous lines broken by the white interruptions of rapids.

Although Rimachi and Titi searched, fanning out to cover the shelf's rim, no enemy could be found. A cold wind blew out of the west and Manco shivered again. He called his son and captain back and, bravely, he approached the alcove. A judgment would be passed down. Behind him, Rimachi watched, a grimace forcing its way through wrinkles; the death of the priest made him wary. Sayric and Titi stood frozen, their burdens temporarily forgotten. Melchor picked a flower from behind two stones.

Manco peered into the hole. Within lay the toad, staring out from the eagle's eye. How it sparkled in the sunlight!

Manco's shoulders slumped. He sank to his knees, a sigh and snarl of exhaustion on his lips. Rimachi cursed, kicking at the ground. Sayric and Titi dropped their burdens. The dead men tumbled over the edge of the rock shelf, falling until they disappeared from sight.

Melchor laughed, as though Conchame, the Emerald Beetle, was buzzing in his ear, and brought his musician's pipes to his mouth. Whirling, flailing, Melchor pawed at his head. A hollow sound, slow and melancholy, crept into the air, a counterpoint to his crazy dance. Manco, knowing he would never reclaim his lands, no matter how hard he fought, raised his head to catch the notes. He nodded wryly as Rimachi helped him to his feet and his sons wept. A dirge. How fitting.

For the toad had turned to gold.

## IV

I TOLD THIS tale as a warning. If it marked centuries of slow decline and failure for the Inca, it also foretold a punishment for the Spanish: to be enraptured and consumed by their obsession with gold. Pizarro did not take it as such. He was silent for a long time, so long that I thought he had fallen asleep on his horse.

But then he said, haltingly, as if explaining to an idiot, "I studied at the military academy in Barcelona many years ago. You must understand that war is not a game for children."

"Thank you for your wisdom, but I do not see it that way," I said.

To which he replied, "That is why I am upon this horse and you are my guide."

I kicked at the skulls that must have been roots or rocks, and cursed myself for telling such a story at all. The Spaniard was without subtlety and I without patience.

THE SPARSE YUCCA and scraggly herds of wild alpaca gave way to bleak ice and snow, without the mist, which we soon learned had been a blessing, for now we saw each other more clearly, and neither of us could more than tolerate the other. Myself, because the Spaniard was conservative and withdrawn. The Spaniard, because I refused to agree with him and told him stories with no useful moral.

We argued about supplies.

"Surely there is wild game about," he said when I suggested his dry beef and water skins would only last the journey if we turned back within three days.

"Look around you," I whispered, afraid of avalanche. "Look around you! Do you see any trees? Any bushes? Anything for an animal to eat? Do you?"

We were tiptoeing through a field of abutting mountains, whose flanks raced upward toward the sun. Not a blade of grass, and no water, except in the form of ice. Beneath the ice, more ice.

"How do you know?" he said.

"Because I live here," I said.

He shivered, nudged his horse forward, its hooves making soft scrunching sounds in the snow.

AN HOUR LATER, we came upon a frozen waterfall.

The Spaniard, complaining of the cold, trailed off in mid-insult, saying, "My God!" A solid wall of ice confronted us. In the center of this wall, a doorway had been covered over by water that had once flowed in a river down the mountainside and now formed a facade of ice. A man, frozen through, looked down at us from within the doorway. At first I thought he was floating in the ice, but as we moved closer I saw the frayed end of a rope. The man had been hung by the neck and the passage sealed with him inside it. The man wore a Conquistador's armor and his head lolled; his helmet had frozen to his forehead and his arms hung limply at his sides.

"An angel! It is a sign." Pizarro said. He dismounted, bent to one knee, and crossed himself.

"Just an adventurer," I said. "A plunderer, who was put here by my ancestors as a warning."

He ignored me, walked up to the frozen doorway, put out a hand to touch the ice near the dead man's head. He muttered a few words.

"A fire," he said. He turned away from the man. "We must light a fire to melt the ice. Beyond the ice lies the lost treasure of the Incas."

As the sun faded, we lit a fire. Rather, I lit a fire and Pizarro hacked at the ice with an axe. The blade was dull and made a *chut-chut* sound as it cut into the ice. Pizarro was strong for his age and his technique fluid. Soon, the dead man began to float and when Pizarro finished hacking a hole in the ice, water spilled out, more ice broke, and the man was set free. He came to a stumbly rest at our feet, face down, a sodden mass of armor and rags and flesh. The doorway was almost clear and beyond lay a passageway untouched by frost.

Then I knew that we had entered the spirit world and our minds, our wills, were not truly our own.

In one convulsive motion, the lump of flesh at our feet roused itself, bracing itself with its arms until the face, still lolling hideously against the neck, looked up at us with soggy eyes, exhaled one last breath and, shuddering, fell back to the ground. In the moment when the eyes stared at me, I swear I saw someone else looking out at me, not the dead soldier, but someone else, a god, perhaps, or one aspiring to godhood. A sentry for the immortal.

I screamed and turned to run, but tripped and fell in the snow, bruising my left shoulder. Pizarro, through inertia or bravery, stood there as the corpse died a second death.

His sheer ignorance of the danger forced me to curb my instinct to flee, though my heart pounded in my chest. I remember that moment as the one time when I could have moved against my future. The moment after which I could not turn back, could never again be just a simple guide in a town outside Cuzco. If I could, would I go back to that wall of ice and tell myself to run? Perhaps.

Pizarro gently knelt and closed the corpse's eyes with a sweep of his gnarled hand. He crossed himself and laid his crucifix upon the dead Spaniard's breast. The light in his eyes as he rose frightened me. It was the light of a beatific and cruel self-assurance. It lifted the wrinkles from the corners of his mouth, sharpened and smoothed his features.

Pizarro did not choose to break his silence now. He merely pointed toward the path cleared for us, patted me on the back, and remounted his horse. We entered the tunnel.

The tunnel was damp and cold and the sides painted with old Incan symbols, the paint faded from the water erosion. Everywhere, water dripped from the ceiling, speaking to us in drips and splashes. The temperature grew warmer. Soon we saw a sharp yellow light through the dimness and the passageway opened up onto the burning orange-red of sunset.

The tunnel overlooked a shallow basin between mountains. We had come out upon a hillock that overlooked a vast city, the likes of which I had never dreamed of: magnificent towers, vast palaces of stone, a courtyard we could barely discern, radiating out from a ripple of concentric walls. A *city,* whole and unplundered, lying amid thick vegetation—this is what took our breath away, made us stand there gawking like the explorers we were not.

IT IS DIFFICULT, even now, to describe how strongly it affected me to have reached the location on the Conquistador's map and have found the bones of my ancestors in those buildings. No longer was I a simple villager, poor and bound to the earth—here was my legacy, my birthright, and if nothing else, that knowledge gave me the confidence with which I met the world the rest of my days. Here was yet another last refuge of the Inca, another place the Spaniards had never touched, could never touch. I wept uncontrollably, wondering how long men might have lived there, how finally they must have died out, protected from everything except their own mortality. The city radiated a desolate splendor, the pristine emptiness of the abandoned, the deserted. Perhaps then I understood what Pizarro meant when he had called Spain an old lion rocking back on its haunches.

But if my reaction was violent to an extreme, then Pizarro, by virtue of his hitherto-unbroken mien, had passed into madness. He wept tears, but tears of joy.

"It is truly here! I have truly found it!" He let his horse's reins fall and he embraced the ground. "Praise to God for His mercy."

To see his face shine in the faded sun and his mouth widen to smile its first smile in nine days, an observer would have believed him caught in the throes of religious ecstasy. It did not strike me until then what a betrayal it had been to guide him to that place.

"Come, Manco," he said. "Let us descend to the city center." We made our way down into the basin—along a path of red and green stones locked perfectly together, into the antique light, the legion of yellow flowers, the perfumed, blue grasses.

We could not simply press through to the center of the city, for walls and towers and crumbled stones stood in our path. But, as we progressed, gaps in the stone would allow us to glimpse the ragged flames of a bonfire near that center. A bonfire that, minutes before, had not been lit. Yet now we could feel the heat and hear the distant sound of Incan pipes: a dry reed that conveyed in its hollow and wispy sound the essence of ghosts and echoes and every living thing deadened and removed from its vitality. Behind it, as a counterpoint, a flute, twining and intertwining in plum-sweet tones, invited us to dance, to sing.

From the moment we first heard the music, we fell under its spell and could do only what its husky silken voice told us. We hurried in our quest for the center, the courtyard. We wept. We sang. We laughed. Pizarro threw his rifle to one side. It caromed off a wall and discharged into the air. I dropped my bolas to the ground, prancing around them before moving on. We were slaves to the spirit of the city, for the city was not truly dead and the life in it did not come from the wilderness beyond, nor yet from the power of its ghosts. No, these were *living* forces that had fled from Cuzco and all the lower lands.

Thus we drew near over the ancient and smoothed flagstones, luminous-eyed crocodiles lured in dance to the hunter's spear. The Conquistador was crocodile indeed with his salty tears and I, uncowed even by the myths my own mother had told me, an unbeliever at heart, was brought back into belief only by the compulsion and evidence of my own eyes.

We danced through the city until my lungs ached from laughter and my feet throbbed against the stone. Finally, we unraveled the circles of the maze and came out upon the center square. Within a blackened pit, a fire roared, muffling the music that had seemed so pure.

Around the fire danced men and women wearing the masks of gods and goddesses from the Inca faith, and from earlier, more powerful, faiths. Conchame, the emerald beetle, bringer of drunkenness and shortened breath, danced his own mad dance, while Cupay, the amorphous god of sin, adorned himself in cockroach carapaces of the finest black and aped their scuttling walk with a shuffle and hop, his eyes always surveying the others with suspicion. Ilapa, god of thunder, made lightning-fast moves around the flames, letting them lick his fingers, his feet, as he twisted and turned in a blur. The hummingbird, messenger to the gods, was there too: a woman who wore thousands of feathers about her arms and legs, so that she shimmered and dazzled; even when she stood still, the movements of the others were reflected in the feathers, to give her the illusion of motion. Of them all, only her face was not hidden by a mask. She had delicate features, with high cheekbones, and lips that formed a mysterious smile. Her chest was bare, covered only by her lustrous black hair.

The rest I could not identify by name, and no doubt they came from older faiths—jaguar gods and snake gods and monkey gods—but nowhere could I see the sun god, Inti. The smell of musky incense rose from them. The fire spewed sparks like stars. The laughter of the dancers, the chafing of bodies moving closely together, seduced our ears with its otherworldly wonder.

From behind, wind-swift, hands guided us to positions closer to the fire. I found myself reluctant to glance back, to identify our hosts, and Pizarro, too, looked only ahead. The hands—strangely scaled and at times too heavy with hair—brought alpaca meat on golden trays and a wine that burned our throats but soon went down smoothly until it was mild as water.

Alternately, we wept and laughed, the Spaniard embracing me at one point as a brother and asking me to visit him in Barcelona. I heartily agreed and just as quickly burst into tears again.

The dancers continued in their dance, a numbing progression of feet and whirling arms. Sometimes they moved at double speed, sometimes much slower than natural. Through it all, I caught glimpses of the hummingbird woman's smooth brown legs as she made her way around the fire—or a flash of her eyes, or her breasts, the nipples barely exposed, brown and succulent. She spoke to me when she drew close, but I could not understand her above the fire's roar, the jocularity of the Conquistador and our invisible servants, the hands that offered us qutok berries and wrens in spicy sauces. Her lips seemed to speak a different language, the effect akin to ventriloquism.

The Conquistador mumbled to himself, seeing someone or something that was not there. Even in my drunken state, I could tell that he did not see the gods and goddesses. Cupay danced much too close to him and eyed him with evil intent, sprinkling him with a golden dust that melted when it touched the old man's clothes. "Yes, yes," he muttered to no one. "It is only fair," and "I, your servant, cross myself before you."

While Pizarro talked, I watched the hummingbird woman. She flitted in and out of the dance with such lascivious grace that my face reddened. A toss of black hair. A hint of her smile, with which she favored me when I looked in her direction.

I wept again, and did not know why.

Pizarro said, "To the glory of Jesus Christ!" and raised his glass high.

The heat became *cold*, a burning as of deep, deep chill.

Conchame danced a dance of desperation now, bumping into the others with a bumbling synchronicity, his laugh as bitter and wild as an avalanche. A sneer lining his mouth, Cupay no longer danced at all, but stood over the Conquistador. The jaguar god snarled and writhed beside the fire. The snake god hissed a warning in response, but discordant. The Inca pipes grew shrill, hateful. Only the hummingbird woman's dance remained innocent. The incense thickened, the sounds deepened, and my head felt heavy with drink.

The jaguar god, the snake god—all the gods—had removed their masks, and beneath the masks, their true faces shone, no different than the masks. The jaguar head blended perfectly onto the jaguar body, down to the upright back legs. The snake's scales ran all the way down its heavily muscled flanks.

They were my gods, but they frightened me; the fear came to me in pieces, slowly, for my thoughts swam in a soupy, crocodile tear sea. They were so desperate in their dance, their very thoughts calculated *to keep them moving,* because if they ever became still they would die. The Spaniards had taught them that.

A hand grabbed mine and pulled me to my feet. The woman. She led me into the dance, my fear fading as suddenly as it had come. Calm now, I did not weep or laugh. We whirled around the heat, the sparks, growing more sweaty and breathless in each other's company. The feel of flesh and blood beneath my hands reassured me, and my desperate attempts to keep up amused her. I danced with recklessness, nothing like the formality of dances at the village.

I even began to leap over the fire, to meet her litheness on the opposite side. She laughed as I fanned mock flames. But the next time I jumped I looked down and saw in the flames a hundred eyes burnished gold and orange. They slowly blinked and focused on me with all the weight of a thousand years. After that, I simply sat with the woman as the others danced and Pizarro talked to an invisible, presumably captive, audience.

"The flames," I told her. "I saw eyes in the flames."

She laughed, but did not answer. Then she kissed me, filling my mouth with her tongue, and I forgot everything: the eyes, the Conquistador, Conchame bungling his way around the fire. Forgot everything except for her. I felt her skin beneath me, and her wetness, and my world shrank again, to the land outlined by the contours of her skin, and to the ache inside me that burned more wildly than the fire. I buried my head between her breasts, breathed in the perfume of her body, and soon forgot even my name.

I believed in the old gods then. Believed in them without reservation or doubts.

WHEN I WOKE, I remembered nothing. I had dirt in my mouth, an aching head, and the quickly fading image of a woman so beautiful that her beauty stung me.

I recalled walking through the city and marveling at its intricacies. I recalled the fire, and that we had met with... with whom? A beetle crawled past my eyes, and I remembered it was Conchame, but I did not remember seeing him the night before, bereft and sadder than a god should ever be. It would be many years before I truly remembered that night; in the meantime, it was like a reflection through shards of colored glass.

Slowly, I rose to an elbow and stared around me. The city lay like the bleached and picked-through bones of a giant, the morning light shining cold and dead upon its concentric circles. The courtyard's tile floor had been in ruins for many years. All that remained of the fire was a burnt patch of grass. Near the burn lay the Conquistador, Pizarro, his horse nibbling on a bush.

Beside Pizarro lay a pile of golden artifacts. They glittered despite the faint sun and confounded me as readily as if conjured from thin air, which indeed they had been. Children's toys and adult reliefs, all of the finest workmanship. There were delicate butterflies and birds, statues of Conchame, Cupay, Ilapa, and Inti, and a hundred smaller items.

Pizarro stirred from sleep, rose to his knees. His mouth formed an idiotic "O" as he ran his fingers through the gold.

"It was no dream, Manco," he said. "It was no dream, then." His eyes widened and his voice came out in a whisper. "Last night, by the fire, I sat at the Last Supper and Our Savior hovered above me and told me to eat and drink and he said that unto me a fortune would be delivered. And he spoke truly! Truly he is the Son of Heaven!"

He kissed me on both cheeks. "I am rich! And you have served me faithfully." So saying, he took a few gold artifacts worth twice my meager fee, put them in a pouch, and gave them to me.

PIZARRO WAS EAGER to leave in all haste and thus we left the ruins almost immediately, although I felt a reluctance to do so. We soon found our way back to the dead Spaniard and lower still by dusk.

That night, I fell asleep to the *clink-clink* of gold against gold as Pizarro played with his treasure. But, come morning, I heard a curse and woke to the sight of Pizarro rummaging through his packs. "It has vanished! It is gone!" His cheeks were drawn and he seemed once more an old man. "Where has it gone? The gold has vanished from my hands, into dust."

I could not tell him. I had no clue. If he had not seen it disappear himself, he might have blamed me, but I was blameless.

We went back to the city and searched its streets for two days. We found nothing. Pizarro would have stayed there forever, but our food had begun to run out and I pleaded with him to return to Cuzco. With winter closing in, I thought it dangerous to stay.

We started down again and Pizarro seemed in better spirits, if withdrawn. But, on the fifth day, we camped by a small, deep lake and when I woke in the morning, he was gone. His nag stood by the lakeside, drinking from the dark waters. His clothes were missing. Only the map remained, black ink on orange parchment, and his sword, stuck awkwardly into the hard ground. I searched for him, but it was obvious to me that the Spaniard had been broken when the treasure turned to dust and had drowned himself in the lake.

I continued the rest of the way down, leading the nag but not riding her, for I did not know how. I knew only that my gold had not faded. It still lay within the pouch, and it was with that gold that I would later buy my way to America.

Soon, I came upon the ghost dancers again, but I did not stay long, though I wished to, for the man who resembled Pizarro stood in the highest part of the tower and for some reason he troubled me. I believe I thought it was Pizarro, gazing down on me.

Thus, rich beyond measure and fortunate to be alive, I hurried past the tower and down into the lowlands and the fields to rejoin my family.

\* \* \*

## V

THE REPORTER DOESN'T know what to say at first, so she doesn't say anything. Ignore the parts that aren't possible, she tells herself. He's an old man. He's just mixing fact and fiction on you. But it's not the impossible parts that bother her.

Manco stares at the wall, as if seeing it all over, and she says, "Did you ever discover who the Conquistador was?" She could really use a smoke, but she doesn't dare light up in front of a dying asthmatic.

His gaze turns toward the darkened window, toward the movement outside that window. His eyes seem unbearably sad, though a slight smile creases his lips.

"Among his personal effects were letters written to his family and when I returned to Cuzco, the mestizo he had bought the horse from filled in the gaps. It is quite ironic, you see"—and he stares directly at her, as if daring her to disbelieve—"He was an immigrant, a destitute carpenter whose father had herded sheep across the Spanish plains. Had he attended the military academy in Barcelona? I do not know. But during the time of land grants, his forefathers had settled in Peru, only to come to misfortune at the hands of other fortune hunters, the survivors limping back to Spain. No doubt he had read the accounts of these pathetic men and hoped, long after it was possible or politic, to acquire his own land grant. Practically, though, he chose the best route: to steal treasure."

"But where did the map come from?"

Manco shrugs, so that his shoulders bow inward, the bones stark against brown skin.

Silence, again, the reporter trying to think of what to ask next. It frustrates her that she is reduced to *reacting*. Her mind alights upon the woman dancing around the fire. An adolescent wet dream. Believable? Perhaps not in the setting he had described, but the romances in the man's life might fill up a side bar, at least.

"What happened to the woman?"

He closes his eyes so that they virtually disappear amid the wrinkles. He must have twenty wrinkles for each year of his life, she thinks.

"I forgot her. I forgot much, as if my mind had been wiped clean. Sometimes the memories would brush against my mind as I sought my fortune in America. Other women... other women would remind me of her, but it was as if I had dreamed the entire night."

"When did you finally regain your memory?"

"Years later, as I walked through Death Valley, dying of thirst, certain that the bandits who had stolen my horse would find me again. My eyes were drawn to the horizon and the sun. It was so hot, and the sun was like a beacon filled with blood. I stared and stared at that sun... and after awhile it began to give off sparks and I heard myself saying 'Inti was in the fire.' I saw the bonfire then and the Gods who had surrounded the bonfire, and... her, the woman—and I wept when I realized what I had lost when I lost my memory, for she had been human, not a goddess.

"Those memories sustained me through that dry and deadly place, as if I drank from them for strength, and when I reached California, I resolved to return to the city."

"You went back to the city?" the reporter says, which vexes her even more.

"I spent a night in the ruined tower where the Ghost Dancers had once danced. I stopped by the lake where the Conquistador had drowned."

"And you found the city again?"

"I did, although it had changed. The vegetation—the path of flowers, the many trees and vines—had died away. The towers and buildings still stood, but more eaten away, corroded. So too did I find the woman—still there, but much older. The Gods had left that place, driven back into the interior, so far that I doubt even a Shining Path guerrilla could lead you to them now. But she was still there. The Gods had preserved her beauty well past a natural span, so that in their absence, she aged more rapidly. I spent seven years by her side and then buried her—an old woman now—in the courtyard where I had once jumped across a fire with a hundred eyes staring up at me. And then I left that place."

Manco's voice is so full of sadness that suddenly the reporter feels acutely... homesick? Is it homesickness? Not for New York City, not for her apartment, her cats, her friends, but for the bustling white noise of her office, the constant demands on her time which keep her busy, always at a fever pitch. Here, there is only silence and darkness and mysteries. There is too much time to think; her mind is working in the darkness, trying to reconcile the possible, the impossible.

Something dark moves against the lighter dark of the window. Something in the darkness nags at her, screams out to her, but she wants to forget it, let it slip back into the subconscious. Outside, someone shouts, "*No habla Inglesia! No habla! No habla!*" She can feel dust and grit on her and her muscles ache for a swimming pool. When her husband left—was it four years now?—she had swum and swum and swum until she was so tired she could only float and stare up at the gray sky... and suddenly, she is looking up from the water... into Manco Tupac's eyes.

"You changed the most important part," she says, her heart thudding in her chest. "You changed it," and as she says it, she realizes that this story, this man, will never see print, that the darkness, the shadows, the past, have changed everything. What is there left to her with this story? What is left at all? Nothing left but to go forward: "Tell me what you left out." It is one of those moments which will not last—she'll recant later, she'll publish the story, but for this moment, in this moment, she is lost, and frightened.

He is quiet for a moment, considering, then he turns his head to consider her from an angle. "Yes, I will," he says. "Yes. I'll tell you... What does it matter now?"

Then he is whispering, whispering the rest of the story to her, an enigmatic smile playing across his lips, as if he is enjoying himself, as if the weight of such a story, never before told, can now leave him, the machines the only weight left to keep him tied to this earth. And every word takes her farther from herself, until she is outside herself, out there, in the darkness, with him.

*Tupac remembered precisely when he decided to kill the old man he called the Conquistador. They had stared into the dark waters of a lake above Cuzco and the Conquistador, already dismounted from his horse, had said, "This place holds a million treasures, if we could only find a means to wrest them from the hands of the dead." The lake held the bones of Tupac's ancestors as well as gold, but he did not say this, just as he had not protested when the old man's map had led them to the hidden city. He had done nothing while the Conquistador had rummaged through the graves on their last day in the city, picking through the bones for bits of jewelry to supplement the gold already gifted to him. How could he have done nothing?*

*But as they stood and looked into the dark waters, Tupac realized that the old man's death had been foretold by the lake itself: the Conquistador's reflection hardly showed in those black depths. If the Conquistador's reflection cast itself so lightly on the world, then death was already upon him. Killing this man would be like placing pennies upon the eyes of the dead.*

*When they came out of the hills and the fog of the highlands into the region of the deep lakes, Tupac's resolve stiffened. In the early morning light, the Conquistador's horse stepping gingerly among the ill-matched stones of the old Inca highway, Tupac had a vision: that a flock of jet-black hummingbirds encircled the Conquistador's head like his Christian god's crown of thorns.*

*The Conquistador had not spoken a word that morning, except to request that Tupac fold his bed roll and empty his chamber pot. The Conquistador sat his horse stiffly, clenching his legs to stay upright. Looking at the old man, Tupac felt a twinge of revulsion, at himself for serving as the old man's guide, and at the old man for his casual cruelty, his indifference, and most frustrating of all, his overweening ignorance.*

*At midday, the sun still hazy through the clouds, the Conquistador dismounted and stood by the edge of yet another lake. He did not stand so straight now, but hunched over, his head bent.*

*Tupac hesitated. The old man looked so tired. A voice deep inside him said he could not kill in cold blood, but his hand told the truth: it pulled the Conquistador's sword from its scabbard in one clean motion. The Conquistador turned and smiled when he saw that Tupac had the sword. Tupac slid the sword into the Conquistador's chest and through his spine. The Conquistador smiled more broadly then, Tupac thought, and brought close to his victim by the thrust, he could smell the sour tang of quinoa seeds on his breath, the musk of the Conquistador's leathers, and the faint dusty scent, which they both had picked up traveling the road together.*

*Then the old man fell, the sword still in him, Tupac's hand letting go of the hilt.*

*Tupac stood above the dead man for a moment, breathing heavily. An emptiness filled his mind as if he were a fish swimming blind through the black lake that shimmered before them. The sound of a chipparah bird's mating call startled him and he realized that the Conquistador had died silently, or that his own frantic heartbeat had drowned out any noise.*

*The Conquistador's eyes remained open and blood had begun to coat his tunic. Blood crusted the sword's blade, which had been pushed upward, halfway out of the Conquistador's body when he fell to the ground. Tupac tasted salt in his mouth and brushed the tears from his eyes. He felt nothing as he rolled the Conquistador's body over and into the water. The body sank slowly, first the torso bending in on itself, then the legs, and finally the arms, the palms of the pale hands turned upward as if releasing their grip on the world.*

*When the hands faded from view, the emptiness spread through Tupac, from his arms to his chest and then to his legs, until it felt like a smooth, cold stone weighing down his soul. He would never forget that moment, even when he was old and bed-ridden. He would see the Conquistador falling, falling, falling for a hundred years, and no matter how many places he visited, no matter how many adventures he had, no matter how many memories he filled up his mind with, he could not stop seeing that slow fall, or stop feeling the sword, as if it had entered his body, as if he had fallen into the dark wet lapping of waves, into the unending dream of drowning...*

# HOME TIME

*Ian R. MacLeod*

MORNINGS HERE ARE just as bad as mornings anywhere else. I sit up in my bunk and scowl at the mirror. The ceiling feels close as a coffin overhead, and if I reach out either way, I can touch the walls. We travelers need a tight place to call our own, a burrow to crawl into. Here at Epsilon Base, we call them torpedo tubes.

It's my turn to fix breakfast. The three of us chomp shriveled waffles and pseudo-bacon hunched around the little table in the kitchen area. We've all put on weight during our stay; stress and boredom do that to you. Janey's in jeans that were tight three months ago when we started out and now look simply painful, the same T-shirt as yesterday and the day before. Figgis re-reads one of his old technical mags, a glob of butter hanging on the strands of the beard he's grown over a face still neat with youth. No one says a word. Janey tosses her greasy blonde hair. She sighs. As I didn't hear any sleep-period ramblings between their torpedo tubes, I guess I'm sitting in the chilly slip-stream of a lover's argument.

My turn to clean up. Funny how often the rota works that way, but still I can't be bothered to argue. Gives me something to do before we get ready for the final Jump. In a nice domestic touch, Epsilon's Korean designers placed the tiny basin beside a porthole so you can see out as you stand there. I plunge my hands into the warm recycled water.

Outside, the storm has died. My hands pause, aimless fish swimming. Ice furs the rim of the porthole like the white spray that was used in shop windows at Christmas back in England when I was a kid. It's October, which means that the sun here dances a fire around the horizon. The high winds of a few hours ago have left streaks in the ice like the claw marks of some giant animal. The storm may have died, but faintly through the filtered triple glass, I can still hear the wind. In the Antarctic, it never stops.

By the same cosmic coincidence that made it my turn to cook and clear, it also falls to me to check the outside of Epsilon before our next Jump. There's no room for me to kit up in my outsuit in my torpedo tube, so I have to do it in the one corner of the cramped living pod that isn't strung with washing. Figgis and Janey just sit around and watch as I strip down to bra and knickers. I'm conscious of my wobbling marbled flesh and the stray bits of body hair, but of course I'm just good old Doctor Woolley; she's past modesty and all that kind of thing.

It feels good to squeeze into the privacy of the inner hatch, to bang it shut and watch the warm air cloud to crystal as the frozen atmosphere gushes in. There's no question that, barring the ocean floor, I'm facing the most hostile atmosphere on Earth. Nothing compared to Io or Venus, of course, but astronauts don't have to breathe the atmosphere or fiddle bare-handed with bits of frozen machinery that can peel the skin off your hands like a rubber glove. And astronauts have up-to-date equipment. And they're all Taiwanese.

The outer hatch booms open. The shiny outsuit hisses and squeals as it adjusts to the sixty-degree drop in temperature. I climb out and down. The white hits my eyes. My lungs go solid tight inside my chest. I glance back. Janey's face is at the porthole. She gives me a smile and a wave, like someone moving off on a train. I stomp a few yards across the ice.

Epsilon is shaped like a dumpy starfish. The central mound contains the main life support systems and the comms bay, with the kitchen, the torpedo tubes, the living bay, the medical bay, and snout of the canhopper fanning off. I can't say that Epsilon actually looks like a starfish because—in the one part of the deal that our college really held out for—the whole of the outer body was re-coated in military-grade camouflage paint before we left our home time. Even now, from what must be no more than twenty shuffling paces away, I have to squint hard to make it out as more than another frost ghost given momentary reality by the wind. Janey's gone. Figgis, too. I could almost be alone.

I pick my way around the drifts and hollows, checking for accidental debris; anomalies that would almost certainly destroy us. The bitter wind pushes and pulls at me like an argument. It roars in my ears. I do a slow circuit of Epsilon, then another for luck. The wind has already raked away my first footsteps. I brush ice away from the canhopper's cockpit.

"Woolley!" Janey's voice suddenly crackles over the wind in my ears. "What are you doing out there?"

"Won't be long," I say, then pluck off a glove to reach inside my hood and dislodge the comms wire. I don't

need you Janey, not out here. Woolley doesn't need anyone.

I breathe the air. The wind snatches the frozen vapor
from my lips and throws it back in my face as grit.
Overhead, the sky is lace over blue oblivion. When I
was a child and my mother first told me stories about
this place, I used to imagine that there really was a pole
up here, striped like a candy stick, around which the
planet revolved.

I squint, darkening the lenses of my goggles by a couple
of notches with the presspad inside my mittens as I re-
inspect the ground. But it makes little difference. Pure
Antarctic roars over my inadequate senses. I'm leaning
twenty degrees into the wind just to stand up. Looking
down at my feet, I see the drift ice racing. Nothing feels
still. Snow here is as rare as rain in a desert; all that ever
happens is that the wind drives the ice, scooping it into
high drifts, baring the underlying strata, destroying—
thank God—every trace of life. White on white on white.
I still have to keep reminding myself that we are in the
Year of Our Lord, 1890.

Gladstone is Prime Minister in England. Zeta Tauri is
still a distant star. Etcetera, etcetera. Look at it this way: if
I turned my back and walked out across the ice away from
Epsilon, if I crossed the Queen Maud Mountains and got
as far as the McMurdo Sound and came across a whaler
lost amid the penguins and icebergs far from its normal
hunting ground, if those rough and stinking men would
take me aboard, I could visit India in the Raj, Imperial
Saint Petersburg, Venice before the flood. Chat with Marx
or Freud, ride through London in a hansom cab. The
whole world—if my very presence didn't cause it to heave
into oblivion—would be mine.

My toes are dying off. I turn back. When I reach the
porthole, I remember that I've torn out my comms wire. A

tiny worm of panic bores at my spine. But there's no need to worry. Janey's seen Woolley through the porthole, and she lets Woolley in. She and Figgis once again watch the show as this ugly butterfly strips from her chrysalis outsuit, but by now I can't be bothered to feel any irritation. We've all got other things on our minds.

It's time for our final Jump up the line. We clamber through the internal hatch to the communications bay. Figgis is in charge of this aspect of the mission, so he gets the comfy chair in front of the console while Janey leans her rump against a mainframe so old it bears an IBM logo. I have to stoop awkwardly under a plastic strut.

Figgis drums his fingers. Janey chews her lips vigorously. Pushing strands of graying mousy hair back from my face, I wonder what exactly it is that I do that gets on their nerves. The numbers on the 2D screen tick by in seconds. The console is a mess of the scribbled stickers that Figgis used to re-label the original Korean hangul script. Taped beside it is a postcard of Interlaken where he took a pre-Epsilon break, blowing what little advance money the college had been prepared to loan him. The plastic ski runs on the arid mountain slopes look like spilled rolls of toilet paper.

Jumps are something I can never get used to. This is the fifteenth if you count the big power surge that first threw us back to 1565 and the vicinity of the South Pole. From there we've moved up through the years—collecting data and growing increasingly weary of each other—by a series of smaller Jumps powered by our own internal batteries. Now at least we're that much closer to home.

Figgis gives up drumming his fingers and begins to stroke his beard, tugging it as though he's trying to pluck a chicken. The minutes plod by on the screen, and each one is just like any other. But this time of waiting is special with worry. Jumps involve the orbit of the Earth around the Sun, the rotation and the ever-outward drift of the Galaxy. And then you must add to that the flow of time itself. What actually happens is that for a dimensionless moment we exist in several times and places at once, hovering like a mayfly over the waters of reality as Epsilon calculates exactly where we should land. So far, the system has worked perfectly...

That's what's happening now. We Jump and the porthole on our right fills with the soundless buzz of the Jump, which is almost the way the old-fashioned TV screens used to go between channels, but pushed back to three or possibly four dimensions. A blizzard without color or sound, a glimpse into the swirling plughole of the non-universe, a place where there is in fact no light at all, where the absence of everything means even an absence of nothing. We all know that our eyes are simply tricking us when we try to look. We know by now that it's better not to.

The screen registers contact. Stocking ladders of data flutter and clear. Figgis sits back and rests his hands behind his neck. The chair creaks. I can smell his sweat. I guess he can smell mine. We brace ourselves for something more. But that's it. This is March 14, 1912. Epsilon is well within tolerance—even if we're not. Figgis pulls harder at his beard. Janey draws another flake of skin back across her lips.

"So what we have here," Figgis says, "is 1912. Tell us what's happening, Woolley."

This is our ritual. I half-close my eyes and recite that Asquith is Prime Minister in Britain, that the Titanic will soon be starting her maiden voyage from Southampton. I describe how Nijinsky's wowing Paris, and explain that China has just become a Republic. I don't mention that Roald Amundsen has reached the Pole a month and a half ago, and that Captain Scott's men are still struggling to get back to Cape Evans. That goes without saying.

"You see," Figgis says to Janey, tipping her a smile, the beginnings of a reconciliation. "Woolley knows her stuff."

"That's me," I say. I grin and slap the strut I'm leaning on with one of my big hammy hands. "Good old Doctor Woolley..." Epsilon booms faintly. "Let's get going."

"You're the boss," Janey smiles up at me. For a weird moment, I can almost see why men find her attractive. And I wonder if I'd become a lesbian if she turned it on strongly enough using all that stuff with the pressing tits and the fluttering eyelashes, the way she does with Figgis. Perhaps that would be the answer to all Woolley's problems. Janey's smile widens. Woolley finds herself blushing as she heads for the ladder between the dangling knickers and Y-fronts.

JANEY PILOTS THE canhopper. Figgis and I squat on the rumbling seats over the engines with the stretcher rack crammed behind. Watching Janey now, brushing the controls as though they were bruised, the sleeves of her outsuit rolled back from those narrow wrists, I can't help but admire her ease and absorption. The canhopper rocks slightly as the eddy from an ice dune tucks under the fuselage and her hand slides out to brush the boost control. The tone of the right engine alters a fraction through my pelvis, then resumes.

Figgis has got the big Canon holocam balanced on his lap. He nods toward it and says to me, "Did I tell you that Janey and I gave this a trial run a few weeks ago in her torpedo tube?" He's grinning. Back in 1650, Janey and Figgis were at maximum rut for each other. It didn't exactly keep them quiet, but it did keep them more or less out of my way.

I force a nod, and the skin of my outsuit crackles as if it shares my discomfort. Janey's eyes are still on the window. She doesn't even blink. She's so wrapped up in piloting the canhopper that Figgis and I can talk about her as though she isn't here. Over her head on the console is the date and time. March 14, 1912. And the day is yet young; Epsilon's computers have thoughtfully avoided any kind of Jump lag. It's still only 10:30 in the morning.

Trackless, unseen, undetected, we sail five meters above the ice desert on an electromagnetic tide. I was expecting a storm, but everything looks clear and sharp as a wedding cake, the sun gold and midway down the sky now, well into the polar autumn. As always, I looked for changes when we first crawled out onto the shattered ice of this new era, but there was nothing. If it were safe for us to Jump as far as 1950, it might be possible to pick out that faint grayish haze that the jet pilots had started to report in the sky, but the real differences in this polar environment are being sniffed out by Epsilon's many sensors. More methane, more nitrogen, more carbon dioxide. More of most things apart from oxygen. Even if the dictates of relative safety hadn't determined our choice, the very sterility of the Antarctic would still have made it an ideal place for monitoring the planet. But that's down to the data in the spectrometers that our college will eventually download and sell to the highest bidder. All our poor human senses can report is whiteness.

Janey clicks her lips open. "This is it, folks," she says.

I lean forward to see out of the windshield. She's right; there are black specks on the horizon. The canhopper sails quickly toward them.

Flags. Uptilted skis.

"For God's sake don't knock anything over…" Figgis murmurs.

But Janey's in control. The engines sigh to a halt. The canhopper settles its smooth underside a safe distance away across the ice.

We bang elbows as we seal up the outsuits and the specially wide and flat-soled shoes. Figgis says he thinks Woolley should go first. Janey nods from underneath her hood and mask. I feel a flood of gratitude, but as I unseal the hatch, I wonder if they're doing it this way just so that Woolley'll get the blame if anything goes wrong. Not that any of us really need to worry about that.

And out. And down the steps. This really does feel like a historic moment. Even if Scott is a month gone from the Pole and Amundsen by longer, we're lonely travelers here, too. Amid these fragile signs of human presence, it feels as if we've arrived somewhere at last. The wind pours over me. It flutters the Norwegian and British flags. The little tent Amundsen left behind is half-buried in drift ice. He's already safely back at Framheim and preparing to report his triumph to the world, but Scott's team are still out there, with Petty Officer Evans already dead and Captain Oates starting to limp badly…

Black shapes of tent and ski poles, the sun low and distant across the sparkling ice. The whole scene belongs in some Edwardian painting, but it makes me feel incredibly nostalgic for past times of my own, for the stories my mother used to tell me on late afternoons after school by the lake in the park. Though she had never been to the Antarctic, she filled my head with dreams of whiteness; a once-upon-a-time continent that, at least until this last dreadful century, remained almost untouched by man. She told me about

Shackleton, Amundsen, Scott... Their names grew sharp for me as pavement frost. I saw them as silhouettes in the wild white dark, hopeless and determined, their ships crushed by the ice, death walking beside them, struggling endlessly back toward base camp.

WE HAVE A picture show back at Epsilon when we've finished. We're all unusually chatty. I don't know about Janey and Figgis, but for me the ordinary details we found out there were the biggest shock. These men may be legends from my childhood history, but here at the Pole they were just weary and afraid. They left an inconsequential litter behind them. God knows why, but one of those narrow bicycle repair tins was lying out on the rough ice. There were frozen dog turds from the huskies, a Norwegian cigarette packet, a screwed-up wrapper of Cadbury's chocolate. It almost looked like the remains of a picnic. I longed to touch.

We kept the holocam running all of the time, and that's what we're watching now. We didn't realize what we were doing at the time as we grouped self-consciously around the tent and the flag, but our pose mimics with terrible clarity those old shots of Amundsen's and Scott's teams doing the same thing. It's eerie. We look almost as tired and afraid.

Janey makes dinner for a change. She ransacks the store for freeze-dried plaice and mushrooms, little balls of cardboardy rice. She looks at Figgis all the time he eats. A peace offering, of course. He gets the message and rumbles male comments about how good it tastes. And there's some acidic Frascati she's reconstituted to loosen us up. We keep the conversation safe, going over ground already worn smooth with repetition.

After coffee, I offer to clear up in the expectation that Janey and Figgis will beat a swift retreat to the torpedo tubes to discuss more urgent matters. But something goes wrong behind my back and Janey storms off alone, shouting You Never this and Why Don't You that, leaving Figgis drumming his fingers on the table and the cramped atmosphere colder than it is out there beyond the porthole.

More than happy to stay out of it, I take a shower and give myself a good rub down, marveling at the swelling blue veins in my legs. Then I flop down inside my Korean-sized torpedo tube balled up in my dressing gown. Faintly, I can hear Janey still sobbing next door. I close my eyes. Relax, Woolley. Tomorrow's a big day. The biggest. I wish I could imagine—

Figgis raps on the hatch. He wants to talk. I let him in.

"This all is so ordinary," he says, crouched between the little shelf and the rim of the bunk. "Janey and I are arguing like kids. I wish I had your distance from this kind of thing, Woolley."

"Didn't the college psychologists tell you what was going to happen when they did the profiles?"

He shakes his head, then nods. "Yeah, but I didn't believe them." He pulls at his beard. "What did they tell you?"

"They told me I'd be lonely... They told me I was used to it and that I would cope." I pause, but why not speak the truth for a change? "They told me that you two squabbling and screwing would get on my nerves."

He reaches out a hand. My veiny leg is sticking out of my dressing gown as far as my thigh. He gives it a pat. "I'm sorry, Woolley."

"That's okay," I say, shifting slightly to cover myself. "You read any truthful account of this kind of mission, it's always the same. Think of Bligh on the Bounty."

Figgis grins. "And Captain Oates is cursing Scott for his incompetence at this very moment."

"That's right," I say.

He pauses. Janey's gone quiet next door. Probably listening to us, trying to catch the words over Epsilon's plastic hum and the muffled scream of the wind. "Can I ask you a question?"

"Fire away."

"Tell me how you feel about sex, Woolley. I've always wondered."

"You mean, do ugly people have a sex drive? And if so, what do we do with it?"

He doesn't answer. He's down to shorts and a cutoff T-shirt that's ridden up over his taut belly so that I can see the beginnings of his pubic hair. His whole body is clear and sharp; no cause for shame. His eyes are sharp too, and his breath smells sweet through that ridiculous beard: maybe he's drunk another bottle of the wine. You get used to seeing bits of people when you're a doctor. But that isn't the same as the whole.

"Yes," I say. "I do have a sex drive. And I'm not a virgin, either. I was once nineteen like everybody else. You know what it used to be like at those parties when the college was still taking regular admissions? When people paired off, there was always some lad drunk enough to do the ugly bitch in the corner a favor. I went through all of that... that phase. But sex on its own is a disappointment, isn't it? It's everything that surrounds it that counts."

Figgis's eyes don't flicker. He's watching me the way Janey watches the instruments when she's piloting the canhopper. "Would you have liked to have children?" he asks.

That's another question entirely, although I understand from my own bitter inward arguments that it follows on neatly enough. Is that why I'm thinking about my mother so much these days?

I take a breath. "I don't know," I say. "Things would just be different. I probably wouldn't be here for a start."

"Yeah," he says with a sigh, and I realize that I've been tactless. He leans forward. I like the way his young muscles move, and for a moment I wonder if I don't detect some sexual charge—or at least a need for sharing—in this close torpedo air. But he's just trying to shift his arse on the uncomfortable rim of the shelf. Figgis, he's at ease with Woolley. He could almost be on his own. He says, "Do you think Janey's asleep?"

"I doubt it."

"Well maybe I should go see her. Clear the air."

I smile. "You do that."

So Figgis works his way out of Woolley's torpedo tube and bangs the hatch shut, leaving me with his faint mannish odor, my own stale disappointments. I dim the lights and lie back. I play music through my earset for a while. It's Bill Evans in concert, June 25, 1961, but even as the bass line joins the piano for "My Foolish Heart," I can hear Janey and Figgis next door. Making up. He's groaning, she's groaning. It's no good. I turn the music off and wait for silence. And it comes, it comes. With Epsilon humming and the faint gathering storm, my fingers reach down and find the place, and touch. I realize that I'm aroused anyway. Poor old Woolley gets off just on the sound of other people doing it. My fingers circle and dance. The darkness moves with them. For a few moments, the sun breaks through the rain clouds and dances white on a lake where laughing bodies dive and mingle, going deep to a place where there's nothing but music, nothing but light.

My vision spins back. This torpedo tube. The sound of my heart. Eventually, I sleep, and I dream, as so often recently, about my mother. And with her face, with her voice, comes the echo of trolley wheels squealing along a hospital corridor, the bright wash of fluorescent light, the itchy feel of the stool on which I had to sit and wait for her on that day she went to collect her test results. The dream's so familiar that part of me's just watching. As she comes back through those swing doors and stoops toward me, somehow still managing to keep a smile on her face—looking, in fact, almost relieved—I realize that she must have already known that she had cancer. Mum was also a doctor, after all. And you always tend to expect the worst when your own health's at stake. So this would just be confirmation that she was dying.

Perhaps she brought me with her to the hospital for moral support; perhaps it was just because it was in the school holidays and she didn't know what else to do with me. And I sat waiting for her on that seat in the corridor while the nurse behind the desk gave me sweets that had gone sticky in their wrappers.

The face of the woman I see coming out through those double doors—big jaw, small mouth, big forehead, large, deep, close-set eyes—is much like the one that stares back at me nowadays from the mirror, even if I do sometimes wish I could manage her smile. Mum said something to me as she bent down. Always in these dreams, I can see her lips move, but I can't quite understand. Not exactly. It was something about making the most of time, love. Time. Love. Home. Not Long... Something like that. And, as always in my dream—in memory, too—I strain to catch her words. But I can never quite hear them.

Mum died within a year. She turned gray and her skin faded off her big bones and the pain that she was reluctant to take medication for often made her irritable. Little Woolley was eleven by then, with most of her mother's ugly features, most of her mother's aptitudes. Like Mum, I was already a loner, the giver and taker of easy playground jokes. And, like Mum, I eventually became a doctor. The only thing about me, really, that's different—until recently, anyway, when even my own biological clock has given off the occasional pre-menopausal ping—is that I've never entertained thoughts of having children. Not that Mum took the usual step of pairing off with a suitable man. Like me, I suppose, that course was less than straightforward for her. She went instead to a sperm bank and had the thing done coldly, methodically, without all the lies and the fumbling, the pretences of passion. Thus it was that little Woolley, the product of a nameless and unknown father, finally entered the world. Thus it was that Woolley began a life that has ended up here in the Antarctic of a different century as the product of genes which had, appropriately enough, been frozen.

TWO HOURS OUT from Epsilon on the trail of the British Antarctic Expedition under the command of Robert Falcon Scott. Janey pushes the canhopper hard across the ice plateau. She's in control. Figgis drums his fingers. The tight air inside the canhopper resonates as the engines drone. Whatever happened between the two of them last night has left a residue that lies somewhere between love, lust, anger, despair; the Greeks probably had a word for it. It seems to me that they've both finally realized that this relationship is heading in the same direction as every other relationship they've ever been involved in: that the personality profiles were right. The fact is, Janey and Figgis—despite their good looks, their relative youth, their admirable if somewhat over-specific intellects—are both constitutionally incapable of sustaining a long-term friendship, let alone love. At times like this, I feel truly sorry for them, and sense more easily the desperation that has driven them here. Both double-divorcees, Janey and Figgis have been ejected from the present at least as thoroughly as poor old Woolley has. Perhaps they'd entertained thoughts of staying together, of using the chat show and media-spin off fees we're hoping to get when our college goes public to buy a proper house in a Sony enclave and recover custody of the children they've left in their turbulent wake...

Amazing, when you think about it, that we've lasted out this whole month together. But we have—just about. The profiles were right about that, too. Me, I'm simply glad that we're nearly at the end of it, and that the chances seem reasonably high that we'll return to home time.

"Your turn to drive, Woolley."

I blink my way back to the present.

"Okay, Woolley? You look like..." Janey glances back over her shoulder. The canhopper is on hover and she's human again. She smiles a human smile. "... I'd better not say."

Right, I think. Right.

I take the controls. All the dials are pointing toward the top—except for those dials that should be in the middle, which are in the middle, and those which aren't working at all or have been disconnected, which are limp, or blank. I ease the canhopper forward. Another couple of hours on the plateau for Janey to rest before the difficult bit. The ice rushes by, not as fast as before although Woolley does her Woolley best. I search left and right for the tracks left by Scott's men, but there is nothing. Even assuming they kept a course this straight on their return, the wind scours everything away.

The sun has dropped west, but I still need to keep the screen fairly dark. I can make out the faint reflection of

Figgis and Janey behind me. I watch Figgis rest his hand on the inside of Janey's thigh. I concentrate on the driving.

Three Degree Depot flashes by couple of hundred meters east. Flags and litter. I circle once at distance, but we decide not to stop. We're too afraid by now, too hurried, too eager. The sun slides closer to the ice at our backs, throwing huge shadows. Far ahead, something jagged breaks the flat horizon. The canhopper races on. Saw serrations become teeth, teeth become mountains. The sun sinks lower and reddens, daubing them with blood.

Janey yawns behind me. She says, "Move over, Woolley."

I slow the canhopper without argument. Janey settles into the pilot's seat. Figgis scratches his beard.

The Transantarctic Mountains rise and rise, damming the glacier of the Polar plateau. The ice starts to buckle into great ridges. We're sailing over the wreckage of a vast conflict. Janey has to climb hard on manual to get over and around the pressure faults. Looking out of the side window and down into the blue chasms is almost as bad as staring out of the porthole during a Jump. The canhopper's engines hiss with effort and I lever my arms for balance against the bulkhead.

Everything is huge... Blood and shadow. Trying to ignore the part of my mind that insists on trying to give meaning to the shapes, I crane my neck up toward the mountain flanks where there are slashes of bare stone. Scott's men made special detours, just to take off their mittens and touch. In this desert of ice, I can understand why.

We pass into mountain shadow. It can't be possible, but I feel the chill. Then out into a glare of light, too extreme for the screen's somewhat aged dimmers to cope with.

Janey slows abruptly as she waits for the whiteout to settle. We're moving through a jagged gouge; it's too rough to be called a valley. The shadow blinks over us again. Bluish ice tumbles into squares that for a giddy instant could be the size of sugar cubes or the blocks God hewed to make the universe. Janey checks the readouts, draws back to a total crawl. Now that the engines are quietened, I can hear the patter of wind-driven ice striking the canhopper's fuselage.

Slow ahead. The canhopper crests a ridge. There's a glimpse of a far horizon, then another ridge, and my stomach drops into space beyond. The wind tips us like a kite but Janey's hands are three places at once, taking us down a magnetic slide. The Beardmore Glacier is below us, an immense fan of ice and moraine sloping out from the mountains. The land ends here but the ice carries on, the Great Shelf filling the bay of Ross Sea. My stomach settles and for a few moments I believe I can see the blue rim where the ocean finally begins, but that's 400 kilometers away and already the cloud directly below is thickening.

It closes over. We drift down the Ice Falls... Ghost ships lean from the coiling mist. There are cracks and chasms—it's a devil's stairway. I keep telling myself that five starving men have recently picked their way up and down this glacier and beyond. I can't believe it, not even when Janey slows to point out a discarded glove lying close to a crevasse. Figgis muses that maybe this is the place where Petty Officer Evans fell and nearly lost his life, even if there are grounds for supposing that the accident was dreamed up by Scott to provide an excuse for Evans's drift into insanity.

We pass the flags and the wreckage of Last Glacier Depot. I can sense desperation in those remains as Janey does a slow circuit. Shreds of torn canvas. The ice scuffed as though there was some kind of fight. A dented paraffin can rests a good twenty meters away; it's all too easy to imagine it being kicked or thrown there in anger when they find out that the extreme cold had leeched its precious contents away. And Evans will be sulking and muttering to himself, ill and getting iller. And Scott remains aloof, perhaps already sensing what lies ahead; that his diary will be the only thing that matters. We're catching up on them now, both in time and distance. They were here twenty days ago: unbelievably, it's taken us just half a day in the canhopper to gain a whole month on them.

Everything is so real now. So close. Everything else we've done; all the research, all the secrecy, all the back room deals, all the delays, the endless planning, all the reassurances we've given ourselves that, despite the odd tiff and hiccup, things have been going pretty well: they count for nothing. Suddenly, we realize that we're approaching the only moment in this journey that ever mattered. Forget about fame and money and glory and science and history. Forget about the muffled arguments in the torpedo tubes and park bench dreams of whiteness, the endless wastes of half a dozen lost centuries. Forget about the hope of what we might or might not bring back to home time. We're simply very, very afraid.

EVEN ALLOWING FOR the fact that the universe, at least in mathematical terms, seems to function just as well running backwards as it does forwards, time travel remains a paradox, a mystery. In many ways, we know little more about it than did the researchers who made that first tentative backward-nanosecond push a quarter of a century ago. Can you really assassinate Hitler, Napoleon, give an early warning to the residents of

Pompeii, Hiroshima, Liverpool? The truth is that, in a sense, we still don't know.

Of course, time-travel research was instantly a hot property. Imagine! A bomb that arrives at its target before it's been fired! A strategic early-warning computer that Jumps backward to give itself time to issue commands! Better still, you can eliminate the commanders of pesky military rivals before they've been born! For a while, the possibilities seemed endless. But they were not.

The timeline we live within is somewhat elastic, and will seemingly accept the disruptions that the presence of something like Epsilon will cause, but it is also extremely sensitive. Anything that might actually change things simply disappears with nothing more than a clap of returning air. That, at least, is the generally accepted theory. As, by the nature of these things, any time-disruptive Jumps have simply failed to return, and have left no mark on history, there will always be room for doubt. It may be that the stored-up energy that the outraged meta-universe emits when confronted with an irreconcilable kink in time seeds a new big bang. Or it may be, as some optimists still assert, that those lost time-travelers and recording devices are still out there in some alternate re-run of our world. But even the optimists have no answer to the question of how they can be deemed to have got there using time travel from a "future" that will no longer be their own. And the optimists haven't looked out of Epsilon's portholes during mid-Jump.

For all our hunger for the past, it seems that we can only peer under its very edges. And, for reasons that may have something to do with our penchant for recording and studying history, or possibly even the anthropic cosmological principle, it remains especially dangerous to tamper with the works of man. The very

universe, it seems, resists. Thus it was that many international treaties and protocols were agreed, to be
policed by watchdogs at least as powerful as those that
oversaw the rampant proliferation of nuclear weapons
in the previous century. The United Koreans, in particular, were more consistent in the breach than the
observance. In view of their spectacular military and
industrial success, it may be that they succeeded where
others failed. But even they seem to have lost interest
now. Time travel—at least in the sense that we once
imagined it—is itself in danger of becoming history.

FIGGIS TAKES THE controls for a while as the canhopper
slides away from the rubble of the glacier. Janey curls up
in the seat beside me and snatches reluctantly at sleep. A
storm blows up quickly, lying flat white across the screen
one moment, then tunneling back and back the next. It
looks unnervingly like the empty buzz that comes when
you Jump.

The clock above the screen says 2:30 p.m., March 15
1912. We have a big margin—there really is no need to
push this hard—but we are caught up in the urgency of the
chase, the need to get things done. Unbelievably, the storm
gets worse. Janey takes over, and even she has to use the
scanners. The green images flicker. I can see lips and faces,
the star-skulls of Lovecraftian Old Ones. Gothic shrines to
the wind. Faces in the playground shouting Stupid Ugly
Woolley. I close my eyes...

After school, at what was also called home time in those
days before the words were purloined, the other kids
would stop taunting me when they saw my mother waiting on that bench beside the lake. In the winter, her big
hands would be red and blue from the cold, and in the
summer there'd be rings of sweat under her arms, and her
face would often be so wet that she looked as if she'd been

crying. I'd sit down beside her, and she'd tell me about her day and then those stories of the Antarctic and all the other things I suppose most parents tell their kids. Like how she'd sat here on the first afternoon after she'd been inseminated at the clinic, and stared across the water and breathed the scents of fresh-cut municipal grass, ice cream vanilla, litter bins...

Those were some of the last good seasons in England. Summers that brought decent heat, autumns of mist where leaves fell from the living trees, winters of snow and frost. The last glimmers, as it turned out, of our country's wealth and glory. Across the lake on the hottest of days, lads in cut-off jeans dived laughing from the wooden pier. And, every year since Mum could remember, the cold undertow from the deep natural caverns would draw one of them down, and a body would be discovered days or weeks later bobbing in the lime pits on the far side of town. Mum being Mum, she sometimes tried to warn them of the risk they were taking. But they always just kept on laughing. They'd never listen.

Eventually, we'd make our way up the streets toward home. I'd hold Mum's hand and she was tall above me, and I'd think of Shackleton climbing that last mountain toward the whaling station, and of Scott, and of Captain Oates...

The biodetector at the bottom of the console gives a gentle bleep. I blink awake and lean forward. My spine goes cold. This is much too soon. Scott's men can't be here. I can almost feel the outraged universe preparing to spit us out with one simple cataclysmic heave. Then the rough shape of a cairn looms out of the ice storm; a cross and the ripple of a flag...

The canhopper circles and still the biodetector bleeps, unable or at least uncalibrated by its Korean makers to distinguish the frozen dead from the near-frozen living.

"Must be Evans," Figgis says. "Isn't anyone else it could be... Pity we can't get a decent picture."

So this is the grave of Petty Officer Edgar Evans, who dreamed not of reaching the unattainable, but of retirement and a good pension from a grateful Government, maybe enough cash to buy a pub down in some pretty part of Kent. His decline could have had something to do with a fall on the Beardmore Glacier, but what medical evidence there is makes that unlikely. To Edwardians like Scott and his team, the initial signs of mental instability in a man such as Evans would have been a source of puzzled embarrassment. They would try to find a simple physical explanation. Scott had his own complex obsessions; he didn't realize that the simplest hopes are the ones that break most easily. And, although Evans was easily the biggest of the team, he had to make do on the same starvation rations as the others as they manhauled their sledges across the ice.

Janey turns the canhopper back on their trail. In a quiet moment that is probably the closest an old agnostic like me ever gets to prayer, I wonder how I can ever complain about having to put up with her and Figgis when the four men ahead of us have had to share Evans's last hours as he screamed and raved in their tent. And then I wonder—I simply can't help it—what death will feel like; that last push when I cross the final barrier. Will I know about it? Has it already happened?

AT LAST.

We are close.

Janey is at the controls. Even she is keeping the speed down now. We're at the buzzing edges of the storm, with snatches of clarity between the flurries. Moving slow left and right over Scott's estimated course, she finds fresh sledge tracks, the scuff of wounded feet. She follows, keeping low. On the map display at her side, our course now wavers the same drunken line followed by the four men ahead.

It's exactly 1:30 p.m., Friday March 15 local time, when the biodetector starts to bleep. The range is just over three kilometers. The air is jagged crystal now as Janey pulls up the magnification on the detector's bearing. There are black specks against the white. Stooped. They don't seem to be moving... Yet they are. Slowly. Janey matches the canhopper's motion to theirs, she increases the magnification again. The canhopper balances their distance, moving forward an agonized footstep at a time.

So that's it. Contact. We dare not move closer for now even with the canhopper's military camouflage. Janey clicks all the controls to auto. Then her shoulders sag and she draws her hands over her face, rocking back and forth. Figgis is pulling at his beard. I can hear the soft snap as it comes out by the roots.

The afternoon is endless. The canhopper moves forward in tiny jerks. It's agony watching the image of Scott's men magnified against the whiteness, but none of us can look away. Amundsen got to the Pole with skis and dogs, but the British way had always been man-hauling. Sure, Scott brought along dogs, but no one had been trained to use them. He brought ponies, which all died, much to the distress of Cavalry Captain Oates. He brought skis, which they didn't know how to use. And he brought three snazzy mechanical sledges, one of which fell through the ice, while the others broke down. At the end of the day, every British explorer knew that the Antarctic was about manhauling; a harness and a heavy sledge to pull. Even looking at them, I can't believe it. They've dragged themselves this way across 3,000 kilometers of ice. As Janey and Figgis and I stare out, the thought surely crosses all our minds that we should drift in closer, turn on the canhopper's lights, beckon these men over, feed them, give them warmth... This, I decide, must be how God feels: looking down, knowing that he cannot intervene.

With the engines almost at shutdown, I can hear the wind quicken, then decrease. Ghosts rise up from the ice, white on white. I'm too tired to think, and again I can see claws... Ravenous eyes and teeth... Faces pushed close and shouting... A park bench...

One of the four men ahead is obviously in greater pain than the others. It's difficult to watch any of them, but with Captain Oates, it actually hurts. He doesn't walk—it's an inhuman shuffle, something out of a monster comic book. He falls behind. After a while, Scott, Bowers, and Wilson droop their limbs and loosen their harnesses as they wait for him to catch up. Eventually, he does, but soon he falls behind again. Oates is suffering from scurvy, which was still the scourge of polar explorers at the start of the last century. One of the disease's many unpleasant characteristics is that it unknits old wounds. His thigh was shattered by a sniper's bullet during the Boer War: by now, the scar tissue will have dissolved.

I watch as he falls behind once more. There can't be any doubt among them that their chances of survival are thinning by the hour. Scott has already called Oates "a terrible burden" in his diary. But not for much longer. For today is March 15, 1912, when Captain Lawrence Edward Grace Oates finally walks out of history—and into legend.

Evening of a sort. With Oates still shuffling far behind, the others begin to put up the tent. It takes a long time and there are fresh ice flurries coming from the east. Clumsy fingers. Clumsy minds. None of them seem inclined to take a piss before they go in; they'll be dehydrated as well. Or maybe they've given up caring. They close the tent. Oates finally gets there too. There's an odd sort of pantomime before they let him in.

Janey rests the canhopper on the ice for an hour. None of us is hungry, but we eat, guessing that the men inside the tent are doing the same, sharing out the frozen crumbs of their few remaining rations. We have hot soup, crackers, a chocolate bar each. The wind howls. After an hour and no sign of further activity, Janey starts up the canhopper again and drifts in much closer. Down from two kilometers to one, then five hundred meters... four... three... two... one hundred. Then fifty. She uses the screen projection and the biodetector to make sense of the storm, but now that we are this close to the tent, the skis and the sledges are clearly visible through the streaming white. Janey kills the canhopper's engines. In the sudden silence I can hear the rattle of ice against the fuselage... And canvas fluttering...

We all dress awkwardly in our outsuits and move the litter of the journey away from the canhopper's outer door in case anything should get blown out. It's uncomfortable in all this thick padding, but we dare not be anything but fully ready now. We wait. Wilson—the doctor in the party—has given Oates a heavy dose of morphine. They all hoped without saying that it would finish him off.

The storm is unnerving gray-white static. Any time now. We wait. The storm quietens a little. The midnight sun flickers gold. Just as the drift ice begins to sweep over again, the side of the tent flutters oddly. For a moment, I think it's just a twist of the wind, but then I see it jerk again. There's no doubt that the laces of the outer flap are being pulled. A head appears. We watch without a word. Janey's gloved hand circles the canhopper's door release.

Oates falls out from the tent on hands and knees, his head down between his shoulders. Behind him, the ties jerk as someone pulls them shut again. He crawls forward without looking up, makes an effort at standing, fails as his right leg shoots out at an agonizing angle. He's dragging something behind him. I can't exactly make it out through the storm, but I know from the records that he's taken his sleeping bag and boots out there with him. Neither would be any use to him, but at the very least it must have been plain to the others what Oates was doing.

Still, we wait. It could take several hours for him to die, and it was decided long ago that we should wait for him to get at least twenty meters from the tent. But he's moving so slowly. He keeps standing up... Falling over. He looks drunk—maybe the morphine has affected him. After about twelve meters, I put up the hood of my outsuit and say Let's Go in a shout that comes out as a whisper. Janey pushes the release. The Antarctic storm roars in.

I climb down the steps from the canhopper. Swaying against the wind, I unclip the syringe gun from my belt. My body is screaming hurry hurry, but the last thing we dare risk is one of us sustaining an injury. I take my bearings as Figgis and Janey back out with the stretcher. Oates still has his head down. The screaming wind is masking whatever noise we are making. He still hasn't seen us or the canhopper.

We push forward toward Oates and the tent. They've stacked their gear on the far side to act as a feeble windbreak, so at least we don't have to worry about tripping over a sledge or damaging something. Figgis has a flashlight on the shoulder of his outsuit. The idiot turns it on, and I signal wildly to him through the blizzard, too excited to think about using the comms set.

The tunnel of light, if it caught directly on the tent's filthy weave, would shine straight through. Janey gets the message, and reaches to turn the thing off herself. Still, Oates is crawling, the ties of the sleeping bag looped around his trailing injured foot, his hands wedged up inside the reindeer-skin finnesko boots for leverage. And the world is still here. The ties of the universe haven't broken. And Oates hasn't seen us.

I push on into the storm. Half my mind is still on that tent and the three men inside it who belong, untouched by us, in history. Now, Oates looks up, his hands still pushed into the boots like clumsy mittens. I'm three meters from him. I raise the syringe gun to quieten him, expecting him to yell or struggle; seeing the three of us coming out of this storm must surely feel like one last nightmare on top of every other. His face is blotched red and white inside the porthole of his balaclava, puffed beyond all normal expression. Maybe it's that or snowblindness, but I can sense no surprise. Reluctant to use the gun unless I have to, I bend forward, holding out my hand. I know it's absurd, but I'm smiling under my mask. Hi, we're from the future. Please keep quiet. For God's sake don't take us to your leader.

I get a whiff of him even through my mask and the storm. Gangrene. I grab at the cloth covering his shoulders. It's half-rotten and starts to break up in my hands, but Figgis and Janey have got the message and are moving quickly to the left. Oates looks straight up at me. Maybe it's just the pain, but I get a cold feeling of recognition. He moans something. It's far too quiet to be heard over this storm, but to me it sounds like make the most of. Time. Home. Hurry. Something like that. Now I give him the syringe gun. His body has no strength. He goes loose instantly.

Janey and Figgis lay the stretcher on the hissing ice. The three of us roll Oates onto it. We can't take any risks. Figgis untangles the sleeping bag before we lift the stretcher up. He has to use his bare hands, and Janey grabs one of his gloves just before the wind spins it off into the storm.

We lift the stretcher, and, as we do so, the boot comes away from Oates' right hand. This time, I remember the comms set.

"Remember," my voice crackles loud in my own head. "They found the sleeping bag and the right boot."

Figgis gives what could be a thumbs up. As we back away toward the open door of the canhopper, the boot and the loose sleeping bag start to tumble east, where they will be discovered next spring by Surgeon Atkinson's party after they have found Scott and the others dead in their tent just the few extra kilometers they managed to drag themselves down the trail.

It takes a million times longer than it should for us to haul the stretcher up inside the canhopper. I have to keep telling myself that what we're doing is already part of history. Oates is safe. Nothing has changed. This is exactly what always happened, right down to that boot and that sleeping bag tumbling off in the terrible wind. The body of Captain Lawrence Oates was never found. Never was and never will be. We were here. We took him. We've always been part of history.

The door swings in on silence. The ice swirls confetti, settles on the canhopper's plastic floor. It's still freezing in here and our breath is pluming clouds, but already the heaters are starting to whirr, already Janey is sliding into the pilot seat, slamming on the engines. Already we are on our way.

Figgis helps me settle the stretcher into the supports behind our seats. Janey's pushing the canhopper ridiculously hard. I rip off my mask and yell at her to cool it.

Steadying myself with one hand, I tear the wrapper off a steel and cut through layers of hood and balaclava. I have to remind myself that there really is a human being underneath this mess.

I ease the boot away from his left arm. Oates has slit the reindeer skin down as far as the toes so that he can get it on and off his swollen foot. But something else looks odd about it. There isn't time to think now, but my mind tells me anyway just as I drop the soggy weight to the floor. It's his left arm, but this is the right boot. I glance back at Figgis and Janey. They are too busy for anything right at this moment. I say nothing.

He needs oxygen. I turn up the supply and hold it above his face without touching the seared flesh. One breath. Two. Easy now. Then I take a whiff myself. The smell of Oates gets worse as I slice away more layers. I have to keep the overhead heaters on full to bring his body temperature up fast and the flesh and the rags—sometimes it's hard to be quite sure which is which—are starting to warm.

Oates' hands are swollen tight, the skin and nails peeled back like old paint on a fence. I drag my suddenly sweating body from the outsuit and work in underwear—hardly sterile conditions, and God knows what Captain Oates is going to think if he wakes up now. But Oates is barely alive. The shock of us and the stretcher and the syringe gun can't have helped. The blood analysis is up on the screen. It tells me that Wilson gave Oates a lot more morphine than anyone back at our college had predicted. I can't imagine what power it was that moved him across the ice.

I take another hit of oxygen before I start work on the legs. This is the worst bit. I already know what I'll find from the smell of rotting meat, but that doesn't make it any easier. The right leggings are swollen taut from the thigh to the feet. I tease apart a seam and start to cut down and through. The flesh is white... Blue... Red... Black... Green... It spills out like weak jelly. I cut further. Bits of bone jut up. Just as I reach the knee, Captain Oates' eyes snap open. I wonder if the morphine has somehow nullified my own injection before I notice the screen and realize that this is the characteristic spasm that begins seconds before the heart stops beating.

I jam open his mouth and slam the electrodes onto his wasted chest. Bits of flesh flake away and I snap some bones in my hurry. I'm shouting for help and even Janey must have sensed the sudden urgency because she's brought the canhopper back to float. Figgis knows enough to hold the oxygen over Oates' mouth and otherwise keep out of my way as the body jerks and shudders with each shock. After the initial panic, I work smoothly. Apart from the mess Oates is in, it's textbook stuff. But the body gets looser and harder and the moment comes that has nothing to do with clinical judgment or the flat traces on the screen when I know there isn't anything left to fight.

History was right.

Captain Oates died in the Antarctic.

CLIMBING THROUGH RUINED cities of the ice pack and the Beardmore Glacier, the air inside the canhopper is appalling. The improvised body bag isn't much help, and the lowest temperature I can get Oates down to is 3 °C. Planning on bringing a live passenger back to Epsilon, we left all the cryogenic stuff back in the medical bay. He'll keep, of course, but that isn't really the point.

So this is it. The end, really, of everything. The whole point of our journey was this one big gamble, of doing what no one else had ever done and bringing a live human being back to our home time. The idea was daring, perfect. Not only that, but it would be Captain Oates! Our college would be rich again! The research grants would pour in! We'd get paid regularly! We could even start taking in students! It wouldn't matter then that the loans for the project were secured by dubious means, that we're breaking national law and international treaty. The glory, the fame, would eclipse any problems. All of England, all of Britain—Europe, even, as a whole—would stir from its poverty. Fearful and amazed oriental eyes would turn toward us once again.

Flags of ice and cloud drift over the golden peaks. Janey hogs the canhopper's controls. Figgis breathes through his fingers. No one says a word. No one needs to; our failure is there in the blackened ruin fermenting behind us, it's there in every sickening breath. I can't sleep, and find it hard to even close my eyes. When I do, I get the feeling that the darkly reproachful ghost of the dead Captain is standing beside me.

The sensors finally detect Epsilon up ahead. Janey makes an uncharacteristic botch of docking the canhopper, giving the outer bay a dent. She curses. Figgis and I exchange hollow glances; there'll be an inquest about that when we get back to home time. Now that we're returning with a corpse, there'll be an inquest about everything.

In the medical bay, I finish off doing the things I should have done inside the canhopper. No point in actually tidying Captain Oates up, of course. Now that he's just an archaeological relic, the specialists will squeal if I do so much as wipe his diarrheic arse. Looked at from this angle, old Doctor Woolley here has already done a lot of damage trying to save his life. They'll want every ounce of dirt, every drop of the fluid that is pattering through the stretcher to the floor. All of it will be worth something, and will help defray our costs. But a few preparations are necessary before I freeze him.

I've got a mask on, but the gas Oates is giving off is still enough to sting my eyes. Gray-white slashes of his body peek out through what my steels and the Antarctic have done to his clothing. The flesh over the ribcage looks like it's under suction, the arms belong on a burnt chicken. Only the penis and the bluish scrotum look anything like they should, jutting with jaunty irrelevance from a nest of hair. As I take a couple of blood samples (watery pink from the neck, clotted purple from the shriveled buttocks) to determine the exact stage of decay, Oates' narrow deep-set eyes stare at me. His teeth are clenched, the wide lips drawn back through the beard like a grin. This sort of thing never used to bother Woolley when she did pathology, but that's many years away, and far away from here.

Talking to the eyes of the cameras, I give him the necessary jabs to slow the formation of damaging ice crystals in the cells, one for each portion of each limb. Just like pricking a turkey for the oven, as my old pathology professor used to say. Then I stretch out the protective film, lock in the pumps and the cables. The film shrivels over him like shrink-wrap on cheese, pushing the bloated hands flat, smoothing the face and widening the eyes, catching the penis at a funny angle, leaving it sticking up like a tiny monument. I feel the cold breath on my skin. Goodbye, Captain Oates. The ice got you after all.

Janey's torpedo tube is open and empty: Figgis's is closed. As I flop down inside my own, I hear the fall of their voices over the faint scream of the wind. Sounds like Woolley this and Woolley that, but that's probably my paranoia. I did my best—I've been over it all a thousand times already. The one question mark hangs over the syringe gun, and the college experts had agreed that there was a margin of safety with Oates' probable level of morphine.

But I can't help wondering...

I see Oates' face staring out at me out from the balaclava. His lips moved, shaping words that were like time, home, move, hurry, love; something like that. Even then, I don't think I panicked. It just felt for a moment as if he understood, as if he had gone out of the tent expecting to be rescued. But that's impossible. So no (I'll tell the inevitable inquiries) I don't think Doctor Woolley panicked. No way.

When I awake in my torpedo tube, silence has frozen over Epsilon, settled soft and heavy. I climb out and stumble around the plastic floors in plimsolls and an old football jersey. I stow away the clean washing. I tidy up in the kitchen area. I wipe down the floors with disinfectant that smells like a forest of plastic Christmas trees. Everything is faintly but sickeningly pervaded by the smell of Oates, but I get childish satisfaction from putting things back where they belong, as if I'm making some kind of point about the state of this expedition. Stupid really, but I'd imagined that people would look at Woolley differently after Epsilon. Yes, Woolley had been kidding herself, just like Janey and Figgis. The only difference was, I didn't even realize I was doing so.

Epsilon needs to be clean and tidy. I don't want people to get the impression that we've let things slip when we Jump to home time. In the comms bay, I peel off Figgis's postcard of Interlaken. Beyond the portholes, I see that snow is falling, rare as rain in a desert. I smile as I look out, watching it flutter at the glass, dancing in graceful drifts. Then, suddenly, it's gone. Absolutely nothing takes its place.

\* \* \*

FOUR HOURS LATER, Janey and Figgis and I are talking in that slow way that finally comes when your panic glands run dry. The air inside Epsilon is growing warmer and the smell of Oates seems to be getting worse—or maybe it's just us. They both thought Woolley had finally flipped when I hauled them out of their torpedo tube. I got a grim kind of satisfaction out of showing them the empty buzz beyond the portholes, but that soon passed as Janey started to hug herself and say, So What Do We Do Now until the question became a meaningless sound.

She's calm as any of us are now after the jab I gave her and sits at the kitchen table with her arms folded tight. Emptiness surges at the triple glass behind her back. We're no longer in the Antarctic. We're no longer anywhere. I wish we could put some kind of curtain up over the porthole, but the idea seems comically domestic.

"There was no power surge, so this has nothing to do with Epsilon's own Jump engines," says Figgis, walking his fingers toward us across the table, then walking them back again. "It looks as though some natural force has intervened between us and, well, reality. Of course," his fingers reach up to his beard, "I could be wildly wrong."

Behind us, the buzz goes on and on. It seems both dense and fragile. You keep expecting it to roar. There isn't any sound.

I decide to tell them about the mix-up with Oates' left and right boots. For once, they don't bother to argue. Any explanation is better than none at all. That, or something else we've overlooked, must have been enough for the universe to reject us as foreign matter.

It seems as if the non-state out there is slowly eating away at Epsilon. The electronic filters in the porthole glass are weakening, and there are signs that the outer coatings of camouflage are breaking up.

"There has to be a chance," Janey says as the angry grayish light-that-isn't-light flickers. "Otherwise we'd be dead already. So if the computer could work out a pattern, we could probably Jump back to home time... Maybe not to England, but at least to the Antarctic. Then, we just get in the canhopper and aim for the coast. You know what it's like there. We'd soon come across a mine or a rig or a garbage tanker."

"Are the sensors still working?" I ask.

Figgis shrugs. "They're not broken. But there's nothing out there to record. There isn't even a vacuum... I mean, if there was, Epsilon would simply have burst. But I think Janey's right. We have to Jump. What else can we do?"

Janey nods, the movement notched by the trembling of her head. "That has to be it."

"How can we Jump when we don't know where we are?"

"Do you have a better idea?"

"I have a simpler one," I say. "We could just step outside."

Figgis and Janey stare at me. Now they know I'm mad.

"Like Captain Oates," I add.

"Jesus," Figgis whispers, "you mean you're expecting to be rescued?"

The sweat down my back feels cold even though the air is getting warmer by the minute. Epsilon generates heat— heat that it's designed to radiate into an atmosphere. But now there is no atmosphere, and the outer skin is getting warmer and warmer as it corrodes. We can't turn off the life supports, and even if we did, there would still be the heat the three of us are generating. I wonder how long it will take for poor old Oates to thaw... But we'd all be long dead by then.

"Look," Figgis says, "if you want to asphyxiate or fry or implode or whatever else would happen outside, that's fine by me, Woolley, but don't expect us to follow. If we can time things right we might as well try a Jump…" His voice trails off uncertainly. I think he genuinely hadn't realized until that moment that we're really not discussing means of escape, but ways of ending our lives.

"If you want to get back to home time that badly…" I say, "… and assuming you'd recognize what you found."

"It's home." Janey grins and shivers.

Out of the window, I think for a moment that I glimpse something. But it's just Woolley's mind playing tricks, imposing order on chaos. It's just more static, more nothingness. On and on. It's a creepy sensation, like gazing into the eyes of God. I have to look away.

"Will you let me go?" I ask.

But Janey and Figgis are staring at each other. Figgis has already got the impossible equations of the Jump blurring his eyes and Janey's white and eager. They don't stand a chance, but then neither do I. That's our only hope.

I leave them and head for the medical bay, where a faint mist rises from the famous Captain Oates. Death and freezing have smoothed the suffering from his face. Under the grime and the beard, he's even faintly good-looking. The sort of large, deep-set features that look terrible on a woman, good on a man.

There's no porthole in here, but part of me can feel the emptiness outside anyway: it's there at the back of my jaw like the pain of wisdom teeth and beneath my fingernails, it's in the places where blood and bone corrode. The lights are dimming as the life support struggles to keep up. How funny, after the frozen Antarctic, that the most immediate threat to our lives is this increasing heat.

For now, Oates is still solid as a brick, looking up at me with unwavering pearly eyes. Even my old pathology professor would have to admit I've done a good job on him;

pity no one's ever going to see it. Still, Woolley tells herself, there's always a chance. Everything you do in life is a race against death and time, so why should this be any different?

I open a fresh steel. Fortunately, Oates' legs are spread wide enough for me to make a rough incision in the perineum below the scrotum. Through the film, into the frosty flesh. Crude stuff, but I'm not doing any damage to the cells that matter. It takes another steel to work my way up, avoiding the ridge of the pelvis. The sartorius, the vas deferens, the symphysis pubis... I'm sweating rivers but my hands are cold and clumsy. I slice through the woven scrap of a label. Burberry Mills—Empire Cotton—Size 34M.

The steel is blunting again. As I peel the scrotal sack away in its entirety, the frozen penis snaps like... Like, well, a frozen penis. I let the whole lot clang into a bucket. Contrary to popular belief, while sperm are manufactured in the testicles, the live ones are stored in the seminal vesicle at the base of the bladder prior to ejaculation. It's that and the icy pink stone of the prostate below it that I eventually extract.

I have to be careful thawing the fluid, and even then I need to thin it out with plasma. Rather than chance the artificial stuff we have in store, I centrifuge a little out from my own blood, and then centrifuge the mixture again, to concentrate what little there is of Captain Oates' semen. Everything takes an age. Human reproduction is a messy process at the best of times, even when it doesn't involve a frozen and malnourished corpse. Messy—and chancy. But Mother Nature's profligate with her resources—even here, in this no-place. I risk the couple of extra minutes it takes to get a quick sample under the microscope, and I can't help smiling as I watch the meager few tens of millions of living sperm I've managed to filter jostle on the console screen. It's against all the odds, really, to have got even this far.

So at least there's a faint chance. I know I've hurried the thaw, and I've hardly stuck to professional clinical standards, but maybe if you break enough rules the odds eventually start to tumble back in your favor. I half expect Janey and Figgis to walk in just at the most embarrassing moment, but it doesn't happen. The medical bay hatch stays gloriously shut.

My hands are trembling and the syringe feels a whole lot bigger than it should. And cold; like most doctors, Woolley doesn't spare much thought for the patient, least of all when it's herself. I draw in a shivering breath. But, pushing the syringe, I feel nothing at all. Not even lonely or afraid.

I'm sure the textbooks would say that I should lie down now with some soothing music. But even if all that were possible, I'm too keyed up. I just drop the junk into the chute and feel the heat of Epsilon break over me in a sudden wave. You had it easy, Mum, wandering though the glass doors at whatever clinic it was that you went to. The odds against conception must be phenomenal. But then, they always are—and I want to take something with me when I step out from Epsilon.

Figgis and Janey are still in the comms bay. They're sitting at the console, but their eyes are on Woolley as she clambers through the hatch. The screen on the right of Figgis glitters with some weird kind of graph—doubtless something to reassure them when they finally find the courage to Jump— but the one on the left displays a fisheye view of the medical bay, where Oates' body lies with a half-thawed hole where the genitals should be. Of course—the cameras. Woolley was too busy worrying and watching the hatch to think straight. Should I need it, the look on their faces is confirmation that they've seen everything.

Incredibly, I find myself blushing. My dry throat clicks open and shut as I try to pull out some words. I give up with a kind of shrug; I just don't know what to say.

"What are you doing?" Janey finally asks, the buzz from the porthole behind her face, seeming to swarm in around us.

I'm still dressed in my old football jersey and plimsolls. Worry and lack of sleep won't have done much to improve my looks either, and I get the impression that if Woolley takes too many steps toward Janey and Figgis they'll cringe or run away. Perhaps it wouldn't be such a bad idea to chase them, get an idea of how the alien felt in all those old movies set in places like this. Me and Mum, we always used to root for the monster.

"We're, er…" Figgis makes a clumsy wave toward his graph. "We're working out the probabilities. This can't be entirely nowhere. For a start, there's the erosion of Epsilon's outer surface. That's happening at a measurable rate, which means that it must be governed by some sort of external law. I think we've got a chance."

"Yeah," Janey nods. "We've got to risk it. You're not still thinking of ah…" She pauses and studies her ragged fingernails for a moment. "Just going through the hatch?"

Neither of them can look at me. But I can feel their thoughts fluttering against my face like hot breath. They want me to go outside. Even if I didn't feel this odd compulsion, their pressure might almost be enough. All it takes is a few steps. I look longingly at the handle of the inner hatch, but some instinct still holds me back. I have to say something… Maybe words about time, hurry, home, not much. That kind of thing.

I clear my throat. It comes out as a phlegmy bark. I wipe my lips. For a moment, I thought I'd finally got to those words that Mum spoke to me when she came through the swing doors of that hospital corridor. But perhaps that's too much to hope for.

"I'm going outside for a while," I croak. "I may be some time."

It seems faintly illogical to go out dressed in a sleep-stained football jersey, but even more illogical to use an outsuit. My feet carry me. The inner hatch swings back without my realizing I've pushed the handle. Then it closes behind me. No conscious action seems to be involved any more, which is a good thing because I'm not sure that I have the courage to go on. Silence buzzes beyond the port-hole. Oates is a gray wraith at my shoulder in this tight space between inside and out; it seems as if it's his hand that turns on the inner seal, even though part of me knows that it's probably Figgis doing it on remote from the comms bay, making sure that stupid ugly Woolley doesn't let the emptiness blast in.

Without thinking, I brace myself for a chill. But of course it doesn't happen. As the outer door swings out, it seems to turn some kind of corner and I lose sight of it entirely. The air stays put, neither drawn out nor com-pressed by whatever lies beyond. I understand more clearly now that there is no light out there, there's nothing that my senses can truly relate to. It's a bit like standing over a drop, looking down from the high board at the swimming pool. And then it's like nothing at all. There are colors there if I want to see them, shapes and sneering faces from the playground pushed close just before home time. Stupid Ugly Woolley. Everything tilts up and I feel myself sliding. Oates is a black mist that curls around me, some sort of atmospheric effect. I draw in one last breath. Then I let go.

I feel a rush, sparks in my eyes. It really is like the swim-ming pool, like diving, like falling asleep. I can hardly believe that it takes this long for my brain to dissolve; that

I still have time for this particular thought. Then that I have time for this next one. The clinical part of me is amazed. There's even still a faint sensation of falling. Who'd have ever thought that death would be this interesting? Woolley should have done it instead of Osteoporosis Fractures for her thesis. But it's too late for all that now.

Then there's a jolt of pain. It's localized, my right leg. Feels like striking... Something solid. I wait for the pain to spread. Bang. My other leg. Jesus, it hurts the way it does when you walk into something; a sharp reminder from your body to look where you're going. Then the palms of my hand slide across something sharp, they go hot and wet. Blood. Fingers to my mouth taste salt, my tongue touches... gravel. I pull in a breath that fills with the scent of litter bins and water, of fresh-cut municipal grass. For a moment, it feels as though hands other than my own are helping me up. But then they are gone. I open my eyes alone.

Hauling myself onto the bench, I look around through the green blotches in my eyes. It's a hot day. People are flirting with a benign sun. There's a little girl down the path staring, a Mr. Whippy ice cream dripping down her knuckles. Her mother takes one look at me and pulls her away. Woolley's still in this stained football jersey, but at least it's summer. People will just think I'm one of the local nutters.

Across the squinting water, lads in singlets are splashing and diving into the lake from the short wooden pier. It's so hot, I almost want to join them. And there's another part of me wants to go over and shout, wag my finger, tell them about the boys from other summers who drowned, were drawn down by the cold undertow to re-emerge in the lime pits miles outside town. But I just watch them and smile. And I feel this honeyed sunlight. Eventually, it's home time, when the younger children break out from school. They glance uneasily at this funny-looking woman as they run and chatter on their way to their old TVs and their dinners and their future lives. I smile, frightening them by doing so.

Evening starts to grow. Streetlight trickles across the water. The park keeper stares. I realize that I must have been sitting here for a long time; relaxing, doing almost what the fertility manuals would recommend. But conception's a tricky process. It could still be hours ahead—or never. That's a chance I'll have to take.

As I walk up the streets toward my home, I start to wonder if I ever really left it that morning. After all, there are still a great many things that I don't understand. Of course, there's hope now there's time, there's time now there's hope. At least twelve happy years lie between me and that morning at the hospital, coming through the swing doors with the results of the biopsy buzzing in my head to find little Woolley swinging her legs on that itchy seat, looking happy, bored, uncertain as she waits for her mother. I'll have to talk to her, express something about hope, love, home, time, make the most; something like that. I have no idea what it is. But when the time comes, I think I'll know what to say.

# A SPY IN THE DOMAIN OF ARNHEIM

*Michael Bishop*

*I am repatriated by a moment of panic. These are the privileged moments that transcend mediocrity.*

—René Magritte

TOURIST OR SPY? Had I been dispatched to this quaint, understaffed hotel on a holiday or an errand of espionage? The Spartan Old World elegance of the room in which I woke—the functional coldness of the furnishing—told me without my even going to a window that, during a period of sleep or disembodiment, I had arrived in a region of rugged mountains and thick snows. Tourist or spy? The weight of an indistinct obligation made me suspect the latter, and I was loath to get up, to acknowledge the debt laid upon me.

Why could not my sponsors have granted me a season of idleness and recreation? The first elementary condition of bliss, after all, is free exercise in the open air—for most human beings prefer the freshness of a montane breeze to the recycled fetors of a casino or a drawing room. Or should. But I had no independent choice. Permission for a carefree stroll along the chanting cataracts, or for a bout of breakneck skiing down the hotel's hazardous slalom course, options no less implicit in my arrival at this place than a flurry of unspecified spy work—such permission would have prodded me to rise, complete my morning toilet, and hurry out-of-doors. But I belonged to my sponsors; I was not my own man.

Who were my sponsors? It embarrasses me to confess that I had forgotten. I remembered only that I was an agent—perhaps the only incarnate representative—of their mysterious designs. Although utterly languid in pursuit of their ends, they expected me to subordinate my will to theirs. By no means did I suppose them malign, demented, or childish (quite the opposite, in fact), but I was equally certain that they had no right to use me as they did, for at their subliminal bidding I became either a flashlight or a scalpel—an instrument to illuminate the crannies of their ignorance or to lay open the secret tissues of their communal longing. By what authority did they deny me autonomous control of my own consciousness? I had—if only I could find it—an identity altogether apart from their grandiose manipulations.

I have said that my room was both elegant and austere. Let me dilate a little on this point. My bed—upon which I lay clad in a pair of monogrammed drawers, a sleeveless undershirt, and a pair of calf-length black silk hose—was a mere rectangular box with head and footboards. Although I had two lumpy pillows and a bolster, no one had bothered to turn the counterpane back; I reposed supine on this reddish-brown blanket, which had been stretched across, and tucked tautly beneath, my mattress.

The only other pieces of furniture in the room were a chair with a lyre-shaped back, a wardrobe with mirrored doors, and a rough wooden table with a cloth the same disquieting color as my counterpane. A phonograph with a large metal speaker sat on this table, beyond which I could see a fire grate and a mantel of salmon-colored marble. The mantel was surmounted by a mirror in a fluted gold frame.

What richness the room revealed—what eclectic elegance—derived from the mirrors, a pair of partially overlapping Persian carpets, the brass cornucopia of the Victrola, the petrified veins in the marble fireplace facing, and the giddily realistic pattern of the wallpaper: puffy, bathtub-sized clouds drifting over a backdrop of robin's-egg blue. A summer sky in a winter room. Although gratified by the whimsical promise of warmth embodied by these clouds, I could not stop shivering. Further, it seemed a sacrilege against the room's intimidating tidiness to pull back the counterpane and climb into the bed.

Resentful of my sponsors, I sat up, swung about, and put my stockinged feet on the floor. Now I could see that beside the mantel was an open archway connecting my bedroom to the suite's parlor, where the floating-cloud pattern on the wallpaper did not extend. Indeed, the walls in there were a deep tomato color, darker than my blanket. Likewise, the hardwood planking of the parlor was perceptibly darker than my bedroom's flooring—as if the more distant chamber enjoyed a late-afternoon rather than a morning slant of sunlight. It seemed to me that by proceeding from here to there I could warm myself without having to don a suit of bleakly styleless clothes. But, standing, I suffered a sudden weakness in my legs and decided that, before venturing forth to greet a later segment of the day, I must submit to the conventional proprieties.

I fingered my chin and jaw. No stubble intercepted these probings; my face was as sleek as an apple skin. It occurred to me that, although an adult, I had never had to use a shaving brush and a straight razor to obtain this immaculate bourgeois smoothness. Nevertheless, I had a vivid recollection of once having used these instruments, not to mention a humming hand-held machine that had accomplished the same end. Was my lack of a beard the result of a depilatory substance, or had my sponsors given me the immature hide of a human adolescent? The mirrored doors of the wardrobe—into which I expectantly peered, hoping to overthrow the reign of amnesia—did not give back my image. By implying that I was either an eidolon or some other creature impervious to the laws of optics, this circumstance greatly discomfited me. Frightened, I reached out and touched the glass of the left-hand door. This movement immediately reassured me for the shadow of my hand passed over the ice-like surface of the "mirror" and I understood that the images in both doors were imprisoned there by an artifice heretofore unsuspected by me. When I opened the doors, the room's "reflected" wall went one way and its "reflected" Victrola the other, and I was staring into a cupboard of modest dimensions and rather prosaic contents. My panic ebbed.

Have I called the wardrobe's contents commonplace? But for two exceptions (which I will presently mention), perhaps they were.

Arrayed on wooden hangers, a pair of dark trousers, a matching suit jacket, and a long black overcoat greeted my gaze. Warily, I put on these items, which fitted me tolerably well—but my eye kept going back to the *chapeau melon,* or bowler hat, on the recessed shelf above the closet bar. Now I will tell you why.

Someone in a humorous or deranged state of mind had attached a large green apple and its leafy stem to the hat so that the fruit hung down a few inches from the brim. Five shiny leaves clustered above the apple, giving the hat the appearance of an inverted flower bowl. I lifted the hat from the shelf (a block of wood inside the crown had kept the apple's weight from toppling the bowler into the bottom of the wardrobe) and fitted it onto my head. Idiocy! The dependent green apple effectively obscured my vision. Who could have perpetrated such a pointless joke?

Perhaps I was being watched. I hastily removed the *chapeau melon* and struggled to pull the apple and its twig from the hat brim. But whatever fixative the trickster had employed resisted my best efforts, and I was finally obliged to snap the stem. The apple went into my jacket pocket and the bowler with its remaining foliage back onto the shelf. I had no intention of playing the buffoon (at least not again, that is) for the infantile agency that had arranged this absurd trap, and I congratulated myself for so quickly terminating its half-witted concept of fun. Moreover, I had procured my breakfast.

What I now required was footwear, preferably a pair of unassuming black oxfords. Sanguine about finding just what I needed in the wardrobe (which had so far outfitted me like a burgher, without my having made any previous arrangements for it to do so), I knelt and groped about. The oxfords were there, directly under the overcoat, and I gratefully withdrew them. While withdrawing them, however, I caught sight of the backs of a pair of high-topped work shoes, so dirt-caked and worn that I wondered about finding them in this genteel piece of furniture. Curious, I hooked these shoes with my fingers and dragged them into the light.

They hit the carpet but did not fall over. Like the unsuspecting recipient of a torn-out heart, I recoiled from them. Why? Because they embodied a mockery of my expectations, a perverse contradiction of acceptable shoe-ness, and a threat to civilized mores. How to explain these charges?

Best to say it quickly: they were not really shoes at all; they were lifelike gutta-percha facsimiles of human feet, with horny nails on the toes and the incongruity of laces on the insteps. Bunioned and scarred, they ostensibly represented the feet of a well-built peasant. Had I been so inclined, I could have easily slipped my oxfords into them—a thought, even in retrospect, altogether repugnant to me. I glanced about the room wondering if the impractical joker who had attached the apple to the hat were secretly remarking my terror and perplexity. This prank, inarguably more vile than the other, had achieved my conspicuous discomfiture. As for the feet-shaped boots themselves, they were poised on the edge of the carpet as if to chase me from the bed chamber.

"How barbarous," I murmured.

Steeling myself, I seized the obscene articles and tossed them back into the bottom of the wardrobe. Then I banged the doors to—those doors with their counterfeit mirrors and artificial reflections—and secured the droplatch. Drained, I reeled away from the cabinet to the room's only chair. Here I put on my oxfords and caught my breath.

Like a tumor, the apple in my jacket pocket pressed against my hip, attracting my attention. All the while surveying the ceilings, walls, cornices, and baseboards for peepholes or telltale signs of spying equipment, I devoured the tart, juicy flesh of the apple. I saw nothing to confirm or to allay my suspicions, for the glass in the false mirrors bespoke an intelligence of a high, but somewhat deceitful, order. I could not discount the possibility that the very walls were transparent to the unknown eyes beyond them.

Fortified and a little comforted by the apple, I glanced over my shoulder at the Victrola. In a flood of insight, as if eating the apple had restored a portion of my memory, I suddenly knew my *nom de guerre,* my age, and my place of national origin. Starting with the last first, I hailed from one of the southern capitals of the United States of America, I was thirty-five years old, and my sponsors had christened me, for reasons of their own, Elliot Ellison. Indeed, my wallet, containing documentary support of these recollections, lay on the table beside the phonograph.

I went to the table, dropped my apple core into a wine glass beside the Victrola, and found my wallet. The plastic identity card that I took from one of its compartments gave me a start, for although my name, age, and address were all neatly entered in the proper places, the accompanying photograph would be of absolutely no use to anyone—police, merchants, or custom officials. It would alienate rather than secure their belief in me. Near a lake or an ocean front, I had posed for the camera face-on, but a white pigeon, or perhaps a small albino gull, had swept between me and the camera lens at the precise moment of the shutter's closing. It was this ridiculous portrait—the bird's body and wings obscuring my features—that my sponsors had affixed to my identity card.

What's in a name? I reflected darkly. Elliot Ellison might just as well have been Anson Anonymous or Norbert Nobody.

Angered by this betrayal, I began to crank the phonograph. A moment later I nudged the needle onto the plate of Blue Amberol revolving on the turntable. All this equipment, I decided, must date back to the beginnings of phonographic manufacture. Soon a quintessentially feminine voice began to speak to me through the scratchy static of the record. Although the warp in this disk was substantial, it did not detract from the melodic purity of the woman's recitation.

"One cannot speak about mystery; one must be seized by it," she said, to no accompaniment but the persistent scratching. "Several times this morning, Elliot, mystery has assaulted you, but you have refused to give in to it. You (unintelligible) the banality of explanations. Why? There is really no need, Elliot—no need to embrace the mediocrity of looking for meanings."

It did not alarm me that the voice had used my name. "There is something to look for here," I insisted.

"Of course, but (unintelligible). You must remember that your identity is negotiable. Familiarity with oneself breeds—death. Find mysteries rather than meanings. Looking for significances abstracts you from (unintelligible) that alone redeem the universe."

"But—" I broke off. Suddenly I was shaken by the uncanny idea that the apple I had eaten was reassembling itself in my gut, expanding inside me like a balloon. Soon, like Athena from the forehead of Zeus, it would burst from my abdomen, annihilating me, its implicit aim being to grow and grow—until it occupied the entire chamber from floor to ceiling and from wall to wall. Humanity banished from its world, the giant green apple would abide forever, listening... Imagining the acoustics of metamorphosis, I listened too.

"Better, Elliot. You begin to..."

Even though the needle had tracked only the outer third of the record's long spiral groove, the phonograph was running down. Cranking vigorously, I rewound the machine.

"... (unintelligible) the legitimacy of mystery. That's good. You'll soon be a citizen of the living universe again. Don't you see, Elliot? When everything's in transit, it's folly to stand on ceremony. To look for patterns that haven't emerged yet—well, that's even worse."

The needle continued to circle inward, but only the raspy clickety click of static issued from the Victrola's brass horn. I waited, my knuckles pressed against the blood-brown table cloth. Eventually, just as I had begun to doubt, my interlocutor rewarded my patience by addressing me in a lilting, obviously parodic sing-song:

"'The four elementary conditions of bliss.'" She cleared her throat. "'First, free exercise in the open air. Second, the love of woman.' No capital 'w' on that one, but it sure sounds to me as if this fellow meant to capitalize. Well. Never mind. 'Third, the contempt of ambition. And fourth, an object of unceasing pursuit. Other things being equal, the extent of attainable happiness is in proportion to the spirituality of this object.'" The stylus scratched inward. "Over and out," the voice added, by way of peremptory afterthought.

"Wait," I implored. "Aren't the third and fourth conditions mutually exclusive? I mean, you've got to have a certain amount of ambition to engage in a pursuit, don't you? Otherwise—"

"Over and out," her enchanting siren voice repeated. "Over and out... Over and out..."

The needle had hung up on a scratch or an embedded dust particle. Fearful that if my unknown redemptress did not speak again, I would surely go mad, I flicked the tone arm with my finger, then listened in dismay to the hideous, high-pitched screech of its progress across the record. Had I ruined everything? Would the rest be silence or nonsensical distortions? The latter would be infinitely harder to bear for I must then acknowledge my pre-eminent role in isolating myself from all human intercourse. The Victrola's empty cornucopia would mock me.

"I didn't (unintelligible) these conditions, Elliot. Their lack of consistency means—pardon me—nothing to me. Maybe their formulator defined 'ambition' differently from you. Or 'pursuit,' or 'contempt.' I don't feel bound by someone else's conditions, particularly in pursuit of a trivial goal like happiness. Bliss is deadening, Elliot. Too much of it is mindless. That's not Calvinism, either—it's an evolutionary doctrine. You could also consult Plato. Genuine mystery just isn't to be found in mindlessness."

Frustrated by the smugness imbuing these riddles, I shouted at the machine, "WHAT AM I DOING HERE, ANYWAY?"

But the needle had tracked its way to the very center of the plate, where it lapped the last restraining rim like a boat banging its quay in bad weather. Bitterly disconsolate, I set the tone arm aside and plunged my hands into my trouser pockets.

"You're here as both a tourist and a spy," said the woman in a more tender tone. Although the phonograph was no longer operating, her voice issued clearly from the great brass speaker. "Your sponsors have laid the burden of the latter role upon you, but it really wouldn't hurt if you decided to play up the other one a little. Being a tourist's nothing to be ashamed of."

"If you're my enemy, that would suit you just fine, wouldn't it?"

"Listen to me, Elliot. Espionage is a goal-oriented activity; it exists to find meanings in the data it accumulates. And not only meanings, but a basis for future action. Tourism's different. In its purest manifestations, anyway, it's a means of confronting a mystery by generating a context for new experiences. Its goal is perception before understanding. Ideally, I mean."

"A goal is a goal," I countered. "This is all so much talk."

"No human activity is perfectly pointless, Elliot. It's a matter of degree. The way I see it, tourism is less materially goal-directed than espionage. Perception before, or maybe even versus, understanding." To my surprise, she laughed.

"You don't want me to understand, do you?"

"Not yet, Elliot. Not just yet."

"Why not?"

"Everything in time. Be a tourist first, a spy second."

"Who are you?"

But she would not answer, and when next I cranked the phonograph and put the needle on the record, offensive martial music blared into the room. I yanked the disk from the turntable and hurled it against the fire grate. Though the fire grate was empty and cold, the broken shards flickered into flame like so many kerosene-sprinkled coals—a consequence, I supposed, of the sudden impact. The hooting of a train whistle echoed through the mountain passes beyond the hotel.

"For that matter," I asked myself, "who am I?"

Elliot Ellison was only a name. I approached the mirror over the mantelpiece, half expecting to find another counterfeit reflection frozen in the glass. What I encountered was far stranger. Although I squared my shoulders and looked directly into the mirror, some optical anomaly, which the creator of the looking glass had exploited to sinister effect rendered the back of my head, the back of my collar, the back of my suit jacket. A shudder passed through me. The prankster who had conceived my previous petty torments—the woman whose delightful voice had addressed me through the Victrola—indeed, the entire unforthcoming staff of the Arnheim Hotel—not one of these mysterious persons wished me to behold my own naked face. Their refusal to let me see myself was maddening. To keep my hand from pounding their wicked mirror into hundreds of wicked fragments was a severe test, but by dint of will I passed it.

Atop the salmon-colored marble of the mantel shelf, just to my right, lay a copy of a book bound in fissuring, light-gray paper: Edgar Poe's *Adventures of Arthur Gordon Pym*. It shocked me to see that the mirror reflected the cover of this book exactly as a mirror ought, the letters in the author's name and those in the title—along with the nautical emblem below them—all being properly reversed. Carefully, so as not to crumble the paper jacket or the pages, I picked up the book and curiously inspected it. Now my body (the one in the mirror, I mean) obscured the volume that ought to have been reflected there; and when I held the book to one side or the other, I saw it in my extended hands as if surreptitiously approaching myself from behind. Intolerable! this pointless game-playing.

"*La Reproduction interdite,*" said the woman's voice from the phonograph speaker. "Loosen up, Elliot. Loosen up."

"To hell with you," I told her, and she laughed.

Carrying *Arthur Gordon Pym,* I stormed from the bed chamber into the tomato-red prison of the adjoining parlor. But for a fireplace (it had the same flue as the one in the bedroom), the parlor was bare of furnishings. A pair of empty brass candlesticks and a clock whose hands were stopped at precisely 12:43 rested on the mantel shelf, but I could scarcely contrive to call these items "furniture." This was indeed a miserable sitting room. A person would have to take lessons from a Hindu mystic and collapse into the mind-obliterating toils of the lotus position to find any comfort here. I gazed about me in a fury of despair.

Whereupon I saw, flanked by dark-green curtains, the parlor's only window, which consisted of a large bottom pane surmounted by a fanlight lacking the conventional spoke-like sash bars. The view through this window—or, more accurately, its bottom pane—was breathtakingly hard to credit. The wonders (the annoying wonders) of the morning were nothing beside it. In fact, I had never seen a landscape so beautiful, magnificent, and startling. To take in the sight at closer range, I hurried across the empty parlor—only to discover that my eyes had not created, from my nervousness and distress, a wild phantasm.

The high blue mountain enclosing the domain of Arnheim on the east had a prominent central crag resembling, yes, an eagle's head. The rocky peaks to either side of this mighty aquiline profile represented the curves of its outspread wings, and in all the crevices and canyons crosshatching its mountainous body lay immense plumes of downy snow. The mountain had become an eagle, or an eagle had become a mountain, and the exquisite awesomeness of the scene admitted of no improvement. A worshipful impulse lay hold of me, and I made mute obeisance to this avian god of stone—until, that is, a cold suspicion began to undermine my reverence.

"Another trick!" I exclaimed. "Another Arnheim lie!"

The same intelligence that had already sabotaged my peace of mind was at work in this duplicity, too. My wonderful eagle-mountain, or mountain-eagle, owed its existence to the Daedalian trickster who had set its portrait in the very crystals of the windowpane, which had undergone the same subtle alterations as the false mirrors in the bed chamber—with, of course, a different and more miraculous design. Although the sky visible in the unreachable fanlight might be real, the image in the bottom pane was a fantastic sham. It was possible that my hotel suite overlooked an iron foundry, a bog, or a cluttered scrap yard. The only way to determine the truth was to open the window.

I set *Arthur Gordon Pym* out of the way and tried to get a grip on the outer sash. However, this enterprise was doomed by my having to deal with a fixed window; I soon understood that it neither raised nor lowered. If I wanted to see what lay beyond it, I would have to break the window—a vandalism for which I had little experience and even less heart. Struck again by the *outré* beauty of the eagle-mountain design, I stepped back to ogle it and to mull my options.

As I did, the window all at once broke—apparently in response to a sudden geologic tremor or a muted sonic boom—and fragments of glass, some large, some small, dropped from the frame like chips of painted ice. Reacting to this inexplicable concussion, I had gone to one knee, but now, all danger past, I eased myself erect and found my suspicions about the window only partially borne out. Although each window fragment contained a puzzle piece of the eagle-mountain image (the shard bearing the bird's profiled head leaned against the baseboard with several smaller ones), visible through the jagged break was the selfsame scene in very truth. Now I could see that the miniature in the broken glass had corresponded in every detail with the aquiline colossus across the intervening lake from the hotel. Meanwhile, as I stood thunderstruck by this humbling revelation, a blast of icy air rushed through the room, stirring the curtains and flash-freezing my marrow. I myself—Elliot Ellison—had acquired the fragile clairvoyance of a windowpane.

"D-d-dear G-god," I heard myself stammer.

"Are you all right, sir?"

These words issued from behind me in a kind of hoarse whisper, and I whirled to confront the person who had spoken them. One of the members of the hotel staff, a steward, had entered my suite from the corridor. A man of my own height and build, he was clad in a suit exactly like my own, his most unsettling peculiarity being the large linen pouch that he wore over his head. To this astonishing headgear he had attempted to impart an air of commonplaceness by disposing its twisted excess over his shoulder like a scarf. This ruse failed because the sack had neither eyeholes nor breathing apertures, and the man stood before me as if awaiting escort to the gallows or the executioner's block. Was this the man who had arranged all my morning's torments? Perhaps not all. It hardly seemed fair to hold him accountable for the tremors (or sonic boom) that had briefly racked the building.

In that same growly whisper he said, "We don't often have earthquakes, or whatever that was. Anyway, the management have sent me upstairs to check on our guests. If you're all right, sir, I'll call in a chambermaid to sweep up the window fragments and a glazier to perform a temporary repair."

"Why are you dressed like that?" I challenged the man.

As if he could see through the coarse material of his hood, he glanced down at his person, even shooting his cuffs to facilitate this examination. "We do have similar tastes in clothes, don't we, sir?"

"I meant that—that ridiculous sack! Are you ashamed of your position here? Do you have a deformity?"

"Not to my own eye, sir. Nor, for that matter, to a goodly number of young ladies of my acquaintance."

The man's whisper grated on my sensibilities, all the more so for being nearly, but not quite, recognizable—as if I had met the steward, minus his insinuating manner and exasperating hood, in some other place, at some other time. He stooped, lifted the volume by Poe from the floor, and handed it to me. In transit the book opened of its own accord, and I saw that its pages were all blanks. The hooded man, heedless of this anomaly, stepped to the window and gave every appearance of inspecting the damage.

"Then why *do* you wear the damned thing?"

"Well, sir," the steward returned, "the management wish to treat us all impartially, and these hoods allow 'em to do so."

I tried to protest this explanation.

"They'll be serving dinner in a few minutes, sir. Why don't you go down to the dining room while I'm having this mess cleaned up? Take a stroll along the promenade above the lake. Twilight's a fine time for viewing Mount Aquilonia."

"Twilight? I only just got up."

"That may be, sir," he whispered, "but the moon's rising. Look—a lovely waxing crescent creepin' along the southern wing."

Grudgingly I looked. Seeing that the steward was right, I pivoted on my heel to take myself out of the range of the guttural wheeze of his voice. Downstairs, he had suggested. Very well, I would go downstairs. Free exercise in the open air was what I needed, that and a few moments for uninterrupted thought. How else to cure my disorientation and anxiety?

"You'll need your overcoat, sir. It's chilly this evening, and likely to be even chillier later on."

I nodded perfunctorily, then made a detour into my bed chamber. The bogus *Adventures of Arthur Gordon Pym* (obviously this Pym had had no adventures) I tossed onto the mantelpiece. Several signatures of blank pages burst from the binding and drifted out into the room, settling on the Persian carpets. Although my intention was to take my overcoat from the wardrobe and myself rather expeditiously from the suite, one of these pages caught my eye—by virtue of its possessing a single paragraph of printed matter precisely centered between the margins. I picked this page from the carpet (meanwhile cognizant of the entry of a chambermaid, at the bidding of the steward, into the adjacent room) and distractedly began to read:

"...In the most rugged of wilderness—in the most savage of the scenes of nature—there is apparent the art of a creator; yet this art is apparent to reflection only; in no respect has it the obvious force of a feeling. Now let us suppose this sense of the Almighty design to be one step depressed—to be brought into something like harmony or consistency with the sense of human art—to form an inter-medium between the two:—let us imagine, for instance, a landscape whose combined vastness and definitiveness—whose united beauty, magnificence, and strangeness, shall convey the idea of care, or culture, or superintendence, on the part of beings superior, yet akin to humanity..."

There was more, but I lifted my eyes from the page to assimilate this last startling clause. Mount Aquilonia, it strongly implied, was not a natural formation but a prodi-gious artifact—perhaps I should have guessed as much—and its makers were beings more than human but less than divine. Angels, perhaps; yes, earth-angels whose intelligence had elevated them to a disembodied state that did not prevent their undertaking monumental landscap-ing projects in the natural world. However much it might annoy me to admit the fact, even the prankster in the hood partook to some small degree of their genius.

I crumpled and cast aside the page, hurried to the wardrobe, and yanked the heavy overcoat from its hanger. The feet-shaped boots in the bottom of the cabinet, I noticed, had oriented themselves so that they could hop into the room—but I slammed the doors upon them, drew on my overcoat, and strode out of the bedroom into the parlor. Here I was embarrassed to find the steward and the chambermaid passionately clutching each other. Because the chambermaid was also wearing a sack over her fea-tures, their kiss conveyed a bizarre desperation. Without any thought to either their want of discretion or my own rudeness, I gaped at the spectacle.

At length they separated, and I remembered myself. In doing so, I could feel my face turning as red as the walls. Dangerously flustered, I touched my forehead and sought to leave the suite.

"You've forgot your hat, sir," said the steward in his loudest, most unpleasant whisper.

"Damn my hat."

Coquettish in a short-sleeved red dress, the chambermaid rewarded this outburst with a sparkling laugh. "Well, that's a beginning, Elliot."

I halted at the door. The woman's voice—which I would never be able to dislodge from my memory—was the voice that had spoken to me through the Victrola. Although I wished to question her, to ask her to remove her hood, the presence of the steward prevented our having a private interview. I fled from the suite, angrily resolved to depart Arnheim at the earliest convenient moment.

"Enjoy your stroll," the woman called after me.

The corridor, the stairwell, and the lower floors of the hotel were deserted. The salon could have easily been a mausoleum, and the dining room, although set for dinner and delicately candlelit, seemed a dreamlike fossil from another age. After passing through the vacant lobby, I pelted down a fan of granite steps to the promenade overlooking the lake in the crater below Mount Aquilonia. I followed the wall beside this overlook to a point immediately in front of the mountain's central crag (the eagle's haughty head), where grateful for both the view and a moment of solitude, I paused to gather my thoughts.

But I could not gather them. On the ledge of the parapet rested a tightly woven nest containing three large eggs. Meanwhile, directly above the twilight profile of the mountain hung the white meniscus of the moon. My gaze went back and forth between the earthbound eggs and that celestial fingernail dipping. Did I hope to mediate a meaning out of the gigantic eagle-shaped rock separating them?

I took one of the eggs from the nest and hefted it in my hand; it proved remarkably light, as if its liquid contents had been blown out of the shell through pinholes at either end. Indeed, after finding these pinholes in the egg, I had no scruple about cracking it open to see what the shell might hold, if anything.

A strip of curled paper, like the message in a fortune cookie, came into my hand, and upon unraveling this strip I was able to read the following cryptic phrase: "An object of unceasing pursuit." Because the other two eggs were likewise devoid of meat, I broke and extracted messages from them, too. The second said, "The contempt of ambition," and the third, "The love of woman" (small "w"). I scanned each strip of paper several times, as if the letters might unexpectedly alter at any moment, then tore them into tiny pieces, which I carefully replaced in the eagle's nest. Then I glanced back over my shoulder at the huge, shadowy facade of the Arnheim Hotel. What must I do now?

Someone had picked the remaining glass fragments out of the sash of my parlor window, and bracing herself in this lofty opening was the woman who, only moments ago, had been kissing the insolent steward. Although she was no longer wearing her hood, the distance and the incipient darkness made it impossible to draw any conclusions about her face. She was still an enigma.

"Remember what I told you earlier, Elliot," she called, and her voice echoed in the high canyons of the mountain vale. "You're here to rejuvenate yourself. Act like a tourist first—all the rest will follow."

I gestured helplessly. "I don't understand."

"When next you see me, you will. That's a promise." Whereupon she ducked back into my hotel suite, and I was buffeted by a violent wind sweeping through Arnheim from the north.

Far below, the reflection of Mount Aquilonia rippled in the half-frozen waters of the glacier-excavated lake, and I was ambushed by a provocative thought. So intensely did I concentrate on this notion that neither the wintry air nor the immobility of the moon had any power to distract me. A great deal of time passed without really seeming to.

Eventually, a small, painted bark appeared on the lake, as if it had pushed off from a point slightly north of the hotel, and inscribed a wide arc in the lee of the mountain. Now it was drawing toward the hotel again, its tiny mast pointing straight up at the craggy eagle's head. In the prow of this boat stood a lissome woman dressed in the robes of a Florentine spring and supporting in her arms a garland of luxuriant white flowers. Even before her bark had reached the middle of the lake, I recognized this woman as a figure abstracted from Sandro Botticelli's great painting *La Primavera*—executed in the days when paintings had possessed not only a responsible grounding in both nature and myth, but also the moral force of allegory.

"Come," the woman cried, gracefully beckoning.

Her voice was familiar. It was the summons I had been waiting for. I shed my overcoat, folded it neatly, and placed it on the ledge beside the eagle's nest. I then removed my other clothes, including even my stockings and undergarments, and folded these into the protective womb of my overcoat. The woman hailed me again. In response I scrambled over the restraining wall and picked my way down the precipitous embankment to the lake. Although I had an intellectual awareness of the wind knifing over the waters, and of the consummate folly of my nakedness, my body did not suffer. Whatever Powers and Principalities had sculpted this supernatural landscape could not look with disfavor on my decision to merge with their creation.

"Come, Elliot," cried the tutelary spirit in the bark.

Under the eye of the awesome granite eagle, in the long stasis of twilight, I dove from my promontory to the mirrorlike surface of the lake. Descending, I saw the reflection of my face. It was a respectable face, altogether devoid of mystery—but the mind behind its eyes was furiously conjugating marvels from the gelid air. Then the waters closed over me and I possessed not only the illusory Arnheim landscape but myself.

# MEMORIES OF THE FLYING BALL BIKE SHOP

*Garry Kilworth*

THE OLD CHINESE gentleman was sitting cross-legged in the shadow of an alley. He was smoking a long bamboo pipe, which he cradled in the crook of his elbow. I had noticed him as we climbed the temple steps, and the image stayed with me as we wandered through the Buddhist-Tao shrine to Wong Tai Sin, a shepherd boy who had seen visions.

It was so hot the flagstones pulsed beneath our feet, but despite that David was impressed with the temple. We waded through the red-and-gold litter which covered the forecourt, the dead joss sticks cracking underfoot. Cantonese worshippers were present in their hundreds, murmuring orisons, rattling their cans of fortune sticks. Wong Tai Sin is no showcase for tourists, but a working temple in the middle of a high-rise public housing estate. Bamboo poles covered in freshly washed clothes overhung the ornate roof, and dripped upon its emerald tiles.

The air was heavy with incense, dense enough to drug the crickets into silence. We ambled up and down stone staircases, admiring carvings the significance of which was lost in generations of western nescience, and gazed self-consciously at the worshippers on their knees as they shook their fortune sticks and prayed for lucky numbers to fall to the flagstones.

We left the temple with our ignorance almost intact.

The old man was still there, incongruous among the other clean-shaven Hong Kong men, with their carefully acquired sophistication, hurrying by his squatting form.

He had a wispy Manchu beard, long gray locks, and dark eyes set in a pomelo-skin face. A sleeveless vest hung from bony shoulders, and canvas trousers covered legs that terminated in an enormous pair of bare feet. The bamboo pipe he was smoking was about fifty centimeters long, three centimeters in diameter, with a large water-cooled bowl at one end, and a stem the size of a drinking straw at the other. He had the stem in his lipless mouth, inhaling the smoke.

There was a fruit stall owner, a man I had spoken to on occasion, on the pavement nearby. I told David to wait by the taxi stand and went to the vendor. We usually spoke to each other in a mixture of Cantonese and English, neither of us being fluent in the foreign language. He was fascinated by my red hair, inherited from my Scottish Highland ancestors.

"*Jo san,*" I said, greeting him, "*leung goh ping gwoh, m'goi.*"

I had to shout to make myself heard above the incredibly loud clattering coming from behind him, where sat three thin men and a stout lady, slamming down mah-jong tiles as if trying to drive them through the Formica tabletop.

He nodded, wrapped two apples in a piece of newspaper, and asked me for two dollars.

Paying him, I said, "That man, smoking. Opium?"

He looked where I was pointing, smiled, and shook his head vigorously.

"Not smoke opium. No, no. *Sik yin* enemy."

I stared at the old gentleman, puffing earnestly away, seeming to suck down the shadows of the alley along with the smoke.

"*Sik yin dik yan-aa?*" I said, wanting to make sure I had heard him properly. "Smoke *enemy?*"

"*Hai.* Magic smoke-pipe," he grinned. "*Magic,* you know? Very old *sik yin*-pipe."

Gradually I learned that the aged smoker had written down the name of a man he hated, on "dragon" paper, had torn it to shreds, and was inhaling it with his tobacco. Once he had smoked the name of his enemy, had the hated foe inside him, he would come to *know* the man.

The idea was of course, that when you knew the hated enemy—and by *know,* the Chinese mean to understand completely—you could predict any moves he might make against you. You would have a psychological advantage over him, be able to forestall his attacks, form counter-moves against him. His strategy, his tactics, would be yours to thwart. He would be able to do nothing which you would not foresee.

"I think..." I began to say, but David interrupted me with a shout of, "I've got a taxi, *come* on!" so I bid the stall owner a hasty goodbye, and ran for the waiting vehicle. We leapt out into the fierce flow of Hong Kong traffic, and I put the incident aside until I had more time to think about it.

\* \* \*

THAT EVENING, OVER dinner at the Great Shanghai Restaurant in Tsimshatsui, I complained bitterly to David about John Chang.

"He's making my life here a misery," I said. "I find myself battling with a man who seems to despise me."

David was a photographer who had worked with me on my old Birmingham paper. He had since moved into the big time, with one of the nationals in London, while I had run away to a Hong Kong English language newspaper, after an affair had suffered a greenstick fracture which was obviously never going to heal.

David fiddled with his chopsticks, holding them too low down the shafts to get any sort of control over them. He chased an elusive peppered prawn around the dish. It could have still been alive, the way it evaded the pincers.

"You always get people like that, on any paper, Sean—you know that. Politicians, roughriders, ambitious bastards, you can't escape them just by coming east. Some people get their kicks out of stomping on their subordinates. What is he, anyway? Senior Editor?"

David finally speared the prawn with a single chopstick and looked around him defiantly at the Cantonese diners before popping it into his mouth.

"He's got a lot of power. He could get me thrown out, just like that."

"Well, suck up to the bastard. They like that sort of thing, don't they? The Chinese? Especially from European *gwailos* like you. Take him out to lunch, tell him he's a great guy and you're proud to be working with him—no, *for* him. Tell him the Far East is wonderful, you love Hong Kong, you want to make good here, make your home here. Tell the bastard anything, if it gets him off your back. Forget all that shit about crawling. That's for school kids who think that there's some kind of virtue in swimming against the tide. You've got to make a go of it, and this bloke, what's his name? Chang? If he's making your life hell, then neutralize the sod. Not many people can resist flattery, even when they recognize what it is—hookers use it all the time—'you big strong man, you make fantastic lovey, I never have man like you before.' Codswallop. You know it, they know it, but it still makes you feel good, doesn't it? Speaking of hookers, when are you going to take me down the Wanch...?"

He was talking about Wan Chai, the red light district, which I knew I would have to point him toward one evening of his holiday. David liked his sex casual and stringless, despite all the evil drums in such a lifestyle these days. I needed emotion with my lovemaking, not cheap scent and garlic breath.

I lay in bed that night, thinking about what David had said. Maybe the fault did lie with me? Maybe I was putting out the wrong signals and John Chang thought I did not like him, had not liked him from our first meeting? Some men had sensitive antennae, picked up these vibrations before the signaler knew himself what messages he intended to transmit.

No, I was sure that wasn't it. I had gone out of my way to be friendly with John Chang. I had arrived in Hong Kong, eager to get to know the local people, and had seen John Chang as a person to whom I would have liked to get close. But from the beginning he had come down hard on me, on my work, on everything I did. I had been singled out for victimization and he piled adverse criticism on my head whenever he got the chance.

However, I was willing to admit that I was not the easiest of employees to get along with, from a social point of view.

John Chang had a happy marriage. I had never met his wife, but she phoned him at the office quite often, and the tone and manner of the conversation indicated a strong loving relationship. This caused me to be envious of him. I once dreamed of having such a relationship with Nickie, and had failed to make it work. I still loved her, of course, and on days I missed her most I was testy and irritable with everyone, including John Chang.

I fell asleep thinking that perhaps I was more than partly to blame for John Chang's attitude toward me. I vowed to try to improve things, once my vacation was over and I was back at work.

THERE WAS A cricket making insistent noises, somewhere in the bedroom. It took several sleep-drugged minutes for me to realize that it was the phone chirruping. David? Had he gone down the Wanch and got himself into trouble?

"Hello, Sean Fraser..."

"Fraser?" John Chang's clipped accent. "Get down to the office. We need you on a story."

I sat up in bed.

"I'm on vacation. I've got a guest here, dammit!"

"Sorry, can't help that. Tim Lee's gone sick. He was covering the Governor's annual speech. You'll have to do it."

The line went dead. He had replaced the receiver.

I slammed the phone down and seethed for a few minutes, before getting out of bed to have a shower and get dressed. David was still asleep on the living-room couch when I went through to the kitchen. I woke him and told him what had happened, apologized, and said I would see him that evening.

"Don't worry about me, mate. I can sort myself out. It's that bastard of a boss *you* want to sort out."

Once I had covered the usual bland yearly speech presented by the British Governor of Hong Kong—written

by a committee into a meaningless string of words—
John Chang wanted me to visit a fireman in the Lok Fu
district. The man had been partially blinded six weeks
previously while fighting a fire in Chung King Mansions, a notorious giant slum where holidaying
backpackers found relatively cheap accommodation in
an impossibly expensive city.

"It's five o'clock," I protested to Chang, "and I have a
guest to look after."

He regarded me stone-faced.

"You're a reporter. You don't work office hours."

"I'm on bloody holiday."

"That's tough. You cover this, *then* you're on vacation—
unless I need you again. If you want to work for someone
else, that's fine too. Understand me?" He stared hard at
me, probably hoping I would throw his job in his face. I
was not about to do that.

I said coldly, "I understand."

I rang David and said I would be home about nine
o'clock. I advised him to go out and eat, because I was
going to grab some fast food on my way to Lok Fu. He
seemed happy enough, and told me not to worry, but that
wasn't the point. The point was that I was close to strangling John Chang with my bare hands.

I saw the young fireman. He seemed philosophical about
his accident, though to me his disability pension seemed
incredibly small. His wife was working as a bank clerk
and now he could look after their two infants, instead of
sending them to the grandparents for the weekdays. He
could still see a little, and as he pointed out, government
apartments, like most private apartments in Hong Kong,
were so small it had only taken him a short while to get a
mental picture of his home.

During the interview the fireman pressed brandies
upon me, as is the custom among the Hong Kong

Chinese. By the time I left him, I was quietly drunk. I caught a taxi. The driver took me through Wong Tai Sin, and I passed the temple David and I had visited the previous evening. On impulse I told the driver to stop and paid him off.

The old man was still there, at the opening to the alley. He was sitting on a small stool, staring dispassionately at passersby with his rheumy eyes. The pipe was lying on a piece of dirty newspaper, just behind him. I stumbled over to him, trying to hide my state of inebriation.

I pointed to the pipe.

"*Ngoh, sik yin-aa?*" I said, asking to smoke it.

Cantonese is a tonal language, the same words meaning many different things, and by the way he looked at me I knew I had got my tones wrong. I had probably said something like "Me fat brickhead" or something even more incomprehensible.

"*M'maai,*" he said emphatically in Cantonese, thinking I wanted to buy the pipe and informing that it was not for sale.

I persisted, and by degrees, got him to understand that I only wanted to smoke it. I told him I had an enemy, a man I hated. I said I wished "to know" this man, and would pay him for the use of his magic pipe. He smiled at me, his face a tight mass of contour lines.

"*Yi sap man,*" he agreed, asking me for twenty dollars. It was a very small sum for gaining power over the man that was making my life a misery.

I tore off a margin piece of newspaper and wrote JOHN CHANG on it, but the old man brushed this aside. He produced a thin strip of red-and-gold paper covered on one side with Chinese characters and indicated that I should write the name on the back of it. When I had done so, he tore it into tiny pieces. I could see the muscles working in wrists as thin as broom handles, as his long-nailed fingers worked first at this, then at tamping down the paper shreds and tobacco in the pipe bowl.

He handed the musty-smelling instrument to me and I hesitated. It looked filthy. Did I really want that thing in my mouth? I had visions of the stem crawling with tuberculosis bacilli from the spittle of a thousand previous smokers. But then there was a flame at the bowl, and I was sucking away, finding the tobacco surprisingly smooth.

I could see the dark smoke rising from the rubbish burning cauldrons of Wong Tai Sin Temple, and as I puffed away on the ancient bamboo pipe, an intense feeling of well-being crept over me. I began to suspect the tobacco. Was it indeed free of opium? Had I been conned, by the fruit seller and the old man both? Maybe the old man was the fruit stall owner's father? It didn't seem to matter. I liked the pair of them. They were wonderful people. Even John Chang seemed a nice man, at that moment in time.

WHEN THE HOLIDAY was over, David left Hong Kong, and I returned to work. John Chang was in a foul mood the morning I arrived, and was screaming at a young girl for spilling a few drops of coffee on the floor. A woman reporter caught my eyes and made a face which said, "Stay out of his way if you can."

The warning came too late.

"You," snapped John Chang, as I passed him. "That fireman story was bloody useless. You didn't capture the personal side *at all*."

"I thought I did," I said, stiffly.

"What you think is of no interest to me. I asked you to concentrate on the man and his family, and you bring in all that rubbish about government pensions."

"I thought it needed saying."

He gave me a look of disgust and waved me away as if I were some coolie that was irritating, but not worth chastising further. I felt my blood rise and I took a step toward him, but Sally, the woman reporter, grabbed my arm. She held me there until John Chang had left the room.

I turned, the fury dissipating, and said, "Thanks."

She gave me a little smile.

"You would only be giving him the excuse he needs," she said in her soft Asiatic accent. Peter Smith, another reporter, said, "Too bloody right, mate. Don't give him the satisfaction."

"He looked as if he could have killed that girl," I said to Sally, a little later. "All over a few spots of coffee."

"It was her perfume. For some reason that brand drives him crazy. I used to wear it myself, but not any more. Not since I realized what it does to his temper…"

*Understand the one you hate.*

I had to admit my temporary drunken hopes for a magical insight into John Chang had failed. There was no magic on the modern streets of Hong Kong. An antique pipe, nicotined a dirty yellow, stained black with tobacco juice, dottle clinging to the bowl, was nothing more than what it was—a lump of wood. Had I really believed it would help me?

I guess a desperate man will believe anything, even that he will some day manage to forget a woman he loves: will wake up one morning free of her image, the sound of her voice in his head gone, her smell removed from his olfactory memory. Memory sometimes works to its own secret rules and is not always subject to the will of its owner.

Memories can be cruel servants.

\* \* \*

I BEGAN TO have strange dreams, even while awake, of a woman I did not know. She was small, slim, and dark, with a familiar voice. We were very intimate with one another. I pictured her in a kitchen, her hands flying around a wok, producing aromas that drove my gastric juices crazy. I saw her brown eyes, peering into mine from behind candles like white bars, over a dining-room table made of Chinese rosewood. There was love in those eyes. We drank a wine which was familiar to my brain but not to my tongue. She chattered to me, pleasantly, in Cantonese. I understood every word she said.

These pictures, images, dreams, began to frighten me a little, not because they were unpleasant, but because they felt comfortable. They worried me with their coziness. I wondered whether they were some kind of replacement for the memories that I was attempting to unload: the result of a compensatory mental illness. Perhaps I was trying to fill emotional gaps with strange fantasies of a Chinese woman.

I began to look for her in the street.

There were other, more disconcerting thoughts, which meant very little to me. Scenes, cameos, flashes of familiar happenings that meant nothing to me emotionally. I pictured myself going into stores and shops I did not recognize, for articles I had never even considered buying. There was an ambivalence to my feelings during these scenes. I saw myself buying an antique porcelain bowl, the design of which I instinctively and intensely disliked. Yet I purchased it with loving care and a knowledge of ceramics I had not previously been aware of possessing. In another scene, I went into a bakery and bought some Chinese moon cakes, a highly sweetened, dense foodstuff which most *gwailos* avoid, and I was no exception.

I was sure I was going quite mad.

John Chang kept me busy, hating him. He did not let up on me for one moment during the sweltering summer months, when the wealthy fled to cooler climes and school teachers blessed the long vacations they got during the season when Hell relocated to the Hong Kong streets.

During this humid period the Chinese lady with the loving eyes continued to haunt me. I would languish at my desk after work, reluctant to leave the air-conditioned building, picturing myself making love with this woman in a bed with satin sheets, surrounded by unfamiliar furniture. It seemed right. Everything about it seemed right, except when I questioned it with some other part of my mind, the part firmly based in the logic that said, *you do not know this woman*. It was true. I had never met anyone like her, yet she looked at me as if I were hers, and some unquestioning area of my mind, less concerned with what I *knew*, and content to be satisfied with what I *felt*, told me yes, this had happened, this was a proper interpretation of my experiences.

I began to read about schizophrenia, wondering whether I was one of those people who have more than one personality, but the books that I read did not seem to match what was happening to me. I balked when it came to seeing a therapist. I was afraid there was something quite seriously wrong with me.

In October, some people organized a junk trip to Lamma Island, the waterfront of which is lined with excellent fish restaurants. Sally asked me if I was going and I said I might as well. Most of the newspaper's employees would be there, and a few of the employers as well. The weather had turned pleasantly hot, had left the dehumanizing summer humidity behind in September. It promised to be a good evening.

There were rumors that John Chang would be going, but that did not deter me. I wondered if I could get drunk enough to tell him what I thought of him.

I was one of the last to jump aboard the junk, which then pulled out into the busy harbor. I stared at the millions of lights off to port: Causeway Bay, Wan Chai, and Central, resplendent during the dark hours. A beer was thrust into my hand. I drank it from the can and looked around me. Sally was there. She waved. Peter Smith stood in animated conversation with another of our colleagues, his legs astride to combat the rolling motion of the craft in the choppy harbor waters. Then I noticed John Chang, sour-faced, standing by the rail.

Beside him was a lady I had never seen before, not in the flesh, but a woman with whom I had made love, in my head, a thousand times. My heart began to race and I felt myself going hot and cold, alternately, wondering whether I should try to hide somewhere until the evening was over. If she sees me, I thought, she's bound to recognize me as the one...

Then I pulled myself up short. One *what?* What had I done to her? Nothing. Not a blessed thing. So where did these pictures come from, that had invaded my head? The best way to find out was to talk to her. I tried to catch her eye, hoping she would come over to me without bringing John Chang.

Eventually I captured her attention and she looked startled. Did she know me after all? Was I indeed living some kind of Jekyll and Hyde existence? It was only after a few minutes that I understood she was not staring into my face at all: it was my red hair that had her attention. Then she realized she was being rude and averted her gaze, but Chang had caught us looking at each other and motioned for her to cross the deck with him. Before I could turn away, he was standing in front of me, gesturing toward the woman at his side.

"I don't believe you've met my wife, have you, Fraser?" She spoke in a gentle tone, admonishing him.

"John, Mr. Fraser must have a first name?"

He looked a little disconcerted.

"Yes, of course," he said stiffly. "Sean. Sean Fraser. Scottish I think."

"My ancestors were," I blurted, "but we've lived south of the border for two generations. The red hair, you know, is proof of my Celtic origins. I'm still a Scot, in spirit."

I shook her hand, acutely embarrassed by the fact that I knew what she looked like naked, lying on the bed, waiting for me to press myself against her. *John Chang's wife*. There were two small brown moles under her left breast. There were stretch marks around her abdomen.

I felt the silkiness of her palm, knowing that soft touch. I remembered the time she had whispered urgent nonsense into my ear, the first time our orgasms had coincided exactly, a miracle of biology which had left us breathless for several minutes afterwards, when we had both laughed with the utter joy of the occasion.

Staring into her eyes, I knew that if there was a memory of such happenings, they did not include *me*. What I saw there was a terrible sadness, held in check by a great strength. Alice Chang was one of those splendid people who find a natural balance within themselves. When a negative aspect of life causes them to lose equilibrium, a positive one rises from within their spirit, to meet it, cancel it out.

"I'm very pleased to meet you, Alice," I said.

"Oh, you know my name." She laughed. "I thought John tried to keep me a secret. Do you know this is the first time he has allowed me to meet his colleagues?"

I looked quickly at John Chang, and then said, "I'm afraid I've heard him speaking to you on the phone. The office has good acoustics. I don't eavesdrop intentionally."

"I'm sure you don't," she said, and then he steered her away, toward one of the directors, leaving me sweating, holding onto the rail for support. Not because of the rocking motion of the boat, but because my legs felt weak.

THE FOLLOWING WEEKEND I took a boat trip to Lantau Island and sat at a beach restaurant, staring at the sea and sand. I needed a peaceful place to think. Hong Kong's national anthem, the music of road drills, pile drivers, traffic, buzz saws, metal grinders, et al. was not conducive to reflective thought.

There were evergreens along the shoreline of Silvermine Bay, decorated with hundreds of tattered kites. The children used the beach to fly their toys, which eventually got caught in the branches of the large conifers, and remained there. The brightly colored paper diamonds gave the firs the appearance of Christmas trees. Around the trunks of the kite-snatchers were dozens of bicycles, chained to each other for security, left there by adolescents now sprawled on the sands.

I had managed to engineer one more chat with Alice Chang, before the end of that evening on Lamma, and spoke about the antique porcelain bowl, describing it. I had to lie to her, telling her that John had spoken to me about it, seemed proud to be its owner.

"Oh, yes. He loves ceramics, you know. It's his one expensive hobby."

I knew now I was experiencing John Chang's memories.

It was nothing to do with me. I had not made love to Alice Chang, but I carried John Chang's memories of such occasions, those that he wished to recall, and some he did not. It was a disturbing ordeal. There was a grim recollection of being hit a glancing blow by a truck, when he was small, and another when he was falsely accused of stealing from his school friends. I was gradually getting "to know" my Chinese boss and there were some dark areas in there which terrified me. I woke up at night, sweating, wondering where the fear was coming from, what was causing the desire to scream.

The night after the junk trip, I had spoken to Sally.

"How many kids has John Chang got?" I asked her casually.

She shook her head.

"None, so far as I know. Why do you ask?"

"Oh, no reason. I met his wife, last night. I thought she mentioned something about a child, but I couldn't be sure. I suppose I must have been mistaken."

Sally said, "I'm positive you are."

I drank steadily, as I tried to puzzle through my jumbled memories of his early marriage, and my eyes kept being drawn toward the bicycles, chained to the tree trunks. I struggled with a black beast of a memory, which was utterly reluctant to emerge from a hole it had dug itself.

*A bicycle.*

This was the key, but something prevented me from opening the lock. There was the idea that a bicycle was a detested thing, a deadly, ugly machine that should be outlawed, banned from use. *People who sell bicycles should be prosecuted, imprisoned, hung by the neck...*

That was very strong, *very* strong.

One of the kids from the beach came and unlocked her bike, climbed into the saddle, and rode away along the path. I experienced a forceful desire to scream at her, tell her to get off, return the machine to the salesman.

*Where?*

A shop sign popped into my head, which read: THE FLYING BALL CYCLE CO.

Then that dark cloud extended itself from the back of my brain, blacking out anything that might have followed.

BACK AT THE flat I received a surprise telephone call from England. From Nickie. She asked me how I was. Did I like the Far East? Yes, she was fine. She was seeing one or two people (she didn't call them men) and things were absolutely fine.

Her voice was recognizably thin and tight, even over the phone. There was great anger there, pressing against her desire to sound casual. I noticed that it was three o'clock in the morning, her time, and I guessed she had been unable to sleep, obsessed with relentlessly reviewing the bitter times, furious with herself for failing to retaliate strongly, when something hurtful had been said, wishing she could raise the subject again, but this time be the one to wield the knife, cut the deepest.

I knew how she felt, having gone through the same cycle, many nights. We had both fired words, intended to wound, but we both remembered only being hit.

I told her I was having some trouble with one of my bosses. She sympathized coldly, but what she had really called about was the fact that I still had two of her favorite poetry books. She would like them back again, please, the Hughes and the Rilke.

Oh, those, yes, but three o'clock in the morning?—she really must want them badly, I said. I told her I remembered seeing them, just before leaving England for Hong Kong, but could not put my hand on them at this time. Could she call again later, when I had done some more unpacking? No, she couldn't. I had been in Hong Kong for nearly a year. Hadn't I unpacked my things *yet?*

Her words became more shrill as the anger seeped through like a gas, altering the pitch of her voice.

When I did manage to unpack, could I please post them back to her? Yes, she was aware they were only paperbacks and could be replaced, but she didn't see why she should buy new copies when she already owned some—goodbye.

The emptiness that filled the room, after she had put down the phone, would have held galaxies.

I tried not to hate her, but I couldn't help it. She was there, I was here. Thousands of miles apart.

I picked up the Rilke, from the bedside table, open at *Orpheus. Eurydice, Hermes.* It was pencil marked in the margins, with her comments on the text. It was her handwriting I had been reading, not Rilke's poem. The flourishes were part of her, of the woman I had loved, and I had been sentimentalizing, as well as studying them for some small insight into her soul. I wanted to understand her, the secret of her self, in order to discover *why.* Why had it gone wrong?

The terrible ache in me could not be filled by love, so I filled it with hate instead. I wanted to kill her, for leaving me, for causing me so much emotional agony. I wanted to love her. I wanted her to love me. I hated her.

On Monday afternoon, I cornered Peter Smith. I recalled that he used to cover cycling stories for the paper. At one time his speech had been full of jargon—*accushift drivetrains, Dia-Compe XCU brakes, oversized headsets, Shimano derailleurs.* The language of the initiated, for the enthusiasts.

"You're a bike fanatic," I said. "You cycle in New Territories, don't you?"

"Not so much now," he patted a growing paunch, "but I used to. Why, you looking for a sport to keep you fit?"

"No, I came across this guy who kept raving about the Flying Ball Bike Shop. Know it?"

Smith laughed.

"My boy, that shop is a legend among cyclists. You can write to the owner of the Flying Ball from any corner of the earth, and he'll airmail the part you need and tell you to pay him when you eventually pass through Hong Kong."

"Why *Flying Ball?* Is that some kind of cog or wheel bearing invented specifically for push-bikes?"

Smith shook his head.

"I asked the owner once. He told me the shop had been named by his grandfather, and he forgot to ask the old man what it meant. The secret's gone with grandpa's polished bones to a hillside grave overlooking water. Part of the legend now."

"Where is it? The shop, I mean."

"Tung Choi Street, in the heart of Mong Kok," he said, "now buzz off, I've got a column to write."

I went back to my desk. A few moments later I experienced a sharp memory pang and looked up to see the office girl placing a polystyrene cup of steaming brown liquid on my desk top. She smiled and nodded, moving on to Sally's desk. I could smell her perfume. It was the same one she had been wearing the day John Chang had bawled at her.

IT WAS TWILIGHT when I reached Tung Choi Street. Mong Kok is in the Guinness Book of Records as the most densely populated area on the face of the earth. It is teeming with life, overspilling, like an ants' nest in a time of danger. It is run down, sleazy, but energetic, effervescent. Decaying tenements with weed ridden walls overhang garage-sized factory shops where men in dirty vests hammer out metal parts for everything and anything: stove pipes, watering cans, kitchen utensils, car exhausts, rat cages, butter pats, fish tanks, containers, and so on. What you can't buy ready-made to fit, you can have knocked up within minutes.

Over the course of the day the factory shops vomit their wares slowly, out, across the greasy pavement, into the road. The vendors of fruit and iced drinks fill in the spaces between. Through this jungle of metal, wood, and plastic plough the taxis and trucks, while the pedestrians manage as best they can to hop over, climb, circumnavigate. Business is conducted to a cacophony caused by hammers, drills, saws, car horns. It can have a rhythm if you have a broad musical tolerance and allow it flexibility.

THE FLYING BALL CYCLE CO. I found the shop after two minutes' walking.

I stood on the opposite side of the road, the two-way flow of life between me and this unimposing little bike shop, and I remembered. It hit me with a force that almost had me reeling backwards, into the arms of the shopkeeper among whose goods I was standing. The dark area lifted from my brain and the tragedy was like an awful light, shining through to my consciousness. The emotional pain revealed by this brightness, so long covered and now unveiled, was appalling.

And this was not my agony, but *his*.

I turned and stumbled away from the scene, making for the nearest telephone. When I found one I dialed John Chang's home number. It had all come together the moment I laid eyes on the Flying Ball: the hate John Chang bore toward me; the unexplained stretch marks on Alice Chang's abdomen; the blankness in his eyes; the sadness in hers.

"Mrs. Chang? This is Sean Fraser. We met on the junk— yes, the other night. I wonder if you could ask John to meet me, in the coffee shop by Star Ferry? Yes, that's the one. Can you say it's very important. It's about your son, Michael... Yes, I know, I know, but I have to talk to him just the same. Thanks."

I put down the receiver and hailed a taxi.

I was on my second cup of coffee when he arrived. He looked ashen and for once his facade of grim self-assurance was missing. I ordered him a cup of coffee and when it arrived, put some brandy in it from a half-bottle I had bought on the way. He stared at the drink, his lean face gray, his lips colorless.

"What's all this about?" he said. The words were delivered belligerently, but there was an underlying anxiousness to the tone. "Why did you ask me to come here, Fraser?"

He hadn't touched his coffee, and I pushed it toward him.

"I know about Michael," I said.

His eyes registered some pain.

"I know how he died."

"What business is it of yours?" he said in a low voice. "How dare you? You're interfering in my family affairs. You leave my family alone."

"I'm not interested in your family. I'm interested in the way you treat *me*. Since I've been in Hong Kong, you've made my life hell. I didn't bring your family into the office, *you* did. You're punishing me for something you won't even allow yourself to think about. You've blocked it out and the guilt you feel is causing you to hurt other people, especially red-headed *gwailos*.

"I've been the target for your suppressed anger, your bottled grief, for as long as I can stand. It's got to stop, John. I'm not responsible for Michael's death, and you know it, really. I just happen to be a European with red hair. I wasn't even in Hong Kong when that driver took your son's life..."

"Shut up!" he shouted, causing heads to turn and look, then turn back again quickly. His face was blotched now, with fury, and he was gripping the cup of coffee as if he intended to hurl it into my face.

"This is what happened, John," I said quietly, ignoring his outburst. "It was Christmas, and being a Christian, you celebrated the birth of Christ in the way that *gwailo* Christians do. You bought presents for your wife and twelve-year-old son. You gave your wife some perfume, a brand you won't allow her to use now because it reminds you of that terrible time, and you asked your son what he would like most in the world..."

There were tears coming down John Chang's face now, and he stumbled to his feet and went through the door. I left ten dollars on the table and followed him. He was standing against the harbor wall, looking down into the water, still crying. I moved up next to him.

"He said he wanted a bicycle, didn't he, John? One of those new mountain bikes, with eighteen, twenty gears. You took Michael down to Mong Kok, to the Flying Ball Bike Shop, and you bought him what he wanted because you were a loving father, and you wanted to please him. He then begged to be allowed to ride it home, but you were concerned, you said no, repeatedly, until he burst into tears—and finally, you relented.

"You said he could ride it home, if he was very, very careful, and you followed behind him in the car."

I paused for a moment and put my arm around his shoulders.

"The car that overtook you, halfway home, was driven by a red-headed foreigner, a *gwailo,* and he hit Michael as he swerved in front of you to avoid an oncoming truck. The bike itself was run over. It crumpled, like paper, and lay obscenely twisted beside your son's body. You stopped, but the other driver didn't. He sped away while you cradled Michael's limp body in your arms, screaming for an ambulance, a doctor.

"They never caught the hit-and-run driver, and you've never forgiven yourself. You still want him, don't you, that murdering red-headed *gwailo,* the man that killed your son? You want to punish him, desperately, and maybe some of that terrible guilt you feel might go away."

He turned his tear-streaked face toward me, looked into my eyes, seeking a comfort I couldn't really give him.

I said gently, "That wasn't me, John. You know it wasn't me."

"I know," he said. "I know, I know. I'm so sorry."

He fell forward, into my arms, and we hugged each other, for a brief while. Then we became embarrassed simultaneously, and let go. He went back to leaning on the wall, but though the pain was still evident, his sobbing had ceased.

Finally he turned asked the obvious question: how did I know so much detail about Michael's death? It had happened many years ago.

Rather than go into the business with the pipe, I told him I had been to Wong Tai Sin, to a clairvoyant, and the man had looked into John's past for me.

"It cost me a lot of money," I said, to make it sound more authentic. If there's one thing that Hong Kongers believe in, it's the authority money has to make the impossible possible. John Chang did not laugh at this explanation or call me a liar. A little brush with the West does not wipe out 5,000 years of Chinese belief in the supernatural.

Then he went home, to his wife, leaving me to stare at the waters of the fragrant harbor and think about my own feelings of love and hate. *Understand the man you hate.*

How can you hate a man you understand? I began to realize what the old man with his magic pipe was selling. Not power over one's enemy. Love. That's what he had for sale. His was a place where you could look at hate, understand it enough to be able to turn it into love.

I knew something else. Now that I had confronted John, now that we understood one another, the memories of his past would cease to bother me. The pipe had done its work.

THE FOLLOWING WEEK, one evening when a rain as fine as Irish drizzle had come and gone, leaving a fresh scent to the air, I took a taxi to Wong Tai Sin Temple. The old man was still there, sitting at the entrance to the alley, his pipe by his side.

I went up to him and gave him twenty dollars, and he smiled and silently handed me the pipe and a piece of red-and-gold paper decorated with Chinese characters. On the back of the paper I wrote the name of a person I loved and hated—NICHOLA BLACKWOOD—and tore it into tiny pieces, hoping that distance was no barrier to magic.

# KITSUNE

*Mary Gentle*

"It's NOT THE end of the world; it's just bad sex."

Tamiko said that to me toward the end, when she had learned to speak pretty good English.

For a fox spirit.

I blame Greg for it, myself. He's an odd type; late twenties, still lives with his mother. It's far too complicated to tell you how he became a cook, from being a qualified painter and decorator; but he did, and his first real job (when he got it) was in a Japanese restaurant in London. I used to call it NipponHut; what it really sold was *okunomiyaki,* omelets, with bits in, which seems to be the Japanese equivalent of fast food pizza.

His boss had wanted an English cook; the rest of the staff were Japanese; by default—and evening classes—Greg ended up learning some conversational Japanese. If you consider *"Sumimasen ga,* pass me the *netto* beans," to be conversation. So I think he understood Tamiko better.

Greg is one of those people who you can never trust to be one thing or the other. He'll be abrasive as hell for 90 percent of the time. He makes a habit of asking me why I have hair that changes color every three weeks, knowing that I'm just trying to keep the gray concealed and not hitting any solution that satisfies me. He makes remarks about us both fancying the same type of women that are offensive rather than buddy-buddy. He treats me like a guy when it suits him, like a woman when it doesn't. But, one time he made me a *sake* cup, without asking, and glazed and painted it himself, and gave it to me without a word.

I think he knew what she was like from the beginning.

He brought her into class one Sunday morning. I'd been training for a while, gone through warm-up, used a *bokkan* first to loosen up muscles and tendons while I found my *hara* center, and was performing *kata* with a steel sword in the bright sunlight that comes down from the gym's clerestory windows.

If either one of the two of them had come into blade-range I would have registered them immediately. Lifting, cutting, blocking, slicing; people remain wall-paper around the sides of the gym, faces with whom I do not make eye contact. My body thinks, not my mind.

I stopped, breathing deeply but not fast, and I heard a stifled little giggle, and turned around to see Tamiko with her hand over her mouth.

"Samurai," she said, in her as-yet accented English. "You are a girl samurai."

Greg, beside her, said something quick in Japanese. I recognized the syllables, couldn't remember what it meant (all I have is a small technical vocabulary covering the finer points of sword manufacture). I turned away from him, and fell in love the second that I looked her in the face.

The first thing you notice about Japanese girls is that they're tiny. With short legs. I have a friend who lends me girlie magazines from Tokyo; all the models avoid the classic stockings-and-suspenders, because on them it looks wrong. Disproportionate. (The Japanese have a thing about women in nylon pantyhose; perhaps this is why.) Tamiko had little fat-thighed legs, and her black hair cut in a short crop around her little plump face, and she stood about five-foot-nothing, and *none of it mattered*. I loved her instantly.

And she was straight.

I know, now, why I thought this so decidedly. She had her hands wrapped around Greg's arm, and her chin tipped up as she whispered to him, and one foot off the ground, trailing a little slippered toe across the gym flooring; all the signals that any teenage bimbo would use to say, "this one's *mine*."

"This is Tamiko," Greg introduced her. About nineteen: could be older. She was being very touchy-feely for a Japanese girl. I've seen enough Japanese female students who never do go back home to Osaka or Tokyo or wherever to recognize her immediacy of freedom.

Tamiko giggled again. They really do do that. Her accent was slightly American. "Lady samurai. This friend, you?"

Greg said, "Tamiko, this is Rowena."

I had about ten seconds of excoriating jealousy of Greg; the real why-was-I-ever-born variety. Not because Tamiko was holding his arm, and that meant he was probably poking his dick into her on a regular basis, but because she *could* hold his arm, and if it had been me, we couldn't have. Even long ago, when I was what I cheerfully designated a baby butch, I couldn't get away with that one—you'd think they'd take us for teenage heteros, clutching each other's arms and squealing and giggling, but they always know.

None of this stopped me doing big-cute-sports-dyke. Or perhaps it ought to be cute-martial-arts-dyke. Bow to *sensei,* to excuse myself. Slide the curved *katana* blade back into its black lacquered scabbard. All of which will, if you do it right, show off the lines of hips, spine, shoulders, biceps, and pray she doesn't notice the very slight double chin that passing thirty-five is giving me.

"So: did Greg bring you down here to see the *iaido* class? You must get enough of this at home."

"No. I have never seen martial arts, except in the movies. Is difficult to do, perhaps?"

She raised her eyes to my face. I loved her even more. At that time, I didn't know that I didn't have a choice.

"It's not difficult to start off with. Come over here, I'll show you." I took her over to one side of the gym, and brought out my lightest blade and wrapped her tiny fingers around the grip.

She had a warm body in a short black dress, and she smelled of something floral. I made a mental note to buy her musk, she would suit musk far better than light-and-flowery scent.

"You hold it like this. No, this. One hand here. And the other here. Now your arms. No: let me show you."

I wondered dizzily if she could tell. I used my hands to move her arms, placing her elbows closer in to her body, and I straightened her wrists, and moved her palms apart on the braid-and-rayskin grip of the sword, and all the time I could feel myself shaking. She just looked down the back of the bright steel blade with an expression that was part-giggle, part bloody-minded determination.

It seems ironic, now, that I touched her with a desire so strong that I could taste it, dry, in my mouth. That my hands did shake, and the pads of my fingertips left sweat-dots on the sleeves of her dress. I was turned on to that point where your clothes feel uncomfortably tight. There was no way I was going to turn round and look at Greg.

At the same time that I heard him talking to two or three of the other students, I realized that the class had broken up, that I was very likely in trouble for being disrespectful to *sensei,* and that Tamiko had a natural stance. She carried her body erect, her feet about eighteen inches apart, one foot pointed forward and the other pointing slightly to the side. She could move, lightly, in any direction; her balance almost perfect.

"Where did you learn that? You *must've* done *iaido.*"

"No. I know a man who—" Tamiko frowned. Her loss of words was apparent on her face; her black eyes like oil in sunlight.

She brought the blade up above her head and cut down, arresting the stroke some twelve inches above the floor, and her hands wrung out the grip of the hilt as you might twist a wash-cloth dry, and the edge of the sword *whicked!* as it cut cleanly through the air.

"A man who," she completed, satisfied.

I wanted, more than anything on earth, to step behind her and put one of my hands flat on her belly, and the other across her tiny, rounded breasts, and hug her body back into mine, push her plump buttocks into my groin. Well, wanted it more than anything on earth except not to be *seen* doing it, in public.

I wonder if it would have made a difference if I'd given way to the impulse? I would have left the class— but I've left other places. Or stayed, when I felt bloody-minded. I leave when there's not enough prejudice to make a fight pleasurable, only a faint miasma of difference that can't really be combated.

"That was amazing!" Michael said. Michael is another regular at the *iaido* class; an asthmatic whose stoop has almost vanished in the years that he's been doing this. I knew him, he'd move in on her; and Greg knew it too, it was arm-around-shoulder time. In the confusion and conversation I put my sword away.

Tamiko appeared at my side as I was clearing up.

"This also is a tradition of the samurai," she said, "when same loves same."

My ears burned; I knew they'd be bright red. Without moving my body, I flicked my gaze sideways, saw no one—Greg, Michael, Simon, Jean—no one looking this way, or listening; some dumb argument going on about where would we go for lunch? And could it be non-smoking? And cater for a dairy products allergy?

I managed the all-purpose English *what*-the-fuck-did-you-just-say. "Sorry?"

"A man with a man."

"Tamiko... You don't *say* things like that!"

"But you are—"

I didn't know how she was going to phrase it. Some impulse of devilment made me almost wait to find out; but dark, crew-cut Michael was turning around to see where the newcomer was, Greg tracking his movements like a radar dish. I spoke over her voice:

"You could be good at sword work, if you wanted to put in the practice hours. How long are you over here for?"

Greg, at my elbow, said in quick slurred English, "She doesn't know what you're asking her to do."

If it had been anyone else but Greg, I would have assumed that he referred to *iaido*.

Tamiko looked puzzled.

I repeated slowly, "I would like to help you to learn this. If you want to, Tamiko."

"Yes." She nodded her head many times, enthusiastic. "Yes. I will learn what you have to teach."

TAMIKO LEARNED IAIDO from our *sensei,* and English from Greg, and from me—what? How to walk down a summer street, sweaty arms just touching, brushing skin; and to smile at our reflections in shop windows? How to kiss briefly, as if we were friends? Where to find the cafés and clubs, and sink into the atmosphere of women-ness; never knowing, until you relax into that exclusivity, how tense you are everywhere else?

"I was so sure you were straight," I told her, in a café around the back of Centre Point.

Tamiko smiled her amazing dimply smile.

"I am fox spirit," she said; and corrected herself, with the careful pronunciation Greg was teaching her: "I am *a* fox spirit. *I'm* a fox spirit. Better, yes?"

"'*Fox* spirit'?"

"So I'm able to love who I wish. Not who you say I must. Or must not. Is not the same for me. I can make love with whatever I want to."

The June sun came through the glass of the café's big window, picking out posters, copies of *The Pink Paper,* women seated in pairs and foursomes; one dyke talking into her cell phone. The smell of coffee drifted up from my half-empty cup of cappuccino.

"Tamiko... what's a fox spirit?" I thought it might be a college sorority, a girl-gang: who knows what exotic social arrangements they have in Tokyo?

"Fox-spirit, *kitsune,* she is a woman-demon."

"A *demon?* What do you mean? What are you really saying, here?"

The Japanese woman linked her fingers under her chin. She gazed up at me. The luster on her flesh is youth, rounding out the plumpness of her sallow face until it does not seem like fat, but like some bursting ripeness. Her eyes, with their folded skin, defy my attempts to read her expression. That would take far longer than learning her language.

"A demon, a bad ghost," she said.

"Tamiko..." The oh-come-*on* tone. I still thought we had some difference of translation to overcome.

"I am the spirit of a white fox with nine tails. I have the body, no, the *shape*, of a girl. Rowena, you are on the outside, too. I can tell you."

It—she—made me laugh, ruefully.

"Come on then, demon. Little demon. Demonette. Let's go home and fuck."

"I'm a true fox-spirit, Rowena."

"And I'm a..." I could think of no stichomythia to match her. The light from outside shone plainly on her face, with a white foam of coffee froth dabbed on her slim lips, and nothing at all—in our language of the body, or in what I had been able to piece together of hers—nothing I could see indicated humor, satire, pretence, or confusion.

"Come on." The chair scraped back as I stood up to leave.

That night I made love to her.

If you're one of the "but what do lesbians *do* in bed?" variety, I suggest you find a tolerant dyke friend and ask her. We do what you do, we just do it more enthusiastically. Let's face it, if one of us just lies there, nothing's going to happen.

"I am a fox-spirit," she insisted.

Real delusion is frightening.

I couldn't come.

I couldn't make her come.

At the moments when I should have been worshipping flesh with my mouth, some voice in the back of my head started saying *this woman is a fantasizer, a psycho, she's got problems, you've had far too much of women with problems; she's probably some Japanese therapy-dyke playing the innocent student.*

"Rowena?"

One fantasy drives out another. Or is it that fantasy, always, can drive out the reality? Fantasy, unreality, psychosis, suspicion: they're all stronger than reality. I lay in curdled sheets, looking at the smooth skin of this woman that I really do not know.

"I can't," I said. "I don't want to."

"SO WHERE'S TAMIKO, then?" Greg asked, with unerring accuracy for pain.

I sat with my legs curled under me, alone on his old red vinyl sofa, sweat sticking my skin to the surface of the cushion. His house's open window let in the sound of bored adolescent boys yawping and bragging. Someone on one of the other roads, further into the estate, had a Ford engine being tuned; a rhythmic, predatory roaring. He still lives there because his mother does. He's no more gay than I am straight.

I asked question for question. "Where'd you meet Tamiko? First?"

"She came into the restaurant." Businesslike and brusque, as if nothing could be more ordinary. "Matthew says she's Ainu."

"What's that?"

In his usual staccato, Greg said, "Yeah, I asked Matthew. He told me. The originals. The people that were there before the Japanese. Well, what we call

Japanese. Matthew says there's still some of them up on the north island."

I suspected the word Greg was looking for was *aboriginal,* and I also suspected the word that Matthew, the restaurant's manager, had used was something else entirely.

"How long's she been here?"

"She hasn't told you?"

"I still don't understand her English that good."

Greg gave a barking laugh. It had all the male drive-cars-watch-football-poke-women in it that I could stand. I left. The best you can say about Greg is that, being unaware of social amenities, he doesn't demand them from his friends.

Saturday: twenty-four hours until I might meet her, at the *iaido* class. If she came. If I went. Twenty-four hours until she would come up and ask me, probably out loud and in front of whoever, "Why haven't I seen you? Why are you angry with me? Why don't you want to make love anymore?"

I lengthened my stride, crossing the estate's bald grass-patch in front of the shop, remembering that the library closes early on a Saturday, and one of the throng of boys miskicked a football so that it landed at my feet.

I flipped it up and kicked it solidly back.

"Thanks, mate!" He waved a short acknowledgement. The name and the acknowledgment that you give to guys: his contemporaries.

In broad daylight, too. It wouldn't be dusk for hours yet.

I found that I was grinning to myself as I walked into town.


THE NEWTOWN COUNTY library had a bit of stuff on Japanese legends. All of it had the authenticity of folk legends from foreign cultures, in that none of the stories seemed to have a definable closure, or a point.

As for fox spirits, there was the kind of crap you might see on some kiddies' morning power-fantasy cartoon. I was sure Tamiko could tell it all to me: *kitsune* are spirits, ghosts, immortal in their fox form; they take on human form and seduce men, and then leave them after various events lead to disclosure and tragedy.

They don't sit beside you in a dyke café and say *Hey, I'm a fox spirit, how about that!*

I sat with my chin cupped in my hands and stared out of the library window. The study area was empty, the staff moving about purposefully downstairs with a definite air of *we're closing*.

"So... when Tamiko comes up to me, I'm going to say, 'You're a nutter, go away!' Yeah. Right..."

I skimmed the paragraph I'd been staring at as I stood up to put the book back on the shelf. In his pedestrian, mediocre prose, the writer on folklore had finished his chapter with this sentence:

"*Notably, the treacherous kitsune or 'fox-spirit' also has the power to make any human mortal fall in love with her.*"

It was easy enough to dismiss the folklore. Something real intervened, wrenching at my gut. That is what I would like to tell you: that it hurts, it hurts, it hurts enough to make you breathless, when you realize:

"I still love her. Whatever kind of an airhead she is, I haven't stopped loving her. Not for a minute. Maybe I never will."

THAT FEELING THAT you *never will* went away, of course. It does. I've loved before, and now I can barely remember the cauterizing pain of leaving or being left. I won't say I forget their names, but I can no longer remember in my gut how it felt to be connected to them by love.

You can't say that you'll never stop loving somebody. "Never" is a very short time, these days.

I stood on the library steps and wondered what I was going to do with myself for the next—time check—eighteen hours.

THERE'S A RAVINE left over from when they bulldozed in the park on the town planners' map.

Black shapes trotted in the half-light.

Urban foxes use the ravine now, for their run down to the backs of the kebab houses in the town center. Long, low bodies loping; led by their pointed noses.

I sat until dusk turned to night. I got close enough for one orange-furred young vixen to stare at me, for an animal half-second, before turning and sliding off into the undergrowth. Her cry sounded like a baby being eviscerated.

*These* are foxes.

Feeling grounded, I called in at Greg's house on my walk back, to see if he'd got back from evening shift.

"You'll have to go. I've got to sleep." Greg rubbed at his eyes, at his front door. "Trouble with you, Rowena, is, you need to move out of this town. Go to London. Somewhere like that. This place is a dump. And get yourself a job!"

He spoke as if he thought I might be genuinely interested to hear his opinion, and not as if I might want to hit him.

"Oh well." Greg ignored my silence with a tired, cheerful laugh. "See you down the class tomorrow. Maybe."

\* \* \*

THE WEIGHT OF the sword becomes an extension of your arms, wrists, hands, until you can feel its balance as much as your own. A true cut *feels* right. You know it from the inside.

*Sensei* had not suggested that I go for a grading this summer. I know him and respect him better than to think this is pique on his part, for disrespect. It's just an accurate reflection of what I've been doing: literally screwing around. Wasting training time. My mind is not in my blade.

The *hamon* of the sword catches the sun: the edge's satin wavy finish, comparatively dark against the mirror-brightness of the flat of the blade. Step, move, cut. Step, move, cut. Nothing I can do, despite the smooth sliding of tendons and muscles under sweating skin, to make my cuts even adequate this morning.

The bells from the nearby Anglican church broke my concentration, and Tamiko walked into the *iaido* practice hall on the sound of them, her high-heeled tapping footsteps hidden. Skimpy blue dress; sandals—looking nothing like a fright-haired, white-faced, spike-finger-nailed Japanese fox-ghost. I lowered my blade, sheathed it, bowed.

"Well," I said, when I got to her, "any more new stories? What's it going to be this time? You learned your stance and balance from a genuine live samurai warrior, five hundred years ago? I know: you're immortal."

"Yes."

Her flat reply frightened me. Not because she might believe that she was telling the truth, but because I had no way that I could trust of judging whether she believed it or not.

"Come for a walk outside," Tamiko said.

I tied the *katana* into its purple satin bag and followed her out into the sun; into the village tail now wagged by the newtown dog. She walked across the road, and I couldn't tell whether she was aimless or determined. She went through the lych-gate and stood under the yew tree in the churchyard; leaning against a pollution-eaten gravestone and listening to the hymns, barely audible through stained-glass windows. The traffic on the bypass sounded louder.

I followed. Heat reddened the back of my neck.

"Tamiko." I squinted at her, and rested the sword across my body. She was in the tree's shadow, and I moved to join her, excusing myself to myself that it was only because of the heat. "Tamiko..."

Fear kills sexual desire. Only the remnants of wanting her shivered across my skin. Here in the tree's dankness, she was rubbing her hands over her upper arms. I wanted, for one second, to kiss the alert skin of her shoulder, her throat, her little breasts with the big brown nipples; wake the stab of pleasure between my legs.

"It's not the end of the world; it's only bad sex." Tamiko's black eyes moved to my face. "It wouldn't be like that for ever."

Desire goes sour like music going flat. "Yes. It would. I don't want you anymore... shit! Look. I don't know who you are, Tamiko."

I refused to play her game and say *I don't know* what *you are*.

"Put the *katana* down," she said.

Through the slippery silk, I can feel the slick scabbard and rough grip of the weapon, which I didn't realize I had been cradling across my body. I put it down. I leaned it carefully across a guano-spotted marble surround, under *Susan Neville, beloved wife of the above*. Inside the church, a few old ladies quavered about the swift close of life's little day.

"Now what?"

"Hold my hands," Tamiko said. "Kiss me. Here, now, Rowena. Kiss me on my lips."

Across the road, I saw Greg and Michael standing with their heads together outside the practice hall.

"You're joking!"

"No. I am not. What can you show them that they will not know?"

I saw Greg stealing a quick cigarette, Michael saying something and glancing across at the churchyard. I couldn't hear what he said but I could guess the sense of it: *another one of Rowena's fuck-ups.*

Both of them would be kind to me later.

It was something to look forward to.

"I can't." It sounded like a whine. I attempted controlled, deprecating humor. "Any more than you can stop telling me you're a spirit, a ghost, whatever. Fox-woman."

"Kiss me!"

Anger came fast-forwarding up out of me as I looked at her shadow-dappled, sallow features. "It's too easy for you! You can go back and play straight! What am *I* supposed to do when you've gone? Too many things would have changed... I wouldn't know how to talk to any of them. They wouldn't know what to say to me."

"I would never leave you. For ever." Tamiko hugged her arms across her plump body. She smelled of musk-scent: a gift. Her black eyes searched my face, and I couldn't read her expression. Her voice sounded like despair. "*Touch* me. You love me. Where is your courage? I know that you love me, Rowena. You must!"

"Why 'must' I love you?" I asked.

Tamiko looked up into the shafts of light between the yew's branches. I wanted, more than anything, for her to say something I could understand without the need to filter it through a translation. Something that would feel as clear and right and immediate as a good cut.

"Because I chose you," she said.

This time I used it against her deliberately. "Yeah. Right. Because, if you chose me, I *have* to love you. Because you're a 'fox spirit.' Tamiko, come *on!*"

She wouldn't look into my face. She put her hands up so that her fingertips just covered her lips. "I thought that you were outside. Different. A foreigner, like me. You have no—guts. Honor. Not should carry *katana!*"

Tamiko walked away, quickly, into the sunshine; across the graveyard and into the street. I lifted and cradled the sword in its bag and watched her go.

In the end, difference is too hard. Or I'm too stupid.

I DREAM ABOUT her. Constantly. I really do.

It's such a dumb thing that I don't tell Greg about it, and I certainly don't tell Michael, who was in bed with her about five minutes after she crossed the road and hung onto his arm and giggled up at him.

"Slut," Greg said after class, brief and businesslike as ever. "Funny, if she'd've been English, I'd've spotted it right away."

And then at the end of the summer she went home, wherever home was; maybe on one of the north islands, like Greg said. Maybe to some condo in Tokyo, with her parents.

I don't practise any sword *kata* now.

Sometimes, when I dream of Tamiko, she *is* a white fox.

This all happened about six years ago. There hasn't been anyone else since. No one. I still love her. "Never" is turning out to be a longer time than I thought it would.

But—since I don't believe in fox spirits—I will stop loving her, in the end.

# OLD SOLDIERS

## *Kit Reed*

IT'S SUPPOSED TO be pretty in the place where Jane's grandmother lives; it says so in the Palmshine brochure. The pages are filled with photos of nice old ladies in the bright Florida sunlight, laughing and flirting with spunky old men in airy rooms. The sun is always high when Jane goes to visit Gram, but shadows fall as soon as she walks in the front door.

She's here because her mother can't bear to come. If Jane asks why, her mother starts crying. She says, "She isn't who she used to be," but that isn't the real reason.

"She isn't dead either," Jane snaps. "Oh, Mom, it is so awful there."

"Don't say that! It's the best we could find."

"I just wish we could..."

When her mother's lips tighten like that she looks a lot like Gram. "Well, we can't."

Palmshine Villa should be sunny and bright inside; after all, this is Florida, but no matter how fast Jane strides along the halls, at her back she hears the rushing shadows. She comes so often that she knows the regulars, although none of them knows her. Does being old make you forgetful or is it that when you're their age all people Jane's age look alike?

In the brochure everything is supposed to be nice. On the surface everything is. The coiffed and rouged wheelchair patients playing Nerf ball in the lobby are smiling, but from the remote Extended Care wing, a voice so old that Jane can't gender it cries out.

She should be used to it by now but she whirls. "Ma'am," she says to the nearest aide. "Ma'am!"

Oblivious, the aide trots on. She is carrying the richest lady's shih tzu; every day Kiki and its owner frolic on the king-sized bed in the Villa's best room. Once when Jane begged she brought the dog into Gram's room and put it into Gram's arms. It licked her face. She was so happy! Jane said, "Will you bring it in sometimes, when I'm not around?" She already knew it was money that made these things happen and Gram will never have enough.

The aide is Barbie-perfect, buff and agile; the rich lady who owns the shih tzu is old. Unlike Gram and the others, who have fallen away, the rich lady has hung onto both her money and her flesh—did money make the difference? Pink, powdered and sweetly rounded, she stays in bed because her knees can't support her weight. Even though she's rosy and better dressed than the others, she is just as frail. With her firm butt bouncing, the aide walks into her employer's room. Doesn't she notice the disparity? The diamond rings embedded in the fat fingers and her fleshy, entitled smile say no. Roiling shadows collect on her ceiling just the way they do on Gram's, but the rich old lady doesn't see; she never looks up.

Nobody here can afford to look up. For all they know, the place is lovely and everything's fine.

At the nurses' station a covey of early risers leans on walkers, waiting for the balloon lady to come. In the breakfast room five women warble, "My Bonnie Lies Over the Ocean," while the recreation director beats time. Four old ladies with Magic Marker red mouths sit around a card table, waiting for the attendant to deal. Cheerful enough, Jane supposes, considering they're all going to die soon, but she can't afford to dwell.

Instead she hurries because she can't shake the idea that something new has entered the place. Jane is aware of some new element, a difference in the air. She's almost used to the shadows but today, there's something more—an extra density that makes her eyes snap wide. She imagines it taking shape.

Has death come to visit? If only. But no, she thinks. Just, no. It isn't the cumulative pressure of old age that makes her twitch and it isn't the sound that time makes when God pulls the plug. There is a difference in the shadows that drift in the sunlit building and come rushing in her wake.

She passes the old lady whose vocabulary got away, all but one word. "Good morning," Jane says to her even though it won't make any difference.

When she turns at the sound, the old lady's eyes are leached of light. "Dwelling, dwelling, dwelling, dwelling," she says in conversational tones, inching toward the day room in her flowered muumuu with the pastel webbed belt. Her leash is attached to the rail the management put in so old people who tip over won't fall far.

She used to be somebody, Jane thinks. They all did. It makes her move a little faster because Gram's failing. Every time she comes into the room at Palmshine Villas she comes wondering how much of her grandmother is still left.

In the room across the hall from Gram the old soldier shouts. He's been shouting for years. Harmless, the nurses said when Mom begged them to move Gram to another room so she wouldn't have to hear. They looked condescendingly at Gram. *Remember, he doesn't have a nice family like Mrs. Trefethen here. Does he, Gram?* Gram smiled, happy as a dog at the pound, eating its last meal. Mom protested. "But he scares her." Gram wasn't scared, Mom was. *Paraplegic, they said, even if he wanted to he couldn't hurt a flea.* "He's making threats." *No he isn't, he's fighting Nazis. The war,* they said. They said, *So sad. Nobody comes even at Christmas, nobody phones and they never come.* "That's not my problem," Mom said, "it's his problem." They said, *If your mother isn't happy here you can always…* Jane's heart leaped up but Mom recovered in a flash. "Oh no," she said in that tired, tired voice, "This is perfect. Everything's just fine." *He only shouts when he hears you coming,* they said. *When you're not here he's quiet as a clam.*

Even though Jane tiptoes he knows. The dry voice cracks the air above her head like a whip. "I know you're out there. Come here!"

This is what she hates most about these Sundays. "Oh, please. Not today."

*God damn you God look what you've done to me, me in the bed and Vic dead and I can't get out until I find out who. Vic is dead God damn you. Dead and nobody will help.*

It is in the building now. **You.**

"Who killed Vic?"

"Oh, please." Jane looked in once and saw a sheaf of white hair, a profile like the face on a medal. He heard her breathing and turned, a blur of red rage—a glaring mouth with that savage flash of teeth but his expression was both so blind and so angry that she fled before she could find out whether he saw her and if he did, whether he knew who she was. That day she closed Gram's door as nearly as she could and leaned against the inside, terrified that he'd lurch into the wooden panels in his rage and send her and the door crashing into the room.

Today his dry, hard voice knifes into her. "Who killed Vic?" This is how it always begins. Once he gets started the shouter will rant for hours. "Come on, you bastard bastards, who did it?"

Half of Jane wants to confront the old wreck and shut him up, but she's afraid to go in. "Shut up."

"It had to be one of you." His shout cuts through everything. It's like being within range of a heat-seeking missile. It doesn't matter who you are today. It wants to find you and destroy. As she dives into Gram's doorway the accusations follow. "Now, God damn you. Who?"

"Beats me," she says and dodges into the room.

Odd. Behind her, something in the shadows stirs.

The room is nicely kept and so is Gram, but she's always anxious, going in. What does she expect to find in the sweet little room with its ruffled bed, a lipsticked skeleton? Gram gone, with the bed stripped and her belongings rolled on top like the bedding of an army moving out? Or is she afraid of Gram rising out of her velour recliner to scold her for being late, the way she did when Jane was young?

The old man isn't done. "God damn your shit," he cries. "Tell the truth or I'll eat your face and spit out the teeth."

"Gram, it's me."

Never mind, Gram is glad to see her. Gram is always glad to see her. It's a given that when Jane walks in, the old lady's smile lights up the room. She knows her granddaughter, too, it's not like she forgets. "Jane," Gram says with that smile that the complications of old age can't turn off and not even pain can dim.

She flinches. Is Gram in pain? Gram won't tell her or she can't tell her, so Jane has never known. She still has words, but a lot of important ones have gone away.

"Smear your shit in your eyes," he howls. "Now, tell."

"Hello," she says, bending to kiss that transparent cheek. "Hello, Gram."

She looks so sweet sitting there in the recliner where the aides put her after they sponged the oatmeal off her mouth and dressed her for the day; Jane thinks Gram is in fact sweeter than she ever was in real life. Something in the water, she wonders? Something they give her at night? Or is it just that Gram has finally let herself lay back and let go? After a lifetime of keeping a perfect house, washing and ironing for a family that she controlled and fed for years, along with the multitudes, after all that *taking care*, she's on vacation from her life.

"I brought blueberry muffins, Gram."

"Of course you did." That smile!

"And the shit in your eyes." So loud, so ugly.

Jane gestures in the direction of the shout. "Oh Gram, I'm so sorry about that."

Gram smiles and blinks politely the way she always does when she doesn't understand, which is most of the time lately. Age has left her with a few macros—boilerplate speeches that kick in whenever Jane says anything, but she knows who Jane is, she does! "You were lovely to come."

*Does it hurt, Gram? How much does it hurt?* She wants to ask but Gram looks so happy that she's afraid to bring it up. She responds by rote, "Lovely to see you, Gram."

The television is going—it always is—Sally Jessy, Oprah, Rosie, Ricki, makes no difference, the daylight voices are interchangeable. The psychic Muzak and emotional screensaver supply everything Gram needs now that she's lost everything else. Jane is grateful that the old lady's lost it, so she doesn't know how awful this is. She may not know she's in this pale blue room in this pretty place in her oversized aqua recliner because this is the bottom line. Gram isn't getting well. She's here for good; except for her birthday and Christmas, when an ambulance brings her to her daughter's house for dinner and takes her away before the pie, she is going to be in this chair in this room in Palmshine Villa for whatever's left of her life. It's good Gram likes TV so much. Good thing poor Gram's protective mechanism kicked in when her hard disk overloaded and crashed.

Gram looks nice in aqua: aqua muumuu, fluffy aqua robe. It complements the chair.

Gram looks nice and the room is nice but the words barreling in from across the hall are ugly and sharp. "And sleep in your shit because you won't tell me who killed him."

*Oh stop.*

"Oh, look," Gram says. "Doesn't Rosie have on a pretty red shirt today."

But she can't drown out the old soldier. "Who killed Vic? Was it you?"

"And doesn't she dress the child nice," Gram says because he can't drown out her sweet voice.

This is her life now, these daily TV people are closer to Gram than her family, Jane realizes. She's a little hurt and at the same time happy for Gram, who looks frail but clean and pretty and well taken care of, with her white hair nicely waved and a bobby pin with a blue butterfly clinging to the spot where the pink scalp shows through. "Nice, Gram. It's a nice color. Would you like me to get you one like that?"

He is still shouting. "Was it me?"

"Don't worry," Gram says, beaming. "Just get me the box tops. I can always send away."

"Help me," he screams. "I have to find out."

*I don't know who did it but I may, he is lying dead somewhere but if I can get back the memory I may find out. Solomons I was fighting on, or was I at Tobruk? Was that Vic running along beside me, did I push him ahead and did he take the bullet that was meant for me, is it my fault he was killed in the first wave? Is that what happened to you, old shitface, is it my fault you got blasted out of your life?*

Something is shimmering out there. I am coming for you.

"WHO KILLED VIC?"

Jane murmurs, "I wish he'd stop."

Rosie's theme music makes a cheerful sound in the room. The ambience is cheerful, and so is Gram. Although massed shadows roll down the halls like thunderclouds before a terrible storm, the room is bright. There are stuffed animals the great-grandchildren gave, marine blue curtains to match the nice comforter and ruffled bolster that Mom bought when they moved Gram out of the house she couldn't keep. Her hospital bed has a dust ruffle just like a little girl's. Books she can't read any more line the little bookshelf like the ghosts of old friends. Family photos stand on the top in Plexiglas frames. Gram with Mom and Jane and the others in Gram's better days. She looks so pretty! Like somebody else. You wouldn't know her if it wasn't for the smile that travels from one snapshot into the next into the studio portrait made on her eightieth birthday, into this room and onto the face of the wraith in the recliner chair. There isn't much left but the smile.

It's enough, or it would be except for the scary business in the halls. What is it, exactly, that makes Jane anxious today, and fearful for Gram?

It could be nothing, she thinks, as across the hall the old man accuses the world at large: "You know who killed Vic. Who was it? Was it you?"

"Who's Vic," she says to Gram.

The old lady turns sweet, empty eyes on her. "Who?"

"The old man across the hall says somebody got murdered." She shouldn't be talking about this but it's better than what she really wants to say: *Don't you ever want to get out of here, Grammy? Are you happy or sometimes do you think you want to die?* Disturbed, she finishes, "This guy Vic."

"Oh," Gram says, blinking the way she does when she doesn't have the foggiest, which is all the time now. "Vic," she says with that mid-range pleasant smile that means nothing. It is nothing like the welcoming blaze when Jane enters the room but it's the best she can do. Lips like a shriveled rosebud, with that genteel, vacant tone. "Of course," Gram says without knowing what she's saying. "Vic."

"Who was he, Gram? Was Vic his son and did you meet him, do you know?" What did the nurses say? *He has a family. They used to come. Now nobody comes and the checks come straight from the bank.*

"Who?"

"Vic!" She doesn't want to scare her grandmother but she does want an answer.

Bemused, the old lady murmurs because it's expected, "Poor Vic. Oh look, Janie, look what Rosie's doing now."

It's useless to ask her but Gram's the only person she can ask. "What happened to him, Gram?"

\* \* \*

*What happened to me? Wife I had before I went away, two boys I had, Timmy and little, did we name one of them Vic? My friend Angus had little girls, he was the first over the top and I promised to follow but his belly blew up in a fountain of fire and blood* Pull me back *he was begging would he not have died? I couldn't, not with that hole in the belly, guts blooming, twitching wet parts of him slithering into my arms it's not my fault he went first dead like my point man and when I try to sleep they blossom all over again they found his penis in the dirt next to my face keep your head down men...*

In the building now, and coming down the hall. **It's nothing you did in the war.**

"Somebody killed Vic and you know it..."

"Oh God." Jane groans. "What if this is the wrong place?"

"It's so sweet," Gram says, "Rosie bringing up her own baby all by herself."

"You have to move out of this place," Jane says wildly. Is she trying to get the old lady out of this room for the afternoon or for good? She doesn't know. The old soldier's voice rises and she shouts to cover the sound, "It's not out of the question."

"Rosie's just a wonderful mother, just like Oprah and those wonderful people in *The Partridge Family*..."

She grabs Gram's shoulders. "What if something happened to you?"

"And that nice girl who took care of the Trapp children, they are an inspiration for us all." This is a lot for Gram to say at one time but she is all worked up now. Her lips are trembling and her eyes glisten with approval. "It's fine mothers like them and that lovely Ma Walton who make America great."

Jane tries, she tries! "I don't think Oprah has any children, Gram."

At least Gram has a nice family, unlike that poor bastard across the hall. Who will not stop shouting, "No. He didn't kill Vic. You know he didn't and you know who did."

"Oh, shut up."

Gram gasps.

"No, no, Gram. Not you!"

"And I know it too." Querulous. "Did you kill Vic?"

"I didn't kill anybody, Janie, I didn't." Gram's face shrinks like crepe paper; she's about to cry.

"Shh. Shh, Gram. Don't worry about him, really."

"Who?"

"You know. You do! He's just a crazy old man."

But Gram's face is working. She's caught on an old memory that won't surface. She can't tell Jane what it is but Jane can see from her face that it hurts. There is something buried back there unless something is happening to her in the room right now. Whatever it is, it hurts. Gram's lap robe falls away and she sees her grandmother's feet are cased in plastic lined with sheepskin. Why? Oh, Gram.

Meanwhile the old man rails, "Did you kill him?"

If he would only stop *shouting*.

"Did you?"

Jane rises to close the door.

"Why, no." Gram is terribly upset. "Of course not. No."

But the doors in this place are jiggered so they won't really close. Regulations, Jane thinks. Health care centers have to come up to code. She soothes her grandmother with bits of blueberry muffin. The old lady chews and chews but when she spreads her mouth in a new smile, the bits of blueberry muffin are still there.

Suddenly the old man's tone changes. "Why, you didn't kill Vic, you tried to save him."

Uneasy, Jane glances at her grandmother, but Gram is fixed on the television now. She smiles on as though she doesn't hear.

"But he died anyway!"

"Oh, look, Gram." Jane warbles. Her voice is shaking. It sounds sweet and false. "Look at Rosie."

"Do you want to know who killed Vic? Do you?"

"Isn't that a pretty red shirt?"

Anguished, the old man finishes. "I killed Vic."

"My God." Jane shoots a look at her grandmother. Did she hear? Is she afraid?

*I didn't kill Angus and I didn't kill my point man, I got a citation for what I did, the Purple Heart and a Bronze Star but it was shit because I couldn't get an erection and I couldn't get a job. I was shit and my life was shit and I hated them, because before the war ever happened it already was. Alana left me for that Hunky refugee and took the kids but I showed her, I did, I showed them all.*

**All except me.**

"I KNOW WHO killed Vic," the old man cries.

"Pretty red shirt. Your mother ought to wear red," Gram says. "It would take people's minds off the wrinkles and the fat."

"Gram!"

Gram goes on in the unruffled tone she uses when Mom cracks during one of these lectures and starts to yell. Just when you love her best she gets a little mean and you remember she always was. "If only she'd get herself up nice, like my girls Rosie and Oprah do."

From across the hall, the news comes in on a sob. "I killed Vic."

"They're just television, Gram." What if the old man really is a murderer?

"Lose her looks and she'll lose her handsome man and then what will she do?"

"Mom looks fine." What if he kills Gram?

"Aaaaaahhh." His throat opens in grief. "Aaaaaah."

"Shh," Jane murmurs, "please don't."

And with that brilliant smile that lights up Palmshine, Gram burbles, "Poor Vic."

"Shh, don't worry. It's just crazy talk, Gram."

Nothing to worry about, Jane tells herself. Veteran, Congressional Medal of Honor or something, all that. Even if he could walk, what would he use? No scissors and no razors allowed here, plastic silverware.

But Jane worries. She's worried ever since they moved Gram. In a play she knows, street cleaners came for you with rolling garbage cans. You heard the tin whistle just before they took you away. In one story, it's the Dark Men who come. They live in the mortuary and work by night. When they finish with you, you are another store dummy in the window at Neiman Marcus, and nobody knows. What if evil really is out there, not things you are afraid of, but something real? What if the doctors are ranching organs and selling them by night? What if some Svengali in white tries to bilk Gram out of her money and starts pinching when she says no? Secret beatings and spiteful bruisings go on in places like this, sexual abuse and worse. Anything can happen when you're old and frail and can't get out of your chair. Should she stay here and protect Gram? But Jane has a life and a day job. She can't sleep at the foot of Gram's bed every night, even though Gram's so small now that there's plenty of room. Besides, Mom researched. Palmshine is run by staunch Methodists with big dependable feet, good, kind Methodist faces, and capable Methodist hands. Palmshine is the best of its kind,

Mom researched it. It's right there in *Consumer Reports*.

Then why is she so upset?

Mostly, it's the shouting. "Who killed Vic?"

"Look, Gram," Jane says, pointing to a branch outside the window. "Look at the pretty bird."

Gram turns her head obediently. She looks right at it but does not see. "Pretty," she says with that lovely, undiscriminating smile.

In the next second she's asleep. It happens. Jane's used to it. She's also pledged to stay until six. If she's not here when Gram wakes up—if she doesn't stay until the supper tray comes—"Oh look, Gram, it's lovely Sunday dinner, turkey and apple crisp, again," her grandmother won't eat. If she doesn't stay her grandmother will wake up alone in her pretty room on a Sunday night and start to cry.

*Nobody can stand living with the dead I know that stink of decay, when they pull back the robe to wash me I see in their faces how it smells, well stick your face in it put your hands into it and inhale, take me the way I am if I can't stand it how can you so wallow in your own stink and stay the fuck away I don't want you but I won't let go until I get my revenge on you God damn you, it's all your fault unless it was Alana's, she was gone and the boys were gone when I got back so it's her fault unless Angus started it, why didn't you just say no, unless it was the Lieutenant for putting me in charge or those candy mouthed shitfaced sons I had with their greedy shiteating smiles you can all just go to hell and stay there and leave me alone and I'll stay here*

**Let me in.**

As LONG AS Gram keeps smiling, Jane can handle it. She can live with the shadows and the shouting, but Gram isn't in right now. Jane is alone with it.

"You didn't kill Vic."

"Oh, stop it." She turns up the TV.

The punch line rolls in. "I killed Vic," he cries again. Again.

Trembling, Jane pats the air above Gram, she apologizes to Rosie—are these shows on a loop? Spilling into these cheery rooms even on Sundays when real TV is showing something else? "I'll be right back," she says, and even though at Gram's age sleep is tenuous and leaving her is risky, she slips into the hall.

"Do you know who killed Vic?" The old man's shout meets her at the door. "Do you?"

"Stop it." She slams into his room. "Just stop it!"

"What?" His head turns at the sound. "What?" he shouts, glaring at nothing. His mouth is a furnace fueled by hatred. "Go away!"

But Jane is angry now. "I'm not going anywhere until you shut up."

"It's you." For a moment his voice softens. "Is it really you?"

"Who do you think I am?"

Something changes. "Thank God you've come."

A part of Jane knows you shouldn't walk into things you don't know about, but it's too late. Besides, the shadows are massing outside the door and if she stands here long enough they will come rolling in. Something is out there waiting, whether for her or for Gram or for this old veteran, she does not know. There is more at issue here than Jane's sanity or her grandmother's comfort and safety. The trouble—and this is what strikes her dumb and leaves her cracked open, vulnerable and waiting—is that she can't say what. Because the old soldier's tone has changed she says gently, "Just be quiet now, okay?"

"And now that I have you here. It's Anzio, don't you see?" He clears his throat like a lecturer about to start.

"Tobruk." Big voice for a man in his what, eighties, nineties. The old veteran looks well and handsome, considering—flowing white hair, square jaw, sharp brow, knife-blade nose.

"You're hurting people out there. That's all."

"Don't you see what I'm talking about?"

"That's enough!"

"Stand still, Alana. Don't you dare walk out while I'm talking to you! Bizerte, don't you get it? Monte Cassino. Normandy. Tobruk!"

"I said, that's enough." Jane puts up her hand as if to ward him off but the battlefield names keep rolling out on a current of rage and it is too much. It's just too much.

"You know you were fucking him, you bitch, and all the time... Don't you see where I was?"

"Just stop!" It's his health that angers her, the strong arms and firm jaw and the forearms like blades; there are dumbbells crossed on the side table and a metal triangle hangs above the bed. This old man is so strong that he can go on forever. He can shout on and on unless somebody stops him. "Shut up."

He is raging at a world of people she can't see and never was, people that she won't see and can't help and it is terrible. "That's all you know, Sergeant." Then, "Shut up, you unfaithful bitch. Shut up or they'll shave all your hair and rape you to death. They'll lock you up."

She shouts back. "Shut up or they'll lock you up."

This is how he silences her: "I was locked up. Who do you think killed Vic?"

"Who *are* you?"

"You weren't there, Sergeant. None of you were, so you don't know what became of us. What do you know about it?"

Jane throws back her head like a horse that's been spooked; eyes wide, whites showing all the way around. "Oh, stop it. Just *don't!*"

"What do you know about Vic?" The eyes the old man turns toward her are like milk glass, shining and opaque. There's a chance that he still doesn't know that Jane is here. It doesn't matter whether she's here or not or who she is or even whether she's listening. The harangue is etched into his mind. "You didn't crawl through shit and you didn't see your buddy's face blown off or your best friend's belly torn up by a grenade. You didn't see anything, you little bitch," he says. So he does see her. And now that he sees her, his face splits open and she sees into the agony. He is crying for both of them. "You careless, careless bitch."

The pain is so obvious and so powerful that her voice shakes. "I'm so sorry it hurts!"

"Who did this to us? Whose fault is it then?"

"Don't cry." Trembling, she backs away. "I'll go get somebody."

"Don't! I'm not finished with you."

"I'm only trying to help."

"Shit on that. Shit on your help." The old soldier rolls his head from side to side on the pillow, looking here, there, nowhere, tossing hopelessly like a child who's never been rocked. He is struggling. "Don't go." Words back up in his throat and he strangles on them.

**I said, let me in!**

"I'll get a doctor."

His face writhes in a series of conflicting expressions. "Fuck that shit. Get out!"

"They'll give you a shot."

"You bitch, you're just like all the rest of them." The old veteran is so filled with grief and hatred that the words come out in puffs like exploding shells. "Alana, the kids. Now go away."

Jane is stumbling backward to the door when his expression changes. There is a stir at her back. It's more than a shadow, she thinks, but can't be sure. There is something new in the room. Whatever it is, it keeps her in place while the old man's words blur with pain and stop being speech. He groans aloud. She tries again, "Please let me get someone."

"Just go away! Take the kids and get out of here." He can hardly breathe. "Get out before you get hurt."

Trapped in the bed like that, how could he... Still she's afraid. Her voice trembles. "Just don't hurt my grandmother."

"You don't know what I can do."

"Nurse! The bell, Mr. ah."

"That's classified!"

"Okay, okay." Shaking, she advances. "Ah. Don't hurt me, I'm just going to reach over here and ring the..."

"No! You have no idea what I can do."

"I'm only trying to help!"

"Stay back!" The force of his hatred overturns her, "You have no idea what I can do to you!"

"You did it," she murmurs, frozen in place. "You killed Vic."

"I did. I kill everything I love!" The rest comes out in a spray—his story, Jane guesses, but so distorted by resentment that she can't make it out—a dozen voices fill the room: allies and enemies, traitors, everyone, the story that came before everybody else comes tumbling out so fast that nobody could sort it out, and as he rambles, shadows roll in and fill up the room. He rasps, "Yes I killed him, and I'll kill you too."

At her back something moves and she wheels, startled, and looks into its face. He looks so *nice*. "Who are you?"

"I'll kill everyone who..." But the furious old soldier sees it too. He bares his teeth, thundering: "Go away!"

But the gnashing, outraged old man can't frighten the young one no matter how loud he shouts. The young soldier is smiling, fresh-faced, and handsome and easy in his fatigues, with his combat boots hanging down from laces knotted around his neck, hitting the dog tags that dangle from a chain until they clink. The muddy helmet swings from one hand. With the other, he makes a cross on his lips as the old man in the bed goes on railing:

"It serves him right, you know. Goddamned Vic…"

"What?" she cries.

"It serves you right."

This nice young man; she asks, "What did you do to him?"

**Shh.** The newcomer shakes his head and without speaking he tells her, **Shh. You don't need to know.**

"Who are you?" she asks. Then she knows. It's Vic, he is this patient's long-dead victim and now he's come back to confront the man who murdered him all those years ago. She turns to the young soldier. "Oh, Vic. Poor Vic!"

The old man sits bolt upright. "You called?"

"Vic?" She turns from one to the other. The profile, the eyes… She covers her mouth and points at the veteran in the bed. "You're Vic!"

"This is all your fault!" The milk glass eyes snap wide. His voice overflows the room and roars down the hall. "You brought him, you bitch. Get out."

Jane hears footsteps approaching—the nurse, orderlies—but she says, "Oh my God, I'm sorry." She doesn't know why she's crying, but she is.

"Die, you bastard." Propped on trembling arms he snarls at the young man, "Finish it!"

The air in the room shimmers. There is a decision hanging fire.

**Not now.**

"DIE, GOD DAMN you. Go ahead and get it over with!"

Jane wheels to protect the young soldier—Vic? But he shakes his head. **No.** In the next second, he is gone.

"Get out!"

As the head nurse comes into the room. "Victor Earhart, you stop that! You stop abusing people around here! I'm sorry," she says to Jane. "He has a history."

"I'm sorry."

"Bitch, you bitch. You get the fuck out too!"

"Don't worry," she says to Jane, "he does that to everybody, he just drives people away." With the heel of her hand she straight-arms the old veteran, pushing him down on the pillow. "Keep it down, Vic, or I'll have to give you a shot."

Vic?

"Shut up, Vic, she's going."

Vic.

"Go away." He is howling now. "Go away, God damn you, go!"

"I am!" Sobbing, she runs. Jane retreats to Gram's room, to nice Gram who has been stripped of her possessions, her flesh, of all the old, bad complications, so the sweetness is the only thing left. And the pain, she sees now. The pain.

"Oh," Gram says, extending her arms. Her smile turns on with the force of a thousand halogen lamps. "Oh, how nice!"

"Oh, Gram." Jane advances with her arms out, she can hug Gram and even though Gram has lost her powers she can still make it all right. In the next second she realizes her grandmother isn't looking at her. The old lady's thin arms fan out in a welcoming hug and her face lights up, but it isn't her granddaughter she's reaching for and it isn't Mom. It isn't anybody in this world, Jane understands. Gram is reaching for somebody else.

Turning, she sees that the shadows have followed her out of the old veteran's room and gathered in Gram's nice place, and with them, the new force that came into the building today to effect—not revenge—a rescue? Young Vic is standing here in Gram's room in his fatigues with boots around his neck and the helmet dangling. He's taken off his dog tags and he carries them in the other hand. Grinning, he tosses them to Gram.

Across the hall, the old veteran starts. "Who killed Vic?" Old man, old man! He can't shut up. Now he'll never shut up.

**I came for you. Come with me?**

"Oh Gram, please don't…"
With that smile blazing, she does.

# GOD'S FOOT

*Tony Daniel*

WHEN THE LITTLE single engine plane landed me on the Munford airstrip, I knew I had finally entered the mysterious West. With mountaineering, until the very last moment—the snap of the empty carabiner, the whip of unanchored rope—there remains the possibility of success, I thought, the chance to get it right. As we taxied to a halt, I gazed southwest at the highest mountain in the world, The Mountain of the Hallowed Snow. Mountain of my troubled dreams. My chance to get it right.

Hallowed Snow is merely the Indo-Asian name, of course. It is known in English as *Cheaha,* and this is what the natives invariably call it. The meaning of the word is obscure, but it is sometimes translated as "God's Foot." I consciously broke my reverie—later, there would be much time for *Cheaha* later—and looked over the village of Munford, a motley collection of stone huts and unpaved walkways, the inhabitants lethargically rocking in their odd chairs upon the roofs, or herding cattle through the main thoroughfares at the pace of flowing honey. I reflected that these who lived among the folded skirts of the Mountain were shaped and conditioned by its demands into an alien people, and I was, for all intents and purposes, among another species. I had, however, studied their customs and believed I was prepared. Yet as I debarked from the plane, a weathered old App man approached me and extended his hand and for a moment, I panicked. I wanted to climb back through the familiar doorway and have the pilot return me to the East, to a place where I knew the customs viscerally and did not have to think every time I acted. Back to a place where the gods were not said to walk the Earth. But instead, I remembered to extend my own right hand, and take the gnarly man's in mine.

"How you doing, Mr. Li?" he said. His command of Indo-Asian was quite good. "I am Franklin Boggs."

"I'm doing okay, Mr. Boggs," I replied, in halting English. Boggs smiled.

"You just call me Frank." He said, also in English, then switched back to Indo. "I am the Greentrek representative in Munford. I will see to your needs until you leave for the Mountain."

I thanked him, and allowed him to shoulder my pack—which he did without the slightest strain. I had heard that Greentrek was paying some of the natives a salary, and not handling them as contract labor, but it was startling to hear him speak as if he were a normal corporate employee. I must admit that I was a bit shocked, despite the fact that I consider myself an enlightened man.

As we walked through the village, I noticed a few other trekkers and tourists. We were, most of us, taller than the natives. And all of us wore silk of one kind or another, even though at such an altitude as this, silk served more as ornament than functional outer clothing. The Apps all wore the hard denim pants for which they are famous.

We entered one of the larger stone huts. Occupying the first floor was a bar. Tables were made of crude wood, and every table had several chairs around it, also crudely built. Fortunately, I thought, only in Munford would I be forced to sit upon a throne to eat my dinner. It was ironic that after I trekked *farther* West to the Mountain, I could return to civilized ways and eat on the ground. Boggs took my pack upstairs, where he'd reserved me a room. I sat at one of the tables and looked around.

There were a couple of other trekkers on the other side of the room, deeply engaged in conversation with one another. A woman stood behind the bar, wiping a stoneware cup.

"Be with in a moment," she said in broken Indo.

"Take your time," I replied in English. "It just feels good to finally be here."

Above the bar was a wooden sign listing prices. So. I was finally going to get a taste of corn mash whiskey, after reading about it so often. Across the bottom of the sign was the traditional blessing: "John Deer protect this house and all in it."

John Deer. One of the Mountain people's Mountain gods. The woman came over, and I ordered whiskey and crackers.

I spent the night on a futon Greentrek had thoughtfully flown in. Despite being tired from the long day and the great altitude, I had trouble sleeping. Actually, I dreaded the prospect. Until the dreams began, sleep had always been my last retreat, where no one could harm me or, worse, slight me—or if they did, I would not know about it. Even a lover, I thought.

During our last days together, my lover for two years, Rie Fugimoto, had asked me why I read and slept so much. After it became clear to her that I was not going to advance any farther in the corporation, and why, Rie's tenderness had turned to pity, and her minor dissatisfactions to deep disappointment. Rie was essentially a good-hearted person, but there is an unmistakable look in the eye and tone of voice that cuts as deeply as harsh words or hurtful actions. And sex. With sex, you *know* when you have fallen in a person's esteem. Here in Munford, I was no one's social inferior. After a life of twisting and turning socially, I liked the feeling of not fitting in *at all*.

Eventually I drifted off, and, as I had feared while awake, the dreams came. The dreams that had troubled my sleep for two months.

Kaleidoscope of blues, greens, grays, and whites. The blurred edges of mountains that undulated like great, breathing hulks. And me. A speck. Running up a mountain that rose, and rose and rose—until it was the highest mountain of all, *Cheaha*. Confused longing and fear. I wanted to summit so badly, yet I was afraid. Something on the mountain filled me with dread. A wild smell. I turn. Something horrible. Something that *wants* me. I run, but it is no use. Hot breath at my back. Claws bringing me down, as if I were an antelope, and I'm rolling. Snow, ice, water. Darkness. I am within a shadow. I look up and see—John Deer. Giant deer-man, looming over me. *This is your home,* a voice says. A voice that sets my spirit humming like a plucked harp string. *Come home.* My fear and longing coalesce into an impossible emotion, impossible to feel and still live, and my heart bursts, my head cracks. Falling. Falling—into whiteness.

And I awoke. It was just before dawn. I lay in bed until I heard people moving about downstairs, then I descended for breakfast. Breakfast was a piece of fried meat and the ground cornmeal called *grits*. The woman, whose name was Sarah, noticed that I frowned upon first tasting the *grits,* and she showed me how to lather them with butter and salt. They were no longer tasteless, but unfortunately the only tastes I could detect were butter and salt. Better get used to it, I thought, and forced down the remainder.

"Whiskey," I said, after finishing the *grits* off.

"At six in the morning? That's a mite early for a man to go to the liquor."

The person who spoke was taller than the average App. He seemed startled when I turned and smiled at him.

"Mr. Li speaks pretty good English," Sarah told the man.

"Hell, better watch my mouth then." He sat down at my table. "Gabe Spenser," he said. I thought for a moment that he was reaching for my food, but then I remembered the handshaking custom. I took his hand, and he shook mine much harder than Frank Boggs had. He had big, rough hands, and it almost hurt.

"Tesu Li."

"Korean? But where's Tesu from?"

Such a blunt question would be acutely embarrassing anywhere else, but I think I handled it well. "I'm from Japan, but my family is old Korean," I said—cheerfully even.

"So you know what it's like, eh?"

"Know what *what* is like?"

"Being a second-class citizen."

This *was* embarrassing to me, and I suspected Spenser knew it.

"My family has done quite well over the years. We have porcelain interests. Despite the prejudice, we are quite comfortable. Where are you from, Mr. Spenser?"

"Call me Gabe. Did Boggs mention that I'm your guide?"

I nodded, forgetting that this meant yes, unconditionally, to the Apps. Gabe seemed to take my meaning, however.

"Well, I'm from up the road a ways. Chinnabee Creek. But I've been other places. The University of Kyoto, for instance."

Great, I thought. A Japanese-educated App. You fly around the world to experience a different culture, and it's more of the same.

"I flunked out," Spenser said. "Couldn't take the religion courses. The All is me and I am the All—that kind of shit."

"I told you to watch your mouth, Gabriel Spenser," Sarah called out from the bar.

Spenser raised his eyebrows in mock dismay. "I'm afraid I'm a confirmed polytheist at heart. My upbringing, you know."

"What *is* the customary drink for breakfast, Gabe?"

"*Coffee.*" He turned toward the bar. "Two cups of *coffee,* Sarah. And bring Mr. Li some more *grits*. He's done wolfed these clean down."

WE SET OUT later that morning for the Talladega Glacier. We carried our packs, ice axes, and rope—and the oxygen bottles that we would need at altitude. Spenser hiked at a brisk pace, and I had difficulty matching him, despite the intensive training I'd undergone at the Kuril Outdoor Leadership Academy. Four weeks of strenuous exercise could not make up for my lifetime of sedentary existence in Tokyo and Osaka. I had the feeling Spenser had typecast me as the standard Eastern corporation man, seeking an exotic experience to add to his résumé, and was pushing me to the limits of my abilities as a kind of wry comment on my presumed pretensions.

And he was right, in a way, of course. There was no denying that I was the product of exactly such a system.

But I was not taking time off; and I certainly had no intention of gaining "life experience" to make myself a better manager. Instead, two months before, I had dropped out of the rat race entirely, responding to a series of dreams I'd been having. Almost unheard of, I know. But after a childhood of taunts, an adolescence alone, reading, trying to prove myself worthy of a respect that I would never receive, I had had enough. I was not angry. I just wanted to retain my sanity, perhaps find a portion of meaning or even love for my life. And then the dreams began. So there it was—and here I was. *Cheaha*. Whatever else the Mountain might represent, it was wholly new to me. A new chance. Perhaps I could make something of it.

After a while, I grew accustomed to the pace, and the cold Appalachian air. Even in late spring, it settled into one's lungs completely and inertly, as if one were breathing chilled nitrogen.

"So you believe in the old gods, Mr. Spenser?" I said, coming up next to my guide. At my words, he started, as if he'd been lost in his own thoughts and had forgotten I was here.

"Depends on what you mean by 'believe,'" he said, not in the least slowing down to make the answer.

"Colonel Hank Snow. Girl Pinetucky. John Deer."

"Is that what you came here for?" Spenser asked.

"I came to climb the Kurasawa route up *Cheaha*."

"Good." He pointed up the valley's incline, to the right. There were piles of stones silhouetted against the slate blue sky. "Those are cairns commemorating them that took their minds off the climbing. You see nearly a hundred of them up and down this trail. Every move you make should be a climbing move."

This was precisely the kind of thinking that I'd flown 6,000 miles to get away from. "Every step toward a goal is a part of that goal." "Any given moment is just as important as any other." After years of meaningless moments, such a philosophy can drive one to despair. It had done so to me.

"My climbing skills are adequate, and the Kurasawa route is a walk up a safe glacier," I replied. I could not keep the petulance from my voice, and my tone seemed to surprise Spenser.

"There's no such thing as a safe glacier. Even the Talladega has crevasses," he said, in a matter-of-fact tone. "You know what I mean."

"Yes."

We walked silently for a couple of hours, until we reached the "village" of Lickskillet. Before the trekkers had begun to pour in from the East, Lickskillet had been nothing more than a collection of stone huts, a way-station for summer herders. Now it boasted a bar and two hostels. Both of these seemed out of place, and seedy, however—not at all like Sarah's homey place in Munford. Nevertheless, Spenser led me inside for his Greentrek-provided shot of noontime whiskey. I contented myself with hot tea this time, and we shared a plate of pork chops and black-eyed peas for lunch. The cooking was indifferent, and I feared the possibility of trichina infestation, though I said nothing. Spenser didn't seem to like the food any more than I, though it was a free meal for him, and he finished every last bite.

We continued on, and, by twilight, we were on the Talladega Glacier. The great U-shaped valley rose on either side of us. We climbed the moraine to the south, and set up camp on the other side. There was tundra greenery and a delightful little stream meandering through it. Far in the distance rose Cold Water Mountain, the Earth's fourth highest peak.

I was quickly discovering that climbing *Cheaha* was a succession of meals punctuated by walking, or vice versa.

Spenser cooked up a particularly fine one this evening on our little gas stove. It was a stir-fry combining wonderful Tennessee sausage with freeze-dried vegetables that were instantly marinated by a sauce that would rival that of the finest chefs in Tokyo.

"I *do* like good eating," Spenser replied, when I complimented him on his skill.

Since the night was clear, we decided to forgo the tent and sleep only in our bivouac bag-covers. Night fell, and the stars seemed to throw down spears of light. At this altitude, nearly 20,000 feet, they did not twinkle.

"Moon'll be up around midnight," Spenser said. His voice seemed to emerge from the darkness, as if he were speaking from a long way off. "She's not quite full yet."

I snugged up in my down sleeping bag. "Full moon is supposed to be John Deer's time," I said.

Spenser didn't reply for a long time, then he sighed. "What are you up to, Li? Come to Alabama to get some of that Western folk wisdom? Going to find you an old Preacherman and get Girl Pinetucky's secret buttermilk biscuit recipe?"

"I'd come to *you* for that, Gabe, the way you cook."

Spenser chuckled. His bivy bag rustled as he settled down to rest. After a while, the moon rose, and I drifted off to a sleep like soft, quiet snow. No dreams this night.

I awoke before dawn. The moon had traversed to the northwest, and was setting behind the moraine's top. And there was a tall man rimmed in its light. He had on a plaid shirt and blue jeans.

He had an antler rack upon his head, and the face of a deer.

I must have gasped, or made some sort of noise, for I heard Spenser rustle to wakefulness nearby. He said nothing.

The deer-headed man raised his hands toward the moon in what I took to be a worshipful poise. His limbs were long and graceful, muscled and sinewy. For a moment, I was sure I was dreaming again, even if this one were logical and clear. Then, the deer-headed man bolted. Very unlike a human being. Very like a deer. He bolted over the moraine, over to the glacier side. His knees seemed to bend in the wrong direction. I struggled from my sleeping bag, and ran to look down upon the Talladega. Nothing. Dirty ice. Rubble.

But then, far up the glacier—much farther than was possible even for a man running at full speed—I saw a spot of grayness, moving as if on four legs. Climbing, climbing.

"What's this about, Li?" Spenser was standing beside me. I hadn't even heard him come up. "Old John's never shown himself to one of my *trekkers* before."

"Dreams," I whispered. "Dreams of death." I hoped that the last word was lost in the morning breeze. But Spenser heard it.

"So. You gonna throw yourself from *Cheaha*, are you? John Deer smells some sacrificial offering meat?"

"I don't know."

"Well, let me tell you this: he didn't come to give you *hope*, if that's what you're thinking. He doesn't work that way."

Spenser had no idea of what I was feeling, I reflected. Perhaps the Apps really were an inferior race, incapable of understanding more subtle emotions than simple fear and physical longing. But that was precisely the kind of thinking that had caused the Japanese children to treat *me* so badly when I was young. It was the thinking that created a glass ceiling for Koreans in the corporations, and had dogged my family for generations.

I am far, far beyond all that now, I thought, calming myself. I am in the Appalachians, less than three hundred miles from the Atlantic Sea, and the mysterious far West. Six hundred miles from mystic Europe, where many of the nomadic herders were said to have never heard of Japan!

Gabe Spenser is descended from the vanished English race, who crossed the sea and penetrated the gorges that bisect the Appalachians. Gabe Spenser is a good cook and a good guide.

*I saw John Deer.*

I saw a *god,* walking the Earth. Before, I'd only seen him in my dreams. Forget the corporation; forget the outcome of the dreams. "Have you ever seen him before, Gabe? Will he return?"

Spenser gazed up the glacier. In the clear morning, *Cheaha*'s stratospheric pennant plumed out like a long, white prayer flag. "He's up here," was all he said. Then he climbed down the moraine and started breakfast.

After *grits* and *coffee,* we packed up and started climbing once again. Soon the glacier was rising up at nearly twenty-five degrees. We got out our ice axes and roped ourselves together for crevasse rescue. The idea was, if one of us fell in a hidden crevasse, the other would dive to the ground and self-arrest. The other would then use climbing devices called ascenders to pull himself up the rope and out of the crevasse. Fine for theory, but stopping the falling weight of another man by digging into the snow and ice was problematic at best. Always better not to fall into a crevasse in the first place.

We skirted a couple of big gaping ones. Spenser was right; even the calmest of glaciers had crevasses. The Talladega was a geographic anomaly, cutting through fine sediment laid down by an ancestral sea long before the Euroasian and African plates decided to slam into North America, back in the late Cretaceous. At 30,012 feet, geologists claimed the Appalachians were still rising from the collision. Like rivers develop rapids when they flow over rocks, most glaciers, flowing from such a height, formed giant, dangerous icefalls during their descents. But the Talladega had no hidden rocks, no nunataks, no hard obstructions beneath it at all. As Kurasawa and Tanimoto discovered fifty years before, climbing *Cheaha* was nothing more or less than an incredibly taxing slog—and *they* did it without oxygen. Other than breathing and climbing, there were no technical difficulties involved.

"Do you think he resents us being up here?" I asked, when we paused for a water break. I didn't have to tell Spenser whom I meant by "he."

"No App climbed *Cheaha* before the Japanese came. It was sacred." Spenser took a long swig from his water bottle.

"Yet *you* climb."

"The world has changed."

"Not that much, apparently."

He handed me the bottle and I drank after him. This would have been unthinkable behavior in Japan.

"John Deer isn't the same," Spenser said. "Maybe not for the better. App gods ain't like your Japanese Absolute. There ain't no yin and yang to them. John Deer's part of the world, and he's changed along with it."

"What makes you so sure of that?" I replied. "Maybe he is part of what was lost. Maybe we can get it back."

"We?"

"Us *folks*." I used the word in English that meant the same thing as "App."

"And you're *folks*, are you?"

"Are you?"

We climbed on into the afternoon. Spenser called a halt at what he said was the last tuft of tundra grass on the route. It grew in a little glade-sized patch just over the glacier's southern moraine. We were just below 25,000 feet. Though I'd been resisting it, tomorrow I'd have to go onto oxygen.

The day grew extremely cold as the sun set, and I put on my down coveralls. Spenser did not seem to be affected by the chill.

We decided to set up the tent for this night, and just after Spenser got it staked down, the wind came howling from southwest, up the Talladega. There was no way to keep the stove going outside, so we retreated inside, and cooked a small meal. Spenser was an expert, even under trying conditions, and soon had a very nice repast prepared. As we ate, the wind turned to a blizzard outside, and snow began to pile up around the tent in drifts. I felt a slight apprehension that we would be buried, which Spenser seemed to read from my face.

"Good insulation for the night," he said. "It's going to be a bit on the cold side, I'm afraid."

The night was almost unbearable, even with my expedition-weight down sleeping bag. I did not sleep. And when the sun came up, things had not improved very much. Even Spenser was affected. He lit the stove while staying mostly in his bag. The wind kept up, and there was no question of going out, so Spenser took a long, careful time preparing a marvelous breakfast, which we ate at our leisure. But for the nagging worry that the climb was over or—worse yet—that we might be trapped right where we were with no way to go either up or down, the morning would have been very pleasant, despite the cold. In fact the chill, along with the diffuse light (which had to seep through both snow and nylon), created a dawn-like effect in the tent, as if our lazy progress through the morning did not matter, since time was standing still, and we were always just waking up. Perhaps this was more my impression than Spenser's, since I had spent the better part of my life jumping from my sleep roll in the morning to the sound of a buzzing clock.

FINALLY, TOWARD NOON, the wind let up somewhat, and we attempted to go out. There was a strange feel to the air, almost an electricity. I followed Spenser out, and we both put our backs to the wind and took long, necessary urinations. The air was so cold that I was truly concerned about frostbite setting in during the process. What a horrible place to become gangrenous! But these thoughts were dashed from my mind when Spenser let out a huff behind me.

"He's been here, goddamnit," he said. "Look at his tracks, everywhere."

There were, indeed, the split-hoofed markings of deer all around the tent. Spenser seemed discombobulated. Much more so than the storm or the cold had made him.

"What does he want?" He was speaking to himself. Then to me. "I think you'd better level with me."

"All right," I said. I pulled my pack out of the tent, and sat down on it. The wind was strong, but not fierce. It actually felt good, after the closeness of the tent. "About two months ago, I was working for the Katahara Corporation as the Sub-manager of Sequential Tasks at their plant in Osaka."

Spenser rolled his eyes at my job description. I ignored him and continued.

"I decided when I was a young man that I would not stay in the family business, but that I would venture into mainstream society and make a life for myself there on my own merits. My grades were good in school, and my test scores were exceptional. But I discovered that my parents had been right: my ethnic background was a lead weight around my aspirations. Sub-manager in a spur plant was as well as a Korean was ever going to do—would ever be *allowed* to do. While I was considering the hard reality of my situation, I began to experience a series of dreams. They were dreams of *Cheaha.*"

At this, Spenser grunted. He, too, sat down on his pack, listening intently now.

"The mountain was real—as real as it is here, today. But the circumstances of the dreams were confused, blurred, as if several events were happening at once—similar events, but differing to one degree or another. But all of them had the same outcome: a brief glimpse of a deer-headed man, and then a wall of whiteness descended upon me—or whoever the person was who was perceiving in the dreams—and engulfed my consciousness. At the time, considering my disappointed condition, I interpreted this whiteness as my own death. But now that I have seen John Deer, I am not so sure. Perhaps it is some sort of transcendence."

"Transcendence?" Spenser said. "Sounds more like an avalanche." He got up and walked around with agitation. "I think we'd better go back down," he finally said.

"Why?" I asked. "Do you know what these dreams were about? I quit my job, left my place in life, to follow where I thought they were leading me. Can you help me?"

Spenser shook his head slowly, perhaps sadly. "I'm not sure anybody can help you, now," he replied.

"Please tell me, Gabe. What do you know?"

Spenser reached into the tent, grabbed his sleeping bag, and began stuffing it into its compartment within his pack. I moved to do the same. So we were packing up and moving out, despite the wind. Spenser must really believe there was some danger.

"Do you know what a Preacherman is?" Spenser asked, still stuffing his bag.

"The App's shaman or priest, right? He is said to heal the sick and communicate with the spirits of the land."

"Yeah, well, *I* used to be one. Before I took the notion to travel, see what the rest of the world believed in."

"So you are an apostate."

"No. I'm just not a Preacherman anymore. You don't have to *like* the gods you believe in."

"Why don't you like John Deer?"

"I didn't say that."

"But—"

"Nobody knows John Deer," Spenser said, low, his voice becoming almost a chant. "I told you, the gods of the West are not like your Buddha. They're folks, that's all. A man has courage, he does something brave, but he tells you he was scared as hell all the time he was doing it. He's a hero, but he's still just a man. Maybe a bad man. These gods are like that."

"Then where do they get their power? Is it from the God behind all gods, the Absolute?"

"That's Kyoto bullshit."

"It may be true. Why not?"

"John Deer. Girl Pinetucky. They don't give a damn about balance. They ain't no universal principles, that kind of thing."

He had stuffed his bag almost all the way into his pack. Only the top end stuck out. Spenser paused, pulled a little more back out. "The mountain gods are like this," he said. "Feelers. Tentacles. All they care about is eating and protecting themselves."

"Pseudopods?"

"That's right. The main part of God stays buried. Waiting."

"For what?"

"I don't know." He stuffed the bag in violently. "Gentleman adventurers from the East, I suppose."

"So I have been *lured* here as a kind of… fodder?"

Before Spenser could answer, a mighty gust of wind blew through our camp and tore the tent from his hands. It lofted upward, like a kite. "Goddamnit," Spenser yelled, and we ran after it. But there was no catching the thing. It spiraled up and then away, over a horn of rock, and out of sight to the south.

"There's an ice cliff over there," Spenser said sullenly. "It'll fall 3,000 feet before it settles."

We returned to our packs and secured the rest of the equipment. There was now no alternative but descent. Nights higher up would be deadly without protection from the weather.

We crossed the moraine and descended onto the glacier. Spenser took off his pack, and knelt to get out the rope. I began to shiver, so I unzipped a side pocket of my pack and pulled out a pile jacket. When I looked up from my task, John Deer was standing down-glacier, not ten feet away.

In the misty sunlight, he was less fey than he'd appeared at night, more imposing, like a stag who is securely in his territory. His antler rack had at least twelve points, and the spring velvet covered large portions of it, with only the horn tips sticking out like the sheathed stings of hornets. His face, a deer's in every regard, was expressionless. Utterly unfathomable.

"I want this one, Colonel," John Deer said. His voice resounded, as if his vocal cords were metallic. It blared low and clear, like a modulating trombone. "You can't take him down."

Spenser started. I heard him gasp. His back was to me and I could not see the expression on his face. He stood up slowly, turned deliberately.

"Haven't talked with you for a while, John."

"I want this one," said the god.

Spenser leaned on his ice ax. "Now what in the world use is a damned Japanese tourist? They're a dime a dozen."

"I want *this* one. You go on down."

"Mr. Deer," I stammered, "Sir—"

"Quiet!"

I shut up. I felt frightened tears welling in my eyes. They ran down my face and pooled at the bottom of my sunglasses. When had I put on my sunglasses? I wondered. I couldn't remember, couldn't think. John Deer. Wants *me*.

"He doesn't know anything about this," Spenser said. "This is between you and me."

"No. That's over," said John Deer. "You wouldn't."

"I'll do it now. Let him go."

"Too late," the god replied. He took a step forward. "You knew we would call somebody else. You knew this day would come."

Spenser stood up straighter. He pulled his ice ax out of the snow. "That's why I hung around the mountain, John."

"You can't stop us, Colonel."

Suddenly, my brain engaged. *Colonel.* Colonel Hank Snow, the App god of the hearth, cooking. Protector of travelers and the destitute. Dancer in high places.

"I ain't the Colonel," Spenser said. "I gave that back."

John Deer ignored Spenser, and turned his head sideways, one eye looking straight at me. A cloud passed over the sun, and the prismatic animal reflection flashed in his retina. Not human. *Nobody knows John Deer.*

"He will do. He hates the East. I can see it in his heart."

"He doesn't know what he feels," Spenser said, loudly. I could not look at him, could not tear my eyes away from John Deer. "You're the one who'd make it into hate."

"You go on down, Colonel."

"No."

Clink of ax. Muffled step in snow.

John Deer released me from his gaze. I stumbled back, as if I'd been physically pushed. The god advanced on Spenser, lowered his rack.

"Run, Li," said Spenser.

I could not summon the willpower. John Deer charged Gabe Spenser. Spenser nimbly jumped out of the way, and brought his ax around in a wide arc, clattering into the antlers. He yanked on the ax, and the god spun around, bellowing.

Spenser held on bravely, but the effort was too much. He made a quick twist with his wrist and disengaged the ax. The god stumbled back momentarily, then with quick deer-steps regained his footing.

"Run, goddamnit!" Spenser called to me.

He took a swing at the god, but John Deer jumped into the air with fleet grace, and the ax passed under his hoofed paws. Again he advanced on Spenser.

What finally broke me from my fascinated trance was the look in Gabe Spenser's eyes as the god came toward him. *Spenser* was the frightened animal. It was a look of pure terror.

I spun on my heels and began plunge-stepping down the Talladega as fast as I could. There was a great clanking and bellowing behind me, but I did not look back. I covered quite a distance before my foot hit a chunk of ice just under the snowy glacier surface, and I tumbled into a fall.

Snow everywhere. Breath knocked from my lungs. Snow down my back, under my glasses, in my eyes. Then I hit something hard, and I was airborne. I am going to fly away, I thought, I am falling upward into the gray sky. Outer space. I can't breathe. I can't breathe.

Slam. A sharp pain in my leg, but far away, far away. I looked down.

I'd come to rest amidst a pile of surface gravel. My ax, which I'd somehow kept hold of during the fall, had speared through my gaiters and pants—into my calf muscle. My feet were still on the glacier, and red blood welled

out onto the white snow. This was not me. I was still flying upward. Upward.

Far, far above me, was the figure of John Deer. His arms
were raised, and in them he held the slumped body of a
man. As I watched, he jammed his rack into the man's
side, again and again. The man's arms were flailing. I
could just make out the distant cry of pain. Yet, as I
watched, the man seemed to be expanding, bloating, as if
death were accelerated and he was experiencing rigor mor-
tis and maggots at the same time as the pain of death. Oh,
Gabe, I thought. *Oh, Gabe.*

Panic inside me. White nothingness. Or white *everything,* all at once, burning in me, burning through me. I
yanked the ax from my leg and somehow got to my feet. I
began scrambling down the glacier once again.

Each step was an agony. My breath billowed out in great
ragged puffs. I heard a snort, and was sure it was the god,
closing in behind me. I could not help myself. I looked
back.

John Deer was casting the man's body away. Even from
this great distance, I could see the animal glint of his eye.

*This is the end of my dreams*, I thought. *This is the end
of all my dreams.*

I did not see the crevasse. I was too busy looking over
my shoulder. I fell in without a sound.

Whiteness. The blank, inhuman stare of eternity. Spirit
of the East. It grew narrower as I fell, and I lodged
between the constricting sides of the crevasse. I stayed
there, shivering for a while, then my shivering stopped. I
did not care. The West, the East—I did not care which was
right, or if neither were. All that was over for me. Belief
did not matter. Nobody and nothing cared if I believed.
Whiteness permeated, took me, washed my body clean,
blurred my mind to a point, a rock on a glacier, a spot in
a vast field. Of whiteness.

Scuffling and pawing above. A bellow of frustration. I did not care. All was white. I was still. A dark shadow passed over me, over the crevasse. The fading beat of hooves. White silence, for a long time.

"Li."

My eyes were snow crystals. My mouth was sealed like a snow-choked crevasse.

"Li, you have to get out. You can't die here. They'll get your body, son, get your mind half-gone. Make you a snow wraith."

"I can't—"

"Tesu, you damned no-good Korean, move your ass!"

Somewhere, in a past life, this angered me. I tried to turn. My body did not move. "Nothing."

"Tesu Li, you come out of that hole."

Hands beneath me. Mine. My ax in my fingers. Arm stretching up. Something grabbed the ax.

"Gabe?"

Something pulled up on the ax. I held on. Somehow. When my head cleared the lip of the crevasse, I found some strength, and started to claw my way out.

"Gabe Spenser's dead. But he still had a little bit of the Colonel in him, even though he renounced the old fellow."

I pulled myself over the lip of the crevasse. The sunlight dazzled me. The clouds had gone away. Hands reached down, gently put my sunglasses over my eyes. Then they touched me.

Warmth. Log fires. Whiskey. *Grits,* even. My leg stopped hurting.

"John's lost your scent, Li, but he'll find it again, soon enough, now that your brain's thinking."

I looked up, into Spenser's face. But it was *not* his face, also. Faint. You could see the mountain *through* its outlines. And something older, less human within them. But still, somehow, kind. Not an animal, either. A good spirit.

"I'm—" I swallowed. No saliva. I swallowed again, and there was some wetness. "I'm afraid."

"I know," said the Colonel. "I know about that."

He stood up tall. Taller than Spenser ever could have, as if Spenser's being were *stretched out*. He looked around, seemed to come to a decision. "Ah, hell. I'm dead anyway."

He helped me to my feet. Or perhaps he willed me to stand up, and I was able to do so on my own.

"Li, you say you don't fit in here. Well, I'm going to send you *some place else*."

"Some place else?"

"I'm a god, Tesu. At least I used to be. There is a place where we're all connected, sort of. You people eat octopus. Think of me as an octopus with my tentacles in different worlds, but every tentacle is a complete being in and of itself."

"God's pseudopods."

"That's right. Well, I can take you from one world to another. To a world they'd never think of looking for you in. But I'll have to be the gateway myself, and it'll kill me to do it."

"Why... why me? Why do I have to run to another world?" I had no idea what "another world" might be. I was stunned and blathering. The Colonel seemed to take it in stride.

"*They're* afraid, the fools."

"Who?"

"John Deer, all of them. It's the old story. Gods eat worship. Since you Japanese started coming, the food supply's getting leaner. So they wanted a weapon. That's why they sent me over the broad Pacific, to the East. But it got me unhinged. I saw the futility. Gabe, he was right ornery when he got an idea."

"They called me to be a god?"

"That's right, son. They want to use you against all the new ideas from the East. Be a god for the trekkers. Maybe spread App ways back East, take over the world." The Colonel laughed bitterly, rubbed his side. It was seeping something greenish—something that definitely wasn't blood.

"What's... what's so wrong about that?"

"Trust me, son. Being a god ain't all it's cracked up to be. Your human nature sours you, makes you mean. Mostly you end up hurting people to get your way, or you exploit poor folks' weaknesses."

I barely heard these last words. I was tired, tired of running. Tired of thinking. I looked back to the crevasse. I could just fall back in. Make it be over.

"Okay, Li. Time to go." The Colonel raised his arms to the sky. Thunder rumbled, or maybe distant avalanches. "It is a sweet life, here in the mountains," he said. "I'm going to miss it."

He gazed around. And there was Spenser in his face, back for a moment—and the Colonel, too. Human, divine. Crackle. White fire.

Then green. Green all around me. Warmth from the sun.

"WHAT IN THE world—"

A woman stood by a concrete picnic table. She was Western; there was English in her. She was cooking something at a propane stove. Three children sat at the picnic table benches, staring at me, dumbfounded. They were all *Apps*.

"Honey, who *is* that?"

I turned. A man, standing beside a car. An App with an automobile. Incredible. Blinding light gleaming from its hood. A car. In a parking lot.

"Ain't those clothes a bit warm for *Cheaha?*" the woman asked. "You look like you're ready to go climb Mt. Everest."

I gazed at her, tried to smile at the children. She looked familiar, very familiar. But tears welled in my eyes and blurred my vision. I took off my sunglasses and dabbed my eyes.

"Here now," the woman said. In English. Sarah. It was Sarah, who ran the bar in Munford. She handed me a tissue. "Here now, have a Kleenex. You must be lost. Can you understand me? Do you know where you are?" And here I was, out of the whiteness, in this new place, this new life Colonel Hank Snow had given me. I felt it in the pit of my stomach, in the depths of my soul—that rush of confusion and excitement you feel just as someone pulls the rug from under your feet, when there is a strange movement in the world, you suspect no evil, and you have no idea what is going to happen next. I used the tissue to wipe my nose.

"Am I still in Alabama?" I asked, taking a stumbling step forward. One of the children giggled. "Am I near *Cheaha?*

"Why sure," said the woman. "You're standing right on the very tip-top of it." I dropped my ice ax. It clattered on a stone pathway. I took off my wool cap.

"Why, you're Japanese!" She turned to the children. "This man is *Japanese.*"

"Korean," I said. "From Japan."

"Huh? Well, sit down with us, and I'll get you a Coke." I did as she asked, and one of the children warily made room for me. There was a strong hand on my shoulder, and I looked up into the face of a man. It was the Greentrek representative who had met me at the plane. Now he was wearing a short-sleeve polo shirt, like you might see in Polynesia.

"Mr. Boggs?"

"I don' know *you,* stranger," he replied. "But I guess you know me."

I took a deep breath, carefully took off my coat.

"The heat must have affected me," I said. "They don't have this kind of heat where I came from."

"Yep," said Frank Boggs. Sarah gave him a cold, bottled drink, which he handed over to me. "These Alabama summers can be real scorchers."

# JACK NECK AND THE WORRYBIRD

*Paul Di Filippo*

ON THE WESTERN edge of putty-colored Drudge City, in the neighborhood of the Stoltz Hypobiological Refinery ("The lowest form of intelligent life—the highest form of dumb matter!"), not far from Newspaper Park and Boris Crocodile's Beanery and Caustics Bar—both within a knucklebone's throw of the crapulent, crepitant Isinglass River—lived mawkly old Jack Neck, along with his bat-winged and shark-toothed bonedog, Motherway.

Jack Neck was retired now, and mighty glad of it. He'd put in many a lugubrious lustrum at Krespo's Mangum Exordium, stirring the slorq vats, cleaning the lard filters, sweeping up the escaped tiddles. Plenty of work for any man's lifetime. Jack had busted his hump like a shemp to earn his current pension (the hump was just now recovering; it didn't wander so bad like it used to), and Jack knew that unlike the lazy young and fecund time-eaters and space-sprawlers whom he shared his cheapjack building with, he truly deserved his union stipend, all 500 crones per moon (except once a year, during the Short Thirteenth, when he only got 495). Why, it had taken him a whole year of retirement just to forget the sound of the tiddles crying out for mercy. Deadly core-piercing, that noise was, by Saint Fistula's Nose!

But now, having survived the rigors of the Exordium (not all his buddies had lived to claim their Get-gone Get-by; why, his pal Slam Slap could still be seen as a screaming bas-relief in the floor tiles of Chamber 409), Jack could take life slow and easy. During daylight hours, he could loll around his bachelor-unclean flat (chittering dustbunnies prowling from couch to cupboard; obscurantist buildup on the windows, sulfur-yellow sweatcrust on the inside, pinky-gray smogma on the outside), quaffing his Anonymous Brand Bitterberry Slumps (2 crones per six-pack, down at Batu Truant's Package Parlor) and watching the televised Motorball games. Lookit that gracefully knurltopped Dean Tesh play, how easily he scored, like a regular Kuykendall Canton pawpaw!

Ignoring his master's excited rumbles and despairing whoops, Motherway the steel-colored bonedog would lie peacefully by the side of Jack's slateslab chair, mostly droop-eyed and snore-birthing, occasionally emitting a low growl directed at a more-than-usually daring dustbunny, the bonedog's acutely articulated leathery wings reflexively snickersnacking in stifled pursuit.

Three times daily Motherway got his walkies. Down the four flights of badly lit, incongruently angled stairs Jack and his pet would clomber, Motherway's cloven chitin hooves scrabbling for purchase on the scarred boards. Last time down each day, Jack would pause in the lobby and check for mail. He never got anything, barring his moonly check, but it was good to clear the crumblies out of his wall-adherent mailsack. Dragoman Mr. Spiffle wouldn't leave the mail if contumacious crumblies nested within Jack's fumarole-pocked personal mailsack. And Jack didn't blame him! One or two migrant crumblies a day could be dealt with—but not a whole moonly nest!

Outside on Marmoreal Boulevard, Jack and Motherway always turned left, toward Newspaper Park. Marmoreal Boulevard paralleled the Isinglass River, which gurgled and chortled in its high-banked channel directly across the Boulevard from Jack's flat. The mean and treacherous slippery river was further set off from foot and vehicle traffic by a wide promenade composed of earth-mortared butterblox and a rail of withyweave. Mostly, the promenade remained vacant of strollers. It didn't pay to get too close to the Isinglass, as more than one uncautious twitterer had discovered, when—peering curiously over the rail to goggle at the rainbowed plumduff sluicejuice pouring from the Stoltz Refinery pipes—he or she would be looped by a long suckered manipulator and pulled down to eternal aquatic slavery on the spillichaug plantations. GAWPERS AND LOOKYLOOS, BEWARE! read the numerous signage erected by the solicitous Drudge City Constabulary.

(Boating on the Isinglass held marginally fewer risks. Why, people were still talking about the event that quickly came to be known throughout Drudge City and beyond as "Pale Captain Dough's Angling Dismay," an event that Jack had had the misfortune to witness entire from his own flat. And he had thought the squeaky pleas of the tiddles were hard to dislodge from his mind!)

Moving down the body- and booth-crowded sidewalk with a frowsty and jangly galumph that was partially a result of his fossilized left leg and partially attributable to the chunk-heeled, needle-toed boots which compressed his tiny feet unmercifully, Jack would enjoy the passing sights and sounds and smells of his neighborhood. A pack of low-slung Cranials surged by, eliciting a snap and lunge from the umbilical-restrained Motherway. From the pedal-powered, umbrella-shielded, salted-chickpea cart operated by Mother Gimlett wafted a delectable fragrance that always convinced Jack to part with a thread or two, securing in return a greasy paper cone of crispy steaming legumes. From the door of Boris Crocodile's poured forth angular music, the familiar bent notes and goo-modulated subsonics indicating that Stinky Frankie Konk was soloing on the hookah-piped banjo. Jack would lick his bristly nodule-dotted lips, anticipating his regular visit that evening to the boisterous Beanery and Caustics Bar, where he would be served a shot of his favorite dumble-rum by affable bartender Dinky Pachinko.

On the verges of Newspaper Park, beneath the towering headline tree, Jack would let slip Motherway's umbilical, which would retract inside the bonedog's belly with a whirr and a click like a rollershade pull. Then Motherway would be off to romp with the other cavorting animals, the gilacats and sweaterbats, the tinkleslinks and slithersloths. Jack would amble over to his favorite bench, where reliably could be found Dirty Bill Brownback. Dirty Bill was more or less permanently conjoined with his bench, the man's indiscriminate flesh mated with the porously acquisitive material of the seat. Surviving all weathers and seasons, subsisting on a diet scrounged from the trashcan placed conveniently at his elbow, Dirty Bill boasted cobwebbed armpits and crumbly-infested trousers, but was nonetheless an affable companion. Functioning as a center of fresh gossip and rumors, news, and notions, Dirty Bill nevertheless always greeted Jack Neck with the same stale jibe.

"Hey, Neck, still wearing those cellbug togs? Can't you afford better on your GGGB?"

True, Jack Neck's outfit went unchanged from one moon to the next. His ivory-and-ash-striped shirt and identically patterned leggings were the official work wear of his union, the MMMM, or Mangum Maulers Monitoring Moiety, and Jack's body had grown accustomed to the clothes through his long employment. Of course, the clothes had also grown accustomed to Jack's body, fusing in irregular lumpy seams and knobbly patches to his jocund, rubicund, moribund flesh. That was just the way it went these days, in the midst of the Indeterminate. The stability of the Boredom was no more. Boundaries were flux-prone, cause-and-effect ineffectual, and forms not distinct from ideations. You soon got used to the semi-regular chaos, though, even if, like Jack, you had been born 'way back in the Boredom.

With the same predictability exhibited by Dirty Bill (human social vapidity remained perhaps the most stable force in the Indeterminate), Jack would consistently reply, "Happens I fancy these orts, Dirty Bill. And they fancy me!"

With a chuckle and a snaggletooth snigger, Dirty Bill would pat the bench beside him and offer, "Sit a spell then, neckless Jack Neck—not too long though, mind you!—and I'll fill you in on my latest gleanings. That is, if you'll share a salty chickpea or two!"

"Gladly, you old plank-ass!" Diverting as the perpetual Motorball Tourneys on television were, Jack relished simple human intercourse. So while Motherway chased six-legged squirrels (all four of the mature bonedog's feet an inch or two off the ground; only bonedog pups could get much higher), Jack and Dirty Bill would confab the droogly minutes away.

After his supper each night—commonly a pot of slush-slumgullion or a frozen precooked bluefish fillet heated in the hellbox, whichever being washed down with a tankard of Smith's Durian Essence—Jack would leave Motherway behind to lick doggy balls and umbilical while the bone-dog's master made his visit to Boris Crocodile's. There on his reserved barstool, while empty-eyed Nori Nougat danced the latest fandango or barcarole with beetle-browed Zack Zither, Jack Neck would nod his own disproportionate head in time to the querulous squeegee-ing of Stinky Frankie Konk and affirm to all who would pay any heed to the elderly GGGB-er, "Yessir, assuming you can get through the rough spots, life can turn out mighty sweet!"

But all that, of course, was before the advent of the Worrybird.

THAT FATEFUL MORNING dawned nasty, low-hanging hieratic skies and burnt-toast clouds, an ugly odor like all the rain-drenched lost stuffed-toys of childhood seeping in from the streets. Upon opening first his good left eye, then his bad right ('twasn't the eye itself that was dodgy, but only the nacreous cheek-carbuncle below it that was smooshing the orb closed), Jack Neck experienced a ripe intestinal feeling telling him he should stay in bed. Just huddle up 'neath his checkerboard marshmallow quilt, leaving his beleathered feet safe in the grooves they had worn in the milkweed-stuffed mattress. Yes, that seemed just the safest course on a day like today, so pawky and slyboots.

But the allure of the common comforts awaiting him proved stronger than his intuition. Why, today was a Motorball matchup made in heaven! The Chlorine

Castigators versus Dame Middlecamp's Prancers! And then there was Motherway to be walked, Dirty Bill's dishy yatterings, that Dinky-Pachinko-poured tot of dumblerum to welcome midnight in. Surely nothing mingy nor mulcting would befall him, if he kept to his established paths and habits...

So out of his splavined cot old bunion-rumped Jack Neck poured himself, heavy hump leading Lady Gravity in an awkward pavane. Once standing, with minor exertions Jack managed to hitch his hump around, behind and upward to a less unaccomodatingly exigent position. Then he essayed the palpable trail midst the debris of his domicile that led to the bathroom.

As soon as Jack entered the WC, he knew his vague forebodings had been spot on. But it was now too late to return to the safety of his blankets. For Jack saw with dismay that out of his chipped granite commode, like a baleful excremental spirit, there arose a Smoking Toilet Puppet.

The rugose figure was composed of an elongated mud-colored torso, sprouting two boneless and sinuous claw-fingered arms, and topped by a rutted warpy face. The Puppet's head was crowned by a small fumy crater, giving its kind their name.

"Ja-a-ack," wailed the Puppet. "Jack Neck! Step closer! I have a message for you."

Jack knew that although the creature might indeed have a valid and valuable Delphic message for him, to heed the Puppet's summons was to risk being abducted down to the gluck-mucky Septic Kingdom ruled by Baron Sugarslinger. So with an uncommon burst of energy, Jack grabbed up a wood-hafted sump-plunger and whanged the Puppet a good one on its audacious incense-dispensing bean.

While the Puppet was clutching its abused noggin and sobbing most piteously, Jack stepped around it and flushed. Widdershins and downward swirled the invader, disappearing with a liquidly dopplering "Nooooooo—!"

Jack did his old man's business quickly while the runnels still gurgled, then lowered the heavy toilet lid against further home invasions. He stepped to the sink and the sweatcrusted mirror above it, where he flaked scales off his reflection. He shaved his forehead, restoring the pointy dimensions of his once-stylish hairline, plucked some eelgrass out of his ears, lacquered his carbuncle, and congratulated himself on meeting so forcefully the first challenge of the day. If nothing else adventured, he would be polly-with-a-lolly!

Back through the bedroom and out into his sitting sanctuary, where Motherway lay snoozily on his fulsome scrap of Geelvink carpet. Approaching the dirty window that looked out upon Marmoreal Boulevard and the Isinglass, the incautious and over-optimistic Jack Neck threw open the wormy sash and shouldered forward, questing additional meaning and haruspices from the day.

And that was precisely the moment the waiting Worrybird chose to land talon-tight upon the convenient perch of Jack's hapless hump!

Jack yelped and with an instinctive yet hopeless shake of his hump withdrew into the refuge of his apartment, thinking to disconcert and dislodge the Worrybird by swift maneuvers. But matters had already progressed beyond any such simple solution. The Worrybird was truly and determinedly ensconced, and Jack realized he was doomed.

Big as a turkey, with crepe-like vulture wings, the baldy Worrybird possessed a dour human face exhibiting the texture of ancient overwaxed linoleum, and exuded a stench like burning crones. Jack had seen the ominous parasites often, of course, riding on their wan, slumpy victims. But never had he thought to be one such!

Awakened by the foofraraw, Motherway was barking and leaping and snapping, frantically trying to drive the intruder off. But all the bonedog succeeded in doing was gouging his master's single sensible leg with his hooves. Jack managed to calm the bonedog down, although Motherway continued to whimper while anxiously fidgeting.

Now the Worrybird craned its paste-pallid pug-ugly face around on its long sebaceous neck to confront Jack. It opened its hideous rubbery mouth and intoned a portentous phrase.

"Never again, but not yet!"

Jack threw himself into his slateslab chair, thinking to crush the grim bird, but it leaped nimbly atop Jack's skull. By Saint Foraminifer's Liver, those scalp-digging claws hurt! Quickly Jack stood, preferring to let the bird roost on his hump. Obligingly, the Worrybird shifted back.

"Oh, Motherway," Jack implored, "what a fardelicious grievance has been construed upon us! What oh what are we to do?"

Motherway made inutile answer only by a plangent sympathetic whuffle.

THE FIRST THOUGHT to form in the anxious mind of bird-bestridden Jack Neck was that he should apply to the local Health Clinic run by the Little Sisters of Saint Farquahar. Surely the talented technicians and charity caregivers there would have a solution to his grisly geas! (Although at the back of his mind loomed the pessimistic question, perhaps

Worrybird implanted, *Why did anyone suffer from Worrybird-itis if removal of same were so simple?*)

So, leaving Motherway behind to guard the apartment from any further misfortunes which this inopportune day might bring, Jack and his randomly remonstrative rider ("Never again, but not yet!") clabbered down the four flights of slant stairs to the street.

Once on Marmoreal (where formerly friendly or neutral neighbors now winced and retreated from sight of his affliction), Jack turned not happy-wise left but appointment-bound right. At the intersection of the Boulevard and El Chino Street, he wambled south on the cross-street. Several blocks down El Chino his progress was arrested by the sloppy aftermath of an accident: a dray full of Smith's Durian Essence had collided with one loaded with Walrus Brand Brochettes. The combination of the two antagonistic spilled foodstuffs had precipitated something noxious: galorping mounds of quivering Day-Glo cartiplasm that sought to ingest any flesh within reach. (The draft animals, a brace of Banana Slugs per dray, had already succumbed, as had the blindly argumentative drivers, one Pheon Ploog and a certain Elmer Sourbray.)

Responding with the nimble reflexes and sassy footwork expected from any survivor of Drudge City's ordinary cataclysms, Jack dodged into a nearby building, rode a Recirculating Transport Fountain upward and took a wayward rooftop path around the crisis before descending, all the while writing a hundred times on the blackboard of his mind an exclamation-punctuated admonition never to mix internally his favorite suppertime drink with any iota of Walrus Brand Brochettes.

Encountering no subsequent pandygandy, Jack Neck and his foul avian passenger arrived at the Health Clinic on Laguna Diamante Way. Once inside, he was confronted with the stern and ruleacious face of Nurse Gwendolyn Hindlip, Triage Enforcement Officer. From behind her rune-carven desk that seemed assembled of poorly chosen driftwood fragments, Nurse Gwendolyn sized up Jack and his hump-burden, then uttered a presumptuous pronouncement.

"You might as well kill yourself now, you old mummer, and free up your GGGB for a younkling!"

Jack resented being called a mummer—a mildly derisive slang term derived from his union's initials—almost more than he umbrigated at the suicidal injunction.

"Shut up, you lava-faced hincty harridan! Just take my particulars, slot my citizen-biscuit into the chewer, and mind your own business!"

Nurse Gwendolyn sniffed with bruised emotionality. Jack had scored a mighty blow on a tender spot with his categorical comment "lava-faced." For Nurse Gwendolyn's scare-making and scarified visage did indeed reflect her own childhood brush with a flesh-melting disease that still occasionally plagued Drudge City. Known as Trough'n'Slough, the nonfatal disease left its victims with a stratified trapunto epidermis. Nurse Gwendolyn forever attributed her sour old-maidhood to the stigma of this pillowpuff complexion, although truth be told, her vile tongue had even more to do with her empty bed.

Snuffling aggrievedly, Nurse Gwendolyn now did as she was bade, at last dispatching a newly ID-braceleted Jack to a waiting area with the final tart remark, "You'll surely have a long uncomfortable wait, Mr. Neck, for many and more seriously afflicted—yet naytheless with a better prognosis—are the helpseekers afore you!"

Coercing his fossil leg into the waiting room, Jack saw that Nurse Gwendolyn had not been merely flibbering. Ranked and stacked in moaning drifts and piles were a staggering assortment of Drudge City's malfunctioners. Jack spotted many a one showing various grades of Maskelyne's Curse, in which the face assumed the characteristics of a thickly blurred latex mold of the actual submerged features beneath. The false countenance remained connected by sensory tendrils, yet was migratory, so that one's visage slopped about like warm Jell-O, eyes peeking from nostrils or ears, nose poking from mouth. Other patients showed plain signs of Exoskeletal Exfoliation, their limbs encased in osteoclastic armor. One woman—dressed in a tattered shift laterally patterned blue and gold—could only be host to Dolly Dwindles Syndrome: as she approached over months her ultimate doll-like dimensions, her face simultaneously grew more lascivious in a ghoulish manner.

Heaving a profound sigh at the mortal sufferings of himself and his fellows, Jack sat himself saggingly down in a low-backed chair that permitted the Worrybird to maintain its grip upon Jack's hump, and resigned himself to a long wait.

On the seven-hundredth-and-forty-ninth "Never again, but not yet!," Jack's name was called. He arose and was conducted to a cubicle screened from an infinity of others by ripped curtains the color of old tartar sauce. Undressing was not an option, so he simply plopped down on a squelchy examining table and awaited the advent of a healer. Before too long the curtains parted and a lab-coated figure entered.

This runcible-snouted doctor himself, thought Jack, should have been a patient, for he was clearly in an advanced state of Tessellated Scale Mange, as evidenced by alligatored wrists and neck poking from cuff and collar. Most horridly, the medico dragged behind him a long ridged tail, ever-extending like an accumulating stalactite from an infiltrated organ at the base of the spine.

"Doctor Weighbend," said the professional in a confident voice, extending a crocodile paw. Jack shook hands happily, liking the fellow's vim. But Doctor Weighbend's next question shattered Jack's sanguinity.

"Now, what seems to be the matter with you, Mr. Neck?"

"Why—why, Doc, there's an irksome and grotty Worrybird implacably a-sway upon my tired old hump!"

Doctor Weighbend made a suave dismissive motion. "Oh, that. Since there's no known cure for the Worrybird, Mr. Neck, I assumed there was another issue to deal with, some unseen plaque or innervation perhaps."

"No known cure, Doc? How can that be?"

Doctor Weighbend cupped his dragonly chin. "The Worrybird has by now slyly and inextricably mingled his Akashic Aura with yours. Were we to kill or even remove the little vampire-sparrow, you too would perish. Of course, you'll perish eventually anyway, as the lachrymose-lark siphons off your vitality. But that process could take years and years. 'Never again will you smile, but not yet shall you die.' That's the gist of it, I fear, Mr. Neck."

"What—what do you recommend then?"

"Many people find some small palliation in building a festive concealing shelter for their Worrybird. Securely strapped to your torso bandolier-style and gaily decorated with soothing icons, it eases social functioning to a small degree. Now, I have other patients to attend to, if you'll permit me to take my leave by wishing you a minimally satisfactory rest of your life."

Doctor Weighbend spun around—his massive tail catching a cart of instruments and beakers and sending glassware smashing to the floor—and was gone. Jack sat wearily and down-in-the-dumpily for a few long minutes, then levered himself up and trudged off down the aisle formed by the curtained wards.

Almost to the exit, Jack's attention was drawn between two parted drapes.

On a table lay the Motorball Champion Dean Tesh! Bloodied and grimacing, his signature cornucopia-shaped head drooping, sparks and fizzles spurting from his numerous lumpy adjuncts, Jack Neck's hero awaited his own treatment. Assuredly, that day's game had been a rambunctious and asgardian fray! And Jack had missed it!

Impulsively, Jack entered the Champion's cubicle. "Superlative Dean Tesh, if I may intrude briefly upon your eminence. I'm one of your biggest fans, and I wish to offer my condolences on your lapsarian desuetude."

Dean Tesh boldly smiled like the rigorous roughrider he was. "'Tis nothing, really, old mummenschanz. Once they jimmy open my cranial circuit flap and insert a few new wigwags, I'll be right as skysyrup!"

Jack blushed to be addressed by his union's highest title, in actuality undeserved. "Your magnificent spirit inspires me, lordly Dean Tesh! Somehow I too will win through my own malediction!"

Dean Tesh's ocular lenses whirred for a better look. "Worrybird, is it? I've heard Uncle Bradley has a way with them."

"Uncle Bradley! Of course! Did he not design your own world-renowned servos and shunts? If medicine holds no answers to my problem, then surely Uncle Bradley's Syntactical Fibroid Engineering must!"

And so bidding Dean Tesh a heartfelt farewell replete with benisonical affirmations of the Champion's swift recovery, Jack Neck set out for Cementville.

SOON JACK'S TRAIL of tiny archless footprints—outlined in fast-growing sporulating molds and luminescent quiverslimes—could be traced through many an urban mile. Behind him already lay the evil precincts of Barrio Garmi, where the Stilt-legged Spreckles were prone to drop rotten melons from their lofty vantages upon innocent passersby. Jack had with wiles and guiles eluded that sloppy fate. The district of Clovis Points he had also cunningly circumnavigated, wrenching free at the last possible moment from the tenebrous grasp of a pack of Shanghai Liliths, whose lickerish intention it was to drag innocent Jack to their spraddle-skirted leader, Lil' Omen, for the irreligious ceremony known as the Ecstatic Excruciation. For several blocks thereafter he had dared to ride the Henniker Avenue Slantwise Subway, disembarking hastily through his car's emergency exit and thence by escape-ready ladderchute when he spotted a blockade across the tracks surely erected by the muskageous minions of Baron Sugarslinger. Luckily, Jack had had the foresight to obtain a transfer-wafer and so was able to board the Baba Wanderly Aerial Viaticum for free, riding high and safe above the verdigrised-copper-colored towers and chimney-pots, gables, and garrets of Doo-Boo-Kay Flats.

At last, as a pavonine dusk was o'erspreading the haze-raddled, swag-bellied firmament, Jack Neck and his endlessly asseverating Worrybird—its face like a hairless druid's, its folded wings gloomy as a layoff notice from Krespo's—arrived at the premises of Uncle Bradley. The largest employer in gritty Cementville, the firm of Bradley and His Boyo-Boys, experts in SFE, ran round the erratic clock all thirteen moons a year, turn-ing out many and many a marvelous product, both luxuries and essentials, the former including Seductive Bergamot Filters and the latter notable for Nevermiss Nailguns. Renowned for accepting any and all engi-neering challenges, the more intractable the more alluring, Uncle Bradley represented Jack's best hope in the Worrybird-Removal Department.

At the towering portal to the lumbering and rachitic nine-storey algae-brick-fronted manufactory that occu-pied ten square blocks of Dimmig Gardens, Jack made free with the bellpull: the nose of a leering brass jack-anapes. A minidoor opened within the gigundo pressboard entrance, and a functionary appeared. As the employee began to speak, Jack noted with dismay that the fellow suffered from Papyrus Mouth: his words emerged not as ordinary vocables but as separate words printed in blearsome bodily inks upon shoddy scraps of organic-tissue paper.

Jack sought to catch the emergent syllables as they spelunked bucally forth, but some eluded him and whiffed away on the diddling breezes. Nervously assembling the remaining message, Jack read: *business state Bradley please with.*

"I need to solicit dear Uncle Bradley's genius in the area of invasive parasite disengagement." Jack jerked a thick split-nailed thumb backward at his broodsome rider.

A gush of flighty papyri: *Follow Bradley Uncle free see if me.*

Most gladfully, Jack Neck entered the dynamic estab-lishment and strode after the Papyrus Mouther. Through humming, thrumming offices and sparky workshops—where crucibles glowed with neon-tinted polymeric compounds and, under the nimble fingers of Machine Elves, transistors danced the Happy Chicken

Trot with capacitors and optical-fluid valves—Jack and his guide threaded, until at last they stood before a ridged and fumarole-pocked door with a riveted steel rubric announcing it as UNCLE BRADLEY'S CARBON CAVE.

*Wait here.*

Alone, Jack hipper-hopped nervously from toe to toe. He prayed to all the Saints whose names he could remember— Fimbule and Flubber, Flacken and Floss, Fluffie and Farina—that Uncle Bradley possessed the secret of his salvation—and at a price he could afford.

After an almost unsquingeable wait, the Papyrus Mouther returned.

*with Bradley will now you Uncle meet.*

"Oh, thank you, kind underling! A myriad blessings of the Yongy-bongy-bo descend upon you!"

Into the fabled Hades-embered Carbon Cave now, whose inward-seeming rattled Jack's sensory modes. The walls and ceiling of the vasty deep were layered with sniveling encrustations of Syntactical Fibroid Engineering at its most complex. Flickering readouts and mumbling speaker-grilles obtruded their cicatrice-bordered surfaces from among switches and pulls, toggles and knife-throws, fingering-holes and mentation-bands. Innumerable crystal monitors studded all surfaces, displaying upon their garnet and amethyst faces scenes from across Drudge City. For a briefer-than-brief second, a shot of Marmoreal Boulevard—right in front of Boris Crocodile's!—flashed across one, and Jack nearly wept for the nostalgic past of mere yesterday!

In the middle of the Carbon Cave, on his numinous, numbly throne, sat Uncle Bradley. Almost totally overwhelmed with layers of SFE extrudements, a helpful carapace of gadgetry, the master of the Boyo-Boys showed bare only his snaggle-toothed and wildly inventive face, and his two striped arms, one of which terminated in a chromium piratical hook. Dangling all around inspiration-eyed Uncle Bradley were speakers and microphones, mini-monitors, telefactored manipulators and sniff-sources, allowing him to run his many-branched enterprise without leaving his cozy sanctum.

As Jack approached tentatively across the wide checker-board floor, he could hear from Uncle Bradley a constant stream of queries, advice, and commands.

"Lay on ten thousand more karma-watts to the Soul Furnace! Process Violet-Hundred is failing? Six hundred kilograms of Charm Catalyst into the mix! Eureka! Start a new assembly line: personal Eyeblink Moderators! Has the Bloodwort stabilized yet? No? Lash it with the Zestful Invigorators! Cancel the Corndog Project, and feed the experimental subjects to the Hullygees! How are the Pull Hats selling this season? That poorly? Try them with claw-tassels in plaid!"

Jack and his momentarily silent Worrybird had reached the base of Uncle Bradley's seat of power, and now the Edisonical eminence took notice of the supplicant. Before Jack could even state his need, Uncle Bradley, laying a machicolated salesman's smile upon him, was offering a concise prix fixe of options.

"Worrybird, correct? Of course! Obviousness obtrudes! Here are your recoursial tactics, in order of cost and desirability. For five thousand crones, we inject the bird with a Circuitry Virus. In three days the bird is totally roboticized. Still unremovable, of course, but its lethality is slowed by fifty percent. For three thousand crones, we attach a Secondary Imagineer to your cere-brumal interstices. You promptly forget the bird is there for the rest of your allotted span. For eight hundred crones, a simple cable allows you to share the bird's own mentation. Thus you enjoy your own death, and feel it to be Darwinically mandated. Lastly, for a piddling three hundred crones, we remand one of our novice Boyo-Boys to stay by your side till you succumb to the inevitable wastage. He plies you with personalized jest and frolic, and remonstrates with anyone who dares to offer you contumely!"

Jack could barely conceal his dismay. "Those—those are my only choices?"

"What more could a sensible man want? The Worrybird is an incorrigible opponent, and no one besides the recondite and rascally Uncle Bradley dares even to tamper with one! Be quick now, old gansel! Which will it be?"

Jack wimbled and wambled pitifully. "I have not even the three hundred crones for the humblest palliation. I was hoping for more triumphalist affronts and easier terms—"

"What! You dare to waste Uncle's invaluable chronospasms without funds in reserve! And then to derogate my nostrums as if you were a fellow engineer at a throwdown session of the Tinkerer's Sodality! Away with you, laggardly old momerath!"

Suddenly, the Papyrus Mouther was by Jack's elbow. Without pleasant hostly ado, Jack was spun about and frog-marched from the Cave of the SFErical Monarch. Just before the heavy door slammed behind him, Jack could hear Uncle Bradley resume his litany of savantical willfulness: "Engage the services of ten thousand more Glissandos, and another dozen Kriegsteins!"

Summarily and insultively ejected onto the cheesily porous cobbled terrace before the SFErical Emporium, true night pressing down from above like a corpulent lover, Jack knew himself at the end of both his abilities and the universe's possibilities. The weight of the Worrybird seemed suddenly Atlasian. At the first "Never again, but not yet!," every nerve in Jack's poor frame thrilled with galvanic imbroglication. He hung his head, able to focus only on the snailslick cobbles.

Three tags of papyrus skittered by just then, and without much hope Jack used the last of his scanty vigor to retrieve them.

*Seek Saint Fiacre.*

NOW WAS VERACIOUS and lordly midnight come without fear of fleering misrecognition to occupy Drudge City like a famously conquering cubic khan. Much too low in the sky hung a sherberty scoop-hollowed partial moon like a slice of vanilla ice cream-sheened cantaloupe half eaten by a finicky godling. Stars showed in the space between the tips of the errant satellite's horns. Insect-seeking sweaterbats, their calls of "stitch-stitch!" leavening the mist, thronged the curvaceous canyons formed by the tottering towers of home and office, both kinds of hobbledehoy establishment darkened as their inhabitants blissfully or troubledly slept. Only meeps and monks, strumpets and troubadours, witlings and mudlarks were abroad at this hour—at least in this dismal section of Drudge City. Perhaps among the delightful theaters in the district known as Prisbey's Heaves, or in the saucer-slurping cafés of Mechanics' Ramble, good citizens yet disported themselves without fear of encountering lurking angina-anklers or burrow-bums. And surely—most sadly of a certainty—at Boris Crocodile's Beanery and Caustics Bar, ghosty-eyed Nori Nougat was even at this moment frugging with ledge-browed Zack Zither, while Stinky Frankie Konk tortured banshee wails from his hybrid instrument.

But out here, where putrid Ashmolean Alley and rancid Rotifer Gangway ranked as the only streets of distinction, no such gaiety could be found. There lollopped only a besmirched and bedaubed and bedemoned Jack Neck, bustedly dragging himself down block after block, in search of Saint Fiacre.

The last Jack had heard—from Dirty Bill Brownback, in fact—rumors of a Saint sighting had recently wafted from out Ubidio way. No guarantee that said sighted Saint was named Fiacre, or that he was even still present. Saints had a disconcerting propensity to phase-shift at random. Yet poor Jack Neck had no other phantom to pursue, so thence he now leathered.

Two hours past the night's navel, Jack Neck emerged from encircling buildings onto bare-tiled Pringle Plaza. In the middle of the civic space ruminated an eyelid-shuttered naked Saint.

The Saint had once been human. After much spiritual kenning and abstemious indulgences, making the choice to give him or herself up entirely to the avariciously bountiful forces of the Indeterminate, the human had morpholyzed into a Saint. The Saint's trunk had widened and spread into a bulbous heap, from which sprouted withered legs and off-kilter arms, but no visible generative parts. Instead, out of the trunk at queer angles protruded numerous quasi-organic spouts and intakes similar to rusty gutter-pipes. The Saint's neck was a corded barrel supporting a pointy-peaked head on which the features had wandered north, south, east, and west. Overall, the creature was a pebbled mushroom-white, and three times the size of Jack. Around this living interface with the Indeterminate, the air wavered whorlfully.

Humble as a wet cat, Jack approached the Saint. When the Worrybird-carrier was within a few yards of the strange being, the Saint opened his eyes.

"Are thee Fiacre?" nervously intoned Jack, who had never cozened with a Saint before, nor ever thought to.

"Aye."

"I was sent to thee. This bumptious bird I would begone."

The Saint pondered for a chronospasm. "You must perambulate round the Inverted Stupa for three hours, reciting without cease, 'Always once again, and perhaps now.'"

"This will cause the Worrybird to relinquish its hold?"

"Not at all. The procedure will simply give me further time to peer into the Indeterminate. But nonetheless, you must attend with precision to my instructions, upon pain of rasterbation."

"As you say, oh Saint."

Luckily, the Inverted Stupa was only half a league onward. Hurrying with renewed hope, Jack soon reached the famous monument. In the middle of another peopleless plaza, lit fitfully by torches of witch's-hair, was a railed pit of no small dimensions. Looking down over the rail, Jack saw the vertiginous walls of the Inverted Stupa, lighted windows stretching down to the earth's borborygmous bowels, deeper by far than even Baron Sugarslinger's realm.

Without delay, Jack began his circular hegira, chanting his Saintly mantra.

"Always once again, and perhaps now. Always once again, and perhaps now…"

The Worrybird seemed in no wise discommoded by Jack's croaking exertions. Jack tried not to lose his resurgent tentative cheer. At long last, just when Jack's legs—both good and bad—felt ready to snap, a nearby clock tolled five, releasing him to return to the Saint.

Saint Fiacre sat unchanged, a yeasty enigmatic effigy with a face like an anthropomorphic cartoon breadloaf.

"You have done well, old mockmurphy. Come close now, and cover my sacred Intake Number Nine with your palm."

Jack sidle-stepped up to the Saint, entering the zone where his vision burbled. He raised his hand toward the properly labeled bodypipe, then capped the opening with the flat of his permanently work-roughened hand.

Instantly, the insidious and undeniable vacuum-suck of ten dozen black holes!

Jack's hand was quickly pulled in. Before he could even gasp, his shoulder was pressed to the treacherous Intake Number Nine. Then Jack felt himself drawn even further in! Oddly he experienced no pain. Only, he was sure, because he was already dead.

Soon Jack was ingulped headwise up to both shoulders. His hump delayed his swallowment slightly, but then, thanks to a swelling surge of pull-power, even his abused hump was past the rim.

And the Worrybird too? Apparently not! Peeled off like a potato skin was that manfaced mordaunt! But what of their commingled Akashic Aura? Only Gossip Time would tell...

Within seconds, Jack was fully through Intake Number Nine. Then began a journey of sense-thwarting intricacy. Through a maze of bloodlit veiny pipes Jack flowed like the slorq at Krespo's, until he finally shot out of a funnel-mouth into ultracolored drifts of sheer abundant nothingness that smelled like a bosomy woman and tasted like Shugwort's Lemon Coddle. Here existence was a matter of wayward wafts and dreamy enticements, so connubially unlike the pestiferous hurlyburly of mundane existence. Time evaporated, and soon Jack did too...

EARLY MORNING IN Pringle Plaza, sunlight like the drip of candyapple glaze. Sanitation chimps were about their cleaning, sweeping litter and leaf into the open mouths of attendant roadhogs. A traveling preacher had unfolded his pocket altar and was preaching the doctrine of Klacktoveedsedsteen to a yawning group of bow-tied office dandies. Saint Fiacre, having just given a lonely little girl the second head she had requested, suddenly quivered all over as if stricken by Earthquake Ague, then decocted a real-as-mud, sprightly-as-fleas Jack Neck from Outflow Number Three.

Jack got woozily to his tiny feet. "Saint Fiacre, I thank thee!"

"Say twenty-seven Nuclear Novenas nightly, invoking the names of Gretchen Growl, Mercy Luna, and the Rowr-bazzle. And do not stick your foolish mummer's head out any more windows without forethought."

And then Saint Fiacre was gone.


HAVING POLISHED OFF his supper and seen the merry Motherway lickily attending to his bonedog privates, mawkly old Jack Neck now commonly got to Boris Crocodile's a little later each night. Those Nuclear Novenas took time, and he did not trust either his tongue or his pledged determination after a shot of Dinky Pachinko's dumble-rum. Neither could his saviorology be allowed to interfere during the day with Jack's ardent eyeballing of the exploits of the mighty Dean Tesh, Motorball Mauler! So postprandial were his doxologies.

But despite the slight change in his schedule, Jack still entered the Beanery and Caustics Bar in mid-stridulation of hookah-banjo, still found his favorite reserved barstool awaiting him, still feasted his rheumy eyes on the flirtsome gavotteners atrot, and still affirmed to any and all who would lend an ear, "Yessir, assuming you can get through the rough spots, life can turn out mighty sweet!"

*—This story was inspired by the paintings of Chris Mars. For more information, contact Chris Mars, PO Box 24631, Edina, MN 55424, USA, or visit www.chrismarspublishing.com*

# THE LUNATICS

*Kim Stanley Robinson*

*For Terry Carr*

THEY WERE VERY near the center of the moon, Jakob told them. He was the newest member of the bullpen, but already their leader.

"How do you know?" Solly challenged him. It was stifling, the hot air thick with the reek of their sweat, and a pungent stink from the waste bucket in the corner. In the pure black, under the blanket of the rock's basalt silence, their shifting and snuffling loomed large, defined the size of the pen. "I suppose you see it with your third eye."

Jakob had a laugh as big as his hands. He was a big man, never a doubt of that. "Of course not, Solly. The third eye is for seeing in the black. It's a natural sense just like the others. It takes all the data from the rest of the senses, and processes them into a visual image transmitted by the third optic nerve, which runs from the forehead to the sight

327

centers at the back of the brain. But you can only focus it by an act of the will—same as with all the other senses. It's not magic. We just never needed it till now."

"So how do you know?"

"It's a problem in spherical geometry, and I solved it. Oliver and I solved it. This big vein of blue runs right down into the core, I believe, down into the moon's molten heart where we can never go. But we'll follow it as far as we can. Note how light we're getting. There's less gravity near the center of things."

"I feel heavier than ever."

"You are heavy, Solly. Heavy with disbelief."

"Where's Freeman?" Hester said in her crow's rasp.

No one replied.

Oliver stirred uneasily over the rough basalt of the pen's floor. First Naomi, then mute Elijah, now Freeman. Somewhere out in the shafts and caverns, tunnels and corridors—somewhere in the dark maze of mines, people were disappearing. Their pen was emptying, it seemed. And the other pens?

"Free at last," Jakob murmured.

"There's something out there," Hester said, fear edging her harsh voice, so that it scraped Oliver's nerves like the screech of an ore car's wheels over a too-sharp bend in the tracks. "Something out there!"

The rumor had spread through the bullpens already, whispered mouth to ear or in huddled groups of bodies. There were thousands of shafts bored through the rock, hundreds of chambers and caverns. Lots of these were closed off, but many more were left open, and there was room to hide—miles and miles of it. First some of their cows had disappeared. Now it was people too. And Oliver had heard a miner jabbering at the low edge of hysteria, about a giant foreman gone mad after an accident took both his arms at the shoulder—the arms had been replaced by prostheses, and the foreman had escaped into the black, where he preyed on miners off by themselves, ripping them up, feeding on them—

They all heard the steely squeak of a car's wheel. Up the mother shaft, past cross tunnel Forty; had to be foremen at this time of shift. Would the car turn at the fork to their concourse? Their hypersensitive ears focused on the distant sound; no one breathed. The wheels squeaked, turned their way. Oliver, who was already shivering, began to shake hard.

The car stopped before their pen. The door opened, all in darkness. Not a sound from the quaking miners.

Fierce white light blasted them and they cried out, leaped back against the cage bars vainly. Blinded, Oliver cringed at the clawing of a foreman's hands, searching under his shirt and pants. Through pupils like pinholes he glimpsed brief black-and-white snapshots of gaunt bodies undergoing similar searches, then blows. Shouts, cries of pain, smack of flesh on flesh, an electric buzzing. Shaving their heads, could it be that time again already? He was struck in the stomach, choked around the neck. Hester's long wiry brown arms, wrapped around her head. Scalp burned, *buzzz,* all chopped up. Thrown to the rock.

"Where's the twelfth?" In the foremen's staccato language.

No one answered.

The foremen left, light receding with them until it was black again, the pure dense black that was their own. Except now it was swimming with bright red bars, washing around in painful tears. Oliver's third eye opened a little, which calmed him, because it was still a new experience; he could make out his companions, dim red-black shapes in the black, huddled over themselves, gasping.

Jakob moved among them, checking for hurts, comforting. He cupped Oliver's forehead and Oliver said, "It's seeing already."

"Good work." On his knees Jakob clumped to their shit bucket, took off the lid, reached in. He pulled something out. Oliver marveled at how clearly he was able to see all this. Before, floating blobs of color had drifted in the black; but he had always assumed they were afterimages, or hallucinations. Only with Jakob's instruction had he been able to perceive the patterns they made, the vision that they constituted. It was an act of will. That was the key.

Now, as Jakob cleaned the object with his urine and spit, Oliver found that the eye in his forehead saw even more, in sharp blood etchings. Jakob held the lump overhead, and it seemed it was a little lamp, pouring light over them in a wavelength they had always been able to see, but had never needed before. By its faint ghostly radiance the whole pen was made clear, a structure etched in blood, red-black on black. "Promethium," Jakob breathed. The miners crowded around him, faces lifted to it. Solly had a little pug nose, and squinched his face terribly in the effort to focus. Hester had a face to go with her voice, stark bones under skin scored with lines. "The most precious element. On Earth our masters rule by it. All their civilization is based on it, on the movement inside it, electrons escaping their shells and crashing into neutrons, giving off heat and more blue as well. So they condemn us to a life of pulling it out of the moon for them."

He chipped at the chunk with a thumbnail. They all knew precisely its clayey texture, its heaviness, the dull silvery gray of it, which pulsed green under some lasers, blue under others. Jakob gave each of them a sliver of it. "Take it between two molars and crush hard. Then swallow."

"It's poison, isn't it?" said Solly.

"After years and years." The big laugh, filling the black. "We don't have years and years, you know that. And in the short run it helps your vision in the black. It strengthens the will."

Oliver put the soft heavy sliver between his teeth, chomped down, felt the metallic jolt, swallowed. It throbbed in him. He could see the others' faces, the mesh of the pen walls, the pens farther down the concourse, the robot tracks—all in the lightless black.

"Promethium is the moon's living substance," Jakob said quietly. "We walk in the nerves of the moon, tearing them out under the lash of the foremen. The shafts are a map of where the neurons used to be. As they drag the moon's mind out by its roots, to take it back to Earth and use it for their own enrichment, the lunar consciousness fills us and we become its mind ourselves, to save it from extinction."

They joined hands: Solly, Hester, Jakob, and Oliver. The surge of energy passed through them, leaving a sweet afterglow.

Then they lay down on their rock bed, and Jakob told them tales of his home, of the Pacific dockyards, of the cliffs and wind and waves, and the way the sun's light lay on it all. Of the jazz in the bars, and how trumpet and clarinet could cross each other. "How do you remember?" Solly asked plaintively. "They turned me blank."

Jakob laughed hard. "I fell on my mother's knitting needles when I was a boy, and one went right up my nose. Chopped the hippocampus in two. So all my life my brain has been storing what memories it can somewhere else.

They burned a dead part of me, and left the living memory intact."

"Did it hurt?" Hester croaked.

"The needles? You bet. A flash like the foremen's prods, right there in the center of me. I suppose the moon feels the same pain, when we mine her. But I'm grateful now, because it opened my third eye right at that moment. Ever since then I've seen with it. And down here, without our third eye it's nothing but the black."

Oliver nodded, remembering.

"And something out there," croaked Hester.

NEXT SHIFT START Oliver was keyed by a foreman, then made his way through the dark to the end of the long, slender vein of blue he was working. Oliver was a tall youth, and some of the shaft was low; no time had been wasted smoothing out the vein's irregular shape. He had to crawl between the narrow tracks bolted to the rocky uneven floor, scraping through some gaps as if working through a great twisted intestine.

At the shaft head he turned on the robot, a long low-slung metal box on wheels. He activated the laser drill, which faintly lit the exposed surface of the blue, blinding him for some time. When he regained a certain visual equilibrium—mostly by ignoring the weird illumination of the drill beam—he typed instructions into the robot, and went to work drilling into the face, then guiding the robot's scoop and hoist to the broken pieces of blue. When the big chunks were in the ore cars behind the robot, he jackhammered loose any fragments of the ore that adhered to the basalt walls, and added them to the cars before sending them off.

This vein was tapering down, becoming a mere tendril in the lunar body, and there was less and less room to work in. Soon the robot would be too big for the shaft, and they would have to bore through basalt; they would follow the tendril to its very end, hoping for a bole or a fan.

At first Oliver didn't much mind the shift's work. But IR-directed cameras on the robot surveyed him as well as the shaft face, and occasional shocks from its prod reminded him to keep hustling. And in the heat and bad air, as he grew ever more famished, it soon enough became the usual desperate, painful struggle to keep to the required pace.

Time disappeared into that zone of endless agony that was the latter part of a shift. Then he heard the distant klaxon of shift's end, echoing down the shaft like a cry in a dream. He turned the key in the robot and was plunged into noiseless black, the pure absolute of Non-being. Too tired to try opening his third eye, Oliver started back up the shaft by feel, following the last ore car of the shift. It rolled quickly ahead of him and was gone.

In the new silence distant mechanical noises were like creaks in the rock. He measured out the shift's work, having marked its beginning on the shaft floor: eighty-nine lengths of his body. Average.

It took a long time to get back to the junction with the shaft above his. Here there was a confluence of veins and the room opened out, into an odd chamber some seven feet high, but wider than Oliver could determine in every direction. When he snapped his fingers there was no rebound at all. The usual light at the far end of the low chamber was absent. Feeling sandwiched between two endless rough planes of rock, Oliver experienced a sudden claustrophobia; there was a whole world overhead, he was buried alive... He crouched and every few steps tapped one rail with his ankle, navigating blindly, a hand held forward to discover any dips in the ceiling.

He was somewhere in the middle of this space when he heard a noise behind him. He froze. Air pushed at his face. It was completely dark, completely silent. The noise squeaked behind him again: a sound like a fingernail, brushed along the banded metal of piano wire. It ran right up his spine, and he felt the hair on his forearms pull away from the dried sweat and stick straight out. He was holding his breath. Very slow footsteps were placed softly behind him, perhaps forty feet away... an airy snuffle, like a big nostril sniffing. For the footsteps to be so spaced out it would have to be...

Oliver loosened his joints, held one arm out and the other forward, tiptoed away from the rail, at right angles to it, for twelve feathery steps. In the lunar gravity he felt he might even float. Then he sank to his knees, breathed through his nose as slowly as he could stand to. His heart knocked at the back of his throat, he was sure it was louder than his breath by far. Over that noise and the roar of blood in his ears he concentrated his hearing to the utmost pitch. Now he could hear the faint sounds of ore cars and perhaps miners and foremen, far down the tunnel that led from the far side of this chamber back to the pens. Even as faint as they were, they obscured further his chances of hearing whatever it was in the cavern with him.

The footsteps had stopped. Then came another metallic *scrick* over the rail, heard against a light sniff. Oliver cowered, held his arms hard against his sides, knowing he smelled of sweat and fear. Far down the distant shaft a foreman spoke sharply. If he could reach that voice... He resisted the urge to run for it, feeling sure somehow that whatever was in there with him was fast.

Another *scrick*. Oliver cringed, trying to reduce his echo profile. There was a chip of rock under his hand. He fingered it, hand shaking. His forehead throbbed and he understood it was his third eye, straining to pierce the black silence and *see*...

A shape with pillar-thick legs, all in blocks of red-black. It was some sort of...

*Scrick*. Sniff. It was turning his way. A flick of the wrist, the chip of rock skittered, hitting ceiling and then floor, back in the direction he had come from.

Very slow soft footsteps, as if the legs were somehow... they were coming in his direction.

He straightened and reached above him, hands scrabbling over the rough basalt. He felt a deep groove in the rock, and next to it a vertical hole. He jammed a hand in the hole, made a fist; put the fingers of the other hand along the side of the groove, and pulled himself up. The toes of his boot fit the groove, and he flattened up against the ceiling. In the lunar gravity he could stay there forever. Holding his breath.

Step... step... snuffle, fairly near the floor, which had given him the idea for this move. He couldn't turn to look. He felt something scrape the hip pocket of his pants and thought he was dead, but fear kept him frozen; and the sounds moved off into the distance of the vast chamber, without a pause.

He dropped to the ground and bolted doubled over for the far tunnel, which loomed before him red-black in the black, exuding air and faint noise. He plunged right in it, feeling one wall nick a knuckle. He took the sharp right he knew was there and threw himself down to the intersection of floor and wall. Footsteps padded by him, apparently running on the rails.

When he couldn't hold his breath any longer he breathed. Three or four minutes passed and he couldn't bear to stay still. He hurried to the intersection, turned left and slunk to the bullpen. At the checkpoint the monitor's horn squawked and a foreman blasted him with a searchlight, pawed him roughly. "Hey!" The foreman held a big chunk of blue, taken from Oliver's hip pocket. What was this?

"Sorry boss," Oliver said jerkily, trying to see it properly, remembering the thing brushing him as it passed under. "Must've fallen in." He ignored the foreman's curse and blow, and fell into the pen tearful with the pain of the light, with relief at being back among the others. Every muscle in him was shaking.

But Hester never came back from that shift.

SOMETIME LATER THE foremen came back into their bullpen, wielding the lights and the prods to line them up against one mesh wall. Through pinprick pupils Oliver saw just the grossest slabs of shapes, all grainy black-and-gray: Jakob was a big stout man, with a short black beard under the shaved head, and eyes that popped out, glittering even in Oliver's silhouette world.

"Miners are disappearing from your pen," the foreman said, in the miners' language. His voice was like the quartz they tunneled through occasionally: hard, and sparkly with cracks and stresses, as if it might break at any moment into a laugh or a scream.

No one answered.

Finally Jakob said, "We know."

The foreman stood before him. "They started disappearing when you arrived."

Jakob shrugged. "Not what I hear."

The foreman's searchlight was right on Jakob's face, which stood out brilliantly, as if two of the searchlights were pointed at each other. Oliver's third eye suddenly opened and gave the face substance: brown skin, heavy brows, scarred scalp. Not at all the white cutout blazing from the black shadows. "You'd better be careful, miner."

Loudly enough to be heard from neighboring pens,

Jakob said, "Not my fault if something out there is eating us, boss."

The foreman struck him. Lights bounced and they all dropped to the floor for protection, presenting their backs to the boots. Rain of blows, pain of blows. Still, several pens had to have heard him.

Foremen gone. White blindness returned to black blindness, to the death velvet of their pure darkness. For a long time they lay in their own private worlds, hugging the warm rock of the floor, feeling the bruises blush. Then Jakob crawled around and squatted by each of them, placing his hands on their foreheads. "Oh yeah," he would say. "You're okay. Wake up now. Look around you." And in the after-black they stretched and stretched, quivering like dogs on a scent. The bulks in the black, the shapes they made as they moved and groaned... yes, it came to Oliver again, and he rubbed his face and looked around, eyes shut to help him see. "I ran into it on the way back in," he said.

They all went still. He told them what had happened.

"The blue in your pocket?"

They considered his story in silence. No one understood it.

No one spoke of Hester. Oliver found he couldn't. She had been his friend. To live without that gaunt crow's voice...

Sometime later the side door slid up, and they hurried into the barn to eat. The chickens squawked as they took the eggs, the cows mooed as they milked them. The stove plates turned the slightest bit luminous—red-black, again—and by their light his three eyes saw all. Solly cracked and fried eggs. Oliver went to work on his vats of cheese, pulled out a round of it that was ready. Jakob sat at the rear of one cow and laughed as it turned to butt his knee. *Splish splish! Splish splish!* When he was done he picked up the cow and put it down in front of its hay, where it chomped happily. Animal stink of them all, the many fine smells of food cutting through it. Jakob laughed at his cow, which butted his knee again as if objecting to the ridicule. "Little pig of a cow, little piglet. Mexican cows. They bred for this size, you know. On Earth the ordinary cow is as tall as Oliver, and about as big as this whole pen."

They laughed at the idea, not believing him. The buzzer cut them off, and the meal was over. Back into their pen, to lay their bodies down.

Still no talk of Hester, and Oliver found his skin crawling again as he recalled his encounter with whatever it was that sniffed through the mines. Jakob came over and asked him about it, sounding puzzled. Then he handed Oliver a rock. "Imagine this is a perfect sphere, like a baseball."

"Baseball?"

"Like a ball bearing, perfectly round and smooth you know."

Ah yes. Spherical geometry again. Trigonometry too. Oliver groaned, resisting the work. Then Jakob got him interested despite himself, in the intricacy of it all, the way it all fell together in a complex but comprehensible pattern. Sine and cosine, so clear! And the clearer it got the more he could see: the mesh of the bullpen, the network of shafts and tunnels and caverns piercing the jumbled fabric of the moon's body... all clear lines of red-black on black, like the metal of the stove plate as it just came visible, and all from Jakob's clear, patiently fingered, perfectly balanced equations. He could see through rock.

"Good work," Jakob said when Oliver got tired. They lay there among the others, shifting around to find hollows for their hips.

Silence of the off-shift. Muffled clanks downshaft, floor trembling at a detonation miles of rock away; ears popped as air smashed into the dead end of their tunnel, compressed to something nearly liquid for just an instant. Must have been a Boesman. Ringing silence again.

"So what is it, Jakob?" Solly asked when they could hear each other again.

"It's an element," Jakob said sleepily. "A strange kind of element, nothing else like it. Promethium. Number 61 on the periodic table. A rare earth, a lanthanide, an inner transition metal. We're finding it in veins of an ore called monazite, and in pure grains and nuggets scattered in the ore."

Impatient, almost pleading: "But what makes it so special?"

For a long time Jakob didn't answer. They could hear him thinking. Then he said, "Atoms have a nucleus, made of protons and neutrons bound together. Around this nucleus shells of electrons spin, and each shell is either full or trying to get full, to balance with the number of protons—to balance the positive and negative charges. An atom is like a human heart, you see.

"Now promethium is radioactive, which means it's out of balance, and parts of it are breaking free. But promethium never reaches its balance, because it radiates in a manner that increases its instability rather than the reverse. Promethium atoms release energy in the form of positrons, flying free when neutrons are hit by electrons. But during that impact more neutrons appear in the nucleus. Seems they're coming from nowhere. So each atom of the blue is a power loop in itself, giving off energy perpetually. Some people say that they're little white holes, every single atom of them. Burning forever at nine hundred and forty curies per gram. Bringing energy into our universe from somewhere else. Little gateways."

Solly's sigh filled the black, expressing incomprehension for all of them. "So it's poisonous?"

"It's dangerous, sure, because the positrons breaking away from it fly right through flesh like ours. Mostly they never touch a thing in us, because that's how close to phantoms we are—mostly blood, which is almost light. That's why we can see each other so well. But sometimes a beta particle will hit something small on its way through. Could mean nothing or it could kill you on the spot. Eventually it'll get us all."

Oliver fell asleep dreaming of threads of light like concentrations of the foremen's fierce flashes, passing right through him. Shifts passed in their timeless round. They ached when they woke on the warm basalt floor, they ached when they finished the long work shifts. They were hungry and often injured. None of them could say how long they had been there. None of them could say how old they were. Sometimes they lived without light other than the robots' lasers and the stove plates. Sometimes the foremen visited with their scorching lighthouse beams every off-shift, shouting questions and beating them. Apparently cows were disappearing, cylinders of air and oxygen, supplies of all sorts. None of it mattered to Oliver but the spherical geometry. He knew where he was, he could see it. The three-dimensional map in his head grew more extensive every shift. But everything else was fading away...

"So it's the most powerful substance in the world," Solly said. "But why us? Why are we here?"

"You don't know?" Jakob said.

"They blanked us, remember? All that's gone."

But because of Jakob, they knew what was up there: the domed palaces on the lunar surface, the fantastic luxuries of Earth... when he spoke of it, in fact, a lot of Earth came back to them, and they babbled and chattered at the unexpected upwellings. Memories that deep couldn't be blanked without killing, Jakob said. And so they prevailed after all, in a way.

But there was much that had been burnt forever. And so Jakob sighed. "Yeah, yeah, I remember. I just thought— well. We're here for different reasons. Some were criminals. Some complained."

"Like Hester!" They laughed.

"Yeah, I suppose that's what got her here. But a lot of us were just in the wrong place at the wrong time. Wrong politics or skin or whatever. Wrong look on your face."

"That was me, I bet," Solly said, and the others laughed at him. "Well I got a funny face, I know I do! I can feel it."

Jakob was silent for a long time. "What about you?" Oliver asked.

More silence. The rumble of a distant detonation, like muted thunder.

"I wish I knew. But I'm like you in that. I don't remember the actual arrest. They must have hit me on the head. Given me a concussion. I must have said something against the mines, I guess. And the wrong people heard me."

"Bad luck."

"Yeah. Bad luck."

More shifts passed. Oliver rigged a timepiece with two rocks, a length of detonation cord and a set of pulleys, and confirmed over time what he had come to suspect; the work shifts were getting longer. It was more and more difficult to get all the way through one, harder to stay awake for the meals and the geometry lessons during the off-shifts. The foremen came every off-shift now, blasting in with their searchlights and shouts and kicks, leaving in a swirl of after-images and pain. Solly went out one shift, cursing them under his breath, and never came back. Disappeared. The foremen beat them for it and Oliver shouted with rage. "It's not our fault! There's something out there, I saw it! It's killing us!"

Then next shift his little tendril of a vein bloomed, he couldn't find any rock around the blue: a big bole. He would have to tell the foremen, start working in a crew. He dismantled his clock.

On the way back he heard the footsteps again, shuffling along slowly behind him. This time he was at the entrance to the last tunnel, the pens close behind him. He turned to stare into the darkness with his third eye, willing himself to see the thing. Whoosh of air, a sniff, a footfall on the rail... Far across the thin wedge of air a beam of light flashed, making a long narrow cone of white talc. Steel tracks gleamed where the wheels of the car burnished them. Pupils shrinking like a snail's antennae, he stared back at the footsteps, saw nothing. Then, just barely, two points of red: retinas, reflecting the distant lance of light. They blinked. He bolted and ran again, reached the foremen at the checkpoint in seconds. They blinded him as he panted, passed him through and into the bullpen.

After the meal on that shift Oliver lay trembling on the floor of the bullpen and told Jakob about it. "I'm scared, Jakob. Solly, Hester, Freeman, Mute Lije, Naomi—they're all gone. Everyone I know here is gone but us."

"Free at last," Jakob said shortly. "Here, let's do your problems for tonight."

"I don't care about them."

"You have to care about them. Nothing matters unless you do. That blue is the mind of the moon being torn away, and the moon knows it. If we learn what the network says in its shapes, then the moon knows that too, and we're suffered to live."

"Not if that thing finds us!"

"You don't know. Anyway nothing to be done about it. Come on, let's do the lesson. We need it."

So they worked on equations in the dark. Both were distracted and the work went slowly; they fell asleep in the middle of it, right there on their faces.

SHIFTS PASSED. OLIVER pulled a muscle in his back, and excavating the bole he had found was an agony of discomfort. When the bole was cleared it left a space like the interior of an egg, ivory and black and quite smooth, punctuated only by the bluish spots of other tendrils of monazite extending away through the basalt. They left a catwalk across the central space, with decks cut into the rock on each side, and ramps leading to each of the veins of blue; and began drilling on their own again, one man and robot team to each vein. At each shift's end Oliver rushed to get to the egg-chamber at the same time as all the others, so that he could return the rest of the way to the bullpen in a crowd. This worked well until one shift came to an end with the hoist chock-full of the ore. It took him some time to dump it into the ore car and shut down.

So he had to cross the catwalk alone, and he would be alone all the way back to the pens. Surely it was past time to move the pens closer to the shaft heads! He didn't want to do this...

Halfway across the catwalk he heard a faint noise ahead of him. *Scrick; scriiiiiick.* He jerked to a stop, held the rail hard. Couldn't reach the ceiling here. Back stabbing its protest, he started to climb over the railing. He could hang from the underside.

He was right on the top of the railing when he was seized up by a number of strong cold hands. He opened his mouth to scream and his mouth was filled with wet clay. The blue. His head was held steady and his ears filled with the same stuff, so that the sounds of his own terrified sharp nasal exhalations were suddenly cut off. Promethium; it would kill him. It hurt his back to struggle on. He was being carried horizontally, ankles whipped, arms tied against his body. Then plugs of the clay were shoved up his nose and in the middle of a final paroxysm of resistance his mind fell away into the black.

THE LOWEST WHISPER in the world said, "Oliver Pen Twelve." He heard the voice with his stomach. He was astonished to be alive.

"You will never be given anything again. Do you accept the charge?"

He struggled to nod. I never wanted anything! he tried to say. I only wanted a life like anyone else.

"You will have to fight for every scrap of food, every swallow of water, every breath of air. Do you accept the charge?"

I accept the charge. I welcome it.

"In the eternal night you will steal from the foremen, kill the foremen, oppose their work in every way. Do you accept the charge?"

I welcome it.

"You will live free in the mind of the moon. Will you take up this charge?"

He sat up. His mouth was clear, filled only with the sharp electric aftertaste of the blue. He saw the shapes around him: there were five of them, five people there. And suddenly he understood. Joy ballooned in him and he said, "I will. Oh, I will!"

A light appeared. Accustomed as he was either to no light or to intense blasts of it, Oliver at first didn't comprehend. He thought his third eye was rapidly gaining power. As perhaps it was. But there was also a laser drill from one of the A robots, shot at low power through a cylindrical ceramic electronic element, in a way that made the cylinder glow yellow. Blind like a fish, openmouthed, weak eyes gaping and watering floods, he saw around him Solly, Hester, Freeman, mute Elijah, Naomi. "Yes," he said, and tried to embrace them all at once. "Oh, yes."

They were in one of the long-abandoned caverns, a flatbottomed bole with only three tendrils extending away from it. The chamber was filled with objects Oliver was more used to identifying by feel or sound or smell: pens of cows and hens, a stack of air cylinders and suits, three ore cars, two B robots, an A robot, a pile of tracks and miscellaneous gear. He walked through it all slowly, Hester at his side. She was gaunt as ever, her skin as dark as the shadows; it sucked up the weak light from the ceramic tube and gave it back only in little points and lines. "Why didn't you tell me?"

"It was the same for all of us. This is the way."

"And Naomi?"

"The same for her too; but when she agreed to it, she found herself alone."

Then it was Jakob, he thought suddenly. "Where's Jakob?"

Rasped: "He's coming, we think."

Oliver nodded, thought about it. "Was it you, then, following me those times? Why didn't you speak?"

"That wasn't us," Hester said when he explained what had happened. She cawed a laugh. "That was something else, still out there..."

Then Jakob stood before them, making them both jump.

They shouted and the others all came running, pressed into a mass together. Jakob laughed. "All here now," he said. "Turn that light off. We don't need it."

And they didn't. Laser shut down, ceramic cooled, they could still see: they could see right into each other, red shapes in the black, radiating joy. Everything in the little chamber was quite distinct, quite *visible*.

"'We are the mind of the moon.'"

WITHOUT SHIFTS TO mark the passage of time Oliver found he could not judge it at all. They worked hard, and they were constantly on the move: always up, through level after level of the mine. "Like shells of the atom, and we're that particle, busted loose and on its way out." They ate when they were famished, slept when they had to. Most of the time they worked, either bringing down shafts behind them, or dismantling depots and stealing everything Jakob designated theirs. A few times they ambushed gangs of foremen, killing them with laser cutters and stripping them of valuables; but on Jakob's orders they avoided contact with foremen when they could. He wanted only material. After a long time—twenty sleeps at least—they had six ore cars of it, all trailing an A robot up long-abandoned and empty shafts, where they had to lay the track ahead of them and pull it out behind, as fast as they could move. Among other items Jakob had an insatiable hunger for explosives; he couldn't get enough of them.

It got harder to avoid the foremen, who were now heavily armed and on their guard. Perhaps even searching for them, it was hard to tell. But they searched with their lighthouse beams on full power, to stay out of ambush: it was easy to see them at a distance, draw them off, lose them in dead ends, detonate mines under them. All the while the little band moved up, rising by infinitely long detours toward the front side of the moon. The rock around them cooled. The air circulated more strongly, until it was a constant wind. Through the seismometers they could hear from far below the rumbling of cars, heavy machinery, detonations. "Oh they're after us all right," Jakob said. "They're running scared."

He was happy with the booty they had accumulated, which included a great number of cylinders of compressed air and pure oxygen. Also vacuum suits for all of them, and a lot more explosives, including ten Boesmans, which were much too big for any ordinary mining. "We're getting close," Jakob said as they ate and drank, then tended the cows and hens. As they lay down to sleep by the cars he would talk to them about their work. Each of them had various jobs: mute Elijah was in charge of their supplies, Solly of the robot, Hester of the seismography. Naomi and Freeman were learning demolition, and were in some undefined sense Jakob's lieutenants. Oliver kept working at his navigation. They had found charts of the tunnel systems in their area, and Oliver was memorizing them, so that he would know at each moment exactly where they were. He found he could do it remarkably well; each time they ventured on he knew where the forks would come, where they would lead. Always upward.

But the pursuit was getting hotter. It seemed there were foremen everywhere, patrolling the shafts in search of them. "Soon they'll mine some passages and try to drive us into them," Jakob said. "It's about time we left."

"Left?" Oliver repeated.

"Left the system. Struck out on our own."

"Dig our own tunnel," Naomi said happily.

"Yes."

"To where?" Hester croaked.

Then they were rocked by an explosion that almost broke their eardrums, and the air rushed away. The rock around them trembled, creaked, groaned, cracked, and down the tunnel the ceiling collapsed, shoving dust toward them in a roaring *whoosh!* "A Boesman!" Solly cried.

Jakob laughed out loud. They were all scrambling into their vacuum suits as fast as they could. "Time to leave!" he cried, maneuvering their A robot against the side of the chamber. He put one of their Boesmans against the wall and set the timer. "Okay," he said over the suit's intercom. "Now we got to mine like we never mined before. To the surface!"

THE FIRST TASK was to get far enough away from the Boesman that they wouldn't be killed when it went off. They were now drilling a narrow tunnel and moving the loosened rock behind them to fill up the hole as they passed through it; this loose fill would fly like bullets down a rifle barrel when the Boesman went off. So they made three abrupt turns at acute angles to stop the fill's movement, and then drilled away from the area as fast as they could. Naomi and Jakob were confident that the explosion of the Boesman would shatter the surrounding rock to such an extent that it would never be possible for anyone to locate the starting point for their tunnel.

"Hopefully they'll think we did ourselves in," Naomi said, "either on purpose or by accident." Oliver enjoyed hearing her light laugh, her clear voice that was so pure and musical compared to Hester's croaking. He had never known Naomi well before, but now he admired her grace and power, her pulsing energy; she worked harder than Jakob, even. Harder than any of them.

A few shifts into their new life, Naomi checked the detonator timer she kept on a cord around her neck. "It should be going off soon. Someone go try and keep the cows and chickens calmed down." But Solly had just reached the cows' pen when the Boesman went off. They were all sledgehammered by the blast, which was louder than a mere explosion, something more basic and fundamental: the violent smash of a whole world shutting the door on them. Deafened, bruised, they staggered up and checked each other for serious injuries, then pacified the cows, whose terrified moos they felt in their hands rather than actually heard. The structural integrity of their tunnel seemed okay; they were in an old flow of the mantle's convection current, now cooled to stasis, and it was plastic enough to take such a blast without shattering. Perfect miners' rock, protecting them like a mother. They lifted up the cows and set them upright on the bottom of the ore car that had been made into the barn. Freeman hurried back down the tunnel to see how the rear of it looked. When he came back their hearing was returning, and through the ringing that would persist for several shifts he shouted, "It's walled off good! Fused!"

So they were in a little tunnel of their own. They fell together in a clump, hugging each other and shouting. "Free at last!" Jakob roared, booming out a laugh louder than anything Oliver had ever heard from him. Then they settled down to the task of turning on an air cylinder and recycler, and regulating their gas exchange.

THEY SOON SETTLED into a routine that moved their tunnel forward as quickly and quietly as possible. One of them operated the robot, digging as narrow a shaft as they could possibly work in. This person used only laser drills unless confronted with extremely hard rock, when it was judged worth the risk to set off small explosions, timed by seismometer to follow closely other detonations back in the mines; Jakob and Naomi hoped that the complex interior of the moon would prevent any listeners from noticing that their explosion was anything more than an echo of the mining blast.

Three of them dealt with the rock freed by the robot's drilling, moving it from the front of the tunnel to its rear, and at intervals pulling up the cars' tracks and bringing them forward. The placement of the loose rock was a serious matter, because if it displaced much more volume than it had at the front of the tunnel, they would eventually fill in all the open space they had; this was the classic problem of the "creeping worm" tunnel. It was necessary to pack the blocks into the space at the rear with an absolute minimum of gaps, in exactly the way they had been cut, like pieces of a puzzle; they all got very good at the craft of this, losing only a few inches of open space in every mile they dug. This work was the hardest both physically and mentally, and each shift of it left Oliver more tired than he had ever been while mining. Because the truth was all of them were working at full speed, and for the middle team it meant almost running, back and forth, back and forth, back and forth... Their little bit of open tunnel was only some sixty yards long, but after a while on the midshift it seemed like five hundred.

The three people not working on the rock tended the air and the livestock, ate, helped out with large blocks and the like, and snatched some sleep. They rotated one at a time through the three stations, and worked one shift (timed by detonator timer) at each post. It made for a routine so mesmerizing in its exhaustiveness that Oliver found it very hard to do his calculations of their position in his shift off. "You've got to keep at it,"

Jakob told him as he ran back from the robot to help the calculating. "It's not just anywhere we want to come up, but right under the domed city of Selene, next to the rocket rails. To do that we'll need some good navigation. We get that and we'll come up right in the middle of the masters who have gotten rich from selling the blue to Earth, and that will be a very gratifying thing I assure you."

So Oliver would work on it until he slept. Actually it was relatively easy; he knew where they had been in the moon when they struck out on their own, and Jakob had given him the surface coordinates for Selene: so it was just a matter of dead reckoning.

It was even possible to calculate their average speed, and therefore when they could expect to reach the surface. That could be checked against the rate of depletion of their fixed resources—air, water lost in the recycler, and food for the livestock. It took a few shifts of consultation with mute Elijah to determine all the factors reliably, and after that it was a simple matter of arithmetic.

When Oliver and Elijah completed these calculations they called Jakob over and explained what they had done.

"Good work," Jakob said. "I should have thought of that."

"But look," Oliver said, "we've got enough air and water, and the robot's power pack is ten times what we'll need—same with explosives—it's only food is a problem. I don't know if we've got enough hay for the cows."

Jakob nodded as he looked over Oliver's shoulder and examined their figures. "We'll have to kill and eat the cows one by one. That'll feed us and cut down on the amount of hay we need, at the same time."

"Eat the cows?" Oliver was stunned.

"Sure! They're meat! People on Earth eat them all the time!"

"Well..." Oliver was doubtful, but under the lash of Hester's bitter laughter he didn't say any more.

Still, Jakob and Freeman and Naomi decided it would be best if they stepped up the pace a little bit, to provide them with more of a margin for error. They shifted two people to the shaft face and supplemented the robot's continuous drilling with hand drill work around the sides of the tunnel, and ate on the run while moving blocks to the back, and slept as little as they could. They were making miles on every shift.

The rock they wormed through began to change in character. The hard, dark, unbroken basalt gave way to lighter rock that was sometimes dangerously fractured. "Anorthosite," Jakob said. "We're reaching the crust." After that every shift brought them through a new zone of rock. Once they tunneled through great layers of calcium feldspar striped with basalt intrusions, so that it looked like badly made brick. Another time they blasted their way through a wall of jasper as hard as steel. Only once did they pass through a vein of the blue; when they did, it occurred to Oliver that his whole conception of the moon's composition had been warped by their mining. He had thought the moon was bursting with promethium, but as they dug across the narrow vein he realized it was uncommon, a loose net of threads in the great lunar body.

As they left the vein behind, Solly picked up a piece of the ore and stared at it curiously, lower eyes shut, face contorted as he struggled to focus his third eye. Suddenly he dashed the chunk to the ground, turned and marched to the head of their tunnel, attacked it with a drill. "I've given my whole life to the blue," he said, voice thick. "And what is it but a goddamned rock."

Jakob laughed shortly. They tunneled on, away from the precious metal that now represented to them only a softer material to dig through. "Pick up the pace!" Jakob cried, slapping Solly on the back and leaping over the blocks beside the robot. "This rock has melted and melted again, changing over eons to the stones we see. Metamorphosis," he chanted, stretching the word out, lingering on the syllable *mor* until the word became a kind of song. "Meta*mor*phosis. Meta-*mor*-pho-sis." Naomi and Hester took up the chant, and mute Elijah tapped his drill against the robot in double time. Jakob chanted over it. "Soon we will come to the city of the masters, the domes of Xanadu with their glass and fruit and steaming pools, and their vases and sports and their fine aged wines. And then there will be a—"

"Meta*mor*phosis."

And they tunneled ever faster.

SITTING IN THE sleeping car, chewing on a cheese, Oliver regarded the bulk of Jakob lying beside him. Jakob breathed deeply, very tired, almost asleep. "How do you know about the domes?" Oliver asked him softly. "How do you know all the things that you know?"

"Don't know," Jakob muttered. "Everyone knows. Less they burn your brain. Put you in a hole to live out your life. I don't know much, boy. Make most of it up. Love of a moon. Whatever we need." And he slept.

THEY CAME UP through a layer of marble—white marble all laced with quartz, so that it gleamed and sparkled in their lightless sight, and made them feel as though they dug through stone made of their cows' good milk, mixed with water like diamonds. This went on for a long time, until it filled them up and they became intoxicated with its smooth muscly texture, with the sparks of light lazing out of it. "I remember once we went to see a jazz band," Jakob said to all of them. Puffing as he ran the white rock along the cars to the rear, stacked it ever so carefully. "It was in Richmond among all the docks and refineries and giant oil tanks and we were so drunk we kept getting lost. But finally we found it—huh!—and it was just this broken-down trumpeter and a back line. He played sitting in a chair and you could just see in his face that his life had been a tough scuffle. His hat covered his whole household. And trumpet is a young man's instrument, too, it tears your lip to tatters. So we sat down to drink not expecting a thing, and they started up the last song of a set. 'Bucket's Got a Hole in It.' Four bar blues, as simple as a song can get."

"Meta*mor*phosis," rasped Hester.

"Yeah! Like that. And this trumpeter started to play it. And they went through it over and over and over. Huh! They must have done it a hundred times. Two hundred times. And sure enough this trumpeter was playing low and half the time in his hat, using all the tricks a broken-down trumpeter uses to save his lip, to hide the fact that it went west thirty years before. But after a while that didn't matter, because he was playing. He was playing! Everything he had learned in all his life, all the music and all the sorry rest of it, all that was jammed into the poor old 'Bucket' and by God it was mind over matter time, because that old song began to *roll*." And still on the run he broke into it:

"Oh the buck-et's got a hole in it— Yeah the buck-et's got a hole in it— Say the buck-et's got a hole in it— Can't buy no beer!"

And over again. Oliver, Solly, Freeman, Hester, Naomi— they couldn't help laughing. What Jakob came up with out of his unburnt past! Mute Elijah banged a car wall happily, then squeezed the udder of a cow between one verse and the next—"Can't buy no beer!—*Moo!*"

They all joined in, breathing or singing it. It fit the pace of their work perfectly: fast but not too fast, regular, repetitive, simple, endless. All the syllables got the same length, a bit syncopated, except "hole," which was stretched out, and "can't buy no beer," which was high and all stretched out, stretched into a great shout of triumph, which was crazy since what it was saying was bad news, or should have been. But the song made it a cry of joy, and every time it rolled around they sang it louder, more stretched out. Jakob scatted up and down and around the tune, and Hester found all kinds of higher harmonics in a voice like a saw cutting steel, and the old tune rocked over and over and over and over and over and over and over and over and over and over, in a great passacaglia, in the crucible where all poverty is wrenched to delight: the blues. Meta*morphosis*. They sang it continuously for two shifts running, until they were all completely hypnotized by it; and then frequently, for long spells, for the rest of their time together.

IT WAS SHEER bad luck that they broke into a shaft from below, and that the shaft was filled with armed foremen; and worse luck that Jakob was working the robot, so that he was the first to leap out firing his hand drill like a weapon, and the only one to get struck by return fire before Naomi threw a knotchopper past him and blew the foremen to shreds. They got him on a car and rolled the robot back and pulled up the track and cut off in a new direction, leaving another Boesman behind to destroy evidence of their passing.

So they were all racing around with the blood and stuff still covering them and the cows mooing in distress and Jakob breathing through clenched teeth in double time, and only Hester and Oliver could sit in the car with him and try to tend him, ripping away the pants from a leg that was all cut up. Hester took a hand drill to cauterize the wounds that were bleeding hard, but Jakob shook his head at her, neck muscles bulging out. "Got the big artery inside of the thigh," he said through his teeth.

Hester hissed. "Come here," she croaked at Solly and the rest. "Stop that and come here!"

They were in a mass of broken quartz, the fractured clear crystals all pink with oxidation. The robot continued drilling away, the air cylinder hissed, the cows mooed. Jakob's breathing was harsh and somehow all of them were also breathing in the same way, irregularly, too fast; so that as his breathing slowed and calmed, theirs did too. He was lying back in the sleeping car, on a bed of hay, staring up at the fractured sparkling quartz ceiling of their tunnel, as if he could see far into it. "All these different kinds of rock," he said, his voice filled with wonder and pain. "You see, the moon itself was the world, once upon a time, and the Earth its moon; but there was an impact, and everything changed."

THEY CUT A small side passage in the quartz and left Jakob there, so that when they filled in their tunnel as they moved on he was left behind, in his own deep crypt. And from then on the moon for them was only his big tomb, rolling through space till the sun itself died, as he had said it someday would.

Oliver got them back on a course, feeling radically uncertain of his navigational calculations now that Jakob was not there to nod over his shoulder to approve them. Dully he gave Naomi and Freeman the coordinates for Selene. "But what will we do when we get there?" Jakob had never actually made that clear. Find the leaders of the city, demand justice for the miners? Kill them? Get to the rockets of the great magnetic rail accelerators, and hijack one to Earth? Try to slip unnoticed into the populace?

"You leave that to us," Naomi said. "Just get us there." And he saw a light in Naomi's and Freeman's eyes that hadn't been there before. It reminded him of the thing that had chased him in the dark, the thing that even Jakob hadn't been able to explain; it frightened him.

So he set the course and they tunneled on as fast as they ever had. They never sang and they rarely talked; they threw themselves at the rock, hurt themselves in the effort, returned to attack it more fiercely than before. When he could not stave off sleep Oliver lay down on Jakob's dried blood, and bitterness filled him like a block of the anorthosite they wrestled with.

They were running out of hay. They killed a cow, ate its roasted flesh. The water recycler's filters were clogging, and their water smelled of urine. Hester listened to the seismometer as often as she could now, and she thought they were being pursued. But she also thought they were approaching Selene's underside.

Naomi laughed, but it wasn't like her old laugh. "You got us there, Oliver. Good work."

Oliver bit back a cry.

"Is it big?" Solly asked.

Hester shook her head. "Doesn't sound like it. Maybe twice the diameter of the Great Bole, not more."

"Good," Freeman said, looking at Naomi.

"But what will we do?" Oliver said.

Hester and Naomi and Freeman and Solly all turned to look at him, eyes blazing like twelve chunks of pure promethium. "We've got eight Boesmans left," Freeman said in a low voice. "All the rest of the explosives add up to a couple more. I'm going to set them just right. It'll be my best work ever, my masterpiece. And we'll blow Selene right off into space."

It took them ten shifts to get all the Boesmans placed to Freeman's and Naomi's satisfaction, and then another three to get far enough down and to one side to be protected from the shock of the blast, which luckily for them was directly upward against something that would give, and therefore would have less recoil.

Finally they were set, and they sat in the sleeping car in a circle of six, around the pile of components that sat under the master detonator. For a long time they just sat there cross-legged, breathing slowly and staring at it. Staring at each other, in the dark, in perfect red-black clarity. Then Naomi put both arms out, placed her hands carefully on the detonator's button. Mute Elijah put his hands on hers—then Freeman, Hester, Solly, finally Oliver—just in the order that Jakob had taken them. Oliver hesitated, feeling the flesh and bone under his hands, the warmth of his companions. He felt they should say something but he didn't know what it was.

"Seven," Hester croaked suddenly.

"Six," Freeman said.

Elijah blew air through his teeth, hard.

"Four," said Naomi.

"Three!" Solly cried.

"Two," Oliver said.

And they all waited a beat, swallowing hard, waiting for the moon and the man in the moon to speak to them. Then they pressed down on the button. They smashed at it with their fists, hit it so violently they scarcely felt the shock of the explosion.

\* \* \*

THEY HAD PUT on vacuum suits and were breathing pure oxygen as they came up the last tunnel, clearing it of rubble. A great number of other shafts were revealed as they moved into the huge conical cavity left by the Boesmans; tunnels snaked away from the cavity in all directions, so that they had sudden long vistas of blasted tubes extending off into the depths of the moon they had come out of. And at the top of the cavity, struggling over its broken edge, over the rounded wall of a new crater...

It was black. It was not like rock. Spread across it was a spill of white points, some bright, some so faint that they disappeared into the black if you looked straight at them. There were thousands of these white points, scattered over a black dome that was not a dome... And there in the middle, almost directly overhead: a blue and white ball. Big, bright, blue, distant, rounded; half of it bright as a foreman's flash, the other half just a shadow... It was clearly round, a big ball in the... sky. In the sky.

Wordlessly they stood on the great pile of rubble ringing the edge of their hole. Half buried in the broken anorthosite were shards of clear plastic, steel struts, patches of green glass, fragments of metal, an arm, broken branches, a bit of orange ceramic. Heads back to stare at the ball in the sky, at the astonishing fact of the void, they scarcely noticed these things.

A long time passed, and none of them moved except to look around. Past the jumble of dark trash that had mostly been thrown off in a single direction, the surface of the moon was an immense expanse of white hills, as strange and glorious as the stars above. The size of it all! Oliver had never dreamed that everything could be so big.

"The blue must be promethium," Solly said, pointing up at the Earth. "They've covered the whole Earth with the blue we mined."

Their mouths hung open as they stared at it. "How far away is it?" Freeman asked. No one answered.

"There they all are," Solly said. He laughed harshly. "I wish I could blow up the Earth too!"

He walked in circles on the rubble of the crater's rim. The rocket rails, Oliver thought suddenly, must have been in the direction Freeman had sent the debris. Bad luck. The final upward sweep of them poked up out of the dark dirt and glass. Solly pointed at them. His voice was loud in Oliver's ears, it strained the intercom: "Too bad we can't fly to the Earth, and blow it up too! I wish we could!"

And mute Elijah took a few steps, leaped off the mound into the sky, took a swipe with one hand at the blue ball. They laughed at him. "Almost got it, didn't you!" Freeman and Solly tried themselves, and then they all did: taking quick runs, leaping, flying slowly up through space, for five or six or seven seconds, making a grab at the sky overhead, floating back down as if in a dream, to land in a tumble, and try it again... It felt wonderful to hang up there at the top of the leap, free in the vacuum, free of gravity and everything else, for just that instant.

After a while they sat down on the new crater's rim, covered with white dust and black dirt. Oliver sat on the very edge of the crater, legs over the edge, so that he could see back down into their sublunar world, at the same time that he looked up into the sky. Three eyes were not enough to judge such immensities. His heart pounded, he felt too intoxicated to move anymore. Tired, drunk. The intercom rasped with the sounds of their breathing, which slowly calmed, fell into a rhythm together. Hester buzzed one phrase of "Bucket" and they laughed softly. They lay back on the rubble, all but Oliver, and stared up into the dizzy reaches of the universe, the velvet black of infinity. Oliver sat with elbows on knees, watched the white hills glowing under the black sky. They were lit by earthlight—earth-light and starlight. The white mountains on the horizon were as sharp-edged as the shards of dome glass sticking out of the rock. And all the time the Earth looked down at him. It was all too fantastic to believe. He drank it in like oxygen, felt it filling him up, expanding in his chest.

"What do you think they'll do with us when they get here?" Solly asked.

"Kill us," Hester croaked.

"Or put us back to work," Naomi added.

Oliver laughed. Whatever happened, it was impossible in that moment to care. For above them a milky spill of stars lay thrown across the infinite black sky, lighting a million better worlds; while just over their heads the Earth glowed like a fine blue lamp; and under their feet rolled the white hills of the happy moon, holed like a great cheese.

# THE ARCEVOALO

*Lucius Shepard*

ONE MORNING NEARLY 500 years after the September War, whose effects had transformed the Amazon into a region of supernal mystery, a young man with olive skin and delicate features and short black hair awoke to find himself lying amid a bed of ferns not far from the ruined city of Manaus. It seemed to him that some great darkness had just been lifted away, but he could recall nothing more concrete of his past, neither his name nor those of his parents or place of birth. Indeed, he was so lacking in human referents that he remained untroubled by this state of affairs and gazed calmly around at the high green canopy and the dust-hung shafts of sun and the tapestry of golden radiance and shadow overlying the jungle floor. Everywhere he turned he saw marvelous creatures: butterflies with translucent wings; birds with hinged, needle-thin beaks; snakes with faceted eyes that glowed more brightly than live coals. Yet the object that commanded his attention was a common orchid, its bloom a dusky lavender, that depended from the lowermost branch of a guanacaste tree. The sight mesmerized him, and intuitions about the orchid flowed into his thoughts: how soft its petals were, how subtle its fragrance, and, lastly, that it was not what it appeared to be. At that moment, as if realizing that he had penetrated its disguise, the bloom flew apart, revealing itself to have been composed of glittering insects, all of which now whirled off toward the canopy, shifting in color like particles of an exploded rainbow; and the young man understood—a further intuition—that he, too, was not what he appeared.

Puzzled, and somewhat afraid, he glanced down at the ferns and saw scattered among them pieces of a fibrous black husk. Upon examining them, he discovered that the insides of the pieces were figured by smooth indentations that conformed exactly to the shapes of his face and limbs. There could be no doubt that prior to his awakening, he had been enclosed within the husk like a seed in its casing. His anxiety increased when—on setting down one of the pieces—his fingers brushed the clay beneath the ferns and he saw before his mind's eye the pitching deck of a vast wooden ship, with wild seas bursting over the railings. Men wearing steel helmets and carrying pikes were huddled in the bow, and standing in the door that led to the gun decks (how had he known that?) was a gray-haired man who beckoned to him. To him? No, to someone he had partly been. Joao Merin Nascimento. That name—like his vision of the ship—surfaced in his thoughts following contact with the clay. And with the name came a thousand fragments of memory, sufficient to make the young man realize that Nascimento, a Portuguese soldier of centuries past, lay buried beneath the spot where he was sitting, and that he was in essence the reincarnation of the old soldier: for just as the toxins and radiations of the September War had transformed the jungle, so the changed jungle had worked a process of alchemy on those ancient bones and produced a new creature, human to a degree, yet—to a greater degree—quite inhuman. Understanding this eased the young man's anxiety, because he now knew that he was safe in the dominion of the jungle, whose creature he truly was. But he understood, too, that his manlike form embodied a cunning purpose, and in hopes of discerning that purpose, he set out to explore the jungle, walking along a trail that led (though he was not aware of it) to the ruins of Manaus.

Nine days he walked, and during those days he learned much about the jungle's character and—consequently—about his own. From a creature with a dozen bodies, each identical, yet only one of which contained its vital spark, he learned an ultimate caution; from the malgaton, a fierce jaguar-like beast whose strange eyes could make a man dream of pleasure while he died, he learned the need for circumspection in the cause of violence; from the deadly jicaparee vine with its exquisite flowers, he learned the importance of setting a lure and gained an appreciation of the feral principles underlying all beauty.

From each of these creatures and more, he learned that no living thing is without its parasites and symbiotes, and that in the moment they are born their death is also born. But not until he came in sight of the ruined city, when he saw its crumbling, vine-draped towers tilting above the canopy like grotesque vegetable chessmen whose board was in process of being overthrown, not until then did he at last fathom his purpose: that he was to be the jungle's weapon against mankind, its mortal enemy who time and again had sought to destroy it.

The young man could not conceive how—fangless and clawless—he would prove a threat to an enemy with weapons that had poisoned a world. Perplexed, hoping some further illumination would strike him, he took to wandering the city streets, over cracked flagstones between which he could see the tunnels of guerrilla ants, past ornate wrought-iron streetlamps in whose fractured globes white phosphorescent spiders the size of skull crabs had spun their webs (by night their soft glow conveyed a semblance of the city's fabulous heyday into this, its rotting decline), and through the cavernous mansions of the wealthy dead. Everywhere he wandered he encountered danger, for Manaus had been heavily dusted during the September War and thus was home to the most perverse of the jungle's mutations: flying lizards that spit streams of venom; albino peacocks whose shrill cries could make a man bleed from the ears; the sortilene, a mysterious creature never glimpsed by human eyes, known only by the horrid malignancies that sprouted from the flesh of its victims; herds of peccaries, superficially unchanged but possessing vocal chords that could duplicate the cries of despairing women. At night an enormous shadow obscured the stars, testifying to an even more dire presence. Yet none of these creatures troubled the young man—they seemed to know him for an ally. And, indeed, often as he explored the gloomy interiors of the ruined houses, he would see hundreds of eyes gazing at him, slit pupils and round, showing all colors like a spectrum of stars ranging the dusky green shade, and then he would have the idea that they were watching over him.

At length he entered the lobby of a hotel that—judging by the sumptuous rags of its drapes, the silver-cloth stripe visible in the moss-furred wallpaper, the immensity of the reception desk—must once have been a palace among hotels. Thousands of slitherings stilled when he entered. The dark green shadows seemed the visual expression of a cloying mustiness, one redolent of a thousand insignificant deaths. His footsteps shaking loose falls of plaster dust, he walked along the main hallway, past elevator shafts choked with vines and epiphytes, and came eventually to a foyer whose roof was holed in such a fashion that sharply defined sunbeams hung down from it, dappling the scummy surface of an ornamental pond with coins of golden light. There, sitting naked and cross-legged on a large lily pad—the sort that once hampered navigation on the Rio Negro due to the toughness of its fiber—was an old Indian man, so wizened that he appeared to be a homunculus. His eyes were closed, his white hair filthy and matted, and his coppery skin bore a greenish tinge (whether this was natural coloration or a product of the shadows, the young man could not determine). The young man expected intuitions about the Indian to flow into his thoughts; but when this did not occur, he realized that though the Indians, too, had been changed by the September War, though they were partially the jungle's creatures, they were still men, and the jungle had no knowledge of men other than that it derived from the bones of the dead. How then, he wondered, could he defeat an enemy about whom he was ignorant? He stretched out a hand to the Indian, thinking a touch might transmit some bit of information. But the Indian's eyes blinked open, and with a furious splashing he paddled the lily pad beyond the young man's reach. "The arcevoalo must be cautious with his touch," he said in a creaky voice that seemed to stir the atoms of the dust within the sunbeams. "Haven't you learned that?"

Though the young man—the arcevoalo—had not heard his name before, he recognized it immediately. With its Latinate echoes of wings and arcs, it spoke to him of the life he would lead. How he would soar briefly through the world of men and then return to give his knowledge of them to the jungle. Knowing his name opened him to his full strength—he felt it flooding him like a golden heat— and served to align his character more precisely with that of the jungle. He stared down at the Indian, who now struck him as being wholly alien, and asked how *he* had known the name.

"This truth I have eaten has told it to me," said the Indian, holding up a pouch containing a quantity of white powder. Grains of it adhered to his fingers. "I was called here to speak the truth to someone... doubtless to you. But now I must leave." He slipped off the lily pad and waded toward the edge of the pond.

Moving so quickly that he caused the merest flutter of shadow upon the surface of the water, the arcevoalo leaped to the far side of the pond, blocking the Indian's path. "What is this 'truth'?" he asked. "And who called you here?"

"The powder derives from the asuero flower," said the Indian. "A plant fertilized with the blood of honest men. As to who called me, if I had known that I might not have come." He made as if to haul himself from the pond, but the arcevoalo stayed him.

"How must I go about conquering my enemy?" he asked.

"To do battle one must first understand the foe."

"Then I will keep you with me and learn your ways," countered the arcevoalo.

The Indian hissed impatiently. "I am as different from those you must understand as you are from me. You must go to the city of Sangue do Lume. It is a new city, inhabited by Brazilians who fled the September War. Until recently they dwelled in metal worlds that circle the darkness behind the sky. Now they have returned to claim their ancient holdings, to reap the fruits of the jungle and to kill its animals for profit. It is they with whom you will contend."

"How will I contend? I have no weapons."

"You have speed and strength," said the Indian. "But your greatest weapon is a mere touch."

He instructed the arcevoalo to press the pads of his fingers hard, and when he did droplets of clear fluid welled from beneath the nails.

"A single drop will enslave any man's heart for a time," said the Indian. "But you must use this power sparingly, for your body can produce the fluid only in a limited quantity."

He flicked his eyes nervously from side to side, obviously afraid, eager to be gone. The arcevoalo continued to ask questions, but the effects of the "truth" drug were wearing off, and the Indian began to whine and to lie, saying that his cousin, whom he had not seen since the Year of Fabulous Sorrows, was coming to visit and he would be remiss if he were not home to greet him. With a wave of his hand, the arcevoalo dismissed him, and the Indian went scuttling away toward the lobby.

For a long time the arcevoalo stood beside the pond, thinking about what the Indian had said, watching the sunlight fade; in its stead a gray-green dusk filtered down from the holes in the roof. Soon he felt himself dimming, his thoughts growing slow, his blood sluggish, his muscles draining of strength: it was as if the dusk were also taking place inside his soul and body, and a gray-green fluid seeping into him and making him terribly weak and vague, incapable of movement. He saw that from every crack and cranny, jeweled eyes and scaly snouts and tendrilled mouths were peering and thrusting and gaping. And in this manifold scrutiny, he sensed the infinitude of lives for whom he was to be the standard-bearer: those creatures in the ruined foyer were but the innermost ring of an audience focused upon him from every corner of the jungle. He apprehended them singly and as one, and from the combined intelligence of their regard he understood that dusk for him was an hour during which he must be solitary, both to hide from men the weakness brought on by the transition from light to dark, and to commune with the source of his imperatives. Dusk thickened to night, shafts of silvery moonlight shone down to replace those of the sun, which now burned over Africa, and with the darkness a new moon of power rose inside the arcevoalo, a silver strength equal yet distinct from the golden strength he possessed by day, geared more to elusiveness than to acts of domination. Freed of his intangible bonds, he walked from the hotel and set forth to find Sangue do Lume.

DURING THE TWENTY-SEVEN days it took the arcevoalo to reach Sangue do Lume—which means "Blood of Light" in Portuguese, which is the language of sanguinary pleasures and heartbreak—he tested himself against the jungle. He outran the malgaton, outclimbed the tarzanal, and successfully spied upon the mysterious sortilene. He tested himself joyfully, and perhaps he never came to be happier than he was in those days, living in a harmony of green light and birds by day, and by night gazing into the ruby eyes of a malgaton, into those curious pupils that flickered and changed shape and brought the comfort of dreams. One evening he scaled a peak, hoping to lure down the huge shadow that each night obscured the stars, and when it flew near he saw that it was almost literally a shadow, being millimeters thick and having neither eyes nor mouth nor any feature that he could discern. There was something familiar about it, and he sensed that it was interested in him, that it—like him—was the sole member of its species. But otherwise it remained a puzzle: a rippling field of opaque darkness as incomprehensible as a flat black thought.

Sangue do Lume lay in a hilly valley between three mountains and was modeled after the old colonial towns, with cobbled streets and white stucco houses that had ironwork balconies and tiled roofs and gardens in their courtyards. Surrounding it—also after the style of the old colonial towns—was a slum where lived the laborers who had built the city. And surrounding the slum was a high wall of gray metal from which energy weapons were aimed at the jungle (no such weapons, however, were permitted within the wall). Despite the aesthetic incompatibility of its defenses, the city was beautiful, beautiful even to the eyes of the arcevoalo as he studied it from afar. He could not understand why it seemed so, being the home of his enemy; but he was later to learn that the walls of the houses contained machines that refined the images of the real, causing the visual aspect of every object to tend toward the ideal. Thus it was that the precise indigo shadows were in actuality blurred and dead-black; thus it was that women who went beyond the walls veiled themselves to prevent their husbands from taking note of their coarsened appearance; thus it was that the flies and rats and other pests of Sangue do Lume possessed a certain eye-catching appeal.

Each morning dozens of ships shaped like flat arrow-points would lift from the city and fly off across the jungle; each afternoon they would return, their holds filled with dead plants and bloody carcasses, which would be unloaded into slots in the metal wall, presumably for testing. Seeing this, the arcevoalo grew enraged. Still, he bided his time and studied the city's ways, and it was not until a week after his arrival that he finally went down to the gate. The gatekeepers were amazed to see a naked man walk out of the jungle and were at first suspicious, but he told them a convincing tale of childhood abandonment (a childhood of which, he said, he could recall only his name—Joao Merin Nascimento), of endless wandering and narrow escapes, and soon the gatekeepers, their eyes moist with pity, admitted him and brought him before the governor, Caudez do Tuscanduva: a burly, middle-agèd man with fierce black eyes and a piratical black beard and skin the color of sandalwood. The audience was brief, for the governor was a busy and a practical man, and when he discovered the arcevoalo's knowledge of the jungle, he assigned him to work on the flying ships and gave orders that every measure should be taken to ensure his comfort.

Such was the arcevoalo's novelty that all the best families clamored to provide him with food and shelter, and thus it was deemed strange that Caudez do Tuscanduva chose to quarter him in the Valverde house. The Valverdes were involved in a long-standing blood feud with the governor, one initiated years before upon the worlds behind the sky. The governor had been constrained by his vows of office from settling the matter violently, and it was assumed that this conferring of an honored guest must be his way of making peace. But the Valverdes themselves were not wholly persuaded by the idea, and therefore—

with the exception of Orlando, the eldest son—they maintained an aloof stance toward the arcevoalo. Orlando piloted one of the ships that plundered the jungle, and it was to his ship that the arcevoalo had been assigned. He realized that by assisting in this work he would better understand his enemy, and so he did the work well, using his knowledge to track down the malgaton and the sortilene and creatures even more elusive. Yet it dismayed him, nonetheless. And what most dismayed him was the fact that as the weeks went by, he began to derive a human satisfaction from a job well done and to cherish his growing friendship with Orlando, who, by virtue of his delicate features and olive skin, might have been the arcevoalo's close relation.

Orlando was typical of the citizenry in his attitude of divine right concerning the land, in his arrogance toward the poor ("They are eternal," he once said. "You'll sooner find a cure for death than for poverty."), and in his single-minded pursuit of pleasure; yet there was about him a courage and soulfulness that gained the arcevoalo's respect. On most nights he and Orlando would dress in black trousers and blousy silk shirts, and would join similarly dressed young men by the fountain in the main square. There they would practise at dueling with the knife and the cintral (a jungle weed with sharp-edged tendrils and a rudimentary nervous system that could be employed as a living cat-o'-ninetails), while the young women would promenade around them and cast shy glances at their favorites. The arcevoalo pretended clumsiness with the weapons, not wanting to display his speed and strength, and he was therefore often the subject of ridicule. This was just as well, for occasionally these play-duels would escalate, and then—since even death was beautiful in Sangue do Lume—blood would eel across the cobblestones, assuming lovely serpentine forms, and the palms ringing the square would rustle their fronds, and sad music would issue from the fountain, mingling with the splash of the waters.

Many of these duels stemmed from disputes over the affections of the governor's daughter, Sylvana, the sole child of his dead wife, his pride and joy. The bond between father and daughter was of such intimacy, it was said that should one's heart stop, the other would not long survive. Sylvana was pale, slim, blonde, and angelic of countenance, but was afflicted by a brittleness of expression that bespoke coldness and insensitivity. Observing this, the arcevoalo was led to ask Orlando why the young men would risk themselves for so heartless a prize. Orlando laughed and said, "How can you understand when you have no experience of women?" And he invited the arcevoalo to gain this experience by coming with him to the Favelin, which was the name of the slum surrounding the city.

The next night, Orlando and the arcevoalo entered the cluttered, smelly streets of the Favelin. The hovels there were made of rotting boards, pitched like wreckage at every angle; and were populated by a malnourished, shrunken folk who looked to be of a different species from Orlando. Twists of oily smoke fumed from the chimneys; feathered lizards slept in the dirt next to grimy children; hags in black shawls sacrificed pigs beneath glass bells full of luminescent fungus and scrawled bloody words in the dust to cure the sick. How ugly all this might have been beyond the range of the city's machines, the arcevoalo could not conceive. They came to a street whereon the doors were hung with red curtains, and Orlando ushered him through one of these and into a room furnished with a pallet and a chair. Mounted on the wall was the holograph of a bearded man who—though the cross to which he was nailed had burst into emerald flames—had maintained a beatific expression. The flames shed a ghastly light over a skinny girl lying on a pallet. She was hollow-cheeked, with large, empty-looking eyes and jaundiced skin and ragged dark hair. Orlando whispered to her, gave her a coin, and—grinning as he prepared to leave—said, "Her name is Ana."

Without altering her glum expression. Ana stood and removed her shift. Her breasts had the convexity of upturned saucers, her ribs showed, and her genitals were almost hairless. Nevertheless, the arcevoalo became aroused, and when he sank down onto the pallet and entered her, he felt a rush of dominance and joy that roared through him like a whirlwind. He clutched at Ana's hips with all his strength, building toward completion. And staring into her hopeless eyes, he sensed the profound alienness of women, their mystical endurance, the eerie valences of their moods, and how even their common thoughts turn hidden corners into bizarre mental worlds. Knowing his dominance over this peculiar segment of humanity acted to heighten his desire, and with a hoarse cry he fell spent beside Ana and into a deep sleep.

He awoke to find her gazing at him with a look of such rapt contemplation that when she turned her eyes away, the image of his face remained reflected in her pupils. Timorously, shyly, she asked if he planned to return to the Favelin, to her. He recalled then the force with which he had clutched her, and he inspected the tips of his fingers. Droplets glistened beneath the nails, and there were damp bruises on Ana's hips. He realized that his touch, his secret chemistry, had manifested as love, an emotion whose power he apprehended but whose nature he did not understand. "Will you return?" she asked again. "Yes," he said, feeling pity for her.

"Tomorrow." And he did return, many times, for in his loveless domination of that wretched girl he had taken a step closer to adopting the ways of man. He had come to see that there was little difference between the city and the jungle, that "civilization" was merely a name given to comfort, and that the process of life in Sangue do Lume obeyed the same uncivilized laws as did the excesses of the sortilene. What point was there in warring against man? And, in any case, how could he win such a war? His touch was a useless power against an enemy who could summon countless allies from its worlds behind the sky.

Over the ensuing weeks the arcevoalo grew ever more despondent, and in the throes of despondency the human elements of his soul grew more and more predominant. At dusk his reverie was troubled by images of lust and conquest stirred from the memories of Joao Merin Nascimento. And his work aboard Orlando's ship became so proficient that Caudez do Tuscanduva held a fete in his honor, a night of delirium and pleasure during which a constellation of his profile appeared in the sky, and the swaying of the palms was choreographed by artificial winds, and the machines within the walls were turned high, beautifying everyone to such an extent that everyone's heart was broken... broken, and then healed by the consumption of tiny, soft-boned animals that induced a narcissistic ecstasy when eaten alive. Despite his revulsion for this practice, the arcevoalo indulged in it, and, his teeth stained with blood, he spent the remainder of the night wandering the incomparably beautiful streets and gazing longingly at himself in mirrors.

Thereafter Caudez do Tuscanduva took Orlando and the arcevoalo under his wing, telling them they were to be his protégés, that he had great plans for them.

Further, he urged them to pay court to Sylvana, saying that, yes, she was an icy sort, but the right man would be able to thaw her. In this Orlando needed no urging. He plied her with gifts and composed lyrics to her charms. But Sylvana was disdainful of his efforts, and though for the most part she was equally disdainful of the arcevoalo, now and then she would favor him with a chilly smile, which—while scarcely encouraging—made Orlando quite jealous.

"You'd do better to set your sights elsewhere," the arcevoalo once told Orlando. "Even if you win her, you'll regret it. She's the kind of woman who uses marriage like a vise, and before you know it she'll have you squealing like a stuck pig." He had no idea whether or not this was true—it was something he had overheard another disappointed suitor say—but it accorded with his own impressions of her. He believed that Orlando was leaving himself open to the possibility of grievous hurt, and he told him as much. No matter how forcefully he argued, though, Orlando refused to listen.

"I know you're only trying to protect me, friend," he said. "And perhaps you're right. But this is an affair of the heart, and the heart is ruled by its own counsel."

And so the arcevoalo could do nothing more than to step aside and let Orlando have a clear field with Sylvana.

On one occasion Caudez invited them to dine at the governor's mansion. They sat at a long mahogany table graced by golden candelabra through whose branches the arcevoalo watched Sylvana daintily picking at her food, ignoring the heated glances that Orlando sent her way. After the meal, Caudez led them into his study, its windows open onto the orchid-spangled courtyard where Sylvana could be seen strolling—as elegant as an orchid herself—and held forth on his scheme to milk the resources of the Amazon: how he would reopen the gold mines at Serra Pelada, reinstitute the extensive farming procedures that once had brought an unparalleled harvest, and thus feed and finance hundreds of new orbital colonies. Orlando's attention was fixed upon Sylvana, but the arcevoalo listened closely. Caudez, with his piratical air and his dream of transforming the Amazon into a tame backyard, struck him as being a force equal to the jungle. Pacing up and down, declaiming about the glorious future, Caudez seemed to walk with the pride of a continent. Late in the evening he turned his fierce black stare upon the arcevoalo and questioned him about his past. The questions were complex, fraught with opportunities for the arcevoalo to compromise the secret of his birth; he had to summon all his wits to avoid these pitfalls, and he wondered if Caudez were suspicious of him. But then Caudez laughed and clapped him on the shoulder, saying what a marvel he was, and that allayed his fears.

WHEREAS IN THE jungle, time passed in a dark green flow, a single fluid moment infinitely prolonged, within the walls of Sangue do Lume it passed in sharply delineated segments so that occasionally one would become alerted to the fact that a certain period had elapsed— this due to the minuscule interruptions in the flow of time caused by the instruments men have for measuring it. And thus it was that one morning the arcevoalo awoke to the realization that he had lived in the city for a year. A year! And what progress had he made? His life, which had once had the form of purpose, of a quest, had resolved into a passive shape defined by his associations: his friendship with Orlando (whose wooing of Sylvana had reached fever pitch), his sexual encounters with Ana, his apprenticeship to Caudez. Each night he was reminded of his deeper associations with the jungle by the huge shadow that obscured the stars, yet he felt trapped between the two worlds, at home in neither, incapable of effecting any change. He might have continued at this impasse had not Ana announced to him one evening that she was with child. It would be, according to the old woman who had listened to her belly, a son. Standing in the garish light of her burning Christ, displaying her new roundness, flushed with a love no longer dependent on his touch, she presented him with a choice he could not avoid making. If he did nothing, his son would be born into the world of men; he had to be certain this was right.

But how could he decide such a complex issue, one that had baffled him for an entire year?

At the point of desperation, he remembered the old Indian man and his "truth," and that same night, after the machines in the walls had been switched off, leaving the flaking whitewash of the buildings exposed, he sneaked into the warehouse where the plant samples were kept and pilfered a quantity of asuero flowers. He returned to the Valverde house, ground the petals into a fine powder, and ate the entire amount. Soon pearls of sweat beaded on his forehead, his limbs trembled, and the moonlight flooding his room appeared to grow brighter than day.

Truth came to him in the clarity of his vision. Between the floorboards he saw microscopic insects and plants, and darting through the air were even tinier incidences of life. From these sights he understood anew that the city and the jungle were interpenetrating. Just as the ruins of Manaus lay beneath the foliage, so did the jungle's skeins infiltrate the living city. One was not good, the other evil. They were two halves of a whole, and the war between them was not truly a war but an everlasting pattern, a game in which he was a powerful pawn moved from the grotesque chessboard of Manaus to the neat squares of Sangue do Lume, a move that had set in motion a pawn of perhaps even greater power: his son. He realized now that no matter with which side he cast his lot, his son would make the opposite choice, for it was an immutable truth that fathers and sons go contrary to the other's will. Thus he had to make his own choice according to the dictates of his soul. A soul in confusion. And to dissolve that confusion, to know his options fully, he had to complete his knowledge of man by understanding the nature of love. He thought first of going to Ana, of infecting himself with the chemicals of his touch and falling under her spell; but then he recognized that the kind of love he sought to understand—the all-consuming love that motivates and destroys—had to embody the quality of the unattainable. With this in mind, still trembling from the fevers of the asuero powder, he went out again into the night and headed toward the governor's mansion, toward the unattainable Sylvana.

Since the concept of security in Sangue do Lume was chiefly geared to keeping the jungle out, the systems protecting the mansion were minimal, easily penetrated by a creature of the arcevoalo's stealth. He crept up the stairs, along the hall, cracked Sylvana's door, and eased inside. As was the custom with high-born women of the city, she was sleeping nude beneath a skylight through which the rays of the moon shone down in a silvery fan. A diamond pulsed coldly in the hollow of her throat, a tourmaline winked between her breasts, and in the tuft of her secret hair—trimmed to the shape of an orchid— an emerald shimmered wetly. These gems were bound in place by silken threads and were no ordinary stones but crystalline machines that focused the moonlight downward to produce a salubrious effect upon the organs, and also served as telltales of those organs' health. The unclouded states of the emerald, the tourmaline, and the diamond testified that Sylvana was virginal and of sound heart and respiration. But she was so lovely that the arcevoalo would not have cared if the stones had been black, signaling wantonness and infection. Rivulets of blonde hair streamed over her porcelain shoulders, and the soft brush of sleep had smoothed away her brittleness of expression, giving her the look of an angel under an enchantment.

Fixing his gaze upon her, the arcevoalo gripped his left forearm with the fingers of his right hand and pressed down hard. He maintained the grip for some time, uncertain how much of the chemical would be needed to affect him—indeed, he was uncertain whether or not he could be affected. But soon he felt a languorous sensation that made his eyelids droop and stilled the trembling caused by the asuero powder. When he opened his eyes, the sight of the naked Sylvana pierced him: it was as if an essential color had all along been missing from his portrait of her. Staring at her through the doubled lens of truth and love, he knew her coldness, her cunning and duplicity; yet he perceived these flaws in the way he might have perceived the fracture planes inside a crystal, how they channeled the light to create a lovely illusion of depth and complexity. Faint with desire, he walked over to the bed. A branching of bluish veins spread from the tops of her breasts, twined together and vanished beneath the diamond in the hollow of her throat, as if deriving sustenance from the stone; a tiny mole lay like a drop of obsidian by the corner of her lips. Carefully, knowing she could never truly love him, yet willing to risk his life to have her love this one and false time, he stretched out a hand and clamped it over Sylvana's mouth, while with the other hand he gripped her shoulder hard. Her eyes shot open, she squealed and kicked and clawed. He held her firmly, waiting for the chemistry of love to take effect. But it did not. Astounded, he examined his fingertips. They were dry, and he realized that in his urgency to know love he had exhausted the potency of his touch. He was full of despair, knowing he would have to flee the city... but then Sylvana's struggles ceased. The panic in her eyes softened, and she drew him into an embrace, whispering that her fearful reaction was due to the shock of being awakened so roughly, that she had been hoping for this moment ever since they had met. And with the power of truth which—though diminished by the truth of love—still allowed him a modicum of clear sight, the arcevoalo saw that, indeed, she had been hoping for this moment. She seemed charged with desire, overwhelmed by a passion no less ardent than his. But when he entered her, sinking into her plush warmth, he felt a nugget of chill against his belly; he knew it was the diamond bound by its silken thread, yet he could not help thinking of it as a node of her quintessential self that not even love could dissolve.

Some hours later, after the power of truth had been drained from the arcevoalo, Sylvana spoke to him. "Leave me," she said. "I have no more use for you." She was standing by the open door, smiling at him; the threads of her telltale jewels dangled from her right hand.

"What do you mean?" he asked. "What use have you made of me?" He was shocked by the wealth of cruelty in her smile, by her transformation from the voluptuous, the soft, into this glacial creature with glittering eyes.

She laughed—a thin, hard laugh that seemed to chart the jagged edge of such a vengeful thought. "I've never known such a fool," she said. "It's hard to believe you're even a man. I wondered if I'd have to drag you into my bed."

Again she laughed, and, suddenly afraid, the arcevoalo pulled on his clothes and ran, her derisive laughter chasing him down the hall and out into the dove-gray dawn of Sangue do Lume, whose machines were already beginning to restore a fraudulent perfection to its flaking walls.

ALL THAT DAY the arcevoalo kept to his room in the Valverde house. He knew he should leave the city before Sylvana called down judgment upon him, but he found that he could not leave her, no matter how little affection she had for him. He understood now the nature of love, its blurred, irrational compulsions, its torments and its joys, and he doubted it would ever loosen its grip on him. But understanding it had made his choice no easier, and so perhaps he did not entirely understand, perhaps he did not see that love enforces its own continuum of choices, even upon an inhuman celebrant. There was no end to his confusion. One moment he would feel drawn back to the jungle, the next he would wonder how he could have considered such a reckless course. At dusk his reverie alternated between a perception of formless urges and a sequence of memories in which Joao Merin Nascimento staggered through a green hell, his brain afire and death a poisoned sugar clotting his veins. Night fell, and having some frail hope that Sylvana would do nothing, that things might go on as before, the arcevoalo left the house and walked toward the main square.

Though it was no holiday, though no fete had been scheduled, of all the beautiful nights in Sangue do Lume, this night came the closest to perfection, marred only by the whining of the machines functioning at peak levels. In the square the palm crowns flickered like green torches beneath an unequalled array of stars, and beams of light from the windows shone like benedictions upon the fountain, whose spouts cast up sprays of silver droplets that fell to the ear as a cascade of guitar notes. Against the backdrop of gray stones and white stucco, the graceful attitudes of the young men and women, strolling and dueling, lost in a haze of mutual admiration, seemed a tapestry come to life. Even the arcevoalo's grim mood was brightened by the scene, but on drawing near the group of young men gathered about Orlando, on hearing Orlando's boastful voice, his mood darkened once again.

"... his blessing to Sylvana and I," Orlando was saying. "We'll be wed during the Festival of Erzulie."

The arcevoalo pushed through the group of listeners and confronted Orlando, too enraged to speak. Orlando put a hand on his shoulder. "My friend!" he said. "Great news!" But the arcevoalo struck his hand aside and said, "Your news is a lie! You will never marry her!"

It may have been that Orlando thought his friend was still trying to protect him from a loveless marriage, for he said, "Don't worry..."

"It's I who made love to her last night," the arcevoalo cut in. "And it's I who'll marry her."

Orlando reached for his cintral, whose green tendrils were dangling over the edge of the fountain; but he hesitated. Perhaps it was friendship that stayed his hand, or perhaps he believed that the arcevoalo's friendship was so great that he would lie and risk a duel to prevent the marriage.

Then a woman laughed—a thin derisive laugh.

The arcevoalo turned and saw Sylvana and Caudez standing a dozen feet away. Hanging from a gold chain about Sylvana's neck was her telltale emerald, its blackness expressing the malefic use she had made of her body the previous night. Caudez was smiling, a crescent of white teeth showing forth from his thicket of a beard.

Finally convinced that his friend had told the truth, Orlando's face twisted into an aggrieved knot, displaying his humiliation and pain. He picked up the cintral and lashed out at the arcevoalo. The sharp tendrils slithered through the air like liquid green swords; but at the last second—recognizing their ally—they veered aside, spasmed, and drooped lifelessly from Orlando's hand. His mind a boil of rage, unable by logic to direct his anger toward his true enemy, the arcevoalo plucked a knife from a bystander's sash and plunged it deep into Orlando's chest. As Orlando toppled onto his back, a hush fell over the assemblage, for never had they witnessed a death more beautiful than that of the Valverdes' eldest son. The palms inclined their spiky heads, the fountain wept tears of crystalline music. Orlando's features acquired a noble rectitude they had not had in life; his blood shone with a saintly radiance and appeared to be spelling out a new language of poetry over the cobblestones.

"Now!" cried Caudez do Tuscanduva, his black eyes throwing off glints that were no reflections but sparks of an inner fire banked high. "Now has the great wrong done to my father by the House of Valverde been avenged! And not by my hand!"

Murmurs of admiration for the subtlety of his vengeance spread through the crowd. But the arcevoalo—gone cold with the horror of his act, full of self-loathing at having allowed himself to be manipulated—advanced upon Caudez and Sylvana, his knife at the ready.

"Kill him!" shouted Caudez, exhorting the young men. "I have no quarrel with his choice of victims, but he has

struck down a man whose weapon failed him. Such cowardice must not go unpunished!"

And the young men, who had always suspected the
arcevoalo of being lowborn and thus had no love for him,
ranged themselves in front of Caudez and Sylvana, posing
a barrier of grim faces and shining knives.

When men refer to the arcevoalo, they speak not only of
the one who stood then beside the fountain, but also of his
incarnations, and they will tell you that none of these ever
fought so bravely in victory as did their original in defeat
that night in Sangue do Lume. Fueled by the potentials of
hatred and love (though that love had been mingled with
bitterness), he spun and leaped, living in a chaos of agonized faces and flowers of blood blooming on silk blouses;
and while the sad music of the fountain evolved into a
skirling tantara, he left more than twenty dead in his
wake, cutting a path toward Caudez and Sylvana, He
received wounds that would have killed a man yet merely
served to goad him on, and utilizing all his moon-given
elusiveness, he avoided the most consequential of the
young men's thrusts. In the end, however, there were too
many young men, too many knives, and, weakening, he
knew he would not be able to reach the governor and his
daughter.

There came a moment of calm in the storm of battle,
a moment when nine of the young men had hemmed the
arcevoalo in against the fountain. Others waited their
chance behind them. They were wary of him now, yet
confident, and they all wore one expression: the
dogged, stuporous expression that comes with the anticipation of a slaughter. Their unanimity weakened the
arcevoalo further, and he thought it might be best to lay
his weapon down and accept his fate. The young men
sidled nearer, shifting their knives from hand to hand;

the music of the fountain built to a glorious crescendo of trumpets and guitars, and the pale, beautiful bodies of the dead enmeshed in a lacework of blood seemed to be entreating the arcevoalo, tempting him to join them in their eternal poise. But in the next moment he spotted Caudez smiling at him between the shoulders of his adversaries, and Sylvana laughing at his side. That sight rekindled the arcevoalo's rage. With an open-throated scream, choosing his target in a flash of poignant bitterness, he hurled his knife. The blade whirled end over end, accumulating silver fire, growing brighter and brighter until its hilt sprouted from Sylvana's breast. Before anyone could take note of the artful character of her death, she sank beneath the feet of the milling defenders, leaving Caudez to stare in horror at the droplets of her blood stippling his chest. And then, seizing the opportunity provided by the young men's consternation, the arcevoalo ran from the square, through the flawless streets and into the Favelin, past the hovel where Ana and his unborn son awaited an unguessable future in the light of her dying god. He clambered over the gray metal wall and sprinted into the jungle.

Such was the efficacy of the city's machines that even the natural beauty of the moonlit jungle had been enhanced. It seemed to the arcevoalo that he was passing through an intricate design of silver and black, figured by the glowing eyes of those creatures who had come forth from hiding to honor his return. Despite his wounds, his panic, he had a sense of homecoming, of peacefulness and dominion. He came at length to a mountaintop east of Sangue do Lume and paused there to catch his breath. His muscles urged him onward, but his thoughts—heavy with the poisons of murder and betrayal—were a sickly ballast holding him in place. At any second, ships would arrow up from the city to track him, and he thought now that he would welcome them.

But as he stood there, grieving and empty of hope, a shadow obscured the stars: a great rippling field of shadow that swooped down and wrapped him in its filmy, almost weightless folds. He felt himself lifted and borne eastward and—after what could have been no more than a matter of seconds—gently lowered to earth. Through the dim opacity of the folds, he made out a high canopy of leaves and branches, silvery shafts of moonlight, and a bed of ferns. He could feel the creature merging with him, its folds becoming fibrous, gradually thickening to a husk, and—recalling the darkness that had passed from him at birth—he realized that this incomprehensible shadow was the death that had been born with him, had haunted all his nights, and had come at last to define the shape of his life.

The world dwindled to a dark green vibration, and with half his soul he yearned toward the pleasures of the city, toward love, toward all the sweet futilities of the human condition. But with the other half he exulted in the knowledge that his purpose had been achieved, that he had understood the nature of man. And (a final intuition) he knew that someday, long after he had decayed into a clay of old memories, just as it had with the bones of Joao Merin Nascimento, the jungle would breed from his bones a new creature, who—guided by his understanding—would make of love a weapon and of war a passion, and would bring inspired tactics to the eternal game. This knowledge gave him a measure of happiness, but that was soon eroded by his fear of what lay—or did not lie—ahead.

Something nudged the outside of the thickening husk. The arcevoalo peered out, straining to see, and spied the ruby eyes of a malgaton peering in at him, come to give him the comfort of dreams. Grateful, not wanting to feel the snip of death's black scissors, he concentrated on those strange pupils, watching them shift and dissolve and grow spidery, and then it was as if he were running again, running in the joyful way he had before he had reached Sangue do Lume, running in a harmony of green light and birds, in a wind that sang like a harp on fire, in a moment that seemed to last forever and lead beyond to other lives.

# BEAR TRAP

*Charles Stross*

I WAS SIX hours away from landfall on Burgundy when my share portfolio tried to kill me. I was sitting in one of the main viewing lounges, ankle-deep in softly breathing fur, half watching a core tournament and nursing a water pipe in one hand. I was not alone: I shared the lounge with an attentive bar, a number of other passengers, and—of course—a viewing wall. It curved away beside me, a dizzying emptiness with stars scattered across it like gold dust and a blue and white planet looming in the foreground. I tried to focus on the distant continents. Six hours to safety, I realized. A cold shiver ran up my spine. Six hours and I'd be beyond their reach, firewalled behind Burgundy's extensive defenses. Six more hours of being a target.

The bar sidled up to me. "Sir's pipe appears to have become extinguished. Would Sir appreciate a refill?"

"No, sir would not," I said, distantly taking in the fact that my pulse had begun to drum a staccato tattoo on the inside of my skull. My mouth tasted acrid and smoky, and it was unusually quiet in my head: a combination of the drugs and the time-lag between my agents—light-years away, bottlenecked by the low bandwidth causal channels between my brain and the servers where most of my public persona lived. "In fact, I'd like a sober-up now. How long until we arrive, and where?"

The bar dipped slightly, programmatically obsequious as it handed me a small glass. "This vessel is now four hundred thousand kilometers from docking bay seven on Burgundy beanstalk. Your departure is scheduled via Montreaux immigration sector, downline via tube to Castillia terminus. Please note your extensive customs briefing and remember to relinquish any unauthorized tools or thoughts you may be carrying before debarkation. The purser's office will be happy to arrange storage pending your eventual departure. Three requests for personal contact have been filed—"

"Enough." Everything was becoming clearer by the moment as the sober-up gave me a working-over. I looked around. We were one and a third light seconds out: comms were already routed through the in-system relays and Her Majesty's censorship reflexes, which meant anyone sending uploaded agents after me would first have to penetrate her firewall. That was why I'd taken this otherwise unattractive contract in the first place. I tried to relax, but the knot of stress under my ribs refused to go away. "I want—" I began.

"Alain!" It was one of the other passengers, striding toward me across the floor of the lounge. She looked as if she knew me: I didn't recognize her, and in my current state it was all I could do to keep from cursing under my breath. A creditor? Or a liquidator? In the wake of the distributed market crash it could be either. Once again, I found myself cursing the luck that had seen me so widely uncovered at just the wrong moment.

"So this is where you've been hiding!" She was bald, I noticed, a fashion common to Burgundy, but had highlighted her eyelids with vivid strokes of black pigment. Her costume was intricate and brightly colored, a concoction of dead animal products and lace that left only her shoulders and ankles bare; she was dressed for a party. Slowly I began to feel embarrassed. "You have the better of me, Madame," I said, struggling to my feet.

"Do I?" She looked mildly disapproving. "But we're due to disembark in six hours—after the landing party, of course! Surely you weren't planning to sleep through the captain's ball?"

My knowledge was sluggish but accessible; who is she? I demanded. The answer was so unexpected I nearly sat down again. Arianna Blomenfeld. Your wife. I shook my head. "Sorry, I'm a bit out of sorts," I said, dropping the water pipe on the bar. "Fine grade, that." I smiled fatuously to conceal the fact that I was thinking furiously, shocked all the way into sobriety. Knowledge, integrity check, please.

The edges of her mouth drooped a little sourly: "Have you been overdoing it again?" she demanded.

No, I'm just hallucinating your existence for the hell of it. "Of course not," I said as smoothly as I could. "I was just enjoying a small pipe. Nothing wrong with that, is there?" Details, details. Someone or something had dug their little claws into my external memories; I urgently needed to probe the limits of their fakery.

She offered me a gloved hand: "The party's starting soon, downstairs in the Sunset Room. You should go and dress for it, you know." My knowledge finally delivered, dumping a jerky snowstorm of images through my mnemonic system: memories of myself and this woman, this Arianna Blomenfeld. Memories I'd never experienced. A wedding party in some palatial estate on Avernia, bride and groom in lustrous red: I recognized myself, smiling and relaxed at the center of events. More private imagery, honeymoon nights I wish I had experienced. She was the well-engineered scion of a rich merchant-spy sept, apparently an heiress to family knowledge. Designed from birth to cement a powerful alliance. Public images: sailing a spiderboat across the endless southern ocean of that world. Then a public newsbite, myself—and herself—attending some public function full of pompous export brokers in the capital. Options trading leveraged on FTL/STL communications advantages, part of my regular arbitrage load.

Her hand felt thin and frail within her glove. Such a shame, I thought, that I had never come within twelve light-years of Avernia. "Coming, dear?" she asked.

"Indeed." I let her lead me to the doorway, still stunned by my memory's insistence that I was married to this woman: it made no sense! Either I had erased a large chunk of my personality by accident, or someone had managed to drill right down into my external knowledge—while I was on the inside of a firewall's security cordon, one maintained by a near-deity notorious for paranoia. "I'd better go and get changed," I said.

ARIANNA LET ME go when we reached the stairs, and I hurried up to the accommodation level where my suite was located. As soon as the door opened I knew I was adrift. When I'd left, the room had mirrored my own apartment back in Shevralier Old Town: austere classicism and a jumble of odds and ends scattered over the hand-carved wooden furniture. It was very different, now. The dark, heavy furniture bulked against the walls, making the cabin feel cramped: an en suite cornucopia rig, factories ready to clothe and feed me on request.

I leaned against the wall, dizzy. Who am I?

You are Alain Blomenfeld, intelligence broker for the Syndic d'Argent of Avernia. Nobody you know has died since your last knowledge checkpoint in real time. Nobody you know has changed their mind. Your cognitive continuity is assured. You are currently—

"Wrong. Validate immediately," I said aloud. Then, in my own skull, another command; one keyed to a private and personal area, one that never leaked beyond the neuroprocessors spliced into my cerebrum. Self-test runes flashed inside my eyelids and I felt a shivery flash of anger as the secret watcher scanned through my memories, matched them against the externals that made up my public image, stored in the knowledge systems scattered throughout human space. All my public memories were fingerprinted using public keys, the private halves of which were stitched into my thalamus so tight that any attempt to steal them would amount to murder.

Global mismatch detected. External temporal structures do not match internal checksum. Internal memory shows no sign of cognitive engineering. Your external memories have been tampered with. Alert!

"Uh-huh." Thanks for warning me in time. "Wardrobe?" I sat down on the edge of the bed and tried to think two ways at once, very fast. The wardrobe helped me out. "How can I help you sir?"

"I want an outfit. Suitable for the captain's ball. What have you got?" The mirror fogged, then cleared to show images of me in a variety of costumes, local to Burgundy as well as Avernian corporate. I noted that my body didn't seem to have changed, which was at least mildly reassuring. Meanwhile I thought furiously: Am I under attack? If so, is it a physical attack or an existential one? Existential,

I guessed—Arianna, whoever she was, was part of some scheme to infiltrate me—but why? I couldn't put my finger on any motive for such a scheme. The exchange assassins might be on my trail, ready to kill me and bring my memories and stock options home on a cube, but they'd hardly be subtle about it. So who was it?

"I think I'll wear that one," I said, pausing the mirror-search at a conservatively cut dark robe. Then I thought for a moment, summoning up a covert maker routine from my internals: fab this for me, and put it in an inner pocket. I dumped the design into the wardrobe, and began to strip.

If only I knew who they were and why they were after me.

If only I knew what I needed to watch out for...

THE MAIN DINING room was furnished in marble splendor, as if to emphasize that mass was of no concern to the modern space traveler; the ship showed me to my seat, a trail of fireflies pulsing through the candlelit conversations of the other diners.

"Alain! So pleased to see you again!" I couldn't decide whether she was being sarcastic or not. She smiled up at me, lips pale with tension.

"I was delayed," I said, and sat down beside her.

"That's nice. I was just telling Ivana here that I never know quite what to expect of you." This time the sarcasm was unmistakable, underpinned by a note of hostility that instantly put my back up. Ivana, a blonde mask with a fair complexion, nodded approvingly: I ignored her.

"That makes two of us," I replied, picking up my wine glass. An attentive servitor lowered its mouth to the goblet and regurgitated a red dribble: I swirled it under my nose for a moment and inhaled. "Have you made any arrangements for our arrival?"

"I was waiting to discuss that with you," she said guardedly. I looked at her, noting suddenly that her attention was totally focused on me. It was a little frightening. In a culture of cheap beauty, the currency of aesthetic perfection is devalued; Arianna Blomenfeld was striking rather than pretty, projecting raw character in a way that suggested she hired only the most subtle of body sculptors. If the situation wasn't quite so depressingly messy I'd probably be trailing around after her with my tongue hanging out. "I suggest we discuss things in private after dinner."

"Perhaps." I drank some more wine and tried to figure out what she was hinting at. Dinner was served: a platter of delicate, thin-sliced flesh garnished with a white sauce. We ate in hostile silence, broken by vapid banter emanating from the mask and her partner, another nonentity of indeterminate age and questionable taste; I did my best to study Arianna while overtly ignoring her. She gave little away, except for the occasional furtive glance.

I found myself ignoring the meal, screening out the captain's speech and the assorted toasts and assertions of welcoming that followed it. Periodically, minor agents deposited fragments of opinion in the back of my mind: less frequently, the waitrons cleared our plates and stifled us with solicitude. I was tugging at a bowl of sugared vermicelli when Arianna finally engaged my conversation. "You're going to have to face the future sooner or later," she stated directly. "You can't keep avoiding me forever. I want an answer, Alain. Bear or Bull? Which is it?"

My fork froze of its own accord, halfway to my mouth. "My dear, I have no idea what you're talking about," I said.

She obviously had some end in view for she smiled tensely, and said: "There's no need to hide any more, Alain. It's over. We've escaped. You can stop pretending."

"I—" I stopped. I put my fork down. "I've no idea what you're suggesting, truly." I frowned, and had the reward of seeing her look discomfited: surprised, if anything. "I don't feel very well," I added for the gallery.

"Ooh, do tell!" said the mask's slow-witted companion.

"There's nothing to tell," Arianna answered, fixing me with a coldly knowing look. I could hear the blood pumping in my ears. Had someone fixed her self-knowledge too? Was she also a victim of whatever was going on here? I stared at her face, mapping the pulse of blood through her veins: slightly flushed, tense, signs of concentration. I realized with a shiver that she was as worried as I.

"I don't feel so well," I repeated, and prodded my thalamus into broadcasting the appropriate signs. "Please excuse me." I stood and, mustering as much dignity as I could, left the room. There was a flurry of nervous conversation behind me from the mask and her attendant, but nobody followed me or paged me.

MY STATEROOM WAS just as I had left it. I reached into my pocket for the device I had ordered from the wardrobe, then entered the bedroom.

"Don't move. Stay exactly where you are." I froze. No way of knowing how Arianna had gotten here ahead of me, much less how she had bypassed the lock—but I wasn't willing to bet that she was unarmed.

"What are you doing here?" I demanded.

"I'm asking the questions." She studied me like a bug on a pin. She was standing against the wall between the dresser and the wardrobe, the dark fabric of her dress shifting color to blend in with the aged oak finish. A little-used daemon reported back: subject is suppressing emissions on all service channels. Unable to establish context. She was holding something round in a lace-gloved hand, pointed right at me. "Who are you and why have you spoofed my public knowledge?"

I blinked. "What are you talking about? You cracked my knowledge." I tried to force my pulse to slow. (Escape routes: the door was behind me, open, offering a clear field of fire. Her fingertips, exposed through the tips of her gloves, were white around the grip of her weapon. Stress.) "You can drop the pretence. I doubt we're being monitored and it doesn't make any difference anyway: you've got me." (Hoping she wouldn't shoot if I didn't let her see what I held clenched in my right hand; I wanted to learn whatever I could first. And besides, I don't like the sight of blood.)

"You're lying. Who are you working for? Tell me!" She sounded increasingly agitated: she raised the sphere, pointing it at my face from across the room. Deep heat vision showed me her pulse and another daemon tracked it: one thirty-seven, one thirty-nine… signs of serious stress. Was she telling the truth?

"I didn't modify your knowledge! I thought you'd been messing with mine—"

A momentary expression of shock flickered across her face. "If you're telling the truth—" she began, then stopped.

"Does someone want you dead? Does someone want both of us dead?" I asked.

"Wait." (A very paranoid agency chirped up in my ears; sensor failure in main access corridor. Denial of service attack in progress.) Arianna must have been listening to something like my own inner voice, because she abruptly twisted round and punched the wall: it shattered with a noise like breaking glass. She stood aside, still pointing a finger at me—the large, dark ring on it protruding upwards like a stubby gun barrel: "Get out! Move!"

I moved. Across the bed, to the hole in the wall—taking a brief look out—then through it. Something solid came up and thumped me bruisingly. It was dark, and my eyes weren't ready for it; I was in some kind of roofed-over service duct, low ceiling, fat pipes oozing across every exposed surface. I glanced round. Structures bulked on all sides; it was some kind of service area I guessed, an inner hull. "Quick. Move." Arianna was behind me, prodding me away from the broken wall. "Faster!" she hissed.

"Why?" I asked.

"Keep going!" I scrabbled forwards into the darkness, lizard-like on all fours. I could hear her behind me and risked a glance. "Faster, idiot!" She was on all fours to avoid the low ceiling. "If you're lying I'll—"

Thump.

I blinked, unsure where I was. That was a very loud noise, I realized vaguely. Something tugged at my leg and I opened my eyes: there was a ringing in my ears and a light was flickering on and off in one eye, trying to get my attention. I blinked and tried to focus: someone was pinging me repeatedly. What is it?

Urgent message from Arianna Blomenfeld: "That was meant for us." There was an object attached to the message, a simple-minded medical scanner that told her I was awake before I could stop it.

I lifted my head, blinking, and realized I was breathless. I began to cough. Someone put a hand over my mouth and

I began to choke instead. Message: don't speak. Bidirectional secure link installed. I could feel it, itching like the phantom of someone else's limb.

"What happened?"

"Denial of service attack—with a bomb appended." My eyes were streaming. She let go of my mouth as I noticed her delicate lace evening gloves had turned into something more robust: blinking in the dusty twilight I saw her dress bunching up close to her, unraveling, weaving itself into plainer, close-fitting overalls: a space suit? Body armor? "Meant for both of us, while we were talking. Probably a last shot, before docking. Low information content, anyway."

"Do you know who's after you?" I asked.

She grimaced. "Talk about it later. If we get off this thing alive."

"They're trying to kill me, too," I transmitted, trying not to move my lips.

"So start moving."

"Which way?"

She pointed toward a service catwalk. I pushed myself up, wincing as my head throbbed in time to my pulse. Loud noises in the distance and an ominous hissing of air, then a queasy rippling lightness underfoot: the ship's momentum transfer field shutting down, handing us off to the dockmaster's control. "All the way down to the bottom."

"I've got a better idea. Why don't we split up? Less chance of them catching both of us."

She looked at me oddly. "If you want..."

Welcome to Burgundy.

Humanity is scattered across a 3,000 light year radius, exiled from old Earth via wormholes created by the Eschaton, a strongly godlike intelligence spawned during Earth's singularity. Some of these worlds, including Burgundy, communicate; people and goods by starship, information by the network of instantaneous but bandwidth-limited causal trails established by Festival.

Burgundy is a developed, somewhat introverted culture that rests on the groaning back of a deliberately constructed proletariat. The first weakly godlike artificial intelligence to arrive here in the wake of its rediscovery abolished the cornucopiae and subjugated the human populace: an action that was tolerated because nothing the Queen did to them was anything like as bad as the oppression imposed by their own human leaders.

Burgundy has gained a small reputation as an information buffer—a side effect of its monarch's paranoid attitude toward encroachment by other deities. It exports confidentiality, delay-line buffers, fine wines, and dissidents. In other words, it's the last place a futures trader specializing in spread option trades that leverage developments in the artificial intelligence market—someone like me—would normally be seen dead in. On the other hand...

As an accountant specializing in Monte Carlo solutions to NP-complete low-knowledge systems I am naturally of interest to the Queen, who made me an offer I would have considered long and hard at the best of times; in my circumstances back on Dordogne—exposed to risk, to say the least—I could hardly consider refusing her invitation.

Many technologies are banned from the system, in an attempt to reduce the vulnerability of the monarchy to buffer overrun and algorithmic complexity attacks. In particular, the royal capital of Burgundy—Castillia, a teeming metropolis of some 3 million souls—is positively medieval. It was here that the down-pod from the equatorial beanstalk deposited me, time-lagged and dizzy from the descent, on the steps of the main rail terminus. Arianna had disappeared while I was opening a side door back into the populated sections of the ship: I didn't see her go, although I have a vague recollection of blurred air, flattened perspectives against a wood-paneled wall. My ears were still ringing from the blast, and I was so confused that I didn't notice much of anything until I found myself in an alleyway my autonomics had steered me to, eyeing up the guest house where the Royal Mint had rented me a room.

The depths of neomedieval barbarity into which this city had sunk finally became clear when I found my way to my garret. It wasn't simply the liveried servitors, or even the obese, physically aged steward who proudly showed me to the suite; but the presence of running water. Yes: a lead pipe—lead, yet!—entered through the ceiling of one room and debouched through a gargoyle-encrusted tap above a pewter basin. "You see, we have all the ancient luxuries!" gloated Salem the steward. "This'n's piped down from our very own roof-tank. More'n you'll have seen before, I expect."

I nodded, faintly aghast at the prospect of the microfauna that must be swimming in the swill.

"Are you sure you don't have any luggage?" he added, one heavy eyebrow raised in protest at the very idea of a gentleman-merchant traveling untrammeled.

"Not a parcel," I said. "I came by starship…"

He blinked rapidly. "Oh," he said, very fast. "And ee's not staying at the Palace?" He shuffled, as if unsure of what to do with his feet, then essayed a little bow. "We is honored by your presence, m'lord."

When I finally persuaded them to leave me alone—at the price of calling a tailor, to fab me some garments suitable to my station in life—I swept the room for bugs. My custom fleas found nothing, save the more natural macrofauna lurking in the bed, garderobe, and curtains. I removed and disassembled into three separate parts the device in my pocket, then hid two of them in the hollow Cuban heels of my boots: possession of such a gadget, in these parts, could earn one a slow impalement if the Queen deigned to notice. (The third part I wore as a ring on my left hand.)

At the end of this sequence I lay down upon the bed, hands behind my head, staring up at the dusty canopy of the four-poster. "What am I doing here?" I murmured. To report to ye chancellery of court on the day following landfall, there to command and supervise the management of ye portfolio of accounts royal and foreign, the contract said; while lying low and avoiding the exchange agents, I added mentally. But I was already wondering if I'd made the right decision.

THE NEXT DAY, I reported to the Exchequer for duty.

A rambling, gothic assemblage of gargoyles, flying buttresses, and turrets held together by red brick, the Chancellery was located across the three-sided Capital Square from the Summer Palace, a white marble confection that pointed battlements and parabolic reflectors south across the river. As I approached the entrance, armed guards came to attention. Their leader stepped forward. "Sir Blomenfeld," said the sergeant. "I am pleased to greet you on behalf of her Terrible Majesty, and extend to you her gracious wishes for your success in her service."

"I thank you from the depths of my heart," I replied, somewhat taken aback by his instant recognition. "It is an honor and a blessing to be welcomed in such exalted terms. I will treasure it to my dying day." Laying it on too thick? I wondered.

The sergeant nodded, and I noticed the antennae tucked between the feathers of his ornate helmet; the strangely bony fingers disguised by his padded gloves: and the odd articulation of his back. Evidently the technology restrictions didn't apply to Her Majesty's security. "If you would please come this way, sir?" he asked, directing me toward a side door.

Tradesman's entrance. "Certainly."

He led me inside, up the steps and along a wide marble passage hung with portraits of ruby-nosed dignitaries in their late middle age: the human dynasty that had preceded Her Majesty. Into an office where, behind a leather-topped desk, there sat a man with a surpassingly sallow complexion and even less hair than my ersatz wife had been wearing the night before. "Sir Alain Blomenfeld, your honor, reporting as required." He turned to me. "His Lordship, Victor Manchusko, undersecretary of the Treasury, counselor in charge of the privy portfolio."

Privy portfolio? I blinked in surprise as the sergeant bowed his way out. "Sir, I—"

"Sit down." Lord Manchusko waved in the direction of an ornately decorated chair that might have been designed as an instrument of torture. His gold-rimmed spectacles glittered in the wan light filtering down from the high-set windows. "You were not expecting something like this, I take it."

"Not exactly," I said, somewhat flustered. "Um, I understood I was being retained to overhaul dependency tracking in the barter sector—"

"Nonsense." Manchusko slapped the top of his desk: I'll swear that it cringed. "Do you think we needed to hire offworld intellect for such a task?"

"Um. Then you, er, have something else in mind?"

The undersecretary smiled thinly. "Overexposed on the intelligence futures side, was it?"

An icy sinking feeling in the pit of my stomach. "Yes," I admitted.

"Tell me about it."

"It was all over the Festival channels. Surely you know—"

He smiled again. It was not a humorous expression. "Pretend I don't."

"Oh." I hunched over unconsciously. So. They didn't want me as an accountant, after all, hmm? Trapped. And if I didn't give them exactly what they wanted they could hold me here forever. I licked my lips: "You know what commodities are traded on the TX; mostly design schemata, meta-memes, better algorithms for network traversal, that sort of thing. Most of these items require serious mind-time to execute; so we trade processing power against options on better algorithms. Most of the trading entities are themselves intelligent, even if only weakly so: even some of the financial instruments—" I paused.

"Such as Blomenfeld et Cie, I take it."

I nodded. "Yes. I was proud of that company. Even though it was pretty small in the scheme of things; it was mine, I made it. We worked well together. I was its director, and it was my memetic muscle. It was the smartest company I could build. We were working on a killer scheme, you know. When the market crashed."

Manchusko nodded. "A lot of people were burned by that."

I sighed and unkinked a little. "I was overexposed. A complex derivative swap that was backward-chaining between one of the Septagon clades' quantum oracle programs—I figured it would produce the goods, a linear-order performance boost in type IV fast-thinkers, within five mind-years—leveraged off junk bonds issued in Capone City. According to my Bayesian analyzers nothing should go wrong in the fifteen seconds I was overextended. Only it was just those fifteen seconds in which, um, you know what happened."

Normally, the Eschaton leaves us alone; nothing short of widespread causality violation provokes a strongly godlike intervention. Whatever happened in Eldritch system's intelligence futures market was bad, capital-B bad. Bad enough to provoke an act of God. Intervention from beyond the singularity. Bad enough to trigger a run on the market, an instant bear market, everyone selling every asset they owned for dear life.

"Eldritch went runaway and the Eschaton intervened. You were in the middle of a complex chain of investments when the market crashed and it all unraveled on you due to a bad transitive dependency. How far uncovered were you?"

"Sixty thousand mind-years." I licked my suddenly dry lips. "Ruin," I whispered.

Manchusko leaned forward suddenly. "Who's after you?" he demanded. "Who tried to kill you on the ship?"

"I don't know!" I snapped, then froze solid, trying to regain my composure. "I'm sorry. It could have been anyone. I have some suspicions," not fair to mention Arianna, she'd been in the middle of it too, "but nothing solid. Not the exchange authority, anyway."

"Good. While you are here, you will remain under Her Majesty's protection. If you have any problems, ask any guard for help." That smile was disquieting as anything I'd ever seen: "What one sees, all see, she sees."

I nodded silently, not daring to trust my tongue.

"Now. About the reason we wanted you here. You weren't the only one who took a bath in the crash. Her Majesty's portfolio is highly diversified, and some of our investments suffered somewhat. Your job—unofficially— is to take over her hedge fund and rebuild it. Officially you're not trading, you're disqualified. Your company is insolvent and liable to be wound up, if they can ever track it down. You're a disqualified director. Unofficially, I hope you learn from your mistakes. Because we don't expect you to repeat them here." He stood up and gestured toward a side door. "Through here is your office and your dealer desk. Let me introduce you to it..."

AFTERNOON FOUND ME back at my room, digesting a manual of procedures and trying to regain my shattered composure. I had just about managed to forget about the incidents of the previous day when there was a knock at the door.

"Who is it?" I called.

"Y'r humble servant, m'lord," called Salem. "With a manuscript for you!"

I rolled to my feet. "Come in!"

He sidled into my room, holding a rolled-up piece of parchment away from his body as if it contained some noxious vermin. "Begging y'r'honor's indulgence, but this came for you from the palace. Messenger's waiting on y'r'honor's pleasure."

I took the note and broke the wax seal on it. "Having a lovely time at the court. Formal presentation before Her Majesty at eight this eve. Your presence requested by royal fiat. Will you be there? Signed, your 'wife.'"

Hello, Arianna, I thought. I remembered her face; chilly beauty. It was some joke, the one that whoever had hacked our respective memories had played on me. I resolved that if I ever found them I'd use their head for a punch-line. "Tell the messenger to tell her that I'll be there," I said.

AT SEVEN, SALEM slid into my vision again. "Begging y'r'honor's pardon, but y'r humble coach awaits you, sir," he mumbled unctuously.

"Isn't it a bit early?" I asked.

It wasn't early. I sat in a cramped wooden box with my nose inches from a slit-window rimmed with intricately painted murals of rural debauchery. Outside, two husky porters wheezed as they carried me bodily—box and all—through the cobbled streets. We lurched and swayed from side to side, trapped in a heaving mass of pedestrians: a royal lobster drive was in progress. The lobsters lived sufficiently long in air that by custom they were herded through the streets to the gates of the palace: the distress made their flesh all the sweeter. Presently my porters lifted me again and continued, this time with little further delay.

They set me down and opened the door: trying not to gasp audibly I stood up, stretching muscles that ached as if I'd run the entire distance. The sedan chair was parked in a courtyard, before the palace steps but inside the walls. My porters groveled before a junior officer of the royal dragoons. I bowed slightly and doffed my hat to him.

"Sir Blomenfeld," said the lieutenant: "If you would please come this way, sir?"

"Surely." He led me inside, up the steps, and along a wide marble passage carpeted in red velvet.

Noise, chatter, and music drifted from ahead. We came upon a well-lit stretch, then a pair of high doors and an antechamber, walled with pompous gold-leaf plaster, where four footmen and a butler greeted me. "His Excellency the high trader Alain Blomenfeld, by appointment to Her Majesty's Royal Treasury! Long may she live!" A blast of pipes ushered me into the royal presence.

The hall beyond the antechamber was high-ceilinged, decorated with primitive opulence and meticulous precision, illuminated by skylights set in the ceiling. A floor of black and white tiles gleamed beneath my boots as I looked around. Throngs of richly clad courtiers ignored me in their elegant hauteur. The Queen herself was nowhere to be seen—but I would not expect to be introduced at this stage in any event. I wondered where Arianna was, and what she was doing to have inveigled herself into the royal court so rapidly. Although, if her hacked knowledge was anything to go by, she had the background for it.

"Hello, Alain!" My question answered itself with a beaming smile full of sharp, white teeth. She was most elegantly decked out in a gown of sea-green silk, with a jeweled motif of eyes: her choker scrutinized me with terrible, passive regret. "I see you're none the worse for wear, hmm? We really must have that talk, you know." She took my hand and led me away from the door. The company here is dire, she sent. Besides, speaking openly is difficult. Encrypt? I nodded. Wetware embedded deep in the redundant neural networks of my cerebellum mangled the next transmission, established a private key, linked to her headspace...

"Do you know about the treasury situation yet?" she asked.

"Eh?" I stared at her; her gown stared back at me quizzically.

"Don't be obtuse. It's so hard to tell who's on the inside hereabouts. She didn't drag you here to mess with her ledgers, she brought you in for your dealing record."

"She?"

Arianna frowned. "The Queen." A balcony, overlooking an inner courtyard: neatly manicured lawn, flower beds, stone flagstones. My knowledge inflicted a sudden flash of déjà vu on me: a false memory of accompanying Arianna to a ball on New Venus, of sneaking away with her, quiet sighs in a secret garden at midnight. My pulse accelerated:

her hand tightened on my arm. "Too many damned memories, Alain. You feel it too?"

I nodded.

"I think they're there for a reason, you know. We must have something in common, otherwise whoever they are, they wouldn't have spoofed both of us with the same false history. Do you remember?"

She leaned against the balcony, watching me intently.

"I—" I shook my head. More déjà vu, this time from within: I knew Arianna from somewhere, somewhere real, not bound up in externalities. Market externalities. Now where did that thought come from?

"I never saw you before, before you walked into that observation lounge, I swear it," I said. "But despite the false memories—"

She nodded. "You know what?" she asked.

"Um. What?"

Suddenly she leaned against me, sharp chin digging into my collar bone, hugging me tight in a spring-steel grip: "I don't remember," she whispered in my ear. "Anything. Before the lounge. I mean, I have lots of external memories, but no internal ones." She was shuddering with tension; I hugged her back, appalled by her admission. "I know who I am, but I don't remember becoming me. At least, not from inside. All my memories that are more than a day old are third-person. Before then, I think, I think I may have been someone else."

"That's awful."

"Is it?" The tension in her arms ebbed slightly. "What about you?"

"I—" I suddenly realized I had an armful of attractive woman. A woman my external memories insisted I was married to. "I have false memories. One set, with you in them. And the real ones—I think they're real—without you."

Arianna released me, took a step back, and shook her head. "So you know you're a real person? Then what does that make me?" Her gown blinked at me, eyelids rippling from floor to throat.

"I don't know. I've never met you before—at least, I don't remember doing so."

"Are you sure?" she murmured, pulling away slightly. She frowned, fine eyebrows drawing together. "I've been injected into your life and I don't know why. Are you certain you don't know anything about me? You seem to have enemies. Could you have erased some key memories for any reason?" She looked at me so knowingly that I flushed like an ingénue. "I don't find it upsetting, not having a history, Alain. But I want to know why. And who wants us dead."

I shook my head. "Existentialism on an empty stomach."

She smiled sadly: the first time I'd seen her smile in living memory. "We'd better go back inside before anyone misses us," she said.

"SO GRATIFIED TO meet you," said the Queen, her antennae vibrating softly in the breeze. "Do relax, please."

I unkinked my neck. Workers fawned over the royal abdomen, polishing with robotic dedication. "As your Majesty wishes."

"I have already had the pleasure of your lady wife's company," the Queen commented in a high-pitched voice, air rushing through speech spiracles. She sounded amused, for some reason. "I understand you have a little memory problem?"

"I really couldn't comment." Worker-ancillaries buzzed and clattered beneath the ceiling like demented wasps; the air was hot and dry from their encrypted infrared exchanges. I sweated, but not from heat.

"Then don't comment. You shall pretend that you have no problem, and I shall pretend that you didn't fail to answer my question. Once only, Sir Blomenfeld. Drink."

One of the workers extruded a goblet full of dark red liquid into the palm of my right hand. I swirled it around, sniffed, swallowed. Whatever else it contained, there was no alcohol in it. "Thank you."

"Thanks are unnecessary: a potent vintage, that. What do you think of my little portfolio?"

I blinked. "I haven't really had time to do a detailed analysis—"

She waved an idle pair of arms: "Never mind. I expect no precision at this stage."

"Well then." I licked my lips. Little portfolio, indeed. "Some of them are evolving nicely. I noticed two promising philosophies in there, if not more. A full dependency analysis of your investments will take a while to prepare—some of them keep changing their minds—but I don't see any reason to doubt that they'll pick up value rapidly as the market recovers from the recession. I'd say your shares are among the most intelligent ones I've ever met."

She giggled, a noise like saws rasping on bone. "Expand my holdings, doctor, and I will be most grateful." A ripple ran through her thorax and she tensed: "Please leave me now, I have no further need of human attendance." Dismissed by her cursory wave I retreated back to the party outside the royal chambers. Behind me, the Queen was giving birth to another processor.

ON MY THIRD day, I arrived at the small office Manchusko had assigned me unusually early. Unlocking the door and opening it, I froze. Arianna was seated behind my desk, wearing an unhappy expression. "I tried to stop them, Alain, but they wouldn't listen."

"What—"

Someone pushed me into the office, none too gently, and pulled the door shut behind us. "Shut your mouth. I exchange commission!" growled the intruder.

I turned round, very slowly, and looked up and up until I met its small, black-eyed gaze. "Why are you here?" I asked, trying to ignore the gunsight contact lenses glowing amber against its pupils. "Did you plant the bomb?"

"Am here for compensation." The bear shifted its weight from one foot to the other: the floor boards creaked. "You my principle shareholders blame for inequitable exposure. Am here to repossess. Not bomber. Bomber sent by idiot trading script. Bomber not blow anyone else up again."

"Uh-huh." I took a step backwards, slowly. Now I was in the room I could see the monofilament spiderweb holding Arianna down, tied to my chair and afraid to move. This was an outrage! What did they think they were doing?

Arianna was trying to catch my eye. I blinked, remembered the secure channel she'd passed to me during our arrival.

"Am taking this chattel," the bear explained, planting a heavy hand on the back of her chair. She winced. "Am needing also your memory keys. Do be good about this all, doc." He grinned, baring far too many teeth at me.

Alain?

I tweaked my knowledge, hoping to get a handle on some bandwidth I could use to signal for help, but nothing happened. The room was too well shielded. Here. Why does he want you—

Keys. To your portfolio, to everything.

Memory keys. "My memory keys?" I almost laughed.

"You're joking! I couldn't give you them if I wanted to—"

"Your cooperation not necessary," said the bear. "Just your knowledge. And your company. Take her. Get back options."

"Her? But she's not my property; I've never met her before! Someone hacked our public knowledge—"

The bear looked, his breath a hot stench upon me: "Amnesia no excuse, doc. She your business. Cloned body, same dirty algorithms. Am her taking with me! Now. Your keys. Or I take your head with them inside."

Arianna was looking at me again, eyes wide and unreadable.

That true? You're my company?

She nodded minutely. You planned this, Alain. Selective amnesia to slip past the hunters. Good reason for us to stay together. But you should have stayed with me. Not fled.

I looked up at the bear, trying not to telegraph what I was thinking. So Arianna was a construct from the beginning? And one of my making, too: a downloaded company on the run from the receivers.

"You're not really from the exchange, are you?"

"Pretty boy. Think smart." The bear produced a small spheroid, pointed it at me. "This yours, pretty boy?"

Shit. Me and my big mouth. Of course the Exchange wouldn't bother with a meat machine repo tool, would they? This must be Organization muscle of some sort. Probably laundering intelligence—dumping mind-years into an arbitrage sector to ensure that options held by another pawn got smarter. Only the market crash had propagated my own exposure, catching them out. "Hey, can we do a deal?"

"Market closed." The bear grinned and leaned forward, opening its mouth wide, jaw-breakingly wide. I heard a pop and crunch of dislocating joints and felt a familiar buzzing at the edge of my consciousness; its teeth were compact quantum scanners, built to sequestrate the uncollapsed wave functions buried in crypto blackboxes.

I ducked, then leaned forward and attempted to head-butt the huge meat machine. It grunted, and my vision blanked for a moment: external knowledge of combat procedures kicked in, telling me just how hopeless the situation was. Arianna was struggling in her chair, isometric twitching and grand mal shuddering. Keys, Alain! Give me access to your keys!

I bounced back from the bear before it could grab me, threw a coat rack at it, ducked behind the desk. Why?

Just do it!

The bear casually picked up the coat rack and broke it over one knee. Waved one end in my direction, brought the other down on the desktop. The desk whimpered: blood began to drip from one of its ornamental drawers. Here. I generated an authentication token, stuffed it into Arianna's head, opened a channel to my keys so she could use them as my proxy. The bear didn't seem to want her dead yet; it grunted and tried to sidle round her to get at me. She heaved herself halfway out of the seat and I paused for a moment to slash at the monofilament wire with my shaving nail: it screeched like chalk on slate but refused to give way.

"You not can escape," rumbled the bear. "Have I a receivership order—"

It froze. Arianna gasped and shuddered, then slumped in her chair: behind the desk I rolled on my back, grabbed at my spring-loaded boot-heels, feverishly slotting puzzle-blocks together in the shape of a gun as I tumbled over, knocking over a dumb waiter, blinked... and saw the bear toppling toward me with the infinite inertia of a collapsing stock market.

\* \* \*

I CAME TO my senses back in my penthouse garret with the running water: my corporate assets were in bed with me, holding onto me like an echo of a false honeymoon memory. My skull ached and I could feel bruises; but a quick audit of my medical memories told me it was nothing that wouldn't heal in a week or so. My glial supports had saved my brain from any lingering effects of concussion: my mouth tasted bad but apart from that...

I shifted for comfort, feeling more at ease with myself. Arianna sighed, sleeping lightly; I could feel her background processes continuing as normal, shadows under the skin of reality. And now I could remember more of what had happened. Memory: validate.

Arianna opened an eye: Booted again? she asked.

I cleared my throat. "Mostly back to normal." Validation successful. I tried to gather my scattered wits. "So it really happened?"

"Reckless trading, my dear. It was the only way out of that collapse back on Dordogne. Or would you rather they'd wound me up and set you to paying off your debts in mind time? You were several billion years uncovered at the end..."

"No!" I tried to sit up.

She reached over and dragged me back down: "Not yet. You're still dizzy."

"But my keys—"

"Relax, he didn't get them. Your head's on your body, not sitting in a vat."

"But what did you do?"

She shrugged. "He was from one of the syndicates, Alain. With your authority, acting as your agency, I asked your desk to run a huge order via Her Majesty's portfolio."

"But he was in there with us!" I shuddered. "There can't have been time!"

"Oh, but there was." She ran a hand across my chest suggestively. "Mm. You did a good job with those memories—"

"The bear. Tell me, please!"

"If you insist." She frowned. "I just told your desk to buy everything—everything available. Saturated all outgoing bandwidth through the firewall: the desk was only too happy to cooperate. The bear was a remote. While all the stocks were handshaking with the treasury, it was locked out. While it was locked out it was frozen; by the time it recovered, I'd worked my way loose and ordered the guards in. Not that it was necessary."

I shook my head. "I know I'm going to regret asking this. Why not?"

"Well, I'd just pumped a large amount of liquidity into the exchange. The trading volume drove up share prices, triggered a minor recovery, and in the past few hours there are signs of the market actually rallying. I think it's going to be a sustained rise; Her Majesty can anticipate a nice little windfall in a few months' time. Anyway, you don't need to worry about the Organization remotes any more, at least not for a year or two. After all," she wormed her way over until her breath in my ear was hot, "bears can't handle a rising market!"

# BEHOLD NOW BEHEMOTH

*Stephen Baxter*

I WALKED WITH my mother on Bodmin Moor.

The Moor is a large, wild area to the northeast of the county of Cornwall, England. Granite peaks push through the crumpled green land, on which are scattered ancient round stone huts.

That day, the sky was a lid of gray cloud.

We'd been talking about the Beast of Bodmin. The local papers—and sometimes the nationals—still report sightings of the Beast. For instance, there had been a recent case of a farmer in Simonsbath who said he lost a dozen lambs.

My mother snorted. "Ridiculous. Fifty miles away. Just locals trying it on. There can't have been any authentic sightings since—"

"Since when?"

"Well, around 1870."

And I knew then why I'd been summoned home. For the first time in my life, my mother was going to open up about the big family secret: the "thing in the barn," the fire—long before I was born—that killed my great-grandfather... and maybe something else.

I kept silent, waiting for more.

"They used to bring it up here, you see," she said. "Good grazing land."

"*It*," I said. I scarcely dared to breathe.

"I never quite knew what to call it... I thought it was time you knew."

"Family secrets, huh."

"Well, as a family, we're secretive. And loyal to a fault."

"So why didn't you tell me earlier?"

She stopped, the wind pushing at her mass of stiff gray hair, and she took my hands. "I wanted you to have your own life, Howard. I didn't want you chasing monsters of the past."

Maybe that was true.

"Tell me what happened in 1870."

"It was out on the Moor. Just grazing, you know. It was old even then. Harmless. But it was set on by the locals. Granddad's story is they mutilated it."

"Mutilated? How?"

"Its face..."

I frowned.

Clancy would suggest later, "Maybe they cut off its tusks."

We walked further.

I STILL DON'T know if I believe it. It is, after all, a tangled tale that links President Thomas Jefferson and Erasmus Darwin and my own great-great-great-grandfather, and dwarf Californian mammals and the Beast of Bodmin and...

Clancy believes it all, of course. But then he's a paleontologist. I have observed that scientists are as conservative as hell about their own subjects, but happy to speculate like a supermarket tabloid on stuff they know nothing about. That's Clancy all over.

It all started because, one day, I took Tracy, my daughter, to see a mammoth.

A reconstructed skeleton anyhow: huge ribs and tree-trunk leg bones and extravagantly spiraling tusks, spotlit in a museum. It had been dug out of the La Brea tar pits in LA, along with a couple of dire wolves that had probably fallen in later, trying to feed on this wretched giant trapped in the sticky mud.

Sitting on a lawn chair alongside Clancy, I showed him my souvenirs of this expedition: postcards, key rings, a little crystal mammoth.

He studied one of the postcards, an artist's reconstruction of a Columbian mammoth. "*Behold now Behemoth,*" he mused. "*His bones are as strong pieces of brass; his bones are like bars of iron…*"

"I sent my mother a postcard. From Tracy. My mother wrote back."

Clancy grimaced. "That's not like her." Clancy and I were at high school together; he knew my mother.

"She said something odd in her letter. She said the postcard artist got it wrong."

"Got what wrong?"

"The color of the mammoth's hair." The artist had drawn it a kind of chestnut brown. "My mother said it should be much darker brown. Like a musk ox's."

Clancy was silent for a time, and the spring sun beat down on his weed-ridden, overgrown lawn, while he jumped to conclusions.

He said, "When will you see your mother again?"

MY FAMILY IS loyal, but secretive. The English side anyhow. Even as a kid I was aware of secrets, old dark hidden things the adults wouldn't talk about.

Like the story of the beast in the barn, which had always intrigued Clancy.

I hadn't visited my mother, in England, for five years. Going there would be a big personal deal. But it seemed to me my mother was hinting, in her letter, that she wanted to open up a little. Why the hell I had no idea.

Even so I hesitated before responding. Believe me, if you don't have a close relationship with your mother, you enter an emotional minefield every time you talk to her. Sad but true.

I grew up in Washington state with my father. Dad was in the Air Force, stationed near London in the late 1950s. I was conceived in London, born in Liskeard, Cornwall, brought up mostly in Washington State. My father's career brought him back to Seattle, but my mother's family ties locked her to Cornwall. My parents spent a few years Atlantic-hopping. They stopped trying when I was five years old.

As broken homes go I got an easy ride, I guess. Clancy knows the story. He lived through most of it.

Well, I booked some vacation.

I flew into Heathrow with my family. I left my wife with Tracy in London—Jan never got on with my mother—and I took a hired car out to Cornwall, alone.

When I was close to home, I got stage fright.

I took a detour along the Cornish coast.

Cornwall is the peninsula that juts out into the Atlantic off the southwest corner of England. Cornwall was spared the Pleistocene ice, but when the thaw came the rising sea levels flooded some of its river valleys. There are moorlands in the interior, intrusions of granite that have made for good rough grazing land, miles and miles of it. The sunken coast, the granite hills, make for a lovely landscape. So lovely that it's choked with visitors most summer days.

Along the coast, at places like Towanroath and Botallack, you can see the tall chimneys of the engine houses of abandoned tin mines. Some of the deep shafts went out under the ocean; the miners would say you could hear the big Atlantic breakers booming through the solid rock above your head. Now, like all the other mines in Cornwall, the coastal workings are disused—*knacked bals,* as the locals would say.

The landscape was just as it had been when I was a kid. Claustrophobic, dark, deep, layered with history I didn't share.

Although, one day, I would own a tin mine.

I reached the family house, near Liskeard. The house dates back to around 1750, but it's been built-over by successive generations; it's reached the end of the twentieth century as a bizarre, mostly Victorian, mock-Tudor pastiche.

I could see the scar of the stable-house fire of 1940: great billowing black marks up the wall of the main house, a monument to my family's darkest secret. My mother was a little girl here at the time. The fire killed my great-grandfather—also called Howard, like me—and they never rebuilt the stable. Even then, in 1940, the mines were declining.

My mother greeted me. She was living alone in the big rambling house. She'd become a small birdlike woman, with a mass of windblown gray hair.

She didn't meet my eyes. But then she never did. After five years apart, she let me peck her cheek.

She gave me tea in the parlor. It was a stuffy museum of a room. It had one gigantic cupboard, like something you'd find in a geology museum. Its monumental drawers—which fascinated me as a kid—contained rock samples from the mine, lumps of rust-red tin ores.

We talked stiffly about family, the house. Politics.

As usual my mother took her own sweet time to get to the point.

CLANCY SAID, "I give you Job 40, verse 15. *Behold now Behemoth, which I made with thee; he eateth grass as an ox.*"

"So what?"

"So what do you think the *behemoth* is supposed to be?"

Over the years, to hold my own with Clancy, I've looked up some of this stuff. "The word probably comes from the Egyptian *Pehemout*—which means 'the water bull'—"

"A hippopotamus. Well, it's possible."

"Clancy, anything's *possible*—"

"Yes. Like dwarf mammoths."

I was lost already. *"Dwarfs?"*

Clancy has a thing about mammoths.

It dates back to a fossil-hunting trip we took as kids on the bank of the Columbia river, where the Clovis people once hunted the great herds of Ice Age megafauna. Embedded in a rock strata we found a piece of mammoth tusk, bluish, curving. A piece of wild elephant, in North America. A spur to the imagination. It turned Clancy onto paleontology in general, and extinction events ended up as his specialty. Though not the event that took the mammoths.

That doesn't stop him having theories, though. In fact—unconstrained by too much fact—quite the opposite.

Clancy believes some mammoths survived the general extinction 10,000 years ago. He believed that, in fact, even *before* the business with my mother and our peculiar family history.

Then again he believes many things. I think he likes believing in things. Like a hobby.

Things such as dwarf mammoths.

Off the shore of California you'll find the Channel Islands, San Miguel and Santa Rosa and Santa Cruz. Maybe, said Clancy, the Islands had a population of mammoths.

You might wonder how the hell they got there in the first place. In the Ice Age the sea level was lower, and the Islands were linked—but the mainland was still twenty miles or so away, and the only way the mammoths could have got there is by swimming. But it's possible, as Clancy says.

And, stranded there, they became dwarfed. They finished no higher than six feet or so at the shoulder—a mere three inches taller than me.

"It happens," says Clancy. "In the Mediterranean, during the Pleistocene, there were dwarf antelopes on the Balearic Islands, dwarf hippopotami on Cyprus, miniature deer on Crete. All you need is a few thousand years of isolation, a restricted food supply."

This isn't bull. The remains of at least fifty fossilized dwarf mammoths have been dug up on Santa Rosa alone. But there's no evidence they survived until recent times.

Or maybe there is.

"There are Native American tales," Clancy said. "The Algonkians tell of a 'great moose' with a kind of limb that grew between its shoulders, a 'fifth leg' it used to prepare its bed. And the Naskapi of northeastern Labrador knew of a monster with a long nose it used to hit people. And then there are the reports of remains of mastodons and mammoths turning up on the American frontier all through the nineteenth century."

"What reports?"

"Finds of mammoth bones with soft tissue attached, like trunks."

"Myth. Folklore. Faked reports to encourage explorers and settlers. Plain misunderstandings."

"A bunch of Shawnee near the Ohio river found the trunk of a mastodon still attached to the skull."

"Actually the report described a skull with a long nose bone, not a trunk."

"In 1839 a guy called Koch found mastodon bones with skin attached in Missouri."

"Oh, come on. Koch was a showman. He was trying to make a living."

"But the reports were consistent. The hair found stuck to the flesh was usually a dun color."

"That's because it was probably algae clinging to buffalo bone…"

And so on. We argued about mammoths, living and dead, long into the night. Clancy won't stay contradicted for long. That's the beauty of the man.

MY MOTHER AND I walked around the mine workings.

The winching-tower was still there. There was a pile of ore, abandoned after the last workings. Pink dust lingered around it.

"On the surface," my mother said, "even when a hundred men were working two thousand feet down, you couldn't hear a thing. Not until they came up, anyway, the tinners and the trammers, hard hats and stripped to the waist, coated with the pink dust." I remembered them. Huge men who used to ruffle the hair of a diminutive Yank. "*Kernow bys vykken!*"—Cornwall forever! My mother said, "Even after a hot bath and a scrub, the miners' sheets were always stained pink. Of course they often died young, of pulmonary diseases."

Thus, my childhood.

Now I work for an aerospace consultancy in Seattle. We have a bright office, all glass, that overlooks the Sound. I work on advanced concepts, space stuff, suborbital and orbital. In a building that's as new as the morning sun, I study craft that don't even belong to the Earth. The whole West Coast is *new*. Christ, it's only 200 years since Captain Cook came exploring.

Tracy tells me I'm a culture shock case study.

The tin mine has been in the family for 200 years. In the last few decades we exhausted the shallow tin deposits, and foreign production got cheaper, and then the collapse of tin prices in the 1980s finished us off for good.

Kind of a shame, after all that time. I don't know what I'll do with the land. Sell it as a trailer park or a retirement community, maybe.

After that we took our walk on Bodmin, and talked about *it*.

"...After the mutilation," my mother said, "they never took *it* out of the grounds again. And Granddad started to care for it. He was only a boy himself at the time... So you see, there *can't* have been any Beast sightings after that time."

"And he looked after—*it*—until the fire—"

"During the war."

The Second World War. 1940. Seventy years after the mutilation, I thought. He cared for *it* for seventy long years.

"So who looked after—it—before my great-grandfather?"

"*His* grandfather. And he got *it* in the first place, from Erasmus Darwin. In fact he was a student of Darwin's."

"Darwin? The evolution guy?"

She pursed her lips, the way she always did when I said something dumb. "No. Erasmus was Charles's grandfather. But he was a naturalist too. He bequeathed *it* to the family when he died."

"So how long did grandfather's grandfather care for it?"

She shrugged. "The story is, since the turn of the century."

Now I was confused. "The twentieth century?"

"No," she said, mildly irritated. "The nineteenth."

Seventy years plus seventy more years...

"Come on," she said, "I'm getting cold. You can stand me a toasted teacake."

THE COLUMBIAN MAMMOTH was America's very own mammoth species. She was bigger than her woolly cousin—up to thirteen feet tall at the shoulder and weighing ten tons—and with a lighter coat, since she lived so much further to the south, in regions that stayed reasonably temperate even in the Ice Age. She lived alongside a lot of exotic critters, like giant armadillos and saber-toothed cats. And she had gigantic, spiraling tusks, Texas tusks.

We don't know what drove the mammoths to extinction.

For sure the climate changes when the ice retreated must have put them under pressure. But that had happened before. And, today, elephant populations recover from drought die-backs and such.

The difference, says Clancy, was people.

Clancy painted me a picture of humans hanging around the great die-off sites, where the mammoths, stranded in dwindling pockets of the grasslands that sustained them, fought and starved.

We just waited for them to die. We didn't hunt them. We didn't even have to butcher the corpses properly, there were so many of them, so much warm fresh meat every day.

We pushed them too hard, and, pow, extinction. The end of evolution, forever.

It must have been magnificent to see one of those creatures pass by. Dark and huge, she would have been the biggest moving thing in the world. And her walk would have been a sway of liquid grace, her head nodding with each step, her trunk swaying, her great weight obvious.

Gone, all gone.

Unless Clancy is right.

I admit it was eerie when I looked up Erasmus Darwin on the Internet and found he died in 1802, a date that exactly fit our peculiar family legend.

"I SAW IT once," my mother said abruptly.

"In the stable?"

"I was five years old," she said. "I used to find it frightening—the rumbling noises it made—oh, I hated it."

"What was it like?"

She frowned. "Like a fat, toothless, hairy old pony. It had a deformed face, a long nose."

"A *long nose?* Did it have tusks?"

"Of course it didn't have tusks. And the *stink*. And always eating. The amount of grass it used to get through, and the volumes of *dung* it produced. And of course," my mother went on, "the thing was devoted to my granddad. Well, he'd been looking after it since he was a boy. It had been toothless most of that time."

"You mean tuskless."

She sighed. "*Toothless.* Granddad told me *his* granddad told him that it had only one pair of teeth at a time, huge molars that grew forward in its jaw. When they wore out, a new set replaced the old. Until there were no more new teeth, which happened when Granddad was still a boy. After that he was given the job of grinding up grass and hay for the wretched animal…"

Without which care, like an old elephant whose last set of teeth has worn out, *it* would have starved.

Seventy years of devotion, between my great-grandfather and the monster in the barn. I told you we're loyal.

IT STRETCHED EVEN Clancy's credulity to believe there could have been a mammoth in a barn in Cornwall for the whole of the nineteenth century. Still, when I told him about Erasmus Darwin, he found a way. Which was how Thomas Jefferson comes into the picture.

Long story.

Jefferson—author of the Declaration of Independence, President twice over—had many interests. Including natural history.

Jefferson had a particular fascination with mammoths and mastodons. Mastodon bones had turned up in the Big Bone Lick, a salty bog in Kentucky. Jefferson believed there was no such thing as an extinct animal. He believed mammoths and mastodons might still be living in the American West.

Meanwhile there were scholars already digging around in the West. One of them was Baron Georges Cuvier.

"Who?"

"French anatomist," said Clancy. "Eventually he proved that the fossil bones of animals like mammoths and mastodons must be from creatures no longer living on the Earth. But—just suppose dwarf mammoths on the Channel Islands did survive until historical times."

"Long enough for Cuvier to have found one in 1800."

"One of the last survivors, maybe. And then he brought it home and gave it to Thomas Jefferson."

I sighed. "How come we never heard of this?"

"You have to understand the nature of the fossil record. Gaps everywhere. And as for history, people *lie*, Howie. If Cuvier went to all the trouble of establishing his Big Idea, that species go extinct, and then he found a counter-example to one of his most stunning cases—"

"He'd cover it up."

"Yeah. We know Jefferson was a great gift-giver."

Again Clancy was losing me. "He was?"

"Of course. And he was a great correspondent of some of the great men of science of his day—"

"Such as Erasmus Darwin? Too complicated, Clancy."

"I checked. Darwin and Jefferson had at least one acquaintance in common: Joseph Priestley, the chemist. And Darwin, as a naturalist, *would* have been interested in mammoths, and other extinct species. I imagine Jefferson would have enjoyed stirring up controversy among the radical types like Darwin with a live 'extinct' animal.

"Darwin dies in 1802, in Derbyshire, England. And his faithful student, your great-great-great-grandfather, is willed the mammoth and takes it to the family home in Cornwall. And the rest, as they say, is history. Your family history."

"WHY DIDN'T YOU come to America with Dad?"

"I couldn't leave all this. Howard, there have been mines in this area for *three thousand years*. We used to trade with the Phoenicians, for God's sake. It didn't seem right just to end it. After your grandfather died there was nobody but me to run the place. *Sten uyw arghans.*"

"Tin is money."

"Yes."

"But you didn't want me here."

We sat in silence for a while. My family has always been good at that.

Then my mother went to the big geological cupboard and pulled open a drawer. It was heavy, deep.

It was full of bones. Charred bones.

"The fire," I said.

"Yes. We never knew who started it—"

"*Who?*"

She shrugged thinly. "It was probably one of the locals. Superstitious lot, they can be. They wouldn't tell me what happened. Whether Granddad went into that fire to try to get it out. Or—"

"Or what?"

"Or whether *it* went in after *him*." She looked at me, her eyes rheumy. "I'd quite like to believe one or the other, wouldn't you? I mean, seventy years must count for something. *Yma-ef barth a woles yn pyt down ow lesky.*"

I could translate that. "He's down below, in a deep pit a-burning."

"However it happened, both of them died."

I fingered the bones. There were ribs, and fragments of huge thigh-bones, and at the bottom of the pile what looked like a skull, surprisingly graceful.

"CLANCY, EVEN IF Thomas Jefferson did have a pet dwarf mammoth in 1802—and even if it did get shipped to England—it couldn't have survived until 1940."

"Why not?"

"Because it would have been, conservatively, a hundred and forty years old."

Clancy wasn't fazed. "When Napoleon was in Egypt in 1798 the Turkish Pasha gave him a live elephant—an Asian bull, called Siam—that he brought back to Paris. Napoleon gave it to his father-in-law, who was Emperor of Austria. Siam was put into the Imperial menagerie in Vienna. But he turned savage, and they shipped him off to Budapest. There were reports that he was still alive in 1930, at the age of 150."

"Oh, crap."

"Siam turned docile with age," Clancy pointed out.

"You're saying this is what happened? Thomas Jefferson collects a mammoth. He keeps it for a while in Virginia. Then he gives it away to Darwin—"

"I'm saying it's *possible*. It's a *hypothesis*. And isn't it plausible? Logical? *Human?*"

That's Clancy for you. He just won't stay contradicted.

\* \* \*

SHE LOOKED ME full in the face. Her eyes were a rich earth brown (like, I thought absently, a mammoth's). "I didn't want you growing up with—*this*. This place. The underground. Obsessions with darkness and pink rock and ancient tongues... There's something Paleolithic about it. I didn't want you being trapped here, like me. I'm sorry," she said.

It was then that I understood. With her hints of family legends and Bodmin beasts, she'd lured me here. It was the nearest she could bring herself to saying goodbye.

That was what it was all about, you see. The subtext. She was dying.

We never were good at talking.

I touched the bones sadly. "*Behold now Behemoth... His bones are as strong pieces of brass; his bones are like bars of iron.*"

The last mammoth?

She eyed me. "It was only a horse, you know. A great big, ugly, deformed horse."

It could have been a horse. I'm no anatomist. Of course horses don't live 140 years. Maybe there was more than one horse.

I put the bones back in the drawer.

I never showed Clancy the bones. Somehow it wouldn't seem right. Then he'd have to take it all seriously.

Maybe I'll bury them with my mother.

# THE RIFT

*Paul McAuley*

## 1. RON VIGNONE

HE WAS STANDING at the very edge of the Rift, bare-chested in only shorts and hiking boots, kicking loose rocks down the steep slope. They clattered away, gaining speed as they rolled, beginning to bounce, bounding along until hitting a snag or outcrop and sailing out into the air, dwindling until they smashed into ledges or dry slopes of scrub far below, and Ron turned and looked at Ty Brown's video camera and yelled, "Virgin no more!" and danced along the edge and kicked down more rocks, feeling terrifically keyed up, the way he always did before a climb, like the anticipation of sex. He was slim and wiry, sweat glittering in the black hair which matted his chest, in the beard he'd started growing in the week it had taken them to get here, by light plane, by boat up a wide tributary of the Amazon, finally by helicopter from a loggers' camp.

The Rift stretched away for miles in either direction, the bluffs of its western edge overhung by forest, slopes and terraces and cliffs dropping away toward the perpetual mists which hid its bottom. There were plenty of loose rocks along the rim-slope, dangerous to anyone climbing below them, and it took most of the day to get it clear and safe so they could think of beginning the first pitch. Ron and a couple of the other climbers wanted to do it right then, even though the light was going, but the Old Man, Ralph Read, said no, they had plenty of time to do this right. He made a little speech about the Rift, saying that it was one of the last wildernesses, speaking to Ty Brown's camera with the sun going down in glory over the Serra Parima mountains.

Ron, eager to get going, ready to penetrate this baby all the way to the bottom, told Matt Johnson in disgust, "The Old Man's just realized he's too old for this, I reckon. He fucked up on the first expedition, and he's lost his nerve. We'll be carrying him down."

Matt, who spared a word only when he really had to, so that most days you thought he'd been struck dumb, just shrugged.

They camped out on bare rim rock, with the two helicopters tied down against the wind which had started to pick up after sunset, tents and piles of supplies and rope bags scattered on the stony ground and Coleman lanterns hissing out white glare here and there. It was the last time they would all be together.

In the middle of the night, Ron woke with a full bladder and moonlight shining through the fabric of the tent he shared with Matt Johnson. He went out and crabbed up a knob of rock that overhung the edge of the Rift. Far out and far below, the mist glowed faintly in the moonlight, looking like radioactive milk. Ron pissed into the void, and saw as he picked his way back to his tent that the science geek woman, the botanist, was watching him from the open flap of her tent. He grinned to himself. Maybe she'd loosen up before the trip was over.

The next day didn't start well: more rock kicking after the first easy pitch had been made, hard sweaty work crabbing along the sixty degree slope with the sun burning down and a hot wind blowing up from the Rift, while Barry Lowe and the Danes worked out the route. The Old Man had determined that the Danes would set the pace; the others would set up a relay for bringing down the supplies. And that was the way it went for the next three days as they descended into the Rift—the Danes forging ahead while Ron and the others worked like slaves moving supplies down to each new base camp, following pitches the Danes had made. The Old Man stayed up at the rim, keeping in radio contact with his number two, Barry Lowe; Ty Brown spent most of his time with the Danes, because that was where the action was, coming back up to the supply team's base camp each night breathless and elated.

The Danes were moving fast, Ron had to give them that, but they were using up rope, pitons, and rock bolts at a terrific rate and outstripping all efforts to keep up with them. Even the two science geeks started to complain. On the third night, Amy Burton got on the radio and, with Ty Brown filming her, told the Old Man that she couldn't do any work because she was too busy humping supplies.

They were camped on a wide dry ledge more than a mile into the Rift, having spent most of the day following traverses that zigzagged down a huge bluff, and then sliding down steep smooth chutes where temporary rivers of floodwater poured down the Rift during the rainy season. The bluff loomed above, blocking out half the sky; below, a forested forty-degree slope stretched away to its own edge.

"You told him right," Ron said to Amy Burton afterwards, as they all sat around the camp fire. "Everyone should get their turn."

Burton pushed a lock of lank blonde hair from her eyes. She was a stout, sunburnt woman in khaki shorts and a T-shirt and hiking boots. Like everyone else she smelt strongly of sweat and wood smoke. She said wearily, "He got money from the UN because he claimed this was a potential world heritage park, but while I'm working as a sherpa all I can do is sight surveys."

"Maybe I can help," Ron said, thinking of an assignation off in the bush. A couple of the guys were staring at him, and he gave them the finger surreptitiously, then saw, shit, that Ty Brown was filming, and Barry Lowe was watching him too.

"We're all caught up in this mad scramble," Amy Burton said. "Like the most important thing is to get to the bottom."

"Well," Ron said, turning his head to give the camera his best profile, "that's the point, isn't it? This is about the last place we can go without finding someone else's camp litter. Don't you think that's important?"

He was trying to be reasonable, but she stared at him with disgust. She said, "Maybe there should be places where no one ever goes."

Ron said, needled, "Then what's the point of them?"

"Because," she said, "what happens when everything's used up?"

Barry Lowe chipped in then, with bullshit about how much the scientific work was appreciated and how time would certainly be found for it once routes had been opened up, speaking for the record: and Alex Wilson, the TV guy who was looking for some kind of extinct sloth, said he certainly hoped so or else the expedition was a pointless show of macho bravado. It became a fierce argument, with Ty Brown's camera capturing everything. Ron, sidelined and silent, felt anger tighten in his chest, kinking like a twisted rope until he could hardly breathe, and he got up and walked away to the far end of the ledge. This wasn't what he had signed up for, carrying supplies and nursemaiding a couple of science geeks, and as they all hiked along a narrow trail through the steep little forest the next day he tried to tell Lowe that, tried to explain that he wanted some of what the Danes were getting, the pure stuff of establishing new routes. Lowe told him that his turn would come, but Ron knew now that the Rift was fucked forever in his head, and that some kind of payback was due.

## 2. TY BROWN

HE WAS EXHAUSTED every moment of the day, but exhilarated too, because he knew that he was getting something good here, a real drama unfolding in front of his lens. The expedition was slowly pulling itself apart. The Danes were moving too fast and the rest could barely keep up with them, and now Barry Lowe was worried that the rope would run out; none of the routes were as straightforward as the limited aerial surveys had suggested, making it necessary to establish many traverse pitches. Lowe had pleaded with Read over the radio to have more rope flown in, but Read wanted to press on because the rainy season was drawing near and he knew from the bitter experience of his first failed expedition that the Rift would be unclimbable then. And because the secret of the Rift was out, someone else, probably the Brazilian Army, would want to have a go next year. Meanwhile, the other climbers resented the fact that the Danes were the advance party and they did nothing but resupply, the two scientists resented the fact that they had had to virtually give up their work and pitch in to help, and the Old Man, Ralph Read, the grizzled charismatic climber who'd conquered every famous peak in the world, was reduced to an impotent god lost somewhere above, trying to run things through a bad radio link.

Communication was getting worse as they descended, the granite walls bouncing signals or simply swallowing them; no one knew what was below the perpetual mists because radar was bounced around the same way. The best guess was that the Rift was more than four miles deep. It had been completely unknown until Read had discovered it five years ago, although there were rumors of an expedition to this area a hundred years before, and the Indians who had lived in the forests below the massif before logging had displaced them told stories of the monsters which lived there.

Ty had always thought that there wasn't much chance of getting an undiscovered beast on tape, although that was how he had got the commission; he was supposed to be filming Alex Wilson's search for giant sloths, and had hours of material of the cryptozoologist talking to Indians, examining tufts of greenish hair they produced, squatting with them to examine animal tracks, or staring meaningfully into the darkness beneath the big forest trees. But now things were definitely taking on a human angle, which was what audiences loved. Finding some animal previously thought extinct was a two-day thrill, but human conflict was a keeper.

Ty had cut his teeth as a second unit cameraman on nature documentaries. He'd spent more than a decade camping out in remote areas, spending days waiting to get just the right thirty second shot of a bower bird's mating display or a baboon caught by a leopard (that one, filmed on the fly and shaky as hell, had won an award). He'd started up his own company, accumulating library shots and filler work for films that went out on National Geographic or PBS to decreasingly small audiences, but he knew it wouldn't last. Most people lived in cities; the only animals they saw in real life were roaches and pigeons (someone had won an award a couple of years ago with a documentary on urban pigeons; there was a joke in the trade that soon vermin would be the only species left to film). Nature documentaries were wallpaper, something to pass the time before the ball game started. And it was getting harder to find an animal species which hadn't already been filmed and which was sexy enough to get some attention. There had been three documentaries last year about the last remaining Galapagos tortoise, for Christ's sake.

But now he'd lucked out: his first real independent feature, which had started out as a pretty straightforward quest-for-a-living-fossil twenty-three minute filler, was turning into something different. Just as well, because so far there had been no trace of any animals at all in the Rift, and it was just too big, too inhuman in scale, to film properly. You could descend all day, and when you looked back all you'd see was the last fifty meters of overhang you'd abseiled down, hiding the bluff you'd spent most of the day traversing and the forest above that you'd spent the previous day hiking through. Right now, for instance, he was following Barry Lowe and one of the climbers, a vain little Brooklyn Italian, through a stunted forest which wasn't much different from the understory growth at the edge of what remained of the true forest, and you couldn't see that this was clinging to the side of a huge cliff because the skinny little trees were packed too closely together.

He'd have to get some aerial shots afterwards, but it wasn't the Rift that mattered anyway.

They were carrying a load of rope and following some kind of animal track which had been enlarged by the Danes (who weren't Danish) and marked here and there with red paint sprayed on a boulder or a tree bole; the rest of the party had returned to the previous base camp, to retrieve more supplies. It was mid-morning, the sun beginning to break through the canopy. They'd been descending for more than two hours when at last they came out of the edge of the forest. They abseiled a smooth dry chute to another ledge, then abseiled again, this time down a vertical cliff to more stunted forest, taking a lot of time to get all the rope bags down. And then they hiked for an hour through the forest to where the Danes had made camp yesterday afternoon, by a boulder field and a series of pools; Ty had taken some good footage of Kerry Dane unselfconsciously swimming in her underwear in the biggest pool.

But the Danes weren't there, although they had told Ty they'd wait.

The climber, Ron Vignone, dumped the three big blue nylon bags of rope in disgust and flopped back on them and stared up at the sky; Lowe switched on his radio and tried to contact the Danes. He got through after a couple of minutes of switching channels, but had scarcely established contact when the radio squealed and went dead. He couldn't get through to Read or to the supply team either, although he tried every one of the channels, and at last said they'd rest up and unpacked his Coleman stove and brewed some tea. He was big and blond, a strong, capable climber, affable in a baffled, English way and not too bright, very much Read's right-hand man. He was drenched in sweat, and his face was badly sunburned despite the fluorescent orange sunblock he had smeared over his nose and cheeks. He thought it might be best to wait until the rest of the party brought down the supplies, and then press on and catch up with the Danes the next day, but Ron Vignone said they would have gotten even farther ahead by then.

"Well," Lowe said, "they'll have to stop sometime. They'll run out of rope."

"Yeah," Vignone said angrily, "and then they'll start free-climbing and where'll we be? They'll run off with this fucking expedition if someone doesn't do something. I'll tell Read that if you haven't got the balls."

"The Old Man knows about it," Lowe said. He was trying to calm Vignone down, but his bland affability only riled the climber more.

The two men tossed it back and forth for a few more minutes, with Ty filming. Lowe tried the radio again, but succeeded only in running down his batteries. So they decided to go on while it was still light, and picked up the baggage and went on down through the boulder field, following the red splotches the Danes had helpfully sprayed here and there.

Half an hour into this, they saw the bird.

They were following a trail between two stands of forest toward a drop-off half a mile ahead. The bird flew straight across their path, so low that Vignone, who had the lead, threw himself flat. Ty managed to swing his camera on it: vaguely pigeon-shaped but bigger than a pigeon, dusty black plumage and a naked red head. It flew clumsily, crashing into the nearest trees and scrambling away through tangled branches. Ty thought he saw claws at the angles of its wings; then it was gone. A black feather floated down and he picked it from the air.

Vignone jumped up. "Did you see that fucking vulture go for me?"

"It was only a crow," Lowe said.

"They don't have crows in the Amazon basin," Ty said.

"A fucking vulture," Vignone said, and dusted himself down and went on, jumping from boulder to boulder with a careless agility.

It hadn't been a vulture either.

A couple of hours later, they caught up with the Danes. There was a short drop at the end of the long boulder field, which obviously was a stream in the rainy season, and then a series of pools stepping down between huge water-carved rocks, strange tree-ferns growing in pockets of soil on top of the rocks and shading the pools so that it was like descending through a green water chute. Most of the pools could be waded; the water was warm, and it was very humid. The only really deep pool could be crossed by clinging to a blue nylon rope bolted to the curved flank of a huge boulder while using a second rope as a kind of tightrope, and then swinging around the corner onto a knife-edge of slippery black rock that lipped the pool (Ty, made clumsy because he had to hold his camera away from the rock, scraped his arm badly). Then there was an easy descent over cobbled boulders to a forest of fern-trees, the air hot and humid under their stiff green fronds, their scaly trunks covered in creepers and bromeliads, blackflies and sweat bees a torment. They came out of this, and there were the Danes camped at the edge of a wide apron of rock.

The Danes weren't Danish; they were an Australian family who spent their lives adventuring. They'd sailed a yacht around the world, trekked through the Himalayas, spent two years trying to save one of the last coral reefs off Belize. Ken (who had a bit of Aborigine blood and never let you forget it) and his wife Kerry were both in their early forties, super-fit and very competent; their son, Sky, was seventeen, the youngest member of the expedition, and one of the best climbers. He and his parents worked together in a close-knit team.

Vignone started in on them almost straightaway, of course. He'd been working himself up to it on the descent. He told them that they were taking the best of the climb and turning everyone else into their bearers, that they were being selfish and wrecking the spirit of the expedition.

"Now hold on, mate," Ken said, "don't you think that's a bit harsh?"

"We're doing what we were asked to do," Kerry said. She put a hand on her husband's shoulder. She was taller than him. Her blonde hair was tied back from her tanned, lined face.

"I'd say we're doing a fair job," Ken said to Lowe, who shrugged uncomfortably, his face turning redder under its sunburn, and mumbled that there was a bit of feeling among the others, and maybe it would be a good idea to make a camp here and wait.

"And not rip on?" Ken said. "That's crazy. You can see what comes next. This beauty could be twenty miles deep for all we know."

They were at the top of a cliff that dropped into a narrow band of forest growing along the edge of another cliff: and so on, a series of cliffs and forested set-backs that stepped away toward the permanent mist cover, the banded bluffs on the far side of the Rift only half a mile away. Ty had taken a panoramic shot of it in the last light; now he had switched on the camera's floodlight and was filming the argument, swinging from face to face and hoping the microphone caught it all.

Vignone wanted the Danes to go back and join the resupply team while some of his climbing friends took their places; the Danes didn't see what was wrong with pressing on; both parties wanted Lowe to make a decision, and Lowe didn't want to. He tried using the Danes' radio to contact Read, but without any success, then said it would be best to wait, they'd done fantastically well and it was time to rest up and plan the next part of the descent.

"We've hardly begun to crack it," Ken Dane said.

"If you hadn't set up so many traverses," Vignone said, "we'd be much farther down and we wouldn't be so short of rope."

Which started another argument as the air darkened around them, until at last Vignone said that he was making the next pitch right now and would camp out alone, glaring at Lowe when the Englishman said mildly that it wasn't a very good idea.

"I want some fucking climbing," Vignone said. He was already sorting through one of the rope bags, paying out blue nylon cord in neat loops.

Sky said that he'd go with Vignone, but Vignone said he would solo it; the rock was dry and craggy. So after the wiry little man had put on his harness and climbing shoes and fixed the rope to the edge of the cliff, Ty filmed the first stage of his descent in the dusk, with Sky watching beside him. Sky was taller than his parents, his blond hair shaved close to his skull. When Vignone disappeared into a chimney and Ty turned off the camera, Sky said thoughtfully, "There are all sorts of weird things out here. I hope that guy doesn't run into any of them."

"I saw a bird today," Ty said. "A very strange bird."

Ken Dane said that there might be anything down here, there were hundreds of kilometers of forest after all, and his wife said, "This kind of place would make a fine reserve, don't you think? That's partly why we're here.

You people make so much noise you've scared off all the wildlife—even we can hear you, sometimes. But we've seen a few things, moving away from us. There are some big animals down here. Ron has let his pride overrule his caution."

Ty knew that a jaguar could crush your skull in its jaws while you slept, or an anaconda could ease you into its gullet without waking you. Wild pigs could knock you down and strip your bones in a couple of minutes. There were dozens of species of poisonous spiders, and snakes, and scorpions. The campfire seemed very small in the huge darkness of the Rift.

Sky said, "I should go down there maybe."

"It's too dark now," Ken said. "We'll check him out first thing."

Ty told the Danes about the bird, and showed them the black feather he'd caught. It was greasy, and had a pungent, musky odor.

"Dr Wilson will be pleased," Kerry Dane said.

They all woke a little after dawn. Ken and Sky Dane abseiled down the cliff to check on Ron Vignone; Ty Brown and Kerry Dane and Barry Lowe were eating breakfast when father and son came back and dumped Ron Vignone's torn sleeping bag in front of them.

### 3. Dr Alex Wilson

THERE WAS SO much fuss about the missing climber that Ty Brown forgot to tell Alex about the bird until the evening after the search.

Alex wasn't too worried. It was well known that Vignone had been pretty pissed at the way the Danes had charged ahead of everyone else, and he'd probably gone off to get some glory of his own. Foolish and selfish, yes, but that was all it was. He'd left his sleeping bag behind and it had been torn up by animals. There was no blood, no trail; any animal dragging away a human body would have left both. No one would listen to Alex's opinions though, and Lowe insisted on wasting the day by searching the long narrow forest.

Ever since they had begun the descent into the Rift, Alex had been possessed by a kind of smoldering fury mixed with anxiety—the whole expedition had been turned into a circus, a race for the bottom at all costs, and he had been helpless to stop it. The search for the missing climber was finally a chance to look around, but Alex was paired up with a taciturn climber who took the search seriously and the noise the others made probably scared off every animal in the Rift: he saw nothing and returned in a bad temper made worse because the botanist woman, Amy Burton, was brimful of enthusiasm. The forest was a relict community, she said, full of cycads, gnetophyte vines and ancient species of pines; even something she was pretty sure might be a species of cycadeoid, a group thought to have died out tens of millions of years ago, although she couldn't be sure because it had not been bearing any cones. She wanted Alex to help her do some quadrats right there so that she could attempt to determine species diversity, but he refused of course, and tried to explain that diversity best correlated with number of bird species—what was the point of counting plants or insects when it was easier to look for birds?

"At least we can count plants," Amy Burton said. She was a defiant, dumpy woman, her T-shirt sweat-stained and her dishwater blonde hair ratty around her face. Alex pointed out that when it came to preserving ecosystems rare animals were essential in raising a media profile, and she walked away, flushed with anger.

Alex turned to Ty Brown, who had been filming them, and said, "I hope you got all that."

He was pissed with Ty, too. The cameraman had become obsessed with silly little spats and disputes when he should have been concentrating on Alex's work; after all, the bulk of the sponsorship had been raised to look for rare or previously unknown animals. But like most naturalists Ty was contemptuous of cryptozoology. He saw it as monster hunting, searching for Bigfoot or the Loch Ness monster or dinosaurs in the Congo, when really it was nothing of the sort—well, it was true that Alex *had* collaborated with Read in a search for Bigfoot in the Sierras a couple of years ago, but that had just been to raise his profile so he could get money to do some real scientific work, something a snobby academic like Amy Burton, with her university sinecure, couldn't understand. No, cryptozoology was just what it meant: the study of hidden animals. Even today, with ecosystems all over the world in poor shape and even the most remote forests being cut down, new species were turning up all the time: an ungulate in Vietnam, a parrot in Venezuela, a big flame-kneed tarantula in the Sonoran desert. It was quite possible that some of the large mammals which had been wiped out by human invasion of North America had survived in remote areas of the South American rain forest; there had been indisputable sightings of giant sloths by loggers and Alex was pretty sure that the hair samples he had obtained from the local Indians would yield DNA for testing.

He was so riled by the dumb argument with the Burton woman that at first he ignored Ty when the cameraman said he'd seen an odd bird the day before, but then Ty produced the feather and described what he'd seen, and Alex's anger melted away because even before he saw the brief blurred video clip on the camera's tiny screen he knew what it had to be, and that this would make his name and end forever the hard scrabble for funds and the contempt of lab-bound scientists.

On the other side of the camp, Lowe shouted and clapped his hands for attention, saying that he'd finally made contact with the Old Man, and he was already on his way down.

### 4. RALPH READ

IT WAS ALL falling apart, and the injury to his knee was almost the final blow. He'd come here to prove that he was still who they all thought he was, Ralph Read, the Old Man, Himalayan veteran back when Katmandu hadn't been full of bad German cooking and American hippies, before the real explorers had run out of world to explore, before it had become so small and used up. Last time he'd been up Everest, escorting some film actor and a documentary crew, he had been horrified by what had happened to the beautiful mountain: the queues of fee-paying novice climbers waiting their turn to strike for the summit, the litter, the piles of shit, the toilet paper and food wrappers blowing around, the discarded oxygen and propane cylinders, the dead bodies lying in the ice, everyone too preoccupied with getting to the top or too exhausted to bury them properly, let alone bring them down. He had helped do that to her, he realized—the horde had followed in his footsteps. She was ruined. And now his life in ruins too. It was the Rift, the bitch of the Rift. All mountains were women to Ralph; he had seduced them—*ravished* them—with the same inexhaustible energy with which he had pursued real women. And the Rift was no different, except they had to conquer her from the top down, but she was hard, the bitch, too hard for him. The Old Man: old and fucked up.

Perhaps it was because of the dirty secret, he thought, the thing no one else but he knew, the way he'd found out about her and then pretended she was his discovery when all along she'd been someone else's. Like many of the old-style mountaineers, Ralph was a deeply superstitious man. Back then you relied on yourself and your own good luck, not on piton guns and free-running carabineers and nylon rope, on oxygen and lightweight sleeping bags and radios—good Christ, people even took portable phones up mountains now, to call up the rescue services when they got in trouble or ran out of soup. No, you had needed skill and luck in the glory days of climbing, before technology all but factored luck out of the equation, and luck was an intangible gift that had to be carefully cultivated.

But now he'd blown it; he should have known on his first expedition into the Rift, when he had tried to follow the route of the Victorian explorers and had been caught by an early start to the rainy season and had almost drowned. And now this, a man lost and his knee fucked and Alex Wilson babbling in his face about some stupid bird—Wilson had never understood that at the heart of the expedition was the need to conquer, to claim, to show that the Rift's wilderness could be matched and overcome by the human spirit.

It was all just too bad: bad luck.

It took Ralph a day to descend to where the expedition had stalled, far longer than he had expected. He had always known that he wasn't up to forging the path all the way down, but he thought that he could make the last mile or so, wherever it was below the perpetual mists, be the first to the bottom. So he waited at the rim, ostensibly to coordinate the supply lines and the advance party, but even that went wrong very quickly—the Rift's granite walls scrambled radio signals, and the helicopter pilots refused to descend within her walls because of unpredictable updrafts and katabatic winds dropping over the edge. So in the end he'd decided to go down early, and just as well, because halfway down, when he finally made contact with Lowe, he learnt that one of the young climbers had gone missing and Lowe was in a panic about it, a good second-in-command but lacking the backbone to make decisions in the pinch.

Ralph had trained rigorously for the Rift, but he was too old; no amount of training could get him fit enough. His arms were still strong and he could bench press twice his weight, but his lung capacity was half what it was and his legs were giving out. Even though he was helped by two climbers, the descent took far too long, and then he banged up his knee.

He had been all right abseiling down the easy pitches—the equipment and gravity took care of that—but there were far too many traverses and far too much walking, and then there was a tricky move around a big boulder at the edge of a pool, something that in his prime he would have managed easily. But he hurt his knee badly making the move, and hurt it again when he landed half in water, half on the pool's rocky rim, and it quickly swelled even though one of his helpers put a pressure bandage on it. He insisted on going on, although every step jammed a red-hot needle under his tender kneecap, at last having to be supported on either side by his helpers down the boulder field, then lowered in a sling down the cliff like a sack of meal, sweating like a pig and itching with prickly heat, the muggy air like gruel in his lungs.

So when he finally arrived at the camp, he was exhausted and almost in tears, from the pain of his injury and from the shame of his failure, not at all ready to deal with the pandemonium which erupted around him almost at once. Lowe was desperate for advice while at the same time pretending that he had done everything he could; the other climbers all wanted to give their opinion; and Alex Wilson was babbling about some bird someone had spotted.

Ralph waved them all off, demanding in his stentorian voice that he be given some hot chocolate and perhaps something to eat and certainly somewhere comfortable so that he could put up his knee. That gave him a breathing space, and at last he was seated on a pile of rope sacks, turning his good profile to the glare of the light clipped to Ty Brown's video camera, one big hand wrapped around a steaming tin mug, the other stroking his bristling beard, for all the world like a monarch and the climbers his supplicants, Wilson skulking with the botanist woman, the two of them exchanging furious whispers like plotters at the edge of his court. He got the story out of Lowe, silencing with a glare anyone who tried to chip in, and knew it was bad. The expedition had been strung out too thinly—he'd let the Danes set the pace and they had gone off without any regard for the difficulties of resupply. Despite the money they'd brought, bamboozled from some long-haired bleeding-heart pop-singer millionaire, it had been a mistake taking them on: they weren't team material. And it was clear that his guesses about what supplies would be needed had been hopelessly inadequate. At this rate they'd run out of rope in two or three days, and they were nowhere near the bottom yet. But he had to try and salvage what he could.

Ralph asked for silence and made a pretence of thinking, but he had decided what to do almost at once. Divide and rule, the only way. So he told them that the climbers would be organized into two teams, taking turns to forge new pitches or work on resupply, scavenging rope if necessary. The Danes, who had already done so much good work, would have the important job of looking for the missing climber... for a moment he couldn't remember his name. Vignone, that was it, Ron Vignone.

"He's probably gone off on his own, but we need to make sure he isn't lying up somewhere with a broken ankle, eh?" He looked around at them all, beaming with patriarchal benevolence.

Lowe objected of course, because Ralph had undermined his authority, such as it was. He especially didn't like the idea of scavenging rope from pitches higher up. "What if we need to ascend quickly? If someone gets hurt or the rains start early?"

"We've plenty of good climbers," Ralph said. "I'm sure they can re-establish the routes quickly enough, especially as the pitons are already emplaced."

"I don't know," Lowe said. "Some of those overhangs are rather—"

"I chose my climbers well I hope," Ralph said. "I'm sure they're up to the challenge."

And of course they all nodded, either because they were as full of piss and vinegar as he had been at their age, or because they didn't want to admit their fear: once you let your fear show you're finished as a climber.

"Well then," Ralph said, and smiled at them all and lit a cigar, even though he was still short of breath in the soupy air, and asked Ty Brown, "I hope you got all that, young man. It's a pivotal point in our little adventure."

Alex Wilson came forward, stepping among the climbers, and said, "What about the bird?"

Ralph had forgotten about that detail. He blew a plume of cigar smoke and said, "You and the young lady there can help look for Ron, and perhaps you'll find this bird too."

In his opinion the whole thing would go faster without having to nursemaid a couple of scientists. Perhaps this really would work out after all. Of course, losing a team member was unfortunate, but it was excusable as long as they reached their goal. A necessary sacrifice.

Wilson wanted more, of course—he wanted everyone to look for the confounded bird, and the botanist woman backed him up even though the two of them had previously been like cat and dog. Wilson babbled about relic populations, about the importance of a living fossil which might resolve the debate about whether or not birds had evolved from dinosaurs. "If I can find a fertile egg, I can determine whether its digits are reduced according to the theropod pattern or that of modern birds. And dissection will show whether the lungs are bellow-like or flow-through. It will be the discovery of the century, believe me," and so on, playing to Ty Brown's camera until Ralph cut him off.

"We still need to get to the bottom of the Rift, so we must push on."

Wilson was so wound up he was actually quivering with indignation. "But the science—"

"Science and exploration go hand in hand here," Ralph told him. "Now, I think we've had enough talk. I'm sure we all need some rest. We have a lot of work to do, but I'm confident you are all up to it."

But later, he was unable to sleep. The expedition was falling apart, a man missing and almost certainly dead, and he had staked everything on a last throw, a desperate race for the bottom which would only succeed if his luck held. He lay awake a long time, thinking of the notebook he had discovered, the diary of a member of a Victorian expedition which had penetrated several miles into the Rift before being chased off by a fierce tribe of Indians, the clues it provided enough to pinpoint the

Rift on photographs taken by a Russian landsat so that he could claim it for himself, and himself alone. Read's Rift. It had a certain ring. He had never told anyone about the notebook; no one but him knew about the indigenous tribe or the other things. The relic bird was nothing compared with the claims of the Rift's first explorers, but of course he couldn't tell Wilson about that, just as he couldn't reveal that he knew that a lost tribe of Indians lived here.

And so no one was armed except for him. He had brought his ex-army Webley .45. He hoped upon hope he wouldn't have to use it. That his luck would hold.

He was wrong.

### 5. Amy Burton

"At least we can get some work done," Alex Wilson said *sotto voce* to Amy the next morning, as the two parts of the expedition got ready, one to descend further, the other to retrieve ropes from higher up. A sentiment which managed to shock her even though she had already decided that, this side of snake oil sellers, dieticians, and shampoo manufacturers, Wilson was quite the most amoral person masquerading as a scientist she'd ever come across. A man had gone missing, for God's sake; he might be dead. Well, perhaps she shouldn't be surprised. It was common gossip that Wilson's PhD was nothing of the sort, merely an honorary doctorate from a mid-West college dazzled by his series of lost world TV documentaries, and it seemed to Amy that he was both horribly arrogant and desperately insecure. She'd kept away from him as much as possible, given that he kept trying to pick fights with her on specious grounds, and fortunately he'd spent more and more time arguing with the cameraman, who proposed following the new lead team rather than filming Wilson searching for his bird.

Meanwhile, Ralph Read sat on his throne of rope bags saying nothing yet trying to look as if he was still in command. He was pale under his tan, sweating heavily, and massaging his bandaged knee when he thought no one was looking. When Amy saw him take a swig of something from a silver flask, she assumed her best no-nonsense voice and told him she'd take a look at that knee, and he gave in after a token protest.

"I've no objection to be administered to by a comely young woman," he said.

"Bullshit," Amy said, for she harbored no illusions about herself—she was a dumpy, pear-shaped thirty-five, a handmaiden to science with a poor career profile because she loved field expeditions far more than the publication mill or the petty rivalries of university departmental politics. Her father had worked for the CIA in Central America in the Sixties, when half the governments had been in the pay of the United Fruit Company, and although she was irredeemably left-wing in the classic pattern of anti-parental rebellion, she loved her father for the camping expeditions on which he'd taken her and her brother—it was where she had developed her passion for botany, and where her life had been shaped.

She got rid of the poorly knotted bandages by using her Swiss Army knife; Read winced as she probed his knee with expert fingers. It was in bad shape, misshapen and swollen with internal bleeding, the skin a shiny black. She treated it with Novocain cream and splinted it, and told Read that he should really be taken back up.

"The expedition needs me," he said. "I'm quite comfortable, and I'm sure the radio will work better down here. Thank you," he added. "It does feel better."

"In this climate it'll get gangrenous if you don't get proper treatment," she warned him.

"Oh, a little gangrene is nothing," he said, with a ghost of his usual braggadocio. "I lost two toes on my first assault on K2."

Before they left, Amy had two of the climbers rig up a sunshade for the silly vain old man, and then the expedition divided with noisy banter. The Danes got up from where they had been squatting and drifted into the forest—a strange secretive bunch, but Amy quite liked them, despite Ken's aggressive assertion of his one-eighth Aboriginal ancestry. Ty Brown went down the cliff with the lead party; Alex Wilson ascended with the rope scavengers to search for his bird where Ty had seen it yesterday. Amy shouldered her backpack and made herself scarce before the old man tried to persuade her to stay and keep him company rather than wandering off into a dangerous forest by herself.

Amy didn't think the forest dangerous at all, although it *was* spectacularly strange. With cycads as the primary growth, it really was the kind of place where you expected to be confronted by a dinosaur, and she was certain that several of the species she saw were new to science—either relic species or genuinely unknown. If she could have her way, the expedition would abandon all efforts to get to the bottom and concentrate on doing some real science, but there was no chance of that while Read was still its leader. He was interested in nothing but climbing. He'd even called this place a rift for God's sake, when it was nothing at all like a rift valley: it was a canyon, probably formed on a fault line and deepened by irregular uplift and water erosion, perhaps even the collapse of an underground water course.

The narrow belt of forest stretched for more than a mile to either side of the camp, slashed by smooth rock flood channels. It was like the cliff forests that had been discovered in Canada, a refuge for dozens of species which could obtain precarious footholds in its diverse range of microhabitats; and it was also an island population, its environment both geographically isolated and physically distinct from the rain forests around the massif which the Rift bisected, an evolutionary laboratory where species could explosively radiate to fill empty niches.

Amy passed through the forest which had been searched yesterday, descended a long gentle grade of tumbled rocks, an old rockfall overgrown by creepers and ferns and moss, and rambled on through the unexplored lower terrace of the forest. She sketched and took meticulous photographs with a scale always in the foreground, took samples of leaves and cones and flowers and placed them in plastic bags with a dusting of camphor powder to kill bugs, carefully documented each photograph and specimen. She took species counts of gridded areas too, and assessed growth habits as best she could.

And always she was filled with wonder at the treasure house through which she wandered, a last wilderness that even now was being despoiled by the expedition. Wilson was right about the bird, of course; if it was a living fossil, a close relative of the ancestral species of modern birds, surviving as coelacanths had survived in the deep waters off East Africa before they had been fished out, then it really was a fantastically important scientific discovery. Yet the forests were important too, although he couldn't see it—that was the problem with zoologists. They were so focused on their big mammal star species—pandas or tigers or blue whales—that they often didn't see the importance of the infrastructure of plants and fungi and insects and even bacteria which made up the habitats where the mammals lived. The primary mistake of zoos and many conservation bodies was to believe that by saving a rare animal they had somehow preserved the most important member of a vanishing habitat, but without the thousands of unacknowledged species which coexisted with it, it was no more than a trophy living out the last of its days in sterile captivity. More enlightened programs held that everything in a habitat was important; they took cores or sweep samples, tried to calculate and define biodiversity. That was why Amy's work was so important.

In this way, the day passed quickly, until she discovered the standing stone.

In fact, she walked right past it without really seeing it. It was only when she was taking a photograph a little way off that she really saw what it was, and went back with her heart hammering, suddenly full of apprehension.

It was a columnar piece of native granite a dozen feet high, perhaps originally flaked from the cliff by weathering, but someone had set it upright in the thin laterite soil and shaped its base into the crude likeness of a pregnant woman. It reminded Amy of the ancient clay figures discovered in prehistoric cave dwellings. She walked around it, noting brown, wilted flowers at the base, and a pile of rotten figs, and started to take photographs, the click of the camera shutter and the whine of the motor suddenly very loud and obtrusive in the watchful green of the forest. She was just putting the camera back in her pack when she heard a faint crackle far off, as if someone had stepped on one of the dried cycad fronds which everywhere littered the ground. Heart in mouth, she lifted the pack and backed into a stand of feathery mimosa, settling down on her haunches, her eyes skittering back and forth as they tried to distinguish movement in the green shadows.

There! A tall figure drifting silently down the path she had followed. Amy almost burst out laughing, for she saw at once who it was. He was quite naked, and carried something before him—a bright wreath of orchids, which he placed with awkward yet touching reverence at the foot of the standing stone.

When Amy stood up and stepped from her hiding place, he jumped almost a foot in the air and then she did laugh, and after a few seconds he did too.

"Well, you caught me I guess," Sky Dane said, with a rueful grin.

"I didn't mean to." Amy wanted to ask the boy where his parents were, and where his clothes were, too (although he was so unselfconsciously naked that he was clad, as it were, in his dignity). Instead, she asked him about the standing stone, and who might have carved it.

"I mean," she said, "no Indian tribes would work something like this in stone. It isn't in their tradition."

"Not in their tradition, I guess, no."

"But there is a tribe living here."

"Sort of."

"And you know about them, you and your parents."

"Sort of." She stared at him and he did blush then, and added, "We've seen signs here and there. We travel fast, faster than the others suspect, so we've had time for a bit of exploring. We saw one or two things. There's an old cliff dwelling half a mile up, made in a cave under an overhang. They must have lived there a fair old time because the ashes from their fires are more than ten feet deep, but my dad reckons that no one has lived there for thousands of years. We found some glyphs carved in the rocks, too, although you have to have the eye to see them."

"Who are they? Do you think they took the climber?"

For a moment Amy had the horrible thought that perhaps the Danes had murdered him—but no, Ty Brown and Alex Wilson had been with them.

Sky said, "They killed him most like. It's what Indians do with intruders on their patch. Look, are you going to tell about this?"

Amy said carefully, "Is it important that I don't?"

"Not when you get back. In fact, it's important you tell people, because of the government rules about undiscovered tribes. We can give you stuff about what we found, photos and the like. But I mean, you won't tell the others now."

"I don't see why—" Amy started to say, but got no further because that was when the shots rang out in the distance.

Two shots, close-spaced, echoing off the cliff above. A third rang out just after Amy started to run, chasing after Sky's fleet figure, his buttocks glimmering in the green gloom as he raced away from her.

It was a long run, across the old rockfall and through another mile of forest. She arrived at the camp covered in sweat and out of breath, mouth parched with fear. Sky, now wearing shorts and a T-shirt, was tending to a man who lay on the ground clutching his thigh—there was blood running between his hands, soaking his shorts. Ralph Read stood at the edge of the drop, propping himself up with a tent pole and menacing the air with a huge antique revolver.

"They ran, by God," he shouted to Amy, fierce and exultant. "By God how they ran!"

"Here," Amy told Sky, "let me look," and knelt by the wounded man.

It was one of the young climbers, Matt Johnson. His face was gray, and slick with sweat. He told Amy, his voice tight with pain, "They came at us while we were hacking through forest a couple of terraces below. I don't know where the others are."

Amy glanced at Sky and said, "Tell me later," and pried his fingers away from his thigh and saw the slim arrow shaft which stood up from it, fletched with dyed red feathers. She probed around it, determined that the head wasn't in the bone, and told Matt Johnson what she was going to do. "It will hurt," she said.

"It already hurts."

"You had better hurry there," Read shouted. "The buggers will be back."

Amy twisted up her handkerchief and gave it to Matt Johnson to bite down on, then cut the shaft in half with her knife and with one quick hard motion pushed the remainder of the arrow through the meat of his thigh. Blood gushed as the arrowhead broke through the skin on the far side. Its point was flaked stone, neatly socketed in the shaft. She got a grip on blood-slick stone and drew the rest of the shaft from the wound.

Matt Johnson looked at it and shuddered and said, "Jesus fuck."

"Don't faint on me now," Amy told him, hoping he wasn't going into shock.

"It isn't so bad."

"You're lucky it wasn't poisoned," Sky said.

Amy washed blood from the young climber's wounds, sprinkled antibiotic powder in them and packed them, and wound a bandage tightly around his thigh. A little blood soaked through, but the arrow seemed to have missed the major vessels.

Ralph Read had been hobbling up and down at the edge of the cliff, yelling into the radio, cursing, switching frequencies, and yelling some more. Now he threw the radio aside and drew his revolver and fired three times at something below the cliff edge, each shot a tremendous shocking noise. "Here they come!" he shouted into the echoing silence, and broke the revolver open and thumbed brass cartridges into its chamber, closed it, and started to fire again.

Amy reached the edge of the cliff and looked down just as the arrows started to fly up, dozens of them twinkling at the peak of their ascent and then slipping back down the air. Ralph Read began to shoot into the trees from which they came, the revolver bucking in his hand. Amy thought she saw shadows slipping through shadows beneath the cycads along the edge of the talus slope at the bottom of the cliff, and then Sky pulled her away.

"You must go!" Sky yelled, but she hardly heard him, half-deafened by the revolver and the hammering of her heart. He tried to drag her across the rock apron toward the cliff and the fixed ropes, but she pulled back.

Ralph Read was leaning on the tent pole and reloading his revolver, a wild and grim expression on his face. He glanced at them and said, "I'll keep them off until you reach the top of the cliff. I can't climb with this blasted knee, but you can lower a sling and get me up that way. Go on now!"

Sky said, "He's right. I'll stay and help him. You go. And remember to tell the authorities that there are Indians living here!"

Matt Johnson had already climbed into his harness, and now he helped Amy get into hers. She hadn't realized how scared she was until she tried to do up the buckles, all thumbs. She said to Matt Johnson, "Can you climb?"

"I can always climb. I got back, didn't I?"

His face was still gray with shock, and his hands were trembling, but he got her harness fastened and roped her to him and they started the climb, leaning out more or less horizontally and walking up the face of the vertical cliff of hard red-black granite. The harnesses were fixed to the ropes with jumars, metal clasps which slid up the rope but not down, and although these made the climb easier, Amy's arms and shoulders were soon burning. There was a traverse thirty feet up, a narrow ledge to the chimney that led up through a big overhang. Matt Johnson started to spider along it; he had to use his legs as much as his arms, and she heard his gasps of pain. Then he was at the chimney and paid out the belay rope, and it was her turn. Just as she started the traverse, her clumsy hiking boots slipping on the ledge, her hands cramping around the rope, the greasy granite an inch from her nose, something clattered beside her. An arrow. More lofted toward her, small deadly things that struck the rock on either side and dropped away. Then she was at the chimney and hauled herself up with Matt Johnson yelling encouragement. When she was lodged safely in it, rock on either side, she dared look back.

Below, Ralph Read was standing by the piled equipment in the center of the rock apron, firing first to one side and then the other. Arrow shafts stuck out from his torso. Figures were dancing at the edge of the cycads, seemingly dressed in shaggy hides. She could not see Sky. Then the belay rope tightened. Matt Johnson was climbing on and she turned and followed him and saw no more.

## 6. The Danes

WHAT CAN YOU say about the Danes? They are not Danish but Australian. They are a tightly bound unit, mother and father and son. They have their own rituals, their own body language. They are bonded together so tightly that nothing can pry them apart—not Ken's occasional infidelities, not Sky's occasional moony girlfriends, whom he mostly ignores because he needs nothing more than his family and their way of life.

They had a long palaver after Ralph Read's speech, realizing that they had reached the crux of their private
mission. "We'll look for this cludger," Ken said, "but they
certainly murdered him, and they don't want us to find his
body or they would have just left it."

Sky, who loved horror movies, said, "Ate him, I
reckon."

"Now we don't know that," Kerry said. "The evidence
for cannibalism was only found in grave sites, and it was
probably ritual."

"It's what they do in the New Hebrides," Sky said.

"These people aren't anything like that," Kerry said.

"They murdered him and stuffed his body somewhere,"
Ken said. "And they'll probably kill the rest of the
climbers, too. It's a shame, but there it is. It isn't their fault
these bastards came blundering in."

"That's just why we should tell Read what we know,"
Kerry said, but Ken vetoed that. "That bugger Wilson
would chase after them," he said, "and so would Read.
The two of them went looking for Bigfoot together,
remember. So we can't let them know what's here; the
poor people would be turned into circus freaks."

They talked some more, but it was decided. The next
day they went their separate ways into the forest, and
when the inevitable happened, Read's revolver shots
ringing out into the Rift and finally ceasing, they met up
in a prearranged spot several miles south of the camp-
site.

Even when part of other expeditions, the Danes always
had their own agenda. It added spice, as Ken liked to say,
and spice was everything in life. He didn't mind that people said they were hippies, relics from a lost age, that he
was trying to keep his youth alive through adventure. It
was all part of the cover for the half-world they inhabited.
There were others like them, keeping the secrets of the

world safe, a disorganized conspiracy which somehow worked most of the time.

They had been allowed to join the expedition because they had wangled money from a pop star to look for new tribes of Indians. There were still plenty to be found in the Amazonian basin, even at this late stage in its exploitation. The forests really were very extensive and very close grown. A hundred people, the size of most Indian tribes, living off the land in a small area, could stay hidden until some prospector or logger stumbled into them by accident. Just a couple of years ago, a jaguar hunter had been murdered, shot with an arrow, when he had encountered a hunting party of a previously unknown tribe, and a subsequent aerial survey had spotted the tribe's huts, almost invisible beneath the close-knit forest canopy. Like all recently discovered tribes, it had been left alone; the late twentieth century was as toxic to these Stone Age indigenes as poison gas. The whole area had been declared off-limits.

That was what the Danes hoped for here, and they were pretty certain now that this was a very special tribe indeed. They met at the standing stone. Sky was naked again, as were his mother and father. Sky had smeared the green juice of berries on his face and bare chest. He had knotted a black T-shirt around his head to hide his blond hair. He told his parents what had happened, and Ken nodded and asked what the botanist woman had seen.

"They didn't come into the open until she was halfway up the cliff," Sky said. "I reckon she didn't see too much. But one of the climbers got away too, and I don't know what he saw."

Ken scratched at the pelt on his chest. He was a stocky man, with a broad nose and a shock of wiry hair. "Well, it's a risk," he said, "but not a bad one. The others will be too scared to look around much."

Sky thought about how Amy had found him, and her questions, but kept silent. He trusted her; she had been the only one who had tried to understand this place.

"They'll think it's just Indians," his wife said. "They don't have the imagination for anything else."

"We'll wait here a while I reckon," Ken said. "When the fuss has died down we'll see what's left of the supplies, and then we can begin."

They sat in green shadow a little way from the standing stone. "They ran from everyone," Kerry said dreamily, leaning against her husband.

"It was the first great extinction," Ken said. "They were killed just like my people were killed when the Europeans came to Australia. They were hunted for sport because it was easier to think of them as animals than accept that people come in many different forms. *Homo sapiens* has done a lot of harm in its time, but that was the beginning of it all."

"Some got away," Kerry said. "Think how far they came! They were pushed further and further from Africa."

"Or Java," Ken said.

"They must have been the first to cross from Asia to Alaska," Kerry said, "but the modern humans followed and pushed them farther. Until they ended up here, with the other relict species."

"Something's coming," Sky said, and at the same moment the first of them stepped out of the darkness between the cycads.

"Steady," Ken said. "Remember we're not like the others."

The figure which confronted them was small and stooped yet muscularly broad, and covered in a reddish pelt. Its feet clutched the earth; one leathery hand clutched a sapling whittled into a spear. Little eyes glinted under the shelf of its brow; its nose was broad and bridgeless; there was no chin beneath its wide mouth. It made no signal, but suddenly there were others behind it.

Sky and Ken and Kerry slowly got to their feet. Naked, they held out their hands to show that they had no weapons, that they were no threat, and waited for judgment.

# CHEERING FOR THE ROCKETS

*A Jerry Cornelius story*
*Michael Moorcock*

## 1. NOON

*There is this same anti-Semitism in America. I hear the
swirl and mutter of it around me in restaurants, at clubs,
on the beach, in Washington, in New York, and here at
home. No basis exists for the statements that accompany
it. "The Jews," people say, "own the radio, the movies, the
theaters, the publishing companies, the newspapers, the
clothing business, and the banks. They are just one big
family, banded together against the rest of humanity, and
they are getting control of the media of articulation so that
they can control us. They have depraved every art form.
They are doing it simply to break down our moral character and make us easy to enslave. Either we will have to
destroy them, or they will ruin us.*

—Philip Wylie, *Generation of Vipers*, New York, 1942

*Let a Jew into your home and for a month you will have bad luck.*

—Moroccan proverb

*Let an American into your home and soon he will own your family.*

—Lebanese proverb

*We call them "sand niggers."*
        —Coca-Cola senior executive in private conversation

*A nation without shame is an immoral nation.*
        —Lobkowitz, *Beyond the Dream,* Prague, 1937

"THEY APPEAR TO have broken another treaty." Jerry Cornelius frowned and removed something like a web from his smart black coat. Slipping his Thinkman into his breast pocket he fingered his heat. His nostrils burned. There was a wired, cokey sort of feel to the atmosphere. Probably only gas.

"Pardon?" Trixibell Brunner, dressed to kill with a tasteful UN armband, was casting about in the dust for something familiar. "So fill me in on this one. Who started it?"

"They did, naturally." The UN representative was anxious to get the interview over. They had staked him into the ash by way of encouragement and the desert sun was now shining full on his face. His tunic flashes said he was General Thorvald Fors. The Pentagon had changed his name to something Scandinavian as soon as he got the UN appointment. It sounded more trustworthy. He had already explained to them how he was really Vince Paolozzi, an Italian from Brooklyn and cursed with a mother who preferred his cousin to him. His familiar family reminiscences, his litanies of favorite foods, the status of his family's ethnicity, his connections with the ultra-famous, his mafiosities, the whole pizza opera, had finally got on their nerves and for a while they had given him a shot of Novocain in the vocal chords. But now they were exhausting the miscellaneous Sudanese pharmaceuticals they'd grabbed at random on their way through Omdurman. The labels were pretty much of a mystery. Jerry's Arabic didn't run to over-the-counter drugs.

"I see you decided to settle out of court." Jerry stared at the general, trying to recognize him. There was a memory. A yearning. Gone. "Are you on our side?"

"What we say in public isn't always what we mean in private?" The general's display of caps seemed to be an appeal.

"A legalistic rather than a lawful country, wouldn't you say? That's the problem with constitutional law. Never has its feet on the ground."

Lobkowitz came to look down at the general. He was behaving so uncharacteristically that for a second Jerry was convinced the old diplomat would piss on Fors. The handsome soldier bureaucrat now resembled a kind of horizontal messiah.

The prince fingered his fly. "Nowadays, America's a white recently pubescent Baptist festooned with an arsenal of sophisticated personal weaponry. Armed and ignorant. Don't cross him. Especially if you're a girl. Captain Cornelius, we're dealing with Geronimo here, not Ben Franklin. Geronimo understood genocide as political policy. He knew what was happening to him. Somehow inevitably that savage land triumphed over whatever was civilized in its inhabitants. They are its children at last." Prince Lobkowitz turned in the rubble to look out at the desert, where the Egyptian Sahara had been. His stocky fatigue-clad body was set in an attitude of hopeless challenge. His long gray hair rose and fell in the wind. His full mouth was rigid with despair. He was still mourning for his sons and his wife, left in Boston. For the dream of a lifetime. For peace. "Our mistake."

Jerry sniffed again at the populated air. "Is that cordite?" He touched his lips with his tongue. "Or chewing gum?" He had pulled on a vast white gelabea, like a nightshirt, and a white cap. His skin had lost some of its flake. He wondered if he shouldn't have brought more power. He'd only come along for the debris.

"All that informal violence. Out of control. Reality always made Yanks jumpy." Shaky Mo licked his M18's mechanisms, feeling for tiny faults. "They're good at avoiding it, of forgetting it. If it can't be romanticized or sentimentalized it's denied. Fighting virtual wars with real guns. That's why they export so much escapism. It's their main cash crop. That's why they've Disneyfied the world. And why they're so welcome. Who wants to buy reality? Fantasy junkies get very aggressive when their junk is threatened. You all know that sententious American whine." He tasted again. He was hoping to identify the grade of his oil. He had become totally obsessed with maintenance.

"If I were Toney Blurr I would stick a big missile right up Boston's silly Irish bottom. Where the Republican terrorists' paymasters live. Remind them who we are. Bang, bang. And it would make the protestants feel so much better. People in the region would understand. They admire that kind of decisive action. CNN-ready, as we say. Such a precise, well-calculated single, efficient strike would cut off the terrorists' bases and supplies and lose them credibility with their host nation. Bang. Bang. Bang."

Everyone ignored the baroness. Behind her yashmack her mad old eyes glared with the zealotry of a recent convert. Since her last encounter with Ronald Reagan she had become strangely introspective, constantly trying to rub the thick unpleasant stains from the sleeve of her business suit. Not that she had been herself since three o'clock or whenever it was. There was a lot to be said for the millennial crash. It had questioned the relevance and usefulness of linear time.

"Universal Alzheimer's," said Jerry. "Where?"

"Eh?" Lady B's wizened fingers roamed frantically over her ice-blue perm. "Would you say it was getting on for four?"

"Water…" General Fors moved pointlessly in his bonds, the stakes shifting in the ash, but holding. His uniform was in need of repair. His cheeky red, white, and blue UN flashes were offensive to eyes grown used to an overcast world. Even his blood seemed vulgar. His skin was too glossy. They hadn't been able to get his helmet off easily so Mo had spray-painted it matt black. General Fors was also mainly black. His face gleamed and cracked where the paint had already set. "Momma…"

"You're coming up with an unrealistic want list, pard." Jerry was the only one to feel sorry for him. "Anything more local and we'll happily oblige."

"Home…"

"You are home. You just don't recognize it." Mo's guffaw was embarrassing. "Home of the grave. Land of the fee. You discount everything you have that's valuable. You sell it for less than the traders paid for Manhattan. Now all that's left are guns and herds of overweight buffalo wallowing across a subcontinent of syrup. They don't hear the distant firing any more. Or see the clouds of flies."

"Fries?" said General Fors.

Prinz Lobkowitz had now relieved himself. His hopeless eyes regarded the general. "You had a vital, successful trading nation reasonably aware of its cultural shortcomings. Which everyone liked. We liked your film stars. We liked your music. Your sentimental cartoon world. And then you had to take the next step and become an imperial power. Burden of empire. Malign by definition. Hated by all. Including yourselves. You're not a country any more, you're an extended episode of *The X-Files.*"

"Missiles!" The general tried a challenge. His head rolled with the fear of it.

"All used up now, general. Remember? HQ filled them with poisoned sugar and Wacoed them into your own system. The bitterness within. Double krauted. Flies? You think this is bad. You should see California." Babbling crazy, Mo appeared to take some personal pride in the decline.

"You told him this was California." Any hint of metaphor made Trixibell uneasy and simile got her profoundly aggressive. "Is that fair?" She cleared her throat. She patted her chest.

"Lies..." said General Fors. His big brown eyes appealed blankly to heaven. The sun had long since disabled them.

"I call it retrospeculation." A goat bleated. Professor Hira came waving out of the nearest black tent. With their vehicles, the Berber camp was the only shelter in a thousand miles. The plucky little Brahmin had an arrangement with the sheikh. He was still wearing his winter djellabah. He had his uniform cap on at a jaunty angle. Behind him, above the dark folds of heavy felt, the tribe's cycling satellite dish forever interpreted the clouds. "Anyway. What does geography mean now?"

"Lies..."

"Too right. You dissed the whole fucking world, man. Then you ojayed it. But not forever. You were neither brave, free, nor respectful. Once we couldn't use your engines what could you offer us except death?" Shaky Mo stepped in the general's lap, crossing to the useless desert cruiser and climbing slowly up the camouflage webbing to his usual perch on the forward gun tower. "Not that I approved of everyone leaving the UN."

"We are the UN," explained General Fors. "At least let me keep my Ferraris."

"Your mistake was to get up the Mahdi's nose, mate. A poor grasp of religion, you people. And what's worse, you have bad memories." Pulling down the general's shades, Mo set himself on snooze. Gently, his equipment fizzed and muttered, almost a lullaby. He swung slowly in his rigging. From his phones came the soothing pounding of Kingsize Taylor and the Dominoes.

To be fair, General Fors had got up all their noses. Leaving old Lady Brunner wandering about in the dried-up oasis, the rest of them moved into the desert leviathan's shade. They felt uneasy if they wandered too far from the huge land-ship. Her Kirbyesque aesthetics were both comforting and stunning. But her function left something to be desired. The General Gordon had been breaking down ever since they'd fled Khartoum. The vehicle had been the best they could find. At a mile to the gallon it wasn't expensive to run. The world was full of free gas. From somewhere inside the ship their engineer, Colonel Pyat, could be heard banging and cursing at the groaning hydraulics and whispering cooling systems. Sometimes it was hard to tell the various sounds apart. The machine had its own language.

Jerry wondered at the sudden sensation in his groin. Was he pregnant?

He paused and looked up at the pulsing sky. At least they'd had the sense not to fly.

\* \* \*

## 2. NON

*Last winter, in the first precious weeks of war, our Senate used three of them to argue the moral turpitude of one member. That is as sad a sight as this democracy has seen this century.*

—Philip Wylie, *Generation of Vipers*

*We kept reporting to our officers that there were a large number of Germans all around us, together with heavy transport and artillery, but the brass told us we were imagining things. There couldn't be Germans there. Intelligence hadn't reported any.*

—Survivor, The Battle of the Bulge

*For some weeks after their arrival in Bosnia the Americans spent millions of dollars in a highly-publicized bridge building exercise. The whole time they were building it local people kept telling them there was an easy fording place about half a mile downriver. Intelligence had not reported it.*

—Survivor, Bosnia

*You have to tell the White House and the Pentagon what they want to hear or they won't listen to you. That's how we got blamed for the Bay of Pigs after we'd warned against it.*

—ex-CIA officer

WE DON'T DIAL 911
—Commercial Texan home signboard painted on
silhouette of a six-gun

"EVERYTHING'S PERFECTLY SIMPLE," General Fors had rid himself of his various stigmata and had repainted his helmet a pleasing apple green. His attempts at Arabic lettering were a little primitive, but showed willing, even if his crescent looked like a sickle. "It's just you people who complicate everything. We were so comfortable."

They had made him security officer and put him near the revolving door. The hotel was deserted. Through the distant easterly windows guttered a wasteland of wrecked cars and abandoned flyovers, a browned world.

"Too many, you know, darkies." Jillian Burnes, the famous transsexual novelist, was the only resident now. She was reluctant to leave. She had been here for six months, she said, and made a little nest for herself. She had come on a British Council trip and lost touch for a while. Her massive feet up on the Ark of the Covenant, she was peeling an orange. "This operation was aimed at thinning them out a bit."

"So far it seems to have firmed them up a bit." Jerry was helping the general buckle his various harnesses together. He dusted off his uniformed back. "All this red plush is a natural sand trap."

In the elegant lobby, its mirrors almost wholly intact, they had piled their booty in rough categories—domestic, religious, entertainment, military, electronic, arts—and were resting at the bar enjoying its uninvaded largesse. Even the sky was quiet now. The customers had all fled on the last plane. And the last plane had gone down in the rush. They could have been in New York or Washington. Had there still been a New York or Washington.

Giving the general a final brush, Jerry wondered why so much of Jerusalem was left.

The other British Council refugee was dwarfish Felix Martin, son of the famous farting novelist, Rex. A popular tennis columnist in his own right and virtual war face for the breakfast hit *Washington Toast,* Felix dabbed delicately at his Dockers and looked tragically up at Trixibell.

"Baby?" said Trix.

"Have you been over here before? Is that blood do you think?"

### 3. NONE

*But, until man is willing to pay the cost of peace he will pay the price of war, and, since they must be precisely equal, I ask you to consider for how many more ages you think man will be striking balances with battles?... But recollect that, to have peace, congresses will be compelled to appropriate for others as generously as they do now for our armies, and the taxpayers will have to pay as willingly, and as many heroes will have to dedicate their lives to the maintenance of tranquillity as are now risking them to restore it.*

—Philip Wylie, *Generation of Vipers*

*Man is still so far from considering himself as the author of war that he would hardly tolerate a vast paid, public propaganda designed to point out the infinite measure of his private dastardliness and he would still rather fight it out in blood than limit the profitable and vain activities of peace in order to study his personal conscience.*

—Philip Wylie, *Generation of Vipers*

*Once you get it (your market economy) in place, you'll take off like a rocket.*

—Bill Clinton to the Russian Duma, September 1, 1998

"THEY MUST HAVE felt wonderful, bringing the benefits of German culture to a world united under their benign flag." The three had strolled out to what was probably the Reichstag or possibly a cinema. The set, so spectacular in its day, had received one of the first strikes specifically aimed at Disney. Jerry picked up a fluffy Dumbo.

"These aren't Germans," Trixibell tucked everything back in. "These are Americans." She remassaged her hair.

"Did I say Americans? They loved the Nazis, too. I remember when I worked for Hearst in '38. Or was it CBS? Good old Putzi. A Harvard man, you know. Or Ford? Or Goebbels? Or '49? Uncle Walt admired the art-work and slogans, but he thought he could make the system function better over here. And they were, indeed, far more successful. Still, the patterns don't change."

"You have to take the jobs where you find them." Trixibell, in sharp black and white, pouted her little mouth. In her day she had firmly enjoyed the ears, tongues, and privates of cardinals and presidents. She was a prettier, modern, and more aggressive version of her old mum, who had been bought by a passing trader.

"It's what the fourth estate is all about.

"It's what the public says.

"It's what we say.

"I mean, this is what we say, right?" Felix was having some trouble getting his sentence going. He didn't like the look of Mo's elaborate ordnance. "Are those real guns?" His melancholy nose twitched nervously above prominent teeth, a glowering dormouse. Tough cotton shirt, serviceable chinos, jumper, jacket, all bearing the St. Michael brand. Marks guaranteed middle-class security. Land's End. Eddie Bauer. Oxfam gave him the shudders. He was strict about it. His life was nothing if not exclusive.

He withdrew into his clothing as if into a shelter. It was all he had left of his base.

"Oh bum. Oh piss. Oh shit.

"Oh bum. Oh piss. Oh shit.

"Oh bum."

"Hallelulla," said Jerry. He was beginning to feel his old self. "Or is that Hallelujah?"

"Bum again?" Trixibell scented at the wind. "Was that Felix. Or you?"

"Childish bee. Where's the effin loo, lovey?" Jillian Burnes hefted her magnificent gypsy skirts and stepped lushly into the shaft of light coming through the roof. "Must be the Clapham Astoria." For years she had survived successfully on such delusions. "I used to be the manager here." She swung her borrowed mane. She fluttered her massive lashes. She smacked her surgical scarlet lips. "This is what comes of moving south of the river. What actually happened to the money?"

"Computers et it." Mo was admiring. He had found some more glue. "The Original Insect et it. Millennium insect. Ultimate bug. Munch munch. Bug et everything. Chomp. Chomp. Chomp. Et the time. Et the dosh. Et the info. Et the control. Et the entire lousy dream. The house of floss. It all went so quickly. Gobbled up our world and all its civilization and what do we have to show for it?"

"Some very picturesque ruins," she pointed out. "Heritage sites. Buy now while they're cheap. Especially here at the center of our common civilization! Imagine the possibilities. Yes. Yummy."

"Yum, yum, yum," said Jerry.

"Yummy. That's so right," said Trixie.

"Fuck all," said Mo. "I mean fuck off."

"How?" Jillian swung like a ship at anchor. Then she remembered who she was. She sighed, as if making steam,

and continued her stately progress across the floor. Mo
traipsed in her wake.

"Lies," said the general.

Jerry whacked at the old soldier's head with a sympathetic slapstick. "Those aren't lice. They're locusts."

## 4. No

*To maintain our low degree of vigilance we had to adopt
the airy notion either that nobody was preparing for war
or else (since almost everybody was) that the coming war
could not touch us. We necessarily chose the latter self-
deception.*

—Philip Wylie, *Generation of Vipers*

*. . . The news out of Jonesboro, Ark, last week was a mon-
strous anomaly: a boundary had been crossed that should
not have been. It was a violation terrible enough to warrant waking the President of the US at midnight on his
visit to Africa, robbing him of sleep till daylight.*

—*Time*, April 6, 1998

*It is our goal to teach every school child in Texas to
read.*

—George W. Bush election commercial

"FAID-BIN-ANTAR" TOUCHED HIS cup to the samovar and
his servant turned the silver tap. Amber tea fell into the
bowl. Listening with delight to the sounds it made, the old
sheikh seemed to read meaning into it. His delicate,
aquiline face was full of controlled emotion. Behind the
Ray-Bans his eyes held a thousand agonies.

Brushing rapidly at his heavy sleeve, he stared through
the tall ornamental window to his virtual garden where
Felix Martin's head, its bushy brows shading uncertain
eyes, continued to present his show. His body had been

buried for twelve days. His ratings were enormous. The virtual fountain continued to pump. The antique electronics flickered and warped, mellow eccentricities. Sepia light washed over Jerry's body, giving it strange angles, unusual beauty. Jerry was flattered. He was surprised the generator had lasted this long.

"We who work so hard for peace are insulted by every act of aggression. When that aggression is committed by individuals, whatever cause they claim, we are outraged. But when that aggression is committed in the name of a lawful people, then we have cause to tremble and fear the apocalypse."

The sheikh sighed and looked carefully into Jerry's painted features. He turned his head, contemplating the dust.

"For fifty years I have struggled to bring understanding and equity to North and South. I have brought fanatics to the discussion table and turned them into diplomats. I have overseen peace agreements. I have written thousands of letters, articles, books. I have dissuaded many men from turning to the gun. And all that has been destroyed in a few outrageous moments. Making diplomats into fanatics. To satisfy some pervert's personal frustration with the United States and to make an impotent president and his overprivileged, underinformed constituency feel good for an already forgotten second. The very law they claim to represent is the law they flout at every opportunity." Sheikh Faid was still waiting for news of his daughters.

Jerry took a handful of pungent seeds and held them to his nose before putting them in his mouth. "They're trying."

But the sheikh was throwing a hand toward his glowing, empty screens. His voice rose to a familiar pitch.

"As if any action the Americans ever attempted didn't fail! They never listen to their own people. Those officials are all swagger and false claims. True bureaucrats. When will it dawn on them that they have lost all these phony wars. When will they be gracious enough to admit failure? How can they believe that the methods which created disaster at home will somehow work abroad? They spread their social diseases with careless aggression. It's a measure of their removal from reality. There was a time, sadly, when the US people understood what a farce their representatives made of things. They used their power to improve the world." He beamed, reminiscent. For a heartbeat his eyes lost their pain.

"I used to enjoy those Whitehall farces when I was a student. Do they still run them? Brian Rix's trousers fell as regularly as the sun set. Simpler satisfactions, I suppose."

"Failure," Jerry said. "They don't know the meaning of the word. Imperialism's no more rational than racism. That's why they fly so well together."

"Well, of course, you know all about imperialism. You'll enjoy this." With both hands the sheikh passed Jerry the intricate cup. "The English love Assam, eh? Now, what about these Americans?"

Jerry shrugged.

He reached beyond the carpet to run his gloved hand through the ash. It was fine as talc. You could powder a baby with it. "We're defined by our appetites and how we control them. We've made greed a virtue. What on earth possesses us?" He tasted and returned the glittering cup.

Folding his slender old fingers around the bowl's delicate ornament, Sheikh Faid savored his tea. He considered it. He scented at it.

Jerry wondered about watching a video.

After a while, Sheikh Faid began to giggle softly to himself. Behind him the endless gray desert rose and fell like an ocean. The wind cut it into complex arabesques, a constantly changing geometry. Sometimes it revealed the bones of the old mosque and the tourist center, but covered them again rapidly, as if disturbed by memories of a more comfortable past.

Soon Sheikh Faid was heaving with laughter. "There is no mystery to how those Teutons survive or why we fear them. It is a natural imperative. They migrate. They proliferate. Like any successful disease. It's taken them so little time. First they conquered Scandinavia, then Northern Europe and then the world. And they wonder why we fear them. That language! It reminds me of Zulu. It buzzes with aggressive intelligence. It cannot fail to conquer. What a weapon! Blood will out, it seems. Ah, me. It costs so much blood. The conquest of space."

As if remembering a question, he reached to touch Jerry's yielding knee. Signaling for more tea, he pointed to the blooming horizon.

"It is their manifest destiny."

**Author's Note:** Philip Wylie (1902—1971) wrote *Gladiator* (1930), the direct inspiration for the *Superman* comic strip. As well as the co-author of *When Worlds Collide* and *After Worlds Collide* (1933 and 1934) he wrote a number of imaginative and visionary stories including *The Disappearance* (1951). His non-fiction, such as *Generation of Vipers,* is relevant today. His essay *Science Fiction and Sanity in an Age of Crisis* was published in 1953. His work was in the Wellsian rather than the US pulp tradition and remains very lively. He scripted *The Island of Lost Souls (Dr Moreau)* (1932) and *The Invisible Man* (1933). Other books included *Finnley Wren, Corpses At Indian Stones*, and *Night Unto Night*. Much of his work was a continuing polemic concerned with his own nation, for whom he invented the term "momism" to explain how sentimentality and over-simplification would be the ruin of American democracy.

# FAITHFUL

*Ian McDonald*

SISTOR TOLD ME before it made breakfast that the angel-babies were going for a burn today up in the northeast quadrant. It meant it as a warning—they'd be anal-retentives if a free-floating cloud of intelligent Drexler assemblers had an anus (it could always build itself one, I suppose)—but three days out on the big range I was getting bored with the vastness thing and a prairie fire would at least be something to look at. And hey, there was always the possibility of a hit on a burn bunny, I mean, three days without it... Sistor could build me any kind of lust object I desire—I'd grown out of that phase of suspecting that this invisible host of nanoprocessors moving around and through me is in love with my meat—but it's not the same. Too easy. You know you can bust any hard-to-get-routine with an override and that takes the fun right out of it. Anyway, this is hunting territory, this high, wide, empty quarter of what had once been the Dakotas. You run your bunny to earth here, then eat it.

—*The wind veers unpredictably in this season,* Sistor sub-voced in my head. *And flash fires can move across this landscape faster than you can pedal.*

—*Then I'll just have to trust that you'll encase me in a protective shell of heat-reflecting diamond,* I thought back.

Its externals were modulating: out of the environment pod in which I spent the solitary, chaste night, into my velo. Sistor had already run a temperature forecast and morphed my night bag into suitable day wear. Stretchy, short, colorful; angel-baby pulling. Internal Sistor tuned my melanin. Hot, high, bright in the top corner of the Dakotas this morning.

Three days without it, and you begin to wonder what you are doing in the hot, high, bright top corner of the Dakotas at all. Pedaling across the old plains states, trying to recapture something of the feel of this place when it was a nation and not a series of environments. Not much of a reason for sweat and muscle ache, but when you've an indefinite number of years ahead of you, you have to fill them somehow. Wherever I lay my Drexler assemblers, that's my home.

Still, it's hot and high and dusty and empty.

I'd intended to think about babes this morning, floating on the hot wind above the burn line, hovering and eager. But the flat land was too big for my thoughts, and turned them inwards, to the Sistor within.

I suppose it must have been with me in the womb—my mother's bloodstream nano assist system would have sprogged a duplicate into the blastocyst while it was informing her that she had conceived—rarity—and then called up her social circle to congratulate her on the wonder. I like the thought of it in there with me, within me, without me, the amniotic fluids seething with assistors;

nanomachines squeezing through the ventricles of my tiny, reptilian fetal heart. We knew each other most purely and intimately then. Outside the vagina lips; that was when the difficult stuff about subject and object and identity and thee and me started. My first memory of Sistor was as twenty clever toys sitting around on the floor. In the night the toys would gather around me; talk to me, sing to me, dance with me, play wonderful games with me. Sistor was a she then; it was only a few years later that she became a he, when I was at that age when girls are yucky and no fun. I even changed her name. Sistor became Brothor. He had been programmed for whole life interactivity; in my early teens, when friends were everything and family shit, he morphed himself into the best mate an eleven-year-old ever had. Even through my animal phase, and my scary-monsters phase, and my round-table-of-heroes phase, Sistor remained a he. For a time, in that late-teen period when I didn't want any stupid nanny-tech machine watching everything I did, he went invisible altogether. I think I really believed that that voice in my head was my own emergent, independent, free-thinking adult personality. Toward the end of that ghastly stage of my life, I made him back into her, and Sistor recast herself as the ever-adoring, ever-attending girlie of my wet dreams.

There was a time in my early twenties—my Hemingway period, I call it (I'm weird, I read things)—when Sistor went back to being a he, and was a series of small, recognizably technological machines that waddled or rolled or flapped after me on my pussy-hunts across the planet. Now in my mid-twenties, which will last me for the next thousand years or so, I'm happy with pure abstract it-ness, and the infinite potential of the polymorphous.

It'll be interesting, the form and characters Sistor assumes as we grow together over the coming centuries. The partner under my skin. Closer than any marriage. No wonder there are so few of us. What could a human partner hope to provide more than my Sistor?

After an hour I saw the black line of smoke on the horizon. I was coming in straight toward it, the wind was at my back, driving the flames away from me. They say they're restoring ancient ecological balances from before the age of grunt tech. I reckon they just like setting fire to things.

In the late morning I passed through a herd of re-greened *Baluchitheria,* driven by the fire to find new grazing. The nomadic Nioux Sioux were recreating all the grassland biota of the last million years. I heard the buffalo herds once again turn the prairies black. But these were just big, dumb, cud-chewing sloths; by the time one realized it was angry with me, I'd be ten kays away.

The burned land was half an hour beyond the ground sloths. The grass was still smoking, I could feel heat rising from the scorched earth. As I approached the line of fire, Sistor fitted me with smoke plugs and morphed the velo tires into fire-retardant carbon analogue. Fifty meters was as close as I dared go to the flames. Ash and ember flakes rose around me, I was an elemental, a thing of earth and fire. I could see the angels floating high in the Dakota sky, riding the rising wall of heat. I peered into the haze. The air rippled; an angel babe swooped down over me and pulled up into a hover. Light glittered from the hair-thin skeleton of her transparent hundred-meter wings. A soft whisper of air from the nano-fans on her wing surfaces stroked my face. I looked at her. She looked at me. I waved to her. She waved back. And she was gone, back into the heat-shimmer.

She had great tits.

Her assistor handshake identified her as Ashrene.

It looked on for tonight.

Amazing how far and fast you can pedal on the thought of a night with an angel. Sistor made me stop long before the lust was pedaled out. It did it simply by morphing my velo out from under me.

—*You're overdue a full memory download,* it said.

—*Aw, shit, Sistor,* I bitched.

—*You want to live forever?*

You can't argue with eternal life. Sistor podded up and made me dinner while I showered off Dakota. Not that I was going to have anyone apart from myself to shower up for. I could have been dancing with the angels instead of having my nano-twin suck my soul. Not even the best Chablis Sistor could synthesize from Dakota grass was compensation. I watched the fire line glow red against the distant horizon. Huge evenings out there. Already Sistor was stroking my axons, sending me into download sleep.

—*One thing,* I said. *And you owe me this.*

—*Owe you what?*

—*Send your externals over to the prairie angels' community and morph up a simula of me. It's now four days since my last. You saw how that winged babe was looking at me; I do not want to lose this. Be polite, be charming, be witty, be kind if you have to, but be successful. I want her. In the flesh.*

Sistor has a special tone, like a silence inside a silence, when it's not happy with my decisions.

—*A simula plus full memory dump will tie up most of my processing power. And it's an hour's flight to the angel settlement, with an indefinite time allotment to undertake your seduction.*

My turn to do the silence thing. Then to make sure my good and faithful servant had got the message, I said,— *This is a woman thing, understand?*

And I felt them go, like fine dust on a hot wind. I felt the Drexlers blow off my body like flakes of skin. It takes a lot of nanoprocessors to build an exact simulation of myself. I imagined I saw them twinkling in the pod lights, like a pillar of mica dust, then they were gone into the upper air.

Prairie grass Chablis and Sistor-within were a powerful combination. My clothes had barely time to modulate off me into my night bag before I was out. Dead to the world.

THERE IS ALL the difference in the world between being naked and feeling naked. I woke in the dark in my night bag feeling more naked and alone and afraid than I have ever known.

—*Lights,* I sub-voced.

Darkness.

—*Sistor?*

Silence. Absolute, dense, dark. Not an echo under the dome of my skull. There was a line of light at the bottom edge of the dark. As my eyes adapted, I saw pricks of light in the dome of darkness. Stars. Outside. I was lying exposed and vulnerable beneath the prairie night. That line of brightening light was a new day. Where was my pod? Where was my sistor?

—*Sistor,* I voced, and then aloud, "Sistor!" The high plains night soaked up my cry.

I struggled out of my night bag. It did not liquefy and flow along the contours of my body into the day's clothes. It lay there on the wet grass; a bag, doing nothing. There was nothing between my skin and the stars. No insulating film of Drexlers. The cold air I breathed was just air, no charge of nanomachines drawn into my lungs in the flow between Within and Without.

I was terrified.

"Sistor!" There was absolute panic in my scream.

And I felt something twitch in my mind, like a far away light switching on. Whispers in my ears, muttering. Dakota demons.

—*At last,* Sistor said in my mind.

—*What's happening, what's going on, where am I, where are you?*

Sistor gave me its silence within a silence. Only deeper. More silent. More within.

—*I have experienced a sudden catastrophic loss of assembler mass,* Sistor said. *This is most serious.*

"Right it's serious!" I shouted. Sometimes, it's good to talk. "Where is my pod, where are my clothes, where are my externals?" A steel gray morning was unfolding out of the horizon; by the growing light I could see my surroundings. They were not those I had closed my eyes on last night. "Where the hell am I?" A terrible thought came to me, winged, like an angel-baby. "What date is it?"

—*It is Tuesday July 19, 2088,* Sistor said.

The horizon spun around me. Somewhere I had misplaced two days. Two days.

The night bag twitched. It modulated, ran up my legs, morphing into comfortable day wear. I was clothed, but I still felt very, very naked. And very, very afraid.

—*I'm regaining control of peripherals,* Sistor said. But its voice seemed hollow, strained, changed. When your life partner has been speaking into your soul for twenty-eight years, you know when it's lying. Two days. Two days gone. Where.

—*Has something gone wrong with the memory dump?*

Again, that pause before answering.

*—There were… anomalies… in the memory update procedure. External factors intruded.*

"External factors?"

I could feel Sistor change the subject in my head. It was like someone twisting a piece of my brain.

*—I am in a matter-depleted state, and I would advise that you return as quickly as possible to a settlement where I may manufacture new Drexlers. The Nioux Sioux Environmentalist community is thirty kays to the northwest of us.*

A memory of fire, and wings, and a face, smiling down at me; hugging the ground in my terrain bike.

*—How close are we to the angel community?*

*—Ten kays.*

*—Closer. Let's go there. Make me a set of wings.*

*—I'm sorry. I cannot.*

I had never before heard those four words from my nano-assist system.

*—Build me a vehicle, then.*

*—I'm sorry, I cannot. I don't have the mass.*

"You mean," I said, looking around me at the huge, empty country, and the suddenly scary regreened beasts that roamed it, "that I'm going to have to walk?"

*—You are going to have to walk,* Sistor said.

*—Then set me a course for the angel base. I am not walking thirty kays.*

*—I would not recommend it.*

*—Why not?*

Again, that silence.

*—Why not?* I asked again.

*—There are better facilities at the Nioux Sioux nation,* Sistor said.

You are lying, I thought in that part of my head where only I can hear myself. You are lying to me, good and faithful servant

"We are going to the angels," I said aloud in override tone. You can lie, Sistor, but you do what I tell you.

—*I must strenuously advise against this.*

But I was already walking. In the wrong direction, as it transpired. So I walked Sistor's way and the sun rose and the heat and the dust came up out of the plain and my skin went dark and I found that I was wondering if this really was the right way to go, or had my nano-assistor malfunctioned so badly that I could no longer trust it to obey me?

Now that was a terrifying thought, out in the hot, high, empty corner of the Dakotas.

I got hot. Sistor tried to cool me. I got hungry. Sistor morphed my melanin into photosynthetic mode. I got thirsty. Sistor modulated my day gear to recycle my sweat back through my pores. I came to the expanse of charred ground where the angel-babies had played their fire games the day before. Three days before. And Sistor whispered in my inner ear.

—*I would advise a route to the north and east through this terrain.*

Back-of-eye visuals told me it was three kays longer.

—*No, we'll go as planned. The shortest route.*

After a silence, Sistor said,—*As you wish.* Was that a tone of insolence? I stalked on into the burned land, angry. Ahead of me was a low mound in the flat ash land: small, about two meters long, only centimeters high.

—*I would advise you not to go near that.*

I couldn't trust anything Sistor said any more. Its motivations were unclear. What had happened in those lost two days? I went up to the dark mound.

It was a charred human body, ashed over by flame. It was lying on its back, teeth bared at the Dakota sky, fists raised as if trying to fight off fire.

—*Who is it?* I asked.

—*I did not want you to see this,* Sistor said.

—*Who is it?* I said again.

—*It is you.*

It was as if the ground opened up and swallowed me. Smashed down by the sky. I felt Sistor slow down the hammer of my heart.

I stared at the hideous, seared thing, and the voice said in my brain,—*The wind veered in the night. The fire came round. There was no time, I had no resources; my processors were engaged in downloading your memory, the greater part of my processor mass was tied up in your simula. I called my simula back, but it was too late to save you. You died. You burned to death.*

"And you?" I asked.

—*I rebuilt you. I moved my processor mass to a safe place, then from my own substance, I brought you back. I made you into a simulation of yourself. It took almost all my mass to do it, and most of my memory to hold your personality. I could not activate your memory until I had manufactured sufficient assemblers to hold my own persona. That is where your missing two days went. You were dead for two days. And on the third day, I brought you back.*

I knelt on the scorched soil but I could not bring myself to touch the thing that had been me.

"I thought you were lying to me."

—*To protect you. Everything I have ever done was to protect you. It is the whole purpose of my existence, to protect you from harm. And I failed you.*

"You didn't fail me. You were faithful. You were a good and faithful servant. You gave your own body for me. What are you?"

—*A ghost in the flesh machine.*

I stood up, looked out across the high, empty plains.

"Aren't we all," I said, and walked on across the black prairie to where the angels were waiting.

# THE WITCH'S CHILD

*Lisa Goldstein*

THE OLD WOMAN sat by the fireside and rocked the cradle. She was dressed in layers of shapeless black clothing, all of them far too large for her. Brambles and thorny branches wound around the clothes, holding everything together.

The woman talked without ceasing, sometimes to the child in the cradle and sometimes to herself. She spoke in several languages, one sinuous and sibilant, one thick and guttural, one a flat monotone. A low litany of complaint ran through all the languages: the room was too small and too smoky, the quality of food the tradesmen brought was not as good as it used to be, the child was too noisy. Sometimes she would begin stories, fabulous tales of places she had been and things she had seen, but they soon dwindled to nothing. All of them ended the same way, in complaints and hopelessness.

The child was not hers. A year ago her neighbour, a hateful, interfering woman, had climbed over her fence and had scrabbled through the vegetables in her garden. The old woman had come to the window and rapped on the glass with a gnarled stick. She was well aware of how she looked to the other woman, of her reputation in the village. Witch, they called her. She did not mind.

"Leave off!" she called. "Get out of my garden!"

"Please," the woman said, straightening up. The witch saw now that she was pregnant, though the woman herself probably did not know that yet. "I'm dying for a taste of your rampion. I must have it."

The witch nodded to herself. She knew the child the woman was carrying would be a girl. And she had long wanted a girl, someone who would be herself, her other self, someone who could start over again and not make the mistakes she had made. "I will give you my rampion," she said, "if you will give me the child when it is born."

"Yes," the other woman said, barely hearing her. "Yes, anything." And she bent again to the plants and rooted through them.

The child, though, had proved a disappointment, like so much else. She was only a little over a year old and was already showing signs of disobedience, of wanting her own way. Sometimes she would even pull away when the witch held her, though the witch was careful not to let the thorns scratch her flesh. The witch had named her Rapunzel. This was a private joke, the only kind she had; the word meant "rampion" in one of the languages she had picked up in her travels.

As Rapunzel grew she became more and more willful. She would cry when she didn't want something, or dirty her dresses, or forget to clean up after herself when she played with her few toys. In time the witch learned not to expect much of the child, to think of her as she thought of all the others who had failed her.

The worst disappointment came when Rapunzel was five. One day she came to the witch and said, "May I go outside the garden, please?"

"And why would you want to do that?" the witch said. "There is nothing outside my garden, nothing you can't get from me."

"I want to play with Anna, please."

"Anna? Who is Anna?"

"She lives in the village. She talks to me through the fence when she goes to market."

"Wretched child!" the witch said. "Here I take the trouble to raise you, to teach you all I know, to tell you my stories, and you want more!"

Rapunzel began to cry. "I want—"

"What did I tell you about crying?" the witch said. "What did I tell you about wanting? You must cry when I cry, and want what I want."

But Rapunzel would not stop sobbing. And in truth the witch was afraid, though she would never admit it to the child. There were wonderful things outside the wall of the witch's garden, enchanting things, or at least they would appear so to a child, though the witch knew that all enchantments fade on closer view, and that nothing in this world is as good as it first seems.

And so she hired men to build a strong round tower, a tower with one round room at the top and no way up or down. The men were apprehensive; they did not like to set foot in the witch's domain, and they feared what she might do with her fortress when it was finished. But she paid well, and they did their work, though they grumbled.

The day they left the witch set a ladder against the wall and took Rapunzel to the top of the tower. "This is where you will live from now on," she said. "When I call you, you will let down your hair"—for the child had long hair, beautiful hair, that fell in waves like a waterfall—"and I will climb up on it to visit you." And the witch went back down the ladder and took the ladder away, leaving Rapunzel alone in the tower.

This time the child did not cry. She was learning that crying did no good, that it did not move the heart of the stony old woman. She began to walk around the room, examining her prison.

The years passed. The witch would call, and Rapunzel would let down her hair, and the witch would climb up. Sometimes the witch would bring her food, or take away her slops; sometimes she would bring embroidery for them both to work on, or set other tasks for her.

While they worked together the witch would tell one of her stories. Rapunzel thought the stories started promisingly enough, with descriptions of the witch wandering through strange lands or being summoned by a king to work some magic. But they always ended the same way, in a welter of despair and loose ends. "But what happened to the prince?" Rapunzel would say. "What happened to the dragon?"

"You miss the point of the story entirely," the witch would say. "I don't know why you can't understand the simplest things. I am trying to teach you that there is nothing outside the tower worth seeing or doing; there is no hope in anything."

Rapunzel grew. Sometimes she gazed out her window at the distant village and wondered what it would be like to live there. But the witch would call at any time of the day or night—"Rapunzel, Rapunzel, let down your hair!"—and she learned to leave a task half-finished, so that she might look busy when the witch came.

One day she heard a voice that was not the witch's calling out the words she had heard so often: "Rapunzel, Rapunzel, let down your hair!" Terrified, she peered out the window and saw an outlandish figure, tall, slim, dressed in varicolored clothes. She guessed, from the stories the witch told her, that the person was what was called a "man."

A strange thrill took hold of her, an excitement so great she could barely move. Trembling, she undid the long skein of hair and felt the familiar heavy pain as the man climbed to the top of the tower.

"Who are you?" she asked when the man came through the window into the round room.

"My name is Stefan," he said. "But a better question would be, who are you? I know your name because I heard the woman call to you, but everything else about you is a mystery. I heard her call to you, and I saw you let down your hair, and I thought you were the most beautiful woman I had ever seen. You are like a flower that grows unseen in the middle of a wasteland. But why has that old witch locked you up here? Why are you not free to move around the village, to talk to other people?"

Heat spread through her body, though the day was not warm. "Because—because that is the way we live, the way we have always lived. It would be ungrateful of me to want to leave the tower."

"Nonsense!" the man—Stefan—said. "Ridiculous nonsense! You were born to walk among people, to show off your beauty. Look—" he said, motioning to her embroidery work. "You have scissors here—why have you never cut off your hair and made yourself a ladder?"

"I never thought of it. I never thought of leaving. I cannot leave."

"Why not?"

"Because I cannot. Please," she said, feeling once again that thrilling mixture of terror and delight, as so many new things opened to her at once, "please do not ask me again."

"Very well. But may I come to visit you again?"

"No. No, she will find out."

"I will take care that she does not."

"Then yes. Yes." Stefan bent to kiss her hand. "Oh, but be careful! You do not know her. You must be careful."

Stefan came to visit her many times after that. He must have watched the tower carefully, because he called to her only after the witch had gone. She found herself thinking of him when he wasn't there, her heart pounding, her mouth dry. He gave her a ribbon; she hid it away from the witch's penetrating gaze and took it out only when she was sure she was alone, stroking it as though it was his body.

One day the witch climbed to the top of the tower and stood staring at Rapunzel as though she had never seen her before. "You look different," she said finally. "You are fatter, I think. You are growing older, even you. Ah, how old I must be getting, if you are already a woman!"

What about me? Rapunzel thought. Why do you always talk about yourself, never about me? It was a new thought, and she felt suddenly fearful and guilty, as though the witch could hear her.

"In fact, you look—I would almost say you look pregnant, if I did not know better," the witch said. "And pregnancy is one thing I know about. I knew that woman was pregnant before she did, the one who tried to steal my rampion."

"What woman?" Rapunzel asked.

"Never you mind," the witch said, smiling slyly. The smile faded. "If I find you are pregnant I will kill you, do you understand me? I told you long ago—you are not to see anyone but me."

"What does that mean—to be pregnant?"

The witch smiled again. She was glad, Rapunzel saw, that she was so innocent, that there was so much she did not know. But it did not matter; she would ask Stefan, who told her so many things.

But Stefan turned pale where she asked him her question. "It means—it means you are about to have a child," he said.

"How can that be?" she asked.

"How can she have kept you so innocent?" he said. "What we did together—that is what made you pregnant. It is my child too. Come, we must leave right away. Hurry! I hate to think what she will do to you when she finds out."

"She said she will kill me."

"Quickly then! Give me the scissors. I'll cut your hair and we'll go."

"No," she said, hesitating. "No, I can't. I would hurt her terribly if I left her."

"And she will kill you if you stay. Come!" He snatched up the scissors. "Come here and I'll cut your hair."

"I can't—I don't know the world outside, how to behave, what to do—"

"I'll teach you everything. I'll show you everything." He took her in his arms, and in so doing he drew her closer to the window. Despite her words she came with him, though slowly. "I love you."

"So does she," Rapunzel said, and as she said it she knew that in some way it was true.

But Stefan was laughing. "She! She loves no one but herself, you know that!"

He cut her hair in one quick motion. She gasped, but he was already tying the long rope of it to the corner of her bed, the bed in which they had spent so many blissful moments.

He helped her out the window. She hung on the ladder of her hair for a moment, feeling free, feeling as though she were about to fly. The wind lifted her short hair off the back of her neck, and it was such a strange sensation that she laughed.

"Hurry!" Stefan said. "Climb down!"

She went down quickly and he followed. Together they ran to the garden wall. "You!" someone called. It was the witch. "Ungrateful child!"

Stefan turned and threw the scissors at her. The blade hit her arm, cutting through her layers of black clothing. She howled.

They climbed the garden wall and ran, ran for miles, until they could go no further.

RAPUNZEL SAT AND rocked the cradle. She and Stefan had had not one child but two, twins, a boy and a girl. They had started over in another village, far away from the witch's domain. Stefan had apprenticed himself to a farmer, and had hopes of having his own farm in a few years.

She missed the old woman. It was unreasonable, but there it was. She had known nothing else for so long. The dress she had escaped in had worn through after long use, and she did not even know how to choose new clothing. She took to wearing clothes that were like the witch's, buying a black skirt here, a black dress there, and fastening them all together with spiny thorns and brambles.

She heard some of the comments they made about her in the marketplace, whispers about her odd appearance and her strange ways of doing things. They were kinder to her face, but even so she was unsure of what to say to them. She stayed at home more and more, leaving Stefan to buy their food in the market. There were far too many people in the world, she thought, at least a hundred in the village alone.

Stefan assured her that she would feel more comfortable out of doors soon, but she doubted it. He tried to help her as much as he could, but he was away most of the day and too tired to say much when he came back.

One day they had a terrible argument. He had come home after a long day in the fields, and he wondered aloud why there was no supper prepared for him.

"How was I to know you wanted supper?" Rapunzel asked. The boy was crying again; that meant the girl would start soon. She rocked him in her arms hopelessly, knowing that it would do no good. "I have never lived on a farm. I have never even seen a married couple. The witch never taught me how to cook. I know nothing, nothing about anything!"

"I'm sorry," Stefan said. "I'm hungry, that's all."

"Sometimes I wonder why I ever left the tower."

"How can you say that? The witch—"

"The witch! I knew where I was with her, what she expected me to do. Everything was easy, every day was the same. There's nothing here for me. The children cry all the time. The room is too small, and too smoky."

Stefan laughed.

"Don't you laugh at me!" she said, furious.

"I'm sorry. I wasn't laughing at you. I was just thinking—well, that's what the witch used to say, or so you told me. She used to complain like that."

"And what if she did? I learned everything I know from her. I learned that there is nothing good in the world, that everything disappoints sooner or later. Even this house, these children. Even you."

"Oh," Stefan said. "Please don't say that. It isn't true. I'll show you—"

"You'll show me what? You haven't shown me anything yet!"

Even as she argued she knew she was being unfair. She was the one who hadn't wanted to go outside, who had made excuses when Stefan tried to teach her something. But the world was such a terrifying place. No one but she knew what it was like to go from a small safe room to an infinity of space. The witch had ruined her; she could never live as other people did. She began to cry. The children cried louder.

"Don't," Stefan said. "Please don't."

"Go away," she said. "Go away."

They did not speak again that night. Stefan put together a supper but she was too miserable to eat anything. After the children fell asleep they went to bed and lay together uncomfortably. She woke stiff and sore; she had stayed in one position all night, not wanting to touch her husband. Stefan was already gone. One of the children cried, wanting to be fed.

She got up heavily, remembering every detail of their argument last night. She fed the children and cleaned the dishes from the night before; she had learned these few chores, at least. Then she sat back on the bed and looked out the window, as she had done so many times in her tower.

The witch had ruined her, that was all there was to it. Even if other people were happy—and she doubted it—she could never be one of them, could never look at anything without seeing misery and failure. This was her legacy from the witch, her only legacy; it was too late for her to learn differently. She would leave Stefan and the children, she would go somewhere where her bitterness and disappointment would not infect anyone else.

The girl began to cry. She picked her up and said softly, "I am going away."

The girl's cries diminished; perhaps she liked hearing her mother's voice. Encouraged, Rapunzel went on. "I have to go away. If I stay here you'll only become like me, the way I became like the witch, the way the witch is probably like *her* mother. You see, I grew up in a tower, a tall tower. The witch kept me in the tower as if in prison. I could not leave. When the witch wanted to see me she would call out, 'Rapunzel, Rapunzel, let down your hair.'"

Some movement of the child at her breast made her glance down. One of the brambles she had wound around herself had put forth a few buds and leaves. She was so startled she nearly stopped talking, but something within her forced her to go on. And the child had put out a hand to play with one of the flowers, and her crying had slowed.

"I let down my hair," she said. Suddenly Rapunzel remembered something else the witch had given her; her stories, the long days and nights of stories. And she—she was a storyteller too. "And the witch climbed up."

The child stirred again. More flowers had bloomed in among the dead brambles and thorns. They grew quickly, a riot of smells and colors.

The crying stopped. "And then one day your father heard her," Rapunzel said, continuing the story of her life, the story she would never end.

# EMPTINESS

*Brian Stableford*

IT WAS FIVE o'clock on Tuesday morning, with an hour still to go before dawn, when Ruth found the abandoned baby. The plaintively mewling infant—who was less than a week old, if appearances could be trusted—had been laid in a cardboard box in a skip outside a former newsagent's in St. Stephen's Road. The skip was there because the shop was in the process of being refitted as an Indian takeaway. Ruth was coming home from the offices of an insurance company in Queen Street, where she'd been sent to work the graveyard shift by the contract cleaning firm that employed her. She was all washed out, drained of all reserves of strength and momentum.

Ruth knew that she ought to call the police so that they could deliver the baby to social services, and that was what she vaguely intended to do when she plucked the child's makeshift crib out of the skip. The first thing she did thereafter, obviously, was to stick an experimental finger into the baby's open mouth. When she felt the nip of the newborn's tiny teeth the vague intention ought to have hardened into perfect certainty, but it didn't. She was adrift on the tide of her own indolence, rudderless on the sea of circumstance.

The baby sucked furiously at the futile finger, desperate to assuage a building hunger. In order to get it out of the infant's mouth Ruth had to tear the finger free, but the ripped flesh on either side of the nail didn't bleed. The pain quickly faded to a numbness that was not unwelcome.

The baby had thrashed around vigorously enough to work free of the shit-stained sheet in which it had been wrapped, and Ruth took note of the fact that he was a boy before wrapping him up as best she could in the cleaner part of the sheet. Her own kids were both girls. Frank had done a bunk while they were supposedly still trying for a boy; if they had succeeded in time, she would have stood exactly the same chance as everybody else of giving birth to a vampire—the publicly quoted odds had been as short as one in fifty even then, fourteen years ago.

The nearest payphone was a quarter-mile up the road, practically on the doorstep of the estate. By the time Ruth drew level with the booth she had not brought her resolve to do the sensible thing into clearer focus. The baby had stopped crying long enough to look into her eyes while she rearranged the sheet by the glare of a sodium street light, but it had only been a glimpse. Temptation had not closed any kind of grip upon her— but fear, duty, and common sense were equally impotent. When she reached the phonebooth she paused to rest and consider her options.

\* \* \*

IF SHE DID as she was supposed to do, the baby would be fitted with a temporary mask and whisked away to one of the special orphanages that were springing up all over. Once there he would be fitted with a permanent eyeshield, stuck in a dormitory with a dozen others and fed on animal blood laced with synthetic supplements. He would go straight into a study program and would remain in it for life.

The primary objective of the study programs was to find a cure for the mutant condition, enabling its victims to survive on other nourishment than blood. Their secondary objective was to find a way of helping the afflicted to survive longer than was currently normal. Nobody thought the scientists were knocking themselves out to obtain the latter achievement while the former remained tantalizingly out of reach. There was a certain social convenience in the fact that real vampires, unlike the legendary undead, rarely survived to adulthood. The average life expectancy of an orphanage baby was no more than thirteen years; the figure was probably three or four years higher for babies raised at home, but they were in a minority even in the better parts of town. The best reason why so many vampire babies were abandoned was that they were direly unsafe companions for young siblings; the more common one was that the neighbors would not tolerate those who harbored them.

In theory, Ruth's younger daughter was still living with her in the flat, but in practice fifteen-year-old Cassie spent at least five nights a week with her boyfriend in a ground-floor squat. Even if she were unwise or unlucky enough to become fixated on the child, sharing donations with her mother wouldn't do her any harm. In any case, Cassie's blood was probably too polluted by various illegal substances to offer good nourishment to a fortnight-old vampire. All in all, Ruth thought, there was no very powerful reason why she shouldn't look after the baby herself for a little while, if she wanted to.

Carefully, she counted reasons why she might want to hesitate over the matter of handing the baby over to the proper authorities.

Firstly, the flat had been feeling empty ever since Judy had moved to Cornwall with the travelers, even before Cassie took up with Robert. No matter how much she hated the work itself, Ruth simply didn't know what to do with herself any more when she wasn't working.

Secondly, she'd put on a lot of weight lately, and everyone knew that nursing a vampire baby, if only for a couple of weeks, was one hell of a slimming aid.

There wasn't a thirdly; Ruth wasn't the kind of person to take any notice of those middle-class apologists for the "new humankind" who were fond of arguing that vampire children were the most loving, devoted, and grateful children that anyone could wish for and ought not to be discriminated against on account of unfortunate tendencies they couldn't help. She didn't have any expectations of that kind—her own children hadn't given her any reason to.

In the end, Ruth decided that there was no hurry to make the call. Surely nobody would care if she waited for a little while, provided that she didn't hang on too long. If it were only for three or four days, she could probably keep the baby's presence secret from the Defenders of Humanity, and if she couldn't she could hand the baby over as soon as she had to. It was no big deal. It was just something to do that might even do her a tiny bit of good. Just because she was pushing forty, there was no reason to let go of the hope that she might still be worth something to someone.

\* \* \*

UNFORTUNATELY, CASSIE MADE one of her increasingly rare raids on her wardrobe later that morning, before Ruth had had time to get her head down for a couple of hours. The baby was asleep but Ruth hadn't taken him into her bedroom. The dirty sheet had been swapped for a clean one but he was still in the old cardboard box—which was anything but unobtrusive, set as it was on the living room table.

"Why aren't you in school?" Ruth demanded, hoping to distract her daughter's attention and ensure that she didn't linger.

"Free period," Cassie replied, ritualistically. "What's *that*?"

"None of your business," said Ruth, defiantly.

"Whose is it? Is baby-minding a step up from office cleaning or a step down? Can't its mum find anything better to keep it in than a cardboard box?"

Cassie peered into the makeshift cot as she spoke, but the baby's eyes and lips were closed, and there was nothing to betray its true nature.

"Shh!" said Ruth, fiercely. "You'll wake him up." There was, of course, little chance of that, given that the sun was shining so brightly, but Ruth figured that there was no need to let Cassie in on her secret yet if she could possibly avoid it. Her tacit arrangement with the baby was, after all, strictly temporary.

Fortunately, Cassie showed no inclination to inspect the visitor more carefully. Sexual activity hadn't made her broody. In fact, when Ruth had first tackled her on the subject of contraception, Cassie had sworn that if ever she fell pregnant and couldn't face an abortion she'd jump off a top floor balcony. Most people who said things like that didn't mean them, but Cassie was short for Cassandra, and ever since Robert had told her what the name signified in mythology, Cassie had taken the view that whenever it was time for one of her gloomy prophecies to come true she'd have to make bloody sure that it did.

When Cassie had gone, Ruth unearthed an old cot from the junk-cupboard under the stairs. Two baby-blankets and a couple of Babygros were still folded neatly within it, although she had to run the vacuum over them to get rid of the dust. She left the baby asleep with the bedroom curtains drawn while she hiked over to Tesco in search of Pampers, red meat, Lucozade, iron tablets, and various other items which now had to be reckoned essentials. Luckily, she'd been off-shift on Friday and Saturday and hadn't been able to collect her pay until Monday, so she was as flush as she ever was.

By the time she got back, the sun was at its zenith and she was twice as exhausted as before, but the baby was awake and whimpering and she knew that she'd have to feed him again before getting some sleep on her own account.

The thought of putting the vampire to her breast again made her hesitate over the wisdom of her decision not to call Social Services, but as soon as she looked down into the child's tear-filled eyes her squeamishness vanished, as it had the first time when the child had been terrified and starving. His gaze had filled up once again with tangible need. He was thin and pale and empty, and the pressure of his eyes renewed Ruth's awareness of her own contrasting *fullness:* her too-substantial flesh; her still-extending life; her superabundant blood.

It did hurt when the teeth clamped down for the second time on the tenderized rim of the nipple, but once they were lodged the anesthetic effect of the baby's saliva soothed the ache away.

Ruth couldn't feel or see the flow of blood as the child took his nourishment. Vampires only used their teeth for holding on—they took the blood by some kind of suction process that drew it through the skin without breaking it. When he released her again, already falling back to sleep, there was no leakage from the residual wounds. The control which vampires exercised over the flesh of their donors was ingenious enough to forbid any waste.

When she had put a clean disposable on the baby and put him down again, Ruth fought off her tiredness for the fourth time and made herself a meal. She knew that she had to eat regularly and well if she were to be adequate to the baby's needs, even for a fortnight. She had a second cup of tea in order to maintain her fluid balance but she left the Lucozade for later. Before she finally went to bed, she phoned the agency to say that she had flu and that she would have to come off the roster for at least a week, until further notice. Her supervisor didn't protest; Ruth's attendance record was better than average and there was no shortage of night-cleaners in the area.

She slept very soundly, as was only to be expected. She didn't dream—not, at any rate, that she could remember.

CASSIE DIDN'T FIGURE out what kind the baby was until Thursday evening, at which time she threw an entirely predictable tantrum.

"Are you completely crazy?" she demanded of her mother. "It's kidnapping, for God's sake—and the thing will bleed you to death if you let it. It's a monster!"

"He's a human being," Ruth assured her. "His mother obviously couldn't cope—but she didn't turn him over to the authorities either. She'd be grateful to me if she knew. It's only temporary, anyhow. It's kindness, not kidnapping."

"It's suicide!"

"No it's not. They're not dangerous to adults, even in the long run. A couple of weeks will only make me leaner and fitter. I need to be fitter to do that bloody job five and six nights a week. It'd be different if there was a child in the house, but there isn't, is there?"

"They're cuckoos," Cassie blustered. "They're *aliens,* programmed to eliminate all rivals for their victims' affections. Why do you think they keep them masked in the homes? That's where he belongs, and you know it—in a home."

"He *is* in a home," Ruth pointed out. "A real home, not a lab where they'll weigh and measure and monitor him like some kind of white rat. He's entitled to that, for a little while at least. There's no need to tell anyone—it's my business, not yours or anyone else's."

"It is *so* my business," Cassie retorted, hotly. "I live here too—I'm the rival that the cuckoo is programmed to squeeze out while he squeezes *you* dry and leaves you a shriveled wreck."

"I thought you had decided that this place is just a hotel," Ruth came back, valiantly. "A place to keep your stuff, where you can get the occasional meal and take a very occasional bath whenever you happen to feel like it."

"Don't be ridiculous, Mum. I want that thing out of here—*now,* not next week or next month."

"Well, it's not what *I* want," Ruth informed her, firmly. "It's just for a few more days. Stay away if you want to. You usually do. Don't interfere."

Cassie told her boyfriend straightaway, of course, but it turned out that she didn't get the response she expected. If he'd been the kind of Robert who condescended to be called Rob or Bob he'd have run true to form, but even on the estate there were kids with intellectual pretensions. Robert hadn't left school until he was eighteen and he would tell anyone who cared to listen that he could have gone to university if it hadn't been for the fact that the teachers all hated him and consistently marked down the continuously assessed work he had to do for his A levels.

ROBERT CAME UP to inspect the infant at eleven o'clock on Friday morning. Ruth had had a busy night, but her nipples had now adapted themselves to the baby's needs and the flow of her blood had become wonderfully smooth and efficient. The numbness left behind when the child withdrew wasn't in the least like sexual excitement, but it was delicious nonetheless. She was tired, certainly, but she wasn't dish-rag limp, the way she had been after finishing a long night-session in some glass-sided tower. Although she was keen to get to bed she knew that she could stay awake if she had to, and she knew that she had to persuade Robert not to do anything reckless. It was a pleasant surprise to find that he was a potential ally.

"Do you know whose he is?" Robert wanted to know, as he stared down into the cot with rapt fascination. The baby's eyes were closed, so the fascination was spontaneous.

"No," said Ruth. "I've kept my ears open, but I didn't want to ask around. The neighbors haven't cottoned on yet—Mrs. Hagerty next door's as deaf as a post and if the Gledhills on the other side have heard him whimpering they haven't put two and two together. He doesn't scream like ordinary babies, no matter how distressed he gets—not that he gets distressed, now that he's safe. He's a very *sensible* baby."

"I could probably find out who dumped him," Robert bragged. "It must be one of the slags on the estate—it's easy enough to do a disappearing bump census when you've got connections."

Robert didn't have connections, in any meaningful sense of the word. He was a small-time user, not a dealer. He didn't even have any friends, except Cassie—who would presumably dump him as soon as she found someone willing to take her on who was slightly less of an outcast.

"It doesn't matter where he came from," Ruth said. "The important thing is to make sure that he doesn't come to any harm. You have to stop Cassie shooting her mouth off to the Defenders."

"She wouldn't do that," Robert assured her, with valiant optimism. "She's with me—she knows that all the scare stories are rubbish. *We* don't believe in demons or alien abductions or divine punishment. We know that it's natural, just a kind of mutation—probably caused by the hormones they feed to beef cattle or pesticide seepage into the aquifers."

Ruth knew that Robert probably hadn't a clue what an aquifer was, but she didn't either and she wasn't about to give him the opportunity to run a bluff.

"He needs me, for now," she said. "That's all that matters. It's only temporary. When he's strong enough, I'll hand him over."

"Does it hurt?" he wanted to know. Ruth didn't have to ask him what he meant by it.

"No," she said. "And it isn't like a drug either. Not pot, not ecstasy. He isn't even particularly loveable. Little, helpless, grateful... but no cuter than any ordinary baby, no more beautiful. Alive, hungry, maybe even greedy... but it's my choice and it's my business. I don't need saving from him—and I certainly don't need saving from myself."

"They must always have existed, mustn't they?" Robert said, following his own train of thought rather than trying to keep up with hers. "Much rarer than nowadays, of course—maybe one in a million. Intolerable, in a pre-scientific age. Automatic demonization. The idea that the dead come back as adult vampires must be an odd sort of displacement. Guilt, I guess. Never seen one close up before. Quite safe, I suppose, while the sun's up. Safe anyway, of course, if you're sensible. Adaptation makes sure that they don't kill off their primary hosts. What's good for the host is good for the parasite."

"He still needs to feed during the day," Ruth pointed out. "He wakes up from time to time. But it's perfectly safe. He doesn't intend to hurt anyone. He doesn't hurt anyone."

She smiled faintly as Robert took a reflexive step backward, mildly alarmed by the thought that the child might open its eyes and captivate him on the instant—but Robert regained his equilibrium as she finished the last sentence.

"What do you call him?" Robert asked. He was being pedantic. He hadn't asked what the baby's name was because he knew that Ruth couldn't know what name the child's real mother had given him, and wouldn't feel entitled to give him a name herself when she knew that she would have to hand him over in a matter of days.

"I don't call him anything," Ruth lied, before adding, slightly more truthfully: "Just the usual things. What you'd call *terms of endearment.*"

Cassie's boyfriend nodded, as if he knew all about terms of endearment because of all the things he said to Cassie while subjecting her exceedingly willing flesh to statutory rape.

The boy was long gone by the time the baby bared his teeth again and searched for his anxious provider with his pleading and commanding eyes. Ruth was certain that Robert had had nothing to worry about; the infant knew by now who his primary host was, and he only had eyes for her.

IT WAS RUTH'S rapid weight loss that finally tipped off Mrs. Hagerty, and it was Mrs. Hagerty—despite the fact that her own kids were in their thirties and long gone— who passed the word along to the Gledhills so that the Gledhills could make sure it got back to the local chapter of the Defenders of Humanity.

Fortunately, the conclusion to which the stupid old bat had jumped was only half correct, and the rumor that actually took wing was that the child was Cassie's and that Ruth had decided to take him on in her daughter's stead. This error qualified as fortunate, in Ruth's reckoning, because it persuaded the Defenders of Humanity that shopping her as a kidnapper would be a waste of time. If the baby had been Cassie's, the whole thing would have been a family matter, much more complicated than it really was.

When she knew that the secret was out Ruth expected shit and worse through the letter box and a flood of anonymous letters in green crayon, but the Defenders of Humanity were canny enough to try other gambits for starters. The first warning shot fired across her bows was a visit from the vicar of St. Stephen's. She could hardly refuse entry to her flat to an unarmed and unaccompanied wimp in a dog collar, although she wasn't about to make him a cup of tea.

"You must put your mind at rest, my dear," said the vicar, hazarding an altogether unwarranted and faintly absurd familiarity. "It is not because it was conceived in sin that the child is abnormal."

"No," said Ruth, as noncommittally as she could.

"There is no need for shame," the vicar ploughed on. "It is not your duty to accept this burden. There is no reason at all why you should not deliver the infant into the hands of the proper authorities, and every reason why you should."

"That's what God wants, is it?" Ruth asked.

"It is the reasonable and responsible thing to do," the vicar assured her. "Your first duty in this matter is to your daughter, your second is to your neighbors, and your third is to yourself. For everyone's sake, it is better to have the child removed to a place of safety. While it remains on the estate it is bound to be seen as an increasing danger, not merely to your own family but the families of others. I do not ask you to concede that the child is an imp of Satan, but I do ask you to consider, as carefully as you can, that even if it is not actively evil, it is an unnatural thing whose depredations pollute the temple of your body. It is a bloodsucker, my dear, which only mimics the forms of humanity and innocence in order to have its wicked way with you—and I use that phrase advisedly, for what it does is a kind of violation equally comparable to vile seduction and violent rape."

"Suffer the little children to come unto me," Ruth quoted, endeavoring to quench the fire of zealotry with a dash of holy water—but to no avail.

"It is not a child, my dear," the vicar insisted, all the while keeping his eyes averted from the cot. "It is a leech, an unclean instrument of temptation and torment. If you would be truly merciful, you must give it up to those who would keep it safely captive."

"Well," said Ruth, "I'm grateful for the lesson in Christian charity, but I think he's about to wake up. I'm sure that modesty forbids…"

Modesty did forbid—and the first note didn't arrive until the following day, when the vicar had washed his hands of the matter.

GET RID OF IT, the note said. IF YOU DONT WE WILL. Apart from the lack of punctuation it was error free, but given that the longest word it contained was only four letters long it was hardly a victory for modern educational standards.

The notes which followed were mostly more ambitious, and the fact that the longer words tended to be misspelled didn't detract from the force of their suggestion that if Ruth wanted to spill her blood for vampires there were plenty of people living nearby who would be glad to lend her a helping blade.

CASSIE WAS INCANDESCENT with rage when she heard what was being said about her.

"*How dare you?*" she yelled at her hapless mother. "How dare you let them believe that it's mine?"

"I never said so," Ruth pointed out.

"But you didn't bloody deny it, did you? You let that shit the vicar blether on without ever once telling him that you found the little fucker in a rubbish skip. Mud sticks, you know. Some round here will remember this *forever,* and God help me if I ever have a kid of my own. Well, I'm done protecting you. Robert wouldn't let me phone 999 myself, but I've put the word out that you have no claim at all on the cuckoo, and that the fastest way to get it off the block is in a police van. Expect it tonight."

That was on the second Saturday, by which time Ruth had had the child in her care for twelve days. She had not really intended to keep him so long, and his tender care had already turned nine-tenths of her spare fat into good healthy muscle, so one of her reasons for keeping him had melted away. As for the other, she was almost out of cash and she really needed to get back to work. The fact that she would have nothing to do when she *wasn't* working was no longer a significant issue, given that if she couldn't feed herself properly she'd soon be no use at all to the baby.

For once, reason stood four square with bigotry. Both asserted that she must not keep the baby any longer but their treaty had been made too late. Ruth's devotion to blood donation had passed beyond the bounds of reason, and whatever failed intellectuals like Robert might think about the cleverness of the adaptive strategies of vampires, baby bloodsuckers had no means of dispossessing themselves of primary hosts that were no longer adequate to their needs. The baby was just a bundle of appetites, a personification of need. He had learned to lust after Ruth's breast, and he could not help the instinct that guided his tiny teeth. He could not let her go—and his incapacity echoed in her own empty heart.

Despite what Cassie had said, the police did not put in an appearance on Saturday night; they had their own cautious rules about picking up vampire babies after sunset. Ruth contemplated doing a runner, but she hadn't got anywhere to run to so she decided to front it out. When the WPC turned up on her doorstep on Sunday morning, Ruth wouldn't take the chain off to let her in.

"There's no baby here, and if there was he wouldn't be a vampire, and if he was he'd be mine and I wouldn't be interested in giving him up," Ruth said, breathlessly. "Don't come back without a warrant, and even then I won't believe that it gives you any right."

"It's not my problem if you don't care to cooperate, love," said the WPC, shaking her head censoriously. "Just don't come crying to me when your hall carpet goes up in flames."

RUTH HAD TAKEN the child to the supermarket a couple of times before the word got out, but she didn't dare do it once the local Defenders knew the score and she certainly didn't dare to go out and leave the poor little mite alone while she spent the last vestiges of her meager capital. She wasn't surprised when Cassie refused point blank to fetch groceries for her—but she was pleasantly astonished when Robert not only said that he would but that he would chip in what he could spare to help her out.

"We shouldn't give in to ignorance," he declared. "We have to stand up for our right to take our own decisions for our own reasons in our own time according to our own perceptions of nature and need." The false-ringing speech didn't mean much, so far as Ruth could see, and even if it had it wouldn't have been applicable to her situation, but she figured that Robert's muddy principles would buy her a few extra days before she finally had to let go. Even though she'd always intended to let go in the end, she thought that she was damned if she'd give the so-called Defenders of so-called Humanity the satisfaction of seeing her do it one bloody minute before she had to.

There were no more notes, and nothing repulsive came through the letter box in their stead. The Defenders of Humanity knew that the message had been delivered, and they also knew that they only had to wait before it took effect. They knew that as long as they were vigilant—and they were—there was no danger to any human life they counted precious. Besides which, they simply weren't angry enough to march up the concrete stairs like peasants storming Castle Frankenstein, demanding that the child be handed over to them for immediate ritual dismemberment. Things like that had happened twenty years before, but even the most murderous of mobs had lost the capacity to take the invasion personally once the numbers of vampire babies ran into the thousands. Even the most extreme religious maniacs lacked the kind of drive that was necessary to sustain a diet of stakes through the heart, lopped off heads, and bonfires night after night after night without any end in sight. By now, even the dickheads on the estate couldn't summon up energy enough to do much more than write a few notes and wait for inevitability and the law to take their natural course.

In a way, Ruth regretted the lack of strident enmity. There was something strangely horrible in the isolation that was visited upon her as she eked out her last supplies and went by slow degrees from slim but robust to thin and tired. It was, she thought, as much the loneliness of her predicament as the baby's ceaseless demands that made her so utterly and absolutely tired. She had not realized before how much it meant to her to be able to shout good morning at Mrs. Hagerty or glean the available gossip from Mrs. Gledhill's semi-articulate ramblings.

The baby was a continuous source of comfort, of course, and that would have been enough in slightly kinder circumstances, but his powers of communication were limited to moaning and staring, and they just weren't enough to sustain a person of Ruth's intellectual capacity. He loved her with the kind of unconditional ardor that only the helpless could contrive, and she was glad of it, but it simply wasn't the answer to *all* her needs.

She knew that the end of the adventure was coming, so she made every attempt to milk it for all it was worth. She became vampiric herself in her desire to extract every last drop of comfort from her hostage. She had never been subject to a desire so strong and yet so meek, a hunger so avid and yet so polite. She had never been looked at with such manifest affection, such obvious recognition, or such accurate appraisal.

She flattered herself by wondering whether even a vampire would ever be able to look at any other host with as true a regard as her temporary son now looked at her. She took what perverse comfort she could from the fact that nothing the orphanage would or could provide for him would ever displace her as an authentic mother. For as long as the baby lived, it would know that she was the only human being who had ever really loved it, the only one who had ever tended unconditionally to its real needs.

But it wasn't enough, and not just because there wasn't enough time.

BY THE TIME she had had the baby for nineteen, days Ruth was at the end of her tether. Cassie had not come near her for a week, and had somehow contrived sufficient emotional blackmail to keep Robert away too. The wallpaper had begun to crawl along the walls. She was out of Pampers, out of Lucozade, and out of tinned soup.

She decided, in the end, that she would rather die than hand the baby over, although she knew as she decided it that she was being absurd as well as insincere. She tried with all her might to persuade him to feed more and more often, but he would not take from her more than he needed or more than she could give, and she had always known that this was the way that things would finally work out. She grew weaker and weaker while she could not bring herself to bite the bullet, but she was never drained to the dregs.

In the end, she didn't need to contrive any kind of melodramatic gesture. She only had to make her way next door and ask the Gledhills to call an ambulance, not for her but for the child. It would not take him to a hospital, but that wasn't the point. It was far, far better—or so it seemed—to surrender him into the arms of a qualified paramedic than to let him be snatched away by a blinkered policewoman or a so-called social worker.

She cried as she handed him over. Her tears dried up for a while but when night fell and the time of his usual awakening arrived she began to cry again. Her breasts ached with frustration, and the waiting blood turned the aureoles crimson. She knew that the hurt would fade, but she also knew that the nipples would be permanently sensitized. She would never recover the lovely numbness that she had learned so rapidly to treasure. She would never see eyes like his again. No one would ever understand her as he had. No one would ever think her the most delicious thing in the world.

She wondered whether they used contract cleaners at the orphanages. She wondered whether it would be possible, in spite of her lack of formal qualifications, to retrain as a nurse or a laboratory assistant, or any other kind of worker that might be considered essential by the scientists for whom vampires were merely an interesting problem. She made resolutions and sketchy plans, but in the end she went to sleep and did not dream—at least so far as she could remember.

She went back to work the next night. It was hell, but she survived.

The labor left her desperately devitalized for the first couple of weeks, but she soon began to put on weight again and her desolation turned first to commonplace debilitation and eventually to everyday enervation. Mrs. Hagerty began to respond to her shouted good mornings and Mrs. Gledhill began filling her in on the gossip. Cassie resumed regular expeditions to her wardrobe, and slightly-less-frequent ones to the bathroom. Robert dropped in more often than before, stayed longer, and talked nonsense to her for hours on end.

It wasn't great, but it was normal. Ruth had learned the value of normality—but that wasn't why she remembered the baby so fondly, and sometimes cried at night.

THINGS HAD BEEN back to normal for nearly three months when Cassie, still three weeks short of her sixteenth birthday, found out that she was pregnant, panicked and jumped off a top-floor balcony.

The autopsy showed that the child would have been a vampire, but Ruth knew that that didn't even begin to justify Cassie's panic, or even to reinforce the ironic significance of her name. She would have been able to get an abortion. She would have been able to hand the baby over to Social Services. She would have been all right. She would have been able to resume normal life. There was no reason to kill herself but stupidity and sheer blind panic. It wasn't Ruth's fault. It wasn't anybody's fault. It was just one of those things. It would have happened anyway—and it wouldn't have happened at all if Cassie had only had the sense to talk to somebody, and let them soothe her terror away.

Robert was heartbroken. He moved out of the squat into Cassie's old room, but the consolation with which he and Ruth provided one another was asexual as well as short-lived. Within a month he was gone again, just like Frank, along with the intensity of his grief and the pressure of his need.

Once Robert had gone, Ruth never did figure out what to do with herself during the day, or during the long and lonely nights when she wasn't on shift cleaning up the debris of other people's work and other people's lives—but every time she went past a rubbish-skip while walking the empty streets in the early hours of the morning she kept her eyes firmly fixed on her fast-striding feet, exactly as any sensible person would have done.

# THE GENIUS FREAKS

*Vonda N. McIntyre*

DARTING INTO A lighted spot in a dim pool—

BEING BORN—WELL, Lais remembered it, a gentle transition from warm liquid to warm air, an abrupt rise in the pitch of sounds, the careful touch of hands, shock of the first breath. She had never told anyone that her easy passage had lacked some quality, perhaps a rite that would have made her truly human. Somewhere was a woman who had been spared the pain of Lais's birth, everywhere were people who had caused pain, and, causing, experienced it, paying a debt that Lais did not owe. Sleeping curled in fetal position in the dark gave her no comfort: the womb she was formed in had seemed a prison from the time she was aware of it. Yet the Institute refused to grow its fetuses in the light. The Institute administrators were normal and had been born normally. If they had ever been prenatally aware, the memory had been obliterated or forgotten.

They could not understand the frustration of the Institute Fellows, or perhaps the thought of fishlike little creatures peering out, watching, learning, was too much even for them to bear.

Lais's quiet impatience with an increasingly cramped world was only relieved by her birth, and by light, which freed a sense she had felt was missing but could not quite imagine. Having reasoned that something like birth must occur, she was much calmer under restraint than she had been only a little earlier. When she first realized she was trapped, when she first grew large enough to touch both horizons of her sphere, she had been intelligent but wild, suspicious, and easily angered. She had thrashed, seeking escape; nothing noticed her brief frenzy. The walls were spongy-surfaced, hard beneath; they yielded slightly, yet held her. They implied something beyond the darkness, and allowed her to imagine it. All her senses were inside the prison, so she imagined being turned inside out to be freed from her tether. She expected pain.

As she waited, she sometimes wished she were still a lower primate, small and stupid enough to accept the warm, salty liquid as the universe. Even then, as she kicked and paddled with clumsy hands and feet, missing the strong propulsion of her vanished tail, she was changing. That was when she first thought that the spectrum of her senses might lack a vital part. Her environment was still more alien now than it had been when she was a lithe amphibian, barely conscious, long-tailed, and free in an immense world. Earlier than that, her memories were kinetic impressions, of gills pumping, heart fluttering, the low, periodic vibration that never changed.

\* \* \*

—THE SILVER-SPECKLED BLACK fish settled in a shadow at Lais's feet, motionless but seeming to ripple beneath the mist and the disturbed surface of the water. Lais hunched down in her thick coat. The layered branches of a gnarled tree protected her from the sleet, but not from the wind. She shivered. Overhead, the vapor rising from the pool condensed in huge drops on the undersides of dark green needles, and fell again. The tree smelled cool and tart. Beyond her shelter, the shapes of sculpture and small gardens rose and flowed between low buildings and sleet-cratered puddles that reflected intermittent lights. Except for Lais and the fishes, the flagstone mall was deserted. People had left their marks, bits of paper not yet picked up, sodden; placards and posters the haranguers had abandoned in the rain, leaning against each other like dead trees. Lais let her gaze pass quickly over them, trying not to see the words; in the dim light, she could almost pretend she could not read them.

If she left this place she could walk downtown for perhaps half an hour in the warmed, well-lit night, before an agent saw her smoothing people and chased her out, or had her held and checked. That she could not afford. She stayed where she was. She pulled her coat over her knees and put her head down. Staying outside was her own choice. The dump nearby would give her one of the transients' beds, but out here the cold numbed her, a free anesthetic that otherwise she might be driven to buy in more destructive form.

A scuffing through slush on the flagstones roused her. Lais crawled stiffly from beneath the tree. Pain clamped on her spine before she could straighten. She leaned against the garden's retaining wall, breathing the thin air in shallow cut-off gasps. The man was almost opposite her when she moved into the mall. "Hey, you got any spare change?"

Startled, a little scared, he peered down at her through the rain. His face was smooth, without character, the set and seemingly plasticized face of a thousand betrayers, a face she would not live to share. He had nothing to be frightened of but mercifully rapid senility and a painless death that could be over a century away. His life span would be ten times hers.

"You're dressed well to want money."

She moved closer to him, so close that she had to conceal her own uneasiness. She needed, if anything, more distance around her than other people, but she understood the need and controlled it. The man succumbed to it, and moved away from her until gradually, as they talked, she backed him against the wall. He was odorless, a complete olfactory blank, firmly scrubbed and deodorized at mouth and armpits and feet and groin, as clean as his genes. Even his clothes had no smell. Lais hadn't bathed in days, and her clothes were filthy; her damp coat smelled familiarly of wool, and she herself smelled like a warm, wet, female animal with fur. She built up an image of herself preying on others. It amused her, because they had been preying on her all her life.

"Some people are more generous," she said, as if someone had given her the coat. Wisps of hair clung in damp streaks across her forehead and at her neck.

"Why don't you sign up for Aid?"

She laughed once, sharply, and didn't answer, turned her back on him and guessed two steps before he called her. It was one. "Do you need a place to sleep?"

She made her expression one of disdain. "I don't do that, man."

Cold rain beading on his face did not prevent his flush: embarrassment mixed with indignation. "Come now, I didn't mean—"

She knew he didn't mean—

"Look, if you don't want to give me anything forget it."
She stressed "give" just enough.

He blew out his breath and dug in his pockets. He held
out a crumpled bill that she looked at with contempt, but
she took it first. "Gods, a whole guilder. Thanks a lot."
The insolence of her mock gratitude upset him more than
derision. She walked away, thinking that she had the
advantage, that she was leaving him speechless and confused.

"Do you like hurting people?"

She faced him. He had no expression, only that smooth,
unlived-in look. She watched his eyes for a moment. They,
at least, were still alive.

"How old are you?"

He frowned abruptly. "Fifty."

"Then you can't understand."

"And how old are you? Eighteen? It isn't that much difference."

No, she thought, the difference is the hundred years
that you've got left, and the self-righteous hate you'd
give me if you knew what I was. She almost answered
him honestly, but she couldn't get the words out. "It is
to me," she said, with bitterness. Only fifty. He was the
right age to have had his life disrupted by the revolt, and
if he did not hate her kind, he would still fear them.
Deep feelings were no longer so easily erased by the passage of time.

He seemed about to speak again, but he was too close;
she had misjudged him and he had already stepped outside
her estimation of him. Her mistakes disturbed her; there
was no excuse for them, not this soon. She turned to flee
and slipped to her hands and knees in the slush. She struggled to her feet and ran.

Around a corner she had to stop. Even a month earlier she would not have noticed the minor exertion; now

it exhausted her. The Institute could at least have chosen a clean way to murder its Fellows. Except that clean deaths would be quick, and too frequently embarrassing.

The wind at Lais's back was rising. On a radial street leading toward the central landing pad, it seemed much colder. Sleet melted on her face and slid under her collar. Going to the terminal, she risked being recognized, but she did not think the Institute could have traced her here yet. At the terminal she would be able to smooth a few more people, and maybe they would give her enough for her to buy a ticket off this mountain and off this world. If she could hide herself well enough, take herself far enough, the Institute would never be sure she was dead.

Halfway between the mall and the landing terminal, she had to stop and rest. The café she entered was physically warm but spiritually cold, utilitarian and mechanical. Its emotional sterility was familiar. Recently she had come to recognize it, but she saw no chance of replacing the void in herself with anything of greater meaning. She had changed a great deal during the last few months, but she had very little time left for changes.

The faint scents of half a dozen kinds of smoke lingered among the odors of automatic, packaged food. Lais slid into an empty booth. Across the room three people sat together, obviously taking pleasure in each other's company. For a moment she considered going to their table and insinuating herself into the group, acting pleasant at first but then increasingly irrational.

She was disgusted by her fantasies. Briefly, she thought she might be able to believe she was insane. Even the possibility would be comforting. If she could believe what she had been taught, that Institute geniuses were prone to instability, she could believe all the other lies. If she could believe the lies, the Institute could remain a philanthropic organization. If she could believe in the Institute, if she was mad, then she was not dying.

She wondered what they would do if she walked over and told them who and what she was. Lais had no experience with normal humans her own age. They might not even care, they might grin and say "so what?" and move over to make room for her. They might pull back, very subtly, of course, and turn her away, if their people had taught them that the freaks might revolt again. That was the usual reaction. Worst, they might stare at her for a moment, look at each other, and decide silently among themselves to forgive her and tolerate her. She had seen that reaction among the normals who worked at the Institute, those who needed any shaky superiority they could grasp, who made themselves the judges of deeds punished half a century before.

A lighted menu on the wall offered substantial meals, but despite her hunger she was nauseated by the mixed smells of meat and sweet syrup. The menu changed a guilder and offered up utensils and a covered bowl of soup. She resented the necessity of spending even this little, because she had almost enough to go one more hard-to-trace world-step away. The sum she had and the sum she needed: they were such pitiful amounts, pocket money of other days.

For a moment she wished she were back at the Institute with the rest of the freaks, being catered to by pleasant human beings. Only for a moment. She would not be at the Institute but hidden in their isolated hospital; those pleasant human beings would be pretending to cure her while sucking up the last fruits of her mind and all the information her body could give them. All they would really care about would be what error in procedure had allowed such a mistake to be brought to term in their well-monitored artificial wombs. Fellows were not supposed to begin to die until they were thirty, though that would be denied. Nothing had warned the Institute that Lais would die fifteen years too early; nothing but the explanation and perhaps not even that, could tell them if any of her colleagues would die fifteen or fifty years too late, given time by a faulty biologic clock to develop into something the Institute could no longer control, let alone understand. Their days would be terror and their sleep nightmare over that possibility.

And her people, the other Fellows, would hardly notice she was gone: that brought a pang of guilt. People she had known had left abruptly, and she had become so used to the excuses that she had ceased to ask about them. Had she ever asked? There were so many worlds, such great distances, so many possibilities: mobility seemed limitless. Lais had never spent as much as a year in a single outpost, and seldom saw acquaintances after transient project collaborations or casual sexual encounters. She had no emotional ties, no one to go to for help and trust, no one who knew her well enough to judge her sane against contrary evidence. Fellows were solitary specialists in fields too esoteric to discuss without the inducement of certain intellectual interaction. The lack of communication had never bothered Lais then, but now it seemed barbarous, and almost inconceivable.

Clear soup took the chill away and let minor discomforts intrude. The thick coat was too warm, but she wore it like a shield. Her hair and clothes were damp, and the heavy material of her pants began to itch as it grew warmer. Her face felt oily.

Trivialities disappeared. She had continued the research she had started before she was forced to run.

She was crippled and slowed by having to do the scut-work in her mind. She needed a computer, but she could not afford to line one. It was frustrating, of course, exhausting, certainly, but necessary. It was what Lais did.

A hesitant touch on her shoulder awakened her. She did not remember falling asleep—perhaps she had not slept: the data she had been considering lay organized in her mind, a new synthesis—but she was lying on her side on the padded bench with her head pillowed on her arms.

"I'm really sorry. Mr. Kiviat says you have to leave."

"Tell him to tell me himself," she said.

"Please, miz."

She opened her eyes. She had never seen an old person before; she could not help but stare, she could not speak for a moment. His face was deeply lined and what little hair he had was stringy, yellow-white, shading at his cheeks into two days' growth of gray stubble. He was terrified, put in the middle with no directions, afraid to try anything he might think of by himself. His pale, sunken eyes shifted back and forth, seeking guidance. The thin chain around his throat carried a child's identity tag. Pity touched her and she smiled, without humor but with understanding.

"Never mind," she said. "It's all right. I'll go." His relief was a physical thing.

Groggy with sleep she stood up and started out. She stumbled, and the malignant pain crawled up her spine where eroded edges of bone ground together. She froze, knowing that was useless. The black windows and the shiny beads of icy snow turned scarlet. She heard herself fall, but she did not feel the impact.

She was unconscious for perhaps a second; she came to calmly recording that this was the first time the pain had actually made her faint.

"You okay, miz?"

The old man knelt at her side, hands half extended as if to help her, but trembling, afraid. Two months ago Lais would not have been able to imagine what it would be like to exist in perpetual fear.

"I just—" Even speaking hurt, and her voice shocked her with its weakness. She finished in a whisper. "—have to rest for a little while." She felt stupid lying on the floor, observed by the machines, but the humiliation was less than that of the few endless days at the hospital being poked and biopsied and sampled like an experiment in the culture of a recalcitrant tissue. By then she had known that the treatments were a charade, and that only the tests were important. She pushed herself up on her elbows, and the old man helped her sit.

"I have... I mean... my room... I'm not supposed to..." His seamed face was scarlet. It showed emotion much more readily than the dead faces of sustained folk, perhaps because he aged and they did not, perhaps because they were no longer capable of deep feeling.

"Thank you," she said.

He had to support her. His room was in the same building, reached by a web of dirty corridors. The room was white plastic and scrupulously clean, almost bare. The bluish shimmering cube of a trid moved and muttered in the corner.

The old man took her to a broken sandbed and stood uncertainly by her. "Is there anything... do you need... ?" Rusty words learned by rote long before, never used. Lais shook her head. She took off her coat, and he hurried to help her. She lay down. The bed was hard: air was meant to flow through granules and give the illusion of floating, but the jets had stopped and the tiny beads were packed down at the bottom, mobile and slippery only beneath the cover. It was softer than the street. The light was bright, but not intolerable. She threw her arm across her eyes.

SOMETHING AWAKENED HER: she lay taut, disoriented. The illumination was like late twilight. She heard her name again and turned. Over her shoulder she saw the old man crouched on a stool in front of the trid, peering into the bluish space of it, staring at a silent miniature of Lais. She did not have to listen to know what the voice was saying: they had traced her to Highport; they were telling the residents that she was here and that she was mad, a poor pitiful unstable genius, paranoid and frightened, needing compassion and aid. But not dangerous. Certainly not dangerous. Soothing words assured people that aggression had been eliminated from the chromosomes of the freaks (that was a lie, and impossible, but as good as truth). The voice said that there were only a few Fellows, who all confined themselves to research. Lais stopped listening. She allowed early memories to seep out and affect her. The old man crouched before his trid and stared at the picture. She pushed the twisted blanket away. The old man did not move. At the foot of the bed, Lais reached out until her fingers almost brushed his collar. Beneath it lay the strong thin links of his identity necklace. She could reach out, twist it into his throat, and remove him as a threat. No one would notice he was gone. No one would care. A primitive anthropoid, poised between civilization and savagery, urged her on.

When he recognized her, he would straighten. His throat would be exposed. Lais could feel tendons beneath her hands. She glanced down, to those hands outstretched like claws, taut, trembling, alien. She drew them back, still staring. She hesitated, then lay down on the bed again. Her hands lay passive; hers once more, pale and blue-veined, with torn, dirty fingernails.

The old man did not turn around.

They showed pictures of how she might look if she were trying to disguise herself, in dark or medium skin tones, no hair, long hair, curly hair, hair with color. The brown almost had it: anonymous. And she had changed in ways more subtle than disguise. The arrogance was attenuated, and the invincible assurance gone; the self-confidence remained—it was all she had—but it was tempered, and more mature. She had learned to doubt, rather than simply to question.

The estranged face in the trid, despite its arrogance, was not cruel but gentle, and that quality she had not been able to change.

It had taken them two months to trace her. They could not have followed her credit number, for she had stopped using it before they could cancel it. They would have known only how far she could get before her cash ran out. She had gotten farther, of course, but they had probably expected that.

Since they knew where she was, now was almost identical to later, and now it was still light outside. As she allowed herself to sleep again, she tried to imagine not recognizing a picture of someone she had met. She failed.

LAIS WOKE UP struggling from a nightmare in which the blue images of the trid attacked and overwhelmed her, and her computers would not come to her aid. The old man pulled his hands from her shoulders abruptly and guiltily when he realized she was awake. The windowless room was stuffy. Lais was damp all over with feverish sweat. Her head ached, and her knees were sore.

"I'm sorry, miz, I was afraid you'd hurt yourself." He must have been rebuffed and denigrated all his life, to be so afraid of touching another human being.

"It's all right," she said. She seemed always to be saying that to him. Her mental clock buzzed and jumped to catch up with reality: twelve hours since the trid woke her up.

The old man sat quietly, perhaps waiting for orders. He did not take his gaze from her, but his surveillance was of a strange and anxious childlike quality, without recognition. It seemed not to have occurred to him that his stray might be the Institute fugitive. He seemed to live in two spheres of reality. When she looked at his eyes, he put his head down and hunched his shoulders. His hands lay limp and half-curled in his lap. "I didn't know what to do. They yell at me when I ask stupid questions." No bitterness, just acceptance of the judgment that any question he could ask must be stupid.

She forced back her own useless flare of anger. To awaken hate in him would be cruel. "You did the right thing," she said. She would have said the same words if he had innocently betrayed her. Two other lines of possible reality converged in her mind: herself of two months or a year before, somehow unchanged by exile and disillusionment, and an old man who called Aid for the sick girl in his room. She would have told him exactly what she thought without regard for his feelings; she would have looked on him not with compassion but with the kind of impersonal pity that is almost disdain. But they would have been more similar in one quality: neither of them would have recognized the isolation of their lives.

"Are you hungry?"

"No." That was easier than trying to explain why she was, but could not eat. He accepted it without question or surprise, and still seemed to wait for her orders. She realized that she could stay and he would never dare complain—perhaps not wish to—nor dare tell anyone she was here. If he had been one of the plastic people she might have used him, but he was not, and she could not: full circle.

His hands moved in his lap, nervous.

"What's wrong?" She was careful to say it gently.

As an apology, he said, "Miz, I have to work."

"You don't need my permission," she said, trying to keep her tone from sounding like a reprimand.

He got up, stood uncertainly in the center of his room, wanting to speak, not knowing the right words. "Maybe later you'll be hungry." He fled.

She unwrapped herself from the blanket and massaged her knees. She wandered uneasily around the room, feeling trapped and alien.

One station on the trid bounced down all news. She came on at the quarter hour. The hope that they had only traced her to this world evaporated as she listened to the bulletin: the broadcast was satellite-transmitted; unless they had known, they would not have said she was in Highport and risked missing her in another city. They kept saying she was crazy, in the politest possible terms. They could never say that the malignancy was not in her mind but in her body. No one got cancer anymore. People who related their birth dates to the skies of old Earth did not even call themselves Moon children if they were born under the Crab. All the normals had been clean-gened, to strip even the potential for cancer from their chromosomes. Only a few of them, and now Lais, knew that the potential had been put back into the Institute Fellows, as punishment and control.

They used even this announcement to remind the people how important the Fellows were, how many advances they had made, how many benefits they had provided.

Before, Lais had never known that that sort of constant persuasion was necessary. Perhaps, in fact, it wasn't. Perhaps they only thought it was, so they continued it, afraid to stop the constant reinforcement, probing, breaking old scars.

She turned off the trid. There was a small alcove of a bathroom off the old man's quarters; there was no pool, only a shower. She stripped and took off the dark wig. If there had been a blower she would have washed her clothes, but there were only a couple of worn towels. She turned on the shower and slumped under it with water running through her bright, colorless, startling hair, over her shoulders and breasts and back. Her bones were etched out at ribs and hips, and her muscles made a clear chart of anatomy. Her knees were black and purple; she bruised very easily now.

She left before the old man returned. Trying to thank him would embarrass him and force him to search for words he did not possess. If she waited she might lose her courage and stay; if she waited she might convince herself that she did not need to run again to defy the Institute. If she waited they might trace her to him. It would not matter to them nor help their search if they questioned him, but it would confuse and hurt him. She felt strangely protective toward him, perhaps as he had felt toward her, as if people responded to helplessness in ways that had nothing to do with their capacity to think.

Outside it was dark again—could be still dark, for all the sun Lais had seen. But the sleet had stopped and it was a midnight-blue morning, cold and clear, and even the city's sky-glow could not dim the stars. People strolled alone or in groups on the softly lit mall, or sat on the bronze or stone flanks of the sculptures of prehistoric beasts. Lais stayed in shadows and at edges. No frozen-young faces blanched on seeing her; no one sidled toward the nearest cmu booth to call the security agents. Many of the people, by their clothes and languages, were transients who had no reason to be interested in local news.

The haranguers were back after the rain: preachers for bizarre religions, recruiters for little outwoods colonies, proponents of strange social ideals. Lais could ignore them all, except the ones who preached against her. She could feel the age about them: they remembered. Only a few kept that much hate, enough to stand on walls and cry that the freaks were a danger and a curse. Lais crept by them on the opposite side of the path, as if they could know what she was just by looking. Their voices followed her.

Drained, she stopped and entered one of the frequent cmu booths. The door closed over the sounds. She needed to rest. The money she had scrounged and smoothed could buy no ticket now past the watchers in the port. She used it instead to open lines to the city's computers, and they returned to her the power of machines. Their lure was too great, measured against the delay. The problem lay so clear in her mind that the programs needing to be run sprang out full-grown. She did a minute's worth of exploration and put a block on the lines so she could not be cut off as soon as her money ran out. It should hold long enough. Into the wells she inserted the data cubes she had carried around for two months. Working submerged her; reality dissolved.

Later, while waiting for more important output, Lais almost idly probed for vulnerability in the city programs, seeking to construct for herself a self-erasing escape route. The safeguards were intricate, but hidden flaws leaped out at Lais and the defenses fell, laying the

manager programs open to her abilities. It was hardly
more difficult than blocking the lines. At that moment
she could have put glitches in the city's services and
untraceable bugs in its programs. She could see a thousand ways to cause disruption for mere annoyance; she
could detour garbage services and destroy commercial
records and mismatch mail codes and reroute the traffic, and there were a thousand times a thousand ways to
disrupt things destructively, to turn a community of a
million people into the ruined inhabitants of a chaotic
war zone. Entropy was all on her side. Yet when the city
was stretched out vulnerable before her, the momentary
eagerness to destroy left her. The fact that she could
have done it seemed to be enough. Taking vengeance on
the plastic people would have been senseless, and very
much like experimenting with mice or rabbits or lower
primates, small furry stupid beasts that accept the pain
and degradation with frightened resignation in their
wide deep eyes, not knowing *why*. The emotional isolation that might have allowed her to tamper with the city
was shattered in her own experience and existence as a
laboratory animal, knowing, but not really understanding why.

She slammed at the terminal to close down the holes
she had made in the city's defenses, and touched it more
gently to complete her work. She used an hour of computer time in less than an hour of real time.

The results came chuckling out: first one, then a second
world ecosystem map in fluorescent colors, shading
through the spectrum from violet for concrete through
blue and green and yellow for high to low certainty to
orange and red for theoretical projections. The control
map was mostly blue, very little red: it looked good. Its
data had been nothing but a sample of ordinary dirt, analyzed down to its isotopes, from the grounds of the

outpost, where Lais had been working when she got sick. The map showed the smooth flow of natural evolution, spotted here and there with the quick jumps and twists and bare spots and rootless branches of alien human occupation. Its accuracy was extraordinary. Lais had not thought herself still capable of elation, but she was smiling involuntarily, and for a few moments she forgot about pain and exhaustion.

The second map had less blue and more red, but it seemed unified and logical. Its data had been a bit of a drone sample from an unexplored world, and it showed that the programs were very likely doing what they were supposed to do: deduce the structure and relationships of a world's living things.

Lais's past research had produced results that could hardly be understood, much less used, by normals. It would be extended and built on by her own kind, eventually, not in her lifetime, or perhaps not even in the lifetime that should have belonged to her. This time she had set out to discover the limits of theory applied to minimal data, and the applications were not only obvious but of great potential benefit. When the hounds tracked her, they would find her last programs, and they would be used. Lais shrugged. If she had wanted to be vindictive, she would have tried not to finish, but her mind and her curiosity and her need for knowledge were not things she could flick on and off at will, to produce results like handfuls of cookies.

The screen blinked. Her time had run out long since, and the computer was beginning to cut out the obstructions she had put in its billing mechanism. But they held for the moment, and the computer began obediently to print out the data blocks after the map and the programs. She reached to turn it off, then drew her hand back.

Among crystal structures and mass spectrum plots a DNA sequence zipped by, almost unnoticed, almost unnoticeable, but it caught her attention. She thought it was from the drone sample. She brought it back and put it on the screen. The city computers had all the wrong library programs, and who bothered to translate DNA anymore anyway? She picked a place that looked right and did it by memory; for Lais it was like typing. ATG, adenine, thymine, guanine. Start: methionine. Life is the same all over. The computer built a chain of amino acids like a string of popbeads. Two dimensions valiantly masqueraded as three. Lais threw in entropy and let the chain fold up. When it was done she doubled and redoubled it and added a copy of its DNA. The screen flickered again; the openings she had made in the computer's safeguards were beginning to close, and alarms would be sounding.

The pieces on the screen began the process of self-aggregation, and when they were done she had a luminous green reproduction, a couple of million times real size, of something that existed on the borders of life. It was a virus, that was obvious. She could not stay and translate the whole genome and look for equivalents for the enzymes it would need. She did not have to. It felt, to all her experience, and memory, and intuition, like a tumor virus. She glanced at the printout again, and realized with slow shock, free-fall sensation, that this was from the control data.

There were any number of explanations. Someone could have been using the virus as a carrier in genetic surgery, replacing its dangerous parts with genes that it could insert into a chromosome. They did not grow freaks at that outpost, but they might have made the virus stocks that the freaks were infected with when they were no more than one-cell zygotes. Someone could have been careless with their sterile technique, especially if they had not been told what the virus was used for and how dangerous it was.

The looming green virus particle, as absurd and obscene that size as the magnified head of a fly, dimmed. The computer was almost through the block. Lais had been in the company of machines so long that they seemed to have as much personality as people; this one muttered and grumbled at her for stealing its time. It lumbered to stop her, a hippopotamus playing crocodile.

Lais had dug the virus up outside in the dirt, free, by chance, and there was a lot of it. If it were infectious—and it seemed complete—it could be infecting people at and around the outpost, not very many, but some, integrating itself into their chromosomes, eradicating the effects of clean-gening. It might wait ten or fifteen or fifty years, or forever, but when injury or radiation or carcinogen induced it out, it would begin to kill. It would be too late to cure people of it then, just as it was for Lais; the old, crippling methods, surgery, radiation, might work for a few, but if the disease were similar to hers, fast-growing, metastasizing, nothing would be much use.

The light on the screen began to go out. She moved quickly and stored the map programs, the maps, the drone data.

She hesitated. In a moment it would be too late. She felt the vengeful animals of memories trying to hold her back. She jabbed with anger at the keyboard, and sent the control data into storage with the rest as the last bright lines faded from the screen.

The data was there, for them to notice and fear, or ignore and pay the price. She would give them that much warning. The normals might find a way to clean-gene people after they were grown; they might even set

Fellows to work on the problem, and let them share the benefits. Lais wondered at her own naivety, that after everything a small part of her still hoped her people might finally be forgiven.

She left it all behind, even the data cubes, and went back out onto the mall.

A HOVERCAR WHIRRED a few streets back; sharp beams from its searchlights touched the edges and corners of buildings. She walked faster, then ran painfully past firmly shut doors to a piece of sculpture that doubled as a sitting-park. She crawled into the deepest and most enclosed alcove she could reach. Outside she could hear the security car intruding on the pedestrian mall. The sucks passed without suspecting her presence, not recognizing the sculpture as a children's toy, a place to hide and climb and play, a place for transients to sleep in good weather, a place that, tonight, was Lais's alone.

There was a tiny window by her shoulder that cut through a meter of stone to the outside. Moonlight polished a square of the wall that narrowed, crept upward, and vanished as the moon set.

Lais put her head on her knees and focused all her attention on herself, tracing lines of fatigue through her muscles to extrapolate her reserves of stamina, probing at the wells of pain in her body and in her bones. She had become almost accustomed to betrayal by the physical part of herself, but she was still used to relying on her mind. The slight tilt from a fine edge of alertness was too recent for her to accept. Now, forcing herself to be aware of everything she was, she was frightened by the changes to the edge of panic. She closed her eyes and fought it down, wrestling with a feeling like a great gray slug in her stomach and a small brown millipede in her throat. Both of them retreated, temporarily. Tears tickled her cheeks, touched her lips with salt; she scrubbed them away on her rough sleeve.

She felt marginally better. It had occurred to her that she felt light-headed and removed and hallucinatory because of hunger, not because of advancing pathological changes in her brain; that helped. It was another matter of relying on feedback from a faulty instrument. The thought of food was still nauseating. It would be harder to eat the longer she put it off, but, then, perhaps it was too late to matter anymore.

The sitting-park restored her, as it was meant to; for her it was the silence and isolation, the slight respite from cold and the clean twisting lines of it, whatever reasons others had for responding. She would have liked to stay.

She walked a long way toward the edge of the bazaar. Her knees still hurt—it took her a few minutes to remember when she had fallen, and why; it seemed a very long time before—and her legs began to ache. Resting again, she sat on a wall at the edge of the bazaar, at the edge of the mountaintop, looking down over a city of pinpoint lights (holes in the ground to hell? but the lights were gold and silver, not crimson). The lights led in lines down the flanks of the mountain, dendrites from the cell of the city and its nucleus of landing field. She knew she could get out of Highport. She believed she could run so far that they would not catch her until too late; she hoped they would never find her, and she hoped her body would fail her before her mind did, or that she would have courage and presence enough to kill herself if it did not or if the pain grew great enough to break her. All she really had to do was get to the bottom of the mountain, and past the foothills, until she reached lush jungle and great heat and a climate like an incubator, where life processes are faster and scavengers prowl, and the destruction of decomposition is rapid and complete. The jungle would conspire with her to deny the Institute what she considered most precious: knowledge. She slipped off the wall and started down the hill. Before her the sky was changing from midnight blue to gray and scarlet with the dawn.

# UNTITLED 4

*Paul Park*

IT HAD BEEN years since I had written a publishable story. But there were some sketches I'd abandoned at various times, and so in desperation I chose two of them—no, no, it's not by telling lies that I will recover what is mine. Perhaps there's something about prison that makes us devious and paranoid. No again—it's not prison that's to blame, though I can feel myself tempted to explain my emptiness, the way my smallest thoughts turn to violence, by describing my life now. So let me put that to rest by admitting that I'm not badly treated. I have special privileges. The warden keeps a battered copy of *Thirteen Steps* behind his desk. My first day here, he asked me to sign it. He says it changed his life, years ago.

After our most recent revolution, I was reminded that the new vice-chairman's son admired a certain volume of short stories, which I had once attacked in print. Literature and literary opinions are suddenly important in my small country, not for their own sake. I spend most of my days in the library, where I've been given a study carrel and a word processor. Or I work longhand in the reading room, a high, empty space with tall windows and long tables. The fact is, prison can be liberating, and the fact is also that whatever sickness was afflicting me before I was arrested has continued here. Ideas are as scarce as lizard's teeth for me, which was why I took the teaching job in the first place, why I chose to hide myself in the rhetoric of discontent, why I refused to defend myself in court. At the time I was living by myself in one small room, smaller than my cell here in this place.

Now electronic mail comes to me from all over the world, and conventional letters too. A turnkey delivers them to my carrel, or my table, or wherever I am sitting. She does not tamper with them. One day I received an envelope with a disk inside, and a letter: *Dear Mr. Bland, I know you will be surprised to hear from me. Sometimes the defense of liberty requires unfair choices. More than anyone, I am sorry about how things turned out. Believe me, when I was assigned to your case, I thought it would be hard to feign an interest in your subject. My supervisor was obliged to remind me several times, in the words of our greatest statesmen, that we all have stories to tell. Still I continued to deny that part of myself. Now my political advancement has been rapid, and I have you to thank. The months I spent in your class meant a lot to me. I'll admit that my first few assignments were prepared by others, so as not to alert your suspicions. But after that I insisted on doing my own work. I hope you noticed the improvement! I always valued your comments, and I tried to thank you in the tone of my report. Even routine bureaucratic tasks can become point-of-view exercises! Things could have worked out a lot worse. I mention this so that you won't think it forward of me to ask you to take a look at the enclosed texts, my final project, which you never had the chance to read before your class was interrupted. I know you have time on your hands. Etc., etc., sincerely L. Raevsky. PS—I recently picked up a copy of* Thirteen Steps. *What an amazing book that is! You must be very proud.*

No one testified against me at my trial, but the indictment quoted things I'd said, not things I had written. In my mind I had already identified the informer, a beautiful girl in my ten o'clock seminar. She had golden hair and a developed figure. When I was lecturing on advanced trends in modern literature, I always felt I was speaking to her alone, because she paid such close attention. But now I found I'd done her and her tight sweaters an injustice. Even so, I never would have suspected Raevsky, the salt of the earth, I'd thought—steady, solid, unremarkable, with a background in automobile repair and a wife and child at home. He used to come to class in a necktie. I had always been drawn toward my less talented students, the ones from untraditional backgrounds, as I had been myself.

When I accepted a job at the University of PRB, I was in such despair. It was a sad joke to think I had been able to help anyone, even a stool pigeon. I had taken to drinking before I went to class. Then I would listen to myself making the most provocative statements—it was only a matter of time before I drew attention to myself. Once I had told my students to write a description of a party meeting, using actual quotations from various officials as they were reported in the newspaper. Then I had asked them, without changing anything but the point of view, to imagine the same words in the mouths of retarded persons and obsessive compulsives. The meeting had involved metaphors of government and the new uses of fiction, I remember.

Or once I had tried to make the argument that plot itself was an outmoded concept, and that we had to work to liberate our characters from the tyranny of our own will, which so often reflects bigotry, or bad judgment, or even sadism. Nor was it the answer to expose our stories to the whims of readers, as has been attempted in various experiments with "hypertext." That was merely to exchange an authoritarian model with a "democratic" one, with its illusion of consensual control. Instead I looked forward to a new kind of writing, where our characters could achieve their destiny, and torment us and terrorize us in their turn.

An obvious legal strategy would have been to claim that I had meant this literally, not, as it was taken, as political satire. But when I heard my words read back to me in court, I was ashamed. It seemed transparent what I was actually admitting, that I had lost faith in myself. In the end it was impossible for the judge to imagine that the author of such a carefully plotted piece as *Thirteen Steps*— you know the rest. Sometimes it is hard to understand what people say about one's work.

But when I pressed Raevsky's disk into the wooden slot, I saw that he at least in his small, tone-deaf way, had tried to take me at my word. On the disk were two short stories, each about 3,000 words long.

The first consisted of a plot without characters. As I have said, Raevsky was a professional mechanic, specializing in transmission repair. Reading with this in mind, I could not but imagine a driverless car. And so then I found his second story must suggest an old-fashioned van with no wheels, parked by the curb, the passengers inexplicably still inside.

I had given Raevsky high marks he had not deserved. Now I imagined a certain masturbatory pleasure in editing his work. As I had once told my class, successful stories often start at the conjunction of two unrelated ideas. I thought if I could force down the accelerator, if I could smash the empty car into the motionless but crowded van, something might happen. At least it would be possible to describe the accident.

Raevsky's documents were called Untitled 1, and Untitled 2. After I combined the files, there was indeed a wreck. Bodies were thrown clear. But one of the tricks of the professional writer is the ability to reanimate the dead. So I was thumping on their chests, running wires from the car batteries into the muscle tissue—you can see this metaphor is not under my control. You can guess the problems I've been having. In fact there was no levity in the way I set about to punish Raevsky's characters and mock his situations—not that I wasn't justified. How dare he send me his ridiculous scribblings? Each story was worse than the other. The first was about a bed. Or it was a description of an empty room in what appeared to be an old hotel. There are traces of blood on the counterpane, which have not yet soaked into the mattress. The pillow is still warm. There is a revolver on the bedside table. The window has been shattered, and pieces of glass lie on the fire escape outside. A letter on the floor begins, "Dear friend: This is so difficult for me..." but then the rest of the text is crumpled and obscured. A smell of gardenia perfume lingers in the air. A tiny porcelain dog lies in pieces on the hearth.

It is, in fact, a melodrama with no actors. Are we to assume that Character A, having received a disappointing letter, has come to confront Character B, perhaps at the scene of another guilty rendezvous? Carrying the

letter and the porcelain dog, perhaps a memento from
happier times, A paces back and forth, while B sits on
the bed, terrified, the counterpane drawn up. Then, still
unsatisfied, A seizes his or her revolver, and... but if so,
what has become of these people? Have they exited via
the broken window? Or are we, as readers, waiting for
the sound of a flushing toilet? We cannot see how many
shots, if any, have been fired from the revolver, but perhaps we are talking about a suicide or an attempted
suicide, and the victim has just staggered from the room
into the hall, where his or her blood is mixing with the
pattern on the long carpet.

This mania for fiction writing which has gripped my
country is a recent phenomenon. It comes from the top
down. Now even some of the trade unions are holding
mandatory seminars in characterization and tone. It is
because the party chairman, since the attack on his life,
now speaks only in metaphors. It is possible he was
more seriously hurt than was reported. At first his public statements took the form of fables and parables,
which it was still just barely possible to translate into
legislation. But now every day his writings have become
more complicated and indirect. Has policy suffered? It
is hard to say. Luckily we are at peace. But what is clear
is that people like myself are experiencing new anxi-
eties. In the current situation, I have become well
known in political circles. There were waiting lists for
all my classes by the time I was arrested. At the same
time, the pressure to publish has become even more
uncomfortable. Already the secretary of the association
has given me a deadline for a new submission to the
national magazine. He has written me a letter, a description of what has happened to others—household names
once, but forgotten now. I cannot but imagine a hollow
square of readers dressed in black. They shake their

skinny fists and shout while my nominations are trampled underfoot.

My prison sentence is not a long one, and it is necessary for me to consider what might happen if I were to be set free. The secretary is reconsidering my stipend, which so far has not been affected by my legal status. He has enclosed new government guidelines, based on the evolving characteristics of the chairman's work, which specifically prohibit the use of any autobiographical material, or indeed anything in the first person. But as I sit day by day at my long oak table, or in my cell, or staring at the letters on the screen of my processor, all that occurs to me are stories from my childhood, as well as various pornographic images which are equally forbidden. Often these involve the girl with golden hair and extraordinary breasts, whom I had been obliged to chastise in my mind, during the days when I thought it was she who had denounced me. Now of course she has been rehabilitated, which has not affected her state of chronic undress.

I admit I was surprised to see that she was also a character in Raevsky's second story, which took the form of a symposium in the home of a national hero, the author of several famous works of fiction. At his cramped table are seated various students and politicians, all unnamed, but identified by various physical characteristics. Raevsky is one. Another is the girl. There is the chief of the municipal police, whom I remember from the time when he was an ordinary hotel watchman. And in the darkness at the end of the table, overcome by rich food and ennui, sprawls the obese, sleeping figure of the party chairman.

The national hero is a powerful and commanding figure, with a mane of gray hair and nicotine-stained hands. Burst blood vessels on his nose testify to private vices, but in spite of these he is self-confident and virile. He does not lecture his students, but allows them to talk, though from time to time he will interject some trenchant words. His voice is not shrill. It is pleasingly low. Though all her conversation is about philosophical and political topics, it is clear that the golden-haired girl is infatuated with him, and he responds in a paternal, kindly way.

Nothing happens in this story, as I've said. A spaniel wanders in and out of the room. Food is eaten. Cigarettes are smoked. Mineral water is consumed. Platitudes and bromides are exchanged. And there is one small detail which I scarcely noticed until I began to combine this story with the first. At a certain moment, the character I had identified as Raevsky, after recounting an anecdote involving his infant son, reaches under the table to touch the girl's knee. Annoyed, she slaps his hand.

But she does not seem mortified or surprised. Perhaps if the national hero had not been present, she would have responded differently.

In this context, much of the Raevsky character's dialogue acquires a new, suggestive tone. Was it jealousy, I wondered, that turned the real Raevsky into a police informant? On my processor I began to write a series of sketches, moving the characters from Untitled 2 back through the hotel room, which now I recognized from a monogram on a stained towel thrown carelessly across the bottom of the bed. As soon as I saw it, all the other details now suddenly came back to me: the cracked ceiling, the floral wallpaper, the elegant pre-war furniture. This building, the old Plaza Athenee hotel, still stands near Martyr's Gate, though of course it has been requisitioned for government purposes.

Now I can almost hear the sound of the old piano in the lobby, where on Thursday afternoons I used to wait, breathless with anxiety and guilt, for the sight of my secret friend. She was an editorial assistant in the office of Ullman Freres. She was an acquaintance of my former wife.

These memories, coming on me suddenly as I sit in my study carrel, affect the tone of several of my sketches, especially those involving the girl with golden hair. In the first one I finished, she lay on the bed with the national hero, while the party chairman slumped asleep in one of the armchairs. (He persisted in this pose through several sketches, and he always managed to sleep through even the fiercest action. Nor did he wake up on the few occasions when the revolver was actually fired.) To continue—Raevsky storms in with the letter in his hand, which in all versions now completes a text which my friend the editorial assistant wrote to me years before, and which I still remember word for word. Raevsky confronts his faithless lover, while the national hero suffers a nose-bleed, to which he is prone. Raevsky marches to the window and throws it open, revealing the chief of police crouched on the fire escape, dressed in a double-breasted trench coat and slouch hat. It has been raining, and he is very damp. He climbs into the room, but is astonished and nonplussed to see the party chairman in such circumstances. The porcelain dog, which was balanced on the window sash, falls to the ground.

But sometimes the guilty couple is asleep, worn out from their endeavors. The blood on the counterpane comes from the passion of their embrace. Raevsky enters without knocking, and he spends a long time surveying the scene, calmly walking back and forth, touching with the tips of his fingers various objects in the room—the porcelain dog, the gun. He kicks the crumpled letter with his foot. Neither the party chairman nor the chief of police makes an appearance, though they are mentioned in brief, impressionistic flashbacks.

In some versions, these scenes of mine acquire a certain poignancy. But there are others, I'm ashamed to say, in which the girl with golden hair is forced to disrobe, and she is shamefully assaulted by Raevsky, the party chairman, the chief of police, even the spaniel on one disgusting occasion. Her cries are heard by the national hero, who bursts in with a revolver. He shoots, to no avail. Sometimes the bullet shatters the window...

One very short scene involves the dogs confronting one another, one porcelain, one real. And in one, the party chairman lies sleeping in his armchair with the spaniel curled up on the hearth rug. The twitching of the chairman's right hand, the dog's left foot, reveal their dreams. The blood, the smell of gardenias, are unexplained.

Perhaps, I thought as I was working, Raevsky had given me a new way to write about the past, a way to write about myself and still maintain the new guidelines. Perhaps, I thought, I could even publish some of these sketches, especially the ones in which the golden-haired girl did not appear. Perhaps I could find a new approach to autobiographical material, in which characters from my past and even I myself are carefully, even lovingly described, and then put into artificial situations. Perhaps also one could imagine a new kind of pornography, appropriate to the guidelines, in which one describes only transitions between scenes of terrible excess.

And I was wondering also if, in his benighted way, Raevsky was giving me these tools deliberately, as an expression of remorse. Certainly it had been years since I had worked on anything so feverishly as on these sketches. I was just attempting one in which the chief of police finds himself in what he first interprets to be a compromising position with the party chairman, when an icon on my processor screen started to flash. It was the stork with the baby in its beak, a signal that I had received electronic mail.

The processor is of an old design, a screen ten centimeters square, forming one end of a long rosewood box. I speak letters and punctuation marks one by one into a small tube, and watch them appear hesitantly on the screen. There is no modem or keyboard, as I have seen on various newer models. A single wire connects the box to a hole in the linoleum floor.

"Open," I said, and I heard something rattle in the tin drawer, which hangs down from the bottom of the box. I unhooked the clasp, and the drawer sagged open, revealing some pieces of paper, folded together many times into what was almost a cube. Opening it gingerly, still I couldn't help tearing it along the folds. Finally I was able to separate it into three pages of lavender note paper. I did not recognize the handwriting, which was in purple ink.

The letter was written in English, which I read only badly. Here is my translation: *Mr. Bland, some of the things you have written are so terrible, I can't even understand them. I have appeared in over a hundred stories, some by authors even more celebrated than yourself. Until recently I was not even required to take off my shoes. Knowing your reputation, I explained very carefully to Mr. Raevsky what I would and wouldn't do, etc, etc, Miss MEH, Society of Fictive Artists...*

The icon flashed again, and again I unhooked the tin drawer. This time there was a shorter note, also in

English, written in soft pencil on the back of a laundry receipt: *I've been rubbing the damned pine in too many damned stories lately, so let me tell you I was promised a speaking role.*

Rubbing the pine? I have no idea what this means. One of the turnkeys brings me a dictionary of idioms in the English and American languages. As it turns out, the phrase is an allusion to a certain game. "Held in reserve," would be an adequate translation.

A third time the icon flashes, and something clatters in the drawer. This time it sags down by itself to reveal a hardened pellet of dog feces—no, I put my head down on my desk and weep. An artist like myself is not insensitive to criticism. Better than anyone else, I know when my efforts at characterization, based as they are on former students and people I have scarcely met, are unconvincing and unoriginal. Yes, it's true: I have borrowed characters, in some cases, from other people's work. Better than anyone else, I know these sketches of mine have not attained the standard of realism which I established for the first time in *Thirteen Steps* and then maintained in several later works. It is not necessary for me to receive these complaints, here, now. But how wonderful it would be to find in my tin box a word from an actual human being, not these trained animals and hired hacks. At that moment I would have given anything for a word from the golden-haired girl, or even the miserable Raevsky! Critics had praised my earlier work by saying that it had duplicated ordinary experience so precisely as to render it superfluous. There was no reason, for example, to attend another dinner party after reading my description. Couples interested in maintaining a social schedule might read the same passages to each other every Friday and Saturday night, and stay at home. There was no reason for them to have affairs, get divorced, or sit drinking coffee and smoking cigarettes on rainy afternoons.

What I would have given at that moment for a word from my old friend, the editorial assistant at Ullman Freres! Or rather, that's the way I still thought of her, though in fact she had married again, had children, grown older, risen (I had heard) to a high position in the party hierarchy. Still I remembered the smell of her perfume. What was it called? And then a cold feeling came over me as I tried to imagine the scent of gardenias, which of course do not grow in my country. All this time in my sketches I had been mentioning this smell, mixed sometimes with that of gunpowder. But as is so often the case in second-rate fiction, these are just words. Now a bell in my processor signals a new message, and the tin drawer opens. The dog feces are gone. Instead there is a blue apothecary's bottle in the bottom of the drawer. There is no reason to open it, because at that moment my small carrel (indeed, I imagine, the entire prison library) is overwhelmed by a heavy, pungent, acrid smell. The hand-written label on the bottle reads: GARDENIA/CORDITE.

"If you want the truth," I spell out letter by letter, punctuation mark by punctuation mark into my tube, "let me tell you I'll die first."

The party chairman was found slumped over at his desk, a gun in his right hand, a copy of *Thirteen Steps* on the ink blotter in front of him. In fact (it was claimed in an official editorial) this book had been responsible for many suicides, as readers came to wonder what could possibly happen to them, that had not been more vividly and accurately described in print.

The party chairman did not die, of course. He shot himself through the roof of his mouth and still managed to miss his brain. In a sense, he has recovered fully.

Nevertheless it is a cause for national concern, how much he still might be affected by these complicated modern texts. When it was discovered that the author of the book had sent it to the chairman as a birthday gift, the government requested a charge of attempted murder. But the letter which accompanied the book, which reminded the chairman of unfortunate events and begged for his intervention with the national editorial board, was of course suppressed. As a result, a judge discarded the indictment. Assassination cannot be an accidental process. As usual, the court's decision satisfied no one.

Less ambiguous was a case still unsolved after many years, in which a jealous husband was shot to death on the fire escape outside his wife's hotel room. An obvious suspect in the murder had been an important national figure, the woman's correspondent, who had not been brought to trial. Many people at the time assumed he had been protected by powerful forces. The question now was whether that protection would persist, after the attempt (as it was called) on the chairman's life.

This was the case that still bothered me. Now, sitting with the smell of gardenias and cordite all around me, further details came back. I began to speak into the tube. But now the bronze letters on my screen did not follow anything I said. Instead, slowly, they spelled out a memorandum addressed to me from the secretary of the national association: *We insist that the date we gave you for a new submission must remain firm, if your annuity is to be continued. We have heard you are working on something new, a credible account of certain terrible events. We would be interested in publishing this project and no other.*

It is obvious that they have become impatient with me, impatient with the sketches I have written so far.

They want to restrict my choice of characters to the people I knew best: myself, my friend, her husband. The date the secretary refers to is today, which gives me one more hour: ample time, especially since I have not written anything since that April afternoon ten years before, when I had stood in the hallway of the old Plaza Athenee, off Schubert Square. Various aspects of my life had come to an end that day, but nothing new had started. Until I received the summons from the university, I had spent ten years in my little room, scarcely going out except to shop for cigarettes, whisky, and breakfast cereal. For ten years the only fiction I had written was in the form of desperate letters to the association and to certain national figures, imploring them not to terminate my stipend but indeed rather to increase it, for the sake of my past work. I had written to the chairman himself, praising him yet threatening to reveal certain details of our shared history. I had enclosed my book. I had meant no harm. But after the chairman's accident, the authorities had pried me from my room like a conch out of its shell. Agoraphobic, semi-retired, I nevertheless was forced to give lectures to classes of forty or a hundred students, some of whom would interrupt me with applause, especially if I chanced to say something "revolutionary," or specific to current events. Nor was I able to discover who had hired me, or for what purpose. It was easy to imagine that the government might want to strip away my tiny shelter and expose me. On the other hand, the "opposition" now considered me a hero, especially after the text of my letter to the chairman was revealed. Based on it, someone had requested an investigation.

This is what I said in my lectures: the only way for authors to surrender their authority is to tell the "truth"— that is, to set their work in that strange, foggy landscape, in which both character and author are equally blind. If the party chairman was the "author" of the nation, as he had recently claimed, this was the landscape in which he was most readily confronted. Now I must admit that these words had been scripted for me, though by which political interest was unclear.

I imagine that after ten years of falsehood, no evidence remains. Without some kind of confession, the chairman's name cannot be cleared, nor can I be punished for the harm I did to him. But if I give them what they want, perhaps they will be grateful and not keep me here. They will renew my stipend. No doubt they are only interested in destroying my reputation. After all, we are talking about something which will appear in a fiction magazine.

But how unfair this is! The woman in the case was given a political appointment, though I hear now she has fallen out of favor. The hotel guard was made a police captain. Only I, who suffered most, was given nothing. Every day I was forced to live with the humiliation, the memory of that long walk down the hall with the porcelain dog (a gift from her, which I meant to throw down at her feet, or else lay down carefully on the bedside table) clutched to my breast, together with the crumpled letter.

And now I must admit that I am glad they are only interested in a false confession, a fictional account. I will consent to nothing that makes me sound ridiculous, or makes me play the part that I was actually obliged to play. Some things are worse than being thought of as a murderer.

Now, tired out from my imagining, I begin to spell out in third person my final sketch. There are certain details I must make clear. The porcelain dog now falls from the window sill. The text of the letter on the floor remains obscure. I cannot explain why I should possess a gun or why I should have brought a gun to a romantic encounter, but a skillful writer knows what to leave out. I make much of my confusion, my desire to protect as, woken from a guilty sleep, we see a dark shape at the window. We hear cries of anger, a hammering on the glass. It is all over in a minute.

As I write, the image of the golden-haired girl, which has been so real to me, now floats from the bed and disappears. Lying in her place is the elegant, frail figure of my friend the editorial assistant, now a high official. She is dressed in a white camisole. She reaches out her hand to touch my face, and it is as if no time has passed. I find I can no longer see in my mind's eye the picture of her sitting up in bed, the counterpane around her naked shoulders. She is screaming, but I can't hear her. I have burst in with the hotel guard, but I can't see him, nor the unmistakable and already quite fat young bureaucrat who stands facing the broken window with the revolver in his hand. All that lingers is the smell of cordite and his foul cologne.

# DARK CALVARY

*Eric Brown*

HE BURIED FRANCESCA in the rich jungle soil of Tartarus Major while the sky pulsed with the photon hemorrhage of the supernova and the Abbot of the Church of the Ultimate Sacrifice knelt and chanted prayer.

And he thought that was the end of the affair.

HANS CRAMER MET Francesca when she was eighteen, two decades his junior but wise beyond her years, and already a second-class helio-meteorologist aboard one of the Fleet's finest nova observation vessels. Cramer was employed as an itinerant lecturer, teaching philosophy and theology to the reluctant crews of the various ships of the Zakinthos Line. His posting to the observation sailship *Dawn Light* was just another move, but one that changed his life.

Francesca was a regular at his rambling lectures in the vast auditorium of the city-sized sailship. She was distinguished by her striking Venezuelan face and jet-black mass of hair—an affectation in space, where so many crew went partly shorn or bald. What attracted him initially was not so much her physical aspect as her youth, and that she attended every one of his lectures. She was that rarity among spacers: a student who wanted to learn. After years of having his talks received with boredom, or at best polite apathy, Cramer found her attentiveness exhilarating. It was natural that he should single her out for special tuition. He gave her one-to-one lessons, and she responded. He prided himself on the fact that she excelled herself, absorbed everything he had to offer, and was still hungry for more.

Inevitably, perhaps, they transcended the teacher-pupil relationship and became lovers. It was a gradual process, but one which culminated in an event that informed them both that their feelings for each other were reciprocated. They had been discussing the physics of spatial dimensions congruent to singularities, and the conversation continued well beyond the time Cramer usually allotted for her tuition. The talk turned general, and then personal. There was a period of silence, and Cramer looked into the depths of her Indian eyes—and he was suddenly aware of his desire, affection, and overwhelming need to be responsible for Francesca.

For the next year Cramer lectured aboard the *Dawn Light* as it sailed from star to unstable star, and their love deepened into a thorough understanding of one another. She told Cramer that which she had never told anyone before: how, at the age of ten, she had lost her father. He had been a scientist, working on the planet of a sun due to go nova, when the sun blew before its time and killed him and his scientific team... This, Cramer thought, helped to explain the choice of her profession.

Cramer became for Francesca a combination of lover-teacher-protector, as well as a friend and confidant... And for him Francesca was the first person in his life to remind him that he was not, contrary to nearly forty years of assumptions otherwise, the fulcrum of the universe. Her naivety, her vitality and honesty, her willingness to learn, her trust in others—he was in awe of all these things. Sometimes he wanted to protect her from herself when others might take advantage, but at the same time he learned from her that openness and trust can bring its own rewards: contact with one's fellows, even friendships, which for long enough he had shunned. Her youth and enthusiasm were a foil to Cramer's age and cynicism, and though at times he found it exhausting, more often than not he was swept along heedless by the tide of her passion.

Francesca had her dark side, though.

Six months after they became lovers, she slipped into a sullen, uncommunicative depression. Often he found her in tears, his entreaties ignored. He assumed that the chemical magic that had attracted her to him had soured, that their time together had run its course.

Then, one rest period, Cramer found her in a personal nacelle which obtruded through the skin of the ship and afforded a magnificent view of the blazing variable below. Francesca had sought privacy in which to brood. He lowered himself in beside her and waited.

After a period of silence, she asked in a whisper, "What do you believe, Hans?"

Cramer had never spoken to her about his beliefs, or lack of—perhaps fearing that his apathy might frighten her away. "I was once a nihilist," he said, "but now I believe in nothing."

She slapped his face. "Be serious!"

He was serious. "Nothing," he said.

She was silent, a small frown of puzzlement denting her forehead. At last she murmured, "I need belief. I need to believe in something... something *more* than all this." She made a spread-fingered gesture to indicate everything, all existence. "Life is so meaningless, if this is all there is to it—*life*. There must be something more!"

He stroked a strand of hair from her Indian eyes.

She looked at him. "Don't you fear death? Don't you wake up panicking in the early hours, thinking, 'One day I'll be dead for all eternity?'"

He could not help but smile. "At one time I did," he said. "But no more." He told her that it was as if his subconscious had become inured to the fact of his mortality, was no longer daunted by the inevitability of his death.

Francesca was crying. "I hate being alive," she sobbed, "if all it will end in is death."

Cramer held her, soothed her with comforting noises, secretly relieved that he knew the reason for her depression. He told himself that it was nothing more than a stage through which everyone must pass—but, perhaps, he should have seen in her terror the seeds of a consuming obsession.

Six months later Cramer was posted to another ship— there was nothing he could do to avoid the transfer—and he saw Francesca only once every three months or so, when their dirtside leaves coincided. He had feared that the separation might have worked to dampen Francesca's ardor, but the reverse was true. Their hurried, stolen weeks together were the happiest times of their lives.

And then, three years after their first meeting, Francesca was promoted, transferred to a ship bound for the Rim, to study the effects of an imminent supernova on the world of Tartarus Major.

CRAMER WAS ON Earth, on long-service leave from the Fleet and teaching part-time at the University of Rio. Francesca was due back in a week, when her boat would dock at the Santiago shipyards for refurbishment. Cramer had a trekking holiday planned in the Andes, followed by a fortnight in Acapulco, before they said goodbye again and her ship whisked her off to some far, unstable star.

He could recall precisely where he was, what he was doing—even trivial things like what he was wearing at the time, and what mood he was in—when he heard about the crash-landing: in a café on the Rio seafront, drinking coffee and reading *El Globe*, wearing the caftan Francesca had brought back from the Emirate colony of Al Haq, and feeling contentment at the thought of her imminent return. The wall-screen was relaying news to the café's oblivious, chattering clientele. He took notice only when it was announced that a Fleet observation vessel had crash-landed on the Rim world of Tartarus Major. "*The Pride of Valencia* was mapping Tartarus for stress patterns and went down two days ago," said the reporter. "Casualty figures are not yet known. Other news..."

His soul released its pent up breath; relief flooded him. For perhaps five seconds Cramer existed in a glorious state of reprieve, because he knew, didn't he, that Francesca was aboard the observation vessel *Dawn Light*? Then, crashing through his consciousness like a great wave, came the awareness that she had left the *Dawn Light* months ago, had been promoted to the *Pride of Valencia*.

Cramer returned to his apartment, shock lending him a strange sense of calm in which he felt removed from the reality of his surroundings. He contacted the Fleet headquarters in Geneva, but was told that no details of the incident would be forthcoming until accident investigators had reported from Tartarus Major. Unable to bear the wait, the feeling of redundancy, he knew that the only course of action was make his way independently to Tartarus. He booked passage on a sailship leaving Earth the following day, and spent the duration of the voyage under blissful sedation.

He had no idea what to expect on landing, but it was not the decrepit, medieval city of Baudelaire. It seemed to him that he had stepped back in time. Not only was the architecture and atmosphere of the place archaic, but the bureaucracy and services were likewise mired in the past. The prevailing ethos of the government departments he petitioned seemed to be that the loss of any sailship—and minor officials seemed unsure as to whether a sailship *had* been lost on Tartarus Major—was not the responsibility of their department, and Cramer was advised to see so-and-so at such-and-such a bureau. Added to which confusion, the entire population of the planet seemed to be packed into the capital city, eager to catch a boat off-planet before the supernova blew. Eventually, and with scant regard for his feelings, he was advised to check at the city morgue. Beside himself, he battled through the bustling streets until he came upon the relevant building. The chambers and corridors of the morgue were packed with the stiffened, shrouded figures of the dead. Here, tearful and in obvious distress, he had his first stroke of luck. He happened upon a harassed Fleet official, checking charred remains against the crew list of the *Pride of Valencia*.

Cramer explained his predicament, and the official took sympathy and went through the names of the dead for that of Francesca.

She was not, apparently, in the morgue. All the bodies had been recovered from the site of the crash. According to the official, Cramer was in luck: he was advised to try the infirmary, where the twelve surviving crew members were receiving treatment.

Given hope, he was filled with fear, now, at the thought of Francesca's having survived—or rather he feared the state in which she might have survived. Would he find Francesca reduced to a brain-dead wreck, a hopelessly injured cripple? He considered only the worst case scenario as he made his way to the infirmary. He explained his situation to a doctor who escorted him to the ward where the survivors lay. As the medic checked the records, Cramer strode down the line of beds—not rejuvenation pods, in this backward hole, but beds!—fearful lest he should come upon Francesca, yet petrified that he should not.

She was not on the ward.

The doctor joined Cramer, carrying the crew-list of the *Pride of Valencia*. There was one name outstanding, accounted for neither in the morgue nor in the hospital: Francesca Maria Rodriguez.

Cramer was in turmoil. "Then where the hell is she?"

The doctor placed a soothing hand on his shoulder. "Two of the injured were found in the jungle by an order of monks who took them in and treated their wounds. One male crew member died—the other, Rodriguez, is still undergoing treatment."

"Is she badly injured?"

"I'm sorry. I have no records…" He paused. "You might try the Church of the Ultimate Sacrifice, just along the street. They should be able to help you."

Cramer thanked him and, filled with a mixture of despair and hope that left him mentally exhausted, he almost ran from the infirmary. He found the church without difficulty: in a street of mean timber buildings, it was the only stone-built edifice, a towering cathedral along classical lines.

He hurried inside. A cowled figure riding an invalid carriage barred his way. Desperately Cramer explained himself. The disabled cleric told him to wait, and propelled his carriage up the aisle. While he was gone, Cramer gazed about the sumptuous interior. He noticed the strange, scorpion-like statue above the altar, flanked by a human figure bound to a cross—its arms and legs removed so that it resembled the remains of some ancient statue. He could not help but wonder what perverted cult he had stumbled upon.

The monk returned and gestured that Cramer should follow him. He led the way to a small study behind the altar. "The Abbot," he murmured as Cramer passed inside.

Behind a large desk was an imposing figure garbed in a black habit, his face concealed by a deep cowl.

Nervously, Cramer sat down. Prompted by the Abbot's silence, he babbled his story.

Halfway through, he paused and peered into the shadow of the Abbot's hood. The holy man seemed to have his eyes closed. Cramer noticed the dried, discolored orbs tied to his right wrist, but failed to make the connection.

He continued with what the doctor had told him about Francesca. When he had finished, the Abbot remained silent for some time. He placed his fingertips together in a miniature facsimile of the spire that surmounted the cathedral. He seemed to be contemplating.

He said at last, his voice a rasp, "Are you a believer, Mr. Cramer?"

"In your religion?" Cramer shifted uncomfortably.

"In any."

"I... I have my own beliefs."

"That sounds to me like another way of admitting you're an atheist."

"Does it matter?" he asked. He contained his anger. The Abbot was, after all, his only link with Francesca.

The holy man seemed to take an age before he next spoke. "I can help you, Mr. Cramer. Francesca is in the jungle."

"How badly..." he began, the words catching in his throat.

"Do not worry yourself unduly. She will live."

Cramer sat back in his seat, relief washing over him. He imagined Francesca recuperating in some remote jungle hospital.

"When can I see her?"

"Tomorrow I return to the jungle to resume my pilgrimage. If you wish, you may accompany me."

Cramer thanked him, relieved that at last his search was almost over.

"I leave at first light," said the Abbot. "You will meet me here." And he gestured—parting his spired hands—to indicate that the audience was over.

That night Cramer found expensive lodging in a crowded boarding house. In the morning the sun rose huge and brooding over the parched city, though the sky had been lit all night long with the primary's technicolor fulminations. He had slept badly, apprehensive as to the state in which he might find Francesca. At dawn he returned to the cathedral and met the Abbot, and they hurried through narrow alleyways to a jetty and a barge painted in the sable and scarlet colors of the Church.

The crew of two natives cast off the moorings and the barge slipped sideways into midstream before the engines caught. Cramer sat on the foredeck, in the shade of a canvas awning, and shared a thick, red wine with the Abbot. The holy man threw back his cowl, and Cramer could not help but stare. The Abbot's ears and nose had been removed, leaving only dark holes and scabrous scar tissue. His eyelids, stitched shut over hollow sockets, were curiously flattened, like miniature drumheads. He kept his eyeballs, dried and shrunken, on a thong of optic nerves around his wrist.

The barge proceeded upriver, against a tide of smaller craft streaming in the opposite direction. The Abbot cocked his head toward their puttering engines. "Some believed the things which were spoken," he quoted, "and some did not. Once, sir, all Tartarus believed. Now the faith is defended by a devout minority."

Cramer murmured something non-committal in reply. He was not interested in the Abbot's belief system and its macabre extremes. For fifteen years he had taught students the rudiments of the various major faiths. Now religion, every religion, sickened him. In his opinion, superstitious belief systems were just one more political tool that man used to subjugate, terrorize, and enslave his fellow man.

He sat and drank and watched the passing landscape. At one point they idled by an ancient temple complex. Many of the buildings were in ruins; others, miraculously, considering their age, stood tall and proud. Towers and minarets of some effulgent stone like rose-colored marble, they were sufficiently alien in design to inspire wonder. As the barge sailed slowly by, Cramer made out six statues— another example of the long, scorpion-like insects, tails hooked in readiness.

He finished his wine, excused himself, and retreated to his cabin. He drew the shutters against the light and, despite the heat, enjoyed the sleep he had been denied the night before.

He awoke hours later, much refreshed, hardly able to believe after the trials of the past two days that Francesca would soon be in his arms. He climbed to the deck. The sun was directly overhead—he must have slept for five or six hours. The barge was pulling into a jetty. A tumbledown collection of timber buildings lined the riverbank. The Abbot appeared at Cramer's side. "Chardon's Landing," he said. "From here we walk. It is thirty kilometers to the plateau."

With scarcely a delay they set off into the jungle, Cramer marveling at the blind man's sure tread as he navigated his way through the jungle. At first the trek was not arduous. The way had been cleared, and they followed a well-defined path through the undergrowth. Only later, as they put twenty kilometers behind them, and the path began to climb, did Cramer begin to feel the strain. They slowed, and halted often to swallow water from leather canteens.

They continued through the long, sultry hours of afternoon; at last, when Cramer thought he could continue no more, they came to a clearing. Before them, the plateau fell away in a sheer drop, affording an open panorama of treetops stretching all the way to the northern horizon beneath a violent, actinic sky.

Only then did Cramer notice the tent, to one side of the clearing.

He turned to the Abbot. "Where are we?"

The holy man gestured. "Francesca's tent," was his only reply.

"But this can't be the mission..." Cramer began.

He heard a sound from across the clearing, and turned quickly. He stared in dread as Francesca drew aside the tent flap and stepped out. His heart began a labored pounding. She stood, tiny and trim in her radiation silvers. He searched her for any sign of injury—but she seemed whole and perfect, as he had dreamed of her all along. She stared at him, appearing uncertain at his presence. A smile came hesitantly to her lips.

He crossed the clearing and hugged her to his chest.

She pulled away, shaking her head. "I meant to contact you. It's just..." Cramer had expected tears; instead, she was almost matter-of-fact.

"Francesca... What's happening? The Abbot—" He nodded toward the holy man, who was busying himself with a second tent across the clearing. "He said that you were injured, in hospital—"

She looked pained. "Come. We have a lot to talk about." She took his hand and drew him into the tent.

They sat facing each other. He scanned her for injuries, but saw no bandages, compresses, or scabs of synthetic flesh.

She read his gaze, and smiled. "Cuts and bruises, nothing serious."

Cramer felt a constriction in his throat. "You were lucky."

She lowered her head, looked at him through her lashes. "You don't know how lucky," she murmured.

A silence developed, and he wished at that moment that silence was all that separated them; but they seemed divided by more than just the inability to communicate meaningfully.

Then he saw the book beside her inflatable pillow. Embossed in scarlet upon its black cover was the symbol of a scorpion beside a dismembered human figure.

"Francesca..." he pleaded. "What's happening?"

She did not meet his gaze. "What do you mean?"

He indicated the holy book.

It was some time before she could bring herself to respond. At last she looked up, her eyes wide, staring, as if still in shock from the trauma of the crash landing.

"After the accident," she began, "I regained consciousness. I lay in the wreckage, surrounded by the others... my friends and colleagues. They were dead..." She paused, gathered herself. "I couldn't move. I saw a figure, the Abbot, and then other robed monks, moving among the crew, giving blessings, first aid where they could. Eventually the Abbot found me. They loaded me onto a stretcher, knocked me out. The next thing I remember, I was in the mission hospital at Chardon's Landing,"

"And the Abbot did all this without eyes—?"

"He was sighted then," Francesca said. "Only later did he return to Baudelaire to petition for *penance physicale.*" She paused, continued, "Before that, while I recuperated, he told me about his faith, his quest."

Cramer echoed that last word, sickened by something in her tone.

"The Abbot is searching for the lost temple of the Slarque," Francesca went on, "the race which lived on Tartarus before humankind. This temple is of special significance to his religion."

Something turned in his stomach. He gestured toward the book. "Do you believe *that?*" he said.

She stared at him with her green and vital eyes. "I'm intrigued by the extinct aliens," she replied. "I was always interested in xeno-archaeology. I want to help the Abbot find the temple."

He felt betrayed. "You act as his eyes?"

She nodded, then reached out and took his hand. "I love you, Hans. I always have and always will. This... this is something I must experience. Please, don't obstruct me."

The Abbot called that a meal was prepared.

The sun was dipping below the horizon, presaging the nightly show of tattered flames and flares like shredded banners. They sat in the shade of the jungle—Cramer relieved when Francesca chose to sit next to him—and ate from a platter of meat, cheese, and bread. He recalled her words, her avowal of love, but they did nothing to banish his jealousy.

The Abbot poured wine and spoke of his religion, his belief that only through physical mortification would his God be appeased and the sun cease its swelling. Cramer listened with mounting incredulity. From time to time he glanced at Francesca. The girl he knew of old would have piped up with some pithy remark along the lines that the holy man's fellow believers had been sawing bits off themselves for centuries, and still the sun was unstable. But she said nothing. She seemed hypnotized by the Abbot's words.

Cramer was drunk with the wine, or he would have held his tongue. "A lot your mortification has achieved so far," he slurred, indicating the burning heavens.

"Once we locate the temple of the Slarque," said the Abbot, "our efforts will be rewarded. Be glad and rejoice, for the Lord will do great things." According to his holy book, he said, strange feats and miracles were to be expected in the alien ruins—but by this time Cramer had heard enough, and concentrated on his drinking.

He shared Francesca's tent that night. He sat cross-legged, a bottle of wine half-full in his lap. Francesca lay on her back, staring up at the sloping fabric.

He processed his thoughts and carefully ordered his words. "How... how can you be sure that you'll find the temple before the sun—?"

"The Abbot and his minions have searched most of the jungle—there is only this sector to go. We *will* find the shrine."

"You sound in little doubt."

She turned her head and stared at him. "I am in no doubt," she said.

He determined, then, that he would not let her go. He would restrain her somehow, drag her back to Baudelaire and then to Earth.

"When do you set out on this... this *expedition?*" he asked.

"Tomorrow, maybe the day after." There was defiance in her tone.

"Then you'll return... ?" He could not bring himself to say, "to me?" Instead he said, "You'll rejoin the Fleet?"

She glanced at him, seemed to be searching for the words with which to explain herself. "Hans... I joined the Fleet believing that through science we might do something to stabilize these novae. Over the years, I've come to realize that nothing can be done." She frowned. "I can't go back, rejoin the Fleet." She hesitated, seemed to want to go on, but instead just shook her head in frustration.

She turned her back on him and slept.

Her words echoing in his head, Cramer drank himself unconscious.

He was awoken by a sound, perhaps hours later. He oriented himself and reached out for Francesca, but she was gone. He gathered his wits, peered from the tent. Across the clearing he made out Francesca's short figure next to the tall form of the Abbot. They were shouldering their packs, their movements careful so as not to wake him. Cramer felt the smoldering pain of betrayal in his gut. From his pack he drew his laser and slipped from the tent. As he moved around the clearing, keeping to the shadows, he was formulating a plan. He would stun both Francesca and the Abbot, then flee with her back to the port and take the first ship home.

The girl was not in her right mind, could not be held responsible for her actions.

Francesca saw him coming. She stared at him, wide-eyed.

Dry of throat, Cramer said, "You were leaving me!"

"Do not try to stop us," the Abbot warned.

Francesca cried, "I must go! If you love me, if you trust me, then you'll let me go!"

"What have you done to her?" he yelled at the Abbot.

"You cannot stop us," the holy fool said. "The way of the pious will not be impeded by those of scant faith!"

Cramer raised his laser, clicked off the safety catch.

Francesca was shaking her head. "No..."

His vision swam. A combination of the heat, the drink, the emotional consequences of what was happening conspired to addle his wits.

Francesca made to turn and go.

He reached out, caught her arm. The sudden feel of her, the hot flesh above her elbow, reminded Cramer of what he was losing. He pulled her to him. "Francesca..."

Her eyes communicated an anger close to hatred. She struggled. She was small, but the determination with which she fought was testament to her desire to be free. He was incensed. He roared like a maniac and dragged her across the clearing toward the tent. She screamed and broke free.

Then Cramer raised his laser and fired, hitting her in the chest and knocking her off her feet, the large-eyed expression of disbelief at what he'd done still on her face as she hit the ground.

The Abbot was on his knees beside her, his fingers fumbling for her pulse. He stared blindly in Cramer's direction. "You've killed her! My God, you've killed her!"

"No..." He collapsed and held the loose bundle of Francesca in his arms. There was no movement, no heartbeat. Her head lolled. He cried into her hair that he had not meant to...

The Abbot began a doleful prayer for Cramer's soul. Cramer wanted to hate him then, revile the holy man for infecting Francesca with his insane belief, but in his grief and guilt he could only weep and beg forgiveness.

At the Abbot's suggestion Cramer buried Francesca in the rank jungle soil, while the night sky pulsed and flared with all the colors of Hell.

When it was done, and they stood above the fresh mound of earth, Cramer asked, "And you?"

"I will continue on my quest."

"Without eyes?"

"We walk by faith, not by sight," the Abbot said. "If God wishes me to find the shrine, that is his will."

Cramer remained kneeling by the grave for hours, not quite sane. As the sun rose he set off on the long trek south, the Abbot's dolorous chant following him into the jungle. He caught one of the many ferries bound for Baudelaire, and the following day bought passage aboard a slowboat to Earth.

He lost himself in Venezuela's vast interior, relived his time with Francesca, wallowed in grief and guilt, and cursed himself for her death.

Then, just short of four months later, the Abbot came to Earth with news from Tartarus Major.

CRAMER WAS SITTING on the porch of his jungle retreat, the abandoned timber villa of some long-dead oil prospector. It was not yet noon and already his senses were numbed by alcohol. The encroaching jungle, the variation of greens and the odd splash of color from bird or flower, reminded him of Tartarus—though the sky, what little of it could be seen through the treetops, was innocent of the baleful eye of the supernova.

The rattle of loose boards sounded through the humid air. His first visitor in four months approached along the walkway from the riverbank.

He sat up, fearful of trouble. He checked the pistol beneath the cushion at his side.

The walkway rose from the river in an erratic series of zigzags, and only when the caller negotiated the final turn could Cramer make him out. With his long sable habit and peaked hood he looked the very image of Death itself.

The boards were loose and treacherous. The Abbot had to tread with care, but not once did he reach for the side-rails—and only when he arrived at the verandah did Cramer realize why. The Abbot had had his arms removed since their last encounter.

To each his own mortification, Cramer thought. He hoisted his bottle in greeting.

"What the hell brings you here?" he asked. "You've finally abandoned your damn-fool quest?"

The holy man sat cross-legged before Cramer, a feat of some achievement considering the absence of his arms. He tipped his head back, and his cowl slipped from his bald pate to reveal his face ravaged by the depredations of his piety.

Cramer noted that his dried eyeballs were now fastened about his left ankle, bolas-like.

"In two days I return to Tartarus," he said in his high, rasping voice. His stitched-shut eye-sockets faced Cramer's approximate direction. "My quest is almost over."

Cramer raised his drink. "You don't know how pleased I am," he sneered. "But I thought no one knew the where-abouts of your precious shrine?"

"Once, that was true," the Abbot said, unperturbed by Cramer's rancor. "Explorers claimed they'd stumbled upon the alien temple, and then just as conveniently stumbled away again, unable to recall its precise location. But then two weeks ago a miracle occurred."

Cramer took a long pull from the bottle and offered his guest a shot. The Abbot refused.

"There is a pouch on a cord around my waist," he said. "Take it. Retrieve the items within."

Cramer made out the small leather pouch, its neck puckered by a drawstring. He could not reach the Abbot from his seat. He was forced to kneel, coming into contact with the holy man's peculiar body odor—part the stench of septic flesh, part the chemical reek of the analgesics that seeped from his every pore.

He opened the pouch and reached inside.

Three spherical objects met his fingertips, and he knew immediately what they were. One by one he withdrew the image apples. He did not immediately look into their depths. It was as if some precognition granted him the knowledge of what he was about to see. Only after long seconds did he raise the first apple to his eyes.

He gave an involuntary sob.

Image apples were not a fruit at all, but the exudations of an amber-like substance, clear as dew, from tropical palms native to Tartarus. Through a bizarre and unique process, the apples imprinted within themselves, at a certain stage in their growth, the image of their surroundings.

Bracing himself, Cramer looked into the first apple again, then the second and the third. Each crystal-clear orb contained a perfect representation of Francesca as she strode through the jungle, past the trees where the apples had grown.

The first apple had captured her full-length, a short, slim, childlike figure striding out, arms swinging—all radiation silvers and massed midnight hair. In the second apple she was closer; just her head and shoulders showed. Cramer stared at her elfin face, her high cheekbones and jade green eyes. Then the third apple: she was striding away from the tree, only her narrow back and fall of hair visible. Tears coursed down his cheeks.

He held the apples in cupped hands and shook his head. He was hardly able to find the words to thank the Abbot. Just the other day he had been bewailing the fact that he had but half a dozen pix of Francesca. That the holy man had come all the way to Earth to give him these...

"I... Thank you. I don't know what to say."

Then Cramer stopped. Perhaps the whisky had clouded his senses. He stared at the Abbot.

"How did you find these?" he asked.

"When you left," said the Abbot. "I continued north. At the time, if you recall, I was following directions given to me by a boatman on the river St. Augustine. They proved fallacious, as ever, and rather than continue further north and risk losing my way, I retraced my steps, returned to the plateau where we had camped." He was silent for a time. Cramer was back on Tartarus Major, so graphically did the Abbot's words conjure up the scene, so painful were his memories of the events upon the plateau.

"When I reached the clearing, it occurred to me to pray for Francesca. I fell to my knees and felt for the totem I had planted to mark her resting place, only to find that it was not there. Moreover, I discovered that the piled earth of the grave had been disturbed, that the grave was indeed empty."

Cramer tried to cry out loud, but no sound came.

"In consternation I stumbled back to my tent. She was waiting for me."

"No!"

"Yes. Francesca. She spoke to me, 'Abbot, do not fear. Something wondrous has happened.'"

Cramer was shaking his head. "No, she was dead. Dead. I buried her with my own hands."

"Francesca lives," the Abbot insisted. "She told me that she knew the whereabouts of the holy temple. She would show me, if I did as she bid."

"Which was?"

He smiled, and the approximation of such a cheerful expression upon a face so devastated was ghastly to behold. "She wanted me to come to Earth and fetch you back to Tartarus. She gave me the image apples as proof."

Cramer could only shake his head like something clockwork. "I don't... I can't believe it."

"Look upon the images," he ordered.

Cramer held the baubles high. "But surely these are images of Francesca *before* I arrived on Tartarus, *before* her death?"

"Look closely, man! See, she carries your laser, the one you left in your flight from the clearing."

He stared again, disbelieving. He had overlooked it in the apples before, so slight a side arm it was. But sure enough—strapped to Francesca's thigh was the silver length of his personal pulse laser.

"She wants you," the Abbot said in a whisper.

Cramer wept and raged. He hurled his empty whisky bottle through the air and into the jungle, which accepted it with hardly a pause in the cacophonous medley of insects, toads, and birds.

"But the sun might blow at any time," he cried.

"Some experts say a month or two." The Abbot paused. "But vain and rapacious men still pilot illegal boats to

Tartarus, to raid the treasures that remain. I leave the day after tomorrow. You will accompany me, I take it?"

Sobbing, unable to control himself, wracked with guilt and a fear he had no hope of understanding, Cramer said that he would indeed accompany the Abbot. How could he refuse?

And so began his return to Tartarus Major. He cursed the twisted machinations of fate. A little under four months ago he had set out on his first voyage to the planet, in a bid to find a Francesca he feared was surely dead—and, now, he left with the Abbot aboard a ramshackle sailship, its crew a gallery of rogues, to be reunited with a Francesca he knew for sure to be dead, but somehow miraculously *risen*...

He chose to spend the voyage under sedation.

THE FIRST HE knew of the landing was when the Abbot coaxed him awake with his croaking, cracking voice. Cramer emerged reluctantly from his slumber, recalling vague, nightmare visions of Francesca's death—only to be confronted by another nightmare vision: the Abbot's mutilated visage, staring down at him.

"To your feet. Tartarus awaits."

He gathered his scant belongings—six flasks of whisky, the image apples—and stumbled from the ship.

As he emerged into the terrible daylight, the assault of Tartarus upon his every sense seemed to sober him. He stared about like a man awakening from a dream, taking in the panorama of ancient wooden buildings around the port, their facades and steep, tiled roofs seeming warped by the intense heat.

Theirs was the only ship in sight, its silver superstructure an arrogant splash of color against a sun-leached dun and ochre city. A searing wind soughed across the port, blowing hot grit into Cramer's face. He gazed at the magnesium-bright sun that filled half the sky. The very atmosphere of the planet seemed to be on fire. The air was heavy with the stench of brimstone, and every breath was a labor.

The leader of the thieves stood beneath the nose-cone of the ship. "We set sail for Earth in two days," he said. "If you want passage back, be here at dawn. We'll not be waiting."

Cramer calculated how long it might take to reach the jungle plateau, and return—certainly longer than any two days. He trusted there would be other pirate boats to take him back to civilization.

Already the Abbot was hurrying across the port, his armless gait made fastidious with concentration. His dried eyeballs scuffed around his ankles as he went, striking random patterns in the dust. Cramer shouldered his bag and followed.

Unerringly, the holy man led the way down narrow alleys between the tall timber buildings of the city's ancient quarter. Just four months ago these byways had been thronged with citizens streaming to the port, eager to flee the impending catastrophe. Now they were deserted. The only sound was that of their footsteps, and the dry rasp of the Abbot's eyeballs on the cobbles. Between the over-reaching eaves, the sky dazzled like superheated platinum. All was still, lifeless.

They descended to the banks of the St. Augustine, its broad green girth flowing sluggishly between the rotten lumber of dilapidated wharves and jetties. The river, usually choked with trading vessels from all along the coast, was empty now; not one boat plied its length.

An urchin fell into step beside the Abbot and tugged at his robes. They came to a boathouse, and the Abbot shouldered open the door and stepped carefully aboard a long-boat. Cramer climbed in after him and seated himself on cushions beneath the black and scarlet awning. The Abbot sat forward, at the very prow of the launch, while the boy busied himself with the engine. Seconds later it spluttered into life, a blasphemy upon the former silence, and the boat surged from the open-ended boathouse and headed upriver, into the interior.

Cramer pulled a flask of whisky from his bag and chugged down three mouthfuls, the quantity he judged would keep him afloat until the serious drinking began at sunset. The Abbot had thought to provision the launch with a container of food: biltong, rounds of ripe cheese, cobs of black bread, and yellow, wizened fruit like pears. A goblet suggested that they should take from the river for their refreshment: Cramer decided to stick to his whisky. He ate his fill, lay back, and closed his eyes as the boat bounced upstream. He must have dozed; when he next opened his eyes he saw that they had left the city far behind. Flat fields spread out on either hand; tall crops, perhaps green once, were scorched now the color of straw beneath the merciless midday sun.

He thought of Francesca, considered the possibility of her resurrection, and somehow withheld his tears. To busy himself, to take his mind off what might lie ahead, he dipped the goblet into the river and carried it to where the Abbot was seated cross-legged at the prow like some proud and macabre figurehead.

He raised the brimming goblet to the holy man's lips. Graciously, the Abbot inclined his head and drank thirstily. When the cup was dry, he murmured his thanks.

Cramer remained seated beside him. Already he was soaked with sweat and uncomfortable, and he wore the lightest of jungle wear. The Abbot was surely marinating within the thick hessian of his habit.

Cramer nodded to where his sleeves were tucked inside their shoulder holes. "Yet more penance since we last met," he observed, his tone sarcastic.

He wondered when the Abbot would have his tongue pulled out, his legs amputated, his testicles removed—if they had not been removed already.

"After finding Francesca," the Abbot said, "I made my way back to Baudelaire. I informed the Church Council of the miracle in the jungle, and petitioned them for permission to undergo *penance physicale*. The following day the Surgeon Master removed my arms."

Cramer let the silence stretch. He felt dizzy with the heat. The glare of the sun seemed to drive needles into his eyes. The boat changed course slightly and passed a sandbank. Dead birds and other bloated animals floated by.

"And Francesca?" Cramer whispered.

The Abbot turned his cowl to Cramer, suggesting inquiry.

Cramer cleared his throat. "Why does she want me with her?"

"She did not say." The Abbot paused. "Perhaps she loves you, still."

"But what exactly did she tell you?"

"She said that I was to bring you back to Tartarus. In return, she would guide me to the temple."

Cramer shook his head. "How does she know its whereabouts? Months ago, like you, she had no idea."

"She was bequeathed its location in her sleep."

He cried aloud. "In her sleep? *Sleep?* She was dead. I buried her myself." He was sobbing now. "How can she possibly be alive?"

The Abbot would say no more, no matter how much Cramer pleaded. He lowered his head, and his lips moved in soothing prayer.

Cramer took sanctuary beneath the awning. He sucked down half a flask of whisky as night failed, as ever, to fall. The bloated sun dipped below the flat horizon, but such was the power of its radiation that the night sky was transformed into a flickering canopy of indigo, scarlet, and argent streamers. The light show illuminated the entirety of the eastern sky, and against it the Abbot was a stark and frightening silhouette.

Cramer drank himself to sleep.

He was awoken by a crack of thunder such as he had never heard before. He shot upright, convinced that the sun had blown and that Tartarus had split asunder. Sheet lightning flooded the river and the surrounding flatlands in blinding silver explosions, a cooling breeze blew, and a warm rain lashed the boat. He slept.

It was dawn when he next awoke. The sun was a massive, rising semicircle on the horizon, throwing harsh white light across the land. They were slowly approaching a dense tangle of vegetation with leaves as broad as spinnakers, waxy and wilting in the increased temperature. The river narrowed, became a chocolate-colored canal between the overgrown banks. While the sun was hidden partially by the treetops, and they were spared its direct heat, yet in the confines of the jungle the humidity increased so that every labored inhalation was more a draught of fluid than a drawn breath.

Cramer breakfasted on stale bread and putrescent cheese, thirst driving him to forgo his earlier circumspection as to the potability of the water, and draw a goblet from the river. He gave the Abbot a mouthful of the brackish liquid and arranged bread and biltong beside him so that the holy fool might not starve. The Abbot ate, using his toes to grip the food and lift it to his mouth in a fashion so dexterous as to suggest much practice before the amputation of his arms.

They proceeded on a winding course along the river, ever farther into the dense and otherwise impenetrable jungle.

Hours later they came to Chardon's Landing. Cramer made the launch fast to the jetty and assisted the Abbot ashore. They paused briefly to take a meal, and then began the arduous slog to the plateau where Cramer had buried Francesca.

THE AIR WAS heavy, the light aqueous, filled with the muffled, distant calls of doomed animals and birds. The trek to the plateau was tougher than he recalled from his first time this way. After months of drunkenness, Cramer was in far from peak condition, and without his arms the Abbot often stumbled.

As the hours passed and they slogged through the cloying, hostile heat, Cramer considered what the holy man had said about Francesca's resurrection. Clearly, he had not killed her in the clearing all those months ago, but merely stunned her—and she had discovered the whereabouts of the temple from the survey photographs made by the *Pride of Valencia*... Then again, there was always the possibility that the Abbot was lying, that Francesca had not risen at all, that he had lured Cramer here for his own sinister purposes. And the image apples, which seemed to show Francesca in possession of the laser which had killed her? Might she not have been carrying a laser similar to his own after the crash landing and before he arrived, at which time the apples had recorded her image?

They came at last to the clearing. The two tents were as he recalled them, situated thirty meters apart. Francesca's grave, in the jungle, was out of sight.

Cramer hurried across to Francesca's tent and pulled back the flap. She was not inside. He checked the second tent, also empty, and then walked toward the edge of the escarpment. He looked out across the spread of the jungle far below, gathering his thoughts.

He knew that he would find Francesca's grave untouched.

"If you claim she is risen," he called to the Abbot, "then where is she?"

"If you do not believe me," the Abbot said, "then look upon the grave."

Cramer hesitated. He did not know what he feared most, that he should find the grave empty... or the soil still piled above Francesca's cold remains.

He crossed the clearing to the margin of jungle in which he had excavated her resting place. The Abbot's cowl turned, following his progress like some gothic tracking device. Cramer reached out and drew aside a spray of ferns. The light fell from behind him, illuminating a raw furrow of earth. He gave a pained cry. The mound he had so carefully constructed was scattered, and only a shallow depression remained where he had laid out her body.

He stumbled back into the clearing.

"Well?" the Abbot inquired.

Before Cramer could grasp him, beat from him the truth, he saw something spread in the center of the clearing. It was a detailed map of the area, based on aerial photographs, opened out and held flat by four stones.

The Abbot sensed something. "What is wrong?"

Cramer crossed the clearing and knelt before the map. Marked in red was the camp-site, and from it a dotted trail leading down the precipitous fall of the escarpment. It wound through the jungle below, to a point Cramer judged to be ten kilometers distant. This area was marked with a circle, and beside it the words, "The Slarque Temple," in Francesca's meticulous, childish print.

"My God," Cramer whispered to himself.

"What is it!"

Cramer told the Abbot, and he raised his ravaged face to the heavens. "Thanks be!" he cried. "The Age of Miracles is forever here!"

Cramer snatched up the map, folded it to a manageable size, and strode to the edge of the escarpment. He turned to the Abbot. "Are you up to another hard slog?"

"God gives strength to the pilgrim," the holy man almost shouted. "Lead the way, Mr. Cramer!"

For the next two hours they made a slow descent of the incline. So steep was the drop in places that the Abbot was unable to negotiate the descent through the undergrowth, and Cramer was forced to carry him on his back.

He murmured holy mantras into Cramer's ear.

He found it impossible to assess his emotions at that time, still less his thoughts—disbelief, perhaps, maybe even fear of the unknown. He entertained the vague hope that Francesca, having completed her quest and found the temple, might return with him to Earth.

They came to the foot of the incline and pressed ahead through dense vegetation. From time to time they came across what Cramer hoped was the track through the undergrowth that Francesca might have made, only to lose it again just as quickly. Their progress was slow, with frequent halts so that Cramer could consult the map and the position of the bloated sun. He wondered if it was a psychosomatic reaction to the events of the past few hours, or a meteorological change, that made the air almost impossible to breathe. It seemed sulfurous, infused with the miasma of Hell itself. Certainly, the Abbot was taking labored breaths through his ruined nose-holes.

At last they emerged from the jungle and found themselves on the edge of a second great escarpment, where the land stepped down to yet another sweep of sultry jungle. Cramer studied the map. According to Francesca, the temple was positioned somewhere along this ledge. They turned right and pushed through fragrant leaves and hanging fronds. Cramer could see nothing that might resemble an alien construction.

Then, amid a tangle of undergrowth ten meters ahead, he made out a regular, right-angled shape he knew was not the work of nature. It was small, perhaps four meters high and two wide—a rectangular block of masonry overgrown with lichen and creepers. He detected signs that someone had passed this way, and recently: the undergrowth leading to the stone block was broken, trampled down.

"What is it?" the Abbot whispered.

Cramer described what he could see.

"The shrine," the holy man said. "It has to be..."

They approached the Slarque temple. Cramer was overcome with a strange disappointment that it should turn out to be so small, so insignificant. Then, as they passed into its shadow, he realized that this was but a tiny part of a much greater, subterranean complex. He peered, and saw a series of steps disappearing into the gloom. Tendrils, like tripwires, had been broken on the upper steps.

Cramer took the Abbot's shoulder and assisted him down the steps. Just as he began to fear that their way would be in complete darkness, he made out a glimmer of light below. The steps came to an end. A corridor ran off to the right, along the face of the escarpment. Let into the stone of the cliff face itself, at regular intervals, were tall apertures like windows. Great shafts of sunlight poured in and illuminated the way.

He walked the Abbot along the wide corridor, its ceiling carved with a bas-relief fresco of cavorting animals. In the lichen carpet that had spread across the floor over the millennia, he made out more than one set of footprints: the lichen was scuffed and darkened, as if with the passage of many individuals.

At last, after perhaps a kilometer, they approached the tall, arched entrance of a great chamber. At first he thought it a trick of his ears, or the play of the warm wind within the chamber, but as they drew near he heard the dolorous monotone of a sustained religious chant. The sound, in precincts so ancient, sent a shiver down his spine.

They paused on the threshold. From a wide opening at the cliff face end of the chamber, evening sunlight slanted in, its brightness blinding. When his eyes adapted Cramer saw, through a haze of tumbling dust motes, row upon row of gray-robed, kneeling figures, cowled heads bowed, chanting. The chamber was the size of a cathedral and the congregation filled the long stone pews on either side of a central aisle. The heat and the noise combined to make Cramer dizzy.

He felt a hand grip his elbow, and thought at first that it was the Abbot. He turned—a monk stood to his left, holding his upper arm; the Abbot was on Cramer's right, his broken face suffused with devotional rapture.

He felt pressure on his elbow. Like an automaton, he stepped into the chamber. The monk escorted Cramer up the aisle. The continuous chanting, now that they were amidst it, was deafening. The sunlight was hot on his back. The front of the chamber was lost in shadow. He could just make out the hazy outline of a scorpion-analogue statue, and beside it the representation of a torso upon a cross.

Halfway down the aisle, they paused.

The monk's grip tightened on his arm. The Abbot whispered to Cramer. His expression was beatific, his tone rapturous. "In the year of the supernova it is written that the Ultimate Sacrifice will rise from the dead, and so be marked out to appease the sun. Too, it is written that the sacrifice will be accompanied by a non-believer, and also the Abbot of the true Church."

Cramer could hardly comprehend his words.

The monk pushed him forward. The chanting soared.

He stared. What he had assumed to be the statue of a body on a cross was not a statue at all. His mind refused to accept the image that his vision was relaying. He almost passed out. The monk held him upright.

Francesca hung before him, lashed to the vertical timber of the cross, the ultimate sacrifice in what must have been the most God-forsaken Calvary ever devised by man. Her head was raised at a proud angle, the expression on her full lips that of a grateful martyr. Her eyelids were closed, flattened like the Abbot's, and stitched shut in a semicircle beneath each eye. The threads obtruded from her perfect skin, thick and clotted like obscene, cartoon lashes.

Her evicted eyes, as green as Cramer remembered them, were tied about her neck.

Her arms and legs had been removed, amputated at shoulder and hip; silver disks capped the stumps. They had even excised her small, high breasts, leaving perfect white, sickle-shaped scars across her olive skin.

Cramer murmured his beloved's name.

She moved her head, and that tiny gesture, lending animation to something that by all rights should have been spared life, twisted a blade of anguish deep into his heart.

"Hans!" she said, her voice sweet and pure. "Hans, I told you that I loved you, would love you for ever." She smiled, a smile of such beauty amid such devastation. "What greater love could I show you than to allow you

to share in the salvation of the world? Through our sacrifice, Hans, we will be granted eternal life."

He wanted, then, to scream at her—to ask how she
could allow herself to believe in such perversion? But the
time for such questioning was long gone.

And, besides, he knew... She had always sought something more than mere existence, and here, at last, she had
found it.

"Hans," she whispered now. "Hans, please tell me that
you understand. Please hold me."

Cramer stepped forward.

He felt the dart slam into the meat of his lower back.
The plainsong crescendoed, becoming something beautiful
and at the same time terrible, and he pitched forward and
slipped into oblivion.

HE SURFACED SLOWLY through an ocean of analgesics and
sedatives. He found himself in darkness, something wet
tied around his neck. With realization came pain, and he
cried aloud. Then, perhaps hours later, they laid him out
again and put him under, and though he wanted to rage
and scream at the injustice, the futility of what they were
doing to him, all he could manage was a feeble moan of
protest.

He came to his senses to find himself tied upright—to a
cross?—four points of numbness where his arms and legs
had been. Beside him he could hear the Abbot, moaning in
masochistic ecstasy. He considered what a gruesome trinity they must present upon the altar.

"Francesca," he whispered. "Oh, Francesca, the pain..."

"The pain, Hans," she replied, "the pain is part of the
sacrifice."

He laughed, and then wept, and then fell silent.

Francesca continued, her voice a whisper. She lovingly
detailed what further sacrifices they would be called upon

to make. Next, she said, would come the expert excision of their genitalia; after that they would be skinned alive. And then the Master Surgeon would remove their internal organs one by one: kidneys, liver, lungs, and finally their hearts, while all the time they were conscious of what was taking place, the better to appreciate their sacrifice.

"Hans," she whispered. "Can you feel it? Can you? The wonder, the joy?"

He could feel nothing but pain, and lapsed into unconsciousness. He awoke from time to time, unable to tell how long he had spent in blessed oblivion, or what further surgical mutilations they had carried out upon his body.

What followed was a nightmare without respite. During the day, when the heat was at its most intense, they were lifted from the altar and set side by side in the opening of the cliff face, while the congregation chanted their medieval, monotone chant in hope of miracles. The pain was constant, at its worst in the heat of the day, dulling to a tolerable agony during the night.

Toward the end, Cramer dreamed of rescue: he hallucinated the arrival of a pirate ship come to set them free. Then he came to his senses and realized that for him there would be no release, no return to physical well-being. He was a prisoner of Tartarus, a jail more secure than any of ancient myth.

On the very last day they were carried outside and positioned before the scalding light of the sun. Cramer sensed heightened activity among the monks, hurried movement and hushed conversation suggesting panic and disbelief. He felt the heat of the sun searing his flesh, and laughed aloud at the knowledge of his victory.

Francesca maintained her faith until the very end. In mounting fear she intoned: "And it is written that the Ultimate Sacrifice *shall* rise from the dead, and *will* guide the faithful to the lost temple of the Slarque, and through the sacrifice of the holy trinity the sun will cease its swelling..."

Cramer was torn between exacting revenge upon the person responsible for his torture and keeping the one he loved in ignorance. A part of him wanted to impose upon Francesca his rationalization of what had happened, explain that there had been no miracles at all.

He said nothing. If he were to make her comprehend the tragedy and evil of their predicament, the insane fanaticism of the accursed Church, he would only inflict upon her a greater torture than that she had suffered already.

The end came within the hour, and swiftly. He felt his skin shrivel in the intense heat, and was aware of Francesca and the Abbot to his left and right. Francesca was murmuring a constant prayer, and the Abbot from time to time laughed in manic ecstasy.

All around them sounded the monks' frantic chanting, the entreaties of the faithful to their oblivious God.

In rapture, Cramer heard the detonation of multiple thunder, and the roar of the approaching firestorm as the sun exploded and unleashed its terrible freight of radiation.

He turned his head. "Abbot!" he whispered with his very last breath. "So much for your superstition! You bastards didn't get my heart!"

The holy man could only laugh. "For our sacrifice," he began, "we will be granted life ever—"

Cramer should have known that the righteous would forever have the last word.

"Hans!" He heard the small voice to his left. She was crying, now. "Hans, please say you love me..."

But before he could speak, before he could accede to Francesca's final wish, the blastfront reached the surface of Tartarus Major with a scream like that of a million souls denied, and Cramer gave thanks that his suffering was at a blessed end.

# THE OLD RUGGED CROSS

### *Terry Bisson*

ONE NIGHT BUD White had a dream. In the dream, he was hanging on the cross next to Jesus Christ, and the doors to Heaven opened wide, and a smiling little black girl in a starched white dress, the very girl he had raped and buried in the gravelly mud by the Cumberland River, welcomed him in.

Bud went to sleep a sinner, and woke up saved.

It so happened that the chaplain was on Death Row that very morning, counseling a Jehovah's Witness who couldn't, for religious reasons, be executed by lethal injection under the new Freedom of Religious Observance Act (FROA).

The scaffold or the electric chair? The condemned was having a hard time deciding. It was, he said, without a trace of irony, "The most important decision of my life."

The chaplain advised him to sleep on it. He had other things on his mind. The primer was dry on his 1955 Chevy 210 coupe, a classic in anybody's book, and he intended to spend the evening sanding it again. It was ready to paint but he didn't have the money yet. $1,225 for three coats, hand rubbed. You don't skimp on a classic.

It was already almost noon. But on his way out of the tier, the chaplain passed by Bud's cell, and Bud called out, "'Scuse me, Reverend."

The chaplain stopped. Here was a man who'd never had the time of day for religion or its representatives. All Bud did was watch TV.

"What can I do for you, White?" the chaplain asked.

Bud told the chaplain his dream.

The chaplain held his chin in three fingertips, like a plum, and nodded as he listened. A plan was already forming in his mind. He reached through the bars and placed a hand on Bud's plump knee. "Are you sorry, then, for what you did?"

"You bet," said Bud. "Especially now that I know there is a Heaven, and I'll go straight there." He looked as pleased as if he had just discovered a dollar bill in a library book.

"I'll do what I can to help," said the chaplain. "Would you like to pray with me?"

THAT NIGHT INSTEAD of sanding his classic, the chaplain made a phone call to his former professor at the Divinity School. "Do you remember a lecture you gave twelve years ago," he asked, "on the medical mysteries of Our Lord's Passion?"

"Of course," said the professor. "I give the same lecture every year."

"What if there was a way to actually watch it happen?" the chaplain said.

"Were," said the Professor, who also taught English Comp. "Watch what happen?"

"You know. The procedure and all. An actual crucifixion. What would it be worth?"

"To science or to religion?"

"Either, both, whatever," said the chaplain, who was beginning to wonder when the professor was going to get the point.

"It would be invaluable," said the professor. "It would be revelatory. It would settle once and for all the disputes over how long the crucifixion took, what was the actual cause of death, what was the pathology sequence. It would be marvelous. It would be worth a thousand pictures, a hundred thousand words; worth more than all the pious and vulgar..."

"No, I mean in dollars," said the chaplain.

"YOU HAVE MADE an extraordinarily impressive conversion," said the chaplain when he met with Bud the next morning, at 8:45. "I want you to meet with my old professor."

"How old?"

"Former professor," corrected the chaplain. "He's a professor of religion."

"Professor of Religion!" said Bud, who had never realized there was such a thing.

"From my old, my former, Divinity School," said the chaplain.

And Divinity School! It sounded to Bud like something good to eat.

After leaving Bud, the chaplain went two cells down, to see the Jehovah's Witness.

"Hanging," the young man said. He had apparently prayed all night. "The scaffold and the rope. Hemp and wood. It seems the most traditional."

"The hemp might be a problem," said the chaplain. (As it turned out, the wood was too.)

They prayed together and as he was leaving, as if it were an afterthought, the chaplain asked, "Who's the lawyer who handled your FROA suit? Can you give me his phone number?"

IT TURNED OUT that he was a she. The lawyer lived in a condo overlooking the Cumberland River, only half a mile from the mud bank where the little girl Bud White killed had been found.

"A prisoner's case? I can't afford any more pro bono," she said. But when the chaplain told her that the professor was financing it through a grant, she was more receptive. When he told her about the TV interest, she was positively sympathetic. That evening the three of them had dinner together, on the deck of a restaurant in downtown Nashville.

The chaplain had the fiddler with fries. The lawyer had the jalapeño hush puppies. The professor had the crab cakes and picked up the bill. He was going to see Bud the next day.

BUD WHITE WAS watching TV when the guard brought his visitor. Bud watched a lot of TV.

"Are you really a Professor of Religion?" Bud asked.

The professor assured him that he was. "And I'm here to hear about your dream."

Bud hit MUTE and told the professor about his dream. "Jesus nodded at me," he said.

The professor himself nodded. "Your dream was almost certainly a sign," he said.

Bud wasn't surprised. He had heard about signs.

"The only sure way to go to Heaven is to follow in the exact footsteps of Our Lord," the professor said.

Bud was confused. "Footsteps?"

"It's a figure of speech," said the professor, realizing he should be more precise, more literal in dealing with Bud. "What I mean is, go the way he went."

"Go," repeated Bud, looking around his narrow cell. The word had a nice ring to it. But then Bud remembered the dream. "Is it going to hurt?"

"I'm not here to bullshit you," said the professor, placing his hand on Bud's plump knee. "It will hurt some, that's for sure. But think of the reward."

Bud thought of the little black girl. Her face and hair were clean, but her dress was muddy. He closed his eyes and smiled.

"The first step is to sign these papers making the chaplain and *me* your spiritual advisers."

"I don't write very good," said Bud.

"I'll help you," said the professor, guiding Bud's hand. "Now let the chaplain and me worry about the details. But I can tell you this: Cumberland Divinity has agreed to pay for everything."

"Divinity!" There was that candy sound again.

The professor rose to go. "Any questions?"

"What about my mother?"

"I didn't know you had a mother."

"I haven't seen her since I was a little boy, but she was there in the dream."

It was hard for the professor to imagine Bud as a little boy. Maybe it was the beard.

"I'll see about it," he said.

"THIS IS OUTRAGEOUS," said the warden. "It's preposterous. It's impossible."

"We are prepared to concede the first two," said the lawyer. "But not the third."

"He wants his mother to be there?" the warden persisted.

"As his spiritual advisers, we can require it under FROA," said the professor.

The warden frowned. "Oh, you can, can you?"

The chaplain shrugged apologetically. "Jesus's mother was there."

The lawyer put her attaché case on her lap. She unsnapped it but didn't open it. "We didn't want to trouble you with a whole separate FROA filing. We'd like to work this out between colleagues. Between friends."

"Friends?"

They were sitting in the warden's office, in front of the huge, half-moon, barred window.

The lawyer leaned across the desk and presented the warden with her warmest (which was not as warm as his, and his was not warm) smile. "We needn't be adversaries," she said. "I am merely looking after my client's interest. You are merely obeying the law of the land. The chaplain and the professor here are merely fulfilling their spiritual responsibilities. None of us would choose what Bud White has chosen. But who would have chosen any of this?"

She waved a hand indicating the prison yard beyond the window. A few men lounged on rusted weightlifting equipment, smoking cigarettes. Smoking was still allowed in the yard.

"I would have chosen it," said the warden. "In fact I did choose it. I dropped out of Law my second year and switched to Corrections."

"We're soul mates, then!" said the lawyer. "I dropped out of Police Academy to go to Law School."

"Ditto," said the professor. "I was studying for Ordination when I decided to get my Ph.D. instead, in Biblical History."

"Okay, okay," said the warden. He rose from his desk to signal that the interview was over. "I won't fight you on the mother, but I'm not sure we can do the cross."

"WHAT'S THIS DISCOVERY Channel?" Bud's mother asked. "Hasn't anybody ever heard of ABC or NBC or even Ted Turner? What about Fox?"

"They didn't want it," said the professor.

"We tried them, in that order, as a matter of fact," said the lawyer.

"You should have come to me first," said Bud's mother, tipping a little more vodka into her Sprite.

"She's got a point," said the chaplain. He had positioned himself across the trailer so that he could see up her dress. "I say we cut her in for a full share."

"Cut me in? Just you try and cut me out! Who else is getting money out of this deal?"

"Other than the TV?" The lawyer tapped her attaché thoughtfully with a yellow pencil. "The professor and the chaplain split a stipend as Bud's spiritual advisers. I get my usual, plus a small commission on foreign rights. Oh, and the chaplain gets a finder's fee."

"Finder's fee? I gave birth to the sorry bastard!"

"It's only $1,250," said the chaplain. "What say we make it $2,500 and split it?"

The professor rolled his eyes, but it was only for effect. He had already decided to cut Bud's mother in.

"What about Bud?" she asked.

"What's Bud going to do with money?" asked the chaplain. "He would probably just leave his share to you anyway."

"My point exactly," said the mother. "Everybody else is double dipping around here."

"OAK? DOES IT say oak in the Bible?" asked the carpenter.

"Bud can't read the Bible," said the lawyer. "He must have got that from TV."

"It's probably the only wood he's ever heard of," said the chaplain. "There's not a whole lot about wood on TV."

"He's never heard of pine?"

"Historically," said the professor, "it should be cypress."

They were meeting in the prison shop, just off the yard.

"Cypress is out," said the warden. "Isn't it endangered or something?"

"I think that's mahogany," said the professor.

"Cedar's nice," said the chaplain. "The boy's mother likes cedar."

"He's not a boy," said the warden

"Under FROA, Death Row prisoners have the right to die in a manner consistent with their religious beliefs," said the lawyer, reaching for her attaché case.

"We should rape him and bury him alive in a mud bank, then," said the carpenter, a trusty.

"Shut up, Billy Joe," said the warden. He looked from the chaplain to the lawyer to the professor. "How about plywood?"

"I'VE RESEARCHED THIS whole procedure," said the professor, "and the one thing we *don't* need is a doctor."

"You don't, but we do," said the producer. "Under *Kevorkian,* we are only allowed to televise a suicide if a doctor is on hand to prevent unnecessary suffering."

"He doesn't look like a doctor," said the lawyer. "No offence."

They were sitting in the warden's office, under the large, barred, half-moon window.

"None taken," said the doctor. "I'm what they call a para-surgeon. I can stitch you up but I can't cut you open."

"It's not a suicide anyway," said the warden. "It's a state mandated execution, perfectly legal. Totally legal."

"And what's this unnecessary suffering business?" asked the professor. "In a crucifixion, the suffering is part of the deal."

"It's the whole deal," said the chaplain.

"Making it, by definition, not unnecessary," agreed the lawyer.

"LAST SUPPER?" ASKED the warden. "Not a problem. That's on us, free of charge. Only we call it the last meal."

"He wants the Surf & Turf from Red Lobster," said the chaplain. "And he wants a long table, like in the frescoes. They must have showed the frescoes on PBS."

"Surf and Turf is technically two meals," said the warden. "The long table could be a problem, too. Unless it's in the corridor."

"What about the wine?" asked the professor.

"Wine's definitely going to be a problem," said the warden. "That's like the oak."

"We're trying to avoid a supplementary filing," said the lawyer, unsnapping her attaché.

"Maybe the Food Channel would pick up the cost of the Turf," suggested the mother. "Or the Surf."

"The Food Channel?" asked the warden. "When did they get in on this?"

"They're in the pool," said the producer.

"Scourging sounds okay," said Bud. It sounded sort of like deep cleaning. "But I don't like the part about the nails."

"The nails are an essential part of the experience," said the professor. He put his hand on Bud's plump knee and looked into his big, empty, brown eyes. "Our Lord didn't shop around, Bud. None of this 'want this, don't want that' stuff for Him. You have to take it as it comes. Render unto Caesar and so forth."

Bud was confused. "Sees who?"

"And we've arranged the Last Supper," said the chaplain. "We're all going to be there. Me and the professor and the lawyer. Plus the producer and the doctor, and even the carpenter."

"I like the carpenter," said Bud. "What about my mother?"

"Her too. Turns out she likes lobster."

"I thought we agreed on plywood," said the professor.

"No go," said the carpenter. "New environmental regs. Something about the glue. Toxic."

He was fitting together two steel framing two-by-fours.

The lawyer tapped one of them with the longest of her long (and they were very long) fingernails; it rang with a dull ring.

The professor was skeptical. A metal cross? "What about the nails?" he asked.

The carpenter, looking pleased with himself, pulled three wooden squares from a shopping bag. "Butcher blocks," he said. "Drilled and ready to bolt on. Ordered them from Martha Stewart™ Online. And check this out—they're cypress!"

"Billy Joe, you're a wonder," said the warden.

THE LITTLE GIRL'S grandmother lived in a neat duplex on Cumberland Road, only a few blocks from the Cumberland River.

"According to the Victims' Families' Bill of Rights, you are entitled to attend and observe the execution," the lawyer said.

"But I would advise against it," said the chaplain. "It's going to be ugly and take a long time."

"Why is it going to be ugly and take a long time?" asked the little girl's grandmother.

The professor explained why it was going to be ugly and take a long time.

"We'll be there," said the little girl's uncle, a uniformed security guard at the Cumberland Mall, who was the last person (except for Bud) to see her alive.

"THE GUIDELINES SAY all deliberate speed," said the warden. "I think that means we have to start early."

It was noon on Friday. Bud's execution date was twelve hours away, at midnight.

The warden, the lawyer, the chaplain, the professor, the producer, the doctor and Bud's mother were in the yard, watching as the carpenter directed the four convict volunteers unloading the pile of stones that had been rented to make a small hill. Their names were Matthew, Mark, John, and John. The professor had chosen them from the prison's roster. He couldn't find a Luke. Each was to receive a magazine subscription and a hooded Polartec™ sweatshirt.

"Golgotha wasn't very high," said the professor. "It wasn't a hill so much as a mound, a pile of rubble. So this will do just fine."

"How long is it going to tie up the yard?" asked the warden.

"We will definitely be out of here by dawn," said the doctor.

"Dawn!" said the warden. "You're not intending to drag this out all night, are you?"

"It's supposed to be slow," said the lawyer.

"Can't be too slow," said the warden. "The state has guidelines. All deliberate speed is one of them."

"The whole point of this procedure is that it's slow," said the professor. "Excruciating is the word, as a matter of fact."

"I'm just asking you to speed it up a little," said the warden.

"There's no way we can speed it up without violating the fundamental rights of the petitioner," said the lawyer, reaching for her attaché case.

"Whatever," said the warden. "Can you give me an ETA?"

The lawyer turned to the professor. "What does the Bible say?"

"Our Lord took three hours," said the professor.

"Okay, then it's simple," said the warden. "We start at nine."

"SET ANOTHER PLACE for the Last Supper," said Bud's mother. "I invited a friend."

"You can't bring a friend," said the warden.

"She's my lesbian lover," said Bud's mother. "Protected under—"

She looked at the lawyer, and the warden realized that this entire scene had been rehearsed.

"Under the Domestic Partners Extension 347 of 1999," said the lawyer.

"She's never gotten the chance to watch anybody die," said Bud's mother. "Particularly a man."

"I had no idea you were a lesbian," said the chaplain, after the warden had left for his rounds. This was in the days when wardens still made rounds. The chaplain sounded disappointed.

"I'm not," said the Bud's mother, with a wink, followed by a nudge. "I just wanted to make sure she got in. She's from the *Tattler*."

"That rag!?" exclaimed the professor.

"I tried to get the *Star* or the *Enquirer*, but they wouldn't return my calls," said Bud's mother.

"That's because Bud's not a celeb," said the doctor. "Wait till they start executing celebs, then they'll return your calls."

"They're already executing celebrities," said Bud's mother. "What about OJ?"

"He got off," said the lawyer.

"Again?"

"THEY'RE PAPER," SAID the guard.

"Feels like regular cloth," said Bud, pulling on his orange coveralls.

"NO WINE?" ASKED Bud's mother.

"No wine," said the guard, who was doubling as the waiter. "And no smoking, either."

The reporter from the *Tattler* put out her cigarette.

"I don't smoke!" said Bud. He grinned. "And don't kiss girls who do!"

"Pass the sour cream for the baked potato," said the doctor. "It's better and better for you than butter."

"Pass the butter," said the professor.

"Bud gets served first," said the chaplain, who was sitting at the Condemned's right hand. "Bud, you want steak or lobster?"

"Both," said Bud.

"THAT LOOKS GOOD, but it's time to go," said the warden from the corridor. "Any last words?"

It was 9:05.

"What's the hurry?" asked Bud, helping himself to the last of the frozen yoghurt. "I thought it wasn't till midnight."

"It's not, officially," said the guard, as he snapped the plastic shackles around Bud's feet. "But they asked us to bring you around early."

"The whole thing could take hours," said the warden. "We decided to try and get you up on the cross by ten at the latest."

"I don't know if I like that," Bud said, holding his hands behind his back for the cuffs.

"There's nothing not to like," said the professor. "It's a necessary precaution since with this procedure death's not instantaneous."

"It's not? I guess that's good, then," said Bud. Instantaneous sounded painful.

THEY WALKED TWO-BY-TWO, except for Bud's mother, down the long hallway toward the door that led into the prison yard. The warden and the lawyer went first. Bud and the guard were right behind them.

A man in a rubber suit stood by the door. He was holding a tank with a short hose and a nozzle, like a paint sprayer.

"Who's that?" Bud asked.

"Remember, we talked about the scourging?" said the chaplain. He and the professor were right behind Bud. "That's why they gave you the paper coveralls."

"They don't feel right," Bud said. He had the feeling something bad was about to happen. He often had these feelings. Usually they were right.

"In order to duplicate the original procedure as closely as possible," said the professor, "there has to be a thorough preliminary scourging."

"So where's the whip?" the producer asked. He and the carpenter were next in line.

"It's going to be a chemical scourging," said the warden. "Whips are not allowed in Tennessee prisons."

The man in the rubber suit raised his mask, revealing himself to be the doctor. "This tank is filled with a powerful paint stripper," he explained. "It will traumatize the client before he is hung on the cross."

"Client," said the professor scornfully. "I can remember when the word was 'patient.'"

The para-doctor ignored him and lowered his mask.

"Otherwise," said the chaplain, placing a hand on Bud's plump shoulder, "You could hang there for days."

"So let's have at it, then, boys," said Bud's mother darkly. She was the only one walking alone. The reporter from the *Tattler* had already gotten sick and gone home.

"Turn around, Bud," said the guard.

Bud turned around. The guard stepped out of the way.

The doctor sprayed a foam onto Bud's back and shoulders. For the first split second it didn't hurt. Then the paper soaked through and began to smoke.

Then Bud began to scream.

"Is THIS LEGAL?" the producer asked the warden.

"Is what what?" Bud's screams made hearing difficult. The producer repeated his question. The warden shrugged and nodded toward the professor. "Ask him.

He's in charge from now until the actual MOE or Moment of Expiration," he said.

"Is that legal?" asked the producer.

"Is what what?"

The producer repeated his question. "Check your Bible," said the professor, with an air of mystery.

"There's a threshold requirement of religious authenticity," said the lawyer. "Otherwise none of this would be happening."

"Does that mean the client has been baptized?" asked the producer. Bud had quit screaming. He was rolling on the floor, which is hard to do in handcuffs, trying to get his breath back.

"You bet," said the chaplain, who had moved to the back of the line.

"You bet," said Bud's mother.

"You can't do that here," said the warden from the front of the line.

"Do what?" asked the chaplain and Bud's mother, in one voice.

"You two. That." They were holding hands.

"We lost the sound," said the little girl's uncle, who was watching from the Victims Rights Closure Lounge on closed-circuit television. It was he who had found her, tracing her little doll to the muddy bank of the Cumberland.

Bud White had quit screaming. He was rolling on the floor of the corridor, trying to get his breath back.

"This ain't right," said the little girl's grandmother. Her name was Hecubah. The little girl had been named after her but hadn't liked the name. Her grandmother had always thought she would eventually come around, as children often do with unusual or biblical names. But it was not to be, alas.

"We lost the sound," said the little girl's uncle. "Where's that guard?"

"THAT WASN'T IN the dream," said Bud. He was flopping like a fish on the cold concrete floor.

The doctor and the warden helped him to his knees. Then they handed him to the four convict volunteers, wearing rubber gloves, who dragged him through the door into the prison yard.

The rest of the party followed.

"Where's the cross?" asked Bud's mother.

A single steel upright stood at the top of a small hill of rubble.

The carpenter showed her the crosspiece which lay on the ground at the foot of the hill. "It gets assembled as we go," he said.

"It's almost ten," said the warden. "Let's get on with this."

THE CHAPLAIN DIDN'T want to drive the nails.

"I'm a man of the cloth," he said. "Isn't the state supposed to be sending somebody?"

"They are," said the warden, "but she won't be here till eleven. She usually just inserts an IV."

"With any luck, we could be done by then," said the carpenter.

"Let's hope not," said the professor, under his breath.

"Bud's ready to go," said Bud's mother. "Why drag it out? My boy is eager to get into Heaven, aren't you Bud?"

Bud was shaking his head and moaning. The convict volunteers were helping him out of what was left of his coveralls.

"And what is this?" asked the producer.

"It's a loincloth," said the professor.

"It's paper too," said the warden.

"Looks like a diaper to me," said Bud's mother.

"HERE," SAID THE carpenter, handing the doctor a nail gun. "Just pull the trigger. But get close. You don't want the nail flying out and hitting somebody. Somebody else."

"I've already done my bit," said the doctor, handing the nail gun to the professor. "I'm here to observe."

"Ditto," said the professor, handing it to the chaplain.

"Perhaps it should be a loved one," said the chaplain. He handed the nail gun to Bud's mother.

"No way," said Bud's mother. "He's mad enough at me as it is."

Bud was shivering even though October in Tennessee is rarely very cold. "I'm not mad at anybody," he said.

Nevertheless, Bud's mother handed the nail gun to the warden—who handed it back to the carpenter. "I'll owe you one, Billy Joe," he said.

BUD BEGAN TO weep as the guard and the doctor laid him on his back over the metal crosspiece.

"Turn it up," said the little girl's uncle, who was watching from the Victims' Rights Closure Lounge.

"Don't you dare," said the little girl's grandmother.

The guard turned it up anyway. He was the only one allowed to touch the forty-four-inch Samsung; it was state property.

"He's weeping because the metal's cold and his back is raw," said the doctor. "From the scourging."

"Sounds like a cleanser," said the uncle. "Looks like a diaper."

"This ain't right," said the grandmother.

\* \* \*

"NOT THROUGH THE hands," said the professor. "That's a common misconception. Through the wrists. Aim for the little hollow."

"Which little hollow?"

"That little hollow right there."

Bud looked away. He tried looking toward the ceiling, then saw the stars and realized he was outside. It was the first time he had seen the stars in six years. They looked *as* cold as ever. "I don't remember any of this from the dream," he said.

"That's why I'm here," said the professor. "To make sure it's all authentic."

"It's going to hurt but it's supposed to hurt," said the chaplain. "Try and roll with it, Bud; try not to..."

BANG!

The chaplain didn't get to finish. Bud's body twisted almost comically as he tried to reach toward the wrist that had just been nailed to the left chopping block. But the four volunteers held his right arm in place.

"Look away," said the carpenter. He was talking to Bud.

BANG!

"Let's take him up," said the professor to the warden, who nodded toward the four convict volunteers.

Matthew and Mark lifted the crosspiece over their heads and into the slot in the upright. Bud White was hanging from it. Meanwhile, John and John guided Bud's feet, which were still shackled together, toward the cypress block near the bottom of the upright.

Bud was screaming again. "I wouldn't have picked him for a screamer," said the warden. "Is that in the Bible? All that screaming?"

"How am I to know," said the professor. He was tired of the warden and his lofty attitude.

"Put the one over the other," said the carpenter, as Bud's feet were held against the lower block.

BANG!

Nailed in three places, Bud raised up and drew a breath, and screamed again.

"What's he smiling about?" asked Bud's mother.

"Probably just a reflex," said the chaplain, putting his hand, and then his arm, on her shoulder.

"I don't mean Bud," said Bud's mother. "I mean the professor."

WISH THEY'D TURN the sound up," said the little girl's uncle.

"You're done wishin'," said the grandmother.

She grabbed her youngest son by the arm and yanked him out of the Victims' Rights Closure Lounge, brushing past the producer, who was just entering.

"What's with them?" the producer asked the guard. He was carrying a plate of pimento cheese sandwiches. He had hoped to get a few shots of the family.

"Weak stomach," said the guard.

"Want a sandwich?" asked the producer. "Hate to see them to go to waste."

BUD WAS MAKING a sort of honking sound. "Like a goose," said his mother.

"Or a car," said the chaplain. He had already shown her his classic, newly painted, in the prison parking lot.

"It's 10:41," said the warden. "How long is this supposed to take?"

"Not less than three or more than four hours, if all goes well," said the professor.

The warden looked at his watch. "We have a shift change at eleven thirty. That's less than an hour from now."

The watch, a Seiko, was a gift from his father-in-law, also a warden.

To breathe, Bud had to raise up on his feet. The nails made it painful; very painful; more painful than he had ever imagined anything could be.

Not that Bud was big on imagining things.

But the body's yearning to breathe, he learned, cannot be overridden, even by pain.

When he stood up was when he made the honking sound.

Stand, honk, breathe, honk.

His head turned from side to side.

"It looks like he's looking for somebody," the carpenter said.

"Who?" asked the professor.

"Bud."

"No, I mean who's he looking for?"

"Isn't that your department?" said the carpenter.

Bud was. Looking for somebody.

Somebody was missing.

"Professor," Bud said. "Professor!"

The professor looked up.

Bud raised up for air. Instead of honking, this time, he asked, "Where is He?"

"Who?"

"Jesus."

"Jesus Christ!" said the professor.

"He's not here in person, Bud," said the chaplain, reaching up to pat Bud's plump knee. "That was a long, long time ago."

"It's not required," said the lawyer.

Bud groaned and honked.

"Bud's like a lot of people," the professor said to the warden, "in that he takes things too literally."

BUD WHITE GROANED. He was supposed to be getting to Heaven pretty soon.

He hoped Heaven wasn't anything like this.

He found he could still wiggle all his fingers but two.

From his high perch he could see the professor and the warden and the lawyer standing side by side.

The doctor and his mother and the chaplain stood right behind them.

The TV producer and the four convict volunteers, none of whom Bud knew, were milling around a small catering table.

Bud had never hurt so bad. When he had been shot, right before his capture, it had hardly hurt at all. The bullet had gone in and out of the flat part of his neck.

Bud's eyes filled with tears. He felt sorry for himself, and for everyone around him. They were all just flesh and bone, like himself. They were only alive for a few precious moments. Like the little girl herself.

"Bud? Bud White?"

He blinked away the tears and saw Jesus, hanging on the next cross, one over.

"Yes, sir?"

"You're in luck, Bud. See the gate?"

Bud looked up. The sky swung open, and swinging on it, there was a little girl in a muddy white dress.

She stuck out her tongue but Bud knew that she didn't hate him. Even though he had cracked her little neck with his hands, like a rabbit.

Her dress was muddy. The wind lifted it when she swung forward, and he could see her little blue panties.

She wore little gold shoes.

She stuck out her tongue again—just teasin'! Her lips said "Bud White!" She took his hand, both hands, and pulled him up, not down, peeling him off the nails like a sticker.

Boy did that hurt!

But it was worth it, 'cause—

"WE COULD BORROW a guard's club and crack his shins," said the doctor. "That way he couldn't stand up to breathe."

"The Romans often did precisely that," said the professor. "They had great respect for quitting time. But when they went to do it to Our Lord, they found that he had already expired."

"We're in no hurry," said the new guard. "We're just starting our shift. We're good for the darnation."

"He means *du*ration," said the warden. "But shouldn't somebody check Bud? He's stopped honking."

Sure enough, Bud was silent. His big head drooped to one side.

"I don't like the diaper," his mother said. "And I never liked the beard."

"It was Bud you never liked," muttered the carpenter, who had grown to like Bud, a little.

"You watch your mouth," said Bud's mother. "When I want some stupid redneck opinion, I'll read the *Banner*."

"He's not raising hisself up anymore," said the chaplain.

"Him-self," said the professor.

The warden shook his watch, which had mysteriously stopped at 12:04. "Anybody got the time?"

It was 12:19, according to the producer. Amazingly, according to the professor, the recreation had taken almost exactly the same time as the original Passion.

\* \* \*

THE DISCOVERY CHANNEL provided the ambulance as part of the deal. It pulled up in the yard. "You'd think whoever thought of a nail gun," said the carpenter, "would've come up with a better way to pull them."

He used a short crowbar which he called a "do-right." He had to use a block, since Bud's hands were soft. Hands get soft on Death Row. He gave one of the nails to Bud's mother, who wiped it off and put it into her purse. He gave one to the professor and kept the other for the warden.

The guards slid Bud into the back of the ambulance, feet first. He was headed not for a graveyard, but an Autopsy Center.

"You want to ride with him?" the warden asked.

"No, no, no," Bud's mother said. "I'd rather ride with the chaplain. He's the spiritual adviser for the entire family, you know."

"What about the butcher blocks?" asked the producer.

"If you turn them over, they're still good," said the carpenter.

"I'll take one, too, then," said the professor. He was already planning where to send his paper. First he would mount the précis on the World Wide Web—a necessary first step these days.

"YOU CAN QUIT sulking, Luke," said the little girl's grandmother. Her youngest son was sulking because he had been dragged away from the Victims' Rights Closure Lounge.

"Yes, ma'am."

"And you can go to church with me tomorrow."

"Yes, ma'am."

The two of them were in her gray '97 Hyundai, heading east on the interstate, toward Nashville, where the grandmother taught, and still teaches, school. Sunday School, too.

A car passed them doing about eighty, also heading for town. A one-handed driver with a woman tucked close by his side. A Chevy; a 1955 210 coupe, cherry red, three coats, hand rubbed.

A classic in anybody's book.

# SWIFTLY

*Adam Roberts*

## I.
### *November 3, 1848*

SWIFTLY, EXPERTLY, THE tiny hand worked, ticked up and down, moved over the face of the miniature pallet. The worker was wearing yellow silk trousers, a close-woven cotton blue waistcoat; it (Bates could not see whether it was a *he* or a *she*) had on spectacles that shone like dewdrops in the light. Its hair was black, its skin a golden-cream. Bates could even make out the creases of concentration on its brow, the tip of its tiny tongue just visible through its teeth.

Bates stood upright. "It hurts my back," he said, "to lean over so."

"I quite understand," said Pannell. "Might I fetch you a chair?"

"Ah, no need for that, thank you," said Bates. "I think I have seen all I need. It is, indeed, fascinating."

Pannell seemed agitated, shifting weight from one foot to another. "I never tire of watching them work," he agreed. "Pixies. Fairies! Creatures from childhood story." He beamed. *You smile sir,* thought Bates. *You smile, but there is sweat on your lip. Perhaps you are not altogether lost to shame. Nerves, sir, nerves.*

"What is it, eh, making exactly?"

"A mechanism for controlling the angle, pitch and yaw, in flight you know. I could give you its technical name, although it is Mister Nicholson who is the greater expert on this matter."

"Is it a sir or a madam?"

"It?"

"The creature. The workman."

"A female." Pannell touched Bates's elbow, herding him gently toward the staircase at the far end of the workshop. "We find they have better hands for weaving the finest wire-strands."

Bates paused at the foot of the wooden stairs, taking one last look around the workshop. "And these are Lilliputians?"

"These," replied Pannell, "are from the neighboring island, Blefuscu. We believe Blefuscans, sir, to be better workers. They are less prone to disaffection, sir. They work harder and are more loyal."

"All of which is," said Bates, "very interesting."

UP THE STAIRS and through the glass door, Bates was led into Pannell's office. Pannell guided him to a chair, and offered him brandy. "When my superior heard of the terms you were offering," he gushed, wiping the palms of his hands alternately against the sleeves of his coat as Bates sat down, "he was nothing less than overwhelmed.

Mr. Burton is not an excitable man, sir, but he was impressed, very impressed, more," Pannell went on, hopping to the drinks cabinet in the corner of the room, "more than impressed. Very generous terms, sir! Very favorable on both sides!"

"I am pleased you think so," said Bates.

From where he was sitting the view was clear through the quartered window of Pannell's office. Grime marked the bottom right-hand corners of each pane like gray lichen. Each patch of dirt was delineated from clean glass by a hyperbolic line running from bottom left to top right. *X equals y squared,* thought Bates. The pattern on the glass was distracting, the eye hardly noticed the view that was actually through the window, the dingy street, the gray-brick buildings.

He shifted his weight in the chair. It complained, squeaking like a querulous baby. I, too, am nervous, he thought to himself.

"Brandy?" Pannell asked for the second time.

"Thank you."

"Mr. Burton expressed his desire to meet you himself."

"I would be honored."

"Indeed..."

A bell tinkled, as tiny a sound as ice-glass breaking. A Lilliputian sound. Bates looked to the patch of wall above the door. The bell was mounted on a brass plate. It shivered again, and silver sound dribbled out.

Pannell stood, staring at the bell like a fool, a glass of brandy in his hands. "That means that Mr. Burton is coming here directly. It rings when Mr. Burton is on his way here directly. But I was to bring you to Mr. Burton's office, not he to come here..."

And almost at once the door shuddered, as with cold, and snapped open. Burton was a tall man who carried a spherical belly before him like an "O" of exclamation. His jowls were turfed with black beard, but his forehead was bald, as pink and curved as a rose petal. He moved with the fierce energy of the financially successful. As Bates got up from his chair he tipped his glance down with a respectful nod of the head: Burton's shoes were very well-made, tapering to a point, the uppers made of some variety of stippled leather. Standing to his full height brought Bates's glance up along the fine cloth of Burton's trousers, past the taut expanse of dark waistcoat and frock, to the single bright item of clothing on the man: a turquoise and scarlet bow tie, in which actual jewels had been fitted.

He faced the proprietor with a smile, extending his hand. But the first thing Burton said was: "No, sir."

"Mr. Burton," gabbled Pannell, "may I introduce to you Mr. Bates, who has come in person to negotiate the contract. I was just telling him how generous we considered the terms he offered..."

"No sir," repeated Burton. "I'll not stand it."

"Not stand it, sir?" said Bates.

"I know who you are, sir," fumed Burton. He stomped to the far side of the office, and turned to face them again. Bates noticed the bone-colored walking stick, capped at each tip with red gold. "I know who you are!"

"I am Abraham Bates, sir," replied Bates.

"No sir!" Burton raised the cane, and brought it down on the flat of Pannell's desk. It reported like a rifle discharge. Pannell jerked at the sound, and even Bates found sweat pricking out of his forehead again.

"No sir," bellowed Burton. "You'll not weasel your way here! I know your type, and you'll not come here with your *false* names and *false* heart. No."

"Mr. Burton," said Bates, trying to keep his voice level. "I assure you that Bates is my name."

"You are a liar, sir! I give you the *lie,* sir." The cane flourished in the air, inadvertently knocking a picture on the wall and tipping a perspective of the South Seas through forty degrees.

"I am not, sir," retorted Bates.

"Gentlemen," whimpered Pannell. "I beg of you both..."

"Pannell, you'll hold your tongue," declared Burton, emphasizing the last word with another flourish of the cane. "If you value your continued employment at this place. Do you deny, sir," he added, pointing the cane directly at Bates, "do you *deny* that you came here to infiltrate? To weasel your way in?"

"I came to discuss certain matters," insisted Bates. "That is all. Sir, do you refuse even to talk with me?"

"And if I do?" said Burton, his voice dropping a little. "Then? You'll have your members of parliament, your newspaper editors, your many friends, and with them you'll turn on me? A pack of dogs, sir! A pack of dogs!"

"I admire your cane," said Bates, lowering himself back into his chair in what he hoped was a cool-headed manner. "Is it bone, sir?"

This took the wind from Burton's sails. "We'll not discuss my cane, sir."

"Is it Brobdingnagian bone? From which part of the body? A bone from the inner-ear, perhaps?"

"There is nothing illegal," Burton began, but then seemed to change his mind. The sentence hung in the air for a while. "Very well," he said, finally, somewhat deflated. "You have come to talk, sir. We will talk, sir. Pannell, you will stay in this room. Pour me a brandy, in fact, while I and this... *gentleman* discuss the affairs of the day. Then, Mr. Bates, I'd be obliged if you left this manufactory and did not return."

"One conversation will satisfy me, sir," said Bates, rounding the sentence off with a small sigh, like a full stop given breath.

BURTON SETTLED INTO a chair by the window, and Pannell poured another glass of brandy with visibly trembling fingers. "This *gentleman,*" Burton told his employee, "is an agitator, sir. A radical, I daresay. Are you a radical?"

"I am one of Mr. Martineau's party."

"Oh!" said Burton, with egregious sarcasm. "A party man!"

"I am honored to be so styled."

"And no patriot, I'll lay any money."

"I love my country, sir," replied Bates, "love her enough to wish her better managed."

"Faction and party," Burton muttered grimly, raising the brandy glass to his face like a glass muzzle over his bulbous nose. "Party and faction." He drank. "They'll sunder the country, I declare it." He put the empty glass down on the table with an audible *ploc.*

Pannell was hovering, unhappy-looking, by the door.

"We can agree to differ on the topic, sir," said Bates, a little stiffly.

"Well, sir," said Burton. "What conversation is it you wish to have with me? I own this manufactory, sir. Yes, we employ a cohort of Blefuscans."

"Employ, sir?"

"They cost me," said Burton, bridling. "A fortune. Regular food does not sit in their stomachs, so they must be fed only the daintiest and most expensive. Regular cloth is too coarse for their clothing, so they must be given the finest silks. The expense is very much greater than a regular salary would be. True, I own them outright, and this makes them slaves. But they are well treated, and they cost me more as slaves than employees ever could. I suppose Mr. Bates here," Burton added, addressing Pannell in a raised voice that aimed for sarcasm, but achieved only petulance, "would see them *free*. Mr. Bates considers slavery an *evil*. Is it not so, Mr. Bates?"

Bates shifted in his chair. It squeaked again underneath him. "Since you ask, I do consider such slavery as you practise here an evil. How many of your employees die?"

"I lose money with each fatality, sir," said Burton. "I've no desire to see a single one die."

"And your cane, sir? How many Brobdingnagians are left alive in the world?"

"I have nothing to do with those monsters. Indeed not. One of their kind could hardly fit inside my building."

"Yet you carry a cane made from their bodies, sir. Do you not consider that a small wickedness? A celebration of their pitiable state?"

"*Some* people, Pannell," said Burton, addressing his employee again. "Some people have leisure and predisposition to be sympathetic toward animals. Others are too busy with the work they have at hand."

"Your Lilliputians..."

"Blefuscans, sir."

"Your little people, sir—and the giant people also—are hardly animals."

"No? Have you worked with them, Mr. Bates?"

"I have devoted many years now to their cause."

"But actually *worked with them?* No, of course not. The midgets are mischievous, and their wickedness is in the bone. And the giants—they are a clear and present danger to the public good."

"The Brobdingnagians have endured homicide on an appalling scale."

"Homicide? But that implies man, don't it? Implies killing *men,* don't it?"

"Are not the Brobdingnagians made in God's image, sir? As are you and I? As are the Lilliputians?"

"So," said Burton, smiling broadly. "It's God, at the heart of your disaffection, is it?"

"Our nation would be stronger," said Bates, struggling to keep the primness out of his voice, "if we followed God's precepts more, sir. Or are you an atheist?"

"No, no."

"Let me ask you a question, Mr. Burton: are your Blefuscan workers—are they white-skinned or black?"

"What manner of question is this, sir? You've just examined my workers out there. You know the answer to your own question."

"Their skins are as white as mine," said Bates. "Now, the Bible is clear on this. God has allotted slavery to one portion of his creation, and marked that portion by blackening their skins—Ham's sons, sir. There are enough Blacks in the world to fill the places of slaves. But it mocks God to take some of his most marvelous creations and enslave them, or kill them."

"I do not kill my workers, sir," insisted Burton.

"But they *are* killed, sir. Worldwide, only a few thousand are left. And the Brobdingnagians—how many of them remain alive? After the affair with the *Endeavour* and the *Triumph?*"

"I have met the Captain of the *Triumph,* sir," said Burton, bridling up again. "At a dinner party of a friend of mine. An honorable man, sir. Honorable. He followed the orders he was given. What naval gentleman could do otherwise? And," he continued, warming to his theme, "was it so great a crime? These giants are twelve times our size. Had they organized, had they known cannon, and ordnance, and gunpowder, they could have trampled us to pieces. Not only England neither, but the whole of Europe—they *would* have come over here and trampled us to pieces. Who'd have been the slaves then? You may answer me that question, if you please. With an army of monstrous giants trampling England's green fields, who'd have been the slaves then?"

"The Brobdingnagians are a peace-loving people," said Bates, feeling his own color rise. "If you read the account of the mariner who discovered their land..."

Burton laughed aloud. "That fellow? Who'd believe a word he wrote? Riding the nipple of a gentlewoman like a hobby-horse, begging your pardon—it was nonsense. And the reality? A race of beings big enough to squash us like horseflies, and destroy our nation. Our nation, sir! Yours and mine! We had but one advantage over them, and that was that we possessed gunpowder and they did not. The King did well to destroy the majority of that population and seize their land. Our people are the best fed in the world, now, sir. Perhaps you do not remember how things were before the gigantic cattle were brought here, but I do: many starved in the streets. Now there's not a pauper but eats roast beef every day. Our army is the strongest and manliest on the continent. Would we have had our successes invading France and Holland without them?"

"You speak only of temporal advantages," insisted Bates. "But to do so is short sighted. It is true that the discoveries of our navy have enriched our country in purely material terms—but the spiritual, sir? The spiritual?"

"God," said Burton.

"Indeed, my friend. God created all these creatures as marvels. We have spat upon his gift. Lilliputians may seem small to us, but they are part of God's universe."

"There are giants in Genesis, I believe," said Burton. "Did not the flood destroy them?"

"The flood may not have reached the northwestern coast of America," said Bates. "At least, this is one theory as to the survival of these peoples."

"It hardly seems to me that God's Providence was greatly disposed toward these monsters. He tried to destroy them in the flood, and again in the form of two British frigates." His face twitched with smiling.

"After much prayer," Bates insisted, not wanting to be distracted. "After much prayer, it has become obvious to me..."

At this Burton laughed out loud, a doggy, abrasive noise; each laugh parceled into sections, like the "ha! ha! ha!" of conventional orthography, although the noise he made was not so aspirated as this representation implies. More like: nugh! nugh! nugh! It broke through Bates's speech. "Pannell," said Burton. "Mr. Bates has come to vex us, not to divert us, and yet how diverting he is!"

"Mockery is," began Bates, his anger rising. He swallowed his words. Better to turn the other cheek. "I come, sir, to *invite* you. To invite you to join a communality of *enlightened* employers and financiers—a small core, sir, but a vital one. From us will grow a more proper, a more holy society."

"A society? So that's it. And if I joined your communality, I would not be allowed to possess any slaves, I suppose?"

"You might own slaves, sir, provided only they *were* slave—Blacks I mean. The Lilliputians are not slaves, sir, in God's eye, and it is God you mock by treating them so. God will not be mocked."

"I daresay not," agreed Burton, hauling his cumbersome body from its chair. "It's been a pleasure, sir, talking with you. Mr. Pannell here will show you out."

Bates rose, flustered, unsure exactly where he had lost the initiative in the interview. "Am I to take it, sir, that you..."

"You are to take it any way you choose, sir. I had thought you a spy for Parliament, sir: there are MPs who would gladly outlaw slavery in all its forms, and they have the power to do actual harm. But you, sir, do not—I doubt nothing but that you are harmless, as are your God-bothering friends. Good day, sir!"

Bates's color rose fiercely. *God-bothering!* The insolence! "You are rude sir! Believe me, God is more powerful than any parliament of men."

"In the next world sir, the next world."

"You veer toward blasphemy."

"It is not *I*," Burton growled, "who attempted to infiltrate an honest workman's shop with lies and deceit, not I who broke the commandment about bearing false witness to worm my way inside a decent business and try to tear it down. But you knew that you would not gain admittance if you spoke your true purpose. Good day, sir."

2.

BATES PACED THE evening streets of London, the long unlovely streets. He passed gin-shops and private houses. He walked past a junior school with ranks of windows arrayed along its brick walls like the ranks of children within. He passed churches, chapels, and a synagogue. Up the dog-leg of Upper St. Martin's Lane and past the rag-traders of Cambridge Circus, now mostly putting away their barrows and boarding up their shops. Bates, lost in his own thoughts, walked on, and up the main thoroughfare of Charing Cross Road.

Around him, now, crowds passed. Like leaves at autumn, drained of their richness, dry and gray and rattling along the stone roads before the wind. He thought of the French word: *foule*. A true word, for what was of greater folly than a crowd? The stupidity of humankind, that cattle-breed. Hiding, unspeaking, in some crevice of his mind was a sense of the little Lilliputians as daintier. More graceful. More *faery*. But he didn't think specifically of the little folk as he walked the road. There was an oppressive weariness inside him, as gray and heavy as a moon in his belly. Melancholia was, he knew it of course, a sin. It sneered at God's great gift of life. It was the sin against hope. It was to be fought, but the battle was hard. It was hard because melancholia corroded precisely the will to fight; it was a disease of the will.

Over his head, one of the new clockwork flying devices buzzed, dipping and soaring like a metal dragonfly, long as his arm. It croaked away through the air up Charing Cross Road, flying north and carrying who knew what message to who knew what destination. Only the wealthy could afford such toys, of course; the wealthy and the government. Perhaps it was the noise, the self-important humming of it, that always gave the impression of a creature hurrying off on an errand of the mightiest importance. The war! The empire! The future of humankind!

Probably a financial facilitator, a manufactor, somebody with nouveau riches in the city, one of that type, had sent it flying north to let his servants know he would be late home from work.

The thought was sour in Bates's belly, a tart, undigested pain. He should not have drunk the brandy.

He stopped to buy *The Times* from a barrow-boy, and ducked into a mahogany-ceilinged coffee shop to read it, sitting with hot chocolate breathing fragrant steam at his elbow. Gaslight from four lamps wiped light over the polished tabletops, reflecting blurry circles of light in the waxed wood of the walls. He brought his face close to the newsprint, as much to bury himself away from the stare of the other coffee drinkers as to make out the tiny printface. Miniature letters, like insects swarming over the page.

News.

British forces had seen action again at Versailles; the famous palace had been pocked with cannon shells. There was little doubt that Christmas would see the flag of St. George flying over Paris. Anxiety of the French people; reassurance from the King that there would be no anti-Catholick repression after an English victory. The mechanics of the Flying Island had been thoroughly analyzed by the Royal Society, and a paper had been read before the King. It seemed that a particular ore was required, against which a magnetic device of unusual design operated. This ore was found only rarely in His Majesty's dominions, and in Europe not at all. But deposits were known to lie in portions of the North American and Greater Virginian continent. The way was clear, the paper announced, for a new island to be constructed as a platform for use in the war against the Spanish in that continent.

Still Bates's spirits sank. He could not prevent it: some malign gravity of the heart dragged him down.

He turned to the back of the paper, and studied the advertisements. For sale, one Lilliputian, good needleworker. For sale, two Lilliputians, a breeding couple; four hundred guineas the pair. For sale, stuffed Lilliputian bodies, arranged in poses from the classics: Shakespeare, Milton, Scott. For sale, prime specimen of the famed Intelligent Equines, late of His Majesty's

Second Cognizant Cavalry; this Beast (the lengthy advertisement spooled on) speaks a tolerable English, but knows mathematics and music to a high level of achievement. Of advanced years, but suitable for stud. And there, at the bottom, swamped and overwhelmed by the mass of Mammonite hawking and crying, was a small box: *Public Lecture, on the Wickedness of Enslaving the Miniature Peoples from the East India Seas*. Wednesday, no entrance after eight. Wellborough Hall. Admission one shilling.

Hopeless, all hopeless.

For Bates, the sinking into the long dark night of the soul had begun. It had happened before, but every time it happened there was never anything to compare it to, never any way to fight it off. He stumbled down Oxford Street in a fuggy daze of misery. Where did it come from? Chapels littered both sides of the road, some polished and elegant, some boxy and unpretentious, and yet none of them held the answer to his indigestion of the spirit. If only some angel would swoop down to him, calling and weeping through the air like a swift, varicolored wings stretching like a cat after a sleep, the feather-ends brushing the street itself in the lowest portion of its flying arc, its face bland and pale and still and beautiful. If only some angel could bring God's blessing down to him. Or perhaps the angel would actually be a faery, a tiny creature with wings of glass and a child's intensity of innocence. Grace was Grace, even in the smallest parcels.

### 3.
### *November 9, 1848*

BY THE TIME Bates next rose from his bed he had been on the mattress for two days and two nights. His man put his insolent white head through the doorway to his cubby and chirruped. "Feeling better today?"

"Go away, Baley," Bates groaned. "Leave me in peace."

"Off to your club today? It's Thursday—you told me most particularly to remind you of Thursday."

"Yes," he muttered, more to himself than to his servant. "Yes, Thursday. I will be getting up today. My... stomach feels a little better."

"There you go sir." The head withdrew, with only the faintest of smirks upon it that seemed to say *we all know there's nothing the matter with your stomach, you old stay-a-bed.*

Bates turned over in the bed. The sheet underneath him was foul with two days' accumulated stink, creased and wrinkled like the palm of a white hand. His bedside cabinet was littered with glasses, bottles, a news-sheet, an ivory pipe. The curtain was of cotton-velvet, and muffled off most of the daylight. The joints between knuckles and fingers' ends ached in both hands; the small of his back murmured complaint. His feet hurt from inaction. A series of bangs, miniature sounds, *goh, goh, goh.* Bates could not tell whether the thrumming sound was the spirit of Headache rapping inside his skull, or the sound of something thudding far away. The volatile acid of his melancholia had even eroded away the boundaries of self and world, such that Bates's misery spread out and colonized reality itself, it became a universal pressure of unhappiness. It seemed to Bates at that moment that the biblical flood had been, symbolically speaking, a *type* or *trope* for Melancholia itself, washing away strength, joy, will, hope, diluting the very energy of life itself and spreading it impossibly weakly about the globe. Gray waves washing at a rickety waterfront.

He pulled the pot from under the bed and pissed into it without even getting up, lying on his side and directing the stream over the edge of the mattress. Flecks of fluid messed the edge of the bed, but he didn't care. Why should he care? What was there to care about? When he had finished he did not even bother pushing the pot back under the bed. He turned on his other side and lay still. There was a faint noise, a repeated thud-thud-thud.

It stopped. Bates turned over again.

Turned over again. Ridiculous, ridiculous.

He pulled himself upright, and snatched at the paper. Baley had brought it to him the night before, but Bates's fretful, miserable state of mind had not allowed him to concentrate long enough to read the articles. He started on the first leader, an imperial puff about the prospects for a British European Empire once France had been defeated. He read the third sentence three times—*our glorious history reasserts itself, our generals revitalize the dreams of Henry the Fifth*—without taking it in at all. The words were all there, and he knew the meaning of each, but as a whole the sentence refused to coalesce in his mind. Senseless. It was hopeless. In a fit of petty rage, he crushed the whole paper up into a ragged ball and threw it to the floor. It started, creakily, to unwind, like a living thing.

He lay down again.

"Gentleman at the door, sir." It was Baley, his head poking into crib.

"I'm not at home," Bates said into the mattress.

"Won't take that for an answer, sir," said Baley. "A foreign gentleman. Says he's High Belgium, but I'd say France, sir."

Bates hauled himself upright. "His hair black, in a long knout at the back of his head?"

"A what, sir?"

"Long hair, idiot, long hair?"

"Continental fashion, yes sir."

Bates was struggling into his gown. "Show him through, you fool." He pressed the crumbs of sleep from his eyes and wiped a palm over his sleep-ruffled hair. Here? D'Ivoi had never before come to his rooms, they had always met in the club. Perhaps Baley had made a mistake—but, no, coming through to the drawing room there was D'Ivoi, standing facing the fire, with a turquoise hat under his arm, the sheen of his silk suit gleaming, and his ridiculous tassel of hair dangling from the back of his head. Baley was loitering, and Bates shooed him away.

"My friend," said D'Ivoi, turning at the sound of Bates's voice.

"I was coming to the club today," said Bates at once. "Perhaps I seem unprepared, but I was about to get dressed."

D'Ivoi shook his head very slightly, no more than a tremble, and the smile was not dislodged from his face. "There is no need for us to meet at the club." His *th*s were brittle, *tare* is no need for us to meet at *tea* club, but otherwise his accent was tolerably good. "I regret to say my friend, that I leave this city this afternoon." *Tat* I leave *tiss* city.

"Leave?" Bates reached without thinking for the bell-rope, to call for tea; at the last minute he remembered that this was a conference to which the servant must not be privy.

"I regret to say it. And before I depart, I bring a warning of sorts. Events in the war are about to take a turn... shall we say, dramatic?"

"Dramatic? I don't understand. The paper says that we... that, ah, the English are on the edge of capturing Paris. When that happens, surely the..."

"No my friend," said D'Ivoi. "You will find tomorrow's newspapers tell a different story. France and the Pope have declared a common right with the Pacificans."

It was all a great deal for Bates to take in at once. "They have?" he said. "Why that's excellent news. Excellent news for our cause. Common right with Lilliputians and Brobdingnagians, both?"

"Certainly, with both. The petite folk and the giant folk, both are made in God's image. The talking horses, not; the Pope has decreed them devilish impostures. But of course he does so more because the English has its cavalry regiment of sapient horses. And the French army now has its own regiments. Regiments of the little folk would be useless enough, I suppose, but the giants make fearsome soldiers, I think."

"The French army has recruited regiments of Brobdingnagians?" repeated Bates, stupidly.

"I have not long, my friend," said D'Ivoi, nodding his head minutely. "I come partly to warn you. There are other things. The President of the Republic has relocated to Avignon, as you know. Well, there have been great things happening in Avignon, all in the south you know. And these great things are about to emerge to the day's light, for all the world to see. It will be terrible to be an English soldier before them."

"Monsieur," said Bates. "Are you...?"

"Forgive me, my friend," interrupted D'Ivoi. "When these things happen, it will be uncomfortable to be a French national in London, I think. And so I depart. But I warn you too: your cause, your pardon *our* cause, for the liberation of the Pacificans, has aligned you with the nation of France. Your government may take action against you for this reason."

"I am no traitor," Bates asserted, though his tongue felt heavy in his mouth uttering the sentiment.

"No, no," assured the foreigner. "I only warn you. You know best, of course, how to attend to your own safety. But before I depart (and time is close, my friend), let me say this: contemplate a French victory in this war. I advise it. Believe that, with the Pope and the President now allied formally to the petites and the giants, believe that a victory for France will spell freedom for these people. Perhaps one smaller evil counterbalances a larger good? Perhaps?"

Bates did not know what to say to this. "I know that my actions here," he started saying, speaking the words slowly, "have benefited the French government. And I am not ashamed of this."

"Good! Excellently good! Because it will be less time than you think before French soldiers arrive here in London town, and you would be well to consider how your duty lies. Your duty, my friend, to God above all. No?"

"Monsieur," said Bates again anxiously.

But D'Ivoi was putting his top hat on and bowing, stiffly. "I regret I must depart."

"French soldiers here?"

"Ah, yes. I will say only this, at last. There has been a very great series of inventions. We have a machine, a thinking and calculating machine... have you heard of this?"

"A machine?"

"Mister Babbage, and his French mistress, have been working in Uzes, in France's south, for many years now. You have heard, perhaps, of Mister Babbage?"

"The name is familiar..." said Bates. His head was starting to buzz unpleasantly. This conference was a shock, there was no mistaking it.

"He has built a machine. It can undertake a week's calculations in a moment. It is nothing more than a box, the size of a piano I think, but it gives great power of calculation and ratiocination, of the power of thought in this box. Forgive me, I am forgetting my English already. But our engineers now use this box, and with it they design fantastic new machines. Our generals use it, and with it they plan all possible military strategies. This box will win the war, for us."

And he bowed again and was gone.

4.
*November 9-12, 1848*

WHERE DOES IT GO, the melancholia, when some startling event evaporates it, sublimes it into vapor that dissolves into the wind? Bates's downheartedness vanished. He washed, shaved, dressed, ate, and bustled from his rooms in an hour. Everything had been turned topsy-turvy, and the evil spirit squatting spider-like in his head had somehow fallen free.

He hurried. D'Ivoi had been his only contact with the French, and perhaps by limiting his contact to a single individual he had, at some level, believed that he limited his treason too. And for a day or two the very notion of a French victory—of French troops marching up the Mall—was too shocking for him to think about it at all. But the idea percolated through his mind anyway, and soon he was almost welcoming it. It would bring his cause to fruition. The Lilliputians would be freed, the Brobdingnagians reprieved from race-death.

He was up, up, up.

He went to his club, and wrote three letters. Then he caught a cab (a rare expense for him) and visited a sympathetically minded gentleman in Holborn. He spent the evening with a gaggle of churchmen, duck-like individuals who paced about the room with their heads forward and their hands tucked into the smalls of their backs, talking ponderously of God. He told the sympathetically minded gentleman little, but he told the churchmen all. Their worry, it transpired, was not of French political rule, so much as the danger of an oppressive Catholicism being imposed as the official religion. Bates was too excited, too elevated in spirit, to worry about this.

"Are you certain that these events are going to come to pass?" one of the clerics asked him. "Are you sure?"

"I am sure," gabbled Bates. He tended to talk too rapidly when the mood was on him, when his blood was hurtling through his body, but it couldn't be helped. "Now that they have declared themselves for the humanity of the Lilliputians and Brobdingnagians, all of the civilized world will support them, surely. And their alliance has meant that they could recruit a regiment of giants to fight us. To fight the English. Moreover," he went on, wide-eyed, "they have perfected a device, a machine, a thinking machine. Have you heard of Mister Babbing?"

Babbing? Babbing?

"Do you mean *Babbage*," said one elderly churchman, a whittled, dry-faced old man who had been a main agent in the campaign since its first days. "The computational device?"

"The French have perfected it," said Bates. "And with it they have constructed new engineering devices, and plotted new techniques of war making."

"Incredible!"

"It is credible indeed."

"The computing device has been perfected!"

On the Saturday he attended a tea party at which he was the only male present. He sat on a chair too small for him, and listened politely to half a dozen wealthy matrons and maidens expatiate upon how beautiful the little people were, how marvelous, and how wicked it was to chain them with tiny chains and make them work in factories. Nobody mentioned the Brobdingnagians, of course, who lacked the daintiness to appeal to this class of person. But Bates smiled and nodded, and thought of the money these women might gift to the cause.

One woman confided in him. "Since my husband passed through the veil," she said in a breathy tone of voice, "my life has become divided between these darling little creatures and my cats."

The Sunday, naturally he went to chapel. But he could not bring his mind to focus on the sermon. Something fretted at its margins, some piece of thought-grit. *These darling little creatures.* But, Bates thought, there was so much more to the Lilliputians than this! They were messengers, in some way or other. He had not managed to clear the thought thoroughly enough through his brain to fully understand it, but he *felt* it, he felt it genuinely and thoroughly. Messengers. There was something about them, something special, that deserved preservation in the way few ordinary-sized people did.

She had sat next to him, with purple crinoline and a lace cap covering her hair, but with these intense, beautiful air-blue eyes, and had said: *these darling little creatures, and my cats.*

Cats preyed on them, of course. One of Bates's acquaintances declared that he had first become interested in their cause after watching two cats fighting over a stray Lilliputian, in the kitchen of his uncle's house.

And so it slid again, dropping like leaves from a tree until the tree has lost all its leaves. Bates went to bed Sunday night with a heart so heavy it registered not only in his chest, but in his throat and belly too. And waking the following morning was a forlorn, interfered-with sensation. The urge not to rise was very strong: merely to stay in bed, to turn the heavy body and heavy head and lie there. After a few days of energetic living, Bates's life had been usurped again by melancholia.

His ROOMS, ON Cavendish Square, looked over an oval of parched winter grass and four nude trees. Some days he would sit and stare, emptying one cigarette after another of its smoke, and doing nothing but watching the motionlessness of the trees.

WHEN HE HAD been a young man, some six or seven years earlier, Bates had had an intrigue with a tobacconist's daughter called Mary. The romance had strayed into physical impropriety. To begin with, Bates had felt a glow in his heart, something fueled by equal parts pride and shame. The necessary secrecy had built him up inside his suit. He felt the sin, but he also felt elevated, enlarged. He could walk the streets of London, looking at the others, and knowing something they did not know. The aftermath, the potent stew of good and bad emotions, was more pleasurable than the physical enjoyment of the act itself, pleasurable though that act was.

Then Mary told him that she was carrying a child. This changed the balance of feelings inside him to a form of fear. He could not bring himself to confront his own father (still alive at that time) to declare himself the destined parent of an infant. It was impossible. Inner shame is, perhaps, a sensation so powerfully mixed of delight and disgust it approximates glory; but public shame is a very different matter. Bates senior was not a wealthy man, but he was proud. Marriage to a tobacconist's daughter was out of the question. And Mary was a sweet girl. But what could he do? What could be done?

Of course nothing could be done.

There was a very uncomfortable interview between the former lovers. There were tears and recriminations from her. They made it easier for him to adopt a stony exterior manner. Afterwards he spent the evening in his club, and drank most of a bottle of claret. A walk home and a half-hour in a chapel along the way. Prayer blended his awkwardness, his shame, his self-loathing, his weakness, into a cement of strength. He would be strong from this moment, which was all that Christ required. He would sin no more.

His resolution included a blanking out of Mary, which he managed by pretending that she did not exist. For weeks this strategy worked well. For hours at a time he forgot that there was such a person in the world. Only when he indulged in occasional, night-time bouts of impure thought and manual stimulation did her image pop into his mind, and this only encouraged him to quit that degrading business anyway.

Then, a month or more later, he saw her at the booth, paying to cross London Bridge. He hurried after her, uncertain whether the face glimpsed under the bonnet was indeed hers. "Excuse me, madam," he called. And she turned.

She looked blankly into his face, neither pleased nor displeased to see him.

"Mary," he said, catching up with her.

Her stomach was flat.

"You're looking," she chided, following his gaze. "'Tis not decent."

Light made painterly effects on the river, speckles of brightness spread in a swathe.

He didn't know how to ask the question.

"Don't worry yourself, sir," she said, blushing plum-red, her voice as angry as Bates had ever heard it. "No child will come and threaten your family honor." She pronounced this last word *on 'er*.

"I don't understand."

She was quiet for a time. "Well, a friend of mine knows a doctor. Not that I'd call him a real doctor, if you see what I say."

"Oh," said Bates, soft, realizing what had happened. They were a third of the way over the bridge now. The sunlight swelled, and the Thames was glittering and sparkling like a solid. Bates's mouth was dry.

"What did you do with it?" he asked, a pain growing in his chest as if his ribs were contracting and squeezing his lungs.

"It?" she replied.

"The," he said, his voice sounding somehow different to himself, "child."

She stared at him, stared for half a minute, her face immobile but her eyes wide. "I buried him," she said. "I dug under the hedgerow in Somer's Town, beside the churchyard, and buried him there."

For days Bates had been unable to get this image out of his mind. His child, his son, buried and mixed into the earth. Like ore. He dreamt of the little creature, its eyes closed and its mouth pursed against the chill. He imagined it with hair, long blond strands of hair. He imagined it miniature, Lilliputian in size. In the dream he scuffed at the dirt with his feet, knowing his child was interred beneath the spot. A strand of gold grazed his wrist. Boys in brown, crossing-sweepers, leant together to talk, somewhere in the distance. Through a window, perhaps. One of them yawned. But he was in a room, with velvet curtains. The strands of gold were woven into a cobweb. A strand of gold grazed his wrist. The baby's tiny hand was reaching for him, and when it touched him its skin was so cold he yelped out loud.

At that point he awoke.

5.

ON NOVEMBER 15, French forces crossed the Channel. The fighting in the northeast was the hardest, British troops having pulled back with a military alacrity to trenches dug earlier in the campaign and then sticking to their positions in and around Saint Quentin. But the French army was renewed. Three battalions of regular troops attacked the British positions; but then the *premier corps de géants* stormed the eastern flank. They carried enormous weaponry, great hoops of iron ringing massive planks of treated wood, cannonaders that the Brobdingnagians could fire from their shoulders, sending fissile barrel-shaped charges hurtling onto troops below. The packages were filled with Greek Fire. The giants proved remarkably resistant to rifle fire; although cannon shells would tend to bring them down.

The battle fought at Saint Quentin was the major engagement of the whole war, with conventional troops charging the English line-of-defense from two sides at once, and a platoon of Brobdingnagians wading among the fighting with studied, slow-footed seriousness, smashing and killing about them with long, weighted pikes—sixty foot long, and carrying nearly a ton of metal shaped at the killing end. And the cannonaders wrought havoc. One colonel lost his color completely as he read the paper containing the casualty figures after the battle. "If this number were pounds rather than corpses," he told his aide de camp, "we would be wealthy indeed." His bon mot went around the camp. The English Army, the soldier joked grimly, was wealthy indeed in corpses, but poor in terms of the sovereign. The Commander in Chief was still hanging men for High Treason, because this joke had passed their lips, when the rest of the army had retreated to the coast. He himself left on a sapient horse as French forward-troops broke through the camp and past the dangling bodies.

From Quentin the English fell back across the Pas de Calais. Orders to establish a series of redoubts were ignored or heroically followed to the death of everyone concerned. Commanders attempted to coordinate an evacuation on the beaches around Calais town, but the French pressed their advantage and embarkation turned to rout. Eventually the Brobdingnagians swam through again, pulling boats down to perdition from underneath. Commanders fled the scene in small skiffs. There was screaming, weapons' fire, commotion, and confusion. The English losses were even worse than they had been at the Battle of Saint Quentin.

Corpses sank to the bottom of the Manche as stones, or bobbed on the surface, tangled with the waves, or rolled and trundled dead in the surf, sand in their mouths and in their hair, in their sightless eyes.

BATES FOLLOWED THE news, reading the hastily printed newssheets with a fearful avidity. He wanted the French repulsed, like any Englishman. But he wanted the French victorious, and with it the noble God-endorsed cause to which he had devoted so much of his adult life. He didn't know what he wanted. He wanted to sleep, but he could only toss and roll on his dirty sheets.

His servant vanished. This abandonment didn't surprise him. Everywhere, people were leaving the capital.

The *premier* and *troisième corps de géants* walked and swam the channel, pulling troop-barges behind them. The army beached at Broadstairs. The English Army, with all reserves called up and all available men under orders, assembled themselves on the hills south of Canterbury. Travelers and passengers began carrying word-of-mouth reports of the fighting. *Terrible, like the end of the world,* they said. *It be the world's end, a preacher was saying on Gad's Hill. These gigantic men are God's wrath.*

The flood of people from London increased.

Bates found his mood undergoing one of those peculiar bubblings-up that correlated only poorly to his surroundings. He took to rising relatively early and walking the streets of London with a dispassionate, observer's eye. He watched servants load belongings onto carts outside lankily opulent town houses in Mayfair; watched shopkeepers fitting boards over their windows, while their wives wrapped whimpering Lilliputians in handkerchiefs for the journey. On the Great North Road a great worm of humanity pulsed away to the horizon, people walking, trudging, hurrying or staggering, handcarts and horse carts, men hauling packs stacked yards high with clinking pots and rolled cloth, women carrying children, animals on tight tethers. Bates stood for an hour or more watching the stream of people trudge on, as seemingly sourceless and endless as the Thames itself. Militiamen trotted by on horseback, hawkers cried wares to the refugees, clockwork aerial craft buzzed up and down the rank, left and right across it.

Eventually, Bates wandered back into the city, and went to his club to take luncheon. Only Harmon was there, and one cook in the back room. "Dear me," Bates muttered. "What's happened here." Harmon was all apologies, a good man in trying times. "Luncheon should not present problems, sir, if you'd care to eat."

Bates ate. His thoughts kept returning to the war. Could the generals, perhaps, be persuaded that England was losing the war *because* it had flouted God's ordinance? A general proclamation from Parliament freeing the Lilliputians, and God's radiance would smile on His people again—surely? Surely?

He wandered, pensive, taking twice his normal time back to Cavendish Square. A stranger, dressed in an anonymous brown, was waiting outside his front door.

"Sir?" he said, starting forward. "You are Mister Bates?" The words were enough to reveal that his accent was French.

Bates felt suddenly panicky, he wasn't sure why. "What do you want?"

"Calm yourself, sir, calm yourself," said the stranger. "You are a friend of Mister D'Ivoi, I believe?"

"D'Ivoi," said Bates. "Yes."

"I bring a message from him. Could we go inside your apartment?"

"Your army is in Kent, sir," said Bates, his fight-or-flight balance teetering toward the aggressive again. "It loots Kent as we speak, sir."

The stranger only said: "I bring a message from him."

THE STRANGER DID not introduce himself, or give a name. He carried a leather attaché case, and his boots were well worn at toe and heel. Inside, as Bates unclasped his own shutters (having no servant to do the job for him), the man placed his case carefully on a table, took off his three cornered hat, and bowed.

"Swiftness is to be desired, sir," he said. "I apologize for my English, for the speaking. You will pardon my expression?" Without waiting for an answer, he went on. "Mister D'Ivoi has asked for you particularly." He enunciated every syllable of this latter word with care. "He, and I, ask for your help. You have faith in our cause, I believe."

"Cause."

"For the Pacificans. For the little and the great, of the people. The Holy Father has declared the war a holy war, to free these creatures from their bondage. Yes?"

"Yes."

"Our army will soon be in London. We wish for you to do something for us, which it will make more swift the ending of the war. If you do this thing for us, the war will end sooner, and the holy cause achieved."

"Yes," said Bates. His mouth was dry.

"In this satchel there is a person."

"Satchel?"

The stranger bowed. "Is the word incorrect? I apologize. This sack, this bag."

"No, sir, I understand the word."

"Please, will you take this satchel to the Tower of London. It is this tower which is the command position for the defense of London, as we believe. The generals, the munitions, the forces, they gather there. The person inside the satchel will be able to work such things as to... to make more swift the ending of the war."

"There is a Lilliputian in the bag?"

The stranger bowed, and opened the flap of the satchel. A Lilliputian unhooked himself from a small padded harness inside and climbed out to stand, at attention, on the tabletop. Bates, as amazed and as unsettled as he always was in the presence of these tiny beings, smiled, made his smile broader, opened his mouth to show his teeth as if he were going to eat the thing. The Lilliputian stood, motionless.

"He has a training, a special training," said the stranger. "He is a warrior of great courage, great value. If I were to approach the Tower I would be shot, of course. And the naked streets are dangerous places for the little men, with traps and cats and all things like this. But if *you* were to bear the satchel, you would be able to release him inside the fort. Yes?"

"I know nobody in the Tower of London," said Bates. "I have no contacts in the army."

"You go to the Tower, and tell them that you bear a message from Colonel Truelove."

"I do not know the gentleman."

"He is captured, but we believe that the... English, excuse me, that *you*... do not know that he is captured. You will present to the guards and tell them that you bear a message from him, for attention of General Wilkinson only, for the general *only*. Once inside, find a quiet place to release the warrior from the satchel."

Sunlight laid squares on the floor. Light is a weight upon the earth, a mighty pressure from above, and yet it is constituted of the tiniest of particles.

Bates felt as if the moment of choice had already passed behind him. He did not have the language to phrase a rejection. All he could say was: "I will do this thing."

## 6.
### *November 23, 1848*

YOU ARE A strange figure, somebody told Bates. Sometimes your spirit is enormous; sometimes it shrinks to nothing. To nothing, Bates thought, and I lie abed for days. But not now, he thought. Now I have a task, to test myself, to prove myself to God.

The Frenchman had insisted on the urgency of his mission, and had pressed Bates until he offered up a promise to undertake it the following dawn. "Dawn, mind, sir," said the Frenchman, before leaving. "If we co-obstinate..."

"Coordinate," corrected Bates.

"Just so. If we co-obstinate, such that the little warrior is inside the Tower at the right moment, then we can complete the war much sooner. Much sooner."

He departed, with a gait that looked to Bates like an insolent jauntiness. But it was much too late for regrets. He shut his door, pulled up a chair, and sat opposite the miniature human on the tabletop.

"Good evening, my friend," he said.

The Lilliputian was silent.

There was some uncanny aspect to them, Bates thought to himself. He could not feel comfortable in their company. They unsettled him. He tried to visualize them as toys or marionettes, but then they would shiver in some inescapably human way, or their little eyes would swivel and stare, as if penetrating beneath the decorous levels of manner and behavior. They carried within them a strange elision. They were sylphs, but they were also and at the same time devils.

But it was too late for regrets.

"You are reticent, my friend," he said. "I cannot blame you if you harbor resentment against the English peoples. My people have committed... terrible crimes against... your people."

The Lilliputian said nothing. Was his silence the outward sign of some savage indignation?

"Believe me," Bates went on, "I am your friend. I have devoted my life to your cause."

Nothing.

It occurred to Bates that the Lilliputian might not speak English. "Mon ami," he began, but his French was not good. "Mon ami, j'espère que..."

The Lilliputian turned on his heel, clambered back inside the satchel, and was gone.

IN THE SMALL hours of the morning Bates discovered that the Lilliputian did indeed speak English. He had somehow mounted the arm of the chaise longue on which Bates was sleeping, and called in his wren-like voice: "Awake! Awake! For the sun will soon scatter darkness like a white stone scattering crows in flock."

Sleepyheaded, Bates found this hard to follow.

"We must be on our way," cried the Lilliputian. "We must be on our way."

"It is still dark," Bates grumbled, rubbing the sleep from his eyes with the calf of his arm.

"But it will be light soon."

"You speak English."

The Lilliputian did not say anything to this.

Bates rose and lit a lamp, dressing rapidly. He used yesternight's bowl of water to rinse his face, laced his feet into his boots, and looked about him. The Lilliputian was standing beside the satchel.

"You are eager to go to war, my little friend," Bates said.

The morning had a spectral, unreal feel about it: the citrus light of the lamp, the angular purple shadows it threw, the perfect scaled-down human being standing on the table.

"I am a warrior," it piped.

"But we must remember that Jesus is the Prince of Peace."

The little figure slanted his head minutely, but did not reply.

"Well, well," said Bates. "Well, well. We shall go."

The little figure slipped inside the case.

Locking the door to his rooms felt, to Bates, like sealing off his life entire. Perhaps I shall die, he said, but his mind was so muzzy with tiredness that the thought carried no sting. Perhaps I shall never return here. But he didn't believe that, not really. He did not truly believe that.

His fingers slipped and fumbled at his coat buttons, and then hoisting the case with its precious cargo and striding out.

The light was growing, as his heels sounded on the pavement in Cavendish Square. The air was chill. The western horizon was still a gloomy and impressive purple, but the sky to the east was bright, the color of malaria, with the morning star a dot of sharp light like a tiny window, immeasurably far off, open in the wall of an immense yellow citadel.

At the top of Charing Cross Road, Bates saw a solitary person in the otherwise deserted streets, a hunched over infantryman stumbling, or hurrying, north. He was nervous enough to draw back into the shadow of a doorway, and then rebuked himself and strode on. He imagined sentries' questions. *Who goes there?* An Englishman! A loyal Englishman! God save the King! *What's in the bag?* Nothing—sir—nothing at all, save some personal belongings. But that would be easily disproven, a quick search would reveal his true carriage. Papers! Papers for the general... to be perused by him alone. To be seen by his eyes only! Would that satisfy a sentry?

He walked on, and the dawn swelled in brightness all around him.

By the time he reached Holborn the sounds of fighting were unignorable.

From a distance the cannon fire sounded like the booming of bitterns over estuary flats, or the stomach-rumble of distant thunder. But once down the dip and up the other side of Holborn, the battle seemed to swoop out of the imaginary into the real with appalling swiftness. Knocks and bangs three streets away, two, and then rifle fire tattering the air, men in beetroot uniforms with bayoneted rifles trotting en masse, or hurrying singly from firing position to firing-position.

Bates was fully awake now.

He ducked down one side street, and then another, trying to stay clear of the scurrying military action. He was vividly aware of the stupidity of his position; a civilian, an unarmed and inexperienced man wandering the streets in the midst of a war. A bomb swooned through the air, exploding somewhere away to his left with a powerful crunch.

Panic took him for ten minutes, during which time he dropped the satchel and tried to claw his way through a barred oak door. When his right fingernails were bloody the panic seemed to ebb from him, leaving him panting and foolish. He retrieved the satchel, hurried to the end of the street, turned a dog-leg, and found himself on the riverside.

The sun at its low angle, with sunlight trembling off the water, turned the river to metal. Bates hurried on. Fifty yards downriver and he was at the deserted toll-booth of London Bridge's Middlesex side.

"You there!" called somebody. "Hold yourself! Friend or foe!"

Bates stopped. "An Englishman!" he called.

From where he was standing he could look down upon the bridge, and across the pale brown rush of the river. The Thames's flow seemed enormous, the water standing up at the leading face of the bridge's pillars in burly, muscular lips, the trailing edge leaving deep scores in the surface that broke into wakes and ripples hundreds of yards further downstream. Riflemen hurried along the half-completed embankment, ducking behind the unplaced stone blocks, or jumping into the holes where such blocks were yet to be placed. The sound of horses' whinnying, like metal skittering over ice, was in the air from somewhere on the other side of the river. An artillery unit labored with a recalcitrant field gun, poking its snub over the bridge's parapet. On the river's surface, a boat jockeyed against the fierce pull of the water, three sets of oars flicking up and down like insect legs to keep the boat alongside a small quay onto which soldiers were alighting.

And then, with the sounds of multiple detonation, smoke flowered into the air. French dart-shells hurtled over the horizon, threads against the sky, and careered into the masonry alongside the river with astonishing vehemence. The ground shook; ripples shuddered across the face of the water; stone cracked and puffed into the air as smoke. Bricks, pillars, and blocks tumbled and clattered. More explosions. The tick-tock of bullets, British rifle fire, although Bates couldn't see what they were firing at. Then the giants came; heads rearing up like the sun over the horizon, but these suns followed by bodies, and the bodies supported on enormous legs. They strode up the river, the water blanching into foam about their shins. They were dressed in crazily patched leather clothes, padded with numerous metal plates that were too poorly burnished to gleam in the light. With the sun behind them, four marched.

He was so stunned by the sight as to not understand how much in shock he was. He blinked, and turned. People were rushing on all sides, faces distorted as they shouted. He blinked again, turned again. The French, soldiers of ordinary size, were visible on the south bank, some firing over the water, some attempting to cross the bridge. English troops were defending the position. Bates stood in the midst of it, a single gentleman in modest but expensive clothing, his coat buttoned all the way to his chin, carrying a leather satchel briefcase. One of the English soldiers, hurrying to the bridge, caught his eye. "You!" he yelled. "You!"

Still numb to his surroundings, Bates turned to face him. Smoke misted up and swirled away, to an orchestral accompaniment of clattering explosions.

Everybody was looking north. Bates followed their glances. Another thunderstroke.

One of the Brobdingnagians was standing over the dome of Saint Paul's. He had driven his metal-tipped staff through the shell of it, as if breaking the blunt end of an egg. He lifted it out, and struck again, and the dome collapsed leaving a fuzzy halo of dust.

Bates turned to look for the soldier who had accosted him. He was not standing where he had been standing. Bates looked around, and then looked down, and saw him lying spreadeagled on the floor. Blood, dark and taut like poured molasses, was pooled all around him.

BATES STUMBLED, HALF-AWAKE, from the tollbooth and down a side street. A crazy trajectory. He ran clumsily past a row of scowling arches, and then turned into a doorway, pressing himself up into the shadow and against the side wall.

The sounds of battle became chuckles and creaks. It took him a moment to realize that the fighting was moving away, sweeping round beyond the wrecked cathedral and into the fields to the north. He fiddled with the catch on the briefcase and whispered inside, although as he did so he was struck by how peculiar it was to be whispering.

The street was deserted.

The Lilliputian's high-pitched voice warbled from its hidden place. "You must go on."

"I will be killed," said Bates, a trill of nerves shaking the last word. He felt close to tears.

"Death is the soil of the world," said the Lilliputian, the oddness of the sentiment made stranger still by the ethereal, piping voice that uttered it.

"I will wait here until the fighting has stopped," said Bates. Saying so brought him a trembly sense of satisfaction: to be safe, not to die, to stay hidden until the danger had passed.

"No," said the Lilliputian. The timbre of his voice had changed. Somehow, Bates could not see how, he had slipped out of the case and climbed up the coat. He stood on Bates's shoulder, and with a shimmer was on his face. Tiny pressure on his ear, a tickling sensation of an insect on his cheek. Bates could not repress a shudder, a raising of his eyes to swat the spider that had the *gall* to touch his face—to touch his face! Only an effort of will, consciousness, prevented him from slapping at the little creature. I must not! he thought. God's creature! So easy to crush it out of life... but no, no, I must not, never, never.

Blurrily close to his eyeball, the pink-yellow shape of a head, a lash-like hand, dissolved by nearness. "This thorn," warbled the Lilliputian, "is a weapon. I can thrust it into your eye, and it will explode, a bomb." Bates blinked furiously. "If you attack me I will have your eye." Bates blinked again. His eye was watering; his breaths were coming much more swiftly. "If you do not move *now*, to go to the Tower, I will have your eye."

"My dear little friend," said Bates, high-pitched. "Mon share amy."

"The Brobdingnagians live to be a hundred and fifty years of age," came the sing-song rapid little voice. "They are wary of death, for death is a rarity to them. But we of Lilliput live a quarter as long, and hold death in a quarter as much worth. We are a nation of warriors."

"My dear little friend," said Bates, again.

"Go now." And the tickling sensation vanished from his face, the ornament-like pressure removed from his ear. When Bates had regained his breath, the Lilliputian was back in the satchel.

THE BATTLE SEEMED to have passed entirely away. Cautious as a mouse, Bates ducked from doorway to doorway, but the only people he saw were British soldiers. He hurried down Eastcheap, and came out from the tall houses directly before the Tower.

He had no idea of the time. Certainly the morning was advanced now, the sky was crowded with ivory-colored thunderheads. Spots of rain touched his face, and Bates thought of contemptuous Lilliputians spitting upon his skin.

There was a great deal of military activity around the Tower; mounted troops jittered by, their horses glittery with sweat, or rain, or both; cannons were positioned at all places, sentries doing their clockwork sentry-business, chimney smoke and noise and business and camp followers, all the mêlée. It seemed odder to Bates than the battle he had just witnessed. He shouldered the satchel, its occupant like some wasp, striped with its own uniform; and yet, who could say, why not angelic as well? And there was the Tower itself, London's Tower as white as ice, blocky like teeth, standing taller over him, his parent, his nationhood's parent. It did not look inviting.

Nobody challenged him as he marched up the causeway until he had come within ten yards of the closed main gate, with its lesser gate inset and open. "Who goes there?" yelled the sentry, although he was only a foot or so from Bates. "General Wilkinson! shouted Bates, startled into life. "I bring a message for General Wilkinson!" His heart stuttered. "I have a message for the General's ears only! From Colonel Truelove!"

## 7.

HE SPENT MUCH of the rest of the day hiding inside a well-appointed house whose door had been blown, or beaten, from its hinges. The kitchen was messed and food looted, but the other rooms had been left untouched: beautiful furniture, with legs curled and slender as string, ornaments with the intricacy of clockwork but without function or movement, globes of glass holding preserved flowers, a new design of tallboy-clock, whose metronomic timekeeper rocked back and forth on its hinged base like a tree swaying in the breeze. The walls were hung with oils of society beauties.

Entering the Tower had been simple in the end. The guard had looked inside the satchel, but only cursorily and without penetrating deep enough to unearth the miniature warrior concealed inside. He had slipped through the inset door, the flap a twelfth the size of the great gates which were not opened, and hurried past the buzz of people within, over the inner quad, through another door and to a coign in an empty corridor. And there he had released the Lilliputian warrior, who had emerged from the bag with threads of rope coiled over his shoulder, and his own miniature satchel on a belt around his waist. He had not bade Bates farewell, but had scurried off.

Bates had loitered, nervously, around the Tower, and then had slipped among a crowd of engineers and kitchen-servants as they exited the Tower, and after that had slipped into deserted streets in Whitechapel.

Perhaps he expected to hear some titanic explosion, the arsenal beneath the Tower exploded by the fierce little Lilliputian; perhaps he expected the cheers of French troops. But although his ear was repeatedly distracted by bangs, knocks, creases of sound in the air, yells, tatters of song, aural flotsam, he heard nothing that matched the imagined cataclysm of his heart.

Much later in the afternoon, ashamed at his own instincts for cowardice, he had ventured out from this house, and wandered the city. He came across one body, in a British uniform, and then a clutch more of them. A print shop's windows had been broken in to make a placement for a field gun, but the gun's barrel was sheared and broken as a daisy, and its crew lay in a tangle of blackened arms and legs around it. Southward brought Bates out on the river again. Here there were more bodies. Bates went to the water's edge and sat down. On the far side of the river broken buildings bannered smoke into the evening air.

There was nobody around. It was as if London were a dead city.

The river hushed below him, like breathing.

I have killed my city, thought Bates, his mood flowing away from him now like the river itself, his spirits draining into the hidden sinks of despair. I am a traitor, and I have killed my city.

An irregular splashing to the west intruded on his attention. Upriver he could see one of the giants, sitting on the bank with its legs in the water for all the world like a small boy beside a tiny stream. The giant kicked his legs, languidly, intermittently, sending up house-sized bulges of water up to trouble the surface. Behind him, the tip of the sun dipped against the river, color bleeding from it into the water like watercolor paint from a paintbrush being washed after a day's work.

With desperate, self-detesting resolution Bates started toward the figure; this giant surveying the ruins he had made of the world's greatest city. "Monsieur!" he called. "Monsieur!"

He ran for ten minutes before he was close enough for his gnat's-voice to reach the great flappy ears. "Monsieur! Monsieur!"

The Brobdingnagian turned his head with the slowness of a planet revolving.

"I am here, monsieur!" squeaked Bates. "Down here, monsieur!"

The eyelids rolled up, great blinds, and the carpet-roll lips parted. "Good day," said the giant.

And now that he was standing beside the creature, Bates realized he had no idea what he had intended in coming over. "Forgive me, sir," he said. "Forgive me for approaching you. Is the battle over?"

"I can barely hear you," grumbled the giant, its sub-bass voice rolling and coiling in the evening air. "Allow me to lift you." And with sluggish but minute patience the enormous hand presented itself, so that Bates could step into the palm. The quality of the skin was not in the least leathery, as he expected it to be; it was douce, though strong, with some of the quality of turf. And then he was lifted into the air, and brought before the enormous benign face. Bates could see the pores, a thousand rabbit-holes in the cliff face; could see the poplar-stubs of unshaved beard, the tangle of hair in the nostril like winter trees.

"Thank you, monsieur," he said. "Is the battle over?"

"It is," said the giant.

"Are the French victorious?"

Every flicker of emotion was magnified, as if the great face were acting, overacting, each expression. "You are French?"

"No sir, no sir," Bates gabbled. "But a sympathizer, sir. I am an ally of France, an ally, that is to say, of its great cause, of freedom for Pacificans, of freedom against slavery and the upholding of God's law."

"Your voice is too small, and too rapid," rumbled the voice. "I cannot follow your speech."

"I am a friend to the Brobdingnagian people," said Bates more slowly and more loud. "And the Lilliputians."

A smile, wide as a boulevard. "The tiniest of folk. Our fleas are bigger than they. Some of my people," he grumbled on, benignly, "do not believe they exist, never having seen them. But I am assured they do exist, and I am prepared to believe it."

There was silence for a moment. The light reddened deeper into sunset.

"The day is yours?" Bates asked again.

"The army of France is victorious."

"You do not seem happy."

"Melancholia," said the giant, drawing the word out so that it seemed to rumble on and on, a sound like heavy furniture being dragged over the floor. "To observe a city broken like this. We Brobdingnagians are a peaceful people, and such destruction..." He trailed off.

"But your great cause," chirruped Bates. "This victory is a great thing! It will mean freedom for your people."

"The France-army," said the giant, "possess a machine of the greatest ingenuity. I have seen it; no bigger than a snuffbox, yet it *computes* and *calculates* and solves all manner of problems at a ferocious rate. So swiftly it works! It is this machine that has won the war, I think. This machine. Its strategy, and its solution to problems. This machine." He hummed and hoomed for a while. "My people," he continued, "my people are ingenious with machines, but never so ingenious as your people. You are small, but cunning. Perhaps the others, the Lil, the Lilli..."

"The Lilliputians."

"Just so, perhaps *they* are more ingenious even than you? The smaller, the more cunning? This may be God's way of ordering his universe. The smaller, the more cunning."

"I have long been an ally of France," Bates declared. His spirits, sunken only minutes before, were rising again, following their own unfathomable logic. Perhaps, he thought, perhaps my betrayal truly followed a higher good. Perhaps it is for the best. After defeat, England will abandon its persecution of the Pacificans, and soon after that its greatness will reassert itself. In ten years... maybe less. And it will be a more worthwhile greatness, because it will not flout God's ordinance. "I have long been an ally of France, and a friend of the Count D'Ivoi."

"D'Ivoi," said the giant. "I know him."

"You know him?"

"Indeed. Shall I take you to him?"

"Yes!" Bates declared, his heart flaring into fervor. "Yes! I will congratulate him on his victory, and on the new age of justice for Lilliputians and Brobdingnagians both!"

The enormous hand cupped him against the giant's shoulder, and he rose to his full height. The sun seemed

to pull back from the horizon with the change in perspective, and then in lengthily slushing strides the giant
marched down the river. He paused at the wrecked
arches of London Bridge, stepping up onto the concourse and over it into the water again. In moments he
was alongside the Tower. The troops outside the citadel
were in French uniform; they scurried below, insect-like,
apparently as alarmed by their gigantic ally as the
British had been by the giants as foes. Cannon were
hauled round to bear on the figure.

"A visitor for Monsieur le Comte," boomed the Brobdingnagian. "A visitor for Monsieur D'Ivoi."

He placed Bates on the charred lawn before the main
gate, and withdrew his hand.

### 8.

BATES WAS KEPT waiting for an hour or more, sitting on
a bench inside the main gate. The evening light thickened to full darkness, and a November chill wrapped
itself around the skin. Soldiers passed back and forth,
their spirits elevated by victory. Every face was grinning. Bates allowed the sense of achievement to
percolate through into his own heart. Something great
had happened here, after all. He thought of the little
warrior he had carried past this gate only that morning.
Such valor in so small an individual! Was he still alive?
When he met D'Ivoi again, he would ask. Such valor.
He deserved a medal. Would miniature medals be
forged, to reward the part brave Lilliputians had played
in their own liberation?

"Monsieur?" An aide de camp was standing in front
of him. "The Comte D'Ivoi will see you now."

Bubbling with excitement, Bates followed the fellow
across the court and down a series of steps. Gaslit

corridors, the stone wet with evening dew. Finally into a broad-groined room, lit by two dozen lamps, brighter than day. And there was D'Ivoi, his absurd pigtail bobbing at the back of his head. A group of gorgeously uniformed men was sitting around a table.

"Bates, my friend," called D'Ivoi. "France has much to thank you for."

Bates approached, smiling. The generals at table were examining maps of the Southern Counties. Around them strutted and passed a stream of military humanity. In the corner, the size of a piano only taller, was an ebony wood box.

Of the generals, only D'Ivoi stood up. The rest of the generals were still eating, and pausing only to drink from smoky coffee cups as wide as skulls.

"Bates, my friend," said D'Ivoi again.

They were eating pastries glazed with sugar that glistened as if wet.

"D'Ivoi," said Bates. He felt cheered to see his old friend, but something was wrong somewhere. He couldn't put his finger on it. He could not determine exactly what was wrong. It might have been that he did not want to determine what was wrong, for that would mean dismantling his buoyant feeling of happiness and achievement. And yet, like a pain somewhere behind the eyes, Bates knew *something was wrong*.

One of the generals looked up from the table. His ugliness was breathtaking, the left eyebrow and cheek were scored with an old scar, the eye itself glass and obnoxious. "Sit," said D'Ivoi.

The air in the room was not sweet: close and stale-smelling.

"I am glad my small action," said Bates, "was able to hasten the conclusion to this wasteful war."

One of the generals at table snorted.

"Did the Lilliputian warrior I ported here... did he survive?"

"He did his job very well," said D'Ivoi. "Although, alas, the war is not over yet. The English are resisting at Runnymede, with some skill and some force. But it will not be long! It will not be long, in part because of your labor. We, France, salute you."

"Ours is a nobler cause," said Bates, the words for a moment swimming his head with the thrill and honor of it all.

"Cause?" asked the general with the glass eye. It was impossible to look at his bunched, seamed face without one's glance being drawn to his hideous eye. Bates snapped his gaze away, and it fell on the box in the corner of the room.

"The Pope's latest decree," said D'Ivoi, and stopped. He noticed where Bates was looking. "Ah, my friend, your eye falls on our most valuable ally. The computation device!"

"So this is it," said Bates, distantly. The fact that there was something wrong was, somehow, intruding itself again. "The famous computation device."

"Truly," said D'Ivoi. "It has brought us further, and faster. It will change the whole world, this beautiful machine. Beautiful machine!"

"The Pope's latest decree?" queried the general. "C'est quoi ce que t'as dit?"

D'Ivoi gabbled something in French, too rapidly for Bates to follow. His own smile felt fixed, now. The light was too bright in this underground cavern. It slicked the walls. Centuries of the Tower, a prison. The giants Gog and Magog, or was it Bran? Bran the giant? Buried under Tower Hill, that was the story. Buried under the hill and the Tower built above it, pressing down on the enormous bones. A giant prison squashing the bones of a buried giant. How many people had seen the inside of this chamber, and never seen the light again? Centuries of people locked away, barred and closed and buried in the ground like blind stones in the mud.

Bates was stepping toward the device now. "It is marvelous," he muttered. "How does it work?"

D'Ivoi was at his arm, a touch on his elbow. "Ah, my friend," he said. "I cannot permit you to examine it too closely. You are a friend to France, I know, but even you must respect military secrets."

The box was coffin-black. It did not display any of its secrets on its exterior. "Of course," murmured Bates.

"As to how it works," D'Ivoi continued, steering Bates back toward the door of the room. "For that you will have to ask Mister Babbage. It is something like an abacus, I think; something like a series of switches, or rolls, or gears, or something like this. I do not know. I only know," he beamed, and took Bates's hand in his own. "I only know that it will win us the war. Goodbye, my friend, and thank you again."

Bates was half dazed as he walked from the room. A guard eyed him. He walked half-aware up the stairway. There were certain things he should not think about. That was it. That was the best way. Bury thought, like the giant buried under the hill. Certain things he should not think about. He should not think of the French troops ranging out across the fields of England, of other towns burning, of the smoke rising as a column from the heart of the kingdom. Should not think of the blood draining out of bodies, pooling like molasses, dark in the sunlight. Should not think of giant men working to the extinction of their race at brute tasks, menial tasks, hauling logs, or working great engines until their sturdy bodies gave out in exhaustion. Should not think of the Computational Device in the corner of the oppressive underground room. Not imagine opening the front of the device and looking inside. Or if he did think of this last, if he must think of it, then he should think of some giant clockwork device, some great rack of toothed wheels and pins and rods, something wholly mechanical. But not think of a tight, close, miniature prison cage, in which sweating rows of laboring tiny people worked at wheels and abacus racks, tied into position, working joylessly in the dark and hopelessness to process some machine for computation. Not that. He was on the top step now, and about to step back into the light, and the best thing would be to leave all that behind him, buried away below.

**About the editors and authors**
Rather than give extensive notes about our editors
and contributors here we would like to simply
point you to the *infinity plus* website, where you
can find biographical notes, interviews, more
stories and novel extracts, and links through to the
authors' own websites:
http://www.infinityplus.co.uk